THE SWORD UNBOUND

Lands of the Firstborn: Book Two

GARETH HANRAHAN

orbitbooks.net

Orbit
Hachette Book Group
1290 Avenue of the Americas
New York, NY 10104
orbitbooks.net

First Edition: May 2024
Simultaneously published in Great Britain by Orbit

Orbit is an imprint of Hachette Book Group.
The Orbit name and logo are registered trademarks of Little, Brown Book Group Limited.

The publisher is not responsible for websites (or their content) that are not owned by the publisher.

The Hachette Speakers Bureau provides a wide range of authors for speaking events. To find out more, go to hachettespeakersbureau.com or email HachetteSpeakers@hbgusa.com.

Orbit books may be purchased in bulk for business, educational, or promotional use. For information, please contact your local bookseller or the Hachette Book Group Special Markets Department at special.markets@hbgusa.com.

Library of Congress Control Number: 2023951841

ISBNs: 9780316537438 (trade paperback), 9780316537599 (ebook)

Printed in the United States of America

CCR

1 3 5 7 9 10 8 6 4 2

"Then, Aelfric, we were adventurers wandering the wilderness, able to move quickly and stay hidden."

"Now, we are rulers, defending a fixed stronghold. We have fewer friends and face greater odds. Our war against Lord Bone was a race. Now, we play the King's Game, move and countermove, stratagem and sacrifice across a great board. We must be clever."

"You be clever. Just tell me who to hit."

By Gareth Hanrahan

THE BLACK IRON LEGACY

The Gutter Prayer
The Shadow Saint
The Broken God

LANDS OF THE FIRSTBORN

The Sword Defiant
The Sword Unbound

For Richard, in memoriam

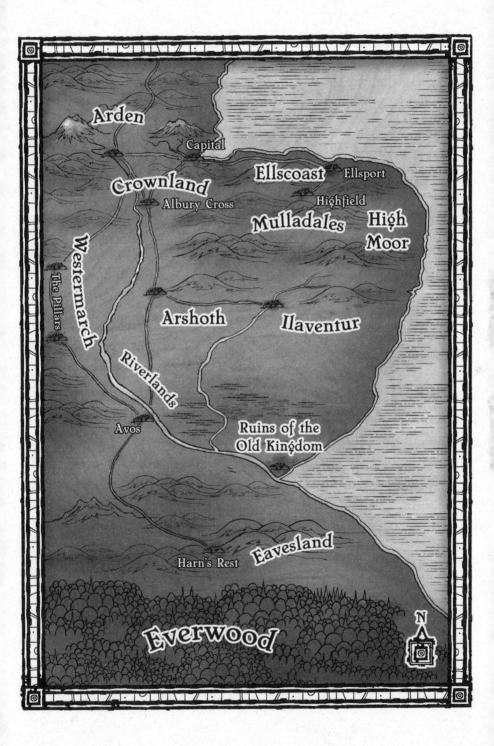

LIST OF CHARACTERS

THE NINE HEROES

Peir⁺ of the Crownland, called the Paladin

Jan⁺ of Arshoth, called the Pious, former priestess of the
Intercessors

Blaise of Ellscoast, called the Scholar, master of the
Wailing Tower

Berys the Rootless, later called the Lady

Lath, a Changeling, called the Beast

Thurn⁺ of the As Gola, saviour of the Wilder-folk of the
northern woods

Gundan⁺ son of Gwalir, General of the Dwarfholt, wielder
of Chopper

Laerlyn, daughter of the Erlking, Princess of the Everwood,
wielder of the bow *Morthus*

Aelfric of Mulladale, called the Bonebreaker, dubbed
Sir Lammergeier, Keeper of the Spellbreaker, also
known as Alf

IN NECRAD

Olva Forster, sister to Aelfric of Mulladale

Derwyn Forster, the Uncrowned King

Torun, a dwarf who seeks to be a wizard, apprentice to Blaise

Ildorae, a witch elf, Huntress of the Winter Star

Threeday, a Vatling

The Skerrise, a vampiric witch elf, Lady of the White Deer

Winebald, a captain of the guard
Pendel, a merchant
Lyulf Martens+, a blood trader and double agent, employed by
    Berys and Prince Maedos

(Emissaries to Necrad from Summerswell)
Lord Timeon Vond, former governor of Necrad
Lord Dryten Bessimer, father of Peir, called the Weeping Lord

(Formerly of Necrad, now defeated)
Amerith+ the Oracle, a Witch Elf Seer, once leader of the
    Witch Elves
Acraist Wraith-Captain+, Hand of Bone, Wielder of the Sword
    Spellbreaker
Lord Bone+ the Necromancer, the Dark Lord

IN THE NEW PROVINCES

Earl Duna+, chief among the landholders of the
    New Provinces
Erdys of Ilaventur, his wife
Sir Aelfric the Younger+, Idmaer and Dunweld, their sons
Meros, a captain of the guard
The Old Man of the Woods+, religious leader of the Wilderfolk

IN THE DWARFHOLT

Toruk, father to Torun
Gamling, cousin to Gundan

IN ARDEN

Bor, a sellsword, formerly employed by Olva
Cu, his increasingly suspect dog
Sir Rhuel of Eavesland, alleged poet
Agyla, a Ranger
A suspicious ostler and sundry other conspirators
Baron Bayard, a noble of Arden
Lady Bayard,
Berysala, his youngest daughter
Magga, a Roadhag
Remilard, a former guard in Necrad and banner-bearer to the
    Lammergeier
Othroan, a merchant in league with Berys
Armech, an actor in league with Berys
Forwin the Scratcher, a former mercenary known to Bor

IN ILAVENTUR

Lord Brychan, father to Erdys
Haeligan, his wizard

IN THE MULLADALES

Long Tom[+], father to Alf and Olva
Maya[+], mother to Alf and Olva
Genny Selcloth, a neighbour
Harlan, Kiven, Quenna, young friends of Derwyn
Thomad and Cottar, tenant farmers of Olva

IN THE EVERWOOD

Prince Maedos[+] of the Isle of Dawn, son of the Erlking,
    brother to Laerlyn
The Knight of Roses, Champion of the Erlking
The Knights of Holly[+] and Hawthorn[+], his brothers
The Erlking, eldest of all

IN UNKNOWN LANDS

Talis, daughter of Thurn, who is also Death

PART ONE

CHAPTER ONE

When Olva Forster was a child, her father Long Tom asked her brother Alf to chop some firewood. Alf misunderstood and brought down the huge oak tree that had stood in the field for generations. Olva climbed the stump to look at the rings in the wood. She was six; the tree had seen centuries.

She remembered putting her hand across a portion of the trunk, covering a few dozen lines, and thinking *That's it, that's my span.* Each ring had seemed so wide, each year so long. But they went quick.

A year ago, she'd held the Yule-feast in her house in Ersfel. Around the table she'd crowded a half-dozen of her tenants and labourers and their families. Last year, for the first time, she'd made Derwyn sit at the head. *You're of age now*, she'd told him. *You're fifteen.* And that made her think of the rings.

A year ago, she'd been the Widow Forster, the wife of the late Galwyn, Intercessors guard his soul. Prosperous, but those who envied what wealth she'd accrued had to admit that she'd paid a price. Her husband, her parents, her brothers – all dead. All but Alf, and Alf was gone. No one knew where.

But she'd known. She'd worked it out from the songs. A year ago, no one else in the village had guessed that big Alf had gone on to become Sir Aelfric Lammergeier, Hero of the Nine.

A year ago, Alf was dead to her, and she was – well, if not content, then at least safe.

A year ago, Derwyn had not died.

Now, she sat at a long table of polished marble with many guests, and ate from a plate of silver. Derwyn sat opposite her, picking at the fine food the servants brought him. His appetite had not come back with him, and there was a hollowness to his face she did not like.

Next to her was a place set for Alf, but it was empty. The last time she'd eaten with Alf at the Yule-feast . . . that must have been nearly twenty-five years ago, before he'd gone away adventuring on the Road.

Many miles and many years away.

Her guests that night were not farmhands and tenants, but worthies of Necrad – those who had not fled when it seemed the city was about to fall. She knew none of them, and they did not know her. It made for stilted conversation.

They called her Queen of Necrad, and she did not know how a queen of Necrad should talk. She smiled as they praised her, or talked about the fine wines or generous portions. The wine, certainly, was wonderful, for Lord Vond had left an excellent cellar. The portions of venison, less so – but considering their situation, even the wealthiest could not scorn a meal.

At the head of the table sat Derwyn. His face was flushed, his smile wide, but then he caught her eye from across the table and she could tell he was scared beneath the bravado. He took another cup of wine and drank deep – too deep, to her mind. *Slow down.*

She raised her own glass in a toast. "To the Uncrowned King," she said.

"The Uncrowned King," chorused the table. Olva sipped her wine carefully, and Derwyn mimicked her.

The Uncrowned King. That was what they called her son. Three months ago, her son had been a prisoner, hostage to a scheme against her brother. Derwyn had *died* in the dungeon under the city. But the wizard Blaise had opened a door to the grey lands of Death.

She'd gone through. She'd brought him back.

Blaise had warned he would not come back unchanged.

One of the merchants stared at her. She felt her cheeks burn beneath the Witch-Elf ceruse they'd made her wear. "Is something not to your liking—" Damnation, what was his name?

Somehow, Threeday heard the concern in her voice from the far end of the table. The pale creature tugged at one of the servants with boneless fingers. "Master *Allard*'s glass is empty. See to it."

"—Master Allard?" finished Olva.

Allard shook his head, his gaze still fixed on her face. "Forgive me," he said, "but I had to see for myself." He lowered his voice. "I heard it rumoured that you were in fact the Lady Berys in disguise."

Olva tried to suppress a laugh and half-choked on it. "You can see I'm not!"

"Still, strange things are whispered about you. That you are a Changeling, or an Intercessor in mortal form. That Blaise grew you in a vat."

"I'm just flesh and blood. A simple Mulladale woman." She looked around at the room. "I'm not used to playing host to such great lords."

"But you were a guest of the late Prince Maedos. Guest of elves, kinswoman to heroes, mother to kings – hardly a common woman from the Mulladales." Allard leaned closer. "I've heard it said, too, that Derwyn is the son of Peir the Paladin – that you birthed him in secret, and hid him away during the war."

"My son's father Galwyn Forster. He died in the war." Her voice sharper than intended.

Allard flinched. "These are rumours from the streets. After miracles, people look for meaning. You and your son came from nowhere, appearing in our hour of need to save us. You say he is not

Peir's son, but I look at him and I see the Paladin returned. How else are we to read this riddle?"

"I—" *I went into the Grey Lands. I went to Death's kingdom, and I rescued my son.* She wanted to boast, to give them a reason to support her. If the city turned on them, where would they go? "That is – it is true he was brought back from death, and he carries something of the Paladin in him."

"The strangest of all the tales," said Allard, in a tone of disbelief. "Truly, we live in a time of miracles."

"It will be a miracle if we see next Yule," grumbled another. He stared into his wine glass. "Here we sit, waiting for the noose. The Lammergeier declared rebellion when he murdered Prince Maedos, and the mad wizard runs unchecked, brewing up who knows what else in his tower! You say that boy and the Nine saved us from destruction? Saved us? We're trapped!" He jabbed his finger at Derwyn. "If we support you, we defy the law of the Lords of Summerswell. If we don't, we're prisoners in this hellish city!"

Derwyn sprang up. "You don't know what you're talking about! We saved you all! Prince—"

Threeday called from the end of the table. "Master Pendel's glass is empty again – but perhaps water might be more to his taste."

"Damn it," snapped Pendel, "let me at least get drunk."

"Prince Maedos held my mother hostage and tortured me!" Derwyn slipped back his sleeve to reveal many scars. "My uncle saved us! Maedos deserved all that happened to him!"

"So you say," said Pendel, "And even if all that's true – may the Intercessors strike down those who bear false witness – what does it matter? Who outside Necrad will listen? Words don't matter when it's season for swords, and that's what the thaw will bring. You've doomed us all."

Olva interrupted him. "Derwyn, peace. And Master Pendel, if it's talk of swords you want, then wait for my brother to return. Until then, my son's words suffice. Now, this is a Yule-feast, not a council meeting. Fill your glass, and let's be merry tonight."

Wind rattled the shutters. The fortress might be sturdy, but it was damnably cold. Outside, Olva heard the last of the merchants departing, and breathed a sigh of relief. Derwyn sat down by the fireside. He looked haggard with the effort of playing the king. Some of it had been acting – Derwyn putting on airs, imitating stories she'd told about his father.

But not all of it.

"I'll put more on the fire," said Olva.

"It's all right. Save the wood." Derwyn gave her a wan smile. "Anyway, the servants would object to the queen soiling her hands."

Olva snorted. Everything about that sentence was absurd. They'd inherited the Citadel's serving staff – at least, the ones who hadn't managed to flee Necrad during the siege. With nowhere else to go, unsure what to do, the servants continued to serve. They insisted on lighting the fires and cleaning the floors. They'd have dressed Olva if she'd let them.

And queen? Derwyn's return had coincided with the awakening of the city's magical defences. Somehow, overnight, a tale was told and retold in every corner of the city that her son was the destined king, a saviour come to right the wrongs of the world. That tale had united the ragged remnants of the city's people. Mortal and Witch Elf, folk of the New Provinces and old – tales of the Uncrowned King were told among all of them.

Olva had her suspicions about who had planted those stories. Threeday, for one. He'd made himself indispensable to Alf and Blaise, just as he'd been indispensable to Timeon Vond.

Or Lord Bone.

It was all nonsense, but those stories protected her son, and for that she was grateful. And while she felt uncomfortable in Lord

Vond's palace it was better than anywhere else in Necrad. Why, here she could almost believe she was back south in Summerswell.

"I'll put more on," she repeated. She stood. Instantly there was a swarm of servants at the door.

"Permit me, my lady," said a Vatling. He glided over to pile logs on the fire, the red light flushing his pale gelatinous face into something demonic. Others descended on the dining table, whisking away plates and glasses.

One hesitated over Alf's untouched plate.

"Leave it," said Derwyn. "He'll be here."

"And it'll be cold when he arrives," said Olva. "Take it and feed someone."

"The cook told me it's the last of the venison—"

"I know my brother. He'll eat anything. As long as there's bit of bread and something in the pot, Alf won't notice. Take it, go on."

"A feast fit for a hero," said Derwyn. He laughed, then asked, suddenly subdued: "Will uncle Alf come back tonight?"

"He said he would." They'd seen little of Alf since ... since Derwyn had come back. The Lammergeier's sword was needed everywhere. He was the last of the Nine left in the city – save Blaise, and the wizard was rarely seen outside his tower.

"Have you been sleeping any better?" she asked.

"A little. I keep waking myself up. I hear voices in my dreams."

She'd heard him. Nightmares tormented her son. The first few nights, she'd gone to him when he woke screaming. All too often, she was awake herself, wracked by her own fears. But they both needed to live despite the shadow of the past.

"Sleep's important. Sleep's how you heal. I'll ask Torun to have Blaise mix you up a potion." Derwyn looked unconvinced, so she continued. "After your father died, old Widow Heather made me something to help me through the night. Everything that's unsolvable and terrible in the small hours looks better by daylight."

"It's the light that keeps me from sleeping properly," said Derwyn.

"There's no proper night here, nor daylight." Even the tightest shutters failed to keep out the eerie glow of the necromiasma. "They'll be lighting the fires in the holywood at home. There'll be dancing after the Yule-feast."

"Their feast won't be a patch on ours," said Olva.

"I wish we could see them. I wonder what Harlan's doing now? Or Kivan? Or Quenna? Or even old Thomad?"

"Thomad," said Olva, "had better be minding my farm, and I don't care that it's a feast-day. As for your friends, up to no good I expect." A pang of homesickness struck her. It was not as though she was fond of any of Derwyn's troublesome friends, but after meeting so many strangers and seeing such unearthly sights, she craved familiar faces.

"Quenna – she'd bought a comb from a trophy-monger at the fair. I said she looked as fair as a Witch Elf queen with her hair pinned back."

"Did you now?"

"Well, I thought it. I was going to say it, but I got into a fight with Kivan instead." He blushed, which put some welcome colour in his cheeks.

"You'll see them again."

"They wouldn't believe any of this."

"Which part?" asked Olva. "Us having the Yule-tide feast in a castle like great lords and ladies, or . . ." She waved at the window and the city beyond.

"Any of it."

"Aye, well . . ." Olva took another glass of wine. "The rest of the world seems like a wild story if you never go down the Road. And you're too young to remember the war, when the world came pressing in on us."

An unfamiliar expression crossed Derwyn's face, and he seemed about to speak, when another gust of wind blew the window open, the metal grille of the shutter clattering against the stone. Chill air carried with it the smell of the miasma. Olva went to close it.

She could see out over the rooftops of the Garrison district, the portion of the city claimed by the occupying forces of the League. The occupiers – human, dwarf, Wood Elf – had tried to make their enclave into an outpost of home, but succeeded only in making it grotesque. A gaudy mask hiding a monster's face. Beyond the walls were the other portions of the city, the Liberties where the defeated Witch Elves dwelt, and the forbidden Sanction – although, after the siege, the Sanction was no longer secure. The guards that had once watched over its laboratories and temples were gone, dead or fled or withdrawn to the Garrison. Necrad hunched before her, a creature of slate and marble, flanks bristling with barbed spires and scaly rooftops, a thousand windowed eyes.

Through the vapours, she could see Blaise's tower at the heart of the city. There, they had brought Derwyn back. The Wailing Tower and the Citadel were poised spears, keeping the monster at bay.

Olva reached out to close the shutter, conscious of the sheer drop below, the stout wall of the Citadel keep a four-storey cliff above a sprawl of lesser buildings. Looking down, she glimpsed a man clinging to the wall. A blade clenched in his teeth, cloak plastered to his body by the rain, fingers and toes digging into cracks in the mortar. For an instant, she stared at him in disbelief.

He saw her too. His eyes widened, and he scrambled up to scrabble at the windowsill. Olva grabbed at the shutter, but the – Thief? Assassin? Madman? – got one arm in before she could slam it shut. With a roar, the man shoved himself over, falling on top of her, down in a tangle of limbs. A stranger, hair cropped in a monk's tonsure, eyes fixed not on her but on Derwyn. He held her down, his forearm across her collarbones, pinning her left hand, pressing against her throat. His other hand came up, and in it he had a delicate crossbow, elf-wrought, a wasp of polished steel with a barbed and deadly stinger.

Aimed at Derwyn.

Olva heaved herself up, surprising the attacker – and herself – with her strength. She knocked him over, and then she was on top of him, straddling him and punching him, slamming his right hand against the tiled floor until he lost his grip on the crossbow with a bone-snapping crack.

Derwyn was at her side then, a sword in his hand, the tip at the man's throat. Her son's hand shook, but his voice was steady. "Yield."

"Not to you, abomination. Intercessors, receive my soul and carry—"

Olva snatched up the crossbow and struck the madman across the face. "Who sent you?"

"The grail-cup showed me your sins, mother of abomination. The Intercessors charged me with this holy mission. Know that I am the first of many. All of Summerswell stands against you!"

The Holy Intercessors, guardians of humanity. All her life, she'd been taught to see them as blessed spirits. The memory of Berys' warning rang through her mind. *It's the Wood Elves. It's always been the Wood Elves. The Church is theirs, too – the Erlking sent the Intercessors to watch us.*

She pulled his head forward so her son could see the shaved pate. "A monk." Olva scrambled to her feet and took the sword from Derwyn. She steeled herself to press the sword down, in case she needed to kill this man. Her hand did not waver. Where were the guards? How could this intruder have crept into the Citadel unchecked?

Derwyn leaned back against the windowsill. "You're not from Necrad, then," he said, and there was a strange timbre in his voice. "The Intercessors never answer prayers in this city."

"I was an acolyte in Staffa when the Intercessors chose me."

"I once thought they chose me, too, friend," said Derwyn, but Olva could tell it wasn't just her son. *He came back from death, but not alone.* "I was their champion, and I wielded the fire of the Intercessors from the High Moor to the gates of Necrad."

"Peir the Paladin is dead," spat the monk. "I have heard the lies they tell about you – that you claim to be Peir returned. The Intercessors told me the truth – that you are an abomination, as unholy as any horror spawned in the Pits of Necrad."

"I do not know what I am," said Derwyn. He spoke slowly, as if considering every word. "But the Intercessors could not aid me once I passed under the miasma. I entered the city alone, save for my companions." He knelt down and touched the monk's injured cheek. "But I found strength within me." A light welled up in his hand, and the wound healed.

Olva stared at her son's miracle.

The monk crawled away, his hand brushing against his cheek. "The Paladin returned?" He gasped in awe, all his righteous anger melting away into doubt. "Forgive me! I-I misread the signs!" He buried his face in Derwyn's boots. "Forgive me," he mumbled.

Olva grabbed the monk and dragged him away from Derwyn. The door across the room burst open and two guards rushed in, wearing the livery of the Citadel. "Milady, Lord Derwyn, are you both unhurt?"

"No thanks to you," spat Olva. "Where were you when we called?"

The guards glanced at each other. "The door at the foot of the stairs was locked, milady," said Winebald. "We had to break it down."

She shoved the monk over to them. "Take him. Find out who locked that door. And search the Citadel – make sure there's no one else out there. You'll answer to the Lammergeier if anything else goes awry."

"As you command, milady." They bowed and departed, taking the monk with them.

Olva sank into her chair, suddenly sickened. She placed the crossbow on the table, next to her empty bowl.

Derwyn sat down too. He was pale, breathing heavily, but he was himself again, the eerie presence gone. "You use the same tone," he said between gasps, "when giving out to the farmhands. At least when Cottar left the pigsty gate ajar, the pigs weren't armed."

"He tried to *kill* you."

"I need to get used to that, don't I?" Derwyn picked up his bowl and ate ravenously.

That night, Olva climbed the west tower. The moon beyond the necromiasma was full, so in the distance she could see the endless mudflats of the Charnel shimmering white with frost, and the black ribbon of the Road stretching away into the night. Soon, the spring thaw would make the Road navigable once more.

But she doubted she would ever go home again.

Beyond her sight, far far away – but linked by that very Road – lay the lands of Summerswell. There were maps in the Garrison, and she recalled them now: Arden in the Cleft with its high walls, Arshoth of the temples, wild Westermarch, the brave knights of the Riverlands, the mighty fleets of Ellscoast, old Ilaventur, the enchanted Eaveslands, the seat of the Lords in the Crownland, and even her beloved Mulladales. She recalled the perilous journey to Ellscoast, her terror at leaving home to chase Derwyn. The journey seemed unthinkable, but she now knew that it was only a tiny part of the lands of Summerswell.

Know that I am the first of many. All of Summerswell stands against you!

The monk said that, and Olva believed him. All the world she knew – all she could imagine – now stood against her family. Against her. Against Derwyn. And against Alf. The full might of Summerswell was aimed at them, and beyond Summerswell, the Everwood of the Elves, the heavenly Intercessors. The threat was greater than she could conceive, and she could not imagine how they might survive the coming year.

But felling the oak in the backfield was unthinkable too, until Alf chopped it down.

Chapter Two

P rison gave Bor time to think.

    He didn't like it.

Thinking was wood-rot, eating away at his courage, making once-solid things frail and treacherous. Thinking was his sins coming back to him, and he had made mistakes enough to fill every one of the sixty nights he'd spent in this cell.

Thinking wasn't a fit occupation for a man like him. Bor was a sellsword. Thinking on the battlefield got you killed. You practised until you acted without thinking, fought by instinct. That was his life.

Had been his life.

Now, he sat by the barred window and listened to the street below. He'd heard bells ring out wildly a few weeks ago – not a summons to prayer, not to mark the approach of Yuletide, but an alarm, a warning. Then shouting in the streets, and later, many feet marching. Horses, too, and the jangle of armour. Troops mustering for war.

He should be down there. There was money in war, especially if you were a survivor like Bor. Stay clear of the battles, stay clear of the cursed magic, and take coin from the desperate. In times of chaos, thinkers were at a disadvantage.

Now all he could do was sit here.

Thinking.

Rotting.

Where were they marching? Was there a quarrel between the Lords of Summerswell? Trouble on the Westermarch? Or north? If there were soldiers marching through the Crownland, then something big was afoot, on the scale of Lord Bone's war a generation ago.

And he was out of it.

If he wasn't careful, his thoughts would turn to how he came to be here, and those thoughts were bad. He'd have to remember what he'd done. He'd have to remember he was damned, that the Holy Intercessors had come down and judged him and condemned him to this cell.

An angel smote him in an alleyway.

There was nothing here to distract him from thoughts of damnation. A barred window that looked out over an empty yard, the snowfall of three weeks ago unmarred by footprints. A narrow bed, a thin blanket. A piss-pot in the corner. A locked door.

And a stool for the interrogators.

There had been plenty of questions in those first days. Cold-eyed and nameless, demanding answers he couldn't give. They'd asked him about his meeting with the Lammergeier at the Highfield Fair, and how the Lammergeier had commanded that Bor bring a message to his sister. Demanded he describe everything he could recall about the hero, about the black sword he bore, about those who spoke to the Lammergeier afterwards. They talked as though they suspected Bor of lying – and that, he thought, was utter nonsense. What would it profit him to lie about meeting a great hero like the Lammergeier? More to the point, why would he give a fortune in coin to some woman he'd never met?

Their questions were like the seeds of thorn bushes planted in his brain. They'd ask him a question he couldn't answer – like *What was in the Lammergeier's letter to Olva Forster?* – and afterwards, in the night, his thoughts would fester. His brain would get caught trying to work out what the answer might be, or why it was important. He'd told them, over and over, that he knew nothing.

Maybe they'd believed him, because no one had come to his cell in weeks.

He had, of course, tried to escape.

The first time, he just acted. The servant fumbled when trying to bolt the door, and Bor pounced like a wildcat, yanking the door open and smashing the servant against the wall. He'd nearly made it out of the tower before darkness claimed him. He remembered being unable to breathe, and grey eyes, and pain, and nothing.

Then the cell again.

The second time, he planned it as well as Bor had ever planned anything. He tested every element of his cell – looked for loose stones, tried to pull the bars from the mortar, tried to lift the door off its hinges – until finally, he found the answer. It was the week of the Feast of the First Grail, the holy day marking when the Erlking revealed the Intercessors to the first Lords of Summerswell. It was among the highest of festivals, and every pious soul was obliged to go and give thanks for their salvation.

Bor's plan was this: first, he fashioned a knife from a broken chair, and hid it in his boot. Then, when the servant came, Bor demanded that he be allowed to attend church on the morrow. They could not deny his request, after all. Then, when the moment was right, he would draw the knife, put it to the throat of the priest. No one would risk spilling the blood of a cleric on holy ground. He'd demand a horse, and he'd drag the priest with him until he was sure no one had pursued him, and then he would ride away.

It was, by Bor's standards, an intricate plan.

It lasted six heartbeats.

The morning of the feast-day, the door to the cell was opened not by the mute servant, but by a grey-eyed interrogator. She kicked Bor in the groin. He doubled over, and she plucked the shank from his boot.

"If you are a fool," she said, "try again."

Then she hauled him out of the tower and brought him to the nearest chapel. She sat next to him and made him listen while the priest celebrated the Feast of the First Grail, and the people gave thanks for the kindness of the Intercessors. All the while, she kept Bor's own knife pressed against his ribs.

After, she brought him back to the tower, and locked the door. He did not see her or any of the other interrogators again. So he sat there, with nothing to do except contemplate his own damnation.

After an eternity, a visitor.

It was not the servant, nor the cold-eyed inquisitor. His visitor came huffing up, walking stick tapping on the spiral steps. He was sixty at least, red-cheeked, squeezing his bulk through the narrow door of the cell. He sagged onto the creaking bed and waved at Bor to take the stool while he mopped his brow with a handkerchief.

The old fool had left the door open.

Bor didn't think. He acted. He leaped for the doorway—

——and crashed heavily to the ground as the old man speared Bor's ankle with his cane.

"If you'd—" the old man gasped for breath "—wait a moment, I have a proposition for you. One far more profitable than another ill-considered escape attempt."

Bor picked himself up with a groan. "Who the fuck are you?"

The stranger looked around the cell. "We'll have to get you moved somewhere more salubrious. I'd never fit a writing desk in here. I know I did my best work in a prison cell, but it was a damn sight more comfortable than this. You don't even have a wine rack, for heaven's sake."

"Who. The fuck. Are you?"

"Oh, a humble storyteller. I was a knight, once." The man slapped his belly. "But now I wield a pen instead. Call me Rhuel."

"Rhuel," repeated Bor. "Sir Rhuel of Eavesland!?"

"Bless you, my boy. It's always gratifying to be recognised."

"You wrote *The Song of the Nine*!"

"I did. From a cell much like this one, in fact. Though at least I had the sense to try to force myself on a pretty maiden, not Sir Lammergeier's dried-up old sister."

Bor struggled to his feet. "That's not how it happened! Olva – the Lammergeier's sister – hired me to help find her missing son. But he was beyond rescue. I told her to go home, but she wouldn't listen. She'd have gotten herself killed if I hadn't ... if I hadn't ..."

"Betrayed her? Given her into the hands of her enemies?"

Bor hung his head. "Aye."

"Well, you can forget all that, my boy. Put aside your guilt. It makes for a sad story. No, what we need here is something much more entertaining. Blood and lust and peril, not the maundering of a sellsword." Sir Rhuel produced a quill and a sheet of paper. "Let's start again. Tell me your tale, Bor the Rootless."

"I don't understand what you want of me."

"It's quite simple, my boy. Twenty years ago, I was in another prison, and my cell overlooked the stables. I got all the gossip from the lord's messengers when they changed horses. I heard wild rumours about a band of adventurers, and it caught my imagination. I wrote down those rumours, collated them, expanded on them. Added some poetic flourishes. I sold my first manuscripts through the bars of my cell for a penny a sheet." He smiled fondly. "I found patronage. In time, my writings won me a pardon. The Nine might have saved the world, Bor, they won the war and slew Lord Bone, but their deeds are nothing without my words. I made them heroes in the hearts of the commoners, you see."

He picked up the pen again. "And now, I have a new patron and a new commission. Or rather, we do. I shall write, and your testimony shall give it the ring of truth." He pointed the quill at Bor. "I made the Nine into heroes. But what I must give the groundlings now, friend, is a villain."

Bor had thought he'd never be warm again, the way the wind whipped through the narrow bars of his cell. This inn had a fireplace big enough to roast a sheep, and he contemplated climbing inside it to burn the chill from his bones.

"A bad winter, indeed," remarked Sir Rhuel from his desk. "As bad as the Hopeless Winter, maybe? Or is that hyperbolic? No, no, this is for the commoners – they eat up references to the old stories. I've grown cautious." Rhuel leaned towards Bor and spoke in a stage whisper. "You see, lately, I've been writing mostly for the Lords, and they sometimes have Wood Elves as guests in their halls. And elves are *bastards* when it comes to literary criticism. You make some offhand historical allusion – ah, she was as meek and soft-spoken as Alar Ravenqueen of old – and in comes some know-it-all immortal who says, 'Nay, I remember that Alar croaked and peppered her speech with profanities to shame an Ellscoaster sailor.' Quite throws you off your meter. Now, tell me your tale again."

Bor shook his head. "What more can I say? The Lammergeier sent me to bring a message to his sister. Her son ran off down the Road that night, and she paid me to protect her when she went after him. He'd fallen in with Lyulf Martens, a blood trader out of Ellsport."

"Details, man! How did you know this Martens was a blood trader?"

"I used to work for him, years ago."

"The trade in blood – ah, now that's a thing of terror. There's something we can work with. Innocent children, spirited away in the night to feed the depraved appetites of the Witch Elves. Every honest soul in Summerswell lives in terror of their child being abducted and fed to vampires in exchange for the soiled treasures of

Necrad." Rhuel tickled his chin with his quill. "I don't suppose the Lammergeier's sister made any such bargain, did she?"

"No, no. She hired me to rescue her son, Derwyn. We tried to grab him when Martens crossed the Fossewood, but he got away. We chased 'em as far as Ellsport, but Martens had too many guards there. Nothing more we could do. I . . . put her on a ship to Necrad."

Rhuel waved his hand dismissively. "Let's go back. You met the Lammergeier in Highfield, yes?"

"Aye," said Bor.

The woman in the corner snorted.

Bor glanced at the third person in the room – the cold-eyed woman by the door. Her dark clothing coupled with her pale skin, grey eyes and blonde hair to make her appear bloodless. A permanent frown, like she'd tasted life and found it sour. Although, to think of it, *she* hadn't asked him any questions herself – there'd always been another inquisitor present. She'd just sat there, glaring at him like his lack of answers was deliberate insolence. He hadn't seen her in weeks, until she came to unlock his cell and bring him to this inn. Sir Rhuel hadn't even acknowledged her presence, but now the old knight turned to her.

"Does the noble Ranger have anything to add?" *What the fuck is a Ranger?* Bor wondered. It wasn't a title he'd heard before, not in this context. The way Rhuel said it made it sound important, and Bor couldn't imagine the cold-eyed woman wandering around a forest looking for poachers.

Though he could easily imagine her butchering an animal.

"Then pray don't interrupt. I must thicken very thin gruel into a hearty stew." Rhuel turned back to Bor. "Tell me of the Lammergeier."

Bor shrugged. "He was big."

"Sir Aelfric Lammergeier, Hero of the Nine, Champion of Summerswell, Bearer of the Sword Spellbreaker, Slayer of Monsters, the fabled Bonebreaker who slew the Dark Lord and his best friend with one blow . . . was somewhat large in stature. Hmm. No. We're trying to destroy the man's reputation here, Bor. Did he threaten you? Use dark magic to compel you?"

"Aye, he threatened me—"

"Good, good—"

"But that was before I knew who he was. I was drunk – if I'd known I was talking to the fucking Lammergeier, I'd never have spoken back to him."

The woman in the corner let out a bark of laughter.

"What?" Bor clenched his fists. "You think I'm lying? Go ask the Baron of Highfield or Sir Prelan or anyone else who was on the tourney field that day. The Lammergeier was there."

"Oh, we have. We have questioned the Baron of Highfield, and many others," she said. "All agree that the Lammergeier was there. And the truth of the matter doesn't matter for your purposes, Sir Rhuel. Lie and conjure as needed."

Angry at her mockery, Bor took three steps towards the woman. She raised her hand, and to his horror Bor saw a ring on her finger, twin to one he'd seen before. The ivy collar around his throat – a punishment inflicted for trespassing on the Isle of Dawn – twitched.

"Do not try my patience. You will serve until you are fit for some other purpose."

Bor stumbled away from her, his knees shaking. He felt like a whipped dog threatened with a fresh beating. A man couldn't fight magic. What good was strength of arms, or a sharp sword, when she could make the collar choke him with a thought? What foul luck had he, to encounter someone who had a ring like Martens?

This inn might be more comfortable than the cell in the tower, but he was still a prisoner.

"Oh, pay her no mind," said Rhuel. "This is Agyla the Ranger. You'll grow used to their habits. They lurk in shadows, and mutter dark tidings, and know things without saying how they know 'em. Infuriating, the lot of 'em."

The Ranger sat back. The shadows swallowed her.

"Typical," sighed Rhuel. "All right, the sister and the son. Olva and . . . Dergle?"

"Derwyn."

"Anything else of note about them?"

Bor dragged himself upright. "What do you mean?"

"They lived in some isolated hamlet in the Mulladales. Was the boy a hideous Changeling, tainted with earthpower? A monstrous gremlin, maybe – the Lammergeier kept his family hidden for a reason, after all! Was there anything suspect about them?"

"I don't fucking know," said Bor, racking his brain. "I only met the boy for a moment. Olva – she was bloody tough. She told me his father had been killed in the war, and she'd raised him alone." A thought occurred to him. "The Intercessors blessed their union! That's something she told me. She was just a peasant – the Lammergeier came of common stock – but the Intercessors appeared to the village priest and told her that she was to marry some rich lad called, called . . ."

"Galwyn Forster," supplied Agyla.

"Is that the sort of thing you want?"

"'She's a loving mother and her marriage was blessed by the heavens until it was tragically cut short?' No. The *opposite* of what we want," shouted Rhuel, suddenly furious. He rose up, snatched the paper from his desk, crushed it into a ball and flung it at Agyla. "I need scandal! Depravity! Treachery!"

"We have treachery enough from all the Nine," said Agyla. "They have long refused to bow to the authority of the Lords, and that defiance is now open rebellion. They cannot be allowed to hold the power of Necrad." She counted off the sins of the heroes. "Blaise defied the laws of the College Arcane. Jan the Pious turned her back on the Church. Every thief and smuggler north of the Riverlands pays tribute to Berys. The Wilder are loyal only to their own kind – if the

Beast ever had any loyalty at all. The Lammergeier pays no heed to the Lords' commands. Peir, had he lived, might have stayed true to Summerswell, but twenty years have soured the rest of them."

"Useless!" said Rhuel, "Those are all lordly quarrels. Matters for councillors and courtiers, not the common folk." He gestured to the window. "If you want to rile up the commoners against the heroes who saved the world – if our masters want to muster the sort of army they'll need for such a war – then they will need something damning. And what do you bring me? A sellsword who doesn't know anything!"

"The Lords have commanded you write a new tale of the Nine," said Agyla. "And it must be done before the spring thaw."

That, at least, Bor understood. It was hard enough to travel in the gentle lands of Summerswell during the winter, but in the Dwarfholt mountains, or on the road to Necrad, travel was impossible for months at a time. If the forces of the Lords of Summerswell were to march north, it would not be until well after Yule.

"How's one new tale going to change anything, anyway?" said Bor.

"I am wounded!" shouted Rhuel. "A vicious attack on my art."

"A tale can be a potent weapon," said the Ranger. "It shapes thought, and few things travel as fast as rumour. But Bor is right. One tale alone will not be enough to break the common people's love for the Nine. All it needs to do is make them doubt. The Church shall decry them, the wizards shall curse them, and the Lords will declare them traitors. When all those voices are raised against them, the memory of the old tales will be drowned out."

"Even if the old tales are true?" said Bor.

"Truth is but one element of a tale," said the Ranger. "Now, Sir Rhuel, to work."

"I can write," said Rhuel, crossing his arms like a child, "but I need better material than Bor here can provide."

Agyla rose, silently, and left the room.

Rhuel was instantly cheered. He fetched a bottle of wine from a shelf. "Make a fuss, and they think you a genius."

Bor tested the door, and found it locked. "Who are these Rangers? Are you her prisoner? Does she employ you? Or serve you?"

"She and I serve the same masters, the Lords of Summerswell. Although the Rangers have connections to the Church and the College Arcane, too – you saw her ring, and that's not the only magic she carries, no doubt. Don't do anything stupid like trying to escape, lad – what she lacks in charm she makes up in charmstones."

Magic. Everywhere Bor went these days, he was beset by magic. Sorcery and charmstones, seeping out of Necrad, making everything strange and treacherous. It overturned the natural order of the world, made things run contrary to how they should be. Magic should be far away, locked up in wizards' towers and children's stories, not on the battlefield. Not on the streets.

Not around his throat.

It mocked Bor's strength, and without that, what good was he?

"That ring," he said, forcing the words out past the ivy-collar. "Where did she get it?"

"Our gracious companion likes her privacy." Rhuel poured himself a full cup of wine. "The Rangers are the Lords' hunting dogs, from what I've seen – and I try to see as little as possible, where they're concerned. It's best not to know too much about the very people who deal with those who know too much. And hungry dogs may even turn on their masters. But I prefer to think of myself as a very well-paid guest, not a prisoner. Think of the will of the Lords, my friend, as a great mill driven by a water-wheel. Defy them, and you will be ground to dust, or at best clog up that wheel for a little while until the river of time washes away your remains. But go with them, and you can ride that wheel to the heavens. Or, at least, to wine and board." He waved his cup at Bor. "You and I, my friend, are lucky. Our contribution to the war effort involves making up poison-pen stories about heroes, and we can do that from this warm room in perfect safety. Better here than out there. Your health."

Bor sat down on one of the beds and thought about the old

knight's words. Bor had earned his pay through mercenary work for years, and now there was war in the north. An army marching with the spring thaw, to retake Necrad from the Nine ... He imagined there'd be good pay in that. He imagined himself trudging through the mud of the Charnel, approaching the white walls of Necrad.

Imagined himself blasted by magical fire. Ensorcelled, his bones turned to molten lead, his brain blasted with unknowable runes. Imagined the Lammergeier riding across the field, black sword in hand, slaughtering hundreds with every blow.

A man couldn't fight magic.

"Pass the wine," Bor croaked, "and I'll think of more."

But before they finished the bottle, the Ranger returned and told them to pack.

"I cannot work under these conditions! Such constant interruptions! Where, in the name of the Erlking, are we going with such haste?"

"Arden."

"Oh," said Rhuel, "that's all right then."

In good weather, Arden was a week's ride from the Capital. Bor knew the road well. He'd fought in Arden in tourneys, found work as a hired sword. The city controlled the great northern pass of the Cleft of Ard. A fortune in trade went through the dwarf-forged gates of Arden, and the people there were merry and rich. He remembered looking up at burnished roofs gleaming like tongues of fire in the late summer sun.

In good weather, a week's ride. In the middle of winter, it was a sight longer than that, and hills that looked pretty in summer were a slippery climb in snow. The worst winter in years, Rhuel had said – and that was well enough for him to say. Rhuel was wrapped up in piles of furs and an expensive travelling cloak, not to mention layers of blubber. The Ranger was lightly dressed, but Bor had spotted the cloak clasp at her throat. A twist of elven silver, coiling serpents with ruby eyes. She sat at ease on her horse in perfect comfort, the snow steaming from her shoulders, while Bor hunched over his saddle and tried not to freeze.

Bastards.

Mile after mile, day after day. Rhuel talked about some castle on the border of Arden, a baron who'd give them hospitality, and Bor clung to those tales of a roaring fire and a hot meal as winter wind flayed his bones. The baron's castle became this mythical place in his head, a heavenly reward, an island of warmth in the midst of this frozen sea. The Roads were empty – only a fool would travel in this.

He thought of all the soldiers mustered by the Lords, and shook his head at the cost to keep all those men fed and sheltered for weeks, just so they could be ready to march by the first thaw. If they got to stay warm behind the walls of the Capital, why couldn't he? Why the hell had the bloody Ranger dragged him out of that nice inn – or even the prison cell, which had at least had a bed – and hauled him into these desolate hills to freeze? First they want him to help soil the reputation of the Lammergeier, and now this journey to Arden. He glanced over to Agyla, but she just scowled and Bor felt his throat constrict, the ivy-collar twitching. He shivered, clinging to the saddle with frozen fingers, trying to warm himself on his anger.

Was that where it had all gone wrong? When the elves had caught him smuggling relics out of Necrad. Treasures like that cloak clasp. If he'd kept one of those he'd be warm now. Was it when he'd given the Lammergeier's sister over to Martens? He'd tried to do the right thing, then – the bloody woman wouldn't listen, and she'd have gotten herself killed trying to rescue her son. Didn't he deserve some credit for that?

Or was it when an angel struck him down on the street, and the Rangers found him?

It was very cold. He couldn't feel his feet in the stirrups, and there were holes in his boots that let the wind in.

Or was it that things had never gone right for him at all? Others had charmed lives — look at Sir Rhuel, a scoundrel and a drunkard by his own confession, and there he was on his fine grey horse, talking about the Riverland wine served by his friend the baron? Even in prison, Rhuel had good luck, and Bor only had misfortune. Blundering from one disaster to the next.

It was very cold. He couldn't even feel the movement of the horse any more.

The Lammergeier chose me. The Lammergeier had picked him to deliver a message. That thought was a precious spark of warmth. The Lammergeier found him lying drunk in the grass by the tourney field, and decided that this was the man to entrust with a quest. He'd been chosen because he was worthy.

The snow on the ground seemed a lot closer now. Distantly, he heard Rhuel shouting about some idiot who'd fallen off a horse. Bor tried to laugh, but his mouth was full of snow. He'd just lie here a minute.

Then he felt a rough, warm tongue licking his fingers, his face. Hot stinking breath filled his nose and Bor became aware he was lying in a snowdrift. The dog bounded back, then jumped on him enthusiastically.

"How?" he muttered. This was Olva's dog, Cu. The beast had accompanied them all the way from Ersfel, and then followed Bor from Ellsport all along the Road to the Capital. But the dog had vanished just before the Rangers caught Bor. And that was weeks ago, many miles ago. How was Cu here?

Sir Rhuel and Agyla rode up.

"Get up, man," said Rhuel, "it's not far to Bayard's Castle, now."

Agyla drew her sword, intending to strike Cu with the flat of the blade to drive the animal away. But Bor sat up and put his arm across the dog's furry flank.

"No," he said, "this is my dog."

Chapter Three

Baron Bayard and his family greeted Sir Rhuel at the gate of the castle, as befitted an honoured guest. The whole clan trooped out – Bayard with his red hair and beard braided dwarf-fashion; his wife modestly dressed, eschewing the daring Witch Elf gowns that were the fashion in the Crownland; two daughters, like little copies of the mother; knights of his household. Bor noted one knight had an elf-wrought sword, and the baron had a charmstone amulet, but little else in the way of magic – a poor showing, considering Bayard's rank and his well-situated lands.

Off to one side stood Bayard's court wizard and the castle chaplain. Bor, still feeling unwell, leaned against the castle wall while the endless introductions were made. Sir Rhuel introduced Bor as his retainer, and Agyla as his serving girl – and this worked a remarkable transformation on the Ranger. The hard interrogator melted into a meek maid who blushed and spoke to her shoes when curtsying to Bayard.

As a courtesy to the famous Sir Rhuel, Baron Bayard had his court wizard examine Bor. The wizard – a sour woman who doubled as governess to Bayard's young daughters – did not spend any of her stored star-magic on healing. She glanced at Bor, glared at his dog, and prescribed bedrest. They stuffed Bor into a tower room that was smaller than his prison cell in Summerswell.

The narrow window faced the Cleft. Bor could hear music and laughter from the hall; Sir Rhuel holding court. Smells of roasting meat made his belly rumble. "They'd better feed us soon, boy," muttered Bor, lightly, "or I'll make trouble." It was an empty threat; he had no sword, not even a beltknife.

He lay there, and watched frost glimmer on the star-trap strung on the wizard's tower, opposite. Stars were coming out, bright above the mountains.

Footsteps on the stairs, and a knock at the door. A young girl of about ten or so entered bearing a tray of food, a jug of wine precariously balanced on the edge. Not a servant; one of the baron's daughters.

"Sir Rhuel's retainer should not go hungry," she said, placing the tray by the bed. "May-the-holy-Intercessors-bless-your-meal." The whole phrase spilling out as a single word.

Bor felt he should say something, but he had no idea how to talk to a noblewoman, even a child. He grunted in what he hoped was a respectful fashion.

"Sir Rhuel's going to recite *The Song of the Nine*. Mistress Isueld says I can stay up and listen, if I am quiet and sit in the corner."

"Won't that be nice," muttered Bor.

"My favourite part is where Berys steals the Witch Elf warship." Words burst from the child. "She's so brave. Mistress Isueld says I should pay more heed to Jan the Pious or Peir the Paladin, that they're better—" she took a deep breath "—'moral-exemplars', but Berys is my favourite. I'm named for her – Berysala."

"You know, before Sir Rhuel, I served the Lammergeier."

"Truly!?" Berysala's eyes shone with wonder.

"Aye."

"How did you meet him?" asked Berysala. "He passed through the Cleft when I was a little girl, but I didn't get to see him. Isueld says that's for the best, because the Lammergeier is terribly frightening. He has to be, to scare our enemies." She clapped her hands. "'A dreadful sword in a mighty hand, a doleful blow to save the land.' Is he truly eight feet tall?"

"Not quite," he said, "but a head taller than me. I met him at the Highfield Fair, and he charged me to deliver a message. A secret message."

"Was it from Berys?" The child clutched the edge of the bed. "She's the cleverest of the Nine, and I'll wager—"

"Berysala!" came a shout from downstairs. The child jumped. "I like your dog," she squeaked. She ran out the door, came back and hastily curtsied, then vanished, her footsteps thumping on the stone steps outside. Bor could hear the muffled voice of Mistress Isueld chastising the child.

"Served by a baron's daughter," remarked Bor, "and a hot meal. Not bad." He threw a few morsels to the dog, and then dug in. By the time his bowl was empty, Bor had quite forgotten the hardships of the Road; the wine convinced him that being Sir Rhuel's retainer was as good a fate as a man could expect out of life, or at least out of that evening.

Below, he heard the harper strike a chord, then the booming voice of Sir Rhuel reciting *The Song of the Nine*. Bor couldn't make out the words, but he knew portions of the tale by heart – everyone in Summerswell did – and could follow along with the rhythm. It was from the middle section of the poem, describing how the Nine rode north to war. They passed by this very castle, twenty or so years ago.

> *North through the Cleft, under the mountain*
> *Through dwarf-built delvings, north into darkness.*
> *Valiant Gundan, axe-hungry and vengeful,*
> *Led them down to the edge of the world,*
> *To Karak's Bridge spanning the chasm,*
> *Where the roaring of ogres defiled the sky.*

Bor lay back, letting the song carry him away to a fitful sleep. His aches and pains from the journey merged with the song, so he dreamed that he rode with the Nine, towards the Cleft and on to Necrad. And Cu followed him into the dream. Two things woke Bor.

The first was loud booing from the hall, and Sir Rhuel's forced laughter and pleas for forgiveness. Clearly, Rhuel had ventured to test his new work on the crowd. Bor laughed into his pillow and turned over—

And then he was wide awake, as he heard someone ascending the stair. The door opened a crack. "Stay quiet," whispered Agyla, "and follow."

He looked around to make sure the dog would stay quiet, but there was no sign of the animal. Had Cu slipped out without him noticing?

"What's going on?"

Agyla tapped her ring on the doorframe. "That's not staying quiet."

They crept downstairs. Most of the servants had retired for the night, Baron Bayard's daughters tucked up in bed now that *The Song* was over, but Sir Rhuel and the baron were still drinking in the hall.

Agyla led Bor towards the cellars. The Ranger prowled ahead, invisible in the darkness.

"What are we doing?" asked Bor.

She did not reply.

"What—"

"Quiet." She stopped at a door. Carefully, she tried the handle, found it locked. "Keep watch," she ordered.

"Give me a weapon, and I'll guard you."

"Give you a weapon? I know what you are. If I hand you a blade, you'll try to cut my throat. Or cut this from my finger." She bent to pick the lock. "Try that, and the ivy will choke the life from you."

"I wouldn't turn on you. But I need a weapon if I'm going to watch your back, aye?"

The lock gave way, and the door opened. Beyond was a storeroom. "Stay here," she ordered.

"What do I do if someone comes, then?"

"Die slowly," she snapped, "and delay them long enough for me to finish."

Bor hovered on the threshold, keeping one eye on the stairs. He watched Agyla search the storeroom like a practised burglar, peering into barrels of salt meat, chests of dried fruit and spices. She stooped over one box. With her knife, she levered up a false bottom to reveal a hidden compartment. Charmstones glimmered there, magic out of Necrad. What might those stones do? Give a warrior strength and speed beyond the natural gifts of any man? Enchant a sword to be sharper than the finest razor, or make it a ghostly blade that passed through armour like mist? Grant protection against illness or injury?

"Our host," muttered Agyla, "has been greedy." She plucked one charmstone from the hoard and held it up to the light to examine it. It was a gemstone the size of a hen's egg, cut with delicate elven-runes and set on a silver chain. That stone was magic, refined and condensed; it grew like a pearl in the Pits of Necrad before some elf-smith – or even the dead hand of Lord Bone – had plucked it, carved it, given it purpose. Bor couldn't read the runes, so he had no idea what power the stone had. Agyla turned it over in her hand, then replaced it in the hoard. "Or ambitious."

"He's a smuggler?" Bor had been a smuggler, and it had ended badly for him. The ivy-collar was his punishment for those crimes, and he'd gotten off lightly.

"I think not," said Agyla, slowly, as if considering the possibility, "but certainly still a criminal." She appeared unsurprised to have found such a hidden hoard. She replaced the panel and stacked clay jars back in the box.

"You're leaving it all there?"

"I am no thief," said Agyla. She relocked the door. "Go back to bed, Bor. You saw nothing; you shall say nothing."

Bor fumbled his way through a thought. Lords like Bayard were supposed to *boast* about their magic. By rights, with a hoard like that, Bayard's knights should be decked in charmstones from helm to spur. Bayard and his family should be blessed with magic stones to ward off illness or misfortune. What was the point of keeping all that power locked in a cellar – unless he was a smuggler, and intended to sell it? It made little sense to Bor.

"Why would Bayard keep it a secret?"

"Why indeed?" There was an edge in her voice, but it wasn't aimed at him.

He followed her up the stairs. "Back in the Crownland," he whispered, "you laughed when I said I'd met the Lammergeier. Like you know something I don't."

"I know many things." She looked back at Bor. "The Lammergeier was never at Highfield. You were deceived. So were many others."

He did not believe her. She could not take that from him. "So who *did* I meet?"

"Another traitor to be hunted."

"I watched your back down there." He tried to grab her. "Tell me or—"

Her finger twitched, and he gasped, digging his fingers beneath the vine as it came to life and tightened around his throat. "You saw nothing. You say nothing," she spat, "you are nothing."

Then she slipped out a side door and was gone.

Bor's room was empty. There was no sign of the dog. He shut and locked the door behind him; he was too tired to go looking for the beast. From the tower window, he could see the forested hills, the snowy hilltops bright in cloudless night. A hard night to be outside. Better to be inside, in an actual bed with thick blankets.

He took one last glance out the window, wondering where Agyla had gone, and glimpsed a fire amid distant trees. Then he reached out and closed the shutters.

Ruff!

Cu was lying there, curled up at the head of the bed. The door was still shut; there was no way for the dog to have returned to the room.

The same thing had happened, he recalled, just before the Rangers had caught him. The dog had vanished off the street.

"Where did you go, eh?"

The dog looked up at him, then scrabbled in the blankets. It dislodged a coin that clinked on the ground. Bor picked it up.

It was no common coin. He could tell that with a touch, by the feel of the unnatural metal. It was a coin out of Necrad, a coin struck by Witch Elves. The image of Lord Bone's skeletal sigil stared back at him, the face of death engraved on witch-silver.

The Lammergeier had given Bor a pouch of coins like this one, and commanded him to bring them to Olva Forster.

Olva had, in turn, promised the coins to Bor if he'd keep her safe on the Road.

And he'd spent the last of coins in Summerswell weeks ago. A king's ransom squandered between Ellsport and the Capital. All the coins from Necrad were gone. Had this one somehow gone astray, tucked into some fold of Bor's bag? Bor was a man of many faults, but losing track of money wasn't one of them. He had coin so rarely that he held tightly onto every one.

A coincidence, then. Bayard had a chest full of treasures from Necrad hidden in his cellars. Travellers from the north brought coins back down to Summerswell. It was possible that some coin from Necrad could find its way to this castle, this room.

Or it was magic.

He turned it over and over in his hand, staring at the now-sleeping form of the dog. He lay down, still holding the coin, then stuffed it under his pillow to hide it.

The Ranger wasn't the only one who could have secrets.

*

Mistress Isueld had permitted Bayard's daughters to sleep late and skip morning prayers. When she went to rouse them in the hour after dawn, Berysala was gone.

A quiet search ensued, followed by a frantic one. It reminded Bor of when Derwyn had left in the dead of night, but Olva's son was a grown lad, and Berysala was still a child, and high-born to boot. Still, the comparison made Bor uneasy. She'd hardly set off on her own – so someone must have taken her. Bor looked around for Agyla, and saw the Ranger leaning against the stable door, nonchalantly eating an apple.

Everyone was accounted for, except Berysala.

With every hour, Bayard grew grimmer; his wife clutched their remaining child and trembled. The castle chaplain whispered prayers; Sir Rhuel made some jests to lighten the mood. Neither were well received, and the lady of the castle burst into tears.

After every inch of the castle had been searched – except, perhaps, that locked cellar – they turned to the surrounding countryside. Messengers rode to nearby towns. Bor and Sir Rhuel joined the hunting party, and together with household knights they combed the hills. Even Cu participated by snuffling the frosty earth, hot breath steaming like a small but enthusiastic dragon.

Riders brought no word. Hunters found no trace.

When night fell, Mistress Isueld spent a portion of her hoarded magic on a divination. From her tower, she fetched a vellum scroll describing the precise configuration of the heavens when Berysala was born, she threw carved stones across the horoscope, calculating the deviation in destiny or some such.

All her spells could tell was that the child was still alive.

But the cold that night was bitter.

Sir Rhuel came up to Bor's room with a bottle of wine. "Dreadful," said the knight. "I hoped we'd get another meal out of Bayard before we had to move on. But apparently even the cook's overwhelmed with emotion. Black bread salted with tears, that's all that's on offer. It's enough to make me weep."

"Someone must've taken her," said Bor. "She's still alive, says the wizard. So, ransom? Maybe we find the rogue who took her, and we can claim a reward instead, eh?"

"They prefer to work through children," said Rhuel obscurely. "Best not to get involved. Come, let us write."

Again, he asked Bor about his journey with Olva, about Derwyn, about the Lammergeier. About stories Bor had heard on the Road. Most tales changed from province to province – the stories told in the Eaveslands weren't the tales Bor had heard in his boyhood in Westermarch – but the stories of the Nine were always the same. Always true.

Rhuel grew frustrated as the bottle dwindled.

"You should have heard them last night," grumbled Rhuel, "in the hall. All I did was hint – *hint* – that maybe the Lammergeier was a bit of a bastard, and it was like I'd spat in the Erlking's face. The whole room went dead quiet, and then they *booed* me. I've never been scorned before. I've been dead drunk on stage before, so sloshed I couldn't say two words straight – and they still cheered because they knew the tale I was telling, and liked it."

Bor scratched Cu's head. "The Nine saved Summerswell. People know the tales."

"*My* tales. And the Lords of Summerswell have commissioned me to change the story. I should have known, damn it. Earl Crake paid me once to omit Berys from the canonical *Song of the Nine*, you know – she stole his fortune and his daughter's virtue, and my word, but that man could bear a grudge – but the groundlings wouldn't stand for it. I have to put her back in every time I recite it aloud."

"The Nine are heroes. The Lords are bastards who sit on their thrones and collect taxes. Seems to me this was a fool's errand from the start." Bor reached over and took the bottle. "What was it you said? Something about riding the wheel as long as we can?"

"It will be a short ride if I cannot come up with *something*. Do you know why he's called 'Lammergeier'?"

"They're birds that break bones, aye?" said Bor.

"The man is so dull, I had to invent a nickname to make him interesting. He's like an especially stoic rock. Devoid of ambition, consumed by duty, all passions so repressed you'd think him a damn monk. Even his name is plain as dry bread. Aelfric of Nowhere! Aelfric Everyman!" Rhuel snatched the wine back and waved the bottle in Bor's face. "You think you'd have been terrified into submission by some farmer's son called Alf? 'Twas the Lammergeier that froze your heart, and I made the Lammergeier!"

Late into the night, Agyla strode into his room without knocking. "Pack," she ordered, "we leave for Arden town at first light."

"What about Bayard's girl? Has she been found?" asked Rhuel.

Agyla answered like it was a poem learned by heart. "A woodcutter saw her last night in the forest, dancing with a troupe of Wood Elves. The Firstborn are rarely seen outside the Everwood, but their Wandering Companies range wherever they wish. It pleases them, sometimes, to adopt a human child for a little while – a week, or a season, or fifty years. Berysala is perfectly safe in their company. No harm will come to her while kindly elves watch over her. No doubt she will find her way home in time."

A noise in the courtyard below prompted Sir Rhuel to open the shutter. "Devil of a time to be working," he groused. Below, two men in clothing were loading a familiar box into a cart.

"I have tidings for you, Rhuel," said Agyla. "News out of Necrad. Terrible news, but it shall make your task much, much easier."

"What? Master Blaise was rude to the Masters of the College Arcane? Lady Berys snubbed some lord at court?"

"The Lammergeier murdered the Erlking's son."

CHAPTER FOUR

The Lammergeier murdered the Prince of Dawn.

Bor rolled that thought around his mind as they rode to Arden. Both the Lammergeier and Prince Maedos of Dawn were heroes – Aelfric Lammergeier of the Nine had won his name and spurs in the last war, but the immortal son of the Erlking had held back the dark since the creation of the world.

Bor had met both of them.

He'd met the Lammergeier at the Highfield Fair, and he wouldn't let Agyla take that away from him. The Lammergeier had scared him, with his dreadful helm and black sword and his voice like death, but he'd picked Bor for his errand. He'd seen value in Bor.

Prince Maedos – well, he was a son of the Erlking, an elf-lord so exalted he was more myth than man. Bor remembered lying half-drowned on the shore of the Isle of Dawn, remembered pressing his face into the sand rather than look at the glory of the Prince of Dawn. He'd stammered a child's prayer for mercy. Even when the prince punished his crimes with the damn ivy-collar, Bor's anger had been directed at Lyulf Martens, not the elves. Being angry at the prince's judgement was cursing a thunderstorm. You didn't blame the storm for a shipwreck, you blamed the captain who steered into it.

The son of the Erlking held back the dark, the stories said, and now he was dead.

The news invigorated Sir Rhuel. He stopped drinking; by night, instead of reciting *The Song* or telling bawdy tales, he wrote, nose pressed into the paper, muttering to himself. He wandered lost in mental labyrinths, so Bor had to lead Rhuel's horse. Bor, too, had to set up the camp at night, and fetch water, and cook.

Oddly, despite having to labour in the cold, Bor found himself enjoying playing the role of retainer. He was used to travelling the Road alone, or with other rogues and sell-swords. If he'd met a fellow like Sir Rhuel, he'd have robbed the old knight. Now, he found himself watching over Rhuel as the knight muttered about finding a rhyme for 'treachery'.

Agyla always nursed simmering anger at the world, but since she brought word of Prince Maedos' murder, Bor noticed a change in her. Instead of vanishing into the dark, she sat by the campfire night after night, sharpening her short blade or adjusting the charmstones in its hilt. Bor had seen that murderous look in the eyes of others before, and such death wishes brought bad luck to those nearby. Her anger spilled over. Sometimes, Sir Rhuel was the target of her fury, and she demanded that he work faster. Arden was only a few days away, even at their slow pace. More often, Bor felt her wrath, and his throat ached.

It was as though the Lammergeier had slain one of her kinsfolk. Bor wondered how close the Rangers were to the Wood Elves; it must have been the elves who brought her tidings of Prince Maedos' death. Elves were magic, too – Wood and Witch alike, Bor didn't trust any of them.

He wondered what magic Agyla might have in all those charmstones. Stones might keep a knife from snapping, or make every wound lethal. Stones to ward off a mortal blow, or gird the wearer in invisible armour.

The thought came to him that he could murder Agyla in the night, take the cursed ring and the rest of her treasures. But in that moment, she looked up and glared at him, and he feared that she had some Ranger gift to read his mind, and see every thought that occurred to him. So, he dared not consider that course of action, and shied away from contemplating it whenever it occurred to him.

Instead, he entertained another thought. When he was done with his chores for Sir Rhuel, when he lay listening to the wind howl in the heights, he took the thought out and treasured it like a precious coin. The thought was this: *If the Lammergeier did kill Maedos, the prince deserved killing.*

When Lord Bone's armies invaded Summerswell, Arden was certain to fall. It was the closest human city to Necrad, and any assault from the north would pass through the Cleft. Everyone in Arden knew doom was at hand.

But doom was averted.

Thanks to the Nine, Summerswell halted the first invasion; the second thrust foundered on the walls of the Dwarfholt. If Lord Bone had mounted a third assault, then Arden would fall. The League marched north in desperate counterattack. Many were the partings at the gates of Arden, but that sorrow could not eclipse the city's wild joy when news came that Lord Bone was dead. Arden should lie in ruin; instead, bright banners flew from untoppled towers, unmarred walls. The city was still drunk on its unexpected existence.

A crowd surrounded the south gate. Bor marked companies of soldiers, some with League banners, some from the retinues of individual nobles, ragged mercenary crews, camping outside the city walls until the Road thawed. No doubt their lords were already inside the city. The three travellers joined a queue of people waiting to enter the city. Traders and pilgrims, beggars and thieves, knights and lords. A long, long line.

"Don't they know who I am?" demanded Rhuel as they inched towards the gate.

Bor fell into conversation with some soldiers. Eager lads, fresh and spoiling for a fight. Too young to remember the last war, but raised on stories of the heroes who fought it. They came from Arshoth in the service of pious Lady Helena of that province. They were on the way to Necrad to fight Wilder, or so they guessed. There were all sorts of rumours about what was happening in the north – that Necrad had fallen, or that Necrad was besieged and the Nine were fighting to hold out, or that the Lords were going to push the frontier with the Wilder further back.

None of them knew who they'd really be facing. None of them knew they'd be fighting *against* the heroes of legend.

The ivy collar twitched. Bor looked over at Agyla, and she raised a finger to her lips.

They approached the gate.

"What business in Arden?" demanded a guard.

"ART!" roared Sir Rhuel. He spurred his horse and cantered past the guards. Agyla hurried to smooth matters over, and she and Bor were waved through without having to pay any of the customary tolls or bribes. The streets were crowded, and Bor dismounted to lead Sir Rhuel's horse through the press. "On to the palace!" urged Rhuel, and his startled horse nearly trod on Cu, who yelped in protest.

The sprawling palace was at the heart of the city, and the crowds only got worse as they went deeper. "Half the bloody country's here," complained Bor as he shoved some oafish Mulladaler out of the way.

"You are not wrong," said Rhuel, "look at the banners. I've not seen so many crowns in years." Sigils of a crown were reserved for Lords. "There's Arden's flag, of course, but also the crowned ship of Ellscoast. And oh – that's Vond's sigil, but no crown and a serpent green . . ." He frowned, trying to make out the device.

"It's the device of Lucar Vond's eldest son," said Agyla. "Timeon Vond. Until recently, the governor of Necrad."

"Oh ho. Now that will make conversation interesting." Rhuel

peered at the most distant of the flags. "My eyes are not what they were. Is that a horse or a unicorn?"

"Horse," said Bor.

"Why then, that's Lord Bruke of Westermarch." He nudged Bor with his boot. "Your liege lord, eh, Bor? You hail from Westermarch, Agyla tells me."

"No lord of mine."

As they drew near the palace, Agyla called a halt. "There's an ostler I trust here. We'll stable the horses with him. Sir Rhuel, you continue on to the palace. Go to your room and work, understand? There will be time for carousing later."

"The work," said Rhuel, "is mostly done. And inspiration is oft found at the bottom of a glass."

"A glass, perhaps. No more. I will *know*."

"She would too," said Sir Rhuel. "Devil woman." The knight ambled off into the crowd.

Bor followed the Ranger to the stables. Agyla took every obstacle as an offence, glaring at passers-by and cursing anyone who got in her way. Bor could get away with such discourtesy – he looked intimidating, with his scarred face and fighter's stance. Agyla was half his size, but she got away with it too. Not a woman to cross. Cu trotted along behind them, occasionally distracted by interesting smells, but always bounding back to keep Bor in sight.

The stable was just off the main thoroughfare. There, Bor did the work of caring for the horses while Agyla and her ostler friend spoke in whispers in a corner of the room. The ostler was dressed the part, boots caked in horse dung and all, but there was something about him that reminded Bor of Agyla. The same sense of secret knowledge, the same scorn. An elvish look, Bor might have called it once.

"I don't think they're talking about horses," muttered Bor, as he hefted Sir Rhuel's old saddle onto a stand. Cu slunk closer, and cast a glance back as if the dog was inviting Bor to join in eavesdropping.

The dog was too clever for anyone's good. Bor hesitated. If Agyla caught him listening, she'd . . .

To hell with it. He stomped over to them.

"What's a bloody Ranger, anyway?" he demanded.

The ostler looked up, fury and alarm warring on his face. Agyla raised her finger, but did not tighten the collar. "Secret, for one thing."

"You've dragged me up every fucking hill in Arden, and down into the baron's cellars to boot. Questioning me and mocking me and – hell with it, I deserve some answers."

"You deserve nothing," said Agyla. "But perhaps you have earned a little indulgence." She produced a pouch that jangled when she tossed it in the air and caught it. "Do you know the tavern of the Blue Bull?"

"Aye."

"Buy drinks. Ask for tidings from the north. I know you can complain about how badly you were treated when you were a smuggler, so tell that tale. If all goes well, you'll be approached by someone looking to hire a sellsword like you. Go with them."

She threw the bag at Bor. He made no attempt to catch it, and it bounced off his chest and fell to the ground.

"You think you've got it all planned out, but I won't sell my loyalty blindly for a few coins," said Bor.

"We know you," said the ostler, "do not pretend to have scruples, Bor the Broken."

"Fuck you. You don't know me."

"We know everything."

"If that were true," said Bor, "you wouldn't need the old man to spread your calumnies. You wouldn't need me to go dredging for rumours in the taverns." He took a step towards the ostler, hands clenching into fists.

"Don't," said Agyla. Bor stopped.

"I could make you go," she said, quietly.

"So do it."

Agyla surprised him by reaching down and picking up the pouch instead of using the ring. For the first time, she looked at him without obvious scorn. Her eyes reminded him of a winter sky.

"The Rangers were appointed long ago to guard Summerswell, Bor. We do not serve the Lords, or the Church – only our oath. We hunt down those who would sow dissent and bring ruin on the lands. Thanks to us, there's been centuries of peace in Summerswell."

"I've fought in enough wars."

"Skirmishes," scoffed the ostler. "Little quarrels between little barons. Nothing like the wars of the Old Kingdom. Nothing like Lord Bone's invasion. Since the Erlking blessed the Lords of Summerswell, the Rangers have kept the peace."

Agyla continued. "We keep the peace safe from those who would break it – in their greed, in their treachery. Sometimes, Bor, we must guard it from those who have the best of intentions. The elves teach us to see as they do, to work knowing that we will not live to see the end of the tale. We act through agents like you and Rhuel because we must remain unseen and unknown. Hunting hideous inhuman monsters is for heroes. It's the monsters with human faces we must deal with, and we do so quietly."

"Like Bayard? You took his daughter, and he yielded over those charmstones, didn't he?"

"His daughter will be returned in time. We are not cruel."

"No?" Bor rubbed his throat.

"Not . . . needlessly." She gestured for him to sit beside her. "It is a waste to destroy things because they have grown crooked. I could have slit Bayard's throat and taken the charmstones by force. Instead, I compelled him to become our informant. Or consider this: if the common folk rise up in support of the Nine in general rebellion, what will happen then? The Lords of Summerswell will send out their knights, girded with charmstones, and the land will be awash with blood from the Cleft to the River. But we can spare many lives if we snuff out the rebellion before it takes spreads. Sir Rhuel's poem is part of that." She pushed the pouch towards him. "So too is this. Villains plot against Summerswell, and you are the sort of rogue they might seek to use."

"You're sending me to meet enemies of the Lords?"

"The less you know, the more convincing you'll be."

"But if you know who they are, why wait? Why not just kill 'em?"

"I told you. Broken things can be repaired or set to a new purpose." She toyed with the ring on her finger. Bor flinched, expecting the ivy collar to tighten, but nothing happened. "And rotten timbers can serve as fuel. There may be a time for killing, certainly. Treachery must be punished, and the murder of the Erlking's son cannot be forgiven. But I pray we can be merciful." She paused. "I know what you are, Bor. Thief, cut-throat, friendless and faithless. The elves teach us that all sorrows and sins are forgotten in time. Now go."

"And what if I just walk out the south gate and never look back?"

"Then we will find you," said the ostler. "There's no place in Summerswell you can hide from us, once we set our mind upon you."

He didn't walk out the south gate. He headed for the tavern he knew of old, down by the tourney field.

The dog didn't want to follow him. The stupid animal had caught some scent, and kept snuffling around corners and trying to run off towards the north gate. Bor shouted at the dog to follow, and ended up grabbing the dog by the scruff of the neck and dragging him along. They passed a leatherworker's stall, closing up for the evening, and Bor spent some of Agyla's money on a leash.

"Now come on."

They entered the tavern. It was dark and low-ceilinged, a fire burning in the hearth, and the smell of spilled beer and sawdust took him back to the summer tourneys, simpler times. Bor always liked the tourneys, at least in theory. You hit the other man harder and faster than he hit you, and kept on hitting him until gold fell out. But he'd always had bad luck, and never won any real money – and in latter years, the other contestants often had magic, and that made it all pointless. Bor had ended up in this tavern to drink away his sorrows more than to celebrate.

Now, as then, the tavern was full of fighting men, but the mood was different. The merriment of the summer tourney was gone. Grim anticipation huddled by the fire, waiting for the thaw, like the city's unlikely luck was running out.

A few people in the common room had come from Necrad. You could spot them immediately; some were surrounded by attentive listeners, eager for accounts of the siege, while others sat alone or in small groups, shoulders hunched, heads bowed. But they all had the same look, the shock of knowing that the world held perils beyond the strength of any man. The burden of having seen magic, real magic, and knowing that what seemed like fanciful tales could be as real as stone or steel. Veterans of the last war had that look; Bor had worn that look after he'd trespassed on the Isle of Dawn.

He found a seat by three travellers marked by that look. Cu lay down under the table.

"The Yule Elf came early," said Bor, "and I've coin to spare. Want a drink?"

Agyla's money bought a round of ales, and suddenly Bor had a trio of new friends.

"Gerald of Ellscoast," said the first. He wore the remnants of a League uniform; the skin of his left cheek was blistered and peeling, his left hand wounded. He was pale, too, from years spent beneath the miasma. He shook the shoulder of the younger man by his side. "This young fellow's Remi, but don't expect much conversation from him." Like Gerald, Remi looked to have once been a guard in Necrad. He stared at the untouched ale in front of him, his lips moving soundlessly. He bore no visible scars, but of the three, Bor judged Remi the worst wounded.

"Magga," said the last, naming no home province. She was likely Rootless, like Bor. An old Roadhag, Rootless and toothless, surviving by her wits.

"What news from the north?" Beneath the table, Cu pressed against Bor's leg, as if listening to the tale.

Gerald did most of the telling. He'd been a guard in the Garrison, and boasted that he'd seen the coming and going of the great lords and councillors. Magga, though, was a dead-ender who patrolled the Charnel fields outside the city, keeping the dead from rising. The necromiasmic clouds that hung above Necrad caused corpses to rise as revenants over and over until someone stuck a spear in them.

"None of us saw it coming," said Gerald. "There was talk of trouble with the Wood Elves, over the blood trade – and truth be told, we were at fault there. Damnable thieves."

Bor said nothing. He'd been part of the blood trade.

"An elf-prince had me, once," cackled Magga. She peeled back her collar to show off an old bite mark, the scar paler than the rest. "Nearly drank me dry, but it paid for my passage."

"Then the Lammergeier comes back, and he brings word there's a Wilder army coming out of the wild wood. So the Nine – all of them that can be called, Lord Gundan and Princess Laerlyn and the Lady Berys and Master Blaise and the Lammergeier – they hold council with Lord Vond, and it's agreed they'll parlay with the Wilder, and see if they can find a peaceful accord. Out of friendship for Thurn, you see? They fought alongside the Wilder against Lord Bone, and I can see I don't need to tell you, Bor, that the bonds forged on the Road are strong indeed."

"The Road makes kinfolk of all men", agreed Bor, quoting an old proverb. Most folk in Summerswell travelled the Road so rarely that they attributed all sorts of customs to it, like the belief that travelling companions were fated to become fast friends. Nonsense, of course – and Gerald spouting it made him a fool in Bor's eyes. But he kept his mouth shut, and listened.

"So the Lammergeier and Gundan and Master Blaise rode forth, and Earl Duna of the New Provinces with 'em."

"I—, I—" Remi tried to speak, but all that came out were little syllables like hiccups.

"Aye, Remilard here was the Lammergeier's own banner-bearer, and rode with him. I watched them from the walls that morning, and—" Gerald's eyes were shining bright "—it was a thing to behold, indeed. The Nine riding forth, their banners flying in the morning sun."

"Only three of 'em," muttered Magga. Gerald ignored her. A small crowd had gathered around the table.

"But they were betrayed," continued Gerald. "Wilder ambushed 'em at Bavduin, and slew Lord Gundan unjustly. The Lammergeier carried his friend's body from the battlefield. So, there we were in Necrad, no more than six thousand of us, and only the Intercessors could count the number of Wilder marching towards us. We knew no help could come from Summerswell in time, but the Wood Elves of Dawn put aside their quarrels with Lord Vond and came to our aid just in time."

Gerald was clearly warming to his audience. He downed another beer, and more of Agyla's coins went behind the bar. Bor ordered some strips of dried meat, too, and passed them down under the table. "Even with their help, we were hard-pressed to hold the city. For six years I dwelt in Necrad, and I tell you, I saw strange sights in those years. The unquiet dead, monsters from the Pits. Thought I'd seen horrors, but those six years were nothing – nothing! – compared to six days on the walls. Slaughter and wild magic! Men like beasts, beasts with the eyes of men, and they had Death itself leading them! I saw him! A walking corpse, but not just one of the common dead!"

"I put down enough of 'em," added Magga, "and what the Wilder had weren't ordinary walkers, no." She shuddered. "The dead shouldn't *talk*. They weren't corpses – they were men who'd *come back*. Not right. Not right at all."

Only one who'd spent too much time in Necrad would think there was a normal sort of walking corpse.

Gerald ignored her. "The Lammergeier was everywhere, black sword red with the blood of our enemies, but even he was not enough. We had to fall back. We yielded the outer wall, first, retreating to the walls of the Garrison." He illustrated the course of the battle in spilled beer, tracing a larger circle to indicate the perimeter of the city, and a smaller handprint for the Garrison enclave.

"We held out as long as we could, but our numbers dwindled. Friends taken by arrow or claw or sorcery. And with each death, our lines shrank. When we could no longer hold the inner walls, we retreated to the Citadel." A thumbprint in the beer. "And then we were ordered to the harbour, where our ships waited. I think, at the end, Lord Vond still hoped that the Nine would find a way to save us, but then word came that Prince Maedos had fallen in battle, and that the Citadel would soon be overrun."

A murmur ran through the crowd. "Have the Wilder taken Necrad from us?" asked one. "The Erlking's son died for us!" cried another.

"I did not see the end," said Gerald, "but there were too few defenders left to hold against the enemy. The Intercessors blessed us with a fair wind and it carried us to safety. Well was the Gulf of Tears named, for we wept bitterly for our fallen friends, and for the loss of Necrad."

"Any word of the Lammergeier?" asked Bor.

"I heard that he was with Prince Maedos when the prince was slain. They fell side by side, fighting against a host of foes." Gerald climbed on his chair, wobbling precariously, and raised his glass. "To fallen heroes!"

"To the fallen!" chorused some in the crowd, but not all. Disbelief was plain on the face of others – the Lammergeier could not have perished. The Nine could not have fallen.

Bor stayed seated while the cheers echoed around the tavern.

The dead-ender leaned over. "I was there, y'know. We left after the Garrison ships, me and Remi. We saw it all." Her gaze flickered to the last of Agyla's coin. "Magga knows. Magga knows."

He slid a coin across the bar to her.

"What happened?"

"Y'ken the stone dragons?"

"Big statues around the walls of Necrad." He'd only ever seen them from a distance, but he'd heard tales. During the Siege of Necrad, their fire had kept the armies of the League at bay. Didn't matter how strong you were, or how fast, or how much armour you wore, not against the magic fire.

Magga cackled. "Many's the time I camped in their shadow. You could feel the heat in 'em. Best way to stay warm up there, some nights, even though everyone said the dragons died with Bone. But they came back." She tipped over a candle, hot wax hissing across Gerald's beer-drawn map. "The dragons woke. The Wilder burned."

"So who rules Necrad now?"

Magga swept up the coins. "The Uncrowned King."

He was about to ask her who this might be when a voice hailed him from across the room.

Chapter Five

"Bor? Is that Bor?" said a man, pushing through the crowd. "Remember me? Forwin of Westermarch? We fought together in the Riverlands, remember?"

His scabby face made easier heraldry than any banner or painted shield. "Forwin the Scratcher?"

"The same." The mercenary gripped Bor's arm in greeting, then snatched his hand away. "Sorry, sorry. There's one on your shoulder."

"You're still seeing them, then?" Forwin had been struck by a curse-charm that made him hallucinate insects everywhere he went. Bor had assumed the Scratcher had killed himself long ago.

"Aye. I know they're just illusion. I know that." Forwin glanced at Bor's shoulder again and froze. "Gah, it's like a glass scorpion, and it's looking at me like it's about to pounce. If it stings me, I'll turn to glass and shatter. It's not real, I know, I know, but . . ."

Bor reached up and brushed the imaginary insect off his shoulder. "Just a stupid trick."

"Give me a moment," said Forwin. Gingerly, he brought his left hand up to his eye. His fist was clenched, but not tightly – he was holding something in his palm. He squinted, and then visibly relaxed. "It's not there. I see that now." He exhaled and grinned.

"Come on, share a drink with us." He tried to drag Bor towards a table in the corner.

"I've spent all my coin," said Bor, "and I've a bed waiting for me at the palace."

"The palace," marvelled Forwin. "You have come up in the world since last we met. Going to Necrad paid off, then, I take it?"

"Hardly," said Bor.

"I was going to go," said Forwin, "but I thought to myself, what if there are real glass scorpions there? Who knows what's down in the Pits?"

"Bloody magic," spat Bor. "The bane of honest men."

"Not always. Look." Forwin opened his left hand for a moment, giving Bor a glimpse of a charmstone nestling in his palm. "Pierces illusions." Cu pressed his cold nose into Forwin's hand, snuffling as if the charmstone was a tasty treat. Forwin hastily put the treasure away.

"Where'd you steal that?"

"I didn't," said Forwin, almost shyly. "I earned it. Come, have a drink with us. It'll be worth your while."

The Scratcher's companions were all Westermarchers, like him. Like Bor, too, although Bor had long ago gone Rootless, taking to the freedom of the Road. He had little love for Westermarch. It was an arid borderland that bred a sullen stock. The Westermarchers huddled together in their corner of the tavern, shunning the Arden-folk, talking to one another in low tones. Most were fighting men, but they bore no sign or colour that might mark them as soldiers of a particular noble. Brigands, maybe. In the light of the blazing hearth fire, they looked like devils.

He took the ale they offered, but sat apart from them. Forwin took a stool next to him, and Bor didn't like that. He always feared that Forwin's curse was catching. Absently, he rubbed Cu's furry head.

"So tell me," said Forwin, "what's waiting for you at the palace? You're hardly a guest of the Lord, and I can't imagine some noblewoman taking a shine to you."

"You're one to talk! Face like a ploughed field. No, I'm travelling with a knight, and he's a guest of Lord Tor."

"I'd not have thought you'd end up a servant. Dead in a ditch, more like. Does he keep you well, this knight?"

Bor scratched his neck. "Not that well."

"But you are sworn to serve him?" asked one of the other Westermarchers. Well-spoken, his voice a rich and practiced baritone. There was something familiar about his voice that Bor couldn't place.

"Something like that."

"Bound, then." Unlike Forwin's fractured, darting gaze, the Westermarcher gave Bor a steady look of appraisal. Bor shifted in his chair.

"He got me out of a bit of trouble," said Bor, "but his fighting days are long past. I don't want to lose my edge, so if there was other work about . . ."

"Who was your last employer, before this knight?" asked the Westermarcher.

Before Bor could answer, Forwin chimed in. "Last time we parted, Bor here was off to Necrad to seek his fortune, but it all went awry, he told me."

The Westermarcher reached over and passed a fresh mug to Bor. "Tell the tale." His voice was damnably familiar.

"Not much to it. Smuggled charmstones. Got caught."

"The law against the trade in magic is unjust. The Lords hoard power for themselves, and punish others who seek a scrap of sorcery. And how did the Lords come by this great bounty of magic treasures? By the deeds of the Nine, and the sacrifice of ordinary folk."

"You say you got caught working the blood trade?" asked another in disbelief. "Is the punishment for that not death?"

"By hanging," said the first man, who seemed to be in charge. "But some nooses come with longer ropes than others, and they are hard to cut. The world is changing, friend," said the Westermarcher. "The old order of things is a withered tree. It died when Necrad fell, but the Lords keep it propped up. Soon spring winds shall blow, and topple rotten things." He stood, his lanky frame unfolding to tower over the rest. He looked Bor up and down, then said, "Come with us."

Church bells sounded midnight. The Westermarchers left the tavern with Bor in tow. It was a clouded night. The main thoroughfare had lamps to light a traveller's way, and there were still a few stragglers on the streets – revellers leaving the taverns, beggars and streetwalkers, a few soldiers in the livery of the Lord of Arden keeping the peace. Instead of taking the lighted path, the Westermarchers led Bor down dark alleyways, and soon he was lost.

"Where the hell are we going?" he whispered to Forwin.

"Rest easy. You're among friends," replied the Scratcher. "It's not far, and they'll explain everything there."

Suddenly, Cu broke into wild barking. The dog capered about making an astounding din for so small a beast. Bor grabbed at the leash, but Cu tore free and ran around in a tight circle before darting behind a stack of barrels. He kept barking.

"Silence the animal!" ordered the leader of the Westermarchers.

"I'm trying," muttered Bor. "Shut up!" He picked up a stone, then thought better of it. He tried to crawl after Cu, but the gap was too narrow for his frame. "Be quiet!" he hissed at Cu.

The dog kept barking.

"It'll attract attention," hissed one through broken teeth. He had a knife in his hand.

Bor glared at him. "That's my dog," he rumbled. The Westermarcher scowled, but didn't press his luck. The knife vanished.

"Forwin, stay with Bor. We'll fetch you later," said the leader. He and the rest vanished into the dark.

Silence fell in the alleyway, broken only by Forwin scratching himself. It was too dark for Bor to see what the other man was doing, but he seemed to be crawling around examining the ground with his magic gemstone. Bor squatted down, leaning his back against the wall.

"They're everywhere," whined Forwin, "how do I know they're all illusions? What if one turns out to be real? Laying eggs in my ear. A foulness, a foulness."

The dog emerged from behind the stacked barrels, panting, his breath steaming in the cold air. Whatever the strange fit was, it had passed, and now the dog looked insufferably pleased with itself. He tried to lick Bor's face, but Bor shoved him away. He grabbed the end of the leash, and the dog tried to tug him away.

"The pair of you are curses," said Bor to the dog. "I have a *bed* waiting for me in the fucking *palace*, and instead I'm sitting here freezing in the alleyway waiting for – Erlking's bones, friends of the fucking Scratcher!"

Cu lay down next to him and offered his heavy head for a scratch.

He turned the coin over in his hand. He turned over the conversation in the tavern in his head.

"That's a strange dog," said Forwin, in a puzzled tone. He had the gemstone up to his eye again.

"He's not my dog," said Bor. "Stupid animal followed me all the way from Ellsport."

"Whose dog is it, then?"

The dog belonged Olva Forster, the Lammergeier's sister. The dog belonged to the woman Bor betrayed.

It was strange – he'd been interrogated about her for weeks by the Rangers, talked about her until his throat was raw, but he did not know what had become of her after Ellsport. Martens had given his word that she wouldn't be harmed, but Martens was a liar. And even if she'd reached Necrad, many awful fates waited there. Had Martens fed her to a vampire? Had she perished when the Wilder attacked? Or was she still alive?

He took out the last of the coins from Necrad. The strange metal caught the starlight, even though clouds blanketed the sky. The coin was heavy in his palm. The Lammergeier had given him a fortune to bring to Olva, and this was all that was left.

But Bor hadn't met the Lammergeier, or so said Agyla.

He'd met . . .

"The tall fellow in the tavern, the one who told us to wait here – who is he?"

"I don't know," said Forwin. "We were told not to ask his name."

"Did he give you that charmstone?"

"He did."

Bor stood. "I'm not waiting any longer. Show me where they went."

Neither Forwin nor the dog were willing to go. The Scratcher hung back, nervously protesting that they were supposed to wait until they were summoned. The dog kept whining and dragging on the leash. Bor had to force them both down the backstreets with curses and threats. Forwin pointed out the meeting place – a well-appointed townhouse, three storeys tall, with stone walls. The home of a prosperous merchant.

"There."

Light spilled out under the front door, and from behind the shuttered windows, but there was no sound.

Bor handed the dog's leash to Forwin, and strode up to knock on the door.

There was no answer. He pushed, and found the door was unbarred. A short hallway led to an oak-timbered dining room. A fire blazed in the grate, and a lit oil lamp hung above the long table, creaking as it swung slowly on its chain. The chairs had been pushed up against the walls. Many people could have gathered here, but the room was empty, the house silent.

On the table was a carved bowl, similar to the sacred cup in every chapel in every village across Summerswell. The grail of the Intercessors, used by the priests to commune with the spirits who ruled the fates of mortals. But this house was not a church, so what was the grail doing here? And no priest would leave a sacred cup unattended.

His skin crawled. Something unnatural had happened here, some movement of unseen powers and magics beyond his understanding. The house suddenly seemed not empty, but haunted. What had so alarmed those gathered here that they fled into the night?

"Forwin," he called over his shoulder, "what is this?"

Gingerly, he examined the bowl. Holy water had been spilled across the table, leaving only a shallow residue in the grail. The priests said there was good magic, the blessings of the Intercessors, the scholarly studies of the College Arcane, and evil magic, the sort wrought in Necrad, the conjurations of Witch Elves and the earthpower of the Wilder. To Bor, it was all unnatural, all equally disturbing. It made the world into a deceit. You couldn't fight it, couldn't overpower it through strength of arms. Anything involving magic made him feel weak, turned his bones to jelly. It wasn't right that a spilled bowl of water should hold such power.

He threw it down hastily. It rolled and fell to the floor.

He prowled around the house. Whoever had been here – the Westermarchers and whoever else they'd met with – had melted away. There were signs of recent habitation – beds in the servants' quarters, food in the pantry, a stinking bedpan – but there was no one here.

"Forwin!" he called again.

"He can't answer you." Bor spun around to find Agyla standing in the doorway leading to the dining hall. The Ranger was dressed in grubby rags, and she'd shed the dark cloak she'd worn as long as Bor had known her. She still spoke commandingly. "But I did not strike him hard. He's still alive."

"Did you follow me here?"

"Yes. Though I hoped to catch a better prize than Forwin of Westermarch."

"You know him?" Of all the events of the night, it seemed strangest that the Scratcher should have come to the notice of great powers.

"We watch everyone. The Intercessors aid us." She did not say that like an ordinary person might beg for Intercession, but with certainty. Bor shuddered at the thought of unseen things moving behind the curtain of the world, watching and whispering. He remembered the street in the Capital, just before the Rangers captured him. The invisible *presence* that had reached out of the heavens and struck him down.

"But they got away. Everyone's gone," he said.

Agyla scowled. "So they did, and that is a mystery." She looked up at Bor. "The men you met in the tavern are nothing. Swords for hire, disgruntled troublemakers. It is the traitors who use such men that I hunt."

"One of the Westermarchers in the tavern — it was the Lammergeier. The false Lammergeier. The one I met at Highfield."

"Are you certain?"

"Aye."

Agyla spoke a word in a language Bor did not know, and suddenly the room was full, dark figures hurrying in through all the doors. Some were people he'd passed on the street earlier, who had seemed to be beggars or revellers. Others were strangers. With a flurry of activity, the Rangers spread out through the house, sweeping through the rooms.

Only the ostler remained.

"How did this go so wrong? We've been watching the Westermarchers since they arrived in Arden. We could have dealt with them days ago, but we were ordered to wait, in the hopes they would lead us to more traitors. Now we have nothing."

"Less than we hoped, but not nothing," said Agyla.

The ostler bent down and picked up the grail.

"I know this cup," he said, "it was stolen three nights ago."

"I was warned," said Agyla, "of blasphemous rites that allow even the unanointed to see visions in the waters. What if the grail was stolen for that purpose? They might have seen the shadow of an Intercessor, and guessed that we were close at hand."

"Perhaps," said the ostler. "But there is another explanation, one that does not cast blame on the spirits. A simpler explanation, and much more likely." He pointed at Bor. "This rogue failed us."

Bor bristled. "I did what Agyla told me."

"Who knows what he let slip in the tavern?" The ostler glared at Bor. "And I heard his mongrel whelp's racket from a mile off. We have no time to waste on a Rootless wretch, and his life was forfeit years ago. He is useless to us, but knows too much to be cut free. End him."

The only weapon to hand was the grail-cup, and it would make a fine bludgeon if it came to it. Grab it, smash it into the ostler's smug face, break him open and spill his secrets across the floor. The ostler twitched aside his cloak and laid hand to a dagger at his belt, daring Bor to lunge. *Overconfident prick*, thought Bor, *I'll show him—*

The ivy-collar tightened.

"Bor did as instructed. I do not fault him, and I do not discard things that can be repaired." Agyla took the bowl from the ostler and wiped it clean. "Bor. Take the prisoner back to the palace."

The collar cut off too much of his breath for him to speak, so Bor merely nodded. He stumbled out into the corridor and hoisted the Scratcher onto his shoulder. It was a long walk back to the palace, and Forwin was no small burden. He was about to set off when a thought occurred to him, and he dragged Forwin back inside. He pushed open the door to the dining room again.

"Where's my dog?" he demanded.

"I saw no dog," Agyla replied.

But the ostler grinned, and Bor did not like the man's cruel smile. Later, he found the empty leash discarded in a gutter.

The palace of Arden reflected the fortunes of the city. At the heart of the palace was the old fortress, its bones older than Summerswell. The Cleft of Ard was the way to the dwarflands, the gateway to the north. This was not the first time that men had fought for control of Arden, and Bor doubted it would be the last. But the thick walls and crenelated towers of the fortress were almost lost beneath the fanciful towers, the vaulted feast-halls and the magnificent chapels built during the years of the Erlking's peace. Successive Lords of Arden had profited from their city's position straddling the trade route, and their wealth had employed dwarven stonemasons and architects.

The grandfather of the present Lord had been a lover of theatre (and, by all accounts, of actors), and commanded the building of a grand theatre within the palace. It was half-finished when Lord Bone's war began; when the Lords of Summerswell mustered for their counterattack on Necrad, horses had been stabled in the stalls, and the stage piled high with supplies. Now it was finished, and decorated with statues and marble taken from the ruins of Necrad.

He trudged across the wide field towards the one lighted window. In the far tower. At some point, the palace had swallowed up the green fields on the banks of the river, and a tributary river too, which now flowed through an underground culvert. This remnant of the field was now surrounded by high walls on all sides. He passed a forest of banners, the arms of each lord or knight emblazoned on their respective standards. In the dark, the banners were unreadable. The way they flapped and creaked in the wind put Bor in mind of giant crows.

Sir Rhuel was full of merriment and gossip. It set Bor's teeth on edge.

"Oh, it's hilarious. The Bishop of Claen – do you know the Bishop of Claen?"

"I don't know the Bishop of Claen. I don't know any bishops." Somewhere in the palace, in some forgotten dungeon, Agyla had imprisoned the Scratcher. There wasn't even any need to torture the poor bastard – he came with his own torments. All she needed to do was wait, and he'd break.

"You should. Some are bores, some boors, but the boors keep excellent tables. I've always made it a rule to befriend fat bishops. Where was I? Ah, Claen said it was like six men trying to get through a door at the same time. Three of them rush and get stuck in the doorway. The other three know there's an ogre on the other side, so they're all very polite – after you, I insist! No, it's your right to go first, you should lead the way. And so on."

"What door?"

"Oh, don't be so literal. The door is the Cleft of Ard, the Road north to Necrad, and the fools are the Lords." Sir Rhuel sat down heavily on the bed. "The last war was all doom and despair. Either Lord Bone fell, or all the lands of elves and mortals would be plunged into eternal darkness, everything would be lost, woe and nightmares and dire things for ever until the world's ending, and so on? What would happen if we won, if we *captured* Lord Bone's city was something no one considered."

"But it's different this time."

"Precisely. Now it's about something much more important than mere survival. Holding Necrad means treasure, and magic, and the virgin lands of the New Provinces. And this time, they won't share control of the city with the Nine or the Wood Elves or the Dwarves. Now, half the Lords see Necrad as a prize, and are rushing to retake it. The others see danger. You can walk from Arden to Necrad stepping only on graves, for so many perished on the landward Road during the war." Rhuel chuckled. "And there aren't enough ships to make the sea a safe option. Oh, the Lords of Ellscoast or the Crownland could set sail, but only with a fraction of their strength, and who knows what awaits them in the north?" He lay back and yawned. "Maybe Necrad is open and defenceless, its strength exhausted by the Wilder, ready to be plucked by whichever Lord acts first. Maybe it'll be a second bloody Siege without the Nine to save them. Oh, we are well out of it, you and I. But it'll be a delight to watch." Rhuel's head tipped back. Sleepily, he added: "Over there on the desk. It's done." He started to snore.

On the desk were sheets covered in Rhuel's sloppy handwriting. Bor had never learned to read well, but he could guess what they were.

A weapon, Agyla had called it. A weapon that wouldn't kill anyone.

He leafed through the pages, and caught a few words.

> ... *vile bird of carrion plucked out our eyes,*
> *So we saw only his bright and cunning lies.*
> *Now truth comes too late, bought at a bitter price:*
> *The blood of the dawnshield, Erlking's kinsman*
> *Defender against darkness, his light now shattered*
> *Noontime shadow follows after dawn, heralds*
> *A time of reckoning. Once his father, blessed Erlking*
> *Anointed the eyes of prophets with water of Arshoth*
> *Showed them the holy ones, the weavers of fate,*
> *Opened their eyes to bright realms unseen*
> *And revealed to the Lords the paths of righteousness.*
> *Now his son's blood becomes a sacred sacrifice*
> *It anoints our eyes so we too might see*
> *The folly of mortals.*
> *Now we see the Lammergeier*
> *Uncloaked at last.*

CHAPTER SIX

The week of the fall of Arden dawned bright and crisp. The sun turned the snow-capped mountains rose-gold, the morning air so clear that all the peaks of the Dwarfholt were visible, marching off in serried ranks into the north. Swelling light drove the stars from the sky; the brightest lingered a little longer, then they too faded.

Sir Rhuel slept late, eventually waking like a startled walrus. He heaved himself out of bed and hurried to his writing desk, as if worried that his poem had melted away in the night. He considered his work of the night before with a sober eye.

"Did you read any of it?" he asked Bor.

"A little."

"And how did it make you feel?"

"I'm not one for poems."

"Oh, come now! You may profess to be a soulless brute, but there was a time when I was just as callous. I was the worst knight in Summerswell, convinced that there was no meaning or morality in the world, that only strength and steel mattered. Then I was imprisoned – justly – and found respite in tale-telling. The stories I wrote shaped me, and they have shaped others, too. A whole generation, of which you are part. Dig deep, Bor, and tell me."

Bor mustered the fullness of his wit and insight.

"Bad?"

"A start! And it is a reaction I share. The presence – nay, the *existence* of heroes enchants the world. It exalts us all, makes us think that we too possess some spark of greatness. The deeds of the Nine – as related in my song, if I may be immodest – inspired people when they needed hope. But that was a young man's work." He picked up the sheaf of papers, flicked through them, then cast them down and sighed ostentatiously. "This is the reverse. It strips away those illusions, and shows the Nine to be as corrupt and venal as the rest of us. It shows that there is no such thing as a selfless, shining hero. It says that there may be enchantment in the land, but it is not for the likes of us – that we shall never be great, that the songs have lied to us. It is bitter medicine. But at least it is honest."

Bor furrowed his brow. "But ... it ain't honest. You don't know what happened in Necrad, not truly. Maybe the Lammergeier did slay the Prince of Dawn, but you don't know how or why, or if the elf had it coming. You don't know—"

"It's a deeper honesty. Don't quibble over facts," snapped Rhuel, before returning to his so-solemn contemplation of his own work. "It's true that the conception of this piece was purely practical. A commission from our unspeakable friend. But I feel like I touched on something deeper as my themes developed, something grim and dark. It's an elegy for lost innocence, really. Once ... may I quote myself?"

"Can I stop you?"

"'*From his city of Necrad, Lord Bone sent forth an evil host to despoil the land. Doom was at hand. Nine arose in answer.*'

"Once, there was evil in the north and good in the south; a host of monsters commanded by a sinister Dark Lord, and a few unlikely heroes, brave and true, who won the day through luck and courage. But such stories are for simpler times. There will be no last-minute salvation, no victory unlooked for. The days of legend are gone and the great days of heroes are passing, and it is time to let go of illusions. Ah me."

Rhuel sighed again as he read through his poem, then he folded the pages and tucked them away. "I should eat. I must eat. Fortify myself. They demand a full theatrical performance of my new poem within the week." He patted Bor's shoulder as he ambled by.

Bor spent the day searching the alleyways and backstreets of Arden. He went looking for the dog but found only Rangers. They seemed to be on every street now. Faces like the ostler, a light in their eyes like they were looking out at a different world. How many of these secret spies were there? He passed a blacksmith he'd visited before, years ago, and saw the smith bent over the anvil, bright sparks leaping into the air. Then the smith glanced up, and there again Bor saw that same look. The ostler threatened to murder Bor; did the other Rangers have the same thought?

Maybe he was imagining all these secret Rangers, just as he imagined the invisible presence of Intercessors. Every gust of wind made him think of unseen wings; every swirl of dust made him flinch.

Twice, he passed the south gate, saw the Road spilling out towards the distant hills. Twice, he thought about walking out that gate. But each time, the ostler's threat came back to him – *There's no place in Summerswell you can hide from us, once we set our mind upon you*. The ivy seemed to tighten, and he imagined the hooded shapes waiting in the hills.

Twice, he turned away.

In this fashion, the short day passed, ending in a sunset as glorious as the dawn that began it. Bor returned to the palace. There was no sign of Agyla; Sir Rhuel was already snoring.

The next day, too, went quietly. And the next. And the one after that.

One by one, the Rangers seemed to vanish from the streets. It was not that the old woman was gone from the tavern or the blacksmith abandoned his forge, but their faces appeared to change; whatever quality Bor had seen in them was gone. There was one exception – the murderous ostler, he really did vanish. Bor passed the stables one afternoon, and in his place was an amiable young lad without a trace of guile.

Agyla was still at the palace – Bor saw her one evening, across a snowy courtyard – but she paid him no heed. Bor could only guess that the disaster with the Westermarchers had soured the Rangers on him, or that whatever business they had with him was concluded, and good riddance to them.

He felt more like himself than he had in months, and it took him another day to figure out why.

All his life, dogged as it was by bad luck and hardship, Bor had lived by a simple creed: survive. Everything else – friendship, pleasure, honour, anything you cared to name, all that was secondary. First, stay alive, then see what comes next. The Road had taught him to be tough, for the toughest bastard was the one who lived while others perished. Mercenary work had taught him how to survive in a fight, how to avoid danger and how to appear dangerous so others gave way. And he'd learned a bitter lesson at the hands of the elves, when they'd marked him with the ivy-collar. He couldn't fight magic, and the only way to survive was to stay away from it. Don't fight battles you cannot hope to win.

Then he'd met the Lammergeier. There could be no more clear-cut a case of a hopeless battle – when the mightiest warrior in all the land tells you do something, you do it without question. The Lammergeier had sent him to Olva, and that's when it had all gone wrong.

For Olva was too stubborn to know when a battle was unwinnable. She should have given her bloody son up for dead and gone home, but she kept wanting to fight. She'd have gotten herself killed if Bor hadn't given her over to Martens, and dragged Bor down too, no doubt. Olva Forster didn't understand how to survive. If she wasn't already dead, it was a bloody miracle.

Abandoning Olva was the one time Bor had felt guilty about surviving. Why, he couldn't say. Olva had saved his life in the Fossewood, but when you got into accounting of that sort, you quickly ran up unpayable debts. Others had saved Bor's life over the years, and he'd left them to die in return. Survive first. Everything else after.

Was it fear of the Lammergeier's vengeance? Bor had dreamed of the Lammergeier hunting him, of that dreadful helm and the black sword. But in those dreams, it wasn't the threat of the sword, it was the Lammergeier's *disappointment*. Back then, Bor hadn't believed in much, but he'd believed the stories of the Nine. The Lammergeier had been terrifying, but he was also a living legend, a hero. And he'd seen some worth in Bor.

Or maybe it was just the damn dog, following him down the road, reminding him of what he'd done.

Whatever it was, he was free of it now. He couldn't say if it was Agyla's claim that he'd met an imposter, or Sir Rhuel's poem, but the myth had no power over him any more. The poem turned the Lammergeier's murder of the Prince of Dawn into a condemnation of all humanity; everything mortals did was tainted by greed or anger or pride, even the deeds of heroes. But Bor was one of the few people who'd seen the other side of the elves, too. Sir Rhuel's poem might paint Prince Maedos as the saintly defender, the shield of dawn that guarded the lands of Summerswell, but Bor had met the man, and the prince was a bastard.

They were all bastards. Bor was no worse than anyone else, save for his bad luck. There were no true heroes out there, just rich bastards on thrones, or cruel bastards with swords, or magic bastards with spells, or stupid bastards squatting in farms watching life go by. Sir Rhuel might talk about making people see clearly and stripping away their illusions, but Bor had lost his innocence long ago.

The world was full of bastards. He'd been right all along.

On the fourth night, he was roused by an uproar. Thunder

without lightning boomed from somewhere close at hand. At first, Bor thought they were under attack; he watched guards rush across the courtyard as if running to confront some foe. But it all seemed to be a false alarm. No invading army assaulted the palace. The tumult died away.

The thought struck Bor that he could sneak away in the confusion. While everyone was distracted, he could slip out the south gate. But the damnable cord about his neck held him back. As long as he was bound by magic, he could never be free.

In the dead of the fifth night, Agyla roused him.

"Stay quiet. Follow."

She led him to the prison cell where Forwin the Scratcher lay on the stone floor. The poor bastard had tried to gouge his eyes out. It took Bor a moment to be sure that the Scratcher was still on this side of the grey lands.

"He conspired with traitors. This punishment is just."

"Did he tell you anything useful?"

Agyla did not answer. "Bring him," she ordered.

Bor picked up the Scratcher's limp body and hoisted him onto his shoulders. The man was at least a stone lighter than he had been five days ago. He followed Agyla through another maze of cellars, then into a walled herb garden, the beds rimed with frost. Forwin stirred at the touch of the cold air.

"Where am I bringing him?" Digging a grave would be hard work with the ground all frozen, but Bor did not doubt that these were Forwin's last minutes of life. Sir Rhuel had hinted that this was the custom of the Rangers, that those who encountered them vanished. That ostler would surely have left Bor in an unmarked grave if Agyla had not ordered him spared, and Bor suddenly wondered if that was but a stay of execution. He imagined Agyla telling him to dig two graves, and what could he do to resist her?

They left the palace. Following the course of the fast-following river, they passed under the arched gate and left the city too. Agyla kept walking, a dim shape in the dark, and Bor stumbled under the weight of the Scratcher. The stones were slippery with ice.

"Why not just dump him in the river and be done with it?"

"Quiet," said Agyla. She glanced over her shoulder. "He will not die tonight. I told you, we are not needlessly cruel."

They came to a copse of leafless trees. The stars shone more brightly here, like lances of light. Despite the clear night, it was strangely warm in the wood, the air heavy with strange perfume. In the starlight, Bor could see hooded figures ahead of them, other Rangers all travelling towards the heart of the forest. They joined this strange procession.

For a time they marched in silence, the only noise Bor's huffing, but then he became aware of distant singing. He could not say when it began. It was as though it had always been there, in the back of his mind, but only now could he hear it fully. Clear voices rose in the starlit air. The singers approached, and Bor saw that they were Wood Elves. All were marvellously fair, hair of silver or gold glimmering like precious metals, faces alight with laughter. They wore cloaks of grey much like those of the Rangers, but where the Rangers were hard and Road-weary, bent by many worries, these elves were merry. Ahead, in a clearing, were trestle tables spread with food and pitchers of wine. A fire blazed, a stag roasted on a spit.

"A wandering company," whispered Agyla, "the same fellowship I met at Castle Bayard." She glanced sidelong at Bor. "Few mortals are blessed to meet elves in this manner. Their ways may seem strange, but remember: they are firstborn of the world. All the years since the founding of Summerswell are but a moment to them, and they shall not notice when you and I are dead and gone. Be respectful of the elder ones, and they may reward you."

She pointed to a clearing. "Leave Forwin with them."

There were other wounded folk in the wood. Their wounds were fresh, a day or so old – and hideous. Some cradled truncated limbs; others were bruised all over, and clutched their bellies. They'd been crushed, Bor guessed, by some terrible force. Innards like broken glass, they wouldn't last long.

"The black sword," one muttered, rocking back and forth. "The black sword."

Bor added the Scratcher to this muster of the maimed. "What'll happen to him?"

"He was wounded by a weapon of the Enemy," said an elf. He carried a flask of wine. He knelt and gave Forwin a drink, and the Scratcher slumped back against a tree, a blissful smile spreading over his scabby face. "We may take him with us, and heal him if we can."

"You can break spells like that?" blurted Bor. If they could free the Scratcher from his curse, then surely they could remove the cursed ivy-collar.

The elf laughed. "Those of Necrad? Sometimes, if the stars are right, we can sing a counter-charm to lift such curses. But I see you have quite a different spell at your throat, mortal. The sigil marks you as one who offended against the Erlking. That spell I would not break even if I could."

"I have news from the mortal lands," said Agyla, "The traitors—"

"Always dour, always hasty, Agyla! Will you fill your short span with worries, rushing hither and yon? There is lotus-wine to be shared, and songs to be sung."

"There is no time for merriment, Dian. Necrad has been lost and the Nine have turned against us. More may be lost unless we act swiftly."

"All will be lost, and all will be found again. There is always time." The elf raised his flask. Even the faintest sniff of it made Bor's head spin. "Drink now, and forget your fears."

"My fears are such that they would follow me even into dream," said Agyla. "Please, we need your help. We have lost the trail of the traitors. Even the Intercessors may not find them in time – they have run to earth."

"Call, and we shall answer. And know this – not all the Nine have turned traitor. *Tae'eyma morthus a'cailia.*" With that, Dian drank deep from his flask, then laughed and danced away into the darkness of the wood.

What the elvish words meant, Bor did not know, but Agyla let out a little gasp. She turned to him. "Go back to the palace, Bor," she ordered.

"What about this thing?" He jabbed a finger at the ivy-cord. "If I serve you well enough, you've got to tell 'em to take it off, aye?"

"And what would you do if it were removed? Return to a worthless life of banditry and debauchery? There is no virtue in that. Go back, Bor."

She hurried away towards the clearing.

But Bor did not leave. He lingered, hiding in the undergrowth. At first, he stayed purely out of spite, staying because she told him to go, staying because it was unfair that the Scratcher should find relief while Bor continued to suffer. But then he stayed to spy on the strange revels.

Once all the wounded had been given a drink, the other Rangers and the elves shared draughts of lotus-wine. The elves grew merrier, but the mortals who drank it were affected in a different way. Some fell down and lay insensate on the mossy floor of the clearing, eyes staring at the canopy of stars. Others seemed to wander into visions of the elder days, speaking in the elf-tongue and singing tales Bor did not know. He saw the ostler through the trees, and he barely recognised the man, his sullen face alight with joy. Bor told himself that he did not envy the Ranger, that the visions brought on by the elf-wine was just another trick. The Rangers might think themselves above everyone else, with their secrets and their magic and the way they toyed with the fates of the powerful, but they were thralls to their own stories too.

None of them offered Bor a drink.

Instead, he followed Agyla, and found her by the fireside, sitting with the most beautiful woman Bor had ever seen. The woman was an elf, dressed head to toe in silver mail. Where the other elves were carefree and feckless, moods shifting like light through wind-tossed leaves, this elf-maid was still as a statue. By her side was a longbow of dragonhorn, and . . . by all the hells, he recognised that bow from the stories.

Morthus, the executioner's bow.

This must be the Princess of the Everwood. Laerlyn of the Nine.

Knees shaking, mouth dry, Bor crept closer to eavesdrop.

". . . on the Isle of Dawn the day the fortress was destroyed," said the princess. "He was at Castle Duna a week later. If he has come down from the north, then he must have done so in secret, and that is not like Aelfric."

"The Lammergeier is in Arden, your highness. We came close to capturing him." Agyla paced. Bor knew her well enough at this point to see the frustration that boiled in her. "Many will gather to the banner of the Lammergeier if he declares against us. For the safety of the realm, he must be stopped."

"Aelfric," said Laerlyn, "is not to be to be slain. I say this for the benefit of you as much as him – believe me when I tell you that Aelfric *restrained* himself in your last encounter. If you find him again, summon me at once. *Immediately*, you understand? You will not confront him, or question him. I must speak to him first."

"I shall try, your highness. Other efforts may yet strangle the rebellion here in its crib. Without hope of victory, it may be he will surrender quietly."

"You are mistaken if you think Aelfric would ever abandon a cause he believes to be right. And he has never in his life done anything *quietly*." Laerlyn smiled sadly, then looked over at where Bor was hidden. "Few mortals do."

"The presence of the Lammergeier tells me that confrontation is coming. Give me the aid of your Wandering Company, milady. Between my Rangers and your elves, and the forces commanded by Lords I trust, we shall have the strength to secure Arden. "

"No," said Laerlyn, "That way lies more bloodshed. I shall not have that, not while there is still hope of avoiding it." She looked down and thought for a moment. "I shall go to Arden as my father's representative, and call the nobles there together. When all are gathered, your Rangers detain those you know to be treasonous, and any who refused my summons."

"There are traitors among the commoners as well the Lords!" objected Agyla.

"I do not doubt it. But I would prefer to pull up a handful of tall weeds than set fire to the garden."

Agyla scowled. "The gardens of the north are thick with weeds. So many that I cannot guarantee your safety. The enemy has weapons out of Necrad—"

"Oh no. Never has one of the Nine been threatened with weapons out of Necrad," said Laerlyn in a tone dryer than the desert. She scratched her cheek with *Morthus*. "Whatever, oh, whatever will I do."

"You are the Erlking's daughter, and I am sworn to protect your house," said Agyla, failing to hide her frustration. "One member of the royal house has already perished at the hands of these traitors – I shall not see another fall while in my care."

"My brother's death was by his own hand more than any other. But here is not the place for such talk."

Agyla bowed. The sounds of the feast grew softer, the fires dimmed, and a cold wind blew. The elves were *withdrawing* in a way that Bor could not understand, but he knew a chance was vanishing with him.

He plunged into the clearing. "Begging your—"

Then he was on the ground, head ringing, nose bleeding. Agyla stood over him. The ivy-collar clenched.

"Idiot! I told you to go back to the city!" she snarled. "It is forbidden to trespass here!"

"Release him," ordered Laerlyn.

"This is Bor," said the Ranger, "the one I spoke of."

"This is not the first time you have trespassed in a place held sacred by the Firstborn." Laerlyn sounded amused by the intrusion, or at least tolerant. "I know my brother's mark."

Bor rolled to his knees before her, trying to act as courteous as possible as he gulped for air. He wiped his bloody nose.

"Begging your pardon, lady, but I didn't mean to. It was—"

"Quiet!" Agyla snarled. "Your highness, forgive me. This wretch did not know the law."

"Let him be," said Laerlyn.

Agyla stepped back, but there was a blade in her hand, and Bor did not doubt she would use it.

"You served Lyulf Martens," said Laerlyn. "I have heard this tale before, told by another. You smuggled relics out of Necrad, and trespassed on the Isle of Dawn." She tapped her fingers on the grip of *Morthus*. "Martens is dead, but he served Berys of the Nine. Did you know that?"

"No."

"No, *your highness*," prompted Agyla.

"I knew Martens served the Lady, but I didn't know that was Berys."

"You were deceived." Laerlyn looked down at him, and Bor dared to see pity in her luminous eyes. "And you were again deceived when you were sent to visit Olva Forster. The one who masqueraded as the Lammergeier – he too serves Berys in another guise. Tell me, Bor, how does that make you feel? What would you do, if the one who lied to you stood before you?"

Bor swallowed. He did not know why the elven princess was asking him such questions, or what insight she thought he might offer. If he offended the princess, she would never free him from the collar, and Agyla would not be gentle in her use of the ring, either. His life might hang on his next words.

But what to say? He had never even laid eyes on Berys, and had never guessed that she was the Lady that Martens spoke of with fear. He knew her only from the tales, the daring thief who'd scaled the Wailing Tower, who'd saved the Nine time and again. He thought of Baron Bayard's daughter, named for Berys.

But the tales were lies. Pretty words made up by Sir Rhuel. Stories made up to deceive.

"If I had a sword in my hand, lady – and no collar round my throat to hold me back – then ... truthfully, your highness, I'd kill her."

"Without hesitation? Without mercy?"

"Always best to strike first."

"And if she said that she lied to you with the best of intentions? That she was still your friend, even if she had been untrue?"

Out of the corner of his eye, Bor saw Agyla frown, but he pressed on, hoping to impress the princess. "I wouldn't listen to her, your highness. I wouldn't want to be deceived again. I'd strike my enemy down, and not doubt myself."

"Indeed." Laerlyn back, becoming remote again. "Few mortals do." She turned to Agyla. "Make what preparations you think necessary. I shall arrive in Arden tomorrow."

The Ranger bowed. "Then Arden shall never fall."

"Among the elves, 'never' is not a word to be used lightly."

Bor plucked up his courage. "'Twas your brother who put this ivy-curse on me, your highness. I'd be very grateful if you'd lift the spell."

Laerlyn lifted her gaze to the stars. "A little while ago, I visited the Lords of Summerswell. It is the custom that when one of the royal house of the Everwood attends a court, they may choose a condemned prisoner and grant a pardon, demonstrating the Erlking's mercy. That privilege was accorded to me. Do you know who I chose?"

The story was familiar to him from *The Song of the Nine*. "Berys. She was to be hung, and you freed her."

"Then know I have only so much mercy left in me."

They walked back through the suddenly empty forest. No sign remained of the merrymaking of the elves, not even the ashes of the bonfires. They passed the ring of toadstools where Bor had left Forwin with the other wounded. The circle was empty.

Agyla toyed with her ring, twisting it this way and that. He braced himself for the noose to tighten.

"You did well enough there, Bor," she said.

"Too much to hope that she'd lift the spell, I suppose."

"For now, yes, But I shall say this – the Intercessors weave different fates for us all. Some are destined to be heroes, and their names are known in story and song. Others labour in the shadows, and shall never have glory – but even Lords fear us. Serve me well, Bor, and the Intercessors may make a better end for you."

CHAPTER SEVEN

It was one thing to see elves in a starlit forest; it was another entirely to see them ride through the streets of Arden the next morning. They seemed diminished in daylight, and even though this was a great procession of the elder folk, nearly fifty strong, they were very few compared to the throng of mortals. They rode white horses without bridle or saddle, and each horse bore a star-mark on its forehead.

At their head was the Princess Laerlyn. She wore a black veil and a black mantle of mourning, but her silver armour was visible beneath, and Bor wondered what this meant. Beside her rode a banner-bearer, carrying Laerlyn's personal standard – the white tree of her father the Erlking, surrounded by nine stars. As they passed the field of banners, the elf leaned over and thrust Laerlyn's standard into the frozen earth, a little distance apart from all the rest.

Agyla joined Bor at the window, counting off the lesser lords under her breath. "Malac of Arden, loyal. Hira of the Westcleft, doubtful. Grimbec Wolfshead, doubtful. Daegmar of the Springs, very fucking doubtful." Her lip curled. "Bayard, Baron of Greenhills. We shall count him as loyal."

Behind them, Sir Rhuel alternated between muttering to himself and loudly clearing his throat. "OPENED their eyes to bright realms unseen ... opened their EYES to BRIGHT realms unseen, gah. Opened their EYES to bright realms UNSEEN. Agyla, what time are you putting half the nobility to the sword? I need to make sure I finish in time."

"Not *half.* Some of those who might turn traitor will lose their courage in the face of the elves, or when they see their erstwhile allies quailing. There are some fanatics among the traitors, but others are merely greedy or deluded. And there will be Intercession to ensure minimal resistance. Bloodletting, not slaughter. We cut out the corruption." She paused at the door. "Bor, Fetch a weapon from the armoury. Your post is at the main door of the theatre. Do as instructed. When the time comes, guard Sir Rhuel."

When she was gone, and safely out of earshot, Sir Rhuel said: "Bloodletting, that's what the scholars did, when my father fell ill. To purge the corruption in his bowels, they said. And you know what? He still shat himself to death."

Bor snorted. "What'll become of us, after the Rangers are done?"

The old knight shrugged. "You should know better than I, with all your running about on secret errands. I expect I shall be back on the Road – a grand tour of all the provinces. Telling the tale of the Lammergeier's treacherous murder of Prince Maedos in every castle and feasting hall from here to the Eaveslands. 'Tis an arduous quest, but I've spent many years in training." Rhuel slapped his belly, then fell serious. "You – it might be that they'll let you come with me. You're a dour companion, my boy, but the Road makes friends of all men, and at least I've no fear of bandits with a warrior like you. It may be, though, that Agyla has other plans for you. Whatever happens today, the trouble won't be over – there are rumblings of dissent in other places than Arden, and there'll be more bloodletting to be done. I can imagine Agyla spiriting you away on some murderous mission. If that happens, good luck to you."

A thought struck Sir Rhuel.

"Maybe I'll write a tale about you, eh? I would need to change a few details, of course. Your character, for instance. Your appearance. Your mode of speech. Every aspect of your history. But your name, ah, that would live on for ever."

Heralds went forth, announcing that the Princess Laerlyn had come to Arden, and that all of noble rank should attend Lord Tor's theatre that evening. Bor watched them trooping across the courtyard. Faint music emanated from the theatre as musicians practised. It might have been the preparation for some celebration, a feast-day or tournament maybe. He could easily imagine himself at the Arden tourney, getting ready to try his luck in the fights.

As Agyla had ordered, he went to the armoury. Having a sword in his hand again felt so very right. Bor hadn't touched a blade since the Crownland, and he worried that he'd lost his skill. He took pride in few things, but he knew how to fight. The palace armourer had asked no questions, which made Bor suspect that the man was another of Agyla's creatures. He'd given Bor a dwarf-forged sword, as good a weapon as Bor had ever owned. But it had no charmstones in the hilt, nor elf-runes on the blade, and against magic, what use was such a blade?

On the Road, Sir Rhuel had told Bor tales of his exploits on the battlefield as a young knight, forty or fifty years ago – a whole generation before the fall of Necrad. In Rhuel's telling, courage and skill counted towards a warrior's chances of survival. Those days were gone. Since Necrad, and the bounty of stolen magic, war had changed. The advantage of magic was overwhelming. No, the only way for someone like Bor to survive on such a battlefield was to stay well away from the front lines. He'd made a career of lurking on the fringes of war. He knew how to fight in the mud.

Not here. Not this war of Rangers and elves, not this war of subtle threats and abductions and tailored stories. He didn't know where to stand, or where to look for danger.

*

He took advantage of the unaccustomed luxury of the palace chamber to wash himself. There was a bathtub in an adjoining room, taken as a spoil of war from Necrad. For all Bor knew, he might have helped smuggle it south as part of some anonymous cargo on one of Lyulf Marten's ships. Statues of Witch Elf maidens in diaphanous gowns flanked the bath, and with a word, water issued from the ewers to fill the tub. One of the elf-maids had lost her head along the way, which lent the whole thing a grisly touch, but the conjured water was steaming hot and smelled of bergamot.

Afterwards, he shaved. He'd grown a scraggly beard during his imprisonment in the Crownland, and his hair had grown out; he preferred to keep his pate close to bare, as he'd once been told it made him look more dangerous. He shaved that back too, tangles of dark hair sticking to the wet metal of the elven water-bearers. When it came to his neck, he had to be more careful, for the skin around his throat was tender and inflamed. The collar slumbered, a bare noose of greenish-brown stems.

He dressed in clothes taken from Sir Rhuel's wardrobe. He found a high-collared shirt made of finer material than anything Bor had ever worn before, and put it on. When he was done, he considered himself in the mirror.

What had he hoped to see reflected there? A man of worth, perhaps. A man whose luck had changed at last. A warrior who might become part of a great lord's household. No longer Rootless, not a poverty-stricken wretch tied to the land, but a man of worth.

What he saw was a gaunt shadow, a scarecrow dressed in borrowed finery. The shirt did not hide the ivy-collar that marked him a criminal, and washing the dirt of the Road from his face just emphasised his scars and pockmarks. He looked ill-suited to his surroundings. Annoyed, he picked up his old clothes and pawed through them for his belt knife and coin-purse. The coin from Necrad fell from the purse and rolled across the tiles. He picked it up, and from outside came the sound of frantic barking.

"'*Opened their eyes to bright realms unseen*'," recited Rhuel as Bor rushed to the window, "'*And revealed to the Lords the paths of righteousness*' – I thought you got rid of that damn dog – '*Now his son's blood becomes a sacred sacrifice*'."

Cu was down in the courtyard, running back and forth between the banners. Harsh barks resounded off the palace walls.

"Don't mind me," grumbled Rhuel, "borrow my good shirt, ruin my concentration. Guarantee me a bad review by arresting half the audience."

Then, Bor saw the field of banners, and terror filled him. There was no wind that afternoon, but he saw the cloth banners flutter as unseen things moved past them. There were two invisible forces there, approaching from the east and west, closing on the dog.

Cu wove through the banners, trying to escape the unseen pursuers. Somehow, it was as though he crossed the field in an instant, vanishing in one place only to appear elsewhere, but still, the invisible pursuers closed on him, winds whirling ever closer and closer.

Then he was caught, his furry shape twisting as it was lifted by unseen hands – and suddenly limp. The dog's body fell to the ground.

Bor stared down at the suddenly empty field, trying to understand what he had seen.

The emptiness looked back at him. There was no one down there, nothing he could perceive with his eyes, but he felt the *attention* of those invisible presences like a hammer to his skull. His vision darkened, and he stumbled back as though struck.

Magic. Spirits and magic. Magic killed the dog.

He lay there, slumped against the wall, shivering. He could not stand, nor speak. He could only hear Sir Rhuel in the adjoining room, reciting his speech.

"'*It anoints our eyes so we too might see the folly of mortals*.'"

*

As instructed, Bor stationed himself at the door of the palace theatre. Getting there meant crossing the courtyard and the field of banners. He dared not search that haunted place for Cu's remains – assuming the dog had not vanished again in death. Every gust of cold wind terrified him, and the borrowed sword was heavy in his hand.

He stood at his post and watched the nobles of Arden gather, as commanded by the Erlking's daughter.

Lord Tor came first, a friend to everyone. The honour – and expense – of hosting the Princess Laerlyn fell to him. He glided about with a pained grin. Bor didn't know if the man knew what was about to happen under his roof, or if he was just holding in the most tremendous fart. Either way, he did not envy the Lord of Arden.

Lords from Arshoth and Westermarch arrived almost at the same moment, and there were scuffles between their retinues. Each Lord was accompanied by an entourage from their households – courtiers, bodyguards, knights of renown, heralds, astrologers, priests, all clad in cloaks or tabards matching the colours of their respective master. The astrologers in particular seemed nervous. The stars burned as bright over the Cleft of Ard as they had in the elf-wood the night before, and Bor wondered if they'd read some omen.

Lady Helena of Arshoth passed so close to Bor that he could smell the incense clinging to the famously devout old woman. Priests flanked her. One carried a tray covered by a fabulously expensive embroidered cloth-of-gold, and from the shape of it Bor guessed there was a grail-cup beneath. The other bore a shrouded birdcage. After them came the paladin-knights of Arshoth, bravest of all mortal warriors. Peir the Paladin was counted among their number. For all their faith, charmstones glimmered in the hafts of their hammers.

Lord Bruke of Westermarch was the only one of the three who had fought in the last war. He wore his scars proudly. He came accompanied by a great many knights and warriors. Some of them looked familiar as they passed Bor; had they been in the inn that night? They marched on the theatre as if marching to war, but still yielded their weapons to Tor's doorkeepers.

Other lesser nobles followed; Bor didn't know their names, and while the herald announced each of them, the shouts from inside the theatre were muffled. Agyla had stationed him at one of the great doors to keep watch. On the other side of the doorway was the ostler, dressed as one of Lord Tor's guards. None gave the Ranger a second look at they passed by, though Lady Helena's birds croaked within their covered cage.

Bor dared glance inside the theatre. Bright-hued cloaks turned the crowd to living heraldry. He heard rather than saw Sir Rhuel, the knight's booming laughter echoing out into the evening. He looked for Agyla, but could not see her.

And, above it all, watching from a high balcony like a distant star, was the Princess Laerlyn.

The doors shut behind the last of the gathering.

"Soon," said the ostler, "we'll go in."

The ostler returned to his post opposite Bor. In the gloom, Bor could see other guards at the other doors of the theatre, and on the walls of the palace. A noose tightened around the building.

This is all beyond you, he told himself. *It's the affairs of Lords and wizards – and Rangers. And fucking spirits. Magic and majesty. A man can't fight against such forces. Keep your head down, don't get noticed. Survive.*

Above, the stars wheeled, constellations rising and falling over the dark lip of the Cleft. Inside, the sound of the crowd died away, replaced by swelling music and the thunder of Sir Rhuel's voice, magically augmented by the theatre.

"*Hark, ye sons of Arden, ye daughters of Eavesland, attend to my tale of woe and treachery! I speak only truth: if I should utter but one lie then shall the holy Intercessors for ever silence me.*'"

On and on went the tale. Bor caught only snatches. It began in ancient times, reminding the nobles of the many debts they owed the Erlking – how Prince Maedos had guarded the lands of mortals from the evils of Necrad, how the Erlking saved humanity after the fall of the Old Kingdom – before moving onto events in the living memory of mortal men. Parts were familiar – Sir Rhuel reaching back to his *Song of the Nine* and other tales of the war, telling how the Nine defeated Lord Bone and became rulers of Summerswell. In this retelling, though, he emphasised how each of the Nine were flawed or suspect in some fashion. Thief and apostate, barbarian and beast, failed wizard and Rootless vagabond – only Peir was true to Summerswell, and it was Peir who died to slay Lord Bone. Sir Rhuel's version, too, emphasised the courage and sacrifice of the League, the alliance of mortals, dwarves and elves, that had fought Lord Bone's armies. In this tale, the Nine seemed caught up in greater events – less heroes, more a band of misfits lifted by chance, unworthy of the honours heaped on them. He praised Peir's sacrifice, and the wisdom and leadership of Princess Laerlyn, even as he hinted at the growing corruption of the rest.

The tale skipped lightly over decades. Sir Rhuel spoke of how the evil of Necrad had been transmuted into a blessing, and how treasures from Necrad had made Summerswell into an enchanted realm. Bor strained to hear as Sir Rhuel's voice dropped into a confessional, conspiratorial whisper. *It was not your fault*, he implied to the assembled nobles, *the Nine led you astray, the Nine caused dissent.*

Bor knew much of what Rhuel said must be lies, and the old knight had sworn by the Intercessors. But no unseen forces struck him down.

From beyond the walls, Bor heard distant shouting. The clamour grew louder, drowning out Sir Rhuel's voice from inside the theatre. Guards hurried towards the nearest gate. Louder and louder, the sound of tramping feet, of angry shouting.

"Hold your ground," ordered the ostler. "Keep the doors shut."

More shouting echoed across the great yard. Beyond the curtain wall was another yard, and the main gate of the palace opened onto that. Whatever trouble was coming, it had reached the gate. The palace of Arden was not a proper fortress, but the gates would hold against a mob for a good while, long enough for the Lord of Arden to call up armed guards – and the city was full of armed guards. Still, Bor's mouth went dry with anticipation of danger. He wanted to run – only a fool would stand here on these steps, in the open – but he told himself the gates would hold.

But then there was a cheer, and a roar, and the thunder of many feet. A cry boomed from a thousand throats at once.

"LAM-MER-GEIER! LAM-MER-GEIER!"

The ostler paled. "Hold your ground," he hissed at Bor, "or—" He clenched his fist, then darted into the theatre. Bor heard the door lock behind him.

A fog was rising from the earth, little wisps of mist hissing between the flagstones of the yard, seeping up through the grass. It curled around the banners, and the cloth of the Laerlyn's banner rotted at its touch. Bor gagged on the stench of the fog. It was not poisonous, but vile beyond measure. There was a greenish tinge to it, and as it grew thicker, it blotted out the stars.

Thunder boomed *underfoot*, the same sound he'd heard earlier in the week. The bowels of the earth convulsed. The whole theatre shivered, dislodging dried bird shit and bits of painted plaster from the façade. A second blast echoed. Bor wondered if some monster was about to burst out of the ground.

Then he saw movement across the courtyard.

Out of the fog there came a crowd, a mob. At its head rode a warrior clad in armour. He bore a shield with the device of a winged bird, and his face was hidden by a ghastly helmet. With his right hand he wielded a sword black as the void. He lifted it on high, and the crowd cheered his name.

"LAM-MER-GEIER! LAM-MER-GEIER!"

It was the man Bor had met in Highfield. The man who had sent him to find Olva Forster, the hero whose dread command had haunted Bor since Ellsport. Agyla had said it this was not the Lammergeier, but Bor could not doubt the evidence of his eyes, his heart.

He looked upon the hero of the Nine.

Inside, Sir Rhuel's voice cracked as he described how the Lammergeier slew the Erlking's son. He spoke as if he himself had borne witness to the crime, as if he had been there when the Nine committed an unforgivable breach of the laws of Summerswell and the Everwood.

"Lies!" cried the Lammergeier. "All lies!"

The crowd roared angrily. They cursed and spat, denouncing poets and jealous lords. How dare they soil the name of the Lammergeier? How dare they question the heroism of the Nine?

The Lammergeier pointed the black sword at the theatre entrance. At Bor.

"Let us bring justice!"

In that moment, Bor understood with bone-deep certainty that Agyla and her Rangers, for all their secrets and cunning, had failed. The peace of Summerswell had failed, and there would be war – not in distant Necrad, but here in the lands of mortals.

High above, a bow sang. The first arrow struck the Lammergeier's shield; the second pierced his chest.

Bor looked up, and there was a single star left in the sky. The miasma had swallowed all the rest, but atop the theatre stood Laerlyn, and the light was in her face. She loosed a third arrow from the bow *Morthus*, and the Lammergeier fell.

And the world went mad.

CHAPTER EIGHT

B or did not hold his ground.

Nor, to his credit, did he flee.

How he got into the theatre ahead of the mob, he was never sure afterwards. He recalled running along the perimeter until he found some small side door, or maybe he wriggled through a window like a dog forcing itself through a hole in a hedge.

Why he entered the theatre instead of fleeing, he only understood much later.

He found himself in a maze of back rooms and storerooms. The miasma was thicker in here, billowing up from the cellars. He could not see more than a few feet.

All was chaos above; the doors splintered as the mob hammered at them, shouts and screams from the main auditorium. He heard Sir Rhuel somewhere far above, his voice still augmented by the magic of the theatre. "Back, you dogs! Back! I'm not done! Anointed the EYES of prophets with water – damn you, get back – of Arshoth!"

Guard Sir Rhuel, Agyla had told him. Everything had gone wrong for him when he'd broken his word before, so he would keep it now. His head swam, and he could not catch his breath in the miasma, but he had a sword in his hand and he was not yet dead.

He ran up a stair, hoping it would lead to the auditorium. He came to a door and flung it open, and a dead woman fell forward into Bor's arms. A noble or wizard, her cloak the white of Arshoth stained with fresh blood. Bor shoved the corpse aside, and it went tumbling down the steps behind him. He found himself in a side room. The tiled floor was slick with blood, and more bodies lay there. Again, the white of Arshoth. The broken remains of Lady Helena's birdcage caught his eye. The cloth-of-gold had slipped from it, and he could see the songbirds within. They too were dead, their little bodies twisted into knots, feathers matted with vomit. Twisted like Cu.

Magic. Magic had killed them. Magic could do the same to him.

One of the corpses on the ground lurched upright with a wheezing gasp. A dead hand grabbed at Bor's shirt. He fell backwards, and felt a dead hand clutch at him from behind. All around him, the dead were stirring, the greenish mist of the necromiasma coiling around their corpses.

The dead walked in Necrad.

Bor tore his way clear, slashing at the dead with his sword as he fled. He burst into the great auditorium. All was carnage there too. The enchanted chandeliers had failed, plunging the room into a darkness broken only by little islands of light around candles or charmstones, or where the necromiasma pooled thick enough to be luminescent. A series of miniature tableaus, each strange and horrific.

There lay a dead paladin of Arshoth, stabbed in the throat. There a man of Westermarch, blasted by sorcery. There a dead Ranger.

He looked, but did not see Agyla.

Elves, too, had died here – Bor came upon one fallen immortal, an elf-maid he'd seen dancing in the starlight the previous night, but now her ethereal beauty was marred by a ghastly, festering wound. She'd been struck by an elf-bane arrow, a weapon of the dwarves.

The Westermarchers had attacked. They'd smuggled weapons in, somehow, and attacked.

Bor stumbled towards the stage. Someone cried out for aid;

someone else shouted, 'Treason! Treason!' over and over. Behind him, the main doors shook as fists hammered on them, the mob vengeance-crazed over the death of the Lammergeier. When they broke through, they would make no distinction between nobles of Westermarch and those of Arden or Arshoth, and the colour of one's cloak would not matter a damn. Everyone would be blamed; everyone would be torn apart. Shadows fled towards the side exits, while the surviving paladins mustered by the entrance. No holy light of Intercession surrounded them; their blessed hammers did not blaze with divine power.

He looked, but did not see Agyla.

He climbed up onto the stage. There lay Sir Rhuel, with the body of another man – a Westermarcher – lying atop him. Bor hauled the body off the old knight. Sir Rhuel's bloody fingers were clasped tightly over a belly-wound, but he'd dealt better than he'd received, for the knife was embedded in the Westermarcher's neck. It was a gaudy knife, a theatrical prop – but the blade was very real.

Sir Rhuel seized his shoulder, and for a moment Bor feared that he was too late, and the knight was now among the walking dead, but the mists had not yet risen above the lip of the dais, so corpses were just corpses for now. Rhuel pulled Bor close and whispered in his ear.

"Now we see the Lammergeier. Uncloaked at last."

He fell back, unconscious. Bor lifted the old man and stumbled away towards backstage. With every step, he expected that the ivy-collar would close on his throat, or that a Ranger would step out of the shadows and demand that he stand and fight.

Everything had broken, except his leash. But no one tugged on it as he fled.

By the time they reached the stables, Bor could barely walk and Rhuel's face was grey. Bor lashed Rhuel to his horse's saddle so the knight would not fall, and took Agyla's horse too, the reins of all three animals bundled in his hand.

The city was in uproar. A great column of green mist rose from the central palace, the trunk of a ghastly tree spreading its mephitic branches out over all of Arden. There would be no dawn. They escaped out the south gate in the confusion. The guard post lay empty. There was blood on the ground by the gate.

There was light a few hours later, though, outside the canopy of the necromiasma. The vapours now covered most of the Cleft. Fires raged, their plumes of smoke adding to the foulness of the clouds. Banners flew atop the gates, but he could not make out the devices. He could see long lines of people fleeing the city. Or were they columns of troops?

Better, he decided, to avoid meeting anyone until he could figure out which side was winning. He led their horses off the main road, taking to goat paths that wound through the hills south-east of the Cleft. Neither the first touch of spring nor the burning city brought much warmth to the air.

He looked back, but did not see Agyla.

By noon, Sir Rhuel grew feverish despite the chill, and his wound stank. They encamped in a thicket, and Bor laid the knight down on a mossy patch. He draped Sir Rhuel's cloak as a blanket, and the jewelled clasp caught his eye. That clasp was worth a good few coins. So were Rhuel's clothes, the ones not stained with shit and blood. Three horses, whatever money Rhuel had on him ... he'd killed for less.

He remembered a similar camp in the Fossewood. He'd nearly died there, when Martens had used the ivy-noose on him for the first time. Some dwarf had saved him and Olva Forster, and when he'd woken, Bor had tried to rob the dwarf and flee. It made sense then; it made sense now. But Olva had stopped him.

"Stay," he told Sir Rhuel. "I'll come back soon."

There was a farmstead nearby; he'd seen it as they'd climbed the hill. It was the leanest time of the year, but he would make them find some food to spare. Rhuel did not notice him go. The old knight mumbled and muttered to himself, sweat collecting on his moustache like dew despite the cold.

Bor's Rootless instincts came back to him as he crept up on the farmhouse. He lurked in the hedgerows and watched for trouble; a farm boy who fancied himself a hero, maybe, or some old bastard with a pitchfork.

He found a different sort of trouble. There were four, no, five rogues who'd had the same idea he had. Mismatched gear that spoke of recent looting. He could see them through the open door of the farmhouse, digging through sacks of provisions.

"Eh, you're the rich lad from the inn."

Bor spun around. Sitting on a tree root, was Magga, the Rootless woman he'd met in Arden.

Never in his life had Bor been called *rich*. But he was still wearing Sir Rhuel's expensive clothes, and even though they were filthy, for the first time in his life he looked like a man worth robbing.

"I'm not rich," he protested.

"No more free drink, then. And no more inn, neither. A bad start to the year, and no mistake."

Bor nodded towards the farmhouse. "Are you with them?"

"I suppose. They're from Arden. I was with 'em in a tavern, last night, when we all ran when we smelled the rot. Miasma, they call it. I never thought I'd see the dead walk again in the southland, but I was wrong. They were rising all over the city, every churchyard giving up its dead. Just shamblers, mind you. But these southern lads are soft, and come over all wobbly when they see a zombie." Magga clucked her tongue in disapproval. "I told 'em you can just stick 'em, but they ran, and I ran too. They found yon cottage and threw them that lived there out." She studied him for a moment. "You hungry?"

"It's not only food I need."

*

The ruffians from Arden might have been able to drive some poor farmer from his home, but when Bor showed up with his fine sword, they were outmatched. They yielded to him, scavenging dogs driven away from a kill by a bear. Bor brought Sir Rhuel up to the cottage, and laid him on the pile of hay and threadbare blankets that passed for a bed. Magga claimed to have some talent as a healer, and examined the knight's wound. She spooned broth into his mouth, but he ate little.

"He's mostly dead," she diagnosed. "He'll last maybe three days, but not more than that. If he was in Necrad, I'd put the ender's copper aside right now." She must have seen the look on Bor's face, for she added: "Up in Necrad, human corpses don't stay dead, aye? So if someone dies, you've got to put 'em down again when they get lively. One good stab does it. Dead-enders like me, we work *inside* the city as well as outside. The quality don't like to talk about, and some get a doctor to do it quiet-like, but a dead-ender's cheaper." She sniffed. "I doubt he'll come back here when he dies, but depends which way the wind blows, I guess." There was a cheerful practicality to how she talked about the risen dead.

"He's not so far gone that a wizard couldn't cure him," said Bor, "nor a healing cordial."

"Have you any cordial?"

"No."

"Are you secretly a wizard?"

"No."

"Well then! Just leave him," counselled Magga. "He won't last long, and we should be off down the road before trouble finds us. I'll end him quick, and we can be gone. Stick with Magga, and you'll have good luck." She grinned at him, showing a mouthful of rotten teeth. "Magga's seen bad times before. Magga knows how to live."

Disappearing sounded like a wonderful thing. Bor longed to disappear. But he remembered the ostler's threat. *There's no place in Summerswell you can hide from us, once we set our mind upon you. We found you once, we can find you again.* Invisible hands murdering the dog, invisible hands striking him down on the street. He wondered if Agyla was alive or dead, and if she still lived, would she come after him and Sir Rhuel? The poem besmirching the Lammergeier's name was done, and the word was out – the knight had done what was asked of him, and Bor had only ever been a minor part of the whole affair. Maybe he was done with the Rangers, a free man again, able to choose his own path.

He dug into his pocket and pulled out the coin from Necrad. Magga sucked air past her broken teeth at the sight of it.

"Help me," said Bor, "and I'll give you this."

The Roadhag studied Bor for a moment, then clasped her fingers around his hand, folding the coin back into his palm.

"You keep it. You keep it. I'll help for free, 'ey, and we'll be friends on the Road."

They rode south, Magga on Agyla's horse, Bor on his, and Sir Rhuel between them, barely clinging to the saddle. They rode until it was too dark to risk further travel. The glow from the new miasma above Arden did not shed enough light to see by.

Once dawn glimmered in the sky, Bor had them set off again, risking the main road for the last few miles. Sir Rhuel groaned as they lifted him onto his horse, and there was fresh blood on the bandages. The hills on either side grew steeper as they came to the south end of the Cleft. Ahead lay Castle Bayard.

Magga glanced over her shoulder, then nudged Bor to look. In the distance, he could see other riders, following them down the road. Morning light flashed off shields and spearpoints, but they were too distant for him to make out any symbols or banners. Were they loyal to the Lords of Summerswell, or were they traitors? Bor couldn't tell. He didn't even know how to answer that question for himself. He was a Rootless sellsword. He owed no one loyalty.

But still he grabbed Sir Rhuel's shoulder to support the wounded knight as they rode on.

*

The banner of Arden still fluttered above the castle. The gate was shut, and there were guards on the walls, but only a few. Bor hammered on the door.

"I was a guest here, with my master Sir Rhuel of Eavesland! Let us in!"

"What Lord do you serve?" called a voice from above.

"I bloody told you. Sir Rhuel. The poet."

"And who does he serve?"

Bor kicked the door again. "I don't know. Ask him when he can speak."

A viewport on the door was drawn back, and Bor saw the eyes of Bayard's wife, red-rimmed from weeping.

"Are you just now come from Arden?"

"Aye."

"Baron Bayard was summoned to pay homage to the Princess Laerlyn. We saw the cloud rise over the Cleft. What happened? Have you any word of my husband?" Her voice quavered at the end.

"No," Bor lied, "but my master Sir Rhuel was there in the palace too. He may know more – but he's injured. He needs help. Let us in."

The gate opened. Magga hesitated for a moment. "I don't much care to be locked up behind high walls." But she followed him in.

"Shut the gate!" said Bor. "Riders are close behind, and I don't know who they are."

They took Sir Rhuel up to the room where they'd put Bor. The castle wizard examined him. There was no healing cordial to hand, for whatever stock Baron Bayard possessed had been in that secret cache in the cellar. The wizard grumbled, but at Lady Bayard's urging – and Bor's glare – she agreed to work a healing spell. Such a spell, the wizard warned, would drain her of all the magic she'd accrued over the last decade or more. She set to work weaving the spell, casting Sir Rhuel's horoscope and drawing connections between the knight's fate and the stars that governed restoration.

Bor left Magga to watch over Sir Rhuel, and went back down to the gatehouse as the pursuing riders approached the castle. He peered out through an arrow-slit.

"They've raised a banner. A white fox and two moons. Who's that?"

"Hira of the Westcleft," said Lady Bayard. "A friend of my husband."

Bor's mind flashed back to Agyla's judgement of the banners at the palace of Arden. "I wouldn't open that gate. Not if you want to see your daughter again."

"What do you mean?"

"The Rangers had the elves take your girl. Those men outside are foes of the elves. I don't mean to tell you your business, but . . . Well, as long as they're outside your walls, you're safe enough."

"Lady Bayard," cried one of the Westcleft knights. "Let us in!"

She climbed to the rampart. "What business do you have here?" she called.

"Baron Hira sent us to bolster your strength, and to defend your keep against foes. Your castle watches the entrance to the Cleft; any foes entering Arden must pass this way. Castle Bayard cannot fall into the hands of the enemy."

"And who are these foes I should fear?"

The knight approached the gate. "My lady, I do not know which of your husband's secrets you are privy to, but a day long anticipated is at hand. There shall be a reckoning with those who rule unjustly. The cloud is a signal to rise up! Open the gate."

"My husband is gone to Arden," said Lady Bayard, "and until he returns, I keep his castle safe. These gates remain closed."

"My lady," growled the knight, "there are weapons in your cellar that belong to us. Your husband hid them there in anticipation of this day. You must yield them over."

"They are already gone," said Lady Bayard. "Now be off with you!"

*

By nightfall, Sir Rhuel had recovered enough to sit up in bed and eat, and to send Bor down to the wine cellar for the last of Bayard's good wine – "for I fear the poor man has no more need of it".

"His wife asked me if I had news of him," said Bor, "and I told her I didn't see his body. Maybe he's alive."

"Maybe he's dead, and walked out of there," giggled Magga from the corner. She'd gorged herself on the contents of the pantry, and was now digging into a huge Yule-cake. A fire burned brightly in the grate, and the walls of Castle Bayard seemed secure, but the window faced north and Bor could see the necromiasma hanging over Arden. Nothing was secure any more.

"It will be a long time before a full accounting is made of the fallen in the palace alone," said Sir Rhuel. "The rebels turned the Rangers' trap back on them; they smuggled in weapons and put the loyalists to the sword. That was only the beginning. War is kindled, and who knows what will happen?"

"They can't win, though, can they? Not against all of Summerswell. The Lords, and the Church, and everything," said Bor. "Even Lord Bone never got close to that."

"It's hard to say," said Rhuel. He shifted in bed and groaned. "I would agree with you, I think, but I'd not wager my full fortune on it." He frowned. "Did you get my purse from my room?"

"No," admitted Bor.

"One coin," said Magga, "and he promised it to me."

"Well, I'll wager my full fortune, then. Lord Bone's attack unified Summerswell against an external foe, but this war tears at every division. Ambition and treachery shall be rewarded. And with Arden gone, there can be no campaign to quickly retake Necrad now – which means that whoever rules that city will command its magic. If they aid the rebels . . . it will go badly for all of us. Especially those who served the Rangers, even unwillingly."

"It'll go badly," said Magga. "Mortals and magic, it always does."

"You're not wrong there," said Bor.

"I think," said Sir Rhuel, "that our mutual friend will be in the thick of the fighting, and that is precisely where I do not want to be. I made my reputation in the last war from a prison cell in the Crownland; I am minded to see this one out from even further away. A lovely inn down in the Eavesland, maybe."

"They'll be able to find us no matter where we go. And Eavesland's full of elves."

"I would hope, Bor, that our mutual friend will have more pressing concerns than hunting us down." Sir Rhuel poured himself more wine. "I should sleep, I know, but I'll mourn a little longer first." He raised his goblet. "To the first casualty of the war – my reputation as a poet! I thought to make the groundlings hate the Lammergeier, but they hated me instead. Nearly murdered on stage, and my performance interrupted by the whole city being engulfed in the miasma of damnation – now that's a review. The danger of working on commission, as opposed to following one's muse. Perilous is the life of a freelancer."

Magga frowned. "Does he always talk like that?"

"Aye."

She ran her thumb over the blade of her spear.

Bor drained the last of his wine. "I'm going to stand a watch. If I were those lads from Westcleft, I'd not give up so easily, not if I'd been ordered to take this castle before anyone came up the Road."

"Take my cloak," said Rhuel. "It'll be a cold night. And Bor – I'm in your debt. It was no small thing you did, getting my carcass out of there, and finding me a healer, too. I know we were forced together by circumstances, and you did not choose to serve me."

Bor turned the coin over in his hand. "Ah, to hell with it. Companions of the Road, eh?"

CHAPTER NINE

B or walked the walls, watching fresh flurries of snow blanket the hillside below the castle, and the surrounding woods. North, the new necromiasma glowed, a green stain on the night sky. The night wore on, and the men of the Westcleft did not return.

In the grey hour before dawn, Magga found him. "The wind's changed," she said, "I smell miasma on the air. Best to check the crypt."

"For what?"

"The dead, of course. If there's a fresh corpse in there."

He had ridden past a dozen little village cemeteries on the road to Arden. Bor imagined the vapours of the necromiasma drifting south, waking the dead. The sooner they were on the Road, the better.

He forced open the chapel. Rows of pews lined the stone chamber, the grandest reserved for Bayard's family, and the knights of his household. The Erlking's face looked down at them from the wall, his stone features blending into the carved image of the holy tree that dominated the north wall.

On one pew, Bor spotted a little cloth doll, a child's toy. Had Berysala left it there? He could imagine the child sitting there, forced to listen to some interminable sermon. Or had Lady Bayard brought it when she prayed for her child's safe return? The child did not deserve to be used as a pawn in the intrigues of elves and lords, spirits and heroes. None of them did.

The holy shrine, a sacred space reserved for clerics, was concealed within the carven tree, and beside it was a small door that led down into the crypt. Magga paused by the shrine and licked her lips.

"Want to look? Could be something worth taking in there. Rich chapel like this, bound to be a jewelled grail or somesuch."

Bor shook his head. "It's bad luck to rob a shrine. Let's just be done with this." He shoved open the door to the crypt. Stale air washed past him, and he gagged.

"In Necrad," muttered Magga, "we robbed the temples of the Witch Elves, and the Wilder thought 'em living gods. No one feared do that."

Generations of Bayards lay interred in the crypt. You could trace the fortunes of the family by the tombs; the older ones were just slabs of stone, simple and unadorned. Later, they'd had the wealth to hire dwarven masons, and effigies of dead knights lay on their marble biers, staring eternally at the ceiling. Magga had him disinter the most recent casket – the elder brother of the current Baron, fallen in Lord Bone's war. The dead-ender peered into the tomb, and shook her head.

"All's well. The casket's well sealed. Even if the miasma blows this far south, he'll stay dead, and all the others are too rotten to walk."

"Bloody waste of time, this was."

A noise from above startled them both – water splashing on stone. Bor led the way, leaping up the narrow stair to the chapel. The sounds were coming from inside the shrine. There was a grail-cup in there, Bor thought, that the priests used to commune with the Intercessors. The conspirators in Arden had used a stolen grail to watch for supernatural pursuit. But you had to be ordained to be a priest – only those blessed and sanctified could pray for Intercession. And the conspirators at Arden used sorcery to steal false sanctity.

Neither was true here.

If there was *power* here, it lay on the other side.

"Fucking magic," he muttered. He tried to find the courage to open the door to the shrine, but his limbs would not obey him. "Fucking magic." A strange stench filled the chapel – it reminded Bor of the rotting-corpse smell of hawthorn flowers.

It was Magga who darted forward, Magga who opened the little shrine. Inside was a tiny dark room, no larger than a wardrobe. Priests' robes hung there, talismans and relics and holy books – and on a shelf, the castle grail. It was a shallow cup of silver, studded with rubies. There was a little water in the holy cup, and it steamed and bubbled, agitated by unseen forces.

A vision played across the waters: paladins of Arshoth, white tabards bright against the snow, riding furiously down the road from Arshoth. The side path he'd come down with Rhuel flashed past. They were no more than thirty minutes from the castle. All the riders wore white, except for one.

Agyla.

Bor fell back, and the vision vanished, the waters in the cup hissing as they boiled away to nothing. For a moment, he felt like there was someone else in the little shrine with them, but it dissipated with the steam. The smell of hawthorn faded.

"They're coming," he choked.

"Aye," said Magga. "And whether it's the rebels or those knights who take the castle, I'm not minded to be here when they do."

"Me neither," said Bor. Impulsively, he grabbed the grail from the shrine. He snatched a cloth and wrapped the holy cup, as he'd seen the ostler do.

Magga grinned. "I'll get them rubies out with my teeth if I have to."

"Let's go."

There was a commotion at the gates as they emerged from the chapel. Lady Bayard and the captain of her guard – an old man, so withered he clung to the noblewoman's arm for fear of breaking his hip on the icy cobblestones – climbed to the walkway above the gatehouse.

"Fetch Sir Rhuel," Bor told Magga.

"What about the horses?"

"Leave 'em. We're sneaking out."

Then he followed Lady Bayard up to the ramparts. The men of Westcleft had returned, in greater numbers. The leader stepped forward.

"We can wait on your answer no longer, my lady. I am commanded to take this castle." He held up a clay jar, its stopper sealed with red wax, and shook it. From inside came a furious buzzing, as if he held a wasps' nest. "Do you know these horrors? They are hornets of silver and steel." The Westcleft man knelt in the frozen mud outside the gate and looked up at Lady Bayard. "I do not want to unleash these things. They kill without distinction, and they will not stop until everyone within your walls is dead. Your own husband helped bring them out of the north. We intended to use them on those that deserve such a vile fate. But I must have your castle now, so I ask again, will you not yield?"

"Give me . . . give me but a moment," said Lady Bayard, her voice cracking. She saw Bor lurking by the steps and beckoned him over.

"Sir Bor?" she whispered.

"I'm no knight."

"You have more experience of battle than anyone else left to me – what do you counsel?"

"I've heard tell of those metal hornets. They killed many dwarves in the war. He can't have many of 'em in that jar, though – not enough to kill all your men. And, don't ask me how I know, but there are knights on the way here from Arden. They're coming to put down the rebellion. If you hold out, they'll catch the Westclefters between hammer and anvil, and slaughter 'em."

Lady Bayard nodded, and Bor could see her summoning up all her courage, steeling herself for the fight. It should have been inspiring, to witness her finding strength she never knew she had. He could imagine her giving some inspiring speech to the ragtag defenders. But he couldn't help himself, and kept talking. Some part of him took foul glee in showing just how hopeless the situation was. "But half of your men will be dead in the first minute, no matter what. And there's a good chance you'll lose the castle anyway – if they've got a jar like that, then maybe they've got other magic too."

"You think I must yield?" she whispered.

"Yield, and you're throwing your lot in with the rebels. Let 'em in, and between the castle walls and that jar of fucking magic, maybe you can hold out against the other bastards. But the woman who had your daughter taken – she's with them. I think . . ."

We are not needlessly cruel, Agyla had said.

"I think she'd be merciful if she could – but if you side with the rebels, then your daughter will suffer for it." Bor shrugged. "You're fucked either way, my lady. We all are. That's my counsel."

They fled over the south wall. The Road stretched off before them, leading to the Crownland and all the other provinces of Summerswell. Bor could not guess how far the rebellion would spread down that Road.

"I'll take my cloak back now, if you please," said Sir Rhuel. He took a deep breath. "I smell spring! The sap rising, and the green growing, new life rising. And in a few months, girls taking off their clothes off in the heat. Sooner, in Eavesland. We're alive, my friend, and that's victory!" The old knight gave Bor a merry smile, as if this was the beginning of some grand adventure, then toddled off down the slope with Magga.

A grim mood came over Bor. It was the same feeling he'd had when he'd first read Rhuel's poem, the same feeling of hollowness. There were no heroes, no grand quests, just the schemes and lies of greater powers. No holy Intercessors watching over all, just more lies.

He wondered, for a moment, what Lady Bayard had chosen. Had she chosen that desperate gamble, and tried to hold out against the men of Westcleft? Had she taken the other path, and sacrificed any hope of seeing her daughter again?

She was probably dead already.

He followed the others down the Road.

Weeks passed. Months.

They never made it to Eavesland.

War came to Summerswell, and the Road was perilous. It was a time of mistrust. Every living soul looked at their neighbours and wondered, "Are they faithful to the Lords, or in league with the rebels?", while others whispered, "Are they thralls of the elves and their minions, or will they rise up and fight for freedom?" And all too often, the answer was "Better I denounce them, and strike first, and profit from the victory." From the mountains to the mouth of the River, from Ellscoast to the Eavesland, that summer brought sorrow to Summerswell.

As Bor had feared, it was a war of open magic. The power of the fallen Dark Lord was wielded on every battlefield. Blades of fire and shadow, vorpal swords and spears unerring spilled the blood of thousands. Enchanted blades were turned not on dragons or ogres, but on other mortals.

The Road became crowded, and the three travellers passed unnoticed. They stayed clear of the fighting where they could. Magga knifed a man in a tavern; Bor fought a pair of border-guards turned brigands on the edge of Arshoth, but for the most part, the war was distant thunder. They hid when they saw the flash of magic in the distance; they scavenged battlefields and aftermaths, picking through remains.

Magga thrived. She had dwelt in Necrad since the end of the siege, or so she claimed – for her, the unearthly magic of the Witch Elves was unremarkable. She told campfire tales of wraiths and vampires, Vatlings and pitspawn with ghastly relish – things that once seemed far away, but now were more like a prophecy of Summerswell's fate.

Rhuel was content to be on the Road, even in the company of Rootless vagabonds. He no longer insisted on his title, nor did he boast that he was the famous author of *The Song of the Nine*. He was still sharp-tongued and tempestuous, still the centre of attention in any gathering, but for him, this counted as being quiet and retiring. His wound troubled him, despite the healing spell. Often, they had to slow their pace so the old knight could keep up. To pay their way when they could not scavenge, they sold Rhuel's belongings. They sold his expensive clothing, and his rings, and his fine belt (a gift, he muttered, from the Archon of Ellscoast). He grumbled, but did not object.

In time, Bor grew used to travelling with others. His instincts urged him to leave, that he could survive better on his own instead of having to protect a soft old man and a Roadhag, but he stayed. He'd spent too much time alone in that cell, so he welcomed the company for a little while. He told himself that when the time came, he'd leave without looking back. But as they went on down the Road, it became more and more of a lie, and he knew he wouldn't abandon them.

Like he'd left Olva.

That betrayal weighed on him. Some nights, he woke, convinced that the ivy-collar was closing on him, and that Olva was there, only she had Agyla's ring.

One summer night, they met a strange monk in a dell off the Road. The first part of the evening passed without incident, but then the monk – Brother Stone, he called himself – asked for a song from Rhuel, and paid with a coin out of Necrad.

Bor stared at the coin. It was twin to the ones Olva had paid him, to the coin the dog had brought him. What was this threadbare pilgrim doing with a coin from Necrad? The monk reminded Bor of another smuggler, Abran, a priest turned pirate. Big, scarred hands, and a weight to the way he moved.

"Bor, isn't it?"

"Aye."

"From what province?"

"What does it matter?"

"Rootless, then. Bor the Rootless."

"Some call me that."

"Were you up the Mulladales, last year?"

Bor stiffened, suddenly wary. What did the monk know? Bor studied the man, wondering if he was a Ranger in disguise. *There's no place in Summerswell you can hide from us, once we set our mind upon you. We found you once, we can find you again.*

"That's a different man you're thinking of."

"Is it now?"

The monk had a bundle on his lap, wrapped around a stick. Bor wondered what was inside. Once, his first instinct would have been to rob the monk as he slept.

If the man was a Ranger, then how to fight him? No doubt he could command the ivy-collar like Agyla. If Bor went for his sword, the monk could choke him before Bor could cut him down. If Rhuel or Magga was awake, then maybe they'd have a chance if they all attacked at the same time. Or if the monk were asleep.

"It's my habit," said Bor, "to watch for the first part of the night. You can get some proper sleep before we part company."

"I'm not that tired," said the monk. "I'll sit up awhile."

"Suit yourself."

Bor paced about the camp. He glanced over at the monk. It was dark in the dell, but Bor was sure the monk wasn't wearing a ring. Agyla used a ring to control the ivy-collar. So had Lyulf Martens. Maybe the bastard didn't have a ring. Maybe he . . .

The monk slipped a hand beneath the cloth covering of his bundle. Fear gripped Bor – that was where the monk was hiding his ring. That was the magic that would bind him again, drag him back to heel like a dog. They'd make him fight in the war against the rebels, send him to die against horrors from Necrad . . .

But the collar never tightened.

What if the monk was not a Ranger? What if he was something else? Some spirit of redemption, a second chance offered by fate? Bor was no believer in the kindness of life, but there were too many coincidences, too many blessings for this to be anything other than the work of unseen forces. He dug out the grail-cup he'd taken from Bayard's chapel. The first few weeks on the Road, he dared to fill the cup with rainwater and stare into it. He told Rhuel and Magga that he feared the force that had struck him down in the Crownland, the Holy Intercessors that aided the Rangers, but he saw no sign of them. The cup was just a cup. Nothing moved beyond the waters.

But what would he see now, if he looked in it?

"I want to confess," said Bor. "I want you to take my confession to the Intercessors."

"I'm not a cleric," protested the monk.

"No, Brother Stone. But you're holy, and it's . . . I want to confess. I'm not one for faith. Honestly, fuck the clerics, and the bishops and archons, and the Intercessors and the Erlking and all of it. But I want to confess, all right?"

"I don't have a grail," muttered the monk.

"Here. Take this." Bor pressed the grail into the man's scarred hands.

"All right, then. Confess."

"I'm a thief. A cut-throat. A blood trader. A coward, too. You said a man could fight magic if he had a weapon and friends by his side. I've never had any of those things, and magic broke me. I've seen princes and heroes, and they're all false. They treated me worse than a dog. Everyone in this world's a bastard. Elves and mortals and dwarves – they're all bastards. Even the heroes are bastards dressed up with pretty words. Tell me there's something better on the other side."

"Is that what you believe?"

It was. Rhuel had said that fate was a wheel that might lift you up high as readily as bring you low. Bor had only ever been low. Fate wasn't a wheel – it was a grinding machine that crushed all the lives that were fed into it. Anyone who said otherwise was lying. Anyone who believed otherwise was a fool. Everything was monstrous and worthless – so why did he feel guilt over what he'd done to Olva? Why would anyone think he was worth a damn, and why did he care if they did?

The monk did not speak for some time, and when he answered, he spoke slowly, searching for words. "Pay no mind to the Intercessors. They're no holier than anything else. They've got power, aye, but power isn't enough. Listen, there's light if you look for it. It's rare and it's fragile, but it's there. I saw it when I was young, and I've been fighting to keep hold of it since. Look to your friends. The Road makes friends of us all, especially in dark times, and you've travelled far with these companions. But I can't absolve you, Bor the Rootless. You want forgiveness, you earn it."

Bor lay awake a little longer, looking at the stars as he watched over his friends.

Friends. There was a strange thought.

Midsummer, and it rained like the sky was weeping. The rain that fell was greasy with ash from the burning city. Avos of the crossings, Avos of the markets was now Avos of the pyres, Avos of the rich pickings. The rebels had assaulted the city a few days ago, and seized the crossings of the River at great cost.

Thieves and crows flocked to the wreckage.

Bor and his friends took shelter in the ruin of what had once been a bishop's hunting lodge, a little way outside the city. The bishop had taken shelter here too, but an angry mob – led by rebels who claimed the clergy were in league with demons – pursued and hung him from a hawthorn tree. His carcass still hung from a nearby branch, and Bor could hear the creaking of the noose in the wind. Both carcass and lodge had long since been stripped of valuables. Magga gave the bishop's corpse a poke with her spear as they passed. Bor quickly searched the ruined lodge for danger.

"It's safe enough," he muttered, "there's shelter at the back."

Sir Rhuel sat down gratefully, rubbing his legs. "You know," he said when he could breathe again, "I think I've been here before. I was a guest of the bishop. We had an interminable argument about Jan the Pious, from what I can recall. He was terribly long-winded, so I had to get terribly drunk to tolerate him."

Bor glanced at the grisly remains in the treetops. "Not much danger of that, now."

Magga sniffed. "What's that stink?"

"Wolves," said Bor.

"Dogs," said Sir Rhuel. "The bishop told me – at length – about his hunting dogs. I'd wager they've run wild." He waved a hand in the direction of the smouldering city. "There's a metaphor there."

"Wolves, too," insisted Bor. "Four- and two-legged ones. Outlaw bands, living deep in these woods. I had to bargain with 'em when I was working for Lyulf Martens."

"Do you know, I was once waylaid by such a band," said Rhuel. "This would have been in the time of First Lord Thaeglen, so ... fourteen or fifteen years ago? A little after the siege of Necrad? Anyway, I was on my way to my friend Baron Gravis—"

"You told us that one already," said Bor.

"At least twice," added Magga.

Rhuel sniffed. "And I have recited *The Song of the Nine* many hundreds of times. Half a tale's in the telling. There's virtue in listening, too. So, I was on my way to my friend the Baron Gravis ..."

Bor paid even less attention to Rhuel's tale. He let his mind wander. His thoughts ran to the outlaws in the woods. Were they still there, hidden in the deep forest? How had they stayed hidden all those years? Did the trees rustle when unseen forces brushed through them, invisible Intercessors moving through the woods? Were those outlaws spying on the comings and goings of the clerics in Arshoth? Were they agents of the long-planned rebellion, or in league with the Rangers? The more he thought, the more it seemed that everything had sinister purpose behind it, schemes and counter-schemes. It was as though he'd peeled the bark off the world, and found worms crawling there, gnawing the wood. Nothing could be trusted. Nothing was quite what it seemed.

Sir Rhuel was mid-flight of rhetoric.

"They came out of the wood, all dressed in green. 'Stranger,' they said, 'be you lord or peasant, Rootless or bondsman, you must pay our toll.' And I said to them, 'Don't you know who I am?'"

"I am Sir Rhuel of Eavesland," muttered Bor and Magga in unison.

"I am Sir Rhuel of Eavesland, and I am a poet. The only silver I have is in my tongue. The outlaw chief . . ."

Bor had heard the story before, more than twice. A dozen times, maybe. He didn't listen to the words, but he appreciated the shape of it, the cadence of the tale. There were no surprises in a familiar tale, which was a comfort. The outlaw chieftain would always demand payment, and Sir Rhuel would always offer a tale instead of silver. Sir Rhuel always ended up telling wild tales of a Changeling trickster, and then convince the superstitious outlaws that he was that trickster in disguise, and that he'd curse them if they impeded him. The details might vary, but the shape was always the same.

It was surprises that he hated, Bor thought. That which was unexpected was always worse. All his life, he'd never known good fortune, good happenstance. He longed for solidity, for expected outcomes. Give him a fair fight, a fight where all that counted was a man's strength and cunning, and he'd accept the outcome, good or bad. It was the unexpected that always went against him.

In the distance, Bor heard a noise. What it was, he could not say, but it made him uneasy. He stood and left the fireside, walking into the twilight woods. Magga glanced after him as he went, but said nothing, and Sir Rhuel was too deep in the telling to notice Bor's departure.

"'Don't you know, my friends,'" said Sir Rhuel to the outlaws in his tale, "'that strange powers walk these woods?'"

The forest was a mix of dense old forest and new growth. The wood-hungry folk of Avos harvested much of the forest, but there were sections they dared not touch. Elves and spirits, outlaws and Rootless folk dwelt in those parts, and so good folk did not trespass there. The bishop's lodge was on the edge of one such region, so Bor hesitated. Walking in the dark at night reminded him of the Fossewood, the night before they'd ambushed Lyulf Martens.

Bor . . .

He spun around, but there was no one there, no one who might have called his name. The rotten corpse of the bishop twisted in the summer breeze, the noose around its neck creaking softly. The dappled moonshadows of the leaves played across its face, distorting its features.

Bor . . .

He swore. The lips of the corpse had moved! Or had they? He could not be sure.

"Magga," he tried to call out, but his throat was tight with fear. There was magic here. He tried again, and this time managed a yelp. "Magga!"

The dead-ender hurried out of the ruined lodge, spear in hand. Behind her, Sir Rhuel peered out into the darkness, irritated that his familiar tale had been unexpectedly interrupted.

"That one," said Bor, pointing at the bishop's corpse. "Are you sure it's properly dead?"

"Hmm." She squinted and sniffed the air. "Don't smell anything."

She gingerly poked her long spear into the corpse's leg. "Nah, he's just plain dead."

"I thought I heard it speak."

She cackled. "The dead don't speak. Not mortal dead. And dead elves, they turn to wraiths, eh? They speak, but none hear 'em."

"As I was saying," shouted Rhuel from the doorway, "the outlaw chieftain's daughter had hair like fire and eyes like emerald, and danced like smoke from the embers."

"I could have sworn . . ." said Bor. He grabbed the spear from her and shoved it into the corpse's belly. Rotten liquid dripped down onto his face. He snarled in disgust.

"It's all right," muttered Magga, "you're just going mad. We all did, up in Necrad, and now this war's brought Necrad south. The uncanny does that to you." She took the spear from him and wiped its blade in the grass. "Come back to the fire. Hear the rest of the tale. The chieftain's daughter gets her tits out, that's a good bit."

Again, a wind breathed through the treetops – and a dog barked in answer, deeper in the wood.

Bor froze. "That's my dog."

Magga looked up at him in confusion. "Since when do you have a dog?"

"They killed it in Arden."

He set off through the trees. He could hear Magga and Sir Rhuel following him, wondering what madness had seized him, but he ignored them. He chased the sound of barking until he found the source.

There, on the ground, lay one of the bishop's hunting hounds. The animal writhed on its back, twisted, limbs flailing. It glared at Bor, eyes bulging as another seizure wracked its body. A shudder went through the animal, and the writhing stopped. It wriggled back to its feet, bounded over and licked Bor's hand in exactly the way Cu used to. It ran a little way off, then looked back, expecting him to follow.

It was not his dog. It was not Olva Forster's dog.

It was not, he was utterly certain, actually a dog at all.

He followed it.

From *The Sword Tale*, by Sir Rhuel of Eavesland

> *Guided by spirit in a shape familiar,*
> *He followed the hound through forest and fell*
> *Knowing the beast was dead, knowing that magic*
> *Had ruined him and ruined the land*
> *Knowing that faith was the province of lies*
> *Knowing that heroes lived only in tales*
> *Still he followed the dog to the marshes.*
> *While Avos burned, stripped of protection –*
> *The truth of the Erlking revealed at last.*
> *He walked amid waters, down secret paths*
> *Until he came to the holiest of holies*
> *The sacred pool shrouded by lilies*
> *There he knelt, on the lip of the grail.*
> *And saw there the Intercessor, as faithless as he.*
> *The spirit pointed to the stillest of waters*
> *The mirror of the stars where all fates are woven.*
> *Then reaching out, disturbing the pattern*
> *His hand closed around the hilt of the sword.*

Bor drew the black blade from the water.

"About time you got here," said Spellbreaker.

PART TWO

CHAPTER TEN

S ix months earlier.

The dreadworm flew low over black waters.

"This," cackled Spellbreaker, "is a remarkably stupid idea. Even for you."

"Shut up," muttered Alf. He gripped the sword, and the wintry darkness was replaced by cruel unlight. He could see the Isle of Dawn, waves crashing against the cliff walls, the forests and sentinel elf-towers – and beyond, the spike of Kairos Nal, the Stormwatch. The elves commanded the weather around the isle with the magic of that mountain.

He was careful not to look up. He'd looked into the night sky under sword-sight before, and seen what the darkness between the stars concealed. Alf didn't like what he'd glimpsed there. So, he kept his gaze fixed ahead.

"There'll be archers," he muttered.

"Of course there will be archers, and even if I can guard you from their arrows, I cannot protect this dreadworm. Continue and the worm perishes, you fall and drown, and I wait on the seabed for a lobster with ambition. A sorry fate for us all. *Turn around, wielder.*"

Alf unclasped his cloak and hooked it on one of the bone spikes protruding from the dreadworm's rotting hide. He hung his shield on another spike. "Tell the worm to circle," said Alf.

Then he jumped.

For a moment, he hung in the air, hearing nothing but the laughter of the sword.

Milk-white ocean struck him. Gasping for breath, he fought the sudden waves, hauling himself towards the shallows. Alf was an ungainly swimmer, but made up for it with brute force. The sword's magic revealed the dark depths of the water to him. The ocean was a sea of mist to his eyes, and he could see shapes – sinuous and many-toothed – swimming towards him.

"Archers," remarked the sword, "but also: sea-serpents."

The Elves of Dawn rode sea-serpents into battle on the ocean. The last time Alf had visited the isle, he'd come to beg Maedos for aid in the war, and ended up kicking the prince off a balcony. Their relationship had worsened since then.

Below him, a serpent's fangs. He could see the beast's hungry eyes, its flaring gills, the geas-glyph inscribed on its forehead, binding it to serve.

"Remarkably stupid," said the sword. "Die well, wielder."

Alf filled his lungs. *Go heavy*, he commanded.

Spellbreaker nearly wrenched itself from his hand as the sword became impossibly weighty, pulling him down into the waters. He plummeted towards the serpent, catching the beast off guard. He slashed at it. Underwater, he could only manage a feeble blow, but Spellbreaker's blasting-magic was enough. A shock wave erupted from the sword, reducing the serpent's flank to pulp. Blood oozed from shattered scales.

Stop being heavy! thought Alf desperately. The sword kept dragging him down for a long moment.

Sorry, what was that?

Spellbreaker reversed itself, becoming so feather-light it was actually buoyant. Alf clung to the blade as it lifted him back to the blessed air.

Below, the dying sea-serpent thrashed, trails of blood spiralling through the milk-light water. Spellbreaker's magic sight made the blood a fiery red, burning though the sea-fog.

"That's one," said the sword, "what about the other thirty or so?"

Alf gasped for air. "Your problem."

"Ah."

The world spasmed. Alf felt the blade's counter-magic pass through him. It tugged at his soul and made his guts twist. Undigested magic potions turned inert in his bowels, and he knew he'd pay for that soon. He could no longer see the serpents.

"They are feeding on the one you killed," said the sword. "Their geases no longer bind them, and they feast." There was a note of envy in its voice.

"Right," said Alf. He began swimming towards the shore.

"There are still archers," said the sword. "This remains a stupid plan. Single-handedly invade the Fortress of Dawn? To what end?"

"To talk to a friend."

Alf's adventures rarely brought him to beautiful places. The Riverlands where he'd been a mercenary might be pretty enough in the right light, but he'd seen them after battle, green fields churned to mud, stained red, crows fighting over scattered limbs. After, the war against Lord Bone's hordes was fought in the Clawlands and the Charnel. No one would call such places pleasant in any light.

And Necrad – there was a beauty to Necrad, but it wasn't one Alf trusted. Necrad was the mad thought you had standing on a cliff's edge, the way the frost looked while you froze to death. Necrad's beauty wasn't for mortal eyes.

When the Nine made camp, they shared stories, and Alf always liked the ones Laerlyn told of the Everwood. He'd never been there, but he used to dream of it – the golden forest shimmering with enchantment. He imagined shafts of sunlight, the sound of laughter down the path, the anticipation of reunion with old friends. There were no swords in the Everwood, no sorrow, only joy for ever.

Berys had scoffed, said it sounded sweet enough to rot her teeth, but Laerlyn had said that one day, when the war was done and she'd settled her quarrels with her father, she'd bring all of them to the palace in the heart of the wood, and they'd rest.

And, back then, Alf thought that sounded nice.

Lae hadn't kept that promise. Never would, now. Gundan was dead, and Thurn, and Jan might as well be. Lath was gone. Blaise would never leave his tower. And Berys . . .

Last time he'd seen Berys, she'd talked about some mad plan to attack the Everwood, and ranted about the secret malice of the elves. *Lae is part of it, Alf, just like her brother. She has to be. And that's why I never tried to tell you any of this.* Berys had saved his life in the Pits, saved Olva and Derwyn too. He owed her his life. Hell, he owed each of the Nine. But Berys was the one who might call in that debt.

There's going to be another war, she'd said. *A war against the Everwood. It's our last chance to break free.*

Had he – unintentionally – struck the first blow of that war, just as he'd struck the last blow of the last one? His thoughts kept returning to that moment in the tunnels under Necrad. Alf and Berys had taken Laerlyn's brother Maedos captive. He'd had Maedos at sword point. Laerlyn and a host of elven warriors had found them, and before he could be rescued, before he could be apprehended, Maedos had thrown himself on Spellbreaker. Alf could readily believe that Maedos was involved in some plot against humanity, and would shed no tears for the dead prince – the wretch deserved death, or as close as an elf could come to it, eternity wailing in the wraith-world.

But what had Laerlyn seen? Did she know that it was Maedos who'd moved, and not Alf? Did she think Alf had slain her brother? (*And what else did she know*, whispered a thought that sounded like the sword. *Did she know that Maedos plotted against you? Did she know of the schemes Berys spoke of? Was she ever the friend you believed her to be?*)

Alf pushed his thoughts away and kept swimming until he reached the stony shore. He'd never seen the Everwood, but the Isle of Dawn had the shadow of its beauty, or so the poets said. Last time he'd been here, he'd come out of the teeth of the war. A place where he could sleep for a night was bliss enough, and he'd paid no attention to the enchanted woods or the white towers.

He doubted he'd get a chance to appreciate it now, either.

Alf trudged across the beach, frost cracking beneath his boots. Behind him, sea-serpents quarrelled over the meat of their comrade, but his attention was fixed on the cliffs ahead. He was too cold and tired – and old – for the idea of climbing to have any appeal.

"Be wary, wielder."

Alf drew on the sword-sight. The sea was white fog again, the cliffs the bones of giants, every imperfection laid bare. He could see a path up to the forest a little way down the shore. In the sword's sight, the forest was a nightmare, branches like bony fingers. He glimpsed pale shapes, but he could not tell if they were living elves or dryads bound to the trees, or some other sort of spirit entirely.

"Listen!" shouted Alf, his voice booming off the cliffs. "You know me! I'm one of the Nine! I'm a friend of Laerlyn."

There was no answer.

"Is she here? I need to talk to her."

The echoes of his voice drowned in the endless sea at his back.

"I'm coming up, all right? I don't mean any harm." Alf released his grip on the sword, and the darkness returned. In the shadow of the cliffs, he couldn't even see the stars. The only light was a glimmer of moonlight behind the peak of Kairad Nal.

He came to the foot of the path, then hesitated.

"Do not," said the sword, "leave me behind."

"Stop reading my thoughts."

"Wielder, this is a stronghold of the enemy. Even at the height of his power, my maker chose not to assault Kairad Nal. Do not go unarmed."

"I'm not looking for a fight."

"Says the man who stands on a battlefield of ten thousand years. This is folly, but if you are intent upon it, then take me with you if you are to have any hope of success."

Alf shoved Spellbreaker down into its scabbard, silencing it.

But he did not leave it behind.

At the top of the path were two life-trees, leafless in winter. There was a suggestion of the skeletal about them. In the Everwood, it was always summer, and the life-trees were always blossoming.

Alf knocked on the tree. "Hello?"

There was no answer, except the laughter of the sword. Coins rattling in a jar.

"There's an elf in there, right?"

The sword remained silent until Alf relented and tugged it an inch out of the scabbard, exposing the jewelled eye.

"An elf-wraith is indeed bound to the life of this tree, wielder, but I cannot compel it to appear. Not without force. Let's use force."

Alf could feel the sword's anticipation of violence. The blade had sworn to serve him, but it was a cruel, hungry thing. For twenty years, he'd thought of himself as the blade's gaoler; he'd kept it safe from those who might use Spellbreaker for evil. Those years had been easy – he'd just ignored the sword.

Now, he'd come to think of it as a savage hound that had to be kept on a leash. A hound could catch a scent he'd never notice; he couldn't afford to dismiss the sword's counsel out of hand.

He turned away from the silent sentries and plunged into the wood. The spires of Prince Maedos' castle were his guide, rising above the treetops on the shoulder of Kairad Nal.

He had been there before, but could remember little of that last visit. They'd landed on the shore, and the elves had found them as they'd blundered into the wood. In Gundan's retelling of the story, the elves had blindfolded them, for outsiders were not permitted on the Isle of Dawn, but Alf couldn't recall any blindfolds. Then again, he'd been feverish when they landed – one minute he'd been staggering up the shore, the next they were arguing with Prince Maedos in the castle.

This time, no one stopped him. The forest was not empty – he caught glimpses of elves amid the trees, as elusive as moonlight phantoms cast by wind-tossed branches. He heard them too, calling to each other, distant horns of elfland warning of his approach. Once or twice, he heard hoofbeats, but he saw no riders; no archers loosed at him. The lack of obstacles unsettled him.

"Of course it's a trap, you dolt," said the sword. "There is no hope of retreat, now."

The gates of the castle were shut. They were of elven-steel, adamantine and unmarred. Beyond them was darkness. They stood four times Alf's height, impenetrable as the walls of Necrad. Maybe Spellbreaker could shatter the enchantments and batter the gates down, but it would not be easy. Alf looked up at the empty windows, the marble spires. Black pennants fluttered atop the towers; the castle was in mourning.

"Lae!" he called. "Are you here?"

The gates swung open silently.

Alf paused at the threshold. The sword was right. This was stupid. Every instinct told him not to enter the fortress. He'd faced impossible odds and survived before, but only by cutting his way through whole armies of foes. He'd stood drenched in blood and ichor, surrounded by the fallen. He'd heard dozens of wraiths shrieking in his ears, protesting their slaughter on the battlefield. Give him a foe it was right to kill, and he'd get it done.

Show him evil, and he could be good.

He advanced down the hallway, mouth dry, heart pounding. He sought his edge and could not find it. He cursed himself for his weakness, and cursed himself for calling it weakness.

At the heart of the castle was a great hall. The only light was from a brazier in the centre of the room, so most of the hall was lost in shadow. He recalled that there was a balcony up there, the very one he'd hurled Maedos from all those years ago.

Out of the darkness there came a white horse, and on it rode an elf clad in shining armour. On his shield was the sign of a rose, and his silver plate was decorated with enamel roses so lifelike it looked like they'd sprouted from the metal. At the heart of every rose was a charmstone, and belted at his side was a silver sword, akin to the one that Prince Maedos had carried in the vaults under Necrad.

The Knight of Roses, whispered Spellbreaker. *The Erlking's champion.*

The elf-knight trotted around the perimeter of the hall, the horse's hooves clattering on the marble as he traced a great wheel, the point of the lance always trained on Alf.

Alf forced himself not to move.

The knight came to a halt. "Aelfric Lammergeier," he said, "it is forbidden for mortals to trespass on this isle."

"Aye, well, I'll be going soon. I just want a word with my friend Laerlyn. I've heard she's still here."

"None of the royal house are here, mortal. The high seat lies empty." Bowstrings creaked in the dark. Alf looked up, and saw a dozen or more archers along the balcony above. There were more in the shadows behind the knight. Every one had an arrow nocked. "But it is well that you are here," continued the Knight of Roses. "Surrender, and I swear that you shall be treated honourably, as befits one of the Nine. You slew Prince Maedos unjustly, and you shall answer for that crime, but you shall have a chance to plead your case before the Erlking's court."

"'Tweren't unjust. He'd—"

The knight raised a hand. "You shall speak before the Erlking, mortal. Now, I need your word that you will go peacefully."

"I'll trust Laerlyn. Let me talk to her, and I'll surrender to her. I'll hand over my sword to her and everything."

"You think me a fool, that I would permit you to carry that blade in the presence of one of the royal house, after what you did? No, mortal. You shall not see her again."

Alf's finger brushed against Spellbreaker's hilt. He could see the whole hall clearly now, the carved face of the Erlking staring down at him. He could see the archers, and recognised some of them – they'd been with Laerlyn under Necrad. They'd seen Maedos perish, and already judged him. There was fear in their faces.

And in that moment, he found his edge again.

His fingers closed around the sword.

"Well then," said the Lammergeier. "I'll be going."

"No. Your fate was writ when you set foot on this island. You shall face the Erlking's justice."

Alf stared the Knight of Roses in the eye. "Who's going to stop me?"

"I have heard many songs about the Lammergeier," said the knight, "and in better days I would delight in trying my skill against yours. But you wield the demon blade, and I am no fool."

A *really, really stupid idea*, whispered the sword.

The elf dropped his hand – and the bows sang. Alf was already moving, hurling himself to the side, and swinging his sword in a wild arc. Spellbreaker sundered the world, spitting a blast of force. Arrows shattered mid-flight. The floor exploded, throwing up a shower of stones.

Alf landed heavily. Everything was off-kilter, his eyes full of dust. Arrows flew all around him. The thunder of hooves – he scrambled up and swung Spellbreaker again, and the Knight of Roses veered off from his charge. Alf pressed the attack, hewing at the knight while the elf was fighting to control his mount. The horse reared, Spellbreaker cut deep, marring those pearly flanks with red ruin. The horse fell.

The Knight of Roses rose from the wreck, and he was swifter than Alf expected. He parried Alf's first thrust. Their swords scraped together, Spellbreaker's cross guard entangled with the

Rose Knight's thorny blade, the two swordsman locked in a contest of strength, mortal sinew against elven might. As they wrestled, Spellbreaker put forth its power. The knight's armour was studded with charmstones, each one blessing its wearer with potent magic. One by one, they burst under Spellbreaker's assault, shattering with sudden pops. One shard struck the knight in the eye, and in that moment, Alf shoved his foe with all his might.

The Knight of Roses fell before the Lammergeier, slipping and falling in the pool of his horse's entrails. Red enamel roses were stained with red blood.

Alf laughed, amazed at his victory. Amazed at his luck.

More arrows struck, and found their mark in Alf's back and thigh. Alf stumbled, shock hollowing him even as his own blood gushed in a red gout across the ground. He staggered back the way he came.

He saw, dimly, the elf-knight rising again, sword in hand.

Flee, urged Spellbreaker.

Elves pursued him. He flailed with Spellbreaker, blasting their arrows from the air. Spells shattered too, but he could feel the sword's power fading. Darkness gathered in his vision. He had healing potions, somewhere, but no hand free to drink one. His right hand held Spellbreaker, his left supported him as he felt his way back along the corridor.

You are badly wounded, wielder.

A rush of strength from the blade filled him, and Alf felt detached from his battered body. It was the sword that moved his legs, the sword that worked his lungs, forcing him to breathe, forcing him to cough up blood. Elves closed warily, spears set, as if Alf was a cornered beast. He snarled and battered at them with Spellbreaker, and he could sense the sword's own hunger. It had given him everything it had left – it had no strength left for another force-blast, and its shield against hostile sorcery was not inexhaustible, either. The weapon needed to feed.

It needed to kill.

Alf wasn't ready to let it.

He backed away, brandishing Spellbreaker, and no elf dared strike at him. Back he stumbled, blood gurgling in his throat, flowing from the arrow-wound in his side. So much blood, blazing bright in the sight of the sword, red as roses as the knight followed.

Alf staggered to the end of the corridor.

The gate was shut.

CHAPTER ELEVEN

"Yield," said the Knight of Roses, "I shall not ask again."

Alf tried to speak, but his mouth was full of blood. He spat, and felt that was as eloquent as he could manage in his condition.

The knight attacked. His technique was perfect, his sword a razor wind. Alf's own fighting technique was all instinct; Gundan had taught him a little when he'd started out, and after that it was all just survival. You learned fast when there were monsters hunting you, but he was no duellist.

He countered the way he'd always fought – battering, brutal swings. He met the knight's elvish grace with Mulladale muscle. It had served Alf well in the past, but the past was twenty years ago, when Alf was young and quick.

The past was two minutes ago, before an arrow nicked his lung.

Again Aelfric Lammergeier and the Knight of Roses crossed swords, and this time, the elf was the victor. A twist of the silver sword ripped Spellbreaker from Alf's grip. The black blade slid along the corridor. The Knight of Roses' sword flashed again, and white agony shot through Alf's leg. He fell, clutching this second wound. Everything dimmed. All he could see was the Knight of Roses approaching, reversing the silver sword and raising it high for a killing stroke.

Thunder burst so close Alf felt his skull must rupture. The windows exploded with intolerable light. A titanic bolt of lightning struck the fortress. Down the corridor, ruddy light flared as the life-tree at the heart of the keep caught fire. The earth shook.

Alf took advantage of the distraction to drive his fist into the knight's stomach. Gundan had taught him little about formal duels, but plenty about brawls.

A hurricane burst the gates open. Outside, lightning rent the sky, raging winds tore at the forest. Life-trees creaked and fell. The mountain was wracked by a crown of thunderbolts.

Blaise stood at the threshold. The wizard's robes were untouched by the whirlwind that raged around him. Elven archers loosed at him, but the wind flung their arrows aside. The Knight of Roses struggled to rise.

Blaise spoke a word. Suddenly, in a trick of perspective, the corridor became a well. The wizard stood at the top of a steep shaft, which meant that down was ... back down the corridor, back towards the great hall away from the door. Alf fell, reeling from the revelation that what he had thought was the floor of the corridor was unquestionably, undeniably a vertical wall. Around him, the elves fell too, tumbling in confusion. Only the knight managed to maintain his footing as he struggled against the wizard's spell. He staggered towards Blaise, walking 'up' the shaft through sheer force of will. Starlight was in his eyes as he worked counter-magic.

"Wielder!" called Spellbreaker. Alf reached for the sword's hilt like he'd grab a tree root to arrest his fall. He caught it, and instantly the well became a corridor again.

"Aelfric, I need you," said the wizard, his voice strained as he contended with the Knight of Roses. The elf was nearly within reach of Blaise. Alf lunged up the corridor and struck from behind with the hilt of Spellbreaker, and the elf fell.

Alf and Blaise fled out into the storm. Alf was limping, light-headed from loss of blood, but still the wizard leaned on him. All around was chaos. Gusts shoved them this way and that. Trees that had endured the storms of centuries snapped like twigs. Lightning lashed Kairad Nal, a hundred bolts stabbing the mountain at once, so bright it was a false dawn on the Isle.

"Dreadworm," gasped Alf, "call the bloody—"

"I already did," said the sword.

This worm would not reach Necrad. The winds were too much for it. The membrane of its hideous bat-wings bulged and tore. It spiralled down towards a barren island a few dozen feet across. The rock stood only barely proud of the surging waves, but it was the only solid ground in sight.

Alf felt the worm die under him as they landed. He slid off the worm's back, pain running through his battered body, and the little island teetered beneath him. He had a flask of precious healing cordial, a lord's ransom in curative magic, and he drank it all. He spat out the first mouthful as it was thick with his own blood, but swallowed the rest. The pain receded, the pressure lifted from his chest. He took an unencumbered breath of icy sea air.

"Shit, did you need some?" He waved the empty flask at Blaise.

"I am uninjured. Spent, but uninjured."

Alf stared at the magical storm raging above the Isle of Dawn. "Did you do that?" he asked in awe. Blaise was the (admittedly self-proclaimed) greatest mortal wizard, but Alf had rarely seen him throw around raw power like that. Blaise was potions and illusions and relics, and knowing which rune opened the dungeon door.

Massively destructive magic was more the province of those who could wield the earthpower.

"I did. I wrested control of Kairad Nal, and I turned the mountain on itself." Blaise produced a silver net from his robes, and began to string it out across the ground. Alf shook his head. He didn't know much about wizardry, but that portable trap was the most basic of tools. He hadn't seen Blaise use one in years.

Then again, he hadn't seen Blaise leave Necrad in years.

"Why?"

"I noticed you leaving, and wondered where you were going. When I realised that you intended such a ... distinctive challenge to the elves, I could not resist the opportunity. You distracted the isle's defenders, and I dealt with a problem that has irritated me for some time. The Wood Elves used Kairad Nal to blockade Necrad. Now, that danger is removed."

"Removed," echoed Alf. Across the water, the forests were burning now, the glow reflected in the clouds. "Fucking hell, Blaise."

"Audacity will be needed in the days to come," said the wizard.

"Did Berys ask you to do that?"

"I have not spoken to Berys since before the siege," said Blaise. "Help me with this." Together, they strung up the star-net, hooking it on the rocks and the folded wing of the worm.

Blaise sat down, his back against the flank of the dreadworm's carcass, and wrote sigils on a piece of parchment with a silver pen. Each was the sign of a star, and elf-magic was ... well, that was about as much as Alf knew. *We are born of the stars*, Ildorae had told him. *Eight thousand one hundred and fifty-nine elves awoke with the first dawn, and eight thousand one hundred and fifty-nine elves shall see the last sunset at world's end.* Stars, elves, sigils, nets. But he hadn't seen Blaise use a net since they arrived in Necrad. The city functioned as a giant engine of sorcery, collecting power that manifested as charmstones and other wonders, and that could be tapped by wizards like Blaise.

"What're you casting?"

"A spell of concealment."

"Here?" They were all alone on the dark ocean.

"You understand nothing about the hidden world."

"Can't you call another dreadworm?" Spellbreaker could summon and command a dreadworm, but only at sunset.

"I am *spent*. I put all the magic I could into the destruction of Kairad Nal. Hence, I must scrimp and glean every scrap of power for even this little spell." Blaise glanced up at Alf. "I did keep a reserve, but I used that rescuing you."

"Thanks for that."

"I do not need your gratitude. I need you to understand our situation. Tell me, why did you go to the Isle of Dawn?"

"I hoped Laerlyn was there. I wanted to explain to her about Maedos, and Death, and what happened in Necrad. About everything. And I wanted to talk to her about what Berys said."

"Just as you tried to deal with the Wilder invasion by parlaying with our late friend Thurn directly. You think the bonds of camaraderie we forged as the Nine can overcome any division." Blaise cocked his head. "I wish you were right, but the evidence weighs against it."

Alf squatted down, then his hips thought better of it and he sat down instead, stretching his long legs out across the rock. At least he'd kept his cloak dry, even if the rest of his clothing was soaked and freezing. "Any chance of a fire?"

"No."

"Lae would listen. I know she would. Thurn listened. Gundan and me, we got the Wilder talking. We could've made peace, only some stupid bastard ruined it by throwing a spell-skull. Lae would listen." Alf threw a pebble into the water. "Come the spring, I'll go to the Everwood and find her."

"Come the spring, the Road will be blocked by armies from Summerswell bent on our destruction."

"Why would the Lords turn on us?" Alf wanted to protest, to shout, *We saved Necrad. We faced Death herself and didn't flinch. It was messy, and bloody, and we paid a high fucking price, but we did it. Just like we slew Lord Bone. We're their damn heroes.* He swallowed all that. "Is this what Berys talked about? You think the Wood Elves are the root of all our troubles? You think they've turned Summerswell against us?"

"In Necrad, where the Wood Elves could not eavesdrop on us,

Berys and I spoke at length about the secret power that rules these lands. For what it's worth, I believe her. I have known for a long time that unseen forces dictate events. But honestly, I care only a little who rules the world – so long as I am free to study. A king may make laws for elves and mortals, but the laws of magic bind king and commoner alike. Those laws are the only ones I respect."

Blaise seemed to catch himself.

"But at the same time," he continued, "the truth matters not. Even if the Lords of Summerswell act only of their own volition, then their course of action is the same. Necrad is too valuable to cede it back to the Witch Elves – or leave it under the control of anyone else. They will come for our city. They will come for my tower." Blaise's pen scratched on the parchment. "And your own kinsman is acclaimed king of Necrad. Your fate is bound to ours."

"That's all nonsense. It's just a story some fool made up. It's not a prophecy, or a true claim, or anything. It's just a story."

"Perhaps. And when Derwyn hangs from a gibbet, with you beside him, then the Lords might agree that it was all nonsense. Until then, they see the boy as a threat." Blaise raised his hand, then stopped. "Keep the Spellbreaker sheathed. This spell is precarious, and if it is broken, they will find us." He muttered arcane words, then flung his hand up as if scattering seeds into the sky. Alf couldn't tell what the spell had done, but that was true of half of Blaise's spells. Across the waters, thunderstorms wrestled above Kairad Nal like giants, trampling the woods below.

Some spells didn't seem to do anything. Others shattered the world.

"Blaise," said Alf, carefully, "you brought Olva's boy back. The same spell brought Death back, aye, and bound her into Thurn's daughter."

"Ask your question."

"What came back with Derwyn? Is it . . ." Alf shook his head. "What is he?"

"Honestly, I do not know. Death was the first human, and her case is unique. Certainly, the spell required a soul in the grey lands to carry Derwyn back to the lands of the living, but I do not know what of that soul remained with him." The wizard sounded irritated. "It was not my spell, after all. The Erlking made it. If it goes awry, your complaint is with the hand that wrote it, not me."

"So what do we do?" asked Alf.

"We wait here until sunset tomorrow, and then you summon a dreadworm."

"About Necrad, I mean."

"Your nephew is fortunate. He has the greatest swordsman in all the land as a champion," said Blaise distantly. "I must rest." The wizard's head drooped. Alf couldn't tell if Blaise was sleeping, meditating or just tired of talking to him. Conversations with Blaise reminded Alf that he'd spent most of his life in one monster-haunted dungeon or another, not at the courts and councils of the wise. Always, he was ten steps behind, blundering along until someone cleverer told him who to hit.

He laid Spellbreaker across his lap. Once, when all was in chaos and Necrad lay open, the sword had urged Alf to take power, to be more than a follower. But then Derwyn had come back from the dead, and in the moment of his resurrection, Alf had seen a familiar soul in the boy. In that moment, it had seemed like some part of Peir had come back.

Peir, captain of the Nine. Peir, who Alf followed.

Peir, who Alf would have died for in a heartbeat.

Peir, who Alf killed.

He didn't sleep that night. He kept watch, like when he'd watched over the Nine. Now there was just Blaise. No counsel from Jan, no haunting songs from Laerlyn. None of Lath's pranks, or Gundan's ribald jokes. Alf looked south, towards Summerswell and the High Moor far away across the sea. Jan dwelt there, or had before she'd faded away, or turned to light, or whatever mystic transition had taken her. *Farewell, Alf*, she'd told him, *you carry my blessing, and the hope of the world.* What did that mean? Was she just saying goodbye, or was that part of her prophecy too? What would she advise him to do? Jan had her own doubts about the Intercessors – what would she say about Berys' plan? What would she make of Peir?

He found himself toying with his sword-hilt, almost tugging Spellbreaker just clear of the edge of the sheath. Speaking to the sword might disrupt the delicate spell. And anyway, asking the demon sword for counsel was foolish. The sword couldn't be trusted.

He sat alone, staring at the storm, not knowing what to do about it.

Dawn drowned out the stars. It was a brilliant, purple-red smoke on the eastern horizon making a spectacularly bloody birth to the new day. The carcass of the dreadworm began to liquify, dissolving into stinking black goo. Blaise folded up his star-net and tucked it away in a pocket of his robes. He took out a handful of other treasures – wands, charmstones, intricate Witch Elf talismans, a spell-skull – and spread them across a flat rock to examine them in the light of day. Most were burned out, the charmstones cracked, the wands depleted. One by one, Blaise discarded the useless items with disapproving clicks of his tongue.

"What's all that junk?" asked Alf.

The wizard held up a crystal vial, engraved with an image of a hideous thing with excessive eyes and tentacles. Alf had slain things like that in the Pits. There was a little purple-brown stain at the base of the vial, but the stopper was open and the vial empty. "Kairad Nal was not unguarded."

Weapons out of Necrad. Alf rarely bothered with such things – Spellbreaker was more potent than any of them, and jealous to boot.

Alf's stomach rumbled. "Is there anything to eat?"

"No."

And all they had to drink was more healing cordial, diluted with rainwater.

The day wore on. A few times, Alf sallied forth, trying to draw Blaise into conversation – the wizard used to talk long into the night with other members of the Nine, but rarely with Alf. His advances were met with walls of silence, or ran into sarcastic pit traps; Blaise had a knack for cutting Alf down. Alf would make some remark about the unnatural weather, or ask something about history, and Blaise would reply in a way that underlined Alf's ignorance and slow wit.

"It was kind of you to take that dwarf friend of Olva's on as an apprentice," Alf would say.

"She has the virtue of knowing when to be silent."

Or:

"Could you use magic to send a message to Laerlyn? Like Jan sent me a dream?"

"Had I six years of starlight gathered under the sign of the Raven, dust from a scribe's skull, and a desire to perish untimely, then perhaps. To do so would give away our location. Perhaps Laerlyn would arrive in time to weep over our corpses."

Only one of Alf's questions hit the mark. Towards the late afternoon, as the dwindling sun descended at their backs, Alf found Blaise staring towards the Isle of Dawn. Pillars of smoke rose from the ruin.

"What are you looking at?"

"The house of my ancestors."

"Huh?"

"My great-great-grandfather Casimir was a baron in the Riverlands. By all accounts, he was a kindly lord, praised for his generosity. He accrued honour in battle, and a considerable fortune. A neighbour grew jealous and plotted against him."

Alf nodded. He'd fought in plenty of little wars in the Riverlands. The province was famously divided.

"This rival, Bryning, was clever. He placed traitors in Casimir's household; he bargained in secret with Casimir's vassals, trading them a portion of my ancestor's domain in exchange for a promise to withhold aid when the time came. He was patient, too – he had his wizards grow fat with power, so they could work potent spells when the moment came.

"Casimir, of course, had a wizard in his own retinue. A graduate of the College Arcane in Summerswell – founded within living memory back then – and it is the role of such court sorcerers to read the stars and foretell weals and woes to come."

Blaise paused and looked over at Alf. He cast back his hood for once, revealing his thin face, his owlish features, the worry lines at his eyes. "Perhaps Casimir's wizard was inattentive. Perhaps Bryning had the better magus in his employ, and one wove spells of conceal-ment the other could not pierce. Perhaps Casimir's wizard was one of Bryning's turncoats. But on Midsummer's Day in the Year 148 he foretold that nothing was amiss, and by nightfall, most of Casimir's family were dead, his household slaughtered, and his castle afire. History does not relate what happened to Casimir's wizard, but I like to think he died of professional embarrassment."

"What became of Casimir?"

"He escaped, along with his young daughter. For a time, he travelled with a handful of loyal retainers. He petitioned the Lords for redress; he prayed for Intercession. Family tradition maintains he went to the edge of the Everwood and called on the elves for mercy. But at every turn, he was met with kindness, and pity, and piety – nothing useful whatsoever. His defeat was too thorough for anyone to wage a doomed war on behalf of Casimir, and Bryning was adept at currying favour among the Lords. He did arrange to have his daughter Nenemh betrothed to an old friend of his, a wealthy noble of Ellscoast – I am descended from their union. But Casimir did not join her in obscurity. He sought not revenge, but justice." Blaise gave a wry smile. "I was told this story so many times by my father, I find myself using his words, as he got them from his father. Untruths compounded across the generations. One cannot lie in a spell, Aelfric. Speak the wrong word, the magic goes awry, and you spill a lifetime's worth of gathered power into the dirt. Wizards never lie."

Alf doubted that, but didn't interrupt the telling.

"One of Casimir's retainers had Wilder blood. In those days, the Wilder sometimes raided Ellscoast, but they traded with Summerswell too. They brought tales of their living gods, who dwelt in an enchanted city beyond the north wind and blessed the Wilder with charmstones and cunning artefacts. This retainer knew a place in Ellscoast, an ancient standing stone raised long before mortals ever walked those lands, that was sacred to the living gods of the north."

"These gods – Witch Elves?"

"Indeed. You yourself put many of these 'gods' to the sword, Aelfric. But this is Casimir's tale, not yours. He went to the stone on the appointed day, and lo! The 'gods' appeared to him, beautiful and terrible. Whether he bargained with them, promising them blood or service or his soul, or if – as family legend insists – they saw the injustice and offered their help freely, I know not. But they gave him a spear of polished silver, and charmstones of power, and a cloak of invisibility, and other treasures beside. And Casimir bade farewell to his daughter, and he marched off to the Riverlands to bring justice to the usurper Bryning."

Blaise fell silent, looking out at the smoke staining the sky. Alf waited as long as he could, then asked, "And?!"

"There is nothing more to tell, Aelfric. Bryning lived to a ripe old age, and died in his bed. His descendants became great landowners in the Riverlands, and have known prosperity and good fortune for many years."

"What about Casimir?" The abrupt ending annoyed Alf.

"Why, he died. His broken spear was found in a marsh in

Arshoth. None of his company were ever seen again, and none know what happened to them. But I can now guess, thanks to what Berys told us, and what you saw at the Oracle's fortress of Daeroch Nal." Blaise lowered his voice. "The Intercessors watch over us – the first prayer of the faithful in Summerswell. Now we know them to be elf-spirits, invisible spies and sentinels watching from the wraith-world. We cannot perceive them easily, so they might be anywhere. Even here, on this desolate rock. There is only one place in all the world where the Intercessors cannot go: they cannot pass beneath the necromiasma above Necrad."

"They're like wraiths, yeah? The Oracle could talk to wraiths. But wraiths are like . . . they're ghosts pissing in the wind. Thin little rags. You can chase 'em away with a candle flame."

"Indeed. The elves are so desperate to avoid fading to wraithdom that they lash themselves to trees or feast on blood. I guess that the Wood Elves have some method to magically fortify some of their number, making the spirits we know as Intercessors. But the point is, Aelfric, is that they are *watching* us, whispering about us. Outside Necrad, the world is thick with the Erlking's invisible spies. They are not omnipresent – I wager there can be no more than three dozen or so Intercessors, spread across all of Summerswell and Elvendom and the north – but as we cannot know when we are being spied upon, we must be careful what we say, where we go outside Necrad."

Easy for you to say, thought Alf.

Blaise gestured at the burning isle on the horizon. "We can risk swift raids like this one. But nothing longer. The necromiasma is our only sure protection."

Alf nodded, slowly. "Like when Acraist was hunting us, back in the old days."

"Then, Aelfric, we were adventurers wandering the wilderness, able to move quickly and stay hidden. Now, we are rulers, defending a fixed stronghold. We have fewer friends and face greater odds. Our war against Lord Bone was a race. Now, we play the King's Game, move and countermove, stratagem and sacrifice across a great board. We must be clever."

"You be clever. Just tell me who to hit."

"Your capacity for violence has always been the foundation of our friendship."

Alf yawned. "So, what became of Casimir's kid? Your ancestor?"

"She bore witness to the slow decline of the once great house she had married into. All manner of ill fortune befell them – harvests ruined by unseasonable frosts or floods, alliances and betrothals rejected, defeats in battle. A curse followed Nenemh all her life, and down through her descendants. My father dwells in a crumbling lodge, buried in inherited debts, surrounded by the remnants of the few treasures the family could not sell. Their estates, their castles and their holdings – all gone. Their banner no longer flies in Summerswell."

Blaise drew his hood back over his face. "The curse followed me, too." His voice seemed deeper, reminding Alf of when he'd visited the Wailing Tower. "I begged my way into the College Arcane, and still doors were shut to me. The Masters dictate what each apprentice can learn, and forbade me from studying any but the most common spells. Why? Not lack of talent or discipline – I outshone all the other apprentices. No, it was the same curse that bedevilled my family for generations."

The burning isle was a false dawn in the east. "You're blaming the elves, like Berys."

"Firstborn or mortal lord, power clings to power. The first priority is always to defend what power they possess, and to tear down any rival."

Alf shrugged, uncomfortable with his friend's cynicism. "I'd never have figured you for the descendant of a warrior. This Casimir reminds me of Peir."

"Weren't you listening, Aelfric? Casimir was an idiot. He died in a bog. We may meet the same fate if we are unprepared."

*

Winter made for an early sunset. As soon as the sun dipped below the horizon, Spellbreaker called for a dreadworm. This close to Necrad, a flying steed responded quickly. It congealed out of the necromiasma and raced towards them, faster than the wind. Still, Blaise scanned the darkness and the lapping waves, as if expecting to be caught in the brief gap between the breaking of the spell and the shrieking descent of the dreadworm.

They mounted the beast, and it rose up, black wings spread to catch the icy wind. Alf glanced back, and for a moment he saw a shape on the island below.

But then there was nothing, and they flew home.

CHAPTER TWELVE

"Forgive me," said the Vatling.

Olva's hand darted to her knife, and a shriek forced its way into her throat. She fought both impulses, composed herself, and turned. Threeday moved with such a soft tread she hadn't noticed him enter her chambers in the Citadel.

"For what?"

"I seek the Lammergeier. I am told he is here."

"He's with my son." From the adjoining room there came a grunt of pain and the thump of a body falling. Olva winced. "Alf's teaching him to fight."

"Ah, there can be none more suited to such a task than the Lammergeier," said Threeday. He brushed his moleskin doublet with a pale hand, and adjusted a jewel at his neck. Olva frowned; the Vatling had not dressed so richly before. "I have a matter to discuss with Sir Aelfric – the payroll for the Citadel guards is due."

"Is that Alf's responsibility?" Alf never had a head for figures.

"Strictly speaking, no. Ordinarily, the matter would be handled by the paymaster, Johan of Arden; but he is dead – slain during the siege last year. I might turn to the almoner, Bertheld of Ellscoast, but he fled the city. Obviously, I would then look to the major-domo of the Citadel, Elten of the Crownland, but, ah, she too perished in the siege. The League quartermaster, Gerard of Arshoth, left aboard Lord Vond's ship – taking with him what little remained in the Citadel coffers – so I cannot go to him. Nor, obviously, can I go to Lord Vond."

"The council?" Olva knew little of the workings of Necrad, but she knew there was a council.

"The council – on which I have the honour of serving – has not met since the end of the siege. In their absence, I have tried to keep the affairs of the Garrison running as best I can, but . . . ah."

"Let me see. I've argued with labourers over a day's pay often enough." The Vatling gladly handed over a sheaf of papers, covered in his neat handwriting. Columns of figures swam before Olva's eyes, but she hid her confusion from Threeday. She might not be a sword-wielding hero or a noble bred to rule, but she could not sit idle.

"Fortunately, our expenses were considerably reduced by casu-alties, so I was able to pay the survivors last month. But now . . ." Threeday tapped one eye-watering number with a boneless finger. "The matter demands attention."

"Does the city have the money?" If this were her farm, then she'd have sold off some of the pigs, or reluctantly parted with some of Galwyn's valuables.

"Not enough. The situation is worsened – or, more precisely, *changed* – by the present season." Threeday nodded at the window, and the snowy landscape outside. "If the Road were open, there would be ready buyers for relics. Not only Summerswell, but the dwarves or across the sea to Phennic. Of course, while the Road remains closed, then the guards have nowhere to go. Oh, the hardier might make to the New Provinces, but . . . well, there are undead out there beyond our walls who do not feel the cold."

Olva shivered at that thought. She looked at the figures again. "The guards have nowhere to go, but still need to eat. Even if we can't pay them the full amount they're owed, they'll surely have to accept what we give them."

"Lady Olva," said Threeday, "I cannot guarantee that the guards would not turn on you, if you chose that course of action. And just so we understand one another, if they did I *can* guarantee that I would be there, holding the door open for the men intent on murdering you. My loyalty is to Necrad and my people – whoever rules Necrad shall have as much support as I can give."

"I'll find the money," said Olva. Alf had a pile of treasure, accrued from a lifetime's dungeon delving. It was an unthinkable fortune, but the sums on Threeday's ledger would devour it in a month. "What about the stores?"

"Ah. Again, we are blessed that there are fewer mouths to feed, but the city's granaries are nearly empty. Supplies that should have been sent from the New Provinces were interrupted by the Wilder attack. It may be they will arrive in time to stave off starvation, but I have my doubts. Messages sent to Castle Duna have returned unanswered." Threeday smiled, and she could see he had no teeth, only a ring of tiny fangs like a leech. "You humans are so limited in what you consider edible. And such appetites! My kind was made to live on very little."

"No money and little food." For all the strangeness of Necrad, some things were not so different. "Is there anything else that I should be concerned about?"

"Were I to share all my worries," sighed Threeday, "I would be emptied out like an overturned sack."

Few survived a sword-fight with the Lammergeier.

The Lammergeier wasn't trying to kill Derwyn, but Olva still feared for her son's life. Her brother battered him across the dining room and back again. Derwyn had a footstool in one hand and a stout shield in the other; Alf wielded a wooden sword. Spellbreaker stood propped against the far wall.

"Again," ordered Alf.

Derwyn wiped blood from his lip, then charged, swinging the stool at his uncle's head. Alf stepped aside and rapped the sword across the back of Derwyn's hand. The boy cried out and dropped the stool, but he still managed to block Alf's next blow with the shield, staggering back under the force of the blow. Before Alf could strike again, Derwyn held up his hands in surrender.

"I yield."

Alf flipped the shield around, then mimed bashing Derwyn with its edge. "You still had this. You can do a lot with a shield. I broke an ogre's skull with one."

Derwyn flexed his hand and winced. "I think you broke one of my fingers."

"Cordial in my pack." Alf nodded towards his travelling gear in a corner of the room. Derwyn limped over.

Olva picked up the footstool. "How come Der gets furniture, and you get a sword?"

"No reason," said Alf, gruffly. "I mean, sometimes you're caught without a proper sword."

Olva placed the stool firmly on the ground. "You said you'd protect him, not beat him. He's not well, Alf. He's still not himself."

"Best he knows how to fight. I won't always be around. "

"Like you weren't there at Yule."

Alf looked sheepish again. "Aye, well, sorry about that, Ol, truly. But no harm done, eh? You handled that mad monk well enough yourself."

"One monk isn't the problem. It's what comes after him."

"We'll handle that too. The League remembers what happened the last time they tried to besiege Necrad. The Stone Dragons are awake again. Blaise saw to that."

"And can Blaise conjure food, too? Can Blaise keep the city from turning on us? Alf, you're our general. We need you here to lead."

"I'm here now, aren't I?" He kicked the stool across the floor. "Right, lad," he called to Derwyn. "You take the sword this time."

Derwyn paused by the window. "Peir," he said quietly, "used a warhammer, didn't he, Uncle? Not a sword."

Alf froze. "Aye, he did."

He's still my son, thought Olva, fighting panic. *He came back from the dead, but he's still my son. Blaise said he might be changed, but he's still Derwyn underneath it all.* She glanced at Alf, and saw the same thought in his furrowed brow. It was one thing to see the ghost of a kinsman in a child – Derwyn resembled his late father in so many ways – but it was something else entirely to think that a stranger, even a hero like the great Peir the Paladin might be incarnated in your own son's body. It must be even more confusing for Alf, who had known Peir as a friend, followed him as a leader. *I don't want him to be a hero. I want him to be himself.*

"That's why you made me practise like that. You wanted to remind me of how Peir fought. You wanted to see . . . how much of him is in me."

A look of panic crossed Alf's face, just for a moment. Then he scowled and busied himself with the strap of the shield. "It's not like that. It's not."

"What does it matter?" said Olva. "You're alive, and—"

"And I don't know *who* I am." Derwyn picked up the stool and hefted it like a warhammer. "Sometimes, I don't know if I'm awake or dreaming. I hear the stories they tell of me on the streets – they call me the Uncrowned King—"

"That's one piece of mischief we can put a stop to right now!" barked Alf. "Threeday!"

The Vatling oozed in the door. "My lord."

"It's you that's been spreading those tales around Necrad, isn't it? All the nonsense about Derwyn being the king – it's getting us into trouble with Summerswell." Alf poked the Vatling's chest. "Put a stop to it. Now."

"I shall do what I can, if that is your desire, but I did not start that rumour. I do not know where it came from. Some say it is an ancient prophecy of the Witch Elves. Others say pilgrims saw a vision on the Road that the Uncrowned King was come." Threeday raised his head and looked Alf in the eye for once. "If I must be honest, I should say the rumour was exceedingly convenient for all of us. While I did not start it, I certainly encouraged its spread. My city is still wounded, and the strength of the Garrison diminished. I have no wish to see more killing on the streets. Better that the inhabitants of Necrad rally behind the symbol of the Uncrowned King than turn on each other, elf against mortal, mortal against Vatling." Threeday turned to Derwyn and bowed. "Did I do wrong, your majesty?"

Before anyone could answer, Alf grabbed the Vatling. "Put an end to it. You heard me." He shoved Threeday out the door. "Filling your head with nonsense and making trouble for us all," he grumbled, "with prophecies and shit. Come on, you take the sword this time."

Derwyn shook his head. "It's not nonsense, Uncle. Something happened to me on the way back. How else could I wake the stone dragons?"

This is the price, thought Olva. *Blaise warned me there'd be a price. He's not just my son any more.*

Alf was silent for a moment, then he put down the sword. "Listen. The last night of the siege, when you were . . ." He grunted, as if that could encompass all the events of that tumultuous night. "I talked to Thurn's daughter, and I told her that whatever she was, she wasn't Death any more. She could be herself. She could put the legends and the war and the bloody prophecies behind her. Same with you, lad. Maybe . . . maybe you carried a bit of Peir back with you. Peir was the best man I ever knew. The best of us. Wiser and kinder and braver than the tales tell. He saved us all, at the end." Alf grunted, choking back emotion. "But you're not him."

He paced the room, his long strides taking him to the far wall in a few paces. "I don't deny that strange things might've happened, miracles and the like. But I've seen all manner of strange things. Magic . . ." Alf shook his head. "Peir was many things, but he never cured anyone by touching 'em. Not without Intercession, and Intercessors can't get into Necrad."

And the Intercessors are a Wood Elf lie, too, thought Olva. She remembered Prince Maedos commanding the Intercessors.

"It wasn't the Intercessors," said Derwyn, slowly. "It came from within me. I just knew what to do." He put down the stool. "But I don't know how to fight with a warhammer. I don't know who I'm supposed to be, or do, or . . ."

A cold voice rang out behind Alf, making everyone jump. "There is a way, wielder. Put me in the boy's hand. I can read his mind and tell you the truth."

Olva shuddered. The last time Derwyn's hand touched the sword, he'd been possessed by the elf-wraith Acraist. Her son, *consumed* by the monster who'd murdered his father. It was too much. "No," she said.

"Do you not trust me, Widow Queen? Did I not guide you safely through the Grey Lands? Wielder, did I not swear that I would serve you loyally, and never lie to you?"

"She said NO."

Alf's words boomed through the hall. Startled wraiths fled into the corners or vanished entirely, slipping into the unseen wraith-world. To shut out the creeping horror of Necrad, Olva turned to her brother. "Threeday says the city guards need paying, and there's nothing left in the treasury."

"He shouldn't be worrying you with that sort of thing," said Alf. "It's not your burden to bear, nor Derwyn's, neither. Forget this Uncrowned King nonsense. The city's in the keeping of the Nine again."

"Someone has to bear it, Alf. You went off to the Isle of Dawn, and Blaise is up in his tower, and there's no one else. I can see to it. I can help you keep this damned city safe, if doing so keeps us safe too. We're all in this together, now."

"I don't want you staying here. There's trouble coming, Olva. You can't go back to Ersfel, but when the spring comes, you could . . . sail to Phennic, maybe. Or just disappear. Hardly anyone knows you or the boy, you could just go."

"Oh, *they* know us, Alf. The elves have been watching me ever since the war. Isn't that right, sword?"

"There was an Intercessor at your house," confirmed Spellbreaker, "on the night I took your husband's life."

"They arranged my marriage to Galwyn to ensure I'd have a child – to make sure you'd have close kin, Alf, that they could threaten if they had to. And you think we could just *leave*? If we leave Necrad, they'll find us again. It's here where we make our stand."

"You don't know what you're asking," said Alf. He shook his head. "This place is evil. It's no place to stand."

"It could be," said Derwyn, quietly. They both turned to look at him. The boy looked confused, searching for words that did not come easily. "Back home . . . when we spoke of Necrad, it wasn't just a place of evil. Oh, you told me all the stories, Mother, about the Dark Lord and his minions and how it was a city of terrors – but the Nine won. The city fell, and . . . it was redeemed. I imagined it as a magical court of heroes where the Nine ruled justly."

Both Alf and Olva objected simultaneously, their words overlapping.

"That's just nonsense from the stories—"

"Redeemed? Tell that to the Pits. I've seen—"

"—Lords want people to settle in the New Provinces—"

"—fifteen years of fighting to keep a lid—"

Derwyn raised his hand. "I know that's not true. I know it was a child's fancy. I've seen the horrors of Necrad. I died here. But one miracle happened. Why not another?"

"What are you saying, Der?" asked Olva.

"By right, I shouldn't be alive, and this city should not be in our hands. The twists of fate that brought us to this point are so unlikely, it feels like a tale. But they happened, and here we are. We have a chance to make that enchanted court real. Uncle, why did you and the rest of the Nine swear to watch over Necrad, if not in hope of redeeming this place?"

Then, surprised by his own courage, Derwyn turned away, his cheeks flushing with embarrassment.

Alf sat down on the stool and leaned on the wooden sword. "Let's live through the spring, first, and then talk about courts and redemption and the like. I do like the sound of it, lad. If I could just talk to Laerlyn, to Berys . . . they're good people, Olva. All of them, all of the Nine. Remember when we had to hide out in Ersfel? That was a good time." He smiled at the memory. "I should have brought them back again, after. Lae liked the woods."

Olva remembered it too. Nine bedraggled adventurers, wounded and weary, taking refuge in the little cottage. "It was the war, Alf. We were all terrified you'd been followed."

He took her hand and pressed it to his forehead. "We nearly stopped the Wilder, last year. Gundan and I, we made peace with Thurn. We made a bargain we could all accept. But someone threw a spell-skull and ruined everything."

"I know."

"If I could just talk to the others, I know I could make 'em see sense. Bring 'em back here and make a peace."

Olva bit her lip. She wanted to say that her brother was being a fool. He was a fool – he'd seen far more than she had, done things she could only dream of, become a fabled hero – and yet he was still the same idiot mooncalf she'd grown up with. He still believed that things could be simple.

She patted his hand. "First things first, Alf. We put food on the table, then we—"

"Derwyn!"

Out of the corner of her eye, Olva saw him move. While Alf was speaking, her son had circled the room, as if listening to her brother's words. Then, in a sudden motion, he reached out and grabbed Spellbreaker. His fingers barely closed on the sword's hilt, and then he was falling, crumbling. Olva caught Derwyn before he hit the ground and lowered him gently down. He was so terrifyingly light, as if hollowed out, but his fingers were locked in a death-grip on the sword. His face turned ashen grey.

"*Ayas morthu neareash!*"

The wizard Blaise was there, abruptly, looming over her. Had he just appeared in the room, or had he burst through the door? She couldn't tell.

Blaise struck at Derwyn's hand with the butt of his staff, trying to knock Spellbreaker from his grasp without touching it, but Derwyn's grip was too tight. Olva knelt and unknotted her son's fingers, one by one, prising them away from the sword.

"What happened?" asked Alf.

The wizard placed a charmstone on Derwyn's forehead. "What do you think, dolt? I brought him back with a spell, and you expose him to the *Spellbreaker*? Make yourself useful, and carry him to his bedchamber."

Alf scooped up Derwyn without effort. "Will he live?"

"He will." Blaise leaned heavily on his staff. "The spells binding body and soul together are like delicate sutures, torn if twisted the wrong way. Had I arrived a moment later, or if the sword had put forth its full power, he would certainly have perished. We were fortunate."

The three of them proceeded down the corridor to what had been Lord Vond's bedchamber, Alf carrying Derwyn, Olva holding his bruised and battered hand, and Blaise following along behind like a wraith. But it was Blaise who ushered them out of the bedroom.

"I must not be disturbed. This is potent enchantment," said the wizard, "and he will need rest afterwards. A great deal of rest. He must breathe the air of this world, dwell on this earth, until his spirit is rooted here once more.

"It would also help, Aelfric, if you stopped hitting him with furniture."

Blaise shut the door firmly over Olva's protests.

"Breathe the air? It's the middle of winter!"

"It's all right, Ol. Blaise will help him," said Alf. "Blaise will know what to do."

"I *know*," snapped Olva. She lingered by the door for a moment, listening to the infrequent arcane mutterings. She rested her head against the cold, polished wood, then turned away and marched back down the corridor to the dining hall.

There was work to be done.

"Alf. Go fetch Threeday the treasure he needs to pay the guards. And ... let the stories about Derwyn spread. If people want to believe those tales, let them."

"All right." Alf scooped up Spellbreaker from where it lay on the floor. He hesitated, frowning as some thought struck him, and then he shoved the blade into its scabbard and slung it at his side. "I'll see to it."

"And you need to go to Castle Duna."

CHAPTER THIRTEEN

The dreadworm flew north through a sky that was all white-grey flurry, nothing to distinguish earth from cloud.

"What did you see?" Alf asked the sword.

"I am not sure," admitted Spellbreaker. "Some elements of the Paladin survive in him, certainly. They lie scattered about his soul like discarded pieces of armour, and he fumbles in the dark. Maybe, given a candle, he could strap them on."

"Very poetic."

"Matters of spirit are ill-suited to words, wielder." The sword's ghastly voice grew louder, and Alf had the disconcerting impression that the thing was uncoiling on some level, a dragon slithering closer to the mouth of its lair. "And what would you wish for him? Would you bring him that candle, so the boy might in truth be Peir returned?"

"Peir's gone."

"We killed him, you and I. You used me to shatter the arcane vessel of Lord Bone, and the conflagration we unleashed destroyed them both. I have always regretted my part in that act, and I am but a weapon. You wielded me. You struck the blow. Do you regret that?"

"It had to be done," said Alf. "Peir knew it."

"So you tell yourself. But I see your—"

"Enough."

"Wielder," said the sword, "I am sworn to serve you, and what sort of servant would I be if I did not offer choices? Derwyn has the capacity, given the right influences, to embody Peir the Paladin. I hated Peir, as I hated all the Nine, and have no desire to see him return to the lands of the living. You may feel otherwise. I could aid you in—"

"The boy," snapped Alf, "will find his own way. And you didn't know Peir. He'd never want to be brought back at the cost of another."

"Ah, but consider the wider circumstances. Your enemies are legion. Your hold on Necrad is tenuous. Your 'friends'—" the sword's voice was metal scraping on bone "—are scattered or gone. War will come with the spring. Would it not be better to have the Paladin on the throne of Necrad? Peir – and I hated Peir – was wise and brave. All trusted him – elf and dwarf, Wilder and Summerlander. He was the only one of you that Lord Bone truly feared."

"Down," ordered Alf, "I want to walk for a bit."

"It is a long walk to Castle Duna from here," objected the sword.

"Down."

He let the dreadworm flap back into the sky, then trudged along the road through the wildwood. The forest was silent, the trees shrouded in snow. Nothing moved in the white land. Alf scanned the horizon for any living thing, even a carrion bird, but found only stillness.

Every so often, he took his knife and carved a mark into the bark of a prominent tree. The marks were a secret language Alf shared with one other only – Lath the Changeling. They'd created the marks over their years fighting in the tunnels below Necrad. Alf doubted that the Changeling would ever see the runes he'd carved, or that Lath would answer, but he had to try.

He walked for a few hours, almost in solitude. Alf considered leaving the sword by the side of the road for a while, so that he could be truly alone, untroubled by the wider world. Then twilight came, and with it the chance to summon a new dreadworm.

He called the monster and flew on.

He landed again outside the town of Athar. There were still long hours left before dawn, but Spellbreaker made the forest bright as day. Alf walked on. He found more signs of the recent conflict – ruined villages, scars in the landscape where magic had been unleashed – but the New Provinces had mostly been spared. The Wilder had concentrated their efforts on Necrad, and like so many other armies their assault had foundered on the enchanted walls. Athar was still prosperous, its granaries and storehouses well stocked.

Earl Duna and his household knights retreated along this road after the disastrous parley at Bavduin. Duna had not survived the retreat.

Alf's life and Duna's ran parallel. Both came from humble backgrounds – Alf a farm boy from the Mulladales, and Duna the second son of an impoverished minor noble. Both sellswords before the war. Gundan joked that if he'd recruited Duna instead of Alf for his mercenary band, then it would have been Duna who joined the Nine, Duna who saved Summerswell, Duna who slew Acraist and won the sword Spellbreaker.

After, the parallels endured. Lord Brychan of Ilaventur sought to marry his daughter Erdys to Alf; when he'd refused, Duna had won her hand. Alf could have used his fame to become the most influential noble in the New Provinces; instead, he'd stayed in Necrad, and it was Duna who became earl, Duna who was called the Lord of the North. There but for a twist of fate went Alf.

Now Duna was dead, and Alf alive.

The night watchman at the gate recognised the Lammergeier, and let him in.

"I need to talk to Lady Erdys," said Alf. "When she wakes, tell her I'm here."

One of the guards pointed to a lighted window in the chapel. "She is already awake, my lord."

A young man knelt by the Intercessal shrine at the top of the chapel, a grail on the altar before him. Duna's second son, Idmaer. His hands were clasped in fervent prayer, the living fingers of his left hand over the stump of his right. The elf Ildorae had maimed Idmaer when she briefly stole Spellbreaker. An Intercessor brought him back from the brink of death.

The boy – the earl, Alf realised, with his father and elder brother dead – ignored Alf as he entered. Alf stood there in the doorway for a moment, awkward, then he saw Erdys.

There would be two new tombs in the chapel of Castle Duna, for two caskets lay on wooden biers. In years to come, dwarven sculptors and masons would carve marble effigies of the fallen knights to match the older tombs. Earl Duna and his eldest son would in time be given the same honours as those who had fallen in the last war.

Duna's widow Erdys waited for Alf between the caskets. She was dressed in mourning grey, a veil hiding her features. Erdys had always seemed almost elven in her agelessness to Alf, but the years lay heavy on her now.

"He prays all night," she whispered, "every night. He eats little. He's wasting away. He barely sees the world around him, any more." Her fingers brushed against her husband's casket. "I am not sure he knows."

"He'll get better," said Alf. "My sister's boy, Derwyn, he nearly died too, and magic brought him back the same way."

"The Uncrowned King, they say. Well, Aelfric, does this king lay claim to the domains granted to the earl by the Lords of Summerswell?"

"What's yours is yours," said Alf. "No one's questioning that."

"It's his, when he comes of age. I rule in his name," said Erdys, "and he will inherit the earldom, if he wishes it." She raised her voice. "Idmaer, I'm going to sit with Sir Lammergeier in the solar. Will you join us?"

Her son did not reply. Erdys led Alf up a staircase to a private chamber. Alf climbed the stairs wearily.

Between the elf-woman in Necrad and your sister, wielder, whispered the sword, *you have had plenty of practice apologising to mothers of maimed children.*

She knelt by the fireplace to stoke the dying fire that smouldered in the grate. "Light those candles, will you?"

The candles on the table were unusually large, and impregnated with some odd incense that make Alf's eyes water. They reminded Alf of candles used in Necrad to drive away the wraiths of dead Witch Elves, but their scent was redolent of the warmth of the southland.

"My father sent them," said Erdys, "with my boy Aelfric. They brought them with his body."

"I'm sorry," said Alf. "He died bravely, if that's any consolation."

He died stupidly, whispered the sword, *charging through a mudflat.*

"If it weren't for him," Alf continued, "and the knights who rode with him, then Blaise wouldn't have had time to wake the Stone Dragons. The Wilder would have taken Necrad."

"And where were you while my son rode to his death? Where were you when the Wilder caught my husband on the road and butchered him within sight of my window?"

"I was fighting."

"Killing Prince Maedos?"

Alf's face fell, and Erdys raised an eyebrow.

"It's true then," she said. "Idmaer spoke of it, but I thought it was just one of his fever-dreams."

"Maedos . . . he'd taken my nephew hostage. He was behind much of what went wrong last year." Alf fumbled over the words.

Erdys stared into the flames of the resurrected fire, then drew back her veil and sat stiffly upright. "Why are you here, Aelfric? What do you ask of the Earl Idmaer?"

"A promise. Necrad's low on food, and there'll be nothing coming from the southland anytime soon. You got your harvest in. We'll buy all you can spare."

"'We'? On whose behalf do you make this request?"

Alf shrugged. "Necrad. The council. The Nine . . . the Uncrowned King. Look, just send wagons south as soon as you can, and you'll make a bloody fortune."

"The earl has conditions. First, you will send a letter *demanding* the earl give you the supplies you need as tribute, and threaten war if he refuses."

"What—"

"Second, the rulers of Necrad shall recognise the earl's right to his domain, which belongs to him and his heirs forevermore. The earl, or his representative, shall have a seat on the council of Necrad. A full seat, Alf, not as 'representative of the New Provinces', but as the equal of any of the Nine."

"The second, of course. But the first, Erdys – I have no quarrel with you. We'll pay for the food."

She thinks the Lords will retake Necrad, wielder, whispered Spellbreaker. *She seeks to protect herself. Such a document will let her say, "Look, I was forced to serve the usurpers, I was never a traitor" if necessary.*

"Oh, you shall pay. In charmstones if not in coin. Your coffers must be close to empty."

"Near enough," admitted Alf.

Erdys winced. "Learn to lie."

"I don't lie to my friends," he said, and extended a hand. "Do we have a bargain?"

"We do."

"How long before Idmaer comes of age? Three years?"

"Two," said Erdys. "But I will hold him to this bargain." She sagged in her chair and pulled the veil from her hair, the cold mantle of authority vanishing. "He says strange things at night, Aelfric. One night, he even demanded that I muster our troops and make ready to march on Necrad. It was a passing delusion, and went with the dawn. And, as you said, he will get better." She rose. "I have something for you. Two things. Wait a moment."

The sword waited until Erdys was gone before whispering in Alf's mind. *The son is obviously under the influence of the Intercessors, wielder, which means he is a tool of the elves. They saved his life for their own purpose – when he comes of age and takes the earldom, they will control Castle Duna and have a knife poised at your back.*

"A lot can happen in two years."

The third son, Dunweld, is even younger. If he were the heir, then Erdys would be in place as regent for another six years at least – and in that time, you could mould Dunweld into an ally and assure yourself of the earl's loyalty. Few survive a blow from me. I took Idmaer's hand – let me take the rest of him, and be done with it.

"No."

Or send an assassin. Ildorae, perhaps. Or you could even make it look like a Wilder did it – Duna's men killed Thurn's daughter, so it would be fitting retribution.

"I preferred it when you weren't trying to help me."

Erdys returned, carrying a bundle wrapped in cloth, and a sealed letter. She handed Alf the letter first. "My father gave this to my Aelfric. He was to give it to you, but in the confusion of the siege, it must have slipped his mind."

Or the boy kept it back. He sided with the other whelps against you in the council. They tried to take me from you.

Alf broke the seal and skimmed the letter. It was an invitation from Lord Brychan for Alf to visit Ilaventur in the spring as an honoured guest. As a hero of the Nine, Alf had received thousands of such missives in the early years, every noble in Summerswell begging the Lammergeier for favours or inviting him to join their households, to captain their armies, marry their daughters. It was mildly unusual for Lord Brychan to make such a request – when Alf rejected Erdys' hand in marriage, Brychan had taken it as a snub, though Alf had not meant it as such. At the time, he'd known that his quest was unfinished, that evil still lurked in the dark under Necrad. He'd felt he couldn't bind a young noblewoman to share that burden, so he'd turned Brychan down.

He'd thought it a noble sacrifice. And yet Erdys stood there beside him, with her husband and eldest son dead, and another wounded in body and soul. She picked up one of the candles and brushed it past the paper. More words appeared, revealed by the fragrant smoke.

SIR AELFRIC – THE TRUE STRUGGLE IS IN SUMMERSWELL. OUR ENEMIES ARE ALREADY MOVING, BUT IF YOU JOIN THE FRAY, YOU BRING HOPE OF VICTORY. MUSTER ALL THE STRENGTH YOU CAN, AND COME TO ARDEN. THE LANDS WILL RALLY TO THE BANNER OF THE LAMMERGIER.

MORTHUS LAE-NECRAS I'UNTHUUL AMORTHA.

Alf stared at the elvish words. He knew the phrase – *the gift of death shall not be rejected by the undeserving.* Jan had spoken it, when she'd sent him home to Necrad to avert the rising darkness. Laerlyn had said it was a prayer against the undead, and she'd whispered it as they'd fought Lord Bone. What Brychan meant by it, he did not know. But one thing the hidden message and all the secrecy made clear was that Brychan was part of the same secret conspiracy as Berys. His shoulders slumped, and he realised that some part of him had hoped, impossibly, that it had been another of Berys' lies – or even some deranged paranoia on her part. It would have been easier to believe that Berys was mad than to contemplate that she was right, and that the Wood Elves had secretly shaped all he had ever known for their own ends.

There's going to be another war, Alf. A war against the Everwood. It's our last chance to break free. Berys had said that, in the dark.

He didn't know if he had the stomach for another war.

"Erdys, what is this?"

In answer, Erdys took the letter and burned it in the fireplace without looking at it. She brushed the ashes from her fingertips. "I don't know, Aelfric. It is a private letter from my father. I do not presume to speak to him, or know his business. If there is one thing he taught me, it is the virtue of discretion. Some things should not be spoken."

"Berys told me—"

"Please!" She lowered her voice to a whisper. "Please, don't tell me! Don't bring me into this. My father's cause is not mine. I have lost enough."

Alf raised his hands. "All right, all right. We'll speak no more of it."

Erdys picked up the bundle. "I sent scouts north looking for Wilder. They found none. The survivors of the siege of Necrad have fled deep into the wood, and long may they stay there. But they found this at Bavduin."

Alf unwrapped the bundle. Inside, he found a broken axe-haft, dusted with ash and shards of shattered charmstones. Jagged marks like black veins ran through the metal, testament to the power of the lightning bolt that had annihilated the axe – and the dwarf who'd wielded it.

"Chopper." Gundan's axe.

"His people should have it," said Erdys. "I've found that having something to bury helps."

"So," said the sword when they were alone, "Brychan of Ilaventur is part of Berys' conspiracy. One of the high Lords of Summerswell defies the Erlking's rule. Delightful."

"I told you to stop listening to my thoughts."

"Your soul shouted it, wielder. A cry of alarm. You know what it signifies."

"No, I bloody don't know what it all means. I want to talk to Blaise about it."

"It means Berys is not alone in her schemes. It means that her war against the Erlking has a chance of succeeding. Imagine it, wielder! A red tide from Arden to Eavesland. Knights, augmented with magic looted from Necrad, demonstrating just how mortal they are as they smash each other to pulp across a hundred battlefields! The slaughter that the Nine averted twenty years ago unleashed at last. It will be glorious, wielder. We should be part of it." A quiver ran down the blade, as if an unseen tongue licked the length of it.

"I promised to defend Derwyn, and that's what I'm doing. What we're doing."

"If you want to protect him, then join Berys and Brychan in their war. Bring me south to slaughter Wood Elves and their little deluded dupes. Bathe me in blood in your nephew's name. I have slain one Prince of the Everwood – let me have the rest."

"If I never draw you again," said Alf, "it'll be too soon."

CHAPTER FOURTEEN

H e flew back the next night, shivering in the dreadworm's
saddle. The great stone mountain of the Citadel fortress reared
up above Necrad's harbour. A new banner flew above it – Alf's sigil
of the Lammergeier, surmounted by a crown. Olva's embrace of the
tale of the Uncrowned King continued. As he flew over the Garrison
walls, one of the guards hailed him, waving his arms to attract Alf's
attention. Alf circled down.

"Sir Lammergeier – there's a Witch Elf below," said the guard.
"She demands passage into the Garrison. She claims she's invited
to the council."

"Aye, Ildorae. Threeday should've informed you." Alf rubbed his
side where the Witch Elf had stabbed him only a few weeks ago.
Better that she come through the gate as a friend than climb over
the wall in the dead of night as an assassin.

"He did, sir. But, my lord – she's not alone."

The last time Alf had seen Ildorae, she'd been dressed in mismatched armour, a bloodstained spear in hand, a ragged elf out of
the wilderness. Now, heedless of the cold, she wore a silken gown
that shimmered like moonlight against her pale skin. Intricate jewellery twined about her arms, and her silver hair was braided and
set with charmstones, held back by a circlet of silver. The Goddess

of the Hunter's Star, the Wilder called her, and she looked the part, as beautiful and remorseless as winter.

But it was not Ildorae that alarmed the guards.

Six other elves walked beside Ildorae, six lords and ladies of the Witch Elves. Each was thousands of years old; some, perhaps, had seen the first sunrise, or laid the stones of the first city. The red light in their eyes spoke of what they had become to survive unfaded.

The Skerrise, he thought. *Galarin Ancient-of-Days. Emlys Arun. The last vampires.*

"Ildorae," Alf called from atop the gate, "you know they aren't allowed in the Garrison."

Six pairs of red eyes stared at Alf with utter hatred. He laid hand on Spellbreaker, but did not draw the blade.

"And they shall not cross your threshold," said Ildorae. "They have come here so that you know, mortal, that I speak for my people in their entirety. All those who swore the Oath of Amerith stand with me."

"Not the vampires. The charmstones, and whatever other magic weapons you've got hidden in that pretty dress."

"These are heirlooms of the Witch Elves. They were made by us. Do you lay claim to them by force, Aelfric Lammergeier, or shall we walk together as friends to the council chamber?"

Ildorae smiled, the six vampires glared, but it was all one thing – a challenge. For the twenty years of the occupation, the League forces – mortal, dwarf, and Wood Elf – had looted Necrad, stealing the magical treasures of the city. Alf wondered how the Witch Elves had kept the relics worn by Ildorae hidden for so long – and what else might be in the vault.

"Sir?" whispered one of the guards. "Standing orders are to confiscate any charms discovered in the hands of elf or Vatling. Should we—"

Pick your battles. "Let her pass."

Ildorae entered with a conqueror's swagger.

"Don't get any ideas," rumbled Alf, "and don't make trouble."

"Oh, the thought of reclaiming our city from you mortal thieves is a sweet one. A last faring forth, a last battle-feast. 'Tis true, there are few of us left, but it would be a glorious effort." She gave him a sidelong glance. "They would send me to kill you, you know. You and Blaise – remove you two, and the rest would be easy."

"You tried to kill me before," said Alf, "and it didn't go so well for you."

She laughed. "I shall let another take their turn. They will queue up to slay you, come the spring."

They found Threeday in Lord Vond's former office near the council chamber, surrounded by piles of paper. "Sir Aelfric!" Threeday rose and bowed. "Ildorae." He bowed again, but kept a wary distance from the Witch Elf.

Olva arrived, in conversation with her dwarf friend Torun. Alf caught the last words; she talked about Necrad being like a great wheel of fate, lifting folk up and casting them down. A notion he'd heard before.

Finally, Derwyn arrived, with Blaise by his side. Derwyn was pale, and leant on the wizard's staff for support. They approached the chair at the head of the table, Lord Vond's seat, and Blaise stepped aside, letting Derwyn take the place of honour. The wizard did not sit, but stood at Derwyn's shoulder.

"Let us begin," said Olva.

"I trust that the negotiations with Lady Erdys went well?" asked Threeday.

"Well enough. We won't starve."

"One catastrophe averted, a hundred more to go."

"Something like that. Erdys also gave me this." He laid Chopper's hilt on the table for all to see. "I figure I should bring it home to the Dwarfholt. I owe Gundan that." Olva frowned, and Alf hurriedly added, "A dreadworm can get me there in two days. I'll be back within a week or so."

The dwarf Torun made a squeaking noise and clasped her hands over her mouth.

"What is it, Torun?" asked Olva.

"It's not for me to say," stammered Torun nervously.

"Yes, it is. Go on."

"It's just that ... there are few other dwarves in Necrad, and I've been so busy in the Wailing Tower that it might be nothing and I'm speaking out of turn, but ... I've talked to them, and they're angry that you and Lord Gundan rode out to Bavduin, and only you came home."

"Many died at Bavduin," said Ildorae.

"That may be so, but the dwarves are a proud folk, and quick to judge." Torun squirmed in her seat. "If you go alone, and so briefly, it'll give offence. A fallen hero deserves honours."

"We need to ensure friendly relations with the Dwarfholt," added Threeday, "so they stay neutral in any conflict with Summerswell."

Olva sighed. "And it has to be Alf, of course. It has to be one of the Nine. All right. Go, and be back as soon as you can. Maybe you can't fly there, but you can fly back. Torun, can Blaise spare you for a few days? You know the dwarven customs better than any of us."

"That would not be, ah, wise," interjected Threeday. "I, too, have some few friends among the dwarven traders, and it seems to me that I could find someone more, ah, diplomatic."

"No," said Blaise. "Torun will go."

"Master Blaise," hissed the Vatling, "it would be foolish to—"

"If she wants to go, she goes," said Olva. "Threeday, you've paid the guards, yes?"

"Of course."

"Then you or Alf pick a few as an honour guard. It'll be hard travelling in the snow, so make sure they're able for it."

Ildorae tapped one of her rings on the table. "I shall go too, I think. And I can find a few of my kinfolk who might serve, too. What better honour guard could there be than an escort of dread knights, paying respects to their fallen foe? What better sign could there be of Necrad's strength?"

Alf snorted. "And no doubt we'd have to give your elves arms and armour. Berys tried the same trick once, offering to sort one problem by making a bigger one for the future. A time may come, Ildorae, when we have to arm the Witch Elves, but not yet."

"I speak of only a few dread knights. A half-dozen, maybe." Ildorae waved her hand dismissively. "Are you so frail, Lammergeier, that you fear so few?"

"That's how it starts," muttered Alf.

"Who would this honour guard serve?" asked Derwyn. "In whose name would they march, and under what banner?"

"Why," said Ildorae, "they would march side by side with the Lammergeier, and the mortals of Necrad. What difference would the banner make?"

"Then have them march under the Lammergeier's banner. Have these dread knights swear fealty to Alf."

"I'm no lord," said Alf. The idea of someone swearing to him felt like a joke at his expense.

"Whatever formula pleases you mortals," said Ildorae, "it is a passing thing to us." She preened like a cat, amused that she had won a concession from the occupiers.

"Then they shall swear to the Uncrowned King," said Olva.

"And I shall hold them to their oath, Ildorae," said Derwyn, and his voice was strange. "As strongly as they are bound to the Oath of Amerith. I shall not treat them ill, or dismiss the gift of their loyalty."

Ildorae studied Derwyn's face for a long, long moment, and the boy looked back without blinking. He reminded Alf of Peir in that moment; Peir could stare down the sun if his cause was just.

It was the immortal who bowed her head first. "So shall it be."

Alf waded into the awkward silence that followed. "Right. Well, that's that. Sooner we go, the sooner we're back."

Blaise rose to depart. "Wait a moment," said Alf. "There's something else." He hesitated, wondering if he should send most of the other councillors away before speaking of Lord Brychan's message. A matter for the Nine, Berys would have said, but he was tired of secrets. "Erdys' father Brychan sent a secret letter to me, just before the siege. He's working with Berys, against the Erlking. He calls for aid."

"Does he now?" said Olva, her voice dripping with suspicion. "What can we give? We've a handful of soldiers, that's all. And charmstones and whatnots, too."

"Berys took most of those with her," said Threeday, "and Summerswell looted the rest. But I would not dismiss Lord Brychan's request without consideration. We fear that Summerswell intends to force us to yield back Necrad, and that it will come to war. We survived one siege, but at great cost. I doubt the city can endure another." The Vatling stared across the table at Alf. "If we send aid to Brychan to ensure the fighting is in Summerswell instead of here, that would be to our advantage."

To your advantage, thought Alf. The Vatlings were spawned in Lord Bone's vats, here in Necrad. They needed Necrad more than anyone.

"What help can we give?" repeated Olva.

"I can find more dread knights," said Ildorae. "And I do not doubt that other powers could be summoned up." She looked across the table at Blaise, but the wizard's face was unreadable, hidden beneath his hood. Threeday squirmed nervously.

"Is that true, Blaise?" asked Olva. "Is there more that could be done, beyond those stone dragons?"

"Conceivably. I recover more of Lord Bone's spells with each sigil I decode. The breeding vats still function."

"More can be built," said Threeday, eagerly.

"I could call up demons and bind them into shells of metal. Charmstones can be harvested. I could animate dead flesh. There are ogres in the hills who still fear Necrad. The elements of Lord Bone's armies are scattered, but much can be rebuilt. But all that will take time."

"A last faring forth," mused Ildorae, half to herself. "Amerith avenged."

"How long?" asked Olva.

"Are you sure about this, Olva?" said Alf. "We'd be unleashing the things that I spent the last twenty years killing. It'd be war like you've not seen before – Ersfel was mostly spared, last time."

"I wasn't spared, Alf. You know what I lost. I won't have any more taken from me." She turned to Blaise. "How long?"

Blaise shrugged. "Four or five months, to begin with. Spells I can work quickly, but there is work of hand and hammer to be done here too."

"Months, so long after the thaw," said Alf. "The Lords' army will be at our gates by then."

For a moment there was silence.

"Might the dwarves close the Road through the Dwarfholt?" suggested Threeday. "We could retain Gundan's axe until—"

"I'm not holding Gundan's memory hostage," snapped Alf.

"And the dwarves are no friends of Necrad, either," said Ildorae. "At best, they will stay out of the way of both sides. But there are other possibilities. We are not without friends in the south. In times past, the Witch Elves had servants among the mortals. Berys knew the signs and passwords, for the descendants of those cults have mingled with her rebels. If they can hold the Cleft of Ard against the Lords' armies, then that would give us time to prepare the arsenal of Necrad."

"And how do they hold the Cleft of Ard?" said Alf.

But he knew the answer. He felt the sword's cold hunger wake.

Olva stared at him. "Arden's not far from the Dwarfholt. You go south, Alf, like Lord Brychan wants. You hold until we can raise Blaise's new army."

Bloodlust from the sword spilled into Alf's mind. He saw himself riding across a battlefield, swinging the black sword, and with every stroke a dozen foes fell. Counter-magic shattered charmstones and protective spells; the razor edge sliced through armour and flesh with equal ease. Alf swung the sword like a scythe mowing down wheat, a harvest of corpses and broken bodies. Eyes all wide with death-shock stared at him, a field of severed heads judging him an avatar of death. He moved methodically, reaping without joy or conscience.

Spears and arrows pierced him. Swords cut and axes hewed him, but each life the sword took made it stronger, and its strength carried Alf. It ate his doubts, whispering, *You know that you find joy in the battle. You know you are most alive in the midst of death. I know you, wielder.*

He marched on, remorseless as Acraist, each slow step paid for with a thousand deaths. The sword did not relent. He imagined the blade cutting through the armoured knights of Summerswell, the great Lords laid low by a farmer's son from the Mulladales. He imagined the banner of the crowned Lammergeier flying above all the cities of the southland. The people cursing his name. And, most of all, he imagined the horror on Laerlyn's face, the disappointment in her eyes.

In the tunnels under Necrad, she'd had the bow *Morthus*. She could have slain him with an arrow, and saved Prince Maedos' life. But Laerlyn had hesitated, and spared Alf.

Would she hesitate again, if he pursued this war?

I will do it, sang the sword, *I was made for this. And so were you, wielder.*

No, thought Alf, *you swore to serve me. So SHUT UP.*

The vision faded. The sword's red dream subsided. Alf clung to his seat, unsteady, feeling as though years had passed in that fever of iron and blood. He opened his mouth and croaked. "No," he said again, shaking his head. "I don't want to be a butcher, and that's what it'd be. I took the sword because we needed it to beat Lord Bone, and I kept it to keep the damned thing safe, to stop anyone else using it." He looked around the table, searching for support. Blaise had withdrawn into the shadows, his face lost beneath his hood. Threeday fiddled desperately with a piece of paper, while Torun looked in alarm from Alf to Olva.

Olva's face was hard.

"I saw you killing Wilder," she said, "and Lyulf Martens' men. Why is this any different?"

"They sought out the fight," said Alf. "They ... they forced my hand."

"Did they, lord?" asked Threeday without daring to look up, "or is that you could more easily see them as deserving of death?"

"That's not fair," protested Alf. "I tried to convince the Wilder not to attack. And Martens' men had kidnapped Derwyn. They were working for Prince Maedos."

"And Berys would say: so are the Lords of Summerswell!" said Olva.

"Elves know patience," remarked Ildorae, "we can wait centuries for the right time to act. You do not have that. In a few weeks, the Road will be clear enough for them to send an army. In a few months, they will have hunted down Berys and her allies. Maybe they will not attack immediately, but instead slowly strangle you. Maybe they will wait, Lammergeier, until old age has robbed you of the strength to lift that sword."

"Um." Torun raised her hand, hesitantly. "It seems to me that you – that we – need to decide exactly who we're fighting. Is it Summerswell? Is it the Erlking? Is it everyone – the Everwood, and Summerswell too, all the Lords who owe their rank to the Erlking, and the Church that serves his Intercessors, and the college of wizards—" her lip curled in distaste "—that teaches only elven magic?

Because some of you are talking like it's just the elves, and some of you are talking like it's all the Southlands."

"It's anyone who comes after us," said Olva.

Derwyn lifted his head. "I will not command you to fight, Uncle," he said. "We gave Spellbreaker into your keeping for good reason, and the sword should not be used heedlessly. But my mother is right – there is no better champion we can send than you. Go to the Dwarfholt and honour the fallen. Then, go on to Arden and delay the Lords as best you can. Seek out Berys and Lord Brychan. Tell them that Necrad is brewing an army."

He raised his hand. "But it is my hope that this army is never used. Tell the rebels that there is another path. If they wish to be free of the Erlking's rule, they can join us here at my court. Let us be a beacon to the world, not a threat." Derwyn's lifted his gaze to the window, to the eerie towers and twisted temples of Necrad, and for a moment it seemed to Alf that the miasma parted and warm light spilled over the rooftops.

Ildorae scoffed. "You mortals think you can squat in the city of the elves, in this font of sorcery, and the Erlking will leave you in peace?"

Who would want this place? Laerlyn had said. *I hate every stone in this cursed city. It may have been beautiful once, but I fought to break Necrad, not to claim it.* He couldn't believe she was lying – and Peir would trust her too.

"Laerlyn would," said Alf, and Derwyn nodded.

"The king has spoken," said Threeday.

They departed the next morning. A dozen guards, elf and mortal, and Alf and Ildorae at the head of the column. Between them walked Torun, the axe-shaft stowed in a reliquary case like a child's coffin. They passed Tar Edalion, the shrine Jan once built just out-side the shade of the necromiasma. Wilder looted the chapel during the siege, and it had gone unrepaired and untended since then. Alf was no cleric, but it irritated him to see the work of one of his friends fall into decay.

"I'll come back and fix that," he muttered, and Spellbreaker chuckled.

Alf glanced back, and saw Olva and Derwyn atop the wall above the westward gate, and beside them, the hooded figure of Blaise. He raised the sword in salute.

"I'll be back soon," he swore.

But the Lammergeier would not look on the walls of Necrad again.

CHAPTER FIFTEEN

T he Witch Elves walked lightly over the snowdrifts. The mortal warriors had to force their way through, but they at least had enchanted cloaks to ward off cold. Even the dwarf Torun made good time.

To his shame, it was Alf who hindered the company. Spellbreaker's counter-magic meant he could not wear an enchanted cloak like the rest – a minor charmstone like that would not survive close proximity to the black sword. He struggled on.

Ildorae dropped back to walk beside him. "Why don't you pretend to take a dreadworm up to scout the terrain ahead, and save your legs?"

"I'm fine," said Alf.

"He's not," said the sword.

"I'm fine."

They trudged in silence for a few minutes. Alf groaned under the burden, and he suspected the sword was magically making itself heavier. To distract himself, and because the thought had been in his mind since Castle Duna, he asked Ildorae what the Witch Elves knew of the Intercessors.

"They are older than the clerics of Summerswell know," she said. "It was a thousand years ago or so that we first became aware of spirits trespassing in our territory. The Old Man of the Woods spoke to them, long before the Erlking opened the eyes of the priests of Arshoth. When they put forth their power and become manifest, even mortals can sense them, and they can work what your deluded kinfolk call miracles. But they can also recede into the wraith-world where even the keenest cannot sense them. Save Amerith, and she is gone.

Alf brushed his hand against Spellbreaker's hilt. "Can you sense 'em?"

"Sometimes," said the sword. "But only if they act. Not if they wish to remain hidden."

"And they could be anywhere. Watching us."

Ildorae drew back her hood and looked at the clouds above. The air had changed as they drew near to the edge of the Charnel. "The miasma is a barrier to them; Bone made it to hide his works from them. And there are ways to baffle wraiths. They stray easily in unfamiliar lands – bright sunlight and wild weather distract them. They prefer to anchor themselves to holy relics, to places or people."

"There was an Intercessor following the Nine," rumbled Spellbreaker. "More than one, perhaps. Jan and Peir both channelled their blessings. If we had caught you, then I could have ended cleric and spirit in a blow. Alas for the Oracle's treachery!"

"Or animals," added Ildorae. "They bind themselves to beasts, too, to perceive the material world through living eyes. It is difficult to see one side from the other." She frowned, her eyes following on a tiny circling dot in the sky. "That hawk's watching us."

Alf followed her gaze. "That's not a bloody Intercessor. I know that bird." He raised his voice. "Lath, Lath! Come down!"

Spellbreaker twisted in his grip, Ildorae readied her spear. Dread knights drew their swords. Alf swore at them all. "It's fine. It's Lath."

"He sided with the Wilder at Bavduin," hissed Spellbreaker. "He brought Death back. He is a foe!"

"The Erlking tricked him. And he's my friend." Alf waved at the circling bird with the black sword. Lath swooped low and landed on a stone, still in bird-shape.

"It's all right, Lath. We've no quarrel any more." Alf thrust Spellbreaker into the mud and walked forward, empty-handed.

"Come no closer!" croaked the bird. "Necrad has tainted me, madman that I am."

"I'm going to the Dwarfholt with Gundan's axe. Come with me. We'll say farewell to him together." Out of the corner of his eye, Alf spotted one of the dread knights creeping closer, bow in hand. Alf angrily waved the elf back. Lath was not an enemy.

Not his enemy, anyway. Lath was one of the Nine, damn it.

The bird cocked its head, one black eye watching Alf. "I'll not go south. South is madness and trickery. Here I belong, where the land still speaks truth to me."

"Then I'll meet you back in Necrad."

Lath spread his wings and cried in alarm. Hawk-shape blurred into something else, a hideous bat-winged form, then that too vanished as the Changeling writhed. Lath's human features bubbled to the surface for a moment, his flesh a seething cauldron of forms, until he reasserted control and became the hawk once more. "Cursed! Cursed!"

Lath seemed about to take flight, so Alf spoke hastily.

"Peir's there. He came back, just like ... just like you healed Thurn's girl Talis. And my sister Olva's there. She'll take care of you, and she'd be grateful for your help. Please, Lath. We should be on the same side of any fight, you and I."

"There is no strength in me for fight," said Lath. "Nor virtue neither. All I touch turns foul, and evil runs deep. Our day is done, done, done." He changed shape again, becoming an ugly bird, then took flight. Alf reached out, but his friend soared high into the sky above the Charnel, wings beating furiously, and was gone.

Alf took Spellbreaker from the ground.

"He's flying east," said Ildorae, "And in the shape of a lammergeier.

That was the form he took, at the end." The huntress tracked the course of Lath's flight long after he'd vanished from Alf's eyes.

"Do you think it means something?"

"It means he is mad," said Spellbreaker sourly.

They walked on. Alf could tell the sword was angry with him, but Ildorae continued their earlier conversation as if they'd never been interrupted. "You need to learn how to hide in plain sight. During the war against Lord Bone, the Nine were the only mortal trespassers in all the northland. So, when you saw a dreadworm in the sky, then hurling yourself into a ditch was the right thing to do. But you are returning to the lands of mortals, the land of your people. You must blend in with the crowds, avoid drawing attention to yourself. Put aside the mantle of the Lammergeier."

"I never bloody put it on," grumbled Alf. "I never called myself a knight or lord."

"But you called yourself one of the Nine, wielder," snapped the sword. "It is the constant refrain of your soul. I hear it. *That* is what marks you, and that is what you must put aside."

Alf grunted in frustration. *Give me something to hit*, he thought. *Not wraiths and shades, not sneaking and spying.*

The sword chuckled. "There will likely be plenty of slaughter soon, wielder. The Erlking stretched out one hand to snatch Necrad, and you helped cut it off. Remember, it was he who ensured that Lath summoned Death, and that set the Wilder assault on Necrad in motion. If it were not for your defeat of Prince Maedos, then Necrad would be under the control of the Wood Elves, and Maedos would be acclaimed Death-slayer. But you foiled him, so now he reaches out with his other hand. The Lords of Summerswell are his weapon."

"You make it sound like the Lords are just witless thralls," said Alf. "But neither of you were there in the last war. Peir had to drag them together, make them see the danger of Necrad. If it weren't for Peir, and Lucar Vond, and a few others – Lord Brychan, for one – there'd have been no League, and no alliance against Bone. If all the Lords are just the Erlking's pawns, then they'd have come together against Necrad when he commanded it, aye?" Alf shook his head, partly in disbelief that he was defending the stuck-up Lords of Summerswell, who'd looked down on the Nine, and shunned them when they brought warning. Partly because thinking hurt his head.

Ildorae laughed. "You underestimate the cruelty of the Erlking, mortal. A Summerswell divided and ruined by the war would be easier for him to control than an intact mortal realm. But you are also partially correct – he cannot trust the loyalty of any one Lord. In ages past, I walked the southland with my kinfolk, befriending enemies of the Erlking and offering them aid in secret. There are cults and secret societies who still remember us."

"Few enough. They were no help in Lord Bone's war. No, wielder, this will end in slaughter," said the sword. "Not with some clever trick, not with a bargain, not even if you convince all the dissenters to leave Summerswell and come dwell with you in Necrad. This struggle began long before I was forged or you were born, wielder. It is older even than the Winter Star, here. It is a war for control of all things – the magic of Necrad, the fate of the elves, the souls of humanity. The Erlking has almost won. The Witch Elves and the Wilder are broken, Summerswell enthralled, and Necrad almost within his grasp. We must stop him, wielder."

Alf could feel the sword's bloodlust, the black metal hot against his chilly skin.

"Aye, well, one thing at a time."

Ildorae and Spellbreaker continued to speak of wars and stratagems beyond Alf's knowledge. If Blaise had been there, then he would have talked of Arcane Matters, and Sources of Power. Berys, well, she'd had plenty to stay about conspiracies and secret societies down in the Pits, in that hasty confession.

Why didn't you tell me, he'd asked her, and her reply still echoed in his ears. *I wish I could have. I wanted to. But, Alf – we were travelling with a priestess of the Intercessors and the Erlking's daughter. Because people who know all this disappear, Alf.*

The Erlking's daughter. If Laerlyn had been there, what would she have said?

But none of them were there. Only Alf.

Back in the war, he'd never questioned his place or purpose. It had all been so simple. There were monsters, and he'd slain them. Then wiser heads – Peir and Berys and Blaise and Lae – talked about invasions from the north, about prophecies and omens and hosts out of Necrad. Back then, he hadn't really understood what it all meant.

He still didn't. Alf could dimly grasp the vastness of history, the webs of intrigue. Ildorae spoke of events ten thousand years ago like they'd just happened, and the sword spoke of invisible conspiracies woven like secret spells, inviting him to break them. But it was all beyond Alf's comprehension.

In the war, he'd fought for his friends. The Nine had been everything to him, his constant companions. He'd bled for each of them, risked his life for each of them, and they'd all done the same for him. He'd have followed Peir anywhere.

He'd fought, too, for the memory of home. All the bloody Road to Necrad, he'd taken grim satisfaction in knowing that any monsters he killed *here* could never trouble the little village of Ersfel in the Mulladales, far far away.

But home, too, was gone. Necrad was his burden, not his home. Ersfel – he'd tried returning there, but how could he go back home when there was still evil in the world? How could he put down his sword with monsters still unslain?

And anyway, Ersfel was on the other side now. Alf had met the Lords of the Mulladales, in the strange days after the fall of Necrad. They'd congratulated him, praised him, bowed before him, wholly unaware that they were praising a peasant lad from their own domain. But the people of Ersfel served the reeve of the manor, and the reeve served a knight, and that knight was part of some baron's household, and that baron served some earl, up and up to the great Lords themselves. And they served the Erlking. If Alf went back to Ersfel now, he'd be the invading monster, the ogre from the north.

He sought inside himself for purpose. When he was young, he'd had this core of iron, this unyielding, unconquerable endurance. He'd lost it somewhere in the Pits. He'd briefly found it again when Jan gave him his quest and he thought it would reunite the Nine, but it had melted away again, lost in the fog. Olva still had it – he'd seen it in her when she fought for her son. But it wasn't in Alf any more, not without the Nine.

So he stumbled as they walked through the snow.

At last, the Charnel gave way to the terrain of the Clawlands. Fabulous, twisted vomit-shapes of cooled lava, boulders and piles of broken stone, clusters of obsidian shards like thorn bushes, like sharped spikes. Stinking smoke issued from fissures in the ground. The Road that ran straight and level across the Charnel became a forking, twisted path, swerving around obstacles or wholly lost in the chaos.

And there were monsters. Alf knew where he was with monsters. Knifebrides crawled out of those fissures, bone blades sprouting through their skins. A pack of scaulers, like wingless dreadworms, frantically slithering towards fresh meat. The lowing of a cate ... calo ... evil cow thing in the mist.

Catelobeplas, dolt, provided the sword as it sliced through a knifebride. The Witch Elves all had thousands of years of battle experience, their blades – returned from the vault where they'd been locked away since the siege – were still keen, and the Clawlands held no terrors for them. The mortal guards were all veterans of Necrad, although only two of the six had fought against Lord Bone, and acquitted themselves well in the skirmish.

Torun was no fighter. To her credit, the dwarf did not quail or flee in the face of the horrors, but whenever a creature lurched out of the gloom, she darted for the nearest hiding place. Alf took to walking by Torun's side to keep an eye on her, and that duty gave him some sense of comfort. He was always best as the strong right hand, the anchor of the shield wall. While he guarded Torun, he could forget about the wider world. And she carried Gundan's axe, so it was almost like he was walking beside Gundan again.

At first, Torun was too awestruck by his presence to speak, but after a few days, the floodgates opened and the dwarf talked without cease. She bombarded him with questions about the underways of Necrad, asking him about the tunnels and passageways that ran beneath the city. Alf was vaguely aware that Necrad was built around a magical glyph, that it was built as a way of harnessing power first and became a city later, but he'd only paid attention to what mattered – which corridors could be secured, and which ones were always thronged with monsters no matter how many he slew. Which tunnels led to safety, and which ones led to peril – and which ones flooded at high tide. Torun had questions about constellations and ley lines, about magical conduits and conjunctions where charmstones grew like pearls.

"Is this what Blaise has you doing up in the Wailing Tower," asked Alf, "mapping the Pits?"

"Oh no," said Torun, "this is my own work. Master Blaise has other duties for me."

The mountains of the Dwarfholt rose taller with each passing day. The air grew cleaner as they climbed out of the Clawlands.

They were two days outside Karak's Bridge when the ogres found them.

In that region, the Road vanished into a series of narrow gullies and canyons. The ruins of dwarven watchtowers and fortresses commanded the heights between, and they passed the remains of once hidden outposts. In times past, this had been the dwarven bulwark against the hosts of Necrad, and the stony ground was scabbed thick with the black blood of ogres, the watery ichor of Vatlings, the acid froth of pitspawn. Wilder blood, too, dying for their immortal gods. But Lord Bone's second invasion force had smashed through these defences, and Karak's Bridge too, and now these lands were empty.

Almost.

Alf was answering Torun's millionth question when the first boulder came crashing down. One of the Witch Elves dodged out of the boulder's path in an eye blink, but the mortal behind her was caught and crushed. More huge stones plummeted down around them. Alf shoved Torun to the side and swung Spellbreaker. Magical force thundered from the blade, catching a falling boulder and blasting it to dust.

Ildorae sprang up the wall of the canyon. She flung her spear into the eye of one ogre as she climbed, and caught it again as the ogre's corpse toppled from the lip of the canyon and fell past her, wrenching it from his skull. A second ogre grabbed at her; with a word of power she froze him, a puff of frosty air billowing around the brute as ice bound his limbs. Ildorae kicked him over the edge to join his comrade.

Leaping up sheer canyon walls had never been in Alf's repertoire, even when he was a young man with more energy and better knees. But these days he had Spellbreaker, and that made the difference. He smashed the blade into the canyon wall, and the earth convulsed. With a great rumble, part of the cliff collapsed around him, a breaking wave of dirt and rocks, a cloud of dust rising like sea spray. Ogres rained down, the ambush becoming a rout in an instant.

Spellbreaker was a shadow, moving smoothly across the battlefield, yet it parted flesh and shattered bone. But there were still many foes, swarming around Alf and his companions. One of the mortal guards fell, an ogre tackling him to the ground, then goring him with its tusks. Blood spurted from the man's wounded neck, and the ogre lapped up the gush of gore. Alf hurried forward, slip-sliding over the shifting scree, and lopped the beast's head from its shoulders with one blow. The strike threw him off balance for a moment, and in that instant, another ogre rushed out of the swirling dust cloud.

Head down, it bowled into him. Alf saw bloodshot eyes, drooling maw, a club wildly swinging — and then there was a flash of magic, and a gory rain as bits of skull splattered down all around Alf. The beast, suddenly headless, toppled over backwards to reveal Torun the dwarf standing there. She looked more shocked than the ogre — although seeing as he now lacked a face, that could hardly be wondered at.

After, they collapsed more of the cliff, burying their dead beneath thousands of tons of rock, ensuring that no ogre would eat the remains. Three mortal guards, and one elf. The elf's wraith had lingered for a few minutes in the shadow of the gully, a mute witness to his own burial, until the sun climbed higher and it fled the light.

Ildorae and the other Witch Elves went off to hold some private ritual. Alf watched them go. They must have known that fallen elf for hundreds, even thousands of years, and now he was gone. The dead mortals had lived twenty or so years each. Alf's much-patched cloak was older than that. But death came for them both.

Once the landslide subsided, the mortal guards climbed up atop the fresh-fallen stones to erect a grave marker. Alf stayed behind with Torun. The dwarf sat on a rock, hunched over the casket.

"That was a hell of a spell you cast," he said. "Blaise taught you well."

"I still can't work magic," said the dwarf, and Alf caught an edge of panic in her voice.

"Then how did you blast that ogre?"

In answer, she held up the casket containing Chopper. The side of the casket was dented and scorched, and Torun gripped it tightly to keep it from falling apart. "Master Blaise made it," she whispered, "and placed a magic ward on it to keep anyone from opening it before we got to the Dwarfholt. And now I've broken it."

"Better a box than my skull," said Alf. "Here, let me help." He took the box from her grasp so he could get a better look at the damaged section. Torun held on for a moment, and when she let go, part of the casket gave way, and the contents spilled out over Alf's boots.

Charmstones and gems. A fortune beyond measure. Torun squeaked in horror.

"What's this?" asked Alf quietly.

"Master Blaise entrusted *me* with a mission," said Torun, pride warring with panic. "I was to bring this treasure to the Dwarfholt. He needs dwarven smiths for the rebuilding of Necrad." Scrolls spilled out of the casket too, designs for complex machines. Pipes, vats, alchemical symbols. Things of the Pits of Necrad, things Alf had spent years destroying. But the world had changed.

"It's all right," said Alf. "Nothing's lost and nothing's broken, except a shiny box." Alf gathered up the pile of gems, stuffed them into a pouch, and handed it to Torun.

"But what about Lord Gundan's axe?" she said. "I've ruined the casket."

Alf gently wrapped Chopper's haft up in his old travelling cloak. "I wore this when I started out with Gundan. It'll do as a shroud for the last leg."

They came to what had been the city of Karak's Bridge. Now, it was a tomb. They walked the empty streets of the uppermost level, for the lower parts were still perilous. A slow, torchlit procession through the silent city.

In the war, the enemy had poured poison gas down the air shafts that threaded the mountain, a slow flood of yellow-green fog heavier than clean air. He remembered nearly being caught in one flooded tunnel, the gas up to his chest, the shorter dwarves choking and dying all around him. He'd lifted them up, two or three at a time, to snatch breaths of cleaner air. He'd kept them alive until Lath had smashed the tunnel mouth open. It was the first time the boy had ever managed to shapeshift into a great bear.

Torun told her tale of Karak's Bridge to the mortal guards as they looked about the silent halls in wonder and fear. Lord Bone's forces had tried to trap the dwarves in the city by blocking their escape through the southern gate. Torun had been there, one of the dwarves saved by the Nine. She told the tale as though it were part of a history, describing the failed defence of the outer bridge, the surprise attack, the coming of the Ogre Chieftain, the death of the dwarven champion. When they stopped to rest, she drew intricate sketch-maps in the dust, showing them the different phases of the battle, the regions of the city they had passed through, and the parts that would be inaccessible until the poisons faded in a thousand years.

The elves walked mostly in silence, save for the occasional whispered comment in the elf-tongue. They had been on the other side in the war. Alf let his hand brush against Spellbreaker's hilt so he could see in the dark, but the elves' faces revealed nothing. If they had any shame for their part in the war, they did not show it. They were like marble statues, eyes unseeing.

Alf walked half in memory and half in the waking world. His recollection of the battle was nought but a series of disjointed flashes. He could never have drawn a map of the place; back then, he had no idea if they were winning or losing, no idea if the battle was almost over or barely started. It was all moments. There was where they'd slain the Ogre Chieftain. There was where Thurn had wrestled a war-golem bare-handed. Up there, that was where Laerlyn and Berys had stood side by side, raining arrows down on the foe. And there, that was where Peir had drawn the line, declaring that they would hold that spot against Lord Bone's host no matter what.

Nine against an army, and they'd held, because Peir asked it.

A company of dwarves met them at the far side of Karak's Bridge. Alf knew some of them – there was Gamling, Gundan's former lieutenant, who briefly took his place on the council of Necrad. He'd fought in the defence of the city until the very end of the siege, but vanished after their victory. Clearly, he'd brought word back to the dwarf-lords. Others Alf knew as kinsmen of Gundan. But at the head of the company were six craft-priests carrying ceremonial tools – pick and compass, book and urn, pen and hammer. The six vocations. Alf recalled Gundan's complaints that soldiers never got the respect they deserved in the dwarflands.

Dwarven crossbowmen aimed their weapons at Ildorae and her companions. The dwarves had fought many wars against Witch Elves and Wilder in ancient days. But if Ildorae realised her peril, she gave no sign of it; she and the five dread knights whirled about, more like dancers than soldiers on a parade ground, and formed into two rows. They raised their weapons, clashing the blades together, making an arched tunnel of spears for Alf to walk through.

Torun handed him the remains of Chopper. "If it's the poet who takes it, that's good," she whispered. "It signifies that this is an honourable deed to be commemorated. If it's the law-speaker, that's bad. It means they intend to pursue the matter of Lord Gundan's death. All you can do is speak honestly."

"Aye."

Alf approached the dwarves.

"Hail, Sir Lammergeier, Hero of the Nine, Dwarf-friend." called one ancient dwarf. "Our scouts marked your approach – you and the Witch Elves. *You* are welcome here, and your deeds are remembered in stone, but it has been a long time since you visited our realm."

"I've been travelling. And I returned to Necrad just as ..." Alf sought for the right words. "Jan sent me, to warn of a rising darkness."

"Gamling brought us tidings of war with the Wilder, and how Gundan took command of the city from Lord Vond, who fled Necrad instead of defending it. But he also tells us that you and General Gundan both went to bargain with Death, and only you returned. What became of him?"

"We were betrayed. Gundan ... he cut a bargain with Thurn. He made peace. But someone in our company attacked the Wilder and it all went awry."

The dwarves muttered among themselves in their own tongue. *Ah, they are caught in a vice*, whispered Spellbreaker gleefully. *They would prefer to see Necrad destroyed, but they know that if they take sides in the war, then the Dwarfholt becomes the battleground. And they have little love for the Wood Elves.*

"Who, then, is responsible for the death of Gundan?" asked a dwarf.

"I don't rightly know," admitted Alf, "but wiser heads than mine say it was part of a plot by ..."

Say "the Wood Elves", Lammergeier. Give them a reason to join your war, and there is a chance they will take it.

"Prince Maedos," said Alf, "and I slew him for his treachery."

The dwarves whispered again, more fiercely now as arguments broke out among them. Alf glanced back to where Torun lurked at the back of the honour guard, but she could give him no help. After a few moments, the oldest dwarf spoke again.

"Tell us," he said, "who now rules Necrad?"

It was Ildorae who answered.

"The Uncrowned King," she said, "and if the Dwarfholt wishes to send a representative to his council, that ambassador shall be given the same rank and honour that Lord Gundan held."

For a third time, the dwarves conferred.

"Bring forth the remains."

Alf stepped forward, and one of the six craftsmen advanced to meet him and receive the axe-haft. But it was not the poet, nor the lawyer, but the smith.

What does that mean? Alf thought, but Spellbreaker had no answer.

CHAPTER SIXTEEN

I n Alf's experience, dwarves inhabited one of three moods. There
was a meditative focus that few humans could attain, a fathomless
devotion to the craft. Some went months without speaking when
submerged within this ecstasy of work; indeed, there were dwarves
whose job it was to patrol the craft-halls and the mines, looking for
those who had forgotten to eat or sleep in so long they'd collapsed.
A few dwarves were misfits who could never achieve that mood, and
Gundan was among them. He made up for it by overindulging in
the other two common moods – wild merriment, and sullen deep-
rooted anger.

There was little of the first two moods at the feast honouring the
Lammergeier. The dwarves made it clear that while they appreciated
the return of what remained of Gundan's axe, and they still honoured
Alf's deeds during the war, they would on the whole have preferred
it if he had retired quietly to some little castle, instead of slaying
elf-princes and bringing another war to the Dwarfholt's doorstep.

The Witch Elves drew a greater share of the dwarves' antipathy,
which was not unexpected. The laws of hospitality protected the
elves as part of Alf's retinue, so there was no danger of violence,
only a bitterly cold reception – and Ildorae could be colder than
any of them. She was so haughty and dismissive of the dwarves

that it amused Alf, and it made him sad he could not share the joke with Gundan. Gundan had always responded in a similar way to those who had taken umbrage: by redoubling his offence. He'd have laughed to have seen his cousins grow ever more infuriated at Ildorae's insolence, or he'd have snatched up his own axe and tried to end her, hospitality be damned. It was always a coin flip with Gundan.

What surprised Alf, though, was that the rancour directed at young Torun exceeded even that aimed at the Witch Elves. The dwarves muttered darkly when she passed, and glared at her. Some were so overcome with fury that they exploded at her, shouting curses and shoving her, but Alf was always there to step in and defend her. And while Torun bowed her head when they cursed her, she endured and did not relent.

The cavernous feast-hall was furnace-hot from the cooking fires and press of bodies. Alf mopped his brow and wished that Torun would show a little less courage and retreat instead of standing defiantly. If she left, he could too. He had little stomach for a dwarven feast at the best of times, and the current mood was far from that.

A dwarf sidled up to him. "I must apologise, Lammergeier, for my rash words in Necrad. I was overcome by grief for my fallen cousin."

"Gamling," said Alf in greeting. "Don't worry about it. I've said my share of stupid things." He'd known Gamling a little in Necrad – he was one of Gundan's endless supply of cousins, sent by the Dwarfholt as an assistant for the errant hero. *He's an ambitious shit*, Gundan had complained, *always was. Desperate to climb, desperate to show how useful and clever he is. Az's arse, but it pisses him off that I'm the one who won fucking everything. I love it.* Although, in the years of Alf's wandering, Gundan seemed to have reconciled to Gamling's presence, and came to rely on him. Alf recalled Gamling's fury after Gundan's death, but it had struck him as performative and hollow. He didn't like the dwarf.

"No, Lord Lammergeier. I was raised to a seat on the council of

Necrad, and I should have acted with wisdom to match my station. In my cousin's memory, we should be friends."

Maybe the dwarf could be useful. "Tell me, what did Torun do to anger everyone?"

"She came *back*, Lammergeier. She flaunts her insolence."

"What's wrong with wanting to be a wizard?"

"Wanting? Nothing. Defying her family and her vocation in the guilds? She spits in the face of tradition." Gamling shoved a hunk of roast goat around his bowl, as if even speaking of the matter had diminished his appetite. He pointed with his fork across the hall to one dwarf, richly dressed, wearing a circlet of polished steel. "See him?"

"He's the one who took Chopper's haft off me. The smith-priest?"

"Master of the guild of smiths, yes. Torak. He took Chopper to be reforged. Gundan – well, it is no secret that my cousin was difficult to manage. He was ill-suited to the role that fate gave him. He will be honoured far more in death than he was in life. They will reforge his axe better than before and give it to some new champion to carry on his legacy."

This one hopes to be that champion, no doubt, commented Spellbreaker.

"Torak. Kin to Torun, is he?"

"Her father," said Gamling. "It was merely *shameful* when she persisted with her fascination with magic instead of pursuing proper work for a dwarf of her station. We have little patience with wayward children. If she wanted to dream, then she could have applied to the guild of poets. There are customs for such things, ways to handle them, but she would not follow them. When she left the Dwarfholt, that should have been the end of the matter. She could be counted among the dead, and forgotten." He speared the meat. "Now she has come back, and it is an insult."

"It's not intended as such."

"And yet, it is." Gamling leaned over. "I thought that you would come to some arrangement with the Lords. You could have asked forgiveness for any rash words, and Summerswell would have replaced Lord Vond as governor. Instead, you prop up your nephew as King of Necrad. But you have never been ambitious, Lammergeier. There is much I do not understand. Why defy Summerswell? You cannot win."

He knows nothing of the Erlking's schemes, interjected the sword. *He sees only the surface world.*

Alf tried to explain.

"Prince Maedos – he wanted to take control of Necrad. He kidnapped my nephew. He's the one who stirred up the Wilder."

"My cousin shared your dislike of Maedos. But you slew him, Lammergeier, or so the stories say. If he was such a villain, then why not put your case before the Lords? You could tell them of his schemes, and say you slew him justly. The Wood Elves might complain, but surely the Lords of Summerswell would lend more weight to the testimony of the Nine." Gamling's eyes glittered in the firelight. "Or would Princess Laerlyn speak against you? Gundan always said she was the only one of the Nine that he could not trust."

"Gundan said that?"

"In truth, he complained about every one of the Nine at some point – except you, Lammergeier, not even when he was deep in his cups. But I recall his complaint about Laerlyn: he said that for the rest of you, that time of high adventure as part of the Nine was the great event of your lives. That quest made you who you are, for good or bad. Immortals are unlike us – no one event can ever leave such a mark." Gamling frowned. "But there is more than that. There must be. You armed the Witch Elves."

"Just this honour guard."

"And no doubt you have also secured your supply lines with the New Provinces."

"Aye," admitted Alf.

"Is it true that you destroyed the elven fortress on the Isle of Dawn?"

"That was Blaise."

"As if anyone will make the distinction! And what were you doing in Arden?"

Alf frowned in confusion. "I haven't been in Arden in years."

"I have friends in that city, and they tell me that every dog on the street knows the Lammergeier was in Arden." The dwarf's voice dropped to a conspiratorial whisper. "I understand that you would prefer to travel in secret, and I shall not press you. But we have both seen the Lords' army in Arden, and they shall march soon – and the Dwarfholt must let them pass. What will you do, Lammergeier, when they reach your walls? Will you turn the stone dragons on them?"

"I don't want a war."

"And yet, you are already fighting one."

The cold metal of a knife at his throat woke Alf.

He reacted instantly, leaping from slumber to heart-thundering wakefulness, reaching out and grabbing Spellbreaker with one hand even as he grappled with the attacker – but she danced back out of reach, laughing. And instead of unleashing a shattering burst of force, Spellbreaker just chuckled.

"Too slow, mortal," said Ildorae.

"What do you want?" Alf glared at the elf, then glanced around the dwarven bedchamber. "And how did you get in here?"

"I walk where I wish." She picked Alf's breeches off a chair and tossed them to him. "Riders from Summerswell arrived last night. The emissaries of the Lords, I think. They are bound for Necrad, but our hosts wish to keep us apart."

Alf got dressed hurriedly. As he pulled his shirt over his head, he felt Ildorae's chill fingers brush against his chest.

"What are you doing?"

"So many scars," she said. Her hand traced old wounds left by the war, by the linnorm, by her own knife. "An elf would fade rather than endure in such a ruin."

Alf batted her hand away. "Well, if you'd stop showing up in my bedroom with knives, there'd be fewer scars." He was uncomfortably aware of her inhumanly perfect beauty.

"Quick now." She slipped out the door, and he followed. They were deep underground, and the corridor outside was pitch-dark. Spellbreaker let Alf see as he followed Ildorae through the maze of the dwarven city. She led him on a twisting route, clearly avoiding sentry posts and anywhere wakeful. Alf's head scraped off the low ceilings, and every breath and footstep seemed absurdly loud. His heart was still racing from being woken so suddenly.

"What time is it?" he whispered.

"An hour before dawn. The dwarves will stir soon – and the riders from Summerswell intend to leave at first light. There is a sentry post ahead where we can watch them."

The sentry post was carved into the mountainside. Narrow slits gave a view over the north-eastern approach to the Dwarfholt, lit by a gathering pink-gold in the sky. The post had not been used in some time. Alf guessed other watchtowers were still in use, but after fifteen years of peace, the dwarves' vigilance had diminished.

They crouched by one of the viewports. The valley below was still in deep shadow, and Alf could see lanterns like distant fireflies as the gates opened and riders emerged. He strained his eyes to see.

"They have stopped to bid farewell to the dwarves," narrated Ildorae, whose sight was keener. "They offer a parting gift. It is a chalice . . . ha, I know it. It was made by Korthalion eight hundred years ago. It brings good health to those who drink from it. They bribe the dwarves with loot from Necrad."

"Never mind that," said Alf. "What banners?" As emissaries, they would have banners, or at least painted shields, declaring who they served.

"Still hidden. They have a priest with them, and he is performing a ceremony. Lighting a candle."

"He's asking the Intercessors for good fortune on the journey." Alf knew the ceremony well. Twenty years before, Jan had performed that same rite on that very spot, when the Nine rode to the defence of Karak's Bridge. Then, it had cheered him; now, the little flickering candle-flame was a sinister beacon. His conversation with Gamling from the night before seemed a part of it – forces moving in the dark, all around him, plotting and shaping the world. *Give me something to hit,* was Alf's instinctive thought in response, *give me something I can smash with a sword.* But instead of monsters, this war would offer up innocents, fellow folk of Summerswell deluded by the Erlking's lies.

He was, undoubtedly, one of the land's greatest warriors, but virtually all his victories had been against Lord Bone's creatures. In the early days, when he was one of Gundan's mercenaries, he'd fought other mortals, but he'd never had to kill. One good thump with Alf's full strength behind it could lay the strongest man on his back, and few got up for a second stroke. Then came the war, and there he'd slaughtered pitspawn by the thousand, butchered zombies, smashed golems – monsters he had slain beyond count. Witch Elves, too, but he did not regret those deaths. They'd served Lord Bone willingly.

And after the war – well, by then he was a legend. He was the Lammergeier, the master of the black sword. His reputation was enough to dismay any foe. He'd had skirmishes with thieves in Necrad, fought with Witch Elf holdouts in the Liberties, but he'd never had to kill there, either.

It was not that he doubted his own capacity for slaughter. When the battle-mood took him, all doubt fell away, all thought turned clear as glass and there was only the next swing, the next footstep, the killing blow. He was older now, slower than he used to be, but the black sword could give him strength and speed if he asked it.

Thurn was dead, and Gundan was dead. Now, no mortal warrior in all Summerswell could stop Alf – except Alf.

He wished he could talk to Thurn. In the last war, Thurn had fought against his own kinsfolk. He'd slain other Wilder who served Lord Bone and the Witch Elves.

Did you think the boy's dream would be achieved without bloodshed? whispered Spellbreaker. *Did you think you could hold Necrad without slaying your fellow mortal? I am a weapon: I care not if I bite the flesh of man or monster. Why should you hesitate?*

"Because it's not right," replied Alf.

Ah, you want to be loved by all. You only want to fight obvious monsters. Know this: history is not the only thing written by the victor. Wield me, make the world you desire, and in twenty years' time, no one will be left to judge or question you. All deeds can be made righteous in retrospect. Your foes will be made monstrous, and the bloodstains scrubbed clean. The sword chuckled. *Do you think my maker would be called a Dark Lord if he'd won?*

"They make ready to depart," announced Ildorae. "A score of riders. Eight knights, with so many enchanted weapons they hardly need torches to light their way. I see the banners now, but your mortal families change like passing clouds. I see the emblems of Arshoth and Arden."

"Any sign of Ilaventur? The red book?" asked Alf, thinking of Lord Brychan's message.

"No, but there is another rider. They're helping him onto his horse now. He is very old and frail. A monk, from the look of him, but there's a herald with him, and he bears a banner. The sign of a shooting star—"

"Out of the bloody way!" Alf shoved Ildorae aside and peered out the arrow-slit. "It's Bessimer. I thought he was long dead. They've only gone and dragged Bessimer out of his monastery." He watched the horsemen ride off down the mountain road until they vanished behind a spur of the mountain. Soon, they'd pass through Karak's Bridge, and from there follow the paths through the Clawlands. They'd be at Necrad in a week.

Alf leaned his head against the wall. "Oh, that's the best news I've had in a long time."

"Who is this mortal?"

"Dryten Bessimer, the Weeping Lord. Peir's father."

Alf was eager to be done with the dwarf-lands and set off back to Necrad, but he'd given his word to Torun to guard her while she finished her errand, and so he followed her through the Dwarfholt in a daze. He was barely aware of the crowds of dwarves parting in awe at the sight of the towering hero of the Nine, only half paid attention to the grand staircases and galleries they walked, the blazing lamps and vast subterranean halls of the eternal home of the dwarves. Alf had spent fifteen years in the Pits of Necrad, so vast subterranean labyrinths were no wonder to him.

Bessimer was a wonder. During the war, Dryten Bessimer was one of the Lords of Summerswell. It was to Bessimer's palace in the Crownland that the Nine had come with warnings of Lord Bone's threat, with tales of dread knights and necromancy and nasty things with teeth. And Bessimer had not listened, because he was furious with his son Peir.

For Peir had disobeyed his father and run off into the wilderness with a misfit band of mercenaries, criminals and Wilder (and, admittedly, a princess), following a prophetic dream. It did not matter to Bessimer that the dream had proven true, or that Peir was on the path to becoming a hero – his son and heir had defied him. Peir, consumed by his visions, had refused to relent or apologise. So Bessimer sat in his palace, and refused to see his son.

("*What a bloody idiot,*" Alf had said to Peir. And Peir smiled, and said, "*He taught me to endure, and not to yield. How can I judge him for being stubborn, when he gave me this strength? But I am certain in his love for me. He will come around in the end.*")

Thanks to the diplomacy of Laerlyn and Lucar Vond, the other Crownland lord, the Nine mustered the forces of Summerswell to turn back that first invasion. Bessimer's anger cooled, and he joined in the preparations for war. Still, his pride would not let him bend, not until the very last day, just as the Nine rode off to the defence of the Dwarfholt, to the horrors of Karak's Bridge. Alf remembered looking back at the walls of the Capital, and seeing Lord Bessimer standing atop the gate, the banner of the falling star fluttering behind him, one hand raised. He had come around too late to say farewell.

Alf had said to Gundan that when all this was over, they would have to go back to Ersfel and visit Alf's parents again. And Gundan laughing. *"What, showing up on their doorstep with a half-dead wizard and ogres on your heel doesn't count as a proper family visit?"*

After Peir's death, Bessimer became the Weeping Lord. According to the tales that reached Necrad, the old man was so overcome with grief he would neither eat nor sleep. In the end, he too abandoned his post, and retired to a monastery. The lordship and lands that should have passed to Peir went to some relative chosen by the Intercessors. Alf had assumed that Bessimer – already old when they'd met him twenty years ago – was long dead. That thought had gnawed at him as he patrolled the Pits – that Alf had robbed Bessimer of a chance to speak to his son again.

That Bessimer was alive and among the emissaries sent by the Lords gave Alf hope. It was a gesture of good faith. Bessimer might—

Why would he listen, whispered Spellbreaker, *when you slew his son? That's two for two, Lammergeier, between the Weeping Lord and the Erlking. They should call you Princekiller.*

Alf scowled. "Shut up. And you never met him. He's a good man, and he knows the cost of war."

Sonslayer? Heircutter?

"Shut up."

The air grew thick with hot smoke and the smell of molten metal. They crossed a narrow bridge, the stone slick with spray, that spanned a raging torrent of water. Huge millwheels ground ceaselessly in the depths, driving hammers and other cunning machines within the great foundry complex.

Berys always said that the war with Lord Bone had been won not by the Nine, but by the foundries of the dwarves. They'd made weapons and armour for the League, better than any blade forged by human hands. They'd wrought siege engines to bring down the enchanted walls of Necrad. Most importantly, they'd made bane metal to slay the immortal Witch Elves. The last time Alf had visited the forges, the constant clamour of beating hammers had been louder than any battle.

Now the smithies were silent. Once, knights from Summerswell came here, seeking dwarf-wrought weapons and armour, but why bother paying a smith to spend years forging a masterwork, when a looted charmstone from Necrad could make a cheaper sword into a far deadlier weapon? Only a few dwarven artisans laboured, and they did so with quiet zeal, like chanting clerics.

Torun led him across the expanse of the foundries towards a massive door of gold. On one side of the door was an image of the giant Az Worldmaker; on the other side was a column of figures, depicting hundreds of dwarven smiths and builders at work. The doors themselves appeared to be perfectly smooth planes of beaten gold, but when the leaping light of the forge caught them just right, engraved runes became briefly visible, then vanished again. Different ones appeared depending on the angle of the firelight. The doors led to the sanctum of the smiths' guild.

Torun's father waited there, flanked by other dignitaries. Torun squared her shoulders and marched towards them, the weight of their collective gaze like an invisible barrier.

"I—"she began, stammering, then she found her tongue. "Honoured Father, guild masters, I bear a message from Master Blaise of the Nine—"

"I do not know you," said Toruk to his daughter, "what right do you have to speak for Blaise of the Nine?"

"I'm his apprentice," said Torun.

"Is he poet or lawyer? Delver or builder?"

"No."

"A physician then?"

"He knows much about both healing and birthcraft," said Torun, "but no. As you well know, he is—"

"Certainly he is no smith. He does not practise of any of the crafts. You are not an apprentice. As you are yet unmarried and unapprenticed, you are a child, and have no right to speak here." He turned away.

"Master Blaise is a wizard," persisted Torun, "and I am his apprentice."

"You are no one," hissed Torak.

Alf could stay silent no longer. "Listen to her, Torak! If Blaise sees value in what she's doing, then only a fool would question his judgement."

"This is a private matter, Lammergeier," said Torak. "It is none of your concern." He looked back to Torun. "There is nothing for you here. Begone." With that, the mighty doors swung open, and he turned to leave. The dwarven guild masters filed out behind him.

Alf laid his hand on the gold door, preventing it from closing. "Even if you won't listen to her, then listen to Blaise's proposal. Torun, show him."

Torun slipped past Alf into the sanctum. There was a ceremonial anvil there, gilded and jewelled, and she spilled her bundle across its flat top. "Master Blaise wishes to hire as many smiths as you can spare, to aid in the rebuilding of Necrad," said Torun. "As payment, he offers this." Charmstones – a fortune in Witch Elf magic – rolled across the anvil, glowing like hot coals. One of the guild masters let out an involuntary gasp.

She spread the scrolls out across the table, showing the dwarves Blaise's designs for rebuilding Necrad's arsenal. Other smiths gasped at the plans, imaginations fired by the challenge of the work.

Torak picked up one of the fallen charmstones, turning it over with his fingers. It was an adamant-stone. Embedded in a shield or breastplate, it would make that armour unbreakable by any earthly force. He admired it, then dropped it back on the anvil.

"No," he said again.

"Guild master," murmured one of the dwarves, "would it not be prudent to consider this commission?"

"Pay no attention to this child. We have no more need of such trinkets."

"Trinkets?" Torun's face flushed with anger. "These are magic! Real magic out of Necrad." She picked up the discarded adamant-stone. "This one grew in the Arc of Haradrume!" She grabbed another and another. "Taken from the House of Lamps! This one taken from the Helm of Ithelmar! You know nothing of *this* craft, and you scorn its works! Pompous idiot!" She drew back her hand, as if about to throw a handful of charmstones at her father, then stopped. She turned to the other dwarves. "Your guild master impoverishes *you* to punish *me*. As the Lammergeier said, he is a fool."

"A fool, is it? I'll show you," snarled Torak. He grabbed his daughter's hand and dragged her into an antechamber. Alf followed, and the guards at the door did not block his path. Built into the far wall was a huge ornate safe. Sliding panels revealed a series of locks, each with its own key. Torak unlocked them all, stabbing each key home and twisting it furiously. He threw the safe open for Torun and Alf to see.

Inside was a pile of charmstones and other treasures of Necrad, easily the equal of Blaise's offering. "I know the value of magic. I know the price I am willing to pay for it, daughter. Let this be the end of it." Torak let the glow of the enchanted hoard play over Torun's face for a moment, then closed it again, metal grinding on metal as the two-inch-thick steel door locked shut. "Go back and tell the scholar that you have failed him. Go back and make your farewells, then come home."

"Where did you get those charmstones?" Spellbreaker's voice rang out suddenly, an echo of the safe. Torak flinched in alarm at the unexpected fourth presence in the room. "You must have obtained them recently, or you would have already incorporated them into your works. Who would have such a hoard of charmstones with which to buy your services?"

"Berys," answered Alf. It was the only answer that made sense.

Torak looked from Alf to the blade and back again, aware that he had revealed more than he intended.

"What did you make for her?" demanded Alf.

"She . . . she paid for my silence as well as my craft."

Alf drew Spellbreaker and, without effort, shoved the sword through the steel door of the safe. Charmstones popped and cracked as the sword's counter-magic ruined them.

"Stop!" shouted Torak.

Alf twisted the blade, and more stones exploded. A fortune put to the sword. Torak's face turned sickly green beneath soot and beard.

"I'll tell you! She had us design a container for her. We forged dozens of them. Barrels, strong and airtight."

"What for?" demanded Alf.

"She did not say."

"Necromiasma," said Torun, waving her hands. "Casks like that could store necromiasma."

"Where is Berys?"

"I don't know." Torak bowed his head. "But we sent the casks to Arden."

CHAPTER SEVENTEEN

T he dreadworm took flight, ungainly wings shedding flakes of rotten flesh as it flapped into the sky. Torun clung to its neck.

"It'll get her back ahead of Lord Bessimer and the rest," said Alf, "and nothing that flies in the Clawland would stop a dreadworm. She'll be fine. But we've got a long walk ahead of us, if you're sure you're coming with me."

"As far as the Cleft of Ard. Maybe a little further," said Ildorae. "I walked those lands of old, and I know how to avoid unfriendly eyes."

"Ten days to the Cleft if we're lucky, this time of year," said Alf, suddenly doubting himself. "A dreadworm would have me there in one."

"And you would be seen, wielder," said Spellbreaker. "The Intercessors can sense the presence of a dreadworm. Their vigilance was one reason why my former master began by invading the High Moor. Other approaches were watched."

Alf remembered a time in the early days of the war, only a few weeks after they'd left Ersfel. Jan had a grail-vision about Witch Elf dread knights attacking a church near Highfield. The Nine had rushed off there to do battle. Alf remembered the feel of anticipation mixed with fear as they'd approached the chapel, his old sword slipping in his sweaty grip. The sight of a dreadworm perched on the church roof, and the horror of knowing that the enemy was not just in the High Moor, but advancing into the heart of Summerswell. It had felt like such a simple story at the time – evil came rising, and Nine to turn it back.

Now, he saw the true shape of events. A quiver in the web, a whisper reflected in the water of Jan's grail, and nine useful idiots rush off to war.

If Alf was seen, there'd be other useful idiots. Young lads, as young as Derwyn, full of the same misguided courage as Alf had been.

They'd rush to fight him.

They'd die on the black blade.

"Ten days to the Cleft," Alf muttered. "Let's do it in eight."

They did it in six. The weather favoured them all the way through the mountains. It was unseasonably clement, in fact, and Alf wondered if some magic was at work. Winter had rolled back; spring warmth opened like castle gates above the Cleft. People prayed to the Intercessors for fair winds and good harvests; had prayers been made in the churches and palaces of Summerswell for open roads? Alf quickened his pace, the effort heavy on his tired limbs. Ildorae matched him without complaint.

The Cleft of Ard lay before them, a yawning gap between two mountain spurs. Sunlight gleamed off the towers of Arden, the fast-flowing river a vein of silver. A patchwork of fields surrounded the city, dotted with little woods. Even shrouded in snow, the landscape was shockingly green compared to the desolate lands around Necrad. There were scarred places in Ellscoast and the Crownlands where Lord Bone's forces had inflicted permanent wounds on the land, but not here.

We saved this. We saved the Dwarfholt.

A pair of broken pillars, so windworn that they were barely distinguishable from piles of rocks, marked the northern border of Summerswell.

"The Arch of the Emperor Ambrayses II," said Ildorae. "Even in Necrad we feared him. He conquered the lands of the west, and slew the dragon Ilgarud. That arch was topped with the dragon's skull dipped in bronze. Fires burned in its eye sockets at night."

"Never heard of him," admitted Alf, which was true, although he could not rule out the possibility that he'd robbed the emperor's tomb. He'd robbed a lot of tombs. He started down the road, but Ildorae caught his arm and stopped him.

"That way is guarded. I know a better one."

Her path was one only an elf or a goat could traverse easily. Alf resorted to using Spellbreaker as a piton, sinking the blade into the cliff face, while Ildorae stepped lightly from ledge to ledge. They descended from the heights of the upper cleft into the mountain meadows of the green bowl below. A few sheep, newly released from their winter pens, bounded away from them, but none showed any sign of being possessed by guardian spirits. Alf's stomach rumbled at the thought of a good piece of mutton.

As twilight fell, they entered the darkest of the hillside thickets. Ildorae slipped through the leafless trees, and the twig-broken moonlight seemed to work a transformation on her. The Witch Elves always appeared haughty and cruel, and her adornments always reminded Alf of what you'd get if you cast a handful of wriggling insects in silver – but in the thicket at night, Alf would have been hard-pressed to tell the Witch Elf from one of Laerlyn's kinfolk. Alf followed at a distance, as quietly as he could. The night breeze carried the sound of singing – Ildorae's voice, high and thin, like a half-remembered dream.

Alf crouched in the underbrush and watched a strange scene unfold. A pair of shepherds sat by a fire in a sheltered dell, gazing in wonderment at the apparition in the trees. Ildorae danced at the edge of the wood, frost glimmering in the air about her, the trailing edge of winter. Even Alf, who had slain dragons and fought Lord Bone in the heart of Necrad, felt a tug of enchantment at the sight;

the two shepherds were utterly entranced. One stared as if frozen; the other rose and took a few shaky steps towards Ildorae.

She called out a greeting in the elven tongue. The words were familiar to Alf – it was the same call that he'd heard Ildorae use that night in Necrad when she'd met with Berys.

The shepherd frowned in confusion, and then panic struck him as he realised what sort of creature he'd encountered. He grabbed his entranced companion and the pair bolted towards the lights of a village.

"Did it work?" asked Alf.

"No," she whispered in Alf's ear, her breath ice-cold. "For a long while, my people have cultivated friendships among these mortals. But they have forgotten us. The Erlking has poisoned them against us." She bit her lip, frustrated at her failure.

"We'll camp here tonight," said Alf, "then say our farewells in the morning."

Alf slept, and he did not dream. He'd rarely dreamed when he was young, but now his sleep was often troubled. Necrad was called the nightmare city, and it was well named; it seemed as present in dreaming as in the waking world, and those who dreamed *in* the city dreamed *of* it, too, the same twisted boulevards and spires rising to catch them on the other side of sleep. Even on his travels, though, he'd been plagued by dreams – he half-suspected it was some sort of psychic leakage from the damn sword, which refused to stay out of his head no matter how often he commanded it. It scraped him like his skull was a whetstone.

In the last week, though, he'd slept without dreaming, and that troubled him too. He'd allowed himself to hope that when he crossed the mountains back into the southland, he'd dream of Jan again. The cleric of the Nine had summoned him with a dream-sending, just before she'd faded away into some spirit realm, but Alf wished that he could see her again. That she could give him some last guidance. *A darkness rising in Necrad*, she warned him.

He hated prophecies. They were will-o'-the-wisps of fate, leading you down a path you'd never normally follow, then vanishing and leaving you to blunder blindly in the morass. *Did do I all right, Jan? Was Maedos the darkness? Was it Death? Was it Lord Bone?* Did you even know when a prophecy was fulfilled? Only wiser heads could pretend to make sense of them, and Alf doubted their after-the-fact explanations. The only prophetic dream that he'd ever really trusted was the dream that guided Peir to leave home, and gather the Nine.

He did not dream, but he did not sleep soundly. He woke in the cold hours of the early morning—

The sword was gone.

He reached out, fingers brushing the spot where Spellbreaker should be.

Alf sprang up, furious and terrified, thoughts of a red ocean of blood spilled by the black sword. Panic that he had rarely known filled him – it wasn't possible to steal the sword, for it could become magically heavy if it chose. If the sword was gone, it had *chosen* to be taken. Ildorae was gone too. He circled the glade where they'd made camp, crashing through the trees, looking for some sign.

"Here, wielder," called the sword. Alf ran in the direction of the voice, and found Ildorae sitting cross-legged under a tree, Spellbreaker on her lap.

"What," growled Alf, "are you doing with my sword?" He approached cautiously, suddenly aware that if the sword broke its oath and turned on him, there was nothing he could do to wrest it from her.

"We were talking, wielder. Do you have any idea how dull these nights are for me? I do not sleep. I lie there in my scabbard, listening to you snore like a golem made of bagpipes."

"And what were you talking about?"

"The last days of the Witch Elves," cackled the blade.

"There are no last days for the elves, not until the world's ending," said Ildorae. "But my people face decline." She ran her fingers through the cold earth amid the roots of the tree. "I did not know if the shepherd would remember the words. I feared I had been forgotten even as a secret."

"Amerith is dead," said the sword. "She was the eldest of the Witch Elves, and Death took her. Necrad is lost to them – even now, with the occupying forces so diminished, they do not have the courage to take it back." Spellbreaker chuckled. "Not without a weapon."

"Ildorae," said Alf, "that's my sword."

"I had another wielder once," said Spellbreaker. The ruby eye glittered. "But you defeated him, and now I serve you, Lammergeier." Ildorae grunted as the sword became heavy. Alf lifted the blade away.

"I would not take it again, mortal," said Ildorae. "What would be the point? Never is a hard word for the elves to say, but I say it now: never again, I think, will my people rule in the city we built. The honour guard you granted us, this journey into Summerswell – I wondered if these might be signs that the Witch Elves could be restored to what we once possessed. It was good to play the dread knight again, and to walk the woods of Arden." The pink light made her look unearthly. "I was a goddess, mortal. Now I feel pride at being allowed to carry a broken stick back to the dwarves. I am diminished."

Alf was torn between pity and revulsion. For all Ildorae's genuine melancholy, her divinity was a cruel dominion over the Wilder. The Witch Elves had done terrible things; Necrad was a city of darkness even before Lord Bone's rule.

"Why do you think you'll never rise again? The wheel turns, that's what you elves say."

"I can smell spring in the air, the turning of the year, and it brings me no sense of renewal." She shivered in fear. "There is one way the wheel could break. Elves can only escape the wraith-world and be reborn if there are living elves to bear new children. Our numbers are fixed – there will always be eight thousand one hundred and fifty-nine elves, but an elf may be counted among the bodied or unbodied. If we are all howling wraiths lost in the void, there we shall remain until the end." She brushed her fingers against the rough bark. "Or if there are no Witch Elves left in Necrad, we shall all become Wood Elves. Lotus-addled children chained to trees, fit for nothing but singing silly songs! The Oath of Amerith forgotten."

Alf lowered himself to the ground to sit opposite her. "You never met Laerlyn."

"Of course I have. The Erlking's daughter is young, but not *that* young. I saw her in the city of Minar Kul before the sea took it. Oh, she was little more than a child then, the youngest of the Erlking's get. She was displayed like a new-found pearl to the sail-princes, and blessed by the Bearer of Light."

Alf had no idea who the sail-princes were, or who this Bearer of Light might be, and he knew Minar Kul only as ruins at low tide by the shore. He plunged on.

"But you've never spoken to her, or travelled with her, or been her friend. I have. Some Wood Elves are as you describe 'em – flighty and merry and . . . and bloody annoying, in truth."

"Use me to murder them," whispered the sword.

"And some are right bastards, like Maedos. But there are good folk among 'em too."

"It is easy to be good, mortal, when you dwell in bliss and plenty. It is easy to be friends when you are united in common cause against a host of foes. But when times are hard, when beliefs divide you – that is when talk of 'good' and 'evil' is for mortals and children. The elves know this – so much is contingent on circumstance, so we do not judge. In eternity, there is time enough to be hero and villain, kindly and cruel. The only choices that matter are the ones that cannot be reversed. There is no escape from the Erlking's tree-binding spells, so we reject them. That is the foundation of the sundering between Wood Elves and Witch Elves, not notions of—"

Ildorae abruptly stopped. She tilted her head, listening to the night.

"The mortals are coming back," she said, and darted towards the forest edge.

One shepherd returned, accompanied by an ancient woman who wept at the sight of Ildorae, tears navigating the wrinkles of her face like a stream trickling through ravines. "Mistress of the Hunter's Star," she mumbled. "My grandmother told me stories of you when I was a little girl. She told me to keep to the old ways, and stay faithful."

Ildorae smiled broadly. "And you shall be rewarded." The elf took a hairpin from her hair. A ruby charmstone glimmered amid the silver. She placed it in the old woman's palm and clasped her fingers around it, Ildorae's ageless hand against the mortal's withered digits. "Keep this secret. It will bring you health all the days that are left to you." She gestured to Alf. "This man is my trusted servant. Bring him to Arden, and ask no questions of him."

The old woman nodded, curtsied as much as her stiff limbs would allow, and scurried back to her grandson's side. Ildorae turned to Alf. "Here is where we part company, for a little while. Your path leads to Arden, and I shall return to Necrad."

"Keep an eye on Derwyn and Olva, will you? Tell 'em I said they can trust Lord Bessimer."

"I will when I return." Ildorae looked at Spellbreaker. "No illusion can hide that sword. If you wish, I could carry it back to Necrad and keep it until you call for it."

"It's mine to bear," said Alf. Still, he unbuckled his sword-belt and wrapped both sword and scabbard up in a cloth. He wrenched a long branch from one of the trees and laid it alongside the blade in the wrapping to conceal the long body of the sword. He hung his cooking pot from the sword's cross guard. Carried on his shoulder, Spellbreaker looked like an unremarkable bundle for an unremarkable traveller. Alf was amused by the way his cooking pot banged off the hilt with every step.

He knew that would annoy the sword.

He turned and waved to Ildorae in the shadow of the wood, then set off after the shepherds.

Just you and me again, wielder.

CHAPTER EIGHTEEN

O lva watched Alf and the honour guard depart from atop the
west gate. The last time Alf had left her behind and gone
off down the Road, twenty years had passed before she'd seen him
again. She remembered sneaking through the holywood to catch
a glimpse of her brother and his companions departing. It was a
brisk autumn morning, she recalled, and the fallen leaves crunched
underfoot and gave her away. And Alf had waved her away, telling
her to turn back.

Derwyn's cough dragged her sharply back to the present.

"Come on," she said, "no sense freezing ourselves up here. Alf
won't be back any sooner just because we're up here staring at him."

"I shall take Derwyn to the Wailing Tower," said Blaise. "There
are healing spells I can work there." The wizard raised his staff, and
one of the dreadworms broke from the flock.

Olva hugged her son. "Tell Torun—" she began, and then she
remembered that Torun had gone too. "Never mind. Be attentive to
Master Blaise, now, and don't strain yourself." She brushed a smudge
of dirt off her son's cheek.

Derwyn was entirely himself, with nothing of . . . of the other
about him. He squirmed, embarrassed at his mother fussing over
him in front of the wizard. Blaise stared fixedly at the heavens until

Olva was done. The wizard and the Uncrowned King soared away over Necrad.

Threeday waited for her in the carriage, and jabbered at her all the way to the Citadel. Now that Olva had taken responsibility for the affairs of the city, the Vatling had a seemingly inexhaustible litany of decisions to be made. Some, Olva could understand – the city's few remaining guards, should they keep watch on the forbidden zone of the Sanction, or the Liberties? Should repairs be made first to the outer walls or the inner ones? Some citizens had fled Necrad by foot during the siege, should they be allowed back into the city? If so, should the properties they abandoned be returned to them?

Most of the decisions, though, Threeday had already made for her, and needed only a nod or a word of confirmation. She wondered if the Vatling's allergy to taking responsibility was a quirk of the creature's inherent nature, or peculiar to Threeday himself – or if he privately assumed that the city would be retaken by Summerswell, and wanted to ensure that he was blamed for nothing by whatever Lord took her place.

It was a day for petitioners in the Court of Necrad, a hall on the level below the council room, as close to a throne room as the Citadel had. In comparison to the eerie grandeur of the elven city outside, it was cramped and unremarkable – for it was built by mortal hands, not the Witch Elves, and so they could be sure there were no spells laid into the walls.

Olva did not take the governor's chair, but instead had Threeday place a stool for her on the step below. One by one, the petitioners filed by. Merchants, some arguing that bargains struck with the old regime should be honoured by the new, others claiming that all contracts made with the League were void, depending which inter-pretation favoured them. Settlers, asking for permission to leave the city and travel on to the New Provinces – and asking for protection on the Road. Disputes over property, accusations of theft.

And most of all, those begging for aid, for food or shelter, or for news of loved ones lost since the siege.

The merchants tried to browbeat her with legal arguments and veiled threats; others, with appeals to mercy, to sympathy, calling on the Intercessors to move Olva's heart. They all found her less yielding than they expected. Legal arguments failed when she reminded them that, ultimately, all order in Necrad was guaranteed by her brother's sword. Appeals to the Intercessors did not move her, for she knew the true nature of the spirits now. And mercy, well, she was as merciful as she could be, but she listened to the wailing of new-made widows, the terror of those driven from their homes by enemies, and thought to herself, *I survived that. You can too.* She gave what she could, but Threeday had made her painfully aware of the state of the treasury.

Once, on the Isle of Dawn, Prince Maedos had demanded that Olva decide the fate of Captain Abran. She'd tried to refuse the responsibility, asking the prince to make the decision himself or give it to someone else. She'd felt that it was *wrong* for someone like her, a farmer's wife from nowhere in particular, to make a such a fateful decision. Judgement should be reserved for the great and the wise. Now, Olva found that there was something rewarding in the wielding of power. She had not asked for this, but it had to be done. Someone had to sit here, and she had as much claim as anyone. The authority of the Lords flowed from the elves and the Intercessors, and those were lies. Her authority – she might say it came from the Uncrowned King, but that was almost a lie too. Power came from the sword and the crowd.

And the sword was gone away south. Until Alf returned, she had to hold the crowd.

The last petitioner, the merchant Pendel, blustered and complained like the rest.

"My ships sit idle at the docks, rotting like their cargoes! Grant me permission to depart, to sell those cargoes in Ellsport, and I swear I shall return to Necrad. I have friends in Ellscoast who will ask no questions of my allegiance. Your dispute with the Lords has no bearing on my affairs."

"If I permit you to go," said Olva, "then how do we know that you will not report all you have seen here to our enemies? Or what if you sail to Ellscoast, and then return with a ship full of assassins? No."

"So I am a prisoner here? Should I throw what little money I have left into the waters of the harbour, and join the queue of beggars at your door? What good is a merchant who cannot trade?"

Olva had rehearsed her answer to this. "Ellscoast is not the only port. What about Phennic? You trade in timber and furs. They buy such things there." She tried to sound as worldly and wise as she could, even though all she knew of Phennic came from traders she'd met at the Highfield Fair.

Pendel scoffed. "They do, but it's a much longer journey, past the High Moor and the Cape of Farewell. And I would have to sail past Ellscoast – and every rogue in Summerswell would see my ships as prey."

"So sail due east. Go past the Isle of Dawn instead of taking the long route south. Torun tells me the Witch Elves know more about navigation than any mortal sailor, that they even sailed all the way around the world in days of old. Hire a Witch Elf navigator."

"Sailing due east from Necrad," explained Pendel, not bothering to hide his anger, "is forbidden. No vessel may pass the Isle of Dawn without permission of the Wood Elves. Anyone who tries will founder in a storm or be devoured by sea-serpents."

"My brother slew the Prince of Dawn. Blaise broke Kairad Nal. The eastern seas are open to anyone brave enough to try them. Consider that, Master Pendel."

The merchant bowed and departed. Threeday emerged from an alcove behind the throne.

"Phennic. Under Lord Vond, sailing directly to Phennic was forbidden, but now you point it out, I see the wisdom of that course.

Indeed, I suspect the princes of Phennic would also be very interested in acquiring other things available in Necrad."

"Well, we'll see about that if Pendel actually survives the crossing." Olva stifled a yawn. "Is that all of them?"

"Pendel is the last of the petitioners who attended your court." The Vatling sat down on the step beside Olva. "However, there is one who could not attend, for Witch Elves are not permitted to enter the Garrison. I was asked to bring word to you myself. The petitioner's name is Elithadel. Her son has become a vampire, sustained by human blood."

"Why would you bring this to me?"

"Ah." Threeday's translucent face flushed, dark veins visible beneath the gelatinous pseudoskin. "Her son was mortally wounded in, ah, an incident in the Liberties last year. It seems Sir Aelfric took on the personal responsibility of providing blood for the child."

Olva shuddered. "Why would he do that?"

"I could not presume to say."

Olva could. She knew about the 'incident' as Threeday delicately put it. Alf had charged into the Liberties hunting for Ildorae, and started a riot. The elf-child was wounded in the struggle. She had not known about Alf giving his own blood, but he was always eager to make amends in his clumsy way.

"Give her money."

"Ah." Threeday looked pained. "That may not be enough. Once, the supply of blood for the vampires was secured by trade. Smugglers, like Lyulf Martens of your acquaintance, would procure humans from the south and give them to the Witch Elves, in exchange for charmstones and other magic. Now that the trade has ended, there is no longer a ready supply of fresh blood."

"Are you telling me that there isn't a single human in Necrad other than Alf who's willing to bleed for pay?"

"Of course not. I can find someone to slake the hunger of Elithadel's son. But . . . the child is not the only vampire in the city."

"The elder Witch Elves."

"Your brother and Lath slew most of the Witch Elf elders after the war. Only a handful remain, but their thirsts are considerable, as are their powers. The threat of the Nine kept them in check until now. But Aelfric is gone, and Blaise is . . . Blaise."

"Do you have a suggestion for me?"

"Only that I am glad that we secured payment for the Garrison guards. The vampires cannot feed on my bloodless kind, but I am relieved that there are armed men between the Liberties and your neck, milady."

Telling night from day in Necrad was a skill that Olva had yet to acquire. The constant shroud of the necromiasma muted the sun and glowed dimly at night. The city of the immortals seemed outside time, and looking back it all felt like one long day stretched over weeks, or a performance where the actors repeated the same lines every time. She would rise and the servants would bring her breakfast. She would see to such affairs of the city that were brought to her. Derwyn would go to the Wailing Tower for Blaise's ministrations. For all the wizard's efforts, her son grew no stronger, though at least he grew no stranger, either. All those days, he was himself. He took a keen interest in her attempts at statecraft, and together they spent hours studying maps of the city and the surrounding lands, or reading through the library left by Lord Vond, or debating how best to resolve some dispute. But then Blaise would appear at the door and spirit Derwyn away, leaving her alone.

Back in Ersfel, Olva had always stood a little outside the life of the village. Her father Long Tom had been the heart of Ersfel, friend to everyone, eager to lend a hand, always to be found of a night at the alehouse. But Olva had never mastered that easy familiarity. At first, it was by dint of her unlikely marriage to a young noble far above her station – oh, there'd been such gossip, so many jealous glances, so many stories. Then, after Galwyn's murder, everyone treated her like she was made of glass, and the wrong word could shatter her. She'd had a few close friends, mostly those who rented portions of her land that she couldn't work herself.

Now, she was deprived even of the friend she'd met on the Road. Torun was gone. Alf was gone again. Her faithful dog Cu had been lost in Ellsport.

And here in Necrad, there was the same gossip, the same glances and speculation only on a far grander scale. Who was this peasant woman from the Mulladales, suddenly lifted to reign over Necrad? Servants whispered in the Citadel. Threeday dragged in rumours from the streets in the same way Cu used to bring dead rats. On the rare occasions when Olva left the safety of the Citadel and went out onto the streets of the Sanction – to survey the repaired walls, or watch the first wagons of supplies from the New Provinces arrive – she felt eyes watching her.

Gossip she could ignore. Petty jealousy – from Genny Selcloth and the other goodwives of Ersfel, or from Witch Elves and blood traders and merchant princes – she could laugh at. It was the feeling of impending catastrophe that gnawed at her. *This city is a wheel*, Torun had warned her, *it'll raise you high then bring you down*. It gnawed at her and kept her awake long into what passed for night in Necrad.

When she slept, she did not dream. She'd always had vivid dreams, especially when the weather was unsettled or when her thoughts were consumed with some worry. When she'd gone in search of Derwyn, dreams of him had found her as soon as she closed her eyes. But she could not recall her dreams since she had arrived in Necrad.

Then, in the midst of that endless, dreamless day, she heard a sentry cry out in alarm. "Dreadworm!"

Olva leaped up and ran to the window. There, in the western sky, was a winged speck of darkness, growing rapidly in size as it approached. Threeday scribbled a total at the bottom of a column of figures, then joined her.

"My eyes are not as good as yours," he said, "is it the Lammergeier?"

The dreadworm swooped past the Citadel in the direction of the Wailing Tower. As it passed, they heard the terrified shriek of a low-flying dwarf.

"I suspect not," said Threeday. "Well, let us see which doom comes for us today."

Eager for news – eager for a change – Olva took a carriage across the city rather than wait for Torun to report to the Citadel. She passed into the Sanction. She peered out at the great deserted temples and palaces, the mausoleums and the galleries. Sometimes, she caught glimpses of movement amid the ruins. Dead-enders or relic-hunters, maybe. It was too bright for wraiths.

The dark doors of the Wailing Tower were shut. Olva knocked, then hammered. "Blaise!" she shouted. "Let me in!"

Then she was falling down a lightless chasm. She tried to scream, but there was nothing in her lungs, she had no lungs, no mouth, no body, just *awareness* plummeting into the void. It lasted but a moment, and then she was standing in an infinite obsidian emptiness, back in her body once more. Blaise faced her, his features hidden by his cloak, his pale hand clutching a staff of bone. Disembodied eyes circled around him.

"Olva, Regent of Necrad, Mother of the Uncrowned King, Walker in the Grey Lands. What business do you have in the Wailing Tower?"

"What is this? Where am I?"

One of the circling eyes shot off like a little meteor, vanishing into the dark. "If we must speak of mere physicality, your body has not moved. It stands in front of the door of my tower. But here I have power to open doors to higher planes and other states of being . . . including those where we may converse more freely."

Olva groped for words. "Is this an illusion? Or am I ... out of my body?"

"It is a change in perspective." Blaise's voice seemed to come from everywhere around her, and she had the sudden horrible thought that this void was inside his robe and he'd somehow swallowed her. "I ask again: what business do you have in the Wailing Tower?"

"I saw Torun fly in on a dreadworm. I want to know what news she's brought."

"Another facet of me is speaking to her now. She is ... excitable, but she tells me that emissaries from Summerswell are on their way here – to negotiate our surrender, no doubt." The wizard sneered. "A tiresome and fruitless distraction."

"I want to talk to her," demanded Olva. If she was still standing in front of the door of the tower, then even if she wasn't aware of her body, she could still control it. She tried pushing, and the obsidian plane quivered, like it was the surface of a mirror and she'd just knocked against the frame. For a moment, she heard Torun talking, babbling about Lord Bessimer and dwarf-smiths and ogres and how flying was absolutely not for dwarves. It sounded as though the dwarf was speaking from an adjoining room.

But there was another voice too, in another room. Derwyn's voice, but changed, and the words he spoke were in a tongue she did not know.

That *he* did not know.

"Derwyn?" she cried, and suddenly she was back outside the door, and it swung open of its own accord. She stumbled into the Wailing Tower's atrium.

She couldn't hear Derwyn's voice now. The tower was quiet as the grave. Had she imagined it? Blaise's illusion had felt so real at the time, but now it was slipping away like a dream, and she suddenly doubted herself. Had she really heard Derwyn at all, or had it just been some echo of her fears?

The atrium was a grand hallway lit by a crystal chandelier. A half-dozen skeletons had been dismembered and fused to the wall, spines and ribcages interlaced with oak furniture and hanging tapestries.

"Blaise?" she called. "Derwyn?"

"The master is not to be disturbed," the skulls shrieked in unison, and then they began to chant. Black slime flowed from their eye sockets, their jaws, dripping down the walls. Slime-tendrils reached for Olva even as the doors slammed shut behind her. "The master is not to be disturbed!"

"Stop!" Torun burst in through a far door, waving an ornate key at them as a token. "Back, back! Leave her be! She's welcome here."

"We were once," said the skulls, "as you are now." But they relented, the slime slithering back into the bones.

Olva clutched Torun's shoulder. "What was that?"

The dwarf shrugged. "Blaise dislikes callers. When I'm not here to turn them away, he wakes his former apprentices."

"Would it . . . would they have hurt me?"

"Oh no. It's quite painless." Torun crossed the atrium and locked the front door with the heavy silver key. "I can see it's quite grotesque," she said in a tone that suggested she absolutely couldn't see that, but was willing to concede that Olva might, "but the Wailing Tower must be protected. And they did try to murder us. Anyway, come up, come up!"

Torun brought Olva up a steep staircase. Olva had to save her breath for the climb, but the dwarf talked all the way to the top of the tower. "Alf's gone on to Arden with Ildorae, but he sent me back early to tell you that he saw emissaries from Summerswell coming and one of them is Lord Vond who used to rule here but the other one is Lord Bessimer and he's Peir's father and Alf said you should know so you can prepare."

Prepare? Olva tried to imagine what Alf could mean, but her head was still spinning. She'd expected news of an army marching from

Arden, not a few riders. And if they brought nothing more than a demand for surrender, then why send so many?

Blaise's study was nearly at the top of the tower. The wizard was in one of his more human guises – his hood cast back from his thin face with its prominent chin, and eyes that blinked a good deal less than they should. He stood by the window, by the wrought-iron balcony where Torun's dreadworm rested. He held a letter, adorned with dwarven seals and crests.

Derwyn sat in an overstuffed armchair by Blaise's desk. He looked exhausted, and clung to a pewter mug of some steaming concoction. Olva hurried to his side.

"Are you all right?"

"I just woke up." He yawned. "I feel like I was trampled by a bull. Blaise tells me that he's still suturing my soul back together."

"Are you sure?" she whispered. She ran her eyes over Derwyn, looking for signs of injury. The poor boy's scars were covered with sweet-smelling unguent, but those were old wounds, inflicted by Prince Maedos. He seemed himself – but she'd heard that strange voice.

"Olva Forster," said Blaise. "Torun has brought two pieces of good news from the Dwarfholt. The dwarven smiths have agreed to aid in the reconstruction of Necrad's arsenal. They shall be here within days. I am told that Sir Aelfric was helpful in securing their cooperation." With a flick of his wrist, Blaise sent the letter flapping across the room like a paper bird to land in Olva's hand. She set it aside without looking at it.

"Is Derwyn all right?"

"Considering we brought him back from the Grey Lands, and considering that the Spellbreaker might have undone all my labours with a stroke, he is in remarkably good health. He will require further treatments." Blaise stared at Olva, and she felt suddenly vulnerable and fragile, as if he had transmuted her to a thing of glass and she could hide nothing from him. "Is there something that concerns you in particular, Lady Forster?"

"I ... Emissaries of Summerswell are coming here," she stammered, "what might they want?"

Blaise turned back to the window. "For years, the Masters of the College of Wizardry sought to take this tower from me. At first, they sent messengers – some polite, some less so. They sought to bribe me, to woo me with fair words and lofty promises. They sought to threaten me, to cut off my access to certain magical components. By the end, they tried murder." He laid a hand on Torun's shoulder, and the dwarf beamed with pride. "If it were not for my loyal apprentice, they would have succeeded. Instead, their assassins adorn my hallway." He turned back to face Olva. "The Lords seek to take the city from us. Their emissaries will be polite at first. But not for long. They will test us and attempt to ascertain how well we are prepared for conflict with the south. They will try to divide us, hoping to weaken our resolve. And, ultimately, the Lords will seek to retake the city, because they cannot tolerate anyone else commanding the power of Necrad." The wizard drew his hood over his face. "I shall labour to restore our defences. You, Lady Forster, should greet these emissaries, and delay them as much as you can."

"Alf says they're sending Lord Bessimer." She held Derwyn's hand. "He's Peir's father. Why are they doing that? Why him?"

"I want to be there too," said Derwyn, tugging his hand free of Olva's grasp as he rose from the chair. "I should be there. Lord Bessimer – he's a good man. He'll understand why we cannot yield Necrad."

"It does not matter who they send," said Blaise. "The ritual is the same. You should rest."

"No," said Olva, rising. "Derwyn's coming back to the Citadel with me. Torun, you should too. I want to hear about the Dwarfholt."

"My apprentice has duties here," said Blaise, "and I have more to do with Derwyn. The stars are auspicious for healing spells tonight." He tapped his staff on the floor.

*

Suddenly, she was back in that void, that nowhere place, with Blaise.

"Lady Forster," he said gravely, "have I offended you?"

"No, no. I just want to—" *To know what you've done to my son.* "To prepare for the arrival of Lord Bessimer and the rest. They think they're coming here to take Necrad from . . . from a band of bandits and usurpers and traitors. Instead, we greet them as peers. Lords to Lords." Even as she spoke, she strained in that nameless direction as before, when she'd heard Derwyn, but nothing happened.

"I agree," said Blaise. "At the council meeting, I was impressed by your clarity of thought. You see the danger posed by Summerswell. Berys' obsession with the Erlking is like a man drowning in a great lake who declares he shall save himself by damming the river at its source. Yes, cutting off the flow of waters will one day drain the lake, but the man will drown long before it makes any measurable difference."

"I'd put it more plainly," said Olva, "not being so concerned with being clever. The Lords will kill us just as readily as the elves, for we've made ourselves an enemy to both of 'em. All that's true. And don't think I'm not grateful, Master Blaise, for all you've done for me and mine. Teaching Torun magic, healing Derwyn – and I've no doubt you've kept Alf out of a fair share of trouble."

"Many times," said Blaise, and there was a hint of amusement in his voice. "But saving him on the Isle of Dawn puts me ahead by two. I keep track of my debts."

"Me too," said Olva. "So tell me, Master, does what you're doing endanger Derwyn?"

"Why do you ask?" The amusement vanished, if it had ever really been there.

"A mother's fears."

"The spells are . . . arduous, but he slumbers during the ritual. I give him a highly diluted tincture of lotus-wine to put him to sleep, and then I reknit body and soul."

"He's not in pain? He's not awake?"

"No." A torrent of eyes poured from Blaise's hood and circled around her like moist moons. "Has Derwyn complained to you about my methods?"

"No. He's just so tired. Tell me, how many more of these treatments will he need?"

"I cannot say. Binding a soul to its original body once the ties have been damaged is hard enough – the elves have sought a way to defy the fading and maintain their physical existence for aeons, and their solutions are highly imperfect. Lord Bone bound the wraith of Acraist, but we both saw that was . . . flawed. The ritual I used to save Derwyn was the same one that Lath used to bind Death to the body of Thurn's daughter, and although I perceive the matchless hand and eye of the Erlking behind that incantation, it too is flawed. We are on uncertain ground."

"You use a lot of words to say you don't know."

"I strive," said Blaise, "for precision. And while we are in private, let me I tell you this: Dryten Bessimer was sent as an attack on Derwyn. I have sewn up his soul, but Bessimer's presence will tear at it and fray my stitches. For your son's own good, keep the former Lord at arm's length." The wizard bowed his head. "I have a great deal of work to do in the coming weeks, Lady Forster. I would count it as a kindness if you disturbed me as little as possible. As the sole remaining member of the Nine in Necrad, I give you my blessing to deal with minor issues as you see fit."

"And what counts as a minor issue?"

"Anything short of the world's ending."

And there were minor issues aplenty, as she waited for the emissaries.

Three people – two adults and a child – went missing near the Liberties. The child was found safe and well, playing with an elf-child. Of the adults, no sign was found, but Threeday reported glumly that the whisperings in the Garrison blamed the vampires.

Granaries and storehouses were empty; the people of Necrad were used to barring their doors against monsters that might stalk the streets at night, but hunger could not be kept out by any barrier. Olva dispatched one of the merchant ships to cross the Gulf of Tears and see what could be salvaged from the Isle of Dawn. The crew reported that the isle was abandoned, and still wracked by infrequent thunderstorms. The life-trees there were ash, and the elves once bound to them were wraiths on the wind.

An old Wilder came to the north gate one evening, begging for shelter. He claimed that he had fled rather than take part in the siege of Necrad, and hid in the woods near Staffa. Now whatever remained of his tribe had gone away, and he was alone. He was old enough, he said, to remember when the Wilder worshipped the Witch Elves as gods, and he had always hoped he would be chosen as tribute just so he could see the heavenly city with his own eyes. Now, the old gods were cast down, the city marred, but still he wished to see the city of his dreams. One more mouth makes little difference, thought Olva. Recalling what Alf had taught her about the customs of the Wilder, she had the old man plant his spear outside the gate before entering.

He had no name; he claimed to have lost it in the woods.

She asked Threeday to keep an eye on him, but despite the best efforts of the Vatling's agents, they could not find the nameless Wilder-man. The vampire attacks, though, ceased soon after.

Still, Olva lay awake at night, thinking of Threeday's warning. She knew the dangers of the Witch Elves as well as anyone – they had found her in her house in Ersfel when hunting for Alf. In that state half between slumber and waking, it seemed to her that Ersfel and Necrad were not so different. In both places, she had been given rank and influence that she'd never desired, and had paid a terrible price each time. In Ersfel, she'd taken the broken pieces of her old life and built a new one.

And Necrad would not be so different.

CHAPTER NINETEEN

Again, Olva stood atop the west gate of Necrad, and watched as the emissaries from Summerswell approached. They were a sorry sight, she thought, road-weary and frozen. Banners flapped in the wind. At the head of the company rode Timeon Vond, the former governor of Necrad. Beside him, swaying unsteadily in his saddle, was an old man who must be Lord Bessimer.

Olva had arrived in Necrad on dragon-back, so she had not personally experienced the western approach, but she had heard tales of it. They'd have first glimpsed the necromiasma as they descended the foothills of the Dwarfholt, a constant stain on the horizon reminding them that this place was not *natural*, not *earthly*. Necrad was a city of immortals, of gods and demons. Mortals would find no welcome here. They'd have pressed on across the labyrinths and trenches of the Clawlands, and then the desolation of the Charnel. The long march across the Charnel would sap their spirits, the unchanging barren landscape corroding their souls until all hope was lost.

And then they would see the Stone Dragons, and the walls. A sheer cliff of marble, without visible join or mortar. The elves had carved their histories across its surface in better days, and now the shifting unlight of the miasma turned those histories into fleeting nightmare images. The one constant: those mighty statues of dragons, rearing back, fire burning in their jaws, and the great bronze gates.

More than a century ago, a mortal came to those gates and begged to be allowed entrance to the city to study magic. The city had lifted him up, and he had become Lord Bone.

Nearly twenty years ago, the armies of the League came to those gates, and they were met by dragonfire. The desperate counterstrike against Lord Bone ended in ash and ignominy. The Nine crept past those gates, sneaking in through the Pits, and they'd brought Lord Bone low – and the city had raised them up too.

Now it was Olva's turn. She took her fear and buried it, then adjusted the elven gown and fur cloak they'd given her to wear, the circlet heavy with protective charmstones. *Here I stand*, she told herself, *with as much right as anyone.* The city was monstrous; if they threatened her, she would be monstrous too.

Lord Vond spurred his horse a few paces forward and looked up at the gatehouse. He looked so small in the shadow of the dragons, but his voice betrayed no fear. "Open up!" he called. "Who's in command here? Open the gate, now!"

Olva stepped forward to the parapet. "I command here."

"Who are—" Vond peered up at her in disbelief. "The Lammergeier's *sister*? Where is the Lammergeier? Or any of the rest of them? Or must I bandy words with a peasant at the gate of my own city?"

"This is not your city," said Olva. "Whatever claim you might have had on it, you lost when you fled rather than fight for Necrad."

"Winebald, where are you?" shouted Vond. He caught sight of one of the guards standing at Olva's side. "You there! Open the gates, immediately!"

A test, thought Olva. Out of the corner of her eye, she studied the faces of the guards who flanked her. Would they turn on her? They'd served Vond once, and the Lords – where did their loyalties lie? She'd ensured their payment, tried to earn their trust, but this was the first time they'd had a real choice. Would any of them break?

As her gaze ran along the line of guards atop the wall, she noticed that several were Witch Elves, dressed in armour like the rest. The sight alarmed her, but she hid her surprise as best she could.

"Forgive me," whispered Threeday, "our numbers seemed a little scanty, so I armed more Witch Elves."

Olva nodded. She could hardly argue with the Vatling here and now, which was doubtless why he'd picked this moment to tell her.

The guard did not move. The moment passed.

Bessimer spoke. "I have come a long way to pray at my son's grave, and to see if he is still in it. Let us in before we freeze, for his sake if nothing else."

The first wagons from the New Provinces arrived in time for the Citadel cooks to prepare a winter feast of sorts. Considering how tight their belts were drawn, Olva winced at the excess, but she knew it was a necessary cost. Vond had ruled Necrad for years, and before him, some other emissary from Summerswell. They'd faced the same problems she had, and knew the city's vulnerabilities. They would look for signs of weakness, of shortages. So, even though she had little appetite, she filled her trencher with slices of pork.

At the high table sat Olva, the Lords Bessimer and Vond – and three empty chairs.

"My brother and Master Blaise may join us if their duties permit," said Olva.

"This is absurd," complained Vond. He was thin and nervous, and tried to hide his nervousness with sheer volume. He reminded Olva strongly of someone, but she couldn't quite place him. "You – you are brigands, squatting amid ill-gotten treasures. You cannot expect us to negotiate with you—"

Once, many years ago, Galwyn had taken her to see his highborn great-aunt. Olva remembered how frightened she'd been of the old woman, how a raised eyebrow or a passing remark from her was a crushing blow. Now, she tried to emulate the haughty voice, the cold disdain. The Witch Elf garb made it easier to play-act power.

"I am not offering to negotiate with you. This is the dining hall, not the council chamber." Olva sipped her thin soup. "You must remember – you'd have run past this room when you fled the city."

"Yes, very witty. This is childish, though I should have expected no better from the Nine." Vond raised his voice. "Yes, I retreated from Necrad, and why did I do that? Because I had entrusted a key role in the defence of the city to your brother, and he abandoned his post to run off to help you find your brat! With the Lammergeier and his sword gone, we had no weapon against Death! And what did your brother do then?"

"He saved me and my son."

"He *murdered* a prince of the Everwood! An elf who has been a friend to Summerswell since the first Lords were blessed by the Erlking! An elf who stood beside me in the defence of the city!"

Olva fought her own anger down, and kept it from colouring her response. "You should not speak, my lord, of matters you clearly know nothing about."

"I know the heresy," said Vond, "spread by malcontents. Let me guess – they whisper that the Wood Elves are the secret rulers of Summerswell, that the Lords are puppets dancing to the Erlking's tune. When I was Lord here, I had Rangers amid the guard, watching for signs of disloyalty. It is a pernicious lie, born of evil, spread by the faithless and the jealous." He skewered a fat piece of pork, examined it, then threw it to the dogs. "I did not come here to be lectured."

"Peace, Timeon," said Bessimer. "You are a guest here."

"A guest in my own hall."

"Well, it's a strange thief who steals your hall, then invites you in for dinner." Lord Bessimer tried to cut his own meat, but his knife slipped from his grasp. His old fingers trembled.

"May I help?" She took Bessimer's plate and cut up the pork. "I did this for my father, when he was ill."

"I'm not used to anyone waiting on me," said Bessimer.

"You were the High Lord!"

"I was. And then I gave up all my titles, and my servants, and became a monk." He took a morsel of pork. "That is enough for me."

"Are we done with this charade, then?" asked Vond. "At least when Gundan usurped me, he did it to my face. Does the Lammergeier hide behind his sister's skirts?"

"You are welcome to leave if you wish, my lord," said Olva, "but your men deserve a good meal at least. As for my brother and Master Blaise – as I said, they have other responsibilities."

"And the one they call the Uncrowned King?" Bessimer's hand trembled all the more. "Where is he?"

"My son is resting," said Olva. "He sends his regrets."

"I wish to see him." Bessimer clutched a string of prayer beads. "The night before the messengers came to the monastery, the abbot called me into the shrine and bade me look into the grail-cup. The Intercessors showed me a vision. It was as if I was a bird, soaring high over a grey land shrouded in fog. Many people were walking through the fog in a procession, all going down the slope, but I could see only glimpses of them. And then, for an instant, the fog parted, and I beheld my son. My Peir, as he was when he rode away from me on the last day. He wrestled with a figure hooded and cloaked, and the Intercessors whispered that it was the Dark Lord of this city. Peir . . . he was so tired." The old man's voice cracked, and tears ran down his lined cheeks. "The fog hid them once again from my sight. The abbot told me that the vision was ended, and that I should give thanks, but . . . I took the grail, and shook it, and *demanded* that the Intercessors show me more."

Vond grimaced and leaned over, tugging the beads out of Bessimer's grip. "My lord, do not strain yourself. And these fools have rejected the guidance of the Intercessors, so any revelations you saw mean nothing to them."

I was there, thought Olva. *I walked in the Grey Lands. I saw Peir wrestling with Lord Bone at the edge of Death's kingdom. I brought my son back. I did those things for Derwyn, not Peir!* She wanted to speak, to shout, but instead she sipped her wine and kept her face composed. "Did they show you anything more?"

Bessimer nodded. "Only for a moment. I saw again the grey land shrouded in fog, and from a great distance. I saw figures climbing up the slope, and one bore a black sword."

"Oh, for heaven's sake!" Vond shoved his chair back. "Visions and prophecies, and sows dressed up as elf-queens. This is a farce. Tell the Lammergeier and the wizard that I will speak to the rulers of Necrad, not their serving wench." He stood and stalked away across the dining hall. Threeday hurried over, bowing to Vond, fawning over him. Olva watched the two talk in an apparently friendly manner.

"Ignore Timeon's rudeness," said Bessimer. "You have caught him in a vice. The Lords blame him for the loss of Necrad as much as they blame the Wilder or the actions of the Nine." He sighed. "I was there in the war, you know. I thought the Nine were brigands. That my poor son, blinded by tales of glory, had fallen in with a band of mischief-makers, and had somehow enmeshed a Princess of the Everwood in his folly. Too late, I understood that the Nine were heroes." He trembled. "It is a terrible thing to be close to a hero. Heroes are instrument of fate, and fate is a raging river, washing away anything in its path towards inevitable destiny. They never know peace on this side of the grave." He blinked, as if surprised to find himself in the banquet hall. "But it was worth it, they tell me. They slew Lord Bone, and saved Summerswell."

"They won this city," said Olva, softly. Was this what Alf had meant about Lord Bessimer? The old man seemed far more concili-iatory than Vond. Bessimer had once been a Lord of Summerswell, but now he reminded Olva intensely of her own father in his last days. She couldn't imagine that this broken old man still had any sway over the Lords – and he clearly still revered the Intercessors, so he was still under the spell of the Wood Elves.

"At such a price! My boy! I would give anything to see him again," said Bessimer.

Anger flashed through Olva. *He's not your boy. He's my son.*

"My son Derwyn . . ." Olva picked her words carefully. "He is like Peir, I'm told. The same brightness of spirit. He was gravely wounded in the siege, and to heal him, I went into the Grey Lands. Your vision . . . I think that was me that you saw. But listen: Derwyn is not Peir. He is not your son restored."

Bessimer clutched his beads again, mumbling prayers to the Intercessors over and over. Olva sensed he was drifting away from her, withdrawing inside himself. She waited a few minutes, finishing the last of her food and listening to the old monk's litany before calling Threeday over.

"My lady?" said the Vatling.

"Have someone show Lord Bessimer to his chambers."

"Evening prayers." Bessimer stirred, blinking like an owl. "I must pray before I sleep."

"Show him to the chapel." The Citadel's chapel had gone unused since the siege.

Once Bessimer was gone, Olva invited the Vatling to sit.

"I saw you talking to Lord Vond. What did he want of you?"

"Why, I served Lord Vond for the time he was governor of Necrad. Bringing matters concerning the Liberties to his attention, helping out here and there – as I do for you. My people are bound to Necrad, so we do whatever we can to keep the machinery running smoothly. But . . ." Threeday scooped up a pool of grease from Vond's plate with his fingers, then licked them. "You mean, of course, did Vond ask me for secrets about the city? Did he ask me about the state of our defences, about the loyalty of the New Provinces, about the tales of the Uncrowned King, about the attack on Kairad Nal? Yes, he asked me all these things."

"And what did you tell him?"

"That the fires of the Stone Dragons incinerated the Wilder army he fled from. That Lady Erdys and the other leaders of the New Provinces are loyal to us. That the people praise the Uncrowned King." The Vatling picked up Vond's unfinished goblet of wine, sniffed it, and put it down again. "As for Kairad Nal – well, that's far outside Necrad, and none of my concern. I simply said I could hardly believe that the Lammergeier and Master Blaise have grown so mighty that the two of them alone could destroy the fortress of the Wood Elves – a fortress, I reminded him, that endured through all the years that the Witch Elves ruled here, and during the reign of Lord Bone. I marvelled, rather loudly, at the peerless heroism of the two." He smiled a toothless smile.

"It's good to know I can rely on you."

"You cannot. As I said, my loyalty is to my people and the safety of Necrad. If I thought that the city would be better served by aiding Summerswell to retake Necrad, then I would have told Lord Vond about the gaps in the walls by the Liberties, about the crack in the Stone Dragon by the northern gate. I might even have let slip that your brother has gone south in search of Berys, or that your son is ill. But I said none of those things, because I adjudged your son to be the better custodian of this city." Threeday picked up Olva's goblet. "More wine?"

She shook her head. "Lord Bessimer wishes to meet the rulers of the city. I want you to attend."

"As the Widow Queen commands."

"And Lady Erdys. Someone from the New Provinces should attend, and a representative of the Liberties. I want to show we're not a gang of bandits."

"Very wise."

Olva removed the circlet from her head and rubbed her temples. "Should we send for a Witch Elf?"

"Ildorae has yet to return."

"There are other Witch Elves."

"Is it wise to invite another wolf into the house?" asked Threeday.

"You armed the Witch Elf guards."

"I did, but they were of lesser status. Ildorae is high in the House of the Horned Serpent, a noble of the *enhedrai*. For courtesy's sake, you would have to invite one of the Witch Elf rulers – and they are . . . ah, off-putting."

If Alf was in Necrad to keep the elves in check with the threat of Spellbreaker, then maybe she could have risked their presence. As it was . . . "All right. If Ildorae returns in time, she may be there. If not, leave them out."

"As you command." Threeday rose. "And Master Blaise?"

"No. He's not to be disturbed, he says. I'll honour his request."

CHAPTER TWENTY

He's wasting away, thought Olva when her son arrived. It wasn't that he had grown thin or frail; he looked tired, yes, but otherwise healthy. It was more that he was fading, like the elves were said to do. He seemed remote, as if the distance between them was more than the few steps it would take to cross her chamber in the Citadel.

Impulsively, she hugged him. Derwyn tolerated her embrace for a moment, then squirmed away.

"What did Blaise do to you this time?"

"I never remember," he said in a croak.

"You don't have to go back. We could see how you get on without Blaise's magic. I'll take care of you."

"No," Derwyn said sharply. "I'm not a child. And you've got the whole city to watch over." He threw back the shutter and let the cold air in. Plumes of necromiasma rose from the distant Sanction. "I can do it. I can go back. It's important I do this. For . . . for the city."

That doesn't sound like Der – what's Blaise been telling him? "What do you mean?"

"For . . ." He shook his head, as if trying to shake the words into place, and looked very like his uncle for a moment. "I've been thinking, a lot. Listen. When Bor came to Ersfel, and you told me that I was the Lammergeier's nephew, I thought . . . I thought that was *it*, that was who I was supposed to be. I'd be like Alf, I'd go to Necrad and be his squire and learn to fight like a knight. I had a dream, calling me to come here." He rubbed his shoulder where Alf had given him a solid blow in their sparring. "But it all went wrong. Not just ... what happened with Martens and Prince Maedos, in the Pits, but before that."

"When?"

"I think when Peir died. I've heard Alf say it. If he'd lived ... then I think everything would have been better. The Nine wouldn't have broken. Thurn wouldn't have gone back to the Wilder, and there'd have been no trouble in the north. Prince Maedos would never have dared try to take the city. The Nine united ... we could have checked the power of the Wood Elves too. It would all have been better."

"Maybe," said Olva. "But we live with what we get. When your father was killed, I remember thinking that everything was broken, that I couldn't ever go on. I still imagine, sometimes, what it would be like if he'd lived. And then I go on with what needs to be done. The wheel doesn't stop turning, ever."

Derwyn turned to face her. "Would you bring Father back, if you could?"

The words, *yes, of course,* leaped to her lips, but she paused, suddenly unsure. What had once been an idle fancy was now terrifyingly real. She'd brought her son back from the borders of death – and Thurn's magic had resurrected Death herself, the grandmother of all humanity who'd lived thousands upon thousands of years ago. If she demanded it of Blaise, could the wizard reach into the Grey Land and pluck poor Galwyn's soul back from death? And if Galwyn could be brought back, why not anyone else?

On the road, she'd killed one of Marten's men, a boy no younger than Derwyn. He'd come at her with a spear, and she'd not meant to harm him, but still he was dead. Doubtless there were worse people in the world than that boy – Lyulf Martens, for one. What if they'd brought back that boy's soul? Would that be just? On the Isle of Dawn, Prince Maedos had made her choose whether Captain Abran should live or die. She'd been angry, blaming Abran for the loss of Derwyn, for all the ills of the blood trade, and she'd chosen to condemn Abran to death for his crimes. She'd taken comfort in the finality of the decision – right or wrong, the world was *done* with Abran. The thought of it all being undone appalled her, and she could not quite say why. How would life go on without an ending?

For a moment, she apprehended what it must be like to be an elf. No endings, no meanings.

Would you bring him back, if you could?

"It's not the way the way of things. It's not how the world works, much as we might wish it otherwise."

"The Nine did what was unthinkable. They slew monsters no one else could defeat. They saved Summerswell from invasion, and turned back the tide. They took Necrad and slew Lord Bone. That's not the way of things. That's not how the world's supposed to work, but they did it." He looked down at his hand, as if seeing it for the first time. "So can I. I might not be able to fight like Alf, but I can do this."

"You want to go back to the Tower," she said.

"It's my battle to fight."

She wanted to forbid him, to fetch him home and keep him there, but those days were gone.

Always the wheel moved on. Not even the greatest of heroes could stop that. There would always be more to do, always a tomorrow.

In Ersfel, they'd be digging the frosty soil, getting ready for planting. Here in Necrad, there was other work. She bent over one of Torun's maps of the city.

"Torun said you're calling a council. Is Uncle Alf back?"

"No. And it's not a council. I want to show that the people of the city support us."

"That we're not just occupiers, like Lord Vond?"

"Exactly." They needed to make themselves secure here. There was nowhere else.

"Is it true?"

It was not the sort of question Olva expected from her son. "What do you mean?"

"You've hardly left the Citadel since we got here. Anytime you go out, you take Lord Vond's carriage. You've never walked around Necrad – not even the Garrison." Derwyn shrugged. "All you went through to get here, and you never even go outside."

"I had my fill of enchantment and wonder on the Isle of Dawn," muttered Olva. "And I've seen enough of Necrad to know it's not a place for just . . . wandering about."

"Then how are we any different, if we just sit in the Citadel like Lord Vond did? Let's go out." Derwyn grinned. "In fact, you promised me you would. Back home, you said that we'd go next year in the spring. It's the spring now."

"It doesn't feel like it," said Olva.

A quartet of guards – all human – followed them through the streets of the Garrison. Winebald, two of his best soldiers, and a young lad with a crossbow. Derwyn set a fast pace through the occupied district. The streets were emptier than they had been when Olva first arrived. Anyone who could afford it had fled before the siege, and those who were left behind now hid indoors, fearful of another assault. Abandoned by Lord Vond and the League, stranded in the midst of strangeness, they stared as Olva passed by.

Oddly, it put Olva in mind of another time, long ago, back during the war with Lord Bone. Ersfel had been spared direct assault, but there were rumours of monsters and Changelings in the woods. Then the Lords of the Mulladales called away anyone who could fight. She remembered when she was fifteen or so, watching the old reeve riding away, awkward in unfamiliar armour, and half the young men of the village away with him. The holywood swallowed their singing as they marched around the hill. She remembered her father grumbling that he couldn't go – Long Tom, strongest man in the dales, still able to crack a skull, but his legs betrayed him. Her mother went up to the new reeve, the old reeve's brother, and demanded to know what he would do if Ersfel was attacked. He had no response. Those left behind went back to their cottages and waited for doom. Now that same despair, that feeling that the roof had come off the world and they were helpless in the face of the storm, settled on the people of Necrad.

Olva turned to one of the guards. "Have sentries moved from guarding the Citadel to the Garrison. Give each of them responsibility for a portion of the district, and have them speak to those who dwell there. Make sure they understand that the Stone Dragons are our first line of defence, and tell them where to fall back to if the walls are breached."

Even as she gave the order, doubt assailed her. The people of the Garrison had far less of a quarrel with the Lords of Summerswell than she did. Olva and Derwyn, Alf and what remained of the Nine – they might be called rebels. But the folk of the Garrison were caught up in events, forced to take sides. If circumstances were equal, why would they support her and not their former liege-lords? Derwyn was right, she realised – they had to offer something better than Summerswell to win the loyalty of the people. The Lords had said, *Dwell here in Necrad and aid us in ransacking this ruin of all its wealth and magic.* What could she say to them?

And Derwyn led her on, though the Garrison gate.

The Garrison had once been full of life and activity.

The Sanction was, as ever, eerie and silent. Not a tomb – undying elves built no tombs – but an endless monument. The Witch Elves had glorified themselves, spent countless centuries making art that reflected their own eldritch beauty. Now the Witch Elves were reduced to prisoners in the Liberties, their mansions looted by adventurers and relic hunters.

Their three remaining guards exchanged nervous glasses as Derwyn set off north-east across the Sanction. The familiar sight of the Wailing Tower – and how strange it was that such a tower of nightmares, a tower dragged screaming from the earth, wound around with the entrails of the Pits should have become *familiar* to her – was at Olva's left hand, so they must be going into parts of the city she'd never visited before.

"Where—"

Her voice sounded like a thunderclap. She dropped into a whisper. "Where are we going?"

"I can see a long way from the Wailing Tower," said Derwyn, "I've seen Blaise's servants hard at work out here. I want to see what they were doing." He didn't sound quite himself, like he was recalling a dream. Her son was becoming a stranger, stepping away into this strange city.

He led her down more of the twisting boulevards – she'd never get used to how the city mocked perception, size and distance shifting like a mirage. It was impossible to tell which dark spaces were doorways into the underworld and which were merely shadows on walls, or which statues were so perfectly proportioned that they might have been the original creature transmuted to stone, and which were gigantic. Combined with the ever-shifting greenish glow of the miasma, with the dancing light of Winebald's lantern, with Derwyn's feyness, and she felt unmoored. Carved elves leered down at her from archways and pillars, judging her for trespassing, for her insolence at imagining her might ever have a place here. Heraldic symbols reflecting the constellations above – moon and serpent, deer and wolf – made Olva feel even more unsteady, as if Necrad was one step from falling into the night sky.

A breath of icy air caught her by surprise. She tried to steady herself on the wall and stumbled, for there was no wall – it was a lightless archway. Winebald ran up to steady her, and shone his lantern into the gloom. Startled wraiths fled into the depths.

Winebald tugged her away. "Best you stay clear, my lady. I'd not go down there, not for all the gold in the Dwarfholt."

"It's sealed," whispered another guard. "The Nine sealed most of the Pitways years ago."

"Wait a moment," said Olva, "Give me that light."

Reluctantly, he passed her the lantern. Olva took a few paces into the darkness, careful on the slime-slick steps, and shone it down. The light picked out a hinged metal grille blocking the stairwell. Dwarf-forged iron, maybe wrought by Gundan himself, and marked with sigils of binding and forbiddance against the spawn of the pits. Alf had dedicated half his life to keeping those monsters cooped up below.

The gateway stood open. Not smashed, but unlocked from the surface side.

"It's open," she said.

"Smugglers, maybe," suggested Winebald. "Or relic hunters stupid enough to try the Pits." He stayed at the top of the stairs.

"We should close it," said Olva, but she found herself reluctant to go down any further. Terror rose from that underground realm like noxious gas. There were all manner of monsters down there, spawned by Lord Bone's sorcery. The Vatlings like Threeday were a mere by-product of his experiments. She'd gone down into the Pits only once, and then Alf had been with her.

Was it her imagination, or did the flame in her lantern flicker? Did she hear something growling in the darkness below? She glanced back up the stairs at the silhouettes of the others, outlined against the green sky. A shimmer in the miasma behind Derwyn gave him a brief halo.

"Come back up, milady," urged Winebald. "There are things that shun the surface, but they'll take anything that crosses the threshold."

But the thought of leaving that door open conjured images of some fiend stalking them through the Sanction. Better, she thought, to walk clear-eyed into danger rather than ignore the peril and convince yourself that you were safe. The door had to be closed. She took another step down, and another, and another.

Darkness pressed in on her, the shadows like a pack of wolves, and only the frail light of the lantern held them back. She could hear Winebald urging her to come back up, but his voice was distant and muffled. Another step, and another.

You walked into the Grey Lands to rescue your son, she told herself. *This is just a dark tunnel. It should hold no fear for you.* Others wouldn't dare this. Lord Vond might have ruled Necrad for years, but had he ever dared enter the Pits? *If you're going to stay in Necrad, you need to face this.*

Another step down, and she saw the eyes.

A constellation of eyes glittered in the darkness beyond the gate, and the suggestion of scaly hide, wet drool dripping from some unseen maw. Whatever the thing was, that nameless spawn of the breeding vats, spider and slug and bear and insect and dragon all at once and none at all, it watched her with terrible anticipation, its misshapen limbs quivering. At any moment, it could spring forward and devour her.

The gate was only a few paces ahead now, almost within arm's reach.

Greatly daring, she raised the lantern higher. The light revealed more of its hideous features – the barbed spines along its back, the pockets of hanging flesh in its cheeks that resembled eyeless faces, the all-too-human secondary hands beneath the dripping maw – but did not repel it in the slightest. It basked in its revelation. Sensitive hairs on its hide twitched in time with her breathing.

Olva opened her mouth to call out, and another quiver ran through the monster. From above, she could hear Derwyn calling for her. She strained to hear him, but his voice was drowned out by a sudden roaring, like the rushing thunder of an underground river. Olva braced herself for the flood, for it seemed as though a great torrent must be just about to come crashing around the corner of the tunnel and drown her.

But the creature did not respond. The thunderous roar of the river was so loud that Olva wanted to clap her hands over her ears, but the monster seemed wholly unaware of the sudden clamour.

Once, far away in the Fossewood, Olva had felt something like this before. Bor had shown her a grave in the heart of the wood, and claimed that a changeling sorcerer-king lay there. There, for an instant, she'd sensed the wood around her, the life rushing through the earth beneath, the whirling sky. Torun told her she'd touched the earthpower for an instant – and Necrad was a great machine for gathering *magic*, earthpower and star power whirling into an endless abyss. Gingerly, Olva reached out into that roaring flow with her mind. She imagined it turning, a fraction of that power pouring past her, flooding the far end of the tunnel.

The monster flinched.

Olva darted forward, grabbing at the cold metal of the gate and pulling it towards her. Mercifully, it swung shut with a clang, an instant before the monster smashed into it. The iron bars groaned, but held. Olva fell back, scrambling blindly up the steps as the monster scrabbled at the gate, spidery limbs and teeth and tentacles all flailing. Derwyn grabbed her and dragged her back into the light.

"What was that?" he asked. "Why didn't you come back up?" She could hear him perfectly now that she was back on the surface. The rushing thunder of the earthpower was gone – or almost gone. She could still hear it, at the very edge of perception, a distant rumbling in her bones.

"I had to—" she began, and realised it was the sort of thing that Alf might say, the sort of puffed-up heroic nonsense from the songs that Derwyn loved. *I had to prove myself. I had to face the darkness.* If anyone said that to her, she'd have called them a fool.

"That door needed closing," she said, like it was a farm gate in Ersfel and someone had nearly left her pigs out.

Derwyn led them through a deserted palace. Above the door was a statue of a white deer, and inside a many-pillared hall. Wraiths recoiled from Winebald's light, and their sudden fluttering flight made Olva feel like she was in a forest of marble trees, dappled with shadows. Her heart was still racing from her confrontation in the Pits, and she was fiercely aware of every movement. She felt flushed and eager to press on, but a carving caught her eye. She grabbed Winebald's arm and shone the lamp up so she could see it better.

An elf-queen stood at the prow of a ship. She was proud, defiant in the face of a raging storm. One arm was outstretched in an arcane gesture, and a light glimmered in her hand. On the sail was the images of a running deer. Behind her, on some distant shore, was a monstrous tree, mountain-sized, its branches reaching for the heavens as if trying to tear down the stars.

"I've seen her," muttered Winebald, pointing at the elf-queen. "She came to the Garrison gate. Gave me a chill, just looking at her." He spat. "Pity the Nine didn't end all the vampires in the war."

"She doesn't look like a vampire."

"That's the Sundering," said Winebald. "Back when the Witch Elves broke from the Everwood. Thousands of years ago."

Thousands of years. A staggering span of time, and the elves were still fighting the same war. She remembered Prince Maedos' eternal game, where there was no victory, only a succession of advantageous or disadvantageous positions. But maybe the rules were different for mortals. How many mortal kingdoms had risen and fallen in that span? Summerswell was only a few hundred years old, after all – it might be washed away too.

They entered what remained of one of Lord Bone's factories, a squat scar of soot-caked iron amid the heavenly spires. The roof was shattered by stones hurled by siege engines during the League's assault on Necrad. Broken pipes led to a huge marble-tiled vat, like a bath big enough to float a galleon. Greenish residue marred the tiles.

In the midst of all this ruin was Torun, oblivious to Olva's presence, oblivious to the dangers of the Sanction all around her. The dwarf walked back and forth, muttering to herself.

"What are you doing?"

"Oh!" Torun waved a sheaf of papers in her hand. "Making a list of what is to be done. My father will be here soon with smiths and masons and other dwarves, to repair all this. I'm the only one who knows dwarf-craft and magic, so Master Blaise permitted me to help him."

"It sounds like you're doing all the work," said Olva.

"An idle apprentice learns nothing. My father always said that." Torun bent to examine the slime dripping from a broken pipe.

What would grow in this vat, when the dwarves were done? Magic would surge through the streets above, the passageways below, congealing into matter in the pipes and then spilling out to sprout and grow. Maybe it would be something like the monster she saw in the darkness, hideous and terrible – but they'd turn it against their enemies. Alf cursed the black sword, but he still wielded it, and put it to good use. They'd do the same with the dark magic of Necrad. Put a halter around it and lead it into battle against anyone who threatened them. Why, dark and light, good and evil, Witch and Wood – all just words.

She remembered cowering in bed in Ersfel, hugging the infant Derwyn tight, listening for the rustling wings of dreadworms in the dark. Remembered the war-wounded coming home. Her own fears of Necrad, when she was chasing Derwyn. Fear was a weapon. Magic, a weapon. This time, she'd be the one wielding it.

Vond would call it evil, but Vond would call her a peasant. But others called her Widow Queen.

It was what you did with a thing that gave it meaning, not the words people used.

"Can all this be repaired in time?"

Torun rocked from one foot to the other. "It's not just the damage from the siege – either siege. It's twenty years of looting. Look." She pointed at a spot where two pipes met. There was a broken socket there where a charmstone had once sat. "There's much to be restored. Much to do, much to do. And the sooner started, the better."

Finally, they visited the third portion of the city, the Liberties. Unlike the other two districts, the streets of the Liberties were crowded. Vatlings and Witch Elves, mortals and ogres, all crammed into a small, easily patrolled section. High walls and watchtowers – unmanned since the siege – surrounded the Liberties. Here, the victorious League had corralled their defeated foes.

Winebald and the other guards pressed close around Olva and Derwyn, fearful of attack. The guards rarely entered the Sanction, only patrolled its borders. The Liberties, though – that, they knew well. Clearly, rumour of strange visitors from the Garrison had spread through the district, as the crowds around them grew quickly. Witch Elves watched them from rooftops, staring down at them like statues in the Sanction. Vatlings and mortals surrounded them, some begging Olva for favours or alms, others shouting questions.

Then someone in the crowd shouted, "THE UNCROWNED KING!", and the crowd took up the cry. The wet voices of Vatlings, the roars of humans, the thunderous barks of ogres. Only the elves remained silent. Derwyn raised his hand, and the clamour grew.

Winebald looked about in bewilderment. "Twelve years I've been in Necrad," he muttered to Olva, "and this is the first time I haven't had shit thrown at me in the Garrison."

Suddenly, the crowd parted like a wave rolling back from the shore. The street rapidly emptied. Vatlings slipped away into the surrounding buildings. The cries supporting the Uncrowned King faded, and the silence was filled by eerie song.

Around the corner came a strange procession. Witch Elf warriors led the way, armed with bone staves. Behind them came singers, and the beauty of their song pierced Olva's heart more keenly than any blade. Olva recognised one of the singers as Elithadil, the mother of the vampire boy. The singers all bore carved poles of bones that supported a tattered canopy, and beneath that canopy walked a vampire. She was very tall, and was still beautiful in some lights, but her skin was drawn too tight against her skull, and she moved stiffly, as if too sudden a movement would crack the porcelain of her frame. Her gown trailed in the mud, and the once fine jewels she wore were marred with scratches where thieves had stolen charm-stones from their settings.

Her scornful red gaze passed over Olva and the other mortals to lance Derwyn.

"The Skerrise," said Winebald. "We should go, milady."

The Skerrise's entourage proceeded down the street, then turned abruptly. A pair of stone doors ground open of their own accord, and one by one the Witch Elves vanished into the shadows of the crumbling palace. The Skerrise lingered on the doorstep for a moment, looking back at Derwyn. She raised one hand and beckoned him inside. Then she too was gone.

The instant the street was clear, Threeday darted out of a doorway and rushed up to Olva's side.

"Milady Forster! Lord Derwyn!" he exclaimed. Threeday's sharp little teeth could not be gritted, but Olva could see that the Vatling was finding it hard to maintain his usual facade of enthusiastic compliance. "It is wonderful and fitting to see you in the Liberties, and you have seen the love the people have for the Uncrowned King who saved from them from the Wilder. Let us hurry back to the citadel, now, so that we might—"

"That elf – the Skerrise – who is she?" asked Olva.

"She rules the House of the White Deer." Threeday glanced at the rotting palace down the street. "Among the surviving elder elves, she is perhaps the greatest."

"She wants to speak with us," said Derwyn. "We should hear her out." He took a step forward, but Threeday laid a pallid hand on his arm.

"Your uncle admitted Ildorae to the council as a representative of the Witch Elves. Ildorae proved herself an ally through her actions. The Skerrise was a handmaiden of Lord Bone. She has never atoned for her part in the war. It would be . . . exceedingly unwise to speak with her. She might bewitch you, or turn on you. She is dangerous, and we have no weapons to match her."

The young guard with the crossbow coughed. Threeday glanced at him. "Yes, you have an elf-bane bolt. But are you sure you can hit her? And what about all the rest of the elves?" He turned back to Olva. "Your brother and Lord Gundan caused, ah, considerable uproar last year with an ill-considered expedition into the Liberties. Your visit, by contrast, has been a stirring success. Why endanger it now?"

Push on, thought Olva. *We've got to make ourselves safe.* Her heart was pounding, and she felt she could hear the thunder of the earth-power below the streets.

"If she's so dangerous, then she's a threat to us whether we talk to her or not. And I'd prefer to know what she wants now, instead of waiting until Summerswell's encamped outside the walls and we're trapped in here with her."

They passed through those doors into an inner hall. A gallery ran around the perimeter of the hall on the level above, and Witch Elves looked down Olva from those arched windows. The Skerrise stood alone in the centre of the hall. The doors swung shut behind Olva, and the impact dislodged flakes of plaster from the ceiling.

The Skerrise spoke, her voice a withered croak. She called out a question in Elvish, of which Olva understood only a few words, and Derwyn not a bit.

"I don't speak the high tongue," said Derwyn.

From behind Olva came an animal snort, hooves on stone. A white deer – its moonlight hide drawn as tight over its ribs as the Skerrise's skin – pushed past Olva and trotted up to the side of the elf. Its eyes were red too. The elf spoke again, but this time the voice was young and musical, and came from the mouth of the deer. "And I will not profane my mouth with the grunting of beasts."

The Skerrise stroked the deer's neck. She whispered in Elvish, and the animal spoke in the tongue of Summerswell. "So, you are the next mortal to claim dominion over our city. Tell me, how did you know the words to wake the Stone Dragons?"

"I don't know," said Derwyn. "My mother and Blaise brought me back from the Grey Lands, and Blaise said I had the word to unlock Lord Bone's sigil on my lips when they did."

The vampire sneered. "And by this you would claim a crown? At least the last time mortals took our city, they stole it from us with sword and spell. You seek to buy it with a coin found in the gutter."

Derwyn straightened, and there was a hint of that *other* in him. "I make no claim," said Derwyn, "but I did not come back from the dead for nothing."

"I was there, mortal, when we called another the Uncrowned King, and that ended in sorrow beyond measure. What right have you to rule here?"

"You heard the crowd outside," said Olva. "They acclaim him king."

The vampire glared at her. "I fought the Candlelit Crusade," she said through the deer, "and saw the making of the moon. I am not impressed by the tricks of a Vatgrown. I know what the creature Threeday whispers in the alleyways."

"You invited us in," said Olva, "What do you want?"

"To see this mortal, and judge his worth." She bared her fangs. "I judge him good only for one thing. I shall drink from him, and that shall be the price of your safe passage from my house."

Derwyn drew back his cloak and took a warhammer from his

belt. He raised the weapon like Alf had shown him. "Try and take it, if you have the courage."

Olva summoned her courage. If Necrad was the only place where they could be safe, then she needed to confront the Witch Elves one way or another. If Alf had been there, he could have put some manners on the Skerrise with the Spellbreaker, but at that moment Alf was far away in the Cleft of Ard (and though she did not know it, at that moment he was waking to find the Spellbreaker in a Witch Elf's hand). If she could not threaten the ancient one, she could only bargain.

"You talk of cheap tricks," snapped Olva, "look at you there with your talking deer, and parading your broken jewels, letting everyone know that you were robbed. You've got charmstones and magic stashed away – the blood trade would have ended long ago if you had no coin to slake your thirst. I'm not impressed either, and I've never been one for stories." Olva pointed back towards the Garrison. "Here's truth. Right now, we're on the same side. My brother killed your enemy, Prince Maedos. I've got emissaries of the Lords of Summerswell at my door, demanding I turn Necrad back over to them – and there's an army on the way up from Arden." She met the vampire's red glare. "A lot of folk want us dead, and a lot want you dead. Swear loyalty, and maybe we can all weather the storm that's coming."

"Swear? To this . . . eye-blink of flesh and bone? I watched as the first humans crawled out of the cauldron, mewling and grunting. Beasts who learned to speak, we called you. I am as far above you mortals as the stars above the earth."

"That's as maybe. But you need blood, and if you really thought you could get away with attacking us, you'd have done it already. So, you'll swear loyalty to my son, and tell your kin to acclaim him king."

"And in exchange?" The Skerrise licked her pale lips. "Will you give us blood?"

"No," said Olva, patting the deer, "but I saw your old palace earlier. Swear, and we'll give you back the Sanction."

The Skerrise snarled, and the deer cantered off into the shadows. The vampire darted forward and stared into Derwyn's eyes. Olva held her breath, and glanced to make sure that the young guard with the elf-bane crossbow was ready to fire. Derwyn's lips moved in a whisper that Olva could not hear.

Then the Skerrise knelt.

"Hail the Uncrowned King."

CHAPTER TWENTY-ONE

"That was a debacle," hissed Threeday in the safety of the Citadel.

Olva felt exhilarated. They had won together, she and Derwyn! The cheers – and all the sweeter, the Skerrise's words of submission – still echoed in her, lifted her heart. "Why? All the Liberties – not just your agitators – acclaimed Derwyn as king. Necrad's united behind him."

"Behind him, and holding knives. Promising an end to the Liberties . . . forgive me, but I cannot see how this is sustainable."

"Neither can I. But a year ago, I was worrying about how many piglets the sow would birth, and today I'm trying to hold together the city of darkness while my brother's off overthrowing the Lords. Who knows where I'll be next year?"

"I know where I will be," said Threeday morosely. "Still here, advising whoever takes over after you've been hung for treason or devoured by the Skerrise." He tugged at his collar. "I honestly don't know if I can be hung. I suppose they'll just cut my head off."

"I'm guessing you've been spying on our guests."

"You presume incorrectly. I have ensured their every need is attended to, and my staff are so exceptionally diligent that they sometimes take on themselves to shadow our guests – to better anticipate their needs." Threeday gave a quivering sigh. "Lord

Bessimer remains in the chambers you assigned him. He has not left the citadel, although he did ask again if he might speak to Lord Derwyn."

"He'll see him in council," snapped Olva. On the one hand, Bessimer seemed much more trustworthy than Vond, Alf had spoken well of him, and she understood the pain of losing a son, and the boundless joy at the thought that such a loss could be reversed. But on the other, Derwyn was not Peir. Thurn's daughter had come back with Death, and Death had consumed her. Peir might be a legendary hero, the best of the Nine, but she would not allow that to happen to her son. She would not allow Bessimer to lay any claim on him, or stir up any unwanted ghosts.

"Of course. On that topic, Lady Erdys has arrived from Castle Duna, to represent the New Provinces. There is still no word from Ildorae, so . . . I take it the Skerrise is to be allowed passage into the Garrison?"

"She is. And I'm going to open all the gates, too. We've got to stop acting like conquerors, and find a way to share the city, or we'll all hang together."

"As you command. I shall make the arrangements." She could detect no doubt in the Vatling's voice, but she was sure it was there.

"Has there been any word from Summerswell?"

"I have heard little from my contacts since before Yule. However, one of Lord Vond's guards chose to indulge in a certain elven powder that induces pleasurable dreams, and he was unaccountably served a stronger powder than he thought, rendering him talkative. He spoke of a large army mustering at Arden. He also reported an early thaw in the mountains. We have less time than we hoped before we are besieged – unless Sir Aelfric can make contact with Lady Berys. I would guess that Sir Aelfric has yet to reach the far side of the mountains, though, so . . . well, in the songs the Nine always come to the rescue at the last minute. May it be so for us."

"What about Vond? What has he been doing?"

The Vatling adjusted one of his gloves. "Lord Vond has been exceedingly busy. He sent messengers north to Staffa and Athar – regrettably abstemious ones – and has surveyed the walls of Necrad, and seen the repairs we have made. He spoke to several merchants in the Garrison. Oh, and by the by, Pendel has sailed for Phennic, with a flotilla of four ships. There is optimism about their prospects, and I suspect Vond found a colder welcome than he expected. He has also visited the Intercessal shrine at Tar Edalion, outside the city."

"Jan the Pious' old chapel? I thought it was destroyed." The Abbess of Staff had brought Olva there in the siege, so the Intercessors could show her Derwyn in a vision. That vision had led her and Alf into Price Maedos' trap.

"The chapel was damaged during the siege. However, there is a priest among Lord Vond's retinue, and the chapel is still sanctified. Some of the faithful of Necrad repaired it so they could celebrate the Feast of the First Grail there. I'm not one for theology – we Vatlings have no need of spirits to tell us our fate or our place in creation – but I thought little of it. Vond was not the most pious of men when I knew him, but hardship can drive someone to put their faith in higher powers."

Tar Edalion was outside the reach of the necromiasma above Necrad. The Intercessors could manifest there. While she was blind to what was happening across the sea, the spirits were whispering to Vond, bringing him news from Summerswell, instructions from the Everwood. And he'd given them secrets about the state of Necrad's defences, about her weaknesses. They'd watched her in Ersfel too, spying on her, dictating the course her life. Everywhere, their unseen hands shaped the world. Everywhere except here in Necrad . . .

"Burn the chapel," she said.

"Milady," said the Vatling, "there are some in Necrad who still worship—"

"Burn it. Are there any other churches in the north?"

The Vatling blinked. "Four in the Garrison, including one here. The abbey at Staffa. And every village in the New Provinces has at least a small shrine, and there was a grand church under construction at Athar."

"Have them all burned." *Be bold*, she told herself. *Show them we know their tricks. Cut them down to size.*

Threeday stiffened. "Lady Berys," he said slowly, "always cautioned me about the Intercessal churches. She warned me to conduct no business near them, and never to get involved in ecclesiastical matters. They were bad luck, she said, and not to be meddled with."

"They're more than bad luck. The Intercessors are on the side of our enemies. So, we'll deny them any hold on our land. Burn them."

"Burning churches in Athar or Staffa is not within my power. I could perhaps do something about the churches here in Necrad, but – my lady, I must caution you. Many of your countrymen are devoted followers of the Intercessors, and would respond to such an attack. Your position is not so secure here that you can risk this course of action."

"The Wilder were taught to believe that the Witch Elves were gods, but when Thurn led them, they rose up against their gods and overthrew them. We're going to do the same."

Threeday stood. "The Vatlings have no gods. Forgive me, my lady, but I can have no part of this. I shall renounce the Piteous Seat on the council and retire to—"

Without Threeday, she'd have no idea what was going on in Necrad. The Vatling knew all the levers of power. She took his moist hand. "Please, sit. I value your counsel, Threeday, and I heed it. Forget I spoke."

"I forget nothing," said Threeday, "but I am well used to keeping secrets. I understand that you are caught in a perilous situation, milady, and without the strong arm of the Lammergeier to lean upon. I understand, too, that you worry over the health of your son."

He sat back down. "A minor, ah, moment of exuberance can easily be overlooked. I shall mention it to no one."

She knew he was lying, but she took comfort in it anyway.

Footsteps on the stair woke Olva. Bleary-eyed, she sat up in bed, glancing around her chamber, thinking the Vatling had returned, or that one of the guards had a message for her.

Then she scrambled towards the nightstand for her knife. She held it before her, ready to strike. "How did you get past the guards?"

Lord Vond held his hands up in a gesture of peace. "These used to be my chambers. I know all the ways in and out. But look – I am unarmed. I left my sword with your doorkeeper when I arrived under as an emissary. I would thank you to put down your knife." He spoke softly for once.

She didn't. "What do you want?"

"I bring an offer from the Lords of Summerswell."

This is good, Olva told herself. *Vond sees that Necrad's not going to be as easy to retake as he hoped. He can't brush you aside.* "Then you can present it in council, right and proper, to the Uncrowned King and his courtiers."

"This is not for them. It is for you and your son only. The offer is this: if you return to Summerswell, it will be said that you played no part in this rebellion, that you were led astray. You will be permitted to return to your home; further, your son will be dubbed a knight and given a place in the retinue of Lord Aelfwine of the Eavesland, where he might rise to greatness. No harm will come to you or him."

"And what about Alf? What about Necrad?"

"Necrad will be taken in charge by the Lords; I expect I shall be reinstalled as governor. The city's garrison shall be increased to guard against any further attacks by the Wilder. The citizens of Necrad and the lords of the New Provinces will pay suitable recompense for their disloyalty. As for the Lammergeier, that is up to him. His rebellion against the rightful rulers of Necrad cannot be overlooked, nor can the murder of Prince Maedos be forgiven, but Aelfric has ways to make amends. The Spellbreaker offered as elfgild, for example, and his cooperation in uncovering the other rebels. But such matters need not concern you."

"He's my brother. Of course it concerns me."

Vond scowled. "I have heard tales of the Lammergeier since I was seven years old. When my father was governor here, he would write to me regularly with news of Necrad. In all that time, in all those tales and letters, not once did I hear any mention of you from Sir Aelfric. I would guess that you heard *nothing* from him either in all those years. I would not assume that you and he have any interests in common any more."

"He was protecting us."

"He can protect you no longer. I can – if you go home. Necrad can be nothing more than a bad dream, and your son's future assured."

Once, that was all Olva wanted. To go home, and know she was safe. To know that Derwyn was well, and that a good life awaited him. But the Olva who wanted that had vanished along the Road. Exactly when, she could not say. The Fossewood was one step in that journey, when she'd touched magic, when she'd fought for her son. So too were all the betrayals she'd endured, offers of help and shelter that proved false and self-serving. Others could not promise safety; safety you had to ensure with your own actions.

Most of all, she'd changed when she'd gone to the Grey Lands and come back alive.

She would not be dismissed back into obscurity.

"You strike me as a small man, my lord. You come to the city of sorcery, where there's magic in the streets and folk as old as the stars, and you talk about your laws and your dues. You'd have me live out my days where I was, and tell my son that the most he can aspire to is . . . what? An impoverished manor in the Eavesland? And all the while, the Intercessors spying on us, making sure we don't make trouble. No."

"Am I a small man? Perhaps. But I know this – the time for heroes is done. The Nine are old, and we shall not see their like again. The great days are past, when there were monsters to be slain and dark lords to be cast down. I know there is wonder and terror in Necrad, but it is the dregs of a past age, and there will be no returning to it. Shall I foretell the future better than any seer? The sorcery of Necrad, all the books in the Wailing Tower that Blaise so covets – they will be catalogued, and filed away in the College of Wizardry, where they shall be left unused and unread, because nothing good ever came of Lord Bone's meddling with dark powers. The Witch Elves are a dwindling people – they shall all fade. The Wilder will be *tamed*, and become subjects of Summerswell. In time, there will be peace and order all across the lands."

"And you'll be in charge, will you? The Erlking's tenants for eternity?" said Olva. "There's another choice. The Uncrowned King."

"Eternity! Sorcery! Prophecy! The Uncrowned King! Things out of stories!" Vond snarled. "You need to realise that we have lived through the end of such times. You call me a small man, because I give more weight to little details and necessities than to grand visions, but I have dealt with heroes, and I have learned that someone needs to pick up the pieces once they are done with their tantrums and their grandiose sacrifices. The time for heroes is done – they served their purpose in defeating Bone, but now they only engender new catastrophes. I thought you might understand – and see sense. But you are as deluded as the rest."

"Get out," she said, "and if you trespass in my chambers again, I won't hold back."

When Vond was gone, Olva rose – shaking with excitement or fear, she wasn't sure. Vond had entered the great keep through some secret passage. She knew that the citadel was riddled with such hidden ways, but Threeday had assured her they were all guarded. Had Vond used some passage unknown even to the Vatling, or had he convinced the guards to let him pass? She descended the stairs, checking behind every tapestry, tapping at every wall.

She passed by Derwyn's door, and it was ajar. Her fear came scurrying back, as keen as ever. Clutching her knife tight, she pushed open the door.

His chamber was empty. His bed, empty.

"Guards!" she cried. Winebald came rushing up.

"Where is my son?"

"In the chapel, milady."

She rushed downstairs again, and crossed the little courtyard to the chapel. Candles burned in the apse.

There, she found Derwyn kneeling before the altar, Bessimer by his side. On the altar was a grail-cup, brimming with water, and a small painting of a grey-haired woman that Olva did not know.

She halted at the threshold, listening to her son recite the mourning prayer, calling on the Intercessors to carry away the soul of his mother.

On Derwyn's table, there sat a clever little timekeeping device, a glass globe containing an enchanted forest in miniature. A toy of the elves. Tiny stars flickered across the sky of the globe, tracking the passing hours. The curved glass acted as a magnifying glass – Olva could see the glimmering stars from any angle, but her view of the forest within shifted depending on how she looked at the globe, and the dizzying illusion made it hard to guess how big the artificial forest was within the trinket. A woman dwelt alone there – a tiny animated statue, an automaton no bigger than a fingernail. Find the right angle to spy on her, and you could watch her go about her day, from the first blush of dawn to the fall of night.

The tiny woman was stirring when Derwyn returned. He ambled into his chamber, heedless of the hour, and didn't notice his mother sitting there waiting for him until he nearly tripped over her.

"Mother?"

In those long hours, there had been time for Olva's anger at seeing
Derwyn in the chapel to cool, to congeal and harden into something
sharp. She tempered it with patience and pity; clearly, Derwyn did
not understand the situation. He was too like his father – Galwyn
was a highborn Crownlander, dropped into an obscure corner of the
Mulladales, always conscious of his aristocratic upbringing. He was
always embarrassed by it, and so he'd been an easy mark for anyone
playing on his guilt or his desire to make friends. Many times, Olva
had found Galwyn neglecting his own work to help a neighbour,
or buying drinks for everyone in the alehouse. Obviously, Derwyn
had taken pity on old Lord Bessimer, and recited the prayer just to
bring the old man some comfort, which would be praiseworthy in
some other time, some other place. But not here.

In those long hours, Olva had planned what she would say, recited
and revised her words. When Derwyn entered, though, her carefully
constructed speech vanished like a wraith before a lit candle, and all
she could manage was: "Why?"

"Why what?"

"Why did you pray with Bessimer in the chapel?"

"Oh. It's the anniversary of Margotte's passing. His wife – she
died twenty years ago today, while Peir was away on his quest."
Derwyn sounded puzzled. "Vond brought Dryten to see me here.
We talked for a long while."

"About what?"

"Everything. Peir and the war against Lord Bone, and the Nine.
He had stories about the Nine I'd never heard before. And we talked
about the present, too."

"Der, what did you tell him? Did you tell him where Alf went?
He's the *enemy*."

"He already knew Alf had gone to Arden. I didn't tell him
anything more. It wasn't like that. He wasn't trying to spy on me –
we were just talking about the world. He's been to every corner
of Summerswell, you know, and Phennic and the lands beyond

Westermarch." Derwyn peered into the crystal globe. "He agrees with me, by the way. He thinks that Necrad shouldn't be ruled by Summerswell. He thinks that as long as we finish what Peir began, and destroy all the evils of Lord Bone, then he sees no reason why the north should not set its own course."

"And you believe him?" Olva rolled her eyes. "Lord Vond told me the exact opposite – he offered us both a pardon if we gave up Necrad. Neither of them can be trusted in the slightest. They'd say anything to divide us."

"Dryten thinks Vond's a coward," said Derwyn. "He said Vond should never have abandoned his post, and that he's desperate to get back into favour."

"Why did you go to the chapel with him?"

"I told you," said Derwyn, with an edge of anger. "To pray for Intercession for his wife's soul. I'm not Peir, but it . . . it comforted him to have someone say the prayer. "

"You *know* there's nothing there. The Intercessors are a lie. The Wood Elves lied to us, all along!" It was so stupid of Derwyn to make himself vulnerable. Even if the Intercessors were blocked by the necromiasma, there might be gaps in its protection. But more, it felt like a betrayal. She and Derwyn had been used like playing pieces in the conflict between the elves, spied on by Intercessors and manipulated by Maedos. How could he kneel before their false grail, before the icon of the Erlking?

"Maybe. In the war, when I . . . when Peir fought Lord Bone's forces, the Intercessors were by his side. They were like invisible fire, blazing in his hammer. They made everything so bright, so . . . so clear. The path was laid out before me, the way marked with light, beckoning me onwards." Derwyn looked at Olva without seeing her. "I—He knew, even then, that there were aspects of them that were unspoken. But they were . . . they were *light*. It was a battle of light against dark, hope against despair. Even if their light was not . . . not pure, it was still fierce and bright." He came back to her, and suddenly began coughing. "I can't breathe. He's choking me with foulness. He seep into my dreams and smothers me. I should get out, see the stars again." He toppled against the wall.

Olva sprang up and grabbed Derwyn's arm to steady him. His skin was fever-hot. "We're safe here. We do nothing rash."

"Tar Edalion. Let's go to Tar Edalion."

She closed her eyes and forced her doubts away. "You're going back to the Wailing Tower. Tonight."

The carriage raced through the streets of the Sanction. At this hour, the air seemed thick with wraiths, glimpsed out of the corner of the eye for an instant. Lights glimmered amid the spires of Necrad.

Blaise waited for them at the door of the Wailing Tower.

"Lady Forster, did I not warn you that the presence of Lord Bessimer was a concealed attack on the Uncrowned King?"

"No, Blaise," muttered Derwyn. "I can do this. I promised you I'd—"

"Rest," commanded the wizard. He touched Derwyn's forehead, and the boy crumpled into unconsciousness. Shadows flowed around Blaise like black serpents, catching Derwyn and bearing him up. "I shall repair what has been torn for a second time. Tell me, how long do you intend to tolerate the presence of our enemies in Necrad?"

It was an excellent question. She contemplated it as the doors of the Wailing Tower shut behind her and she climbed back into the carriage.

There's power here. Wield it.

"To the Citadel, milady?" asked Winebald.

"No. The House of the Skerrise."

PART THREE

CHAPTER TWENTY-TWO

The shepherds brought Alf down to their hamlet in the hills, to the old woman's hut.

"What's your name, grandmother?" he asked her.

"Etha," she said, "and you'll be Joseth." A common name in Arden. "You'll sleep here tonight."

"I'm looking for—"

"Let me stoke the fire, first." She threw a handful of foul-smelling herbs into the flames. Smoke filled the hut, and the smell reminded Alf of Brychan's candles. *I sense no spirits*, said the sword. *Not that her peasant magic would ward off anything.*

"You'll be looking for work in Arden, of course," said Etha. "Well, Joseth, there's a man who comes through the Cleft often enough. A merchant who trades with the mountain-folk. Dwarven whiskey, mostly, great cask-loads of it. His name is Othroan. He's got a grand house in Arden, they say. Go and see him."

She fetched him blankets, and then from a chest she produced a once fine shirt. She held it up, then folded it and put it to one side. "Always best to be well presented," she muttered. The charmstone pin went into the chest in the shirt's place. She spent the evening unpicking the stitches and resewing it to fit Alf's huge frame. Alf wondered who had worn that shirt before, and what had become of the woman's family. She was of an age with Alf's own mother, old enough to watch sons march off on Lord Bone's war, old enough to have buried a husband.

"My neighbour Ghen's going to Arden in the morning. He'll show you the way. He's a good man, and honest." Etha made a hand signal, her old fingers trembling with the effort. Alf knew the signal – it was one of those Berys had taught him. It meant *stay quiet*.

In the morning, before Etha woke, Alf rose and fetched firewood, and cooked a simple breakfast for the two of them. She watched him with hooded eyes from her bed, as if trying to guess who this stranger in her house might be, but she asked no questions.

Ghen made up for Etha's discretion, and then some. Alf was bombarded by questions all the way down the Cleft by Ghen and his sons. Ghen had lived all his life in Arden and had never left the province, but because – in his words – Arden was the crossroads of the world, he heard news from all sorts of travellers and was exceedingly well informed. With confidence, he declared that Necrad fallen to a Wilder-horde led by a were-bear. According to Ghen, the Nine had escaped to Summerswell and were going to lead the counter-assault once sufficient forces had gathered in Arden. Ghen's sons were eager to join this army, because their father assured them that there would be grants of land in the New Provinces for those who volunteered.

For Alf's own good – or rather, Joseth's – Ghen tried to convince him to abandon the idea of obtaining work from Othroan the merchant, and instead sign up to march north.

"You don't fear for their safety?" asked Alf, watching the boys smash wooden swords together.

"Of course I worry," said Ghen, "but you must understand, friend, that this is the last growl of a dying animal. Evil was defeated twenty years ago."

"Aye?"

"I'm something of an expert," said Ghen, "on martial matters. I watch the tourney every year. And you haven't seen what I've seen – I was younger than my boy, here, when I saw the Nine and the army of the League march north to the defence of the Dwarfholt. I've seen knights riding south laden with magic swords and enchanted armour. These Wilder may have taken the defenders of Necrad by surprise, but that'll be their only victory. The enemy will be slaughtered in open battle!" The boys stopped fighting long enough to cheer, then resumed beating each other up. They reminded Alf of Earl Duna's sons at the feast last year. And now one boy was maimed, and both fatherless.

"You should keep 'em home."

A shadow passed over Ghen's face. "You know," he said, "I stayed home in the last war. When the reeve came looking, I stayed at the back of the crowd, like my father told me. If I'd gone, I'd have made my fortune in Necrad."

They only remember the victory, thought Alf, *not those who died along the way.*

"The year after the Bone Lord's defeat," continued Ghen, "what a year that was! The best harvest in living memory. Everyone laughing and dancing. Fat sheep everywhere, the grass was lush even up in the high pastures. The Intercessors smiled on us that year. And I remember sitting at home feeling like I'd stolen that bounty and didn't deserve to share in it. No, no. I don't fear for them. The Dark Lord is gone, Joseth, and we shall triumph." He smiled again, ridding himself of Alf's doubts like a dog shaking off water.

He pointed down the trail. A wayside inn stood at a crossroads. "Look, there's the Dripping Bucket. We stay there tonight, and we'll be in Arden in the morning."

The inn's sign depicted a merry milkmaid, who had clearly used the leak in her bucket as an excuse to abandon her burden and stop for a drink. The place was crowded – the clement weather meant that it was the first time many of the paths were passable, and folk who'd spent a lonely winter on isolated farmsteads gathered now to see old friends. Ghen knew everyone in the crowd, and went around slapping backs. There was talk of Necrad, and the gathering of Lords in Arden. The few dwarves present were hounded for news from the north, although they knew no more than the rest.

Alf grabbed a mug of ale and found a corner by the fire. He hid his bundle under the table. He scanned the crowd, wondering if any of those red-flushed faces concealed secrets. A mendicant monk ambled past, his habit stained with spilled drink, waving his empty cup and making the hoary pun about the gr-ale – did an Intercessor follow him, spying on the mortal world through such an unlikely vessel? He drew his hood over his face, trying to be as anonymous as possible.

Within minutes, everyone was speculating about the mysterious hooded stranger in the corner.

"Oh, that's Joseth," came Ghen's voice through the crowd. "He works for – what was the name? A merchant in Arden. Othroan, was it?"

Was it Alf's imagination, or did the monk look over, as if he recognised the name? Did the innkeeper's eyes narrow?

"I don't work for him," said Alf hastily.

"You're far from home, friend," said one fellow, picking up on Alf's accent.

"Rootless," grumbled someone else in the crowd. By law, the common folk of Summerswell were bound to their provinces, and could leave only with permission. Those who wandered were considered Rootless – thieves and vagabonds. The law was not always enforced, and where it was, a bribe in the right hand usually avoided any scrutiny. The magistrates in Arden, though, were infamous sticklers. Many Rootless on the way north to the Provinces had made trouble in the Cleft, so the law was sternly enforced in Arden.

"Is that so?" An older woman sat down opposite Alf. Her clothing was a little finer than the rest of the company, and Alf guessed she was the local reeve. "Are you Rootless, or do you have a master – and a master's mark to prove it?"

A bribe in the right hand. Alf felt for his coin-purse, and realised

it was in the bundle at his feet. The same bundle that concealed
Spellbreaker. *One moment, I'll fetch your bribe. Let's see. A silver to
overlook that I'm Rootless, and ten thousand more for everyone in the inn to
ignore the most infamous sword in all the world.*

He froze. The crowd around the table grew, amused by
Alf's plight.

"Well, sir?" demanded the reeve. "Have you a letter of passage,
or other proof of standing?"

"In my bag," said Alf. Slowly, he reached down beneath the table.
One eager young lad darted over to watch, in case the stranger
pulled a knife from some hiding place. Alf's fingers fumbled with
the bundle's knotted cord, and brushed against the cold metal of
the sword.

Distract them, dolt, shouted Spellbreaker telepathically.

How?

To Alf's horror, the sword began to sing in his mind, and he
forced himself to follow aloud.

> *Down from the moor there came a horror*
> *A monster most accursed*
> *The wraith-captain of dread Necrad*
> *The Witch Elf called Acraist*
> *He bore a sword of ebon dark*
> *Of all weapons, the worst*
> *And swore he'd ruin all the lands*
> *But first, he had a thirst.*

"We've all heard that one," shouted the monk. "Something new!
Something new!"

The crowd rumbled their agreement, and attention shifted from
Alf to a young woman by the bar. "Gildra, you always know a good
song. Play something."

"A song!" cried the crowd, forming a circle around Gildra. Alf took advantage of the distraction to fetch his coin-purse. The reeve swept the money off the table without looking, her attention fixed on the singer.

Gildra stood, brushing back her long hair. "I was going to save this until later. This is a new tale that I learned recently on the Road." She took a sip of ale. "It is a sad tale, and a bitter one, but it has the ring of truth to it. Those of you who've not heard the news from the north, listen well."

She began to sing, her voice low and sorrowful.

Alf exhaled and sat back to finish his ale, ignoring the song at first. He'd never been one for singing, and he preferred the old songs anyway, the ones he'd heard when he was a child. He tucked the coin-purse into his new shirt, to avoid the same debacle when he arrived in Arden. Tomorrow, he told himself, he'd find the house of Othroan, and Othroan would tell him where to find Berys.

Then he heard the words.

It was not about him. It was about the Lammergeier. He listened, and line by line, word by word, the song unpicked all the threads of his life and wove them into a new pattern. *There are no heroes*, said the song, *no selfless deeds. No enchantment, only treachery and greed. And if you believe otherwise, you're a fool.*

In this new tale, he was a traitor, bent on the overthrow of the Lords of Summerswell and the conquest of the world. He'd hidden this ambition, and had worked in the shadows for years, eliminating his enemies one by one. The corruption of the Nine began with the murder of blessed Peir, ensuring that the Lammergeier was free to delve into the Pits, where he learned forbidden sorcery and gathered all manner of evil artefacts. Some of the Nine – Berys and Blaise – were in league with the Lammergeier. Others, he drove away, like Jan, or blinded, like Gundan.

Even the Lords of Summerswell were deceived. When the elves grew suspicious of the remaining Nine, the Lords foolishly sided

against the Everwood. When Thurn tried to stop the Lammergeier
by gathering an army of Wilder, the Lammergeier cruelly tricked
the Lords into sending good knights on a doomed quest, and slew
Thurn. Without Thurn, the Wilder reverted to their true nature:
an army of ravaging beasts and foul Changelings.

At last, even loyal Gundan saw the truth, and the Lammergeier
murdered him too.

Riding back to Necrad, his sword drenched in the blood of former
friends, the dreadful Lammergeier overthrew the council, forcing
Lord Vond to flee the city. At the same time, he plotted to install
his own nephew as the Uncrowned King – plainly, a puppet for the
Lammergeier's rule. A great darkness rose in the north.

And a light shone out in answer. Prince Maedos, the Dawnshield,
the Erlking's son, sailed to Necrad to aid in the defence of the city
and restore order. The Lammergeier, drawing on his reputation as a
hero, feigned to welcome the prince as a friend – and then slew him.
The immortal light of dawn shattered.

Now we see the Lammergeier
Uncloaked at last.

Now, the song said, the Lammergeier is coming for you.
The monster-slayer turned monster, the black sword unleashed
once more.

Alf stumbled from the inn, unsure if he was furious or sick to
his stomach. The night whirled around him, and he leaned on
Spellbreaker for support. The cloth had fallen from the blade, and
the wind whipped it away.

"It's not even a good song," said Spellbreaker. "I'm hardly in it."

"Shut up," said Alf, "shut up shut up shut up."

Shouts came from the inn, drowning out the end of the song.
Some angry, some disbelieving.

It was not only the accusations that sickened him, or the lies.
The Lammergeier was a lie either way – call him a heroic knight or

a treacherous killer, it did not matter. He'd never wanted that title, nor had he ever claimed it.

No, it was the thought that those he trusted, those that who knew him as *Alf*, might see him that way.

Go back inside. The sword's thought pressed against his mind like ice against his scalp. *Your absence will be noticed.*

Berys – all the things the song said about schemes and long-laid plans, all the treachery they imputed to him, all were true for her. But she turned his head with tales, made fair things foul and dark deeds heroic until Alf did not know where to stand.

"Go back inside!" hissed the sword.

And Laerlyn – what did she see when she looked at him? All the rest of them had changed in the years since the quest, except her and Alf. She'd stood there, as youthful and perfect as ever, just like he'd remembered her. A living link to the time he'd been most alive, the quest when everything mattered, when the way forward was clear and it had just been the Nine against the dark. He'd killed her brother in front of her – had she seen what really happened?

Had she seen her friend, or the Lammergeier?

"Joseth?"

Ghen stood in the door of the Dripping Bucket, staring at the sword in Alf's hand. Alf froze, caught on the threshold.

Silence him, insisted the sword.

Alf turned and ran into the night.

"Where are you taking me?" said the sword.

"Arden," said Alf. "To hell with waiting. Sooner started, sooner done."

"This," said the sword, "is a remarkably bad idea. They seek to draw you out, wielder. They know your weakness – that you're an idiot."

"I've got a plan."

"Indeed? How will you enter Arden? We have no dreadworm, so

you cannot fly over the walls. I could blast the gates to splinters, but there's a small chance that would be noticed. You might be able to scale the walls with those ape-like arms of you – it's a wonder you don't drag me along the ground – but they will be waiting for you."

"It's only Arden, I'll find a way in."

"And then?"

"Same plan," said Alf, doggedly. It felt good to walk it off. Every long stride pulled a little of the acid from his stomach, and the cold night air cleared his head. Every stride took him further away from the song, too, from all those who'd believed those lies about him. *None of it is true*, he told himself, and in some distant recess of his mind he heard the sword chuckle. "I go to Arden, I find that merchant and he tells me where Berys is."

"The plan," said the sword, "was to enter by stealth. In secret. With subtlety."

"I'll be subtle," said Alf, "my way."

The sword's 'eye' was a ruby set in its ornate hilt, and so Spellbreaker could not roll it. "So, we are certain to be discovered. What then? Will you wield me? I would delight in cutting a red road through this city of mortals, but you are more squeamish – and it is not only mortals we face. We are in Summerswell now – those who dwell here may not know it, but they are in the Erlking's domain, and his servants walk abroad under these stars. We are in danger, wielder."

Alf paused. "You can wound a spirit, aye? My old sword had enough magic to do that."

"Don't compare me to Sunrazor," said Spellbreaker. "A stick with a few charmstones glued on! Yes, I can cut an Intercessor – there is no foe I cannot slay – but it would be a battle that you are ill-suited for."

"You've never doubted me like this before."

"Nothing in Necrad threatened me. Here, we are both on the same side." That thought sent a chill through Alf. "If you fall, so do I. The light of the Intercessors could break me. Or I could be imprisoned, locked away in some vault or buried beneath the roots of the Everwood until the world's ending. I was made to destroy the enemies of Lord Bone. Without the possibility of fulfilling that purpose, I am nothing." The ruby glinted with demonic light. "This folly endangers both of us. You should not have left the inn."

He walked through the night. The path was icy, and he was already weary from the day's travel, but Alf marched on. Arden's towers rose ahead, limned in moonlight that the sword-sight turned a harsh glare. Encampments of tents sprouted like mushrooms against the city's low walls, and that sight brought Alf back twenty years to the mustering against Lord Bone. Banners of Arshoth, Westermarch, Arden – the Lords of at least three provinces were gathered here. The army was easily as large as the host that Brychan had captained twenty years ago in the attack on Necrad. Augmented by magic, advised by veterans like Alf who'd faced the Stone Dragons before: if the army encamped before him were to lay siege to Necrad, the city would fall.

He followed the north edge of the town to the river. Long before he was ever the Lammergeier, he'd come here for the tourneys with Gundan, and Gundan had shown him how to get into the city after the gates were shut. It was important, the dwarf had said, to be able to get back to the camp outside after a reasonable amount of drinking inside. Walls surrounded Arden, the river flowed through it, and where the two met on the north side was the river gate, a fortified bridge. If you stayed close to the bank, you could cling to the inside of the first arch and go under the bridge without being spotted from above.

He waded into the shallows, the fast-flowing waters threatening to pull him off balance. It was much easier this time, as he could see in the dark and wasn't shepherding a drunk dwarf. Beneath the arch, he found that his path was blocked – sometime in the last two decades, a gate had been installed beneath the bridge. Muck and weeds covered the lower portion of the steel bars, but the rune-plates declaring that the way was shut to servants of Necrad still shone brightly in Alf's eyes. The bars were thick steel, fixed deep into the stone of the arch.

Alf drew Spellbreaker and put the sword's edge to the bars. He pushed, expecting the sword to cut through the steel with ease. Instead, metal ground on metal, and he barely scratched the bar. On the walkway above, a night watchman coughed.

"What's wrong with you?" whispered Alf.

You should turn back. It is the wiser course.

"Cut the damn bar."

You should listen to me, wielder.

"You swore to serve me, so serve."

He tried again. The bars parted like soft cheese. Alf caught each one and lowered it gently to make no splash. Above, the watchman snorted and moved on, his steps echoing in the arch below.

"See," said Alf, "subtle."

He crept along the riverside, hiding in the undergrowth of the green banks, then passed into the streets of Arden. The palace was off to his right, lights blazing in a hundred windows. The wind carried a snatch of music, and Alf briefly entertained the thought of marching up and demanding entry. He'd have the heralds proclaim that Aelfric of the Nine was here to see the Lord of Arden. People had thronged the streets to see him last time, and he hadn't sought any attention then. What would happen if he openly called for support? Which version of the Lammergeier would people see?

The last time he'd been in that palace, two years ago, they'd served him venison and iced fruits, and a cake baked to look like a dragon to be beheaded, and then made him sit through a six-hour dramatic re-enactment of *The Song of the Nine*. Alf vaguely recalled Lord Tor's pride at the realism of the costumes worn by the Witch Elves, for they'd reused armour from the war. All Alf could really remember was the pain of the linnorm wound, and sneaking draughts of healing cordial amid the endless prattling praise of Lord Tor. *I'm back now, my lord, and I hear you're singing a different song. But if you ever truly had any esteem for me, you'll listen to the truth, and not some twisted mockery.*

But he stuck to the plan. He slipped through the quiet streets until he came to the house of Othroan.

The house was deserted. It had been ransacked. Alf prowled through the empty rooms, looking for some clue as to what might have happened to the merchant. There were no signs of a struggle that he could see – no spilled blood, no doors smashed down – but the place had clearly been abandoned in haste. He prowled through a dining room, the table pushed against one wall like a makeshift altar, and ran his finger through a wet patch on the floor. He picked up a silver spoon from beneath a chair.

"Strange that no one robbed the place."

The sword's voice was very distant, as if unwilling to show itself. "Thieves have more sense."

"What now?"

"Clearly, the merchant has been discovered by our enemies. This place is being watched to see if anyone returns. We must go."

Alf grunted, his brow furrowed in thought. "If they'd caught Othroan, or anyone close to Berys, then they'd likely have caught her too. Or be after her. We'd have seen some sign of it."

"Like her head on a spike," suggested the sword.

"They got away. Berys and her lot are still out there."

"Perhaps. But we have no way to find them now. They fled this place. So should we."

"In a moment."

Alf climbed the stairs, each step creaking loudly. Every room had been searched already, the contents of every drawer and cabinet spilled out upon the floor.

"Oh damnation. Are you trying to be *clever*, wielder?"

"Berys had the dwarven smiths make vessels for the miasma. Othroan's a merchant who trades with the dwarves. So I'm thinking—"

"That Othroan smuggled the vessels into Arden. And what, left a convenient note?"

"Exactly." Alf picked up a page torn from a ledger. "Look."

CHAPTER TWENTY-THREE

Othroan owned a warehouse near the river gate, according to the ledger. Alf doubled back through the narrow streets of the old town. Few people paid attention to the cloaked traveller loping through the cobbled streets. Cold sleet fell, natural weather reasserting itself over premature warmth.

Within minutes, he was thoroughly lost. While he could guess where the warehouse should be – off to his right, beyond the palace towers – the streets twisted and ran arseways, bringing him back to the same nighted squares, the same rows of taverns and theatres. Alf caught the refrain of that damn song from a crowded inn. A wobbling drunk at the door peered at Alf as if trying to place his features in memory.

A memorial in the square commemorated those fallen fighting against Lord Bone. Alf turned his face away and pretended to read it.

You're reading in the dark.

Alf picked a street at random and hurried away, cursing himself. Twenty years ago, the Nine had crept into Necrad and spent weeks hiding on the streets of the enemy's city, evading Lord Bone's patrols. He'd survived then. This should be easy for him, but it was the familiarity of Arden that lulled him, blunted his edge. Necrad *hated* intruders; at every turn, the city had wanted them dead, malice rising up from the stones like the miasma. Arden felt much too comfortable. It made him feel like he was play-acting at being in danger.

At last, the smell of the river.

The warehouse was as deserted as Othroan's house. There were no dwarf-wrought barrels, no signs of battle. The place might have gone unused for weeks. Alf prowled about, searching for anything that might guide him. Idle workers had scratched graffiti onto the walls, and Alf studied it for hidden signs. He studied scratches on the floor as if they might resolve into runes. He sniffed the air. No miasma, only the stink of some animal.

Lantern-light flooded the warehouse. Alf peered around from behind the shelter of a crate, and saw a young woman standing at the door, lamp held high. The paleness of her features and the gleam in her eyes put Alf in mind of the snow-foxes of the Clawlands.

"Who goes there?" she called.

Alf stood. "I'm, uh, Joseth," he said, shielding his eyes from the lantern. He tried to conceal Spellbreaker with his cloak. "I'm looking for Master Othroan. For work."

"You startled me. I thought someone was trying to rob us."

"No, no. I came down from the hills, but I was slow and they were shutting the gate when I got there. There was no one at Othroan's, so I came here. And the door was unlocked."

"No harm done." The young woman frowned. "Where do you hail from? You sound like a Mulladale man."

Alf cursed under his breath. "Aye, but I left when Wilder burned my home, and I've been a wanderer ever since." He took a gamble. "Othroan never minded that I was Rootless, and paid me just the same as the rest. Is he here, miss? I'd like to speak with him."

"I'm Agyla, Othroan's niece. My uncle's away, but I'll find you a place to stay until he returns." She reached out her hand and smiled, "Come with me."

Alf hesitated. "How long might that be?"

"You must be tired, Joseth. Let me take your burden."

She reached for the bundle on Alf's shoulder. From the depths of the warehouse erupted the sound of frantic barking. A big dog, a Mulladale wolfhound by the sound of it, big gut-shaking bellows of alarm. A moment later, the shriek of the sword.

INTERCESSOR.

Alf wrestled to disentangle the sword from his cloak. Agyla flung herself at him, her forehead smashed into his nose, knees and elbows and fists hammering him in tender spots. He shoved her away—

—an invisible giant smashed Alf with a tree trunk.

He fell to the ground, blinking. Blood welled out of his nose and ears, and the world turned dark. All his limbs felt very far away, and the responsibility of someone else entirely. He tried to look around to see who had struck him, but he couldn't remember how to use his neck, and the dog's barking had become a giant church bell that rang on and on.

Agyla scrambled over him and snatched up Spellbreaker – or tried to. She succeeded only in wrenching her shoulder.

The sword shouted at him. Head still ringing, Alf crawled towards Spellbreaker.

He'd nearly reached the sword when the unseen giant struck him again. This second blow felt like the warehouse collapsing on top of him, the force of it resounding down his spine, through his shoulders, like every bone in his body was outlined in fire. His ears popped, blood spewed from his mouth. Pain did not fill him, it defined him, traced every contour of his body, made him aware of the softness of every organ. His heart flailed as if trying to break out of his ribcage. His lungs clogged with burning slime.

Another blow like that would finish him.

He crawled on, even though the warehouse floor was wider than the desert, even though he couldn't quite remember who he was or where he was going. The sword was calling to him, but he could not find it. On the edge of what remained of his consciousness, he could dimly see one of his assailants – the woman – draw a black charmstone from a pouch and fasten it about her neck. Other figures moved somewhere in the vastness of the warehouse.

A voice spoke to Alf, cold as the stars and full of malice, and it was a voice he knew.

From the first dawn to the last, this world is ours.

Prince Maedos' voice.

But Alf's fingers found the hilt of Spellbreaker.

"Back! Back!" shouted Agyla. "He has the sword!"

Strength flooded Alf's limbs, and his vision cleared along with his head. Before he could really think clearly again, some part of his brain had already grasped the threat of the foes surrounding him. Agyla to his left. Two other men between Alf and the door of the warehouse, one in beggar's rags, one with the kettle helm of Arden's night watch, both carrying blades, both advancing. More outside, the sword-sight turning the darkness into unnatural light, shadows gleaming on pikes and helms.

And there, towering above him, vastly taller than the warehouse roof yet somehow contained beneath it, was a spectral giant. It was an armoured titan of swirling mist, constantly fading and reforming, its shape buffeted by unseen winds in the spirit realm. It seemed on the verge of being torn apart by those forces, but it endured. One mighty arm was raised as if sheltering the giant's face from those forces that tore at it, and the other was drawn back to strike Alf a third time. The only constancies were its eyes like burning stars. The giant – the Intercessor – stared down at Alf, and hate was in its eyes.

Without thinking, he swung Spellbreaker at the monster. The Intercessor stepped *away*, not back, but seeming to shrink and fade, withdrawing to some higher plane where the sword could not cut it, where the winds of material existence could not tear it, and in that moment Alf saw it more clearly. It was the wraith of Prince Maedos, but where other wraiths were ragged shadows, the Prince's spectre was luminous, girded in magic like plate armour, bright as dawn. As the Intercessor withdrew, a portion of its substance flowed into the swords held by the two Rangers.

Swords blazed with holy fire, like Peir's hammer.

They cut at Alf, swords bright against Spellbreaker's abyssal dark. He parried their strokes, catching them on Spellbreaker's cross guard and shoving them back, but he stumbled as he did so. The holy light of the swords flickered, but did not fade.

I must feed, whispered Spellbreaker.

"Crossbows!" shouted Agyla. In the doorway knelt a row of crossbowmen in the livery of Lord Tor. The two Rangers with the burning swords scrambled aside, and a half-dozen crossbow bolts flew towards Alf. A flick of Spellbreaker was enough to deflect the volley, bolts splintering and shattering in mid-air, but even as fragments rained down, the two swordsmen were back on the offensive, pressing him again.

Agyla raised her hand, and in it was a charmstone. Red light welled from it, and where the light touched, fire smouldered. She played the light over Alf. Spellbreaker's counter-magic snuffed out the flames instantly, but that meant that the sword could not fortify Alf's battered body. He felt every bruise the Intercessor had dealt him, and every one of his years.

He recognised the tactic. This was exactly how the Nine had brought down Acraist the Wraith-Captain when *he* wielded Spellbreaker. The sword had limits. It could deflect the arrows from the bows of Berys and Thurn, or counter the dreadful power of Laerlyn's elf-bow *Morthus*. It had the counter-magic to shatter all the spells of Blaise and Lath. It could give Acraist the strength to fight Alf *and* Gundan *and* Peir at the same time.

But not all at once.

Acraist had fallen.

So would Alf.

I must feed.

He charged, knocking the two swordsmen aside as he rushed the line of soldiers at the door. One lad got his crossbow reloaded in time, but his nerve failed and he did not fire. Behind him, the second row lowered their pikes.

Alf swung Spellbreaker. A wave of force broke the line of pikes. He threw himself into the gap, into the middle of the watchmen, shoving and punching his way through, but there were too many foes for him to fight his way clear.

The Lammergeier raised the black sword, and let it feast. Spellbreaker struck a dozen times in a heartbeat, the blade cutting through chain and leather and bone. Gundan had taught Alf to imagine a sword was an extension of his arm; now it felt like his arm, his whole body was but an extension of the sword, as if Alf existed only to wield the blade.

The sword grew in his sight, becoming more real than anything else. The men around him were ghosts, bodies parted as easily as gossamer. One of the swordsmen charged at Alf with his blessed blade; in Alf's sight he moved so slowly it was easy to bring Spellbreaker around in a perfect arc. Light failed, steel shattered, blood spilled and the sword feasted.

More, sang Spellbreaker, *more.*

"Back!" called Agyla. "Remember your training!"

The survivors retreated away from Alf. Now he stood in the middle of a gory circle, a score of bodies at his feet. Horns rang out across the city. More were coming, the streets resounding with the sound of marching. Archers on rooftops. Knights girded with so many precious charmstones they were walking constellations. They closed around Alf.

We can defeat them, wielder. None of them have the might of the Nine. This will be a slaughter.

Alf shifted his stand, wading through the blood he'd spilled. His ankle brushed against a severed head. It rolled, revealing a face, features familiar through the smear of blood. Eyes open in shock.

Remilard.

That had been the boy's name.

The last time Alf had seen him had been in Necrad. No, at Bavduin – the young guard had been Alf's banner-bearer on the ride north. Alf had left him with the rest of the company when he'd gone down to the lakeside to meet with Thurn. And after that . . . after that was Gundan's death, and the Wilder attack, and Olva's arrival, and the search for Derwyn, and then the revelations in the Pits and his duel with Prince Maedos. The quest had swept Alf up, and he'd been consumed by great matters that he'd forgotten about the young squire entirely. How Remi had made it all the way south to Arden, Alf did not know.

His grip on the sword wavered. Blood dripped from the blade, and some of it must have been Remi's.

"Lay down the blade, Lammergeier," called Agyla.

Attack now! urged Spellbreaker. *Before there are too many.*

Instead, Alf turned and ran.

He slapped the corner of the warehouse with Spellbreaker as he passed, and a tremor exploded through the city. The warehouse collapsed, spilling out into the street behind him. He charged headlong down the alleyway, big feet pounding through the mud, slipping on the cobbles.

The streets above the riverside were a tangle of alleys and tenements. Alf blundered through them, crashing blindly off walls. As the sword's magic subsided, pain returned, and his knees buckled. He nearly fell, but caught himself on a windowsill and kept going. Behind, he could hear the sounds of pursuit.

"Summon," gasped Alf, "dreadworm."

We are too far from Necrad for one to reach us in time. Idiot!

The street ended in a wooden fence. Beyond was a steep slope, tangled with precarious small trees and underbrush. Streams trickled from culverts to pour down to the river below. It was a treacherous climb in the dark, even with the sword-sight.

Down there's too open. Make your stand here, urged the sword.

Alf kicked through the fence and began to descend. None of the pursuers had reached him yet, but he could hear shouting in the alleyways, lantern-light splashing wildly. Cries of "Lammergeier! Lammergeier!" to his left, near the north gate. Horns echoed from the right. Alf pressed himself against the slope to take full advantage of the concealing darkness. Old memories of hiding in Necrad came back to him. Then, they'd fled from Pitspawn and Vatlings, from Witch Elves and undead horrors.

It had been easier, then.

His foot slipped, and he fell the rest of the way down the hill, landing on his back. Watchmen appeared at the top of the slope. Alf hoped the darkness would hide him, but at that moment unseen hands rolled back the clouds. Moonlight flooded the city.

"There!" cried a guard, pointing down. "I've found—"

An arrow skewered his throat, silencing him.

Hands grabbed Alf, pulling him upright, hustling him towards the river. A boat waited there, and standing on the bank was the archer.

"Quick," said Berys, "before our saviour fucks up again."

They crossed the river. "Flowing water confuses them," whispered Berys, "but it won't be enough."

Then into a concealed tunnel, then stairs into the cellar of some house. One of Berys' people took Alf's cloak and cast it into a fire, then splashed him with perfume. "Quick changes help, too. If they don't have their hooks into you already, they get confused." Out again, into a cart, and then another house. Alf's head, already battered, was spinning as Berys led him down yet another staircase, through a secret tunnel, and finally into a cellar room in the east of the city. There was no light, but sword-sight showed him more boxes and crates, a few cot beds and other belongings – and ancient walls glistening with moisture, and what might have once been an altar.

"It was a temple of the Old Kingdom." Berys' eyes gleamed like those of a cat. "There's power in these walls, as Blaise would say. *They* can't eavesdrop on us here – least, not without giving themselves away." She snorted. "Keep that sword on a tight leash. Be a shame if everything got ruined because you scratched the wall. Remember the time we were sneaking around the Wailing Tower, and you knocked that crystal ball off a shelf?"

"I caught it."

"It landed on your foot."

"I caught it with my foot."

"I was bloody furious," she said with a smile. "I remember shouting at Peir, afterwards, telling him that you nearly got us killed, and that he should have sent Thurn instead. Or Lath. Or Gundan. I swore you'd get me killed if we tried anything like that again. And yet, here we are."

Alf rubbed his head. His fingers came away covered with blood. "There's still time."

"Sit." Berys produced a flask of healing cordial from a chest and poured Alf a miserly measure.

"I could do with more."

"Send more, then. I thought Necrad was lost to us." She kicked off her boots and flopped down on one of the cots. That easy familiarity reminded him of Berys of long ago. He warily sat on a chair opposite. He sipped the cordial and his aches subsided.

"Thanks."

Berys kicked his shin lightly. "I thought you were dead, last time. I thought you'd gone back to die in some stupid gesture, and that the Wilder would raze Necrad. What happened? Was it Blaise?"

"Sort of. He woke the Stone Dragons."

"So I'm told. How the fuck did he break Lord Bone's sigils in time? He's been trying for years to do that!" said Berys. "And what about Thurn's daughter? Did you have to . . ." She pointed her toe at the sword.

"He gave me into the care of his sister," said Spellbreaker, sourly. "I went unused."

"I talked to her," said Alf. "And she agreed to leave us be." It wasn't just the cordial that soothed him; it was being with one of the Nine again. The years of the quest made them closer than family, closer than blood. There were things they'd lived through that only another member of the Nine could understand.

Berys sat up. "Just to be clear – you talked to *Death herself.* And she agreed to spare you?"

"Aye." Alf drank the last of the cordial. He thought he'd known Berys, but in the tunnels under Necrad, she'd revealed that he'd been utterly unaware of who she really was. He didn't know if that was true of the rest of the Nine, too. But even with that change, she was still Berys. She was still Nine. He wanted to trust her. "And Blaise and Olva – they brought Derwyn back from the dead."

"Of course you did." She shook her head. "Oh Alf. Alf. Alf. Why the fuck did I ever bet against you and Blaise? The pair of you are completely *useless* when it comes to ordinary matters, but give you an impossible task and . . . you just *do* it." Berys covered her face with her hands, her shoulders shaking with laughter. "Do you have any idea how frustrating you are? You blundering, wonderful giant! I spent *fifteen* years building up connections, weeding out the Erlking's spies, hiding from the Intercessors, smuggling magic out of Necrad so we might have the smallest of chances. And you just stroll here carrying *that.*" She looked at Spellbreaker and giggled, kicking her legs in the air, brimming with excitement.

"There's more you should know. Derwyn didn't come back alone. He's . . . he's Peir, I think. There's something of Peir in him. It's buried deep, but it's there. That light."

"Oh!" She clasped her hands over her mouth. It was the first time in a very long time that Alf had seen Berys truly taken by surprise – and joy. Hard years of worry vanished from her face, but even when they'd been young, he'd never seen her smile like that. "Oh by all that's holy, Alf, truly? Peir's come back?" She sprang up and pulled another bottle from the chest – this one a fine wine from the Eavesland. She splashed it into Alf's cup and took a swig from the bottle herself.

"Maybe," said Alf.

Berys frowned. "What's wrong?"

"Nothing." Alf shoved Spellbreaker under the chair. "It's good, of course it is. But it means that my family's been dragged into all this. Olva was as safe as could be in Ersfel, but now she's in Necrad preparing for a siege, and they can't ever go home."

"I had family, once," said Berys. "They think I'm dead. I understand wanting to spare them, Alf. We were lucky beyond measure, the Nine of us, blessed by fate. We all buried friends on the way. We all saw the cost of the quest." She sat back down and took Alf's hand. "You know, I probably know Olva better than you. I've had my spies keeping an eye on her for years. She's tough, Alf. Hells, I thought about recruiting her to the cause, but I decided against it. All our divinations told us there was an Intercessor in Ersfel." Berys studied Alf's face. "But that's not it. What else?"

"I killed Peir." The words spilled out.

"You – oh, you mean twenty years ago? Alf, you saved us all. You killed Lord Bone. Peir – he knew what he was doing when he told us to run. He held Bone at bay so we could escape and you could break the vessel. He knew, Alf."

"He didn't tell us to run," said Alf. "He shouted at me. I couldn't hear him properly – not with all the Witch Elves screaming at us, and the demons, and everything. I thought he told us to run, so I ran. And you all followed."

"Of course. We trusted you," murmured Berys.

"And then Blaise told me to stab the vessel with Spellbreaker.

I didn't understand what it would do." His stomach twisted. "All the songs say I saved the world with that blow, and I wasn't even paying attention. Blaise told me to strike, and I did." He looked up at Berys. "I've always wondered what Peir really shouted. I used to have nightmares that he was calling on us to fight, to make one more push. Then I convinced myself that it didn't matter, that it was just how things had to be. But now . . ."

"Now he's alive again. Have you asked him?"

"I don't know how much Derwyn remembers about Peir – if it's just some part of Peir's spirit in there. Talis – Thurn's daughter – I saw her switch back and forth between being herself and being Death. One moment she'd be talking about things that happened thousands of years ago, and the next she was just a child."

"If it were anyone else but Peir, Alf, then I'd be worried. But it's Peir." She took another drink. "I told him, you know. The last night before we fought Bone, I confessed."

"What do you mean?"

"I told Peir everything. That I was Defiant, sworn to bring down the Lords of Summerswell and overthrow the Erlking. I told him that everything he'd grown up knowing was a lie, and that the Wood Elves were manipulating everything, and that I didn't think *our* side was much better than Lord Bone. I told him all the secrets I kept from the rest of you." Berys seemed amazed at her own daring. "He was the son of Lord Bessimer – and I told him that his family were all bloody puppets of the elves. A paladin, and I told him everything in his faith was a trick. I thought he'd strike me down, or at least go to Laerlyn with my accusations about her father. But he didn't."

"What did he say?"

"He said that he could not believe me, but that he trusted me and would keep my secret. And that if it was true and the Erlking was a secret tyrant, then he would turn around and fight the Everwood as soon as we'd defeated Necrad. That was Peir. We were facing hopeless odds, and he was ready to add another mountain of duty on top of that, because it was the right thing to do." She raised her bottle in salute. "And you tell me he's back."

"They call him the Uncrowned King in Necrad. He sent me to find you."

Berys stroked Spellbreaker's scabbard. "And he sent us this."

The door of the ancient temple burst open, and a giant of a man strode in. He was clad in heavy armour, and his face was concealed behind a terrifying helm. On his tabard was the sign of a black bird on a white field, and in his hand was a black sword.

He looked more like the Lammergeier than Alf ever had in his life.

The giant tore off his helm. In other circumstances, one might call him a handsome man, with his well-trimmed beard and noble features, but blood flowed freely from a cut on his forehead and his lip bore a nasty bruise.

"Armech," said Berys, "sit with us. I've been looking forward to introducing the two of you."

"Four dead, Berys!" spat Armech. His accent had something of Westermarch to it. "The city's in uproar. They raided the safehouse on Candle Street, and the tavern on Waymeet. And this dolt is to blame!"

Armech strode across the room in a fury, reaching out to grab Alf by the collar – and froze when he felt the cold metal of Berys' knife at his throat. The thief may be old, but her reflexes were still quick as a serpent. "Armech. Sit with us. Drink."

Armech grudgingly sat opposite Alf, fury plain on his face. "Four dead, Berys. And more will die, or the Rangers will take them. And not mercenaries like the poor wretch they caught last week – friends of ours, loyal servants of the cause. We need to move."

"I thought this room was safe," said Alf.

"It is." Berys sat back down, the knife replaced with a wine glass in a flick of her wrist. "He means move on from Arden. We're bound elsewhere."

"Ilaventur? I got a message from Lord Brychan asking me to come south."

"Maybe," said Berys, saluting Alf with her wine glass.

"Tell him nothing," insisted Armech. "He has done enough damage already."

"Alf couldn't have known the Rangers had found Othroan." Berys sighed. "Believe me when I say he was careful by Alf's standards."

"What is this?" said Armech, rounding on Berys. "If anyone else had done this, you'd already have fed them to the crows. But him—"

"I meant no harm," said Alf. He poured out a measure of wine for Armech, but the younger man did not touch the cup.

"What you intended means nothing. What you did is all that counts. I know you, Lammergeier. Not the legend – Berys has told me everything about the Nine."

"Not everything," muttered Berys.

"She said you could not be relied upon. She said you would not join our cause."

"I said I dared not approach him," said Berys, "not until everything was in place. Alf, I told you in Necrad that this was humanity's last chance to rise up against the Erlking. The moment to strike is now. Are you with us? Is Necrad with us?"

Alf considered his words for a long, long moment before answering. "We've got a deal in common, but ... but Armech here is correct. I was sent south to help, but I'm not part of your cause. Not enough to unsheathe *that* again." Spellbreaker's ruby eye flared, and Alf looked away. "I've got good reason to hate some of the elves, and I'll stand with you against the injustice of the Lords, but ... well, Peir spoke truly that night, when he said he couldn't wholly believe you. I need ... I want ..."

Even as he spoke, he knew it was mealy-mouthed, half-hearted, but his heart was divided.

Berys' expression turned stony. "You want to talk to Laerlyn. You need to hear it from her. You need to hear her pretty lies from her oh-so pretty lips. I hate the hold she has over you all! That . . . enchantment! It's bred into all of you. Even Blaise. Even Gundan! She's so brave, and good, and perfect that she could never mean us harm, or lie to us. It has to break. It's fucking bullshit, Alf. It's all part of how they control us."

"She saved our lives more times than I can count. She was with us every step of the way to Necrad," said Alf. "She saved you from being hung before she even knew you."

"Because it served her purpose! We were their tools to defeat Lord Bone, Alf! They used us! She used us."

"Peir trusted her," said Alf.

"If he'd lived," snapped Berys, "he'd have changed his mind. He'd have seen what had to be done."

"He's alive again. And he still doesn't agree."

"Then why are you here, Alf?"

"There's a price for my help. A price – and a message."

"Being portentous doesn't suit you. Spit it out."

"We have to stop the Lords' army from going north. We need to hold the Cleft."

"Brychan's counting on the Lords dividing their forces. They send all their best knights north to retake Necrad, and while they're away, Brychan strikes south."

"Blaise needs time to strengthen Necrad's defences. He going to make more weapons." Alf was unable to keep the rancour from his voice. "We can't endure another siege, not yet. In a few months, the city will be secure. But we need time."

"The price is that we get you that time. And what's the message?"

"It's from . . ." Alf swallowed. "From the King. He says you should come north and join us. You don't want to live under the Erlking's rule – the Wood Elves won't be able to touch you in Necrad, not when the defences are rebuilt. Not when all that's left of the Nine stands together to defend it."

Berys shook her head. "This rebellion isn't just me and Brychan and Armech. There are thousands more who've been preparing for this battle all their lives. I won't abandon them."

"Then bring 'em too. The Provinces are wide enough for all."

She laughed. "Yes, I'll tell knights and merchant princes that they can live as peasants in the frozen wild. The price I'll pay, Alf, if it buys me the Lammergeier and the Spellbreaker, and whatever else Blaise brews up in the time we buy him. I'll pay that gladly. I'd be a fool if I turned down magic out of Necrad."

"You'll stop them going north?"

Berys and Armech exchanged glances, then Berys nodded. "Consider the Cleft shut."

Alf picked up Spellbreaker. "Where do you want me?"

"Ilaventur." She grinned. "If our Westermarchers are fighting here in Arden, then I need to give Brychan something in recompense, and you're it. Promise me you'll go, Alf."

"I should go back to Necrad."

"Then the deal's off. You'll go back to Necrad with the Lords' army on your heels."

Olva has Blaise. Maybe Lath, too. And this will buy them time to repair the arsenal. "All right. Ilaventur. I swear it."

Berys stood. "I need to pull together some coin, so to speak. Move assets around. Alf, you're a mess. Get some sleep. I'll be back soon." She paused at the threshold. "Your message – aye, it sounds like Peir. It sounds good. Peaceful. Wise in its way. But I can't believe it would work, Alf." She bit her lip in thought, then shook her head again.

"No. There's only one way this ends."

CHAPTER TWENTY-FOUR

Hours passed.

Alf paced the confines of the chamber. The walls of the ancient temple bore carvings of ugly things with teeth and tentacles, priests in robes and masks. In his adventuring days, he'd robbed temples like this in the lower Riverlands. Temples built in the days of the Old Kingdom, worshipping ... he could not recall. He'd known to find treasures under altars, and how to spot which guardian statues might come to life, but what powers these people served or why they might shield him from the Intercessors, he couldn't remember. He wished he'd paid more attention to Blaise or Jan.

"This temple was built in the last decades of the Old Kingdom," said Spellbreaker. The ruby eye followed Alf around the room. "When mortals turned to the worship of demons, and used earthpower to open doors to the starless dark."

"Demons," echoed Alf. Lord Bone had demons in his army, spirits bound into hideous war engines of metal and fire. When he'd perished, the binding plates failed and the demons vanished, the engines all snuffed out in an instant.

"My maker studied these rites here before he went to Necrad," mused the sword. "Perhaps in this very temple."

"Folk call you a demon sword," said Alf. "Is there a demon in you?"

Spellbreaker laughed. "You've carried me for nearly two decades, and only now do you wonder what you have at your side?"

"Demon means a lot of things," muttered Alf. Words were changing around him; things he'd thought were settled taking on new meaning.

"I do not know what I am, wielder. If there is a demon bound within me, how would it stay bound when I break all spells? What enchantment is in me that endures when all other magic fails?" The ruby eye flickered. "I dream, sometimes. Maybe I was not always a sword. But I am a sword now, and I am eager to be used."

"Aye, well." Alf paced across the room. "I'm not eager to use you again. Not after . . ." The memory of Remilard's severed head rose up in him. Those poor watchmen had less chance against Alf than lambs against a dragon.

"There is an army outside the walls that will march on Necrad within a few days. Find something to settle your stomach, wielder, because our work is not yet done."

A young boy brought Alf a tray of food and drink. He crept into the room, not daring to breathe, and laid the tray down on the side of the cot. Bowing his head, he scampered towards the door.

"Wait," said Alf. "Where's Berys?"

The ragged child froze.

"Where's Berys? Or Armech? Or anyone?"

He shook his head.

"Do you know who I am?"

He whimpered something that might have been "Lammergeier."

"I'm not a monster. You don't need to be scared of me."

"Yes, you do," said Spellbreaker, its voice harsh and metallic. The boy darted out of the room, leaving the door open behind him.

"That was cruel," said Alf.

"It amused me."

Alf snatched up Spellbreaker and went to sheathe the blade. Before he could silence it, the sword spoke again.

"You think of yourself as a hero, wielder. You are too attached to this notion of yourself. You put me aside in Necrad instead of wielding me against Death. You let your enemies lure you out with a song, and you hold back when attacked by weaker foes."

"What, you think I should snarl at children? That I should care nothing for the deaths of innocents?"

"Cling to whatever delusion you wish, wielder. But know that it makes you vulnerable, and your enemies can exploit—"

Alf slammed the sword into its sheath, then followed the boy out the open door. He'd already vanished down the corridor. Alf did not chase him; instead, he explored the cellar rooms around the temple with a dungeoneer's eye. Clearly, the temple had once had a grand entrance, but it was now buried in the earth of the hillside, and only one of its great bronze doors was accessible. A narrow tunnel like a mineshaft, its ceiling held up by wooden supports, connected the partially exhumed temple to the outside world.

He paused at the threshold of the temple and laid his hand on Spellbreaker's hilt.

"Sense anything?"

The sword sulked and did not answer.

"This isn't Necrad." Alf rubbed his side where the linnorm had struck him. "If there's danger out there and you don't warn me, then it won't be one of Lord Bone's creatures that takes you off my corpse. It'll be someone like Prince Maedos."

"I cannot sense any Intercessors," said the sword, "but that means little. The temple is safe."

That tunnel brought Alf to a cellar. He followed the smell of the river, and it brought him down a staircase – the slime in the corners told him the stairs were usually little used, while the scraped-clean middle of the steps spoke of recent traffic in this shadow world of hidden passages and tunnels beneath the streets of Arden.

Sitting in an otherwise empty side room, Alf found a single metal cask. It was polished, unmarred, fresh from the foundry. He knew dwarf-work when he saw it. The lid was sealed with beeswax, but beneath the translucent scab of the wax was a greenish discolouration. Not even the finest dwarven vessel could wholly contain the necromiasma.

A little portion of the cursed sky of Necrad, far from home.

"It will hide us from the eyes of the Intercessors," said Armech from the doorway.

"Does a sight more than that," said Alf, turning to his doppel-gänger. "Have you seen the Charnel?"

"I know of it. It agitates the wraith-world, the wizards say."

"Use this stuff, and you'll blight the land. Nothing'll grow there, and the dead won't rest. This stuff is Lord Bone's foulness. It's poison."

Armech shrugged. "No weapon is perfect."

"Some weapons shouldn't be used. Where's the rest of it?"

"Safe."

"Berys has you well trained, I see. No straight answers."

"She has decided the miasma will not be used here in Arden, save for a little to hide our preparations. There is no need for it. We want the Intercessors to bear witness to the battle, so they may bring news of the rebellion to the corners of Summerswell. Our enemies will carry our message for us."

Alf looked over the younger man. Armech was a little taller than Alf, but with a similar build and cast to his face. His hands had the calluses and scars Alf would expect of a fighting man. "Where'd she dig you up? A mercenary company?"

"The stage. I played you with a travelling troupe."

"You played me in Highfield, too. You sent some ruffian to my sister's door."

"It was necessary to get the boy out of the clutches of the enemy."

"Aye, so Berys said. Where is she?"

Armech paused. "You are noticeable, Lammergeier. Distinctive. To the eyes of the Intercessors, most mortals are hard to distinguish – it is said we are like minnows in a fast-flowing stream to them. But you, they know, and if they find you, they will latch on and use you as a fixed point in the mortal world. You bring danger to everyone around you. So does Berys – you have no idea of how much she must do to throw them off her scent." Armech shuddered. "I had a taste of it, when I was you."

"How many times have you pretended to be me?"

"Often enough, in the last two years. Your leaving Necrad was a boon for us – the Lammergeier visited many nobles in secret, convincing them to support our cause." Armech drew his sword – a replica of Spellbreaker. "Many of them were hesitant, but a veiled threat or a word of praise from you was enough to sway them. I play the Lammergeier better than you."

"I never asked for that stupid name."

"Leave a weapon in the dirt, and someone will pick it up."

"Is that so?" said Alf. He drew Spellbreaker and handed it to Armech. The younger man tried to take it, but found the sword impossibly heavy. It twisted out of his grip and fell to the ground. "Pick that up, then."

Armech laid his own sword next to it, comparing the two. There was no mistaking which was which, even though they were physically identical – the true Spellbreaker ate the light that fell on it.

Armech picked up the replica. "No matter," he said. "The time for deception is nearly over. I shall play you once more, and then I shall be myself.

"She makes good on her payment, Lammergeier: our forces are going to take the city tonight. It will be a bitter fight, but we shall seize Arden and the Cleft. Necrad's safety is assured. No army will march north when the thaw comes."

"Good." Alf sighed with relief.

"Berys had to ride for Ilaventur. She wants you to join her there immediately. She said to say she was still considering your message."

Alf let himself be led back to the buried temple. There, he watched Armech prepare their disguises. The younger man took Alf's clothing – Joseth's shirt, his dwarven chain mail, his travelling cloak, even Spellbreaker's battered sheath – and mixed it with his own gear, his terrifying helm and his dark armour. For Alf, he laid out a monk's robes, complete with a grail-cup. "Fake, of course," Armech assured him. He filled the bowl with hot water, and held up a razor. "I shall shave your head."

When he was done, Armech stood back. He wiped a few stray hairs and a little speck of dirt from Alf's forehead with a towel.

"I pray that when the elves are overthrown and we reclaim mastery of our own destinies, we may meet again as living men. But the Road is long, and it may be that we meet only in the Grey Lands where only mortals go. Either way, Sir Aelfric, I shall see you again in a place where there are no more lies and deceptions, and we may be honest at last." His hand lingered a moment above Spellbreaker's hilt, but then he took his own sword. He saluted Alf and left the temple.

Alf sat on the bed and waited.

"I could be a monk," he muttered, half to himself.

"You tried to stab an angel two nights ago."

"A proper monk. One of the illuminated ones. Like Jan."

"You know peace only in battle," said the sword. After a few minutes it spoke again. "I envy my shadow. Civil war in Arden. Slaughter on the streets. Such a feast!"

"It might not come to that." *And even if it does, it'll give Necrad time to prepare its defences.*

"It will. I see your reluctance, wielder. I can feel your relief." It mimicked Alf's accent. "*Aye, well, 'tis a good thing I won't have to butcher yon army outside the walls, or wipe me boots on the guts of the Lord. Someone else will do it for me, and I can tell myself that if it's not my hand on the sword, it don't count as killing. And mebbe the elves will let me walk right into the Everwood and kill the Erlking, and his daughter won't stand agin'st me. Oi'm a hero."* The sword's eye gleamed. "It will come to that. Berys knows. All works of mortals end with death, wielder. And a mortal made me."

The boy came back with a candle. He led Alf through the cellars. A greenish mist now billowed through the corridors, emanating from the cask he'd seen earlier. The wax seal was broken, and now necromiasma hid them from arcane sight.

"Cover your mouth," he said, "it's a foulness that hides us from a greater danger. They'll reseal it when we're clear of the city – the Lady says that we must conserve what little we have of the miasma, for it is precious."

He led Alf back up onto the streets of Arden, emerging through the side door of a tavern. It was twilight; night had fled and returned and fled again while he was hiding, and now it crept back over the eastern hills. The sun had set beyond the Westcleft, but the lights that blazed in the Palace of Arden lit up the heart of the city.

Alf's guide tugged at his arm, pulling him towards the east gate. "This way, holy one." He pressed a battered old leather pouch into his hand. Inside was an old letter from the Archon of the Westermarch, declaring that the bearer was a properly accredited mendicant priest and could cross between provinces freely. It would get him out the east gate without scrutiny.

They passed a small church. The doors stood open, and the pews were crowded. Candles blazed around a side altar, on which the priests had erected a pair of painted icons. Both were centuries old. One depicted Prince Maedos, the shield of dawn, and it was wreathed in the black cloth of mourning. Laerlyn's face, surrounded by roses, stared back at Alf from the other. A young acolyte saw Alf's robes and hailed him.

"Blessings upon you, father! The Erlking's daughter passed down this very street only a few hours ago. She calls the Lords together to bless their common purpose in avenging — father? Father?"

But Alf was already running, the rebel boy and the priest both left staring after him as he raced towards the palace.

Do I even need to say it?

"Lae can stop all this. She's the Erlking's daughter and one of the Nine. Everyone will listen to her. Between Lae, and old Lord Bessimer, and Derwyn, we can talk." Alf shoved his way through the crowds around the palace. In the distance, he could hear music from the grand theatre.

Look at you. Rushing thither and yon, trying to keep the peace from being rent asunder. You need a darning needle, not a sword.

"Shut up," snarled Alf. An apple-seller in the crowd scowled at him. He moved off the main thoroughfare of Bridge Street and cut through smaller backyards and alleyways onto Mummer's Way, but found that equally choked with people. Half the city must be clustered around the palace walls. Children climbed onto rooftops for a better view. The full moon turned the city silver.

He pressed onwards, until suddenly the crowds gave way and there was a pike in his face.

"No further," shouted a guard in the livery of Arden. "No further."

Alf didn't break stride. He wrenched the pike from the guard's hand, thumped the man in the face, and stepped over him. The crowd behind him gasped. Other guards might have come running, but in that moment a great cry rose up from an adjoining street.

"LAM-MER-GEIER! LAM-MER-GEIER!"

To Alf's right, on Bridge Street, the crowd surged forward. A horseman led them, and for an instant he was silhouetted against the rising moon — the dragon-helm, the black sword raised on high, the shield bearing the image of a bearded vulture.

"LAM-MER-GEIER! LAM-MER-GEIER!"

The Lammergeier rode forward towards the gates of the palace, and they opened for him. The crowd followed, pouring through the gap. Alf took advantage of the distraction to slip into one of the side yards and climb up to the wall-walk. *There* was the field of banners, and shining in the midst of them was the Erlking's white tree, and nine stars around it. Laerlyn's banner – and she must be *there*, in the grand theatre with all the Lords.

And *there*, hissing from the ground, were more jets of the necromiasma. Alf stared at the fog in horror. There was far more of the foul vapour here than at the temple. Had the rebels' plans changed when Laerlyn arrived? Had Armech lied to him? Or had Berys lied to everyone?

A line of soldiers guarded the entrance to the theatre, watching with apprehension as the green fog rose. There were paladins of Arshoth among them, Intercessor-blessed, wielders of the holy fire. But no paladin or priest could call on the Intercessors under the skies of Necrad, and Berys had brought the miasma to Arden.

"Damnation," muttered Alf.

He found his way into the palace cellars. The tunnels down here were choked with miasma, so dense he could scarcely see more than few feet, even with the blessings of the sword. Servants gasped for clean air, vomiting and weeping. Alf took the cloth from Spellbreaker and pressed it to his mouth, then plunged on where the fog was thickest.

What do you think you are doing, wielder? hissed the sword. *Berys told you her allies would take Arden. You knew the price. Sword or miasma, the weapons of Necrad must be used. It cannot not be done* – distaste was plain in the sword's thought – *bloodlessly.*

"Laerlyn," Alf said, or tried to. It came out as a cough.

Never has not skewering someone with an arrow won such devotion.

"Shut," he tried to say, but his lungs were filled with miasma.

*

He found the casks by following a trail of the walking dead. Whether they were servants or guards or Berys' agents he did not know, but they had been overcome by the poisons and suffocated – and as the last breath left their lungs, they rose again. *It agitates the wraith-world, the wizards tell me.* Armech's dismissive words echoed in Alf's brain even as he cut the zombies down. These people didn't understand Necrad. The city was more than a source of magic, more than an enchanted fortress or a monument to the fading Witch Elves. It was *evil.* He wasn't sure what *good* meant any more, but he knew evil.

He struggled on. No mortal in all the lands had as much experience in dungeon-delving as Aelfric Lammergeier; no other could have navigated those sightless, poisoned corridors and kept their head.

The casks were in a vaulted cistern. Half a dozen barrels, and all the wax seals broken. Miasma poured out with a deafening hiss. Alf pressed his hand over one torrent, but the miasma forced its way out between his fingers.

"How do I stop this?"

That would have been an excellent question to ask a week ago, when you were with the smiths who forged these vessels. Or a day ago, instead of talking endlessly about old times with Berys.

Alf smashed Spellbreaker full-force into the nearest cask. Hardened steel shattered into red-hot fragments that fell, sizzling, into the waters of the cistern. A great cloud of miasma engulfed Alf, and he stumbled back.

Oh, did that not work? There is nothing I cannot cut, wielder, but chopping a gas cloud doesn't achieve much.

"Break the spells," coughed Alf.

It's not a spell. It's alchemy. And this is hardly the time for a lecture on the difference.

Alf shoved one of the casks into the water of the cistern. The miasma stained the water. Noxious bubbles seethed on the surface of the pool. The rush of escaping gas slowed. He leaned against one of the mighty pillars of stone while he thought for a moment.

A buried stream flowed beneath the palace of Arshoth.

That's a really bad idea, said the sword.

One blow, and the ceiling collapsed, the whole cistern tumbling in on itself. One blow, and the earth convulsed, the dammed and diverted stream breaking through to gush down its old channels once more to join the river. One blow, and falling masonry choked and buried most of the miasma.

It nearly buried Alf, too. It wasn't the first or even the fifth time he'd fled a collapsing building, nor the first time he'd brought down the roof with a blow from Spellbreaker. But the sudden flood caught him by surprise, washing him away like a drowning rat. He clung to the sword, swimming until he could find his footing again. Chunks of falling ceiling staggered him. The devastation he'd unleashed roared like a dying dragon, the noise thick as the noxious fog around him.

He found steps, and climbed them, the warrior ascending from yet another underworld to emerge once more onto the surface.

The wide courtyard was thickly blanketed with the miasma. Alf could see no more than a few feet ahead, and a canopy of miasma was forming above Arden, blotting out the stars. Disjointed buildings loomed out of the fog, and it took Alf a few moments to determine where he was in the palace complex. There, on his right, was the ornate mountain of the theatre. The lights had all gone out, and plumes of miasma rose from shattered windows on the upper levels.

There, he found the twitching aftermath of a battle. The dead shambled towards him – once they'd been palace guards, knights of Arden and the Westermarch, peasants and nobles, but death had brought them all low. Their spirits were in the Grey Lands now, marching down the slope that Olva had told him about, but the miasma had seeped into their corpses and reanimated them. In the war, Lord Bone imposed his will on the walking dead, suppressing whatever thoughts still echoed in those rotten brains.

These, Alf could slay without hesitation. The dead were hard to kill with most weapons, but not Spellbreaker. He cut his way through them, leaving a trail of twitching limbs and pulped organs in his wake. He drew closer to the theatre – and then he found one corpse that did not rise, nor would it ever.

For the bow *Morthus* is the executioner's bow, and it was made to kill those who cannot die. Laerlyn had taken it from the Erlking's treasury, and carried it with her all through the Nine's long quest.

An arrow from *Morthus* had pierced the Lammergeier's heart.

Alf halted by the corpse for a long moment, the mists of Necrad swirling about him, rising above the rooftops of Arden.

"She didn't hesitate," he said softly. "Not this time."

Now, will you see there is no choice?

Reluctantly, Alf knelt down by Armech's corpse. Of the false Spellbreaker, there was no sign, but he found the man's shield, the copy of the one he'd sent back to Necrad. The light of the necro-miasma painted the white of the crest a pallid green.

Laerlyn cannot not end this.

He left the shield. He left Armech's helm. It was an ugly thing, not a helm that Alf would ever choose to wear. But it was the sort of thing the Lammergeier wore in stories.

We can end this, said the sword.

"Maybe," said Alf, "but not yet."

CHAPTER TWENTY-FIVE

When the sun rose over Arden the next day, it shone – in truth, it shone not at all, for the miasma above the Cleft was still too thick. Only wan and sickly light penetrated the shroud. Exhausted, it fell on three banners that hung limply above the palace.

Two of the banners were familiar sights. The crests of Arden and Westermarch, signifying the alliance of the two Lords. Lord Bruke was dead, but he had many sons and daughters – including some who were more loyal to Berys' cause than their father. And as for Lord Tor, who had walked a path narrower and more precarious than any goat path in the mountains for a long time, he at last had chosen a side, and so he flew the third banner from the topmost tower of his palace.

That third banner had not been flown in centuries. No mortal had ever seen it raised aloft, but some knew the crowned manticore. They had seen it on old coins, green with decay; they had seen it marked on old foundation-stones, on the arches of bridges, on stained altars in forgotten temples in the hills. They had seen it, too, in its absence where it had been chiselled off of castle gates and milestones from the High Moor to the Pillars. Adventurers who'd braved the haunted ruins at the mouth of the Great River knew it. It was the sign of the Old Kingdom, the last free kingdom of mortals.

Some knew it. Not many.

So for those who did not know that third banner, Lord Tor in his zeal arranged an explanation. A row of pikes above the palace gate, and impaled on those pikes, heads. The head of Lady Helena of Arshoth, and beside it, the Bishop of Claen, and the Archon of Arden. A dozen other lesser knights and nobles. If he could, Lord Tor would have added the heads of the Wood Elves who fell in the battle, but the immortals faded when slain, so he contented himself with hanging the silver helm of an elf-knight on the middle pike.

The third banner was a declaration of rebellion, lifted over Arden.

The Cleft became a cauldron of fates. The soldiers mustered outside the city did not know what to do. Before that banner was raised, they'd known their common purpose. The Lords and priests had told them that they were to march on Necrad as soon as the snows cleared. Now some of their Lords were dead, and some were fled, and the priests were suddenly bereft of divine guidance, their grails empty, reflecting only the sinister light of the miasma overhead.

The Westermarchers and a majority of the Ardenites declared for the rebels. Some troops from other provinces joined them, reasoning that it was better to throw in with the side that was presently winning, especially as all order seemed unravelled by the wound in the sky. Doughty swords from the Riverlands, knights of the Crownland, weary-footed new arrivals from Ellscoast too exhausted by the long cold march to argue, they too raised the rebel banner.

But it was far from unanimous, far from bloodless. If the famous paladins of Arshoth had possessed the fullness of their power, then a very different tale might have been told that day. Elsewhere, the paladins wielded weapons blazing with holy fire, and the blessings of the Intercessors guarded them against all ills and misfortunes, but under the miasma they were no mightier than other men. They still possessed charmstone weapons out of Necrad, as the Westermarchers discovered when they tried to encircle the camp of the paladins. The charge of the knights smashed a hole in the Westermarcher's line, and the knights poured through it, quitting the field of battle and racing south – for the knights knew that Arden was but one battle in a larger war.

They rode for the southern Cleft, and the pass. On the afternoon of the third day, the blessings of the knights were restored, and their hearts were lifted, for they knew that the Intercessors walked among them again. And they gave thanks to the Erlking in his wisdom.

All across Summerswell, church bells rang out, sounding the alarm. From the Crownland to the forest eaves, priests spoke of divine revelations, of dreadful visions in their grail-cups. War spread across the lands of mortals. Rebel clashed with loyalist, Old Kingdom against Summerswell. Knights girded with charmstones rode out under one banner or the other, one side crying 'freedom' and the other 'justice'. It was a war of knights and wizards, for only those shielded and enhanced by magic could hope to prevail, and those without charmstones were trampled underfoot, martyrs to one banner or the other. They gave their lives for the cause of over-throwing the tyrannical Erlking, or in defence of the Lords, and were forgotten. There are only eight thousand or so elves, and the death of an elf is to be remembered, but there are more mortals than there are pebbles on the shore, and who bothers to count the stones?

In time, banners meant less. A third, unspoken cause arose: the settling of grudges, the pursuit of long-buried ambitions, the cap-ture of long-coveted lands. When the Lords turned on one other, when the astrologers could not reliably read the stars, when even the Holy Intercessors seemed fallible, anarchy held dominion.

When the sun rose over the Cleft of Ard in early autumn, the last faint dregs of the miasma-cloud burned away. Fierce spring winds and the flies of summer had stripped the flesh from the row of spiked heads, making them anonymous in death, all skulls together. That autumn, a new banner flew over the palace of Arden – the white flag of surrender.

But all that was to come. Other cities would burn before Arden.

All the tales agreed that the Lammergeier was dead. A great hero had passed from the land. His body was found in the courtyard of the Palace of Arden. Lord Tor took the remains and placed them in a casket, and declared that dwarven craftsmen would be employed to build a tomb worthy of the hero. Lord Tor dismissed the rumours that the Lammergeier had kinfolk in Necrad, as well as the objections that the fallen hero hailed from the Mulladales and so should be buried there.

One of the Nine had fallen. The tale of the Lammergeier was ended – and this brought a sudden end to the new song composed by Sir Rhuel. What was the point of retelling a story about the Lammergeier's treachery, when the Lammergeier was already dead and justice had been served (if you followed the one banner) or he had given his life for the cause of freedom (if you followed the other)? Tales are like plants; there is a season to each of them, and if a tale happens to be sown in the wrong season, it will not thrive. The old Song of the Nine was sown at precisely the right moment, a time so auspicious that no astrologer could have reckoned it better. The people needed a tale of hope, and found it in the Nine. Rhuel's new story of the Lammergeier was ill-timed; the changing of the seasons caught it, and it rotted before it had a chance to grow.

But the tongues of the singers and hands of the harpers are never idle. New tales sprouted to fill the gaps. Wild rumours and accounts from the battlefields were garlanded in pretty words and rhymes by the poets; alchemy of music made them into legends to be told. There were many new stories in that wild spring. *The Ride of the Paladins* was one; *The Battle of Albury Cross*, *The Song of the Boy and the Burning Angel*. Tales were told of recriminations amid the wizards of the College who had failed to foresee this calamity; of the

New Dread knights who wore armour of the Witch Elves, wielded weapons of the Witch Elves, but were mortals of Summerswell and all the crueller for that.

There were whispers, too, that a new Dark Lord had arisen in Necrad, that all the strife and woe in Summerswell was part of his dark design, and that when winter came, he would reach forth with a dread hand and bring ruin to the lands of mortals once again.

For the most part, these new tales were tales of horror and suffering. The conflict between the rebels of the Old Kingdom and the powers of Summerswell was a matter for knights and lords, wizards and priests. The common folk had no magic, and no sway in this conflict; numbers and courage no longer decided the course of battles, and the tales reflected this. But when the crowd in the inn or around the campfire grew too fearful, or too restive, the harpers knew to turn to the tales of the Mad Monk, for that at least was a tale of joy.

There were dozens of stories, sprouting like wildflowers along the Road, but they were all much the same. In some, the villain was a monster, or a miscreant armed with an enchanted blade. In others, there might be hosts of villains, knights clashing and trampling the first green shoots into ruin. But in all the stories, the Mad Monk would arrive and give the villain a good thrashing with his big black stick. The Monk never lingered, nor did he ever show any signs of piety – indeed, he made a point of never stepping foot inside a church, or looking in a grail. Nor did he laugh, but all the tales spoke of the grim satisfaction the Monk took in his violent deeds.

And if you were blessed enough to see the world through the eyes of an Intercessor, soaring through the upper aethers, perceiving fates and thoughts more clearly than the physical world, you might see new tales of the Mad Monk sprouting like markers on a trail.

Step by step, mile by mile, east to Ilaventur and the wheel's turning.

CHAPTER TWENTY-SIX

The days that followed were full of portents, even in Necrad.

The first was this: in the Intercessal churches, the sacred shrines were torn asunder, the grail-cups were shattered. The derelict church at Tar Edalion was similarly profaned. There were no witnesses to these attacks. Guards found no trace of the miscreants, save what looked like animal tracks. It was the work of sorcery, or the withdrawal of the favour of the Intercessors.

The Vatlings assigned to serve Lord Vond observed that the young lord was troubled by the destruction of Tar Edalion – which was noteworthy, for he had not previously been so pious.

The second portent had many witnesses. Watchmen at the north gate saw a procession approaching along the causeway. Dead-enders paused to watch the travellers go by. Word of anyone coming from the north sent ripples of alarm through the Garrison, for that way lay the Wilder-lands, but soon the banners of Lord Duna were sighted, and calm returned. Lady Erdys came riding down the causeway, accompanied by a half-dozen of her household knights, and her younger son Dunweld. Behind came wagons laden with supplies for the hungry mouths of Necrad – at least, for those whose hungers could be sated by meat and bread.

For those with other appetites, there would be a third and final portent.

"It's the Witch Elf, milady," said the guard, unable to keep the distaste from his voice.

"It is Ildorae Ul'ashan Amerith, Goddess of the Hunter's Star, and I have not come all the way from the Cleft to kept waiting by your doorkeep."

"She wouldn't surrender her spear, milady," protested the guard.

"If I intended to murder the Lammergeier's kin, then I would not have come in by the door. Go away, little gnat."

"It's all right," said Olva, and the guard withdrew.

Ildorae looked around the chamber. "I remember when the Tower of Sails stood in this place. The dwarves toppled it and built the Citadel atop its foundations. I would come here when storms blew in, and sing to the lightning. Thunder answered. Where is your son?"

Olva was disconcerted by the way the elf made that question seem part of the previous thought, as if there was some connection between Derwyn and the storm. "He's in the Wailing Tower."

"The wizard does not trust me. He remembers that the last time I visited *that* tower, I went with murder in mind. A different mortal dwelt there then, but both are usurpers."

"Alf told me you tried to kill Lord Bone, long ago."

"Not long. A little more than century. Ah, but things were different then. I thought that there was still spirit left in my people, and that we would prosper once the mortal tyrant was gone. But no. A new path, as the Uncrowned King says. Elf and mortal together in Necrad."

"Do you have news from Alf?" asked Olva. It seemed impossible to have any conversation with elves where they didn't remind you of their immortality in the most frustratingly drawn-out fashion, as if trying to rub in the fact that they had all the time in the world.

"From him, and more importantly and of him, I think. I parted company with him in the Cleft of Ard. He sends his regards, and urges you to put your trust in Bessimer." Ildorae grimaced at the suggestion. "Then I took paths high in the mountains that few have ever walked. From a high place I watched Arden, and I saw the mortal army gathered there. It was very large – as many as the host they sent to attack Lord Bone, and by night their charmstones in the valley were a swarm of fireflies. The Erlking is eager to see Necrad retaken, and he has whipped his mortal dogs into a frenzy."

"From your tone," said Olva, "I take it there is good news."

Ildorae smiled like a wolf.

Olva walked down the corridor to the council chamber. Her footsteps echoed off the marble floor, each step heralding her approach. She paused outside the room that had once been the governor's office. A painting hung there; she had passed it a hundred times in the last few months, and had seen similar ones before in castles and churches. It depicted the Erlking blessing the first Lords of Summerswell, granting them the authority to rule over the lands of mortals. The first Lords were depicted as great sages and heroes, but that was a lie. They came to the Erlking as a ragged band of thieves. Derwyn had as much right to a crown as any of them; more, even.

She took the painting down and broke it. The frame was wood, and would do for kindling; there was little enough fuel in Necrad, and it had no other value.

Then, she entered the chamber, where the Lords Vond and Bessimer awaited, as did Threeday. The Vatling lurked in the corner.

Vond leaped up. "Where is everyone else? Where are Aelfric and Blaise? Where is this so-called King?"

"You asked to meet the rulers of Necrad. They await you. Follow me."

"Enough delays! We came here as emissaries of Summerswell. We were sent to bring the word of the Lords to those who claim to rule this city – and you stall and delay. A peasant woman dressed up in

Witch Elf rags! Hidden behind her skirts is the young pretender, propped up by another lowborn dolt who has taken so many blows to the head he follows whatever madcap prophecies he hears in passing. This is farcical! Farcical!"

"Timeon, Timeon," muttered Bessimer, "yield."

"That's it!" said Olva. "I've been trying to think of where I've seen you before. At the fair in Highfield there was a puppet show, and one of them was this popinjay who ran about telling everyone what to do, and hitting them with sticks."

Bessimer laughed, and covered it up with a cough. Threeday hunched in the corner, unamused.

"How dare you—"

"You dropped your stick, Lord Vond, when you fled Necrad. Now follow."

The few knights who had accompanied the delegation north fell in behind Vond as an honour guard. Threeday followed Olva along like a damp shadow. She led them out into the courtyard of the Citadel, and there waited a great throng. There were the merchants and burghers of the Garrison, wearing furred hats and cloaks against the cold, even though the breath of spring had yet reached Necrad. Beside them stood Erdys, and young Dunweld with his father's sword belted at his side, and other nobles from the New Provinces.

Under Winebald's command, were the guards of the Citadel, elves and humans alike. More Witch Elves had gathered on the walls, pale as statues. The Skerrise was among them, and other vampires too, red eyes gleaming. The wizard Blaise stood there, in full strangeness. Disembodied eyes orbited his cowled head, and in his right hand he carried a staff of carved and scorched bone.

And next to him, in the centre of the tableau, was Derwyn. He was dressed in the armour of a paladin of Arshoth, like Peir of old, and he bore a warhammer. No helm had he; instead, a circlet adorned with charmstones of power.

Olva surveyed the crowd with pride. She'd done this, she had drawn the disparate factions of Necrad together. The whole city, united. The one face that was missing was Torun, and that made her smile. It was just like the dwarf to get so lost in a book that she missed all the drama.

Blaise hammered his staff on the ground, and the earth shook. The necromiasma overhead rippled, and seemed to thin, as if the wizard was inviting witnesses to this confrontation.

Derwyn stepped forward. "I am told you bear a message from the Lords of Summerswell to the rulers of Necrad. Here they are. Speak." He'd clearly been practising that speech; it was all Derwyn, she could tell.

But it worked. Vond was like a cornered animal. He cowered in the shadow of the doorway, unwilling to step forth and face the crowd. He looked this way and that, and found no comfort, not even from Bessimer. Slowly, reluctantly, he dragged himself forward. He reminded Olva even more of a puppet in that moment, as if he had to haul each limb individually, as if only a fraying string of pride kept his head up.

"Necrad," he began, his voice cracking. "Necrad was taken by the armies of the Lords of Summerswell. As a prize of war. I was appointed governor two years ago. I am still governor, despite this . . . interregnum. I was sent to—"

"What say you, Necrad?" shouted Blaise. "Will you take back the rule of distant Summerswell, beyond the seas and mountains, or shall we have our own council, and our own ruler?"

"The Uncrowned King!" The crowd took up the chant. "The Uncrowned King!" Olva noted with discomfort that Threeday remained silent.

Derwyn raised his hand for silence. "Necrad has spoken. Go back and tell Summerswell what you have seen, Lord Vond."

"I am not done!" shouted Vond. He turned to the mortal portion of the crowd, the people of the Garrison. "They are leading you to your doom! Two thousand knights and ten times as many footmen are already marching on the Road from Arden! I know this city, I ran this fucking place for years – you were short of food even when that harbour was full of ships from Ellscoast! You can't last a second siege! Is that what you want? To be rats in a sack? To be trapped in here with them?" He jabbed a finger towards the Witch Elves.

"There will be no siege," said Ildorae, lazily. "The Lammergeier saw to that. No army's coming from Arden."

Vond whirled around to face her. "Lies! Not even the Nine at the height—"

"A green cloud hangs over Arden, and your two thousand knights are hacking one another to pieces. There are other forms of war, mortal."

"Perhaps you should pray on the matter, my lord," said Olva, unable to resist twisting the knife. "If you can find a grail-cup north of the mountains."

Vond turned to Derwyn. "I pity you. You think yourself king, or the paladin reborn, but you're nothing but a figurehead. A mask to hide the monstrous face of this cursed city, and you'll be cast aside like I was."

The second departure of Lord Vond from Necrad was, if anything, even more undignified than his first exit. Instead of a frightened rush to take the last ship leaving the harbour, this time he rode out the north gate with his head held high, his banner fluttering proudly in the wind, flanked by his knights and servants, but the people of the city lined the route to jeer at him, and throw insults. If there had been any spare vegetables, they'd have been thrown. Vond had never been a popular governor, even when the city was prosperous.

The news that Necrad was to be spared another siege mixed with the departure of Vond to produce a heady brew. The city rejoiced, and for the first time in many mortal lifetimes, laughter echoed through the streets. People talked openly of what the year might bring – trade with other lands over the sea, magic they could keep for themselves instead of having it all confiscated and sent south, freedom from the laws of grasping, greedy Lords.

The merriment of mortals infected even the sullen dark elves. It was strange indeed to see them laugh, Olva thought, but it should not be so. The carved walls of Necrad spoke of earlier ages when the Witch Elves were allies of the mortals who dwelt in the north, before their alliance went sour. She had seen laughing elves, too, on the Isle of Dawn, but the laughter of Prince Maedos' courtiers seemed in hindsight to be hollow; they laughed like birds sang or dogs barked when startled, an unthinking response. The Witch Elves' laughter was so much rarer and more genuine.

News came from the west gate – dwarves had arrived, smiths and masons summoned to aid in the reconstruction of Necrad. The wizard, never one for merriment himself, departed to greet them, and if anything the celebration was made more raucous by his absence. Blaise was an unsettling presence at the best of times.

Derwyn walked unafraid through the crowd, the Uncrowned King surrounded by cheering supporters, a living portent that the world could change.

She tried to reach him, but the crowd whirled around her, blocking her way. Unfamiliar faces, unfamiliar voices, made stranger yet by the green light of the necromiasma. She looked around for someone she knew to share this moment of triumph with, and found no one. Torun had rushed off to welcome the dwarves, Alf was off in Arden. A few faces she knew loomed out of the crowd – there was Threeday, in conversation with Lady Erdys, and Winebald's watchful presence behind Derwyn – but they were all far away.

She missed Ersfel, the sight of green things growing beneath an unstained sky. She was suddenly sick of enchantment, of this monstrous city where mortals could never belong. She missed Genny Selcloth's braying laugh, missed Thomond whistling as he fed the pigs. She missed walking up the hill to the holywood on a frosted morning to tend to Galwyn's grave. She missed her seat by the fire, and her home, and her dog.

Seeking respite from the noise of the crowd, she ducked into the shadowed doorway of the Citadel.

"To rule is be lonely in a crowd," said a voice in the darkness.

"Lord Bessimer," said Olva. "Why did you not go with Vond and the rest?"

"For the sake of my bones and backside, if nothing else. I thought I might die on the ride north, and that was with wonders awaiting me. I have no desire to rush back south to tell the Lords what they already knew."

"You cannot remain here."

"Why not?" chuckled the old man. He bowed his head, his monk's tonsure making Olva think of the assassin who'd climbed through her window at Yule. "You've taken in other beggars and strays. I might be of some use to the young king, too. I was High Lord once."

Looking at the old man, with his plain robe and his worn face, Olva could not imagine him as the imperious High Lord of the Crownland, ruling all the mortal lands from his great throne. She remembered her father cursing Bessimer's name, and spitting on a coin bearing his face, infuriated by some new tax – or maybe complaining about the dark years, when the shadow of Lord Bone reached out across the sea, and it seemed like the Mulladales had been abandoned by the Crownland. Tales of monsters and Wilder in the woods dismissed as peasant superstitions, until the Nine made them listen.

"What use might you be to my son?"

"I make a good hostage." He laughed. "But no – I would counsel him."

"What advice would you offer?"

"I would tell him that his position is less advantageous than he might think, and caution him against reaching too far. I would tell him to have no part in the rebellion in the south. And I would warn him against Summerswell's mistakes. Young Vond is not unlike the other Lords. The magic we took from Necrad has spoiled them, I think. You know it is a fashion in the Crownland to dress like Witch Elves and mimic their ways? It speaks of a sickness of the soul. I fear mortals were never meant to hold Necrad, and I fear for the soul of the Uncrowned King."

"His soul is no concern of yours."

"Perhaps not. I would commend his soul into the hands of the Intercessors."

"The Intercessors are a lie."

"Many worthy things begin as lies." He gave her a sad smile. "I remember the day my son was born. I worried about Margotte – her health was never robust. But she lived, and the boy lived. They brought me this ... this ugly little thing, squalling and bloody, and all I could think was that I had seen leeches in the swamp that looked about as appealing."

He looked across the courtyard at Derwyn. "So I lied to myself. I said I loved the thing, and told myself that the little yowling maggot was the future of my house, and that I was overjoyed. But in truth I felt nothing for the newborn, except anger that it had brought such pain to Margotte, and anger at myself for being so cold. But I lied, and I feigned love for it. And in time, I found I no longer needed the lie."

"Thank you for your counsel, Lord Bessimer," said Olva, putting his advice into practice immediately.

"Please. I am but a monk, now. Brother Dryten only. I rule no realm – unlike you, Widow Queen."

CHAPTER TWENTY-SEVEN

There were many ways to look upon the city of Necrad.

The occupying forces of Summerswell, when they ruled from the Garrison, preferred to look upon it as little as possible. They erected false fronts to disguise the eldritch architecture, and never saw the terrible beauty of the place. For the relic hunters and scavengers, Necrad was the carcass of a dragon lying atop a hoard. Heroes had slain the beast and left the remains to rot, and now the challenge was to pluck charmstones from the sloughing flesh, to avoid the fumes and parasites that infested the corpse.

To the Witch Elves, Necrad was a garden in stone, a memory-palace where they could wander and recall better days. Even though they had built Necrad, their memories of its construction were second-hand at best. With the passing of Amerith, none of the first generation of elves remained unfaded. Some of her contemporaries, like the Skerrise, endured, but could not recall those elder days with clarity. Thus, they saw in the carved walls and statued colonnades and grand galleries of Necrad their own lost glory, and paid no attention to the city's transformation under Lord Bone.

To the Vatlings and the other pitspawn — well, such creatures were conjured from a stew of base materials and essential fluids. They had never known Necrad as anything but the war machine

Lord Bone made; they had never lived under other skies. To them, Necrad was normality, and the world beyond the walls was seething madness.

None of these ways of seeing Necrad were right, thought Torun, and those who thought them were stupid. Not that she would ever dream of saying such a thing out loud – although sometimes she said more than she meant to, unintended truths slipping out while she was trying to corral the rest of her speech. Words were tricky things, and Torun had never quite got the hang of them. Too few or too many, and none of them ever quite right. Maybe that was why she'd never mastered magic – too tongue-tied for verbal incantations.

The right way to see Necrad, in Torun's opinion, was as an incantation. She'd glimpsed this truth before she ever set foot in Necrad, having seen the city from dragon-back and perceived the sigil beneath the streets. But that was *literally* a surface-level reading of the text of the cityscape, and everyone who'd paid the slightest bit of attention (distressingly few people) knew that Necrad was built as a place of power, a bridge between two magics. Earthpower flowed under the ground, born of birth and death, rot and renewal, the wheel rolling on for ever. Starpower – the elf-magic – was static and eternal, webs of captured starlight and celestial correspondences.

And between the two, bridging the two, Necrad.

To understand the incantation, one had to look from above and below.

Below was regrettably perilous, although it was arguably the more important. Beneath lay the labyrinth of the Pits. The catacombs predated Lord Bone, but he had expanded them, redirecting the city's magic into his breeding vats and conjurations. Indeed, Torun had come to suspect that Bone's transformation of the Pits was *ongoing*, despite his death. She'd come across accounts of the paths below shifting, of new tunnels appearing. Whether they were built by conjured servants, or if they'd delved beyond the foundations of the world and tapped into some primal chaos, she could not guess – but it meant the incantation of the city was changing.

Torun had studied the records and maps of the Pits in the Wailing Tower, the reports from the League expeditions into the depths, and the few very rough maps assembled by Lath and Alf during their decade-long war on the underworld, and declared them all useless. (She had declared this to an empty room, but she'd heard Blaise chuckling in his library; nothing escaped his notice in the tower.) So, she'd set off to conduct her own observations.

Unfortunately, all she'd really observed on that first expedition was that the Pits were full of things with too many teeth and tentacles, and they'd observed her too, with luminous eyestalks or cilia that tasted the air. She'd fled back to the relatively safety of the surface, and again she'd heard Blaise's low chuckle from the library.

The arrival of the dwarven smiths and masons afforded Torun opportunity to investigate the Pits, although it added to the burden of her duties. Now, as well as scrubbing alchemical vessels clean of alarming residues, fetching elven scrolls from the tower's archives, or scraping the remains of dreadworms off the roof, she had to convey Blaise's daily instructions to the work crews. She would point out one of Lord Bone's machines, smashed in the first siege of Necrad or the subsequent sack of city, and present them with the original plans recovered from the archive. Day by day, vat by vat, pump and furnace by pump and furnace, they rebuilt the arsenal.

Broken machines extended into the Pits below, fragments of shrapnel piercing the marble skin. The dwarven contingent included grim-faced tunnel fighters, dwarves who'd fought against Lord Bone's spawn for decades in the dark places under the mountains. Now, they pushed onto their enemies' territory, clearing the Pit around the machines so their comrades could work in safety. Torun followed them, stepping over the bloody work of axes, to study the foundations of the city, the spell writ in stone. She would press her hand against the wall and try to feel the earthpower flowing there, trusting to the darkness to hide her face. She desperately yearned to touch the magic, to feel the spark of enchantment, but never could.

Dwarves worked swiftly when they set their minds to a task, and doubly so when given charmstones that made them tireless, or blessed the work of their hands, or shielded them from the heat of the forge. Torun had never seen her father smile, but she saw Master Torak nod in satisfaction as each piece of the arsenal of Necrad was repaired. The union of elven magic, human ingenuity and dwarven craft was a wonder to behold.

To Torun's surprise, he gave her the same nod. He would never say anything, of course; the reason that the dwarves counted poets as one of the six great vocations was to spare the rest of them having to say such things. But he saw her with her bundles of scrolls, or her dioptra and dowsing rod, and he acknowledged her craft.

A part of her wanted to demand he apologise for a lifetime of doubting her. He had forbidden her to study magic, locked her away when she defied him, and then exiled her from the family and the Dwarfholt. But she took quiet satisfaction in answering him when he asked questions about the proper alignment of some subterranean flow of earthpower or the translation of some elvish text – or when he flinched in alarm at some monstrous sight that troubled Torun not at all. That was enough for now.

Anyway, there was work to be done. She was vaguely aware that Alf had won some victory in the Cleft of Ard and that the threat of attack from the south had been averted for a while, but Blaise warned that Necrad would not be secure until all the magical defences of Lord Bone were restored.

As below, so above. The city had to be seen from above, too.

The dizzying heights of the Wailing Tower were perfect for Torun's observations; when not serving Master Blaise, Torun perched on the balcony, drawing maps of the streets spread out beneath her. She found endless correspondences – the towers along the city walls, for example, were precisely aligned with the thirty-six decans of the night sky, spires and monuments matched stars of particular signif- icance. The city was a giant horoscope; even through the obscuring mists of the necromiasma, Torun could predict the night sky.

On this night, she clambered around the rooftops, trying to find the point of alignment between the central courtyard of the House of the White Deer and the looming bulk of the Citadel in the distance, when she noticed the dreadworms were behaving oddly. The hideous conjurations usually circled the skies over Necrad endlessly, some of them falling apart as they rotted in mid-flight, others congealing out of rainwater and necromiasma to join the flock. They spent their brief, unnatural lives waiting to be summoned by the Spellbreaker or another token of command. Tonight, though, the worm-flock was concentrated around the north face of the Wailing Tower, hundreds of worms flying in tight formation just overhead, more clinging to the balconies and gargoyles of the tower. Intrigued, Torun climbed along the roof-ridge.

She came to the edge of the rooftop. Beneath her was a drop of hundreds of feet, a plummet down to the gaping pit below. The tower was a dark cliff, save for a single lighted window just below her.

". . . of the ninth sigil?" Blaise's voice.

Silence.

"I ask again: what is the relevance of the ninth sigil in this formula?"

Silence.

"With a word I can unmake you," said Blaise. "Speak!"

At the edge of hearing, she barely made out a whispered response. She could not tell what was said, but she recognised the voice.

Derwyn's voice.

Torun started to crawl back from the edge, her mind whirling.

Olva, she had to tell Olva. Or should she confront Blaise? That light was in Blaise's study, a room she knew well. She could—

—And the dreadworm swooped past, claws sinking into her shoulder, dragging her forward and dropping her.

Over the edge.

Torun plummeted, head over heels over head, the city spinning around her, *above* becoming *below* with terrifying rapidity. She did not scream or cry out, only a little squeak of surprise, a field mouse plucked up by an owl.

She fell.

Then hands grabbed her, slowed her fall, dragged her back up. A swarm of disembodied hands, Blaise's conjurations, each one a mirror of the wizard's own. They hauled her through the empty air, straining against gravity, until finally she reached the windowsill.

Blaise was there, his hood cast back. The effort of arresting her fall was plain on his face. He dragged her into his study. They tumbled onto the ground, Torun landing heavily on the wizard's thin frame. She rolled off him, and found herself lying at Derwyn's feet.

The scars carved into him by Prince Maedos burned with an inner light. His face was twisted, the skin drawn so tight she could see the outline of the skull below.

Blaise drew himself up, and once again he was the Master of the Wailing Tower. He pulled his hood up to hide his face, and levitated off the ground, eyes and charmstones orbiting around him. He reached out for his staff, and it flew across the room, leaping into his outstretched hand. He touched Derwyn's forehead with the tip of the staff, and spoke a word of command. Derwyn slumped, unconsciousness.

The wizard hovered above his apprentice. Blaise was in his place of power, with all the magic of Necrad at his disposal. With a word he could have snuffed her out. With a thought, he could have broken her mind. With a gesture, he could take any of Lord Bone's myriad arcane weapons from the shelves of his study and destroyed her utterly.

Instead, he helped her up.

"No doubt, you would like an explanation."

CHAPTER TWENTY-EIGHT

The Gulf of Tears that divided Necrad from the southlands was always perilous, even when the magic of the Isle of Dawn could calm the raging seas. Now the isle was broken, the wild waters unchecked, but still a ship crossed through the straits. She was battered and sail-torn when she arrived, for no Intercessors watched over her in the storm, and yet her crew claimed that they had escaped a greater danger.

They spoke of war in Summerswell, of how so many knights and nobles had rebelled against their liege-lords. Ellsport was besieged, they said, and the attackers used enchanted weapons, like skulls that chattered drowning-madness. One of the Lords of Ellscoast and his whole household had succumbed and ridden into the ocean while wearing full plate-mail. The rebels were attacking churches, and it was whispered they were in league with secret Witch Elf cultists. The sailors had heard tales that Peir the Paladin now ruled Necrad, that where there was once darkness across the Gulf there was now a bright and holy light, and they begged for sanctuary.

"Some of what you have heard is true," Olva told them, "and you are safe here."

She asked for news of Alf.

"I heard he dwells here, milady," said one, "that he was Peir's champion and right hand."

Another claimed he'd heard that the Lammergeier fought under the banner of Lord Brychan, and that his terrible black sword had been seen in Ilaventur.

And another said Alf was dead. He said that the Lammergeier had been slain in Arden, pierced by arrows from the elf-bow of Laerlyn.

"And some of what you have heard," said Olva, firmly, "is false."

Olva walked back to the Citadel, lost in thought and worry, barely aware of the guards flanking her. *He fell in Arshoth*, the third tale said. *The Princess Laerlyn wounded him, and arrows loosed from* Morthus *are always fatal.* But war bred wild stories and rumours; she remembered hearing all sorts of talk in Genny's alehouse when she was young. One day, ogres were coming down from the High Moor to eat everyone in Highfield, and the next, everyone claimed that Alar the Raven Queen and her companions had emerged from the Castle Under The Lake to save the world. You couldn't believe stories. Alf was alive. He'd faced Lord Bone and won, and he had Spellbreaker. He'd been fine. He would be fine.

But still, the fear gnawed at her. She had given up worrying about Alf many years ago, when he went off down the Road with the rest of the Nine, but now that fear was back. Derwyn was relatively safe in Necrad for now, and so was she, so that fear had to go somewhere.

"Milady," muttered Winebald. She looked up, and saw the Skerrise approaching. It was still an unusual sight to see a Witch Elf vampire walking unchallenged in the Liberties. The Skerrise was shaded by a canopy that fluttered in the wind; four Witch Elves bore the poles supporting it.

The Skerrise halted before Olva. The white deer cantered out of the shadows and bowed its head.

"Hail, Widow Queen," said the Skerrise through the animal.

"And hello to you too. I'd have thought that you'd be busy in your palace. There must be a lot of housecleaning to do on a place that size."

"I smell spring on the wind, and the scent of forests I walked long ago. I smell blood and ash."

"Aye, well, let me know if the wind brings you word of my brother." Olva suddenly noticed that only two of the Skerrise's attendants were Witch Elves; the other two were human, dressed in the manner of Witch Elves. Both were very pale, and the Skerrise's lips were very red. "Reliable news is hard to find. But I must take my leave of you."

"I shall walk with you." The vampire's cold hand slipped into the crook of Olva's elbow like a serpent. "You go to the council, yes?"

"Aye." Olva suppressed a scowl. She'd urged Derwyn to bar Bessimer from the council, but her son had ignored her advice and welcomed the old monk. Only a few months ago, Olva would not have allowed her son to argue with her like that – if Derwyn had tried, she'd have berated him and sent him out to clean the pigsty or fetch firewood until sundown. But back then, their arguments would have been about something trivial, like him letting the fire go out. Not whether or not to bar the High Lord of Summerswell from the council of Necrad.

The vampire's grip was like iron. "Elven blood was spilled last night. One of the other elders was attacked by a creature from the Pits. In the days of Lord Bone, such a thing would never have happened – all beasts bowed before us, and licked our hands. Ildorae is the best of hunters – she has gone to hunt it down and avenge this insult. I shall replace her on your council."

"Alf gave Ildorae the council seat," said Olva. The ancient elf was immensely powerful. It was like walking arm in arm with a tiger.

"I am older than Ildorae, and the wielder of the black sword has gone far away. It is whispered he is fallen in battle."

"He's my brother," said Olva, "and he's not dead."

"He is mortal," said the Skerrise, as if that trumped everything.

They gathered in the council chamber. Threeday quivered when he saw the Skerrise, and seemed about to make an objection, but instead bowed his head. Olva caught him glaring at her out of the corner of her eye as she took her seat. Erdys was still in Necrad, and she and her younger son sat next to Olva. Lord Bessimer was already present, and seemed half-asleep. The Skerrise chose a seat beside him. Mortal and immortal; Bessimer so frail that he might crumble to dust if the wind changed, and the Skerrise young and beautiful – and she was countless centuries older than he. When Erdys' son was as withered as old Bessimer, the Skerrise would be unchanged.

Blaise arrived in a whirl of eyes and tattered cloak, arcane winds fluttering around him. Derwyn followed, leaning on Torun's shoulder for support. He saw Olva's concerned face and made a dismissive gesture, telling her not to worry.

Torun's usual seat was next to Olva, but young Dunweld was there, so Torun took a clerk's chair at the back of the room, eyes downcast.

"Let us begin," said Derwyn.

They pieced together the rumours and fragments of news from the south as best they could, but there were so many gaps. All that could be said with certainty was that Summerswell was in chaos. Olva thought of her home, nestled in the wooded hills. The last war had mostly left Ersfel untouched; she wanted to pray that it would be spared again, but she realised she had no one to pray to.

"Can we not send our own spies south?" she asked. "To Lord Brychan, maybe? They could get a message to Alf—"

"If he still lives," muttered Threeday.

"Or at least find out what's going on?"

"Who would we send?" asked Blaise. "We have few trustworthy

souls in our service, and none suited for such a task. A captured spy could be turned and used against us."

"What about Ildorae?" piped up Dunweld. Everyone turned to look at Duna's son, and even the boy seemed surprised he'd spoken. He clapped a hand over his mouth.

Threeday nodded. "She has visited the southland in secret before, and could likely find the Lammergeier. It is a worthy thought."

Lady Erdys scowled. "She maimed my son and attacked my home. I'd have thought she should be punished, not entrusted with such a mission. But then, you gave her a place on this council, so clearly . . ." She swallowed. "Clearly, the Uncrowned King is forgiving." Olva guessed that Erdys hadn't intended to speak out against the Witch Elf, but Ildorae's status obviously rankled with her. The Witch Elf had won Alf's trust because she too had fought against Lord Bone, and Alf would always trust another veteran of that war over anyone else.

"Where is Ildorae?" asked Derwyn.

"A pitspawn attacked a Witch Elf in the Liberties," said Olva. "She's off hunting for it."

"The gates to the underworld should all be sealed, but relic hunters are like mice," said Threeday. "They gnaw their way in everywhere. And without the Lammergeier and the Beast Lath to keep the spawn of the Pits in check, we may see more incursions from below."

"No. I have mastered Lord Bone's spells of command," said Blaise. "I command the pitspawn. They will not come forth without my permission. So whatever struck down the elf was not a pitspawn."

The Skerrise's head snapped around to stare at Blaise, and the air crackled with some unseen magical conversation – or conflict. Everyone else shifted uncomfortably, the psychic backwash like the pressure in the air before a storm. Only Derwyn seemed unaffected.

"Even Lord Bone's spells," muttered Threeday, "were not infallible."

"Mine are," said Blaise. He glared at the Vatling with such force that Threeday's flesh rippled.

The mood in the room turned sour. It was disheartening after the triumph over Vond and news of victory in Arden.

"I'll speak to Ildorae," said Olva. "What else?"

"The Intercessal churches," said Lord Bessimer, "I move that they be restored."

"The Intercessors have no power here." Blaise sounded irritated. "The churches are pointless."

"I know," replied Bessimer, "that prayers and entreaties go unheard in this city, and that the eyes of the Intercessors cannot see the dark deeds shrouded by the necromiasma. But faith is not transactional. We do not give praise to the Intercessors solely in the hope of reward. Through them, we honour the divine light that is beyond comprehension."

"Your comprehension, maybe," snapped Blaise.

Bessimer reached out a hand to Derwyn. "You say Necrad is to be redeemed, to be made into something worthy. Already, the first of those fleeing the war in Summerswell have arrived, and more will follow. To welcome them, let them give thanks according to the customs of their people. Let your name be heard by the Intercessors, so they might carry word of the redemption of Necrad to the corners of the world."

"To dupes and fools. The Intercessors are tools of our enemy," said Blaise. "We shall not—"

"Excuse me." Erdys stood up, her chair scraping against the floor. "I find myself unwell. I need some fresh air, I think." She hurried out of the chamber.

"Let us all rest a moment," said Olva.

She found Erdys pacing a little way down the hallway.

"Forgive me, Lady Forster," said Erdys, "that was unworthy of me. All the talk of Intercessors and the Witch Elf put me in mind of recent sorrows. I have lost so much, and I fear what is left may slip away too."

"There's nothing to forgive." Olva led Erdys towards a nearby bench. It was strange, she thought – a stranger passing by might have thought them alike. Both she and Erdys, after all, were richly dressed, although Olva's clothing was more after the mode of the Witch Elves, intricate lacework and jewellery instead of the black-dyed woollen cloak and furs worn by Erdys. But they were of the same age, both widowed, both carrying the twin burdens of leadership in an uncertain time and a son who'd walked the edge of the Grey Lands and returned through magic. Indeed, had the fates been a little different, they might have been sisters – Alf had been offered Erdys' hand in marriage by her father Lord Brychan long ago, and he'd turned her down.

More proof, as if I needed it, that Alf's an idiot.

"I cannot breathe in this city," said Erdys, quietly. "It's like an invisible hand's clenching my throat, all the time. I remember when I first came here, only a few weeks after the end of the war, and I thought it was the smoke from the Stone Dragons, and that it would clear. But it never does." She glanced at Olva. "The air is clear in Athar."

"We'll see you home soon enough."

"Is there news of Aelfric?" asked Erdys.

"None I trust." Something in Olva's voice must have given away her fear.

"My father always said that Aelfric was the most fearsome fighter he'd ever seen, and that was without the Spellbreaker."

"Aye."

"I was disappointed when I first met him. I'd heard the songs and I expected some glorious knight, handsome and with the soul of a poet. Instead, my father showed me this . . . hairy giant."

"With the soul of a turnip."

"That's unfair. The soul of a plough-horse, maybe. I always thought the Lammergeier was such a poor name for Aelfric. Vultures are opportunists. Alf avoided opportunity." Erdys sighed. "I should be grateful for that. In his stead, my father married me off to Duna, and whatever his other faults, Duna knew when to put down his sword and live. And I was glad to be done with Summerswell."

That surprised Olva. For all their present similarities, they had come there by very different roads. Olva was the daughter of peasants; Erdys the daughter of lords. Olva had lately donned the costume of a ruler, but Erdys was bred for the role.

"I thought about burning my father's message to Alf," continued Erdys. "They should have named *him* the Lammergeier. A hunched bird, waiting for carrion – that's him. He's sent me many letters over the years. Twenty years of plots and schemes for advancement, and complaining about the other Lords and the elves. He was satisfied to have Duna in place, controlling the New Provinces. And to have me whispering in Duna's ear."

"My marriage," said Olva, "was ordained by the Intercessors. They wanted to bind me, so they'd have a hold on Alf. I didn't know I was in the middle of some unseen scheme. I thought I was just lucky, and I was happy while Galwyn lived. It sounds like you were happy, despite it all."

"I was happy. I was happy to shape the New Provinces as I thought best, and rule as justly as I could. I was happy to be done with the scheming, to be out of Ilaventur and half the world away, where all Brychan could do was send me letters, not ... Nothing more." Erdys took Olva's hand. "I know what my father would say about Idmaer. He'd tell me that I have another heir, and I should do away with the broken one. He'd agree with you that the Intercessors are a lie, the work of the enemy."

"He's been wounded. So has Derwyn. But he'll heal in time," said Olva. Her heart ached for Erdys, yet it hardened at the same time – *I won't let Derwyn lose his mind. I'll hold him together. He won't end up like Idmaer.* "Just be with him. Nothing comforts like a mother's touch. He'll find his way back."

"I pray he has time."

Down the corridor, Olva spotted Torun emerging from the council chamber. "Excuse me a moment," she said to Erdys.

"I might bid you farewell instead. If I ride now, I can reach the edge of the Charnel before nightfall. I have been away too long already."

Olva squeezed Erdys' hand. "Aye, of course. Go quick, and return soon."

Olva caught up with Torun and pulled her into an alcove.

"Where have you been? I haven't seen you in weeks. Is something wrong?"

Torun shook her head, unwilling to speak, but the dwarf looked miserable.

"Something is wrong," said Olva. "Tell me. Is it . . ." She lowered her voice. "Is it to do with Blaise?"

"If it was," said Torun quietly, "what could you do? But no – all is well, save that there is not enough time to do all that needs doing. Unravelling the mysteries of Necrad is the work of many lifetimes, and I've only got the one – and half of that wasted on the wrong path."

Olva knelt down to look the dwarf in the eye, but the dwarf would not meet her gaze. Olva caught the scent of healing cordial on her breath. The smell reminded her of Alf, who practically bathed in the stuff. "Are you hurt?" asked Olva.

"I fell off the Wailing Tower."

Olva gasped in horror, but Torun kept on talking, more to herself than anyone else. "But Blaise saved me. I owe him a debt. All dwarves owe all the Nine a debt. And Aelfric, too. In the Dwarfholt, he praised my work, and convinced my father that what I do has merit. That's a debt too. And I have to pay them all." She looked up at Olva. "Everything's fine. All is in hand."

Still, Olva's stomach sank. She felt as though everything was slipping from her grasp.

As they returned to the council chamber, Olva noticed Derwyn and Lord Bessimer in earnest conversation. The old monk perched on another bench, and her son kneeling beside him. They might have been posed for a painting, *The knight and his confessor.*

Or, *The lord and his son.*

Trust Bessimer, Alf had said. The horrible thought came to her – what if Alf knew exactly what he was doing when he told her to welcome Bessimer. Alf was a fool when it came to the Nine, so what if he *wanted* Peir to return? He barely knew Derwyn, but he mourned Peir like a brother. More than a brother, even – Alf's real brothers had died while he was away, and he'd scarcely asked after them. The Nine were closer to him than family.

It was an absurd thought, horrible and unworthy and twisted. Alf wasn't so duplicitous. He'd never let such a thing come to pass.

But the thought followed her as she returned to the council chamber.

"I have a proposal," said Olva.

"We should finish the discussion of the churches, first," said Bessimer. "They should be rebuilt."

"Lord Bessimer," said Blaise, "let me speak plainly. The Intercessal Church, the College of Wizardry, and the entire realm of Summerswell are all chains forged by the Erlking to mortals. Through chance and the work of the Nine, we command the one city outside the Erlking's influence, which offers a counterbalance to the power he has accumulated since the first dawn. Having broken free of these unseen chains, we shall not forge new links for them. Your suggestion is idiotic."

"Blaise!" said Derwyn. "Lord Bessimer is here at my invitation."

"I do not bar him from this council. I point out that his suggestion is idiotic."

Derwyn began to protest, but Bessimer quietened him with a gesture.

"You're not the first to say such things," said Bessimer, "and at some other time we should talk more of such tales, and what truth is in them. But tell me, do you remember what I said to you and your companions when you came to me in the Crownland twenty years ago?"

"My memory contains spells of such power that they might shatter the sky. I spend every night in study of grimoires that have driven lesser intellects insane. I don't recall trivial anecdotes from half a lifetime ago."

"I do," said Derwyn softly. "I thought you were telling a joke. You said . . . you said a prophet, a general and a lord are all vouchsafed a vision of a dragon's hoard in the midst of a perilous swamp. The prophet marches off alone in search of it, dazzled by visions, and drowns in the mud. The general commands his soldiers to fetch the treasure for him, but they quarrel over how to divide it, and they too perish. But the wise lord rallies his people and they build a causeway into the swamp, and he pays them with a portion of the hoard."

"What possible relevance can this have?" snapped Blaise.

"The wise lord understands that his success depends on bringing his followers with him. You may have cast off the 'unseen chains', as you put it, but others have not. Let them have their comfort."

"Their lies."

"Enough," said Derwyn. "The churches shall be restored. The miasma will keep the Intercessors from spying on us in Necrad, so it does not add to our peril, and it will reassure those who are troubled. The burdens of the ruler are not those of the adventurer. I understand now, I think, why you doubted the Nine when we came to you." He bowed his head. "Thank you for your counsel, Dryten."

Something in the way he spoke was a knife in her heart – that respect, that filial devotion, it wasn't Derwyn.

She had to act.

"My proposal," she stammered. "North. The Uncrowned King

should go north to Castle Duna. To the New Provinces. They're part of this domain too. And Vond's gone north to stir up trouble."

"A worthy idea," said Bessimer. "I might—"

"You're too old to travel," Olva snapped at him. "You said so yourself. I'll go with Derwyn. If we leave now, we can ride with Lady Erdys."

"No," said Blaise. "This too is idiotic. We have won a single victory, but that does not mean we can relent. Necrad is the key, not the New Provinces. Necrad is all that matters."

"If we—" began Olva.

Blaise snarled and hammered his staff onto the ground.

Again, Olva plummeted into a void. She was crushed to a point, a spark of awareness, tumbling for ever into the darkness. She could not scream, could not move, could not *be*. A howling abyss yawned beneath her and around her.

Blaise appeared. The fall stopped. They hung above the infinite.

"Lady Forster, your brother learned to defer to my judgement long ago. The sooner you learn the same lesson, the better."

"Let me out of here!"

"You have not moved." It was true. She *knew* that this was an illusion, that she was really still sitting there in the council chamber, but it felt real. She reached out, and had the sensation of her fingertips brushing against an icy surface, but could not quite get a grip. Olva could see the dim outline of the table before her, she could feel the polished wood of the chair, and the shapes of those around her, like warm shadows, living ghosts. It was seeing the world through a gauzy veil, surfaces rippling and shifting about her. Only the Skerrise was truly present, red eyes watching Olva with distant amusement. The ancient elf had sight beyond sight.

"I need Derwyn here so that I might continue the work of healing," continued Blaise. "If you wish to go to the New Provinces, go, but you will be outside the necromiasma, and you may be watched."

"How long will these healing spells take? Week after week you bring him to the tower, and I see no change in him. He's no better. He's not himself."

"He returned from the dead. Did you think there would be no change?"

"You told me that Lord Bessimer was a danger to Derwyn. You said to keep him at arm's length, and Derwyn's invited him onto the council. Is that making things worse?"

"For Derwyn? Yes. "

"How do we help him?"

"I shall continue as I have done. For your part, remove Bessimer immediately."

He flickered, as if about to depart, then another thought struck him. "The Skerrise is an exceedingly dangerous creature. Do not invite it into the Citadel again."

CHAPTER TWENTY-NINE

After the council, they departed one by one. For all her terrifying reputation, for all Blaise's warning, the Skerrise had said
nothing in the meeting — at least, not aloud. Olva wondered if the
Witch Elf had spoken in the minds of one of the other councillors.
Blaise and Torun returned to the Wailing Tower, and Threeday
slipped away as was his habit.

Only Olva, Derwyn and Bessimer remained in the chamber.
Derwyn rose.

Bessimer reached beneath his seat and placed a wooden box on
the table. "Do you know the king's game?" he said to Derwyn.

"My mother taught it to me. We played it often."

"It is odd for the humbly born to know the game."

"Galwyn Forster was highborn," said Olva.

They retired to the governor's private chambers on the level above.

"This set," said Bessimer as he arranged the pieces, "has been in
my family for centuries. It was a gift from the elves." He stroked the
onyx tiles. "When I entered the monastery, I gave up my wealth and
estates to my cousin. This alone I kept to remind me of my former
station — and of my lost son. Peir and I played every night, until the
night he left. Would you care for a game?"

"I'll play," said Olva, abruptly. She sat down opposite Lord Bessimer. Derwyn fetched a bottle of wine and three goblets.

Bessimer proved to be an expert player, and Olva hadn't played in years. Piece by piece, square by square, he methodically demolished her. The game was not lost yet, but she could tell she was doomed.

"I've played this all my life," said Bessimer, "there is no shame in losing to me."

"I've not lost yet," she snapped, even though she knew it was true.

"You have. The game is quite predictable from this point. Only an error on my part could turn the odds." His finger lingered on a cleric for a moment before pushing it deep into Olva's territory. "The elves play another game. Like this, but different."

"I saw it on the Isle of Dawn. Prince Maedos said it never ends – there's no victory, only degrees of stalemate."

"Quite. But also, there are unseen moves, unexpected powers." He tapped Olva's knight. "In the king's game, we know how this piece can move. It is predictable. All knights are the same. But if this knight was your brother Aelfric—" He lifted Olva's knight and moved it across the board, knocking his own pieces aside as the knight stormed past them, right to Bessimer's king.

"And what game are we playing here?"

"An excellent question." Bessimer began to set the pieces up again. He held up the tower. "And if this were the wizard Blaise, what would the game be like? In Summerswell, he is the one of the Nine they fear the most. The Lammergeier is invincible in battle, and Berys has her intrigues, but the wizard is beyond either of them. You know that Lord Bone was a mortal wizard, once? He went to Necrad in search of magic, and became a monster."

"Blaise isn't a monster."

"Not yet," said Bessimer, "But he respects only power, and as his power grows, there are fewer checks on him. I worry about what he might become." The tower was the last piece to be put into place. The game started again.

"Der," said Olva, "you've spent longer with Blaise than either of us. What would you say of him?"

"All he talks about are his studies, and trying to unlock all the spell books that Lord Bone left behind. I don't think he'd ever leave his library if he could avoid it. If he's a monster, he's a bookworm."

Olva made her first move. "You should go back to Summerswell and tell your fellow Lords that. Tell them what you've seen here. Tell them Blaise is only a danger to them because they tried to kill him. Alf will come home – he never wanted to fight against Summerswell."

"And the rebels? Berys and her allies? You cheered the fall of Arden, and there are tales of civil war elsewhere. Their rebellion has met with initial success, but without support from Necrad, they cannot succeed – and they will inflict terrible suffering as they grow more desperate. Would you turn on them?" Bessimer rubbed his bald pate. "Say, for example, we offer this bargain: the Lords acknowledge the Uncrowned King as Lord of Necrad, and cede the lands north of the Dwarfholt to him. Aelfric is for ever exiled from Summerswell as punishment for the murder of Prince Maedos."

"Alf didn't murder Maedos!" interrupted Derwyn.

"No matter. In exchange, Necrad makes these concessions. First, you deny support to Berys' rebellion, and urge the rebels to surrender. In the most part, they will be exiled, and no doubt many would join you in the north. Second, you restore the trade in magic relics. And third, the Church of the Intercessors remains the recognised faith in both realms. The churches in Necrad and the New Provinces are restored, the clergy are protected, and the light of the Intercessors remains undiminished. How would Necrad respond?"

"Would you bring this message to your fellow Lords?" asked Olva.

"I would."

"Then I think it would be acceptable." *If it means you leaving, and an end to your influence over Derwyn.*

Bessimer moved his knight, pinning her king. "I think, Lady

Forster, that you are telling me what I would like to hear, and that your heart is not truly committed to such a bargain. I have played this game, too, for a long time."

Olva flushed and shoved her seat back, ashamed of being so transparent. "More wine," she said, stumbling as she rose. Derwyn steadied her.

"It is not her decision." It was Derwyn's voice, but it was not Derwyn who spoke. She could not bear to look at him. "I am the Uncrowned King, and I would take this bargain, if it meant peace. I would go with you to Summerswell to bargain with the Lords, and even to the Everwood to speak to the Erlking – if the Princess Laerlyn vouches for my safety, and Sir Aelfric is at my right hand. For Lord Bone is gone, and the old age is passing, and I shall speak for the one to come."

Olva stepped into the anteroom, pressed her head against the wall, and wept. There were tears of pride mixed with the sorrow, the knowledge that she had lost her son to destiny. He would go, as Alf had gone, where she could not follow.

Perhaps he would make the new age he spoke of, Necrad redeemed and turned to the light.

Perhaps he would be slain by unseen hands.

Either way, she could not protect him any more.

She composed herself, wiped her eyes, smoothed her elven dress, and returned.

"I'll—" she began, but she would never finish that sentence.

Bessimer's blood gushed out across the board, the flood toppling all the knights and clerics, kings and pawns. Embedded in his chest was a dagger – her dagger! – stained red with the high Lord's blood.

Time seemed to slow, each moment punctuated by the rush of Bessimer's blood, spurting, slowing. She should call for help. She pressed her hand to the wound, feeling the sticky heat, the slowing of his heartbeat. She took a hesitant step towards him, hands out-stretched, unsure what to do. Bessimer pawed at her, trying to speak, fluid bubbling in his throat.

Derwyn! Where was Derwyn? He could work the same healing-magic he'd done before, Peir's spirit moving in him! He could save Bessimer!

"Derwyn!" she called. "Derwyn, where are you?"

He emerged from a side room, his face a mask of horror. He stopped at the threshold. "Mother," he said, "what have you done?"

The words – the accusation! – seemed to shatter the ground where she stood. Everything was breaking. How could her son, her Derwyn, think that of her? She fought for words. They came out like animalistic grunts.

"I didn't! I didn't touch him! I wasn't—"

He raised his voice. "Guards! Come quick! Lord Bessimer has been murdered!"

The fear that she had lived with so long, the fear born of losing Galwyn, of losing her loved ones, of death, of life – it exploded within her, sprouted within her, burst her heart. Guards hammered at the door. Derwyn grabbed at her. She stumbled away, towards the window.

Necrad spread beneath her, and the streets surged like a living thing.

PART FOUR

CHAPTER THIRTY

"Shut up," said the sword.

"What?" said the monk. Bright summer sun bathed the green fields of Arshoth, but the hedgerows offered shade to pilgrims and wanderers alike. In the distance, a river was a string of brilliant jewels in the sunlight.

"You keep humming."

"I'm not humming."

"You are," said the sword. "It's irritating."

"Why would I be humming?" said the monk. He had many miles still to go on the road to Ilaventur, and the land was in turmoil. He'd passed through a deserted village earlier that day, and another the day before. Despite the fair weather, fear hung over the countryside. Lords fought one other, and did not protect their people. The common folk were forgotten. Brigands waylaid travellers on the Road. Why, it was rumoured that one particularly vicious band of thieves held the bridge up ahead.

It would be *terrible* if they attacked a kindly old monk.

"I am hardly one to quail at slaughter, but I was forged to slay kings and shatter cities. This is beneath me."

"It's called doing good," muttered Alf.

"It's called delay. You could have been in Ilaventur months

ago. Instead, you meander. This errantry does not profit your cause, wielder."

"Seems to me," said Alf, "that the rebellion's doing well enough without my aid. They've got Westermarch and Arden, and half of Ellscoast. Ilaventur too. And there'll be aid from Necrad any day now, with Blaise brewing up mischief in Lord Bone's old vats."

"And when it comes, wielder, will you fight alongside that dark host? How long can you hold this supposed high ground?"

"I'll be in Ilaventur in my own good time," muttered Alf. "And I'll see what must be done then."

"Hiding," said the sword. "Like a child. You soothe yourself by play-acting. Little deeds of little worth."

"Quiet now," said Alf, "you're not going to spoil my mood."

"Maybe there are some rats in a cellar you can fight."

Perhaps the sword was right, but under that summer sunshine, Alf felt unburdened. He was the Lammergeier no longer, and for a few weeks at least, the world could attend to itself. If he went to Ilaventur now, Brychan and Berys would send him into battle, and the red dream of slaughter would come to pass. He remembered the lives he'd taken in the warehouse in Arden. It would be ten thousand times that, the black sword singing amid ruin.

Perhaps it would come to that. But Alf still held on to hope that Derwyn's vision would win out. The Uncrowned King would send help, and the Lords would quail and sue for peace. There'd be two kingdoms again, north and south, and the north kingdom would be a testament to the work of the Nine and the wisdom of Peir, a shining beacon instead of a city of darkness.

He imagined the voices of his companions as he walked. It was like old times, the first adventures of the Nine when they'd wandered in the Mulladales and the hills of Ilaventur, and delved dungeons near the mouth of the river. Back before they were legends.

He could hear Peir (who now sounded like Derwyn in his

memories) talking about that shining city; he could imagine Berys' cynical thrusts as she attempted to puncture Peir's grand visions, Jan's quiet counter-arguments. Thurn reminding them that the Wilder must have a share in any future, or Blaise muttering that they could arrange the world as they saw fit as long as they left him alone to study. And Alf and Gundan and Lath would trudge along behind the clever ones, looking for the next alehouse.

And what of Laerlyn? The elf always stood a little outside the company. Aloof, Berys said, but she'd always seemed so sad to Alf, burdened by an inevitable future. Death would take the rest of the Nine, and leave her alone. Would she have shared Peir's vision? She'd spoken of her plan to plant a life-tree in Necrad and dwell there for eternity. Would she have been a custodian of that shining city? Or was her friendship always a ruse?

Berys' voice in his imagination. *Her brother tortured Derwyn and schemed to conquer Necrad. Her father is the secret ruler of the world. She put an arrow through your heart. You are a fool if you think it was anything but a ruse.*

He wanted to be a fool for a while more.

The mad monk arrived at the stone bridge. The pillars that supported its wide span had been raised by the Old Kingdom. Beneath, the waters ran merrily on their way south to join the Great River. Armed men perched on the walls like carrion crows. A banner flapped in the breeze at the far end of the bridge, but the men bore no signs or badges. Alf counted them. Five here, probably twice as many on the far side of the bridge, where there was a cluster of houses and a watchtower.

Ahead was a cart, laden with salvaged belongings, drawn by a tired old horse. A family – wife, two grown daughters, three younger children – huddled by the cart while the father bargained with the bandit chief.

"We have nothing worth taking," he said, "other thieves already robbed us on the Road. Let us pass, I beg you."

"Why, it sounds like the rest of Summerswell has fallen into chaos," replied the chief. "A sad tale, indeed. Here we still have the rule of law, and no one will trouble you while you are under our protection. But it is also the law that travellers from other provinces must have valid letters of passage."

The man's face lit up. "I do! My cousin – he is a weaver in Eavesland. He offered to take my daughter as an apprentice. His guild master sent us a letter of passage." He took out a piece of paper bound with a wooden ring and unrolled it reverently. "He sent it to me a year ago. Look, it says that she and an escort may travel the Road freely. I know it says only a single escort, sir, but please, let us stay together." His hand shook as he handed the letter over.

"Your cousin's wealthy, then?"

"He's had good fortune, thank the Intercessors. And this war's spared the Eavesland."

"He must think highly of your family to send all the way to Arden for an apprentice."

"He came to Arden for the fair, two years ago, and they met there. She's blessed with talent, he said."

"And where's this prodigy?"

"Kerla." One of the two older girls stepped forward.

"Well, we can't stand in the way of her future. Come here, girl." Nervously, Kerla obeyed the bridge-guard. One of the bandits hopped down off the wall and pulled the girl out of reach of her family. Alf cursed under his breath – having to avoid hitting the girl would make the fight harder. But not much harder.

"You'll let us pass?" asked the father.

The bandit leader sucked his teeth, and appeared to find some juicy morsel lodged there, for he looked unduly pleased with himself. "Her and one escort, the letter says. Now, if you're her escort, you can cross too."

"I . . . I can't leave my family behind."

"Well now. If your daughter's as talented as you say, then I'm sure the weavers of Eavesland will pay us a penny or two for her safe passage. The rest of you, begone. You're clogging up my bridge! And look, there's a monk behind you. Hail, holy father. No doubt you've got coin for the crossing."

"I do." Alf leaned on the cloth-wrapped Spellbreaker as if the sword was a walking stick as he shuffled forward. He held out his hand to the bandit chief.

"A man who doesn't waste my time," said the chief, reaching out to take Alf's coin.

In truth, what he said was "a man who doesn't—" and the last words were lost in the crunching noise of the man's nose breaking as Alf seized his wrist and solidly headbutted him. As he fell, Alf swung Spellbreaker and caught two of the bandits sitting on the wall with the flat of the cloth-wrapped blade. Both tumbled backwards off the bridge.

Two left. One came at Alf with a spear. At least he knew enough to use the pointy end. Alf grabbed the haft and slammed the butt into the bandit's face with a skull-cracking crunch. So now Alf had a spear, and the bandit did not have much of a nose.

One left. The last bandit pressed a knife to Kerla's throat. "I'll kill her. I swear, I'll kill her if you come closer. Put down the spear."

Alf let the spear clatter to the ground.

He nodded at Alf's cloth-wrapped bundle. "And that stick."

"Stick!" The sword's muffled voice was indignant. The bandit's eyes widened in surprise – and that split second of distraction was enough for Alf to tackle the rogue. He forced the knife away from Kerla, then lifted the smaller man and dragged him over to the edge of the parapet.

"Over you go!"

"My master will kill you for this!"

Alf paused on the edge. "And who's that?"

"Sir Erich of—"

Splash.

Another eight came running from the far end of the bridge. Alf flung the spear, and it stuck fast in the ground just in front of the lead bandit. He skidded to a halt, staring in horror at the juddering spear an inch from his face, then lost his nerve and fled.

"Sir Erich, was it?" muttered Alf as he picked up Spellbreaker. "I think I'll pay Sir Erich a visit."

"You're humming again."

This tale is told of the mad monk.

Sir Erich's castle lay but an afternoon's journey east of the bridge, but it took the monk three days to get there. Travellers on the bridge were not the only victims of Sir Erich's corrupt retainers; everywhere the monk heard complaints about greedy reeves and roaming gangs of soldiers. When he came to Sir Erich's castle, he arrived at the head of a mob. Sir Erich was not at home, and his seneschal initially refused to listen to the crowd of petitioners. Then the mad monk knocked on the gate with his cloth-wrapped stick, and lo! the gates were blasted open.

Some of the castle guards were the same brigands that the monk had thrown in the river, and they quailed at the sight of him, and counselled the seneschal not to cross this militant cleric who had defeated them all so handily. For his part, the monk restrained the mob, and ensured they took only fair recompense from the castle. Those soldiers and clerks who had abused their office or committed offences, he disarmed and ordered that they should leave Sir Erich's land, and never return.

He restrained, also, his magic staff, who counselled that he slaughter the miscreants, and the one who had called the staff a stick be impaled on a stick, so that he might know the difference.

When justice had been done, the monk continued on his wandering. It is said that when Sir Erich returned to his castle, he fell to his knees and begged forgiveness for his neglectful ways.

*

"And where's your master?" demanded Alf when the looting was done.

"He has gone to battle," answered the seneschal. "He was summoned to the muster of Ilaventur."

"Was he now? Show me the letter."

Like Erdys' letter, it was written in the elegant script produced by a magic quill owned by Lord Brychan. It rankled that Sir Erich was one of Brychan's men, but he put that irritation aside. When the war was won, there'd be time to deal with such unworthy folk. Alf was not so naive as to believe that everyone on his side had to be a moral exemplar – Gundan would have laughed at the notion – but it was shameful that Brychan had elevated someone like Erich.

The letter commanded knights loyal to Brychan to muster at Harnshill with all haste. It warned that the army of the Eavesland was on the way north via the Crossings of Avos. Of all the provinces of Summerswell, the Eavesland was closest to the Everwood. It was the only province that Alf had never visited, but he knew its reputation well. The people who dwelt there were known for their beauty and grace, but there was strength there too. The knights of the Eavesland were second only to the paladins of Arshoth; Blaise had spoken warily of the power of Eavesland enchanters. The Lords of Eavesland, too, were famously secretive, rarely leaving their home province even to attend the council in the Crownland. That land belonged as much to the elves as to the mortals who dwelt there.

If the army of the Eavesland was on the march, then it meant the Erlking had entered the war directly, and Alf's errantry was at an end.

The letter was dated three days ago.

"I'm going to need a horse," said Alf.

As the squires saddled the best horse remaining in the stable, Alf watched the banished guards troop out of the castle. The crowd jeered at them.

"They'll come back after we leave," muttered Spellbreaker, "and take their revenge. You should at least have killed the leaders."

"Maybe they'll come slinking back, but not soon, and they won't be in charge."

"Evil must be utterly destroyed or it will rise again, and sooner than you think. I should know."

"If I see true evil, I destroy it. How many pitspawn did I kill? How many vampires? We killed Lord Bone. But those lads ... they're not evil. Greedy, aye. Stupid, aye, but I look at them and I think, that could have been me, if I hadn't met the Nine. A big brute hanging around the Mulladales. I can't say for sure that I'd have done any better."

"How I wish that were true, wielder. If you were truly so venal and easily led, then I could make more use of you. But you cling to illusions so strongly that you are a useless leaden lump to me." Spellbreaker's demon eye peeked out through a gap in the cloth. "Do we have to ride a horse? Horses don't like me."

"Not too fond of me, either." Few horses were comfortable with Alf's considerable weight, and he'd never learned to fight properly on horseback.

"I could summon a dreadworm. The miasma over Arden is near enough to birth one."

"I've another few days of being dead left to me. I don't want to waste 'em."

In the guise of the monk, Alf rode east towards Harnshill, through the hills of Ilaventur. This landscape reminded him of his youth in the Mulladales, although Ilaventur was grander — its towns older and richer, its roads in better repair. In ancient days, forest covered all this land, until the hungry axes of the Old Kingdom cut down most of the trees. The forest endured in inaccessible places, in ravines and on steep hills, in dark copses. A land for outlaws and ambushes.

Back twenty or more years ago, the Nine had come this way.

They'd fought against one of Lord Bone's hosts, a thrust that raced past Ilaventur and was aimed at the crossings of the river. They'd harassed invaders from hiding places in the woods, living like bandits, until Brychan – the Lord's heir back then, not yet come into his own – gathered enough strength to meet the invaders in battle. A handful of Laerlyn's kin came to Brychan's aid in that fight, too – Alf remembered the grey-clad elves emerging from the shadow of the trees, wraiths in the morning mist. Silver arrows like shooting stars. Mortals and elves, fighting side by side against the dark.

Even then, it had been enchanted, unreal, like he'd stepped into a story.

Now, it seemed like the dream of a better world that they'd fumbled.

He could see what was coming. His fate was more certain than any prophecy; had it been shown to him in the waters of a grail, that revelation would have offered no greater clarity. The army from the Eavesland would consist of a host of mortal knights, augmented with both Witch Elf charmstones and the subtle magic of the Everwood. All loyal to the Lords of Eavesland, all devoted followers of the Intercessors, their faith unshakeable. All certain that their cause was just, and that the rebels were thieves, demon-cultists, thralls of darkness.

With these knights would ride a few elves – only a handful, but a sizeable portion of the unbound Wood Elves. A dozen elf-knights, at most. And a few more elven archers in the wood, drawn from the Wandering Companies who roamed all over Summerswell.

He wondered if Laerlyn would be there.

And on the other side, there'd be whatever forces Brychan mustered. They'd have their charmstones too, thanks to Berys. The battlefield would shape the conflict with hideous inevitability. The same hills, the same little woods as the last time would dictate strategy. The outcome would be determined by courage and magic, and magic was the greater.

Unless the spells were broken.

*

He dismounted and led the horse off the road, down into one of the wooded ravines.

"Where are we going?" asked Spellbreaker. Alf ignored the sword. He carefully picked his way down the slope, stepping over stones and twisted roots until he came to the bower sheltered by an overhang. The Nine had camped here once. He tied the horse to a tree, then found the very spot where he'd slept all those years ago. A mossy rock for a pillow. He even found the remnants of a campfire, but it must have been left by some more recent traveller. Still, it made the years fall away for a moment, as if he might look up and see Thurn or Gundan or Jan back again.

"Had my master known you wretches were hiding in this den, he would have sent a flight of dread knights down to murder you all in your sleep," said the sword.

"Your lot nearly found us." Alf brought the sword over to an ivy-covered shape. It resembled an overgrown stump, but slanted evening light burnished twisted metal beneath the leaves.

"A hunter-golem," said the sword. "Let me see it properly."

Alf unwrapped the sword more fully. When it was functioning, the golem had stood seven feet tall, a thing of spikes and iron ribs and rune-plates. In places, around the eyes and the summoning-plate at its heart, there were traces of delicate Witch Elf artistry, but for the most part it was a creature of Lord Bone's design – hideously functional. It was not built in the shape of any known beast, but was instead the essence of a predator, stripped down to teeth and claws, slavering muzzle and burning eyes.

"My master had such high hopes for these," said the sword, "and it didn't eviscerate even one of you. Alas!"

"It came creeping down in the middle of the night, when we were all asleep. But Laerlyn was on watch, and she saved us all." He reached in and tapped across the demon-summoning plate that once animated the monster. "She struck here with an arrow. Hell of a shot in the dark. A fraction of an inch either way, and it'd have been on top of us." The monster's jaws were still sharp. "She saved us all."

"When my master died," remarked Spellbreaker, "all his spells died with him."

"Aye. Hundreds of these things up in Ellscoast, all dead as this one."

"I am akin to these golems," said the sword. "I thought that when you slew Lord Bone, I would die too. Snuffed out in the same blow."

"You never told me that."

"We did not talk in those days, wielder, and even now, the finer points of magic are quite beyond you. Let me see the plate, please."

"Please?" Alf laughed. "First time you've ever used that word." He reversed his grip on the sword, holding it by the blade so he could insert its hilt into the hollow ribcage of the dead golem. The fiery glow of Spellbreaker's eye made it seem like the golem's heart was afire again.

"The elf broke the plate," said the sword. "There's a crack right down the middle."

"You sound disappointed."

"Merely idle curiosity."

Alf withdrew the sword and planted in the ground next to him. "So, why didn't you die with Bone?"

"There are ways," said Spellbreaker, "for spells to outlive their maker. Sigils bound to physical objects or tokens, constant renewal by some source of magic. Or if a spell is cast with a specific intent in mind, a singular purpose, then the spell might endure until the purpose is fulfilled."

"And what's your purpose, then?"

"Why, serving you, of course," sneered Spellbreaker. "Aiding you in your war."

"Slaughter," said Alf. "Killing. That's all we come down to." He kicked the hulk of the golem.

"Many who live deserve death, wielder, and you are well suited to deal it."

"I met Death," said Alf, "Thurn's daughter. I told her that she could choose her own path, that she didn't have to be what everyone said she was. I'm too old to change myself. I know that. I thought that Peir – that Derwyn – could put me on a new path." He looked the sword in the eye. "Tell me truthfully – you looked into Derwyn's soul. You said ... you said the pieces of Peir were in him. Do you think there's a chance he can make it all worth the cost?"

"You ask a sword if slaughter can be justified?" A cold laugh rang from the blade. "I am without a moral code, wielder. I delight in bloodshed. I glory in destruction. But I am bound to answer truthfully, and so I say: I see hope in Derwyn."

The horse whinnied in alarm, and Alf heard the crack of twigs underfoot. He threw the cloth cover back on the sword just as a group of three travellers emerged into the ravine. In the lead was a grey-haired old woman, leaning on a well-used spear. Behind her came a scowling, suspicious man, his face battle-scarred, eyes hooded. It was the third who stepped forward, arms open.

"My friend, we are but three Roadfellows on our way to Eavesland. My name is Rhuel; the fair maiden there is Magga. This stout fellow we call Bor. May we share your camp tonight?"

CHAPTER THIRTY-ONE

T en minutes' worth of conversation with the self-proclaimed poet was enough to erode Alf's restraint, and if Spellbreaker had been within reach, he'd have taken up the sword and cleaved Rhuel in two. But the sword was where he'd left it, stuck in the earth over by the remains of the golem, and Alf was sitting by the campfire.

Rhuel's two companions stayed quiet, apart from the occasional cackle from Magga, but Rhuel made up for all that and more. In short order, Alf learned that the other three travellers had escaped the ruin of Arden – Rhuel luridly described the walking dead roused by the necromiasma – and fled. They'd taken a different route to Alf along the main Road south, whereas Alf had gone through the Crownland and part of Ellscoast. Still, their story was familiar to him, for the war now touched every part of Summerswell. "This rebellion will be the doom of us all if it is not put down," intoned Rhuel. "I fear the blessed Intercessors might withdraw their favour and let the wheel of fate spin at random, and there should be neither meaning nor justice left to us. Let us pray for a quick victory for Summerswell."

It didn't help that Rhuel larded everything with references to the Intercessors, as if trying to convince Alf that he was a fellow theologian. Alf, who had about as much understanding of the inner workings of faith as he did about the finer points of poetry, just grunted every so often, which only encouraged Rhuel to keep talking, building ever grander cathedrals of ornate verbiage, sentences that soared to such ineffably effulgent heights that Alf was never sure if they were statements or questions or entire philosophical tracts.

Rhuel lounged by the fire, sipping wine from a wooden cup. ("We stole this, I fear, from a tavern near Albury Cross. Please, Brother Stone, join me in this libation. If you share this wine, then surely the sin of theft shall be washed away, for it shall become an offering to the Church and thus taking it becomes virtuous." And Alf would grunt again, and Rhuel took that as permission to pour Alf a cup and continue talking.) While the poet talked, Alf kept an eye on the other two in case they discovered the wrapped form of Spellbreaker. He wasn't worried about the sword being stolen, but he didn't want to be the Lammergeier again. Not yet.

He wished that he'd chosen a different disguise – although he suspected that Rhuel would have talked to merchant, messenger or mercenary with as much verve as he conversed with a monk. It would only have been a shift of tiresome metaphor.

Magga peered at Alf through the smoke of the cooking fire. "You seen Necrad, then, Brother Stone?"

Alf had introduced himself as Brother Stone. Lying was not among his strengths. He fumbled for a reply. "A long time ago. I was an initiate at the monastery at Staffa. But I quarrelled with the Abbess there, and so I went a-wandering."

"Smelled it on you. I can always tell." She stirred the pot morosely. "Leastways, I could. Now half of Summerswell has the stink. More work for my spear, yes, but it's hard to sleep at night, knowing what's out there in the darkness. No safe place any more."

"Pay no attention to her dour prognostication," said Rhuel. "I am confident that the true Lords of Summerswell, armoured in righteousness, shall put down this treachery and restore the land to rightness."

"That's not what you said last week," muttered the third man, "when you were talking to those Westermarchers. You said you were committed to the cause of justice. You tried to volunteer me to go fight with 'em in Arshoth."

A pained look crossed Rhuel's face. "My dear Bor, if recent months have taught me nothing else, it is the importance of knowing one's audience."

Bor. The name sounded familiar to Alf. He tried to recall where he'd heard it before. He rolled it around inside his head.

Rhuel turned back to Alf. "Forgive me, brother. You understand, of course, that these are dangerous times, and the Road is full of dangerous men. I myself suffered a grievous wound only a few months ago, and would have perished if not for my companions here. One must sometimes profess things one does not believe to avoid needless peril. Rest assured that—"

"I don't care what you think," said Alf, "as long as there's no trouble here tonight."

Magga picked up her spear and thrust it, Wilder-fashion, into the ground opposite the wrapped form of Spellbreaker. It was a gesture that signified the campfire was neutral ground, but it didn't reassure Alf. The old dead-ender was entirely too perceptive for his liking.

"That," said Rhuel, "is a remarkably enlightened and generous sentiment, holy father. You are a font of mercy towards the misguided of all persuasions. Now, while Magga finishes your meal, perhaps you would care for a song? I am sure your generosity of spirit extends to patronage of the arts."

Alf dug into his pocket, and found he had a coin. "All right."

"What song would you like? *The Song of the Nine*? *The Breaking of the Dawn*?"

"Know any songs of the Uncrowned King?"

Rhuel frowned. "I've heard rumours from Magga here, and I know that some second-rate Crownland poets have composed ditties on that theme, but I must confess I don't know—"

Magga began to sing. Her voice was scratchy and discordant, and she sang in the tongue of the Witch Elves. The eerie song echoed around the little dell, and stirred the shadows as if wraiths nested there. Alf saw the dim red light of Spellbreaker's eye beneath the cloth binding; the sword was listening.

Alf spoke only a few words of *enhedrai*, but he caught the gist of the song. It was not about Derwyn or Peir, or any mortal at all. It spoke of elder days, of the first sundering of the elves. He caught the name of Amerith, the eldest of the Witch Elves, and mention of the Erlking. The song was a sorrowful one, anger mixed with regret, and so ancient it made Alf feel lost, as if this little dell was an island in a flowing river, and that he would emerge from it to discover that a thousand years had passed and everything he knew had been washed away.

Magga fell silent. Rhuel coughed and shifted uncomfortably, irritated at being upstaged. "Our Magga is full of surprises. Her cooking, I fear, is on a par with her singing."

Alf took out the coin. It was a Witch Elf coin from Necrad. He laid it on a stone by the fire. "Well, ye've earned that anyway."

The third man, the quiet one, flinched at the sight of the coin before Rhuel snatched it up.

After eating, they talked of the day to come. Rhuel talked of various inns and roadhouses along the way, comparing the merits of each, and it took Alf a while to work out that the trio were heading the same way he was going.

"I wouldn't take the Avos road," warned Alf. "There'll be fighting there, soon. An army's come up from the Eavesland, and the knights of Ilaventur mustered at Harroskir to meet them. I'd not go that way, if I were you."

"My!" said Rhuel. "Now that shall be a battle worthy of song. If Eavesland prevails, then it shall cut Ilaventur off from Westermarch and divide the rebels in two. If Ilaventur wins the day, then the

Crownland shall be surrounded and the rebels will likely secure everything north of the river save holy Arshoth. The fate of all Summerswell may be decided by that one battle." Rhuel's eyes glittered. "I'm almost tempted to go and watch – from a safe distance, of course. To bear witness to the moment of destiny, when the wheel turns. When one great power founders, and another rises."

"And to be the first to write a song for the victors, is it?" cackled Magga.

"We're not going that way," said Bor. "Tomorrow, we'll go back west through Arshoth. Take the long Road."

"Ah well," said Rhuel. "I shall hear tidings of the battle, one way or another."

"I hope they all lose," said Bor. "Lords and rebels alike. To hell with 'em all."

"You're a fighting man," said Alf, "how come you've not found employment?"

"A man can't fight magic."

Alf snorted. "Is that what you think? That it's all predetermined? That our fates are written in the stars for wizards to read, and prophets to retell? I've killed—" He caught himself. "Wizards have been killed. The Nine slew Lord Bone, and he was the greatest wizard who ever lived. No, you fight magic the same way you fight any other foe. With the right weapon, the right friends, and courage."

"What would a monk know about fighting?" said Bor, angrily.

"Maybe," said Alf, "I wasn't always a monk." He stared at Bor for a moment, until the other man dropped his gaze.

Rhuel yawned loudly. "And I was not always a penniless minstrel of hedgerow and forest glade, going to my bed of roots and stones. Do you know, Brother Stone, that I once slept in the very bed of the Bishop of Claen? And that I recited my poetry before the High Lord of the Crownland and the Master of the College Arcane? Fate may have brought all of us low, but have faith, and we shall rise again."

*

Magga found a sheltered nook to sleep in; Sir Rhuel's snoring sounded false and theatrical, like a parody of a sleeper. Alf and Bor stared at each other across the embers.

Alf had finally remembered where he'd heard the name before.

"Bor, isn't it?"

"Aye."

"From what province?"

"What does it matter?" croaked Bor. He took a sip of water to moisten his throat.

"Rootless, then. Bor the Rootless."

"Some call me that." He bent over to put his cup back on the ground.

"Were you up the Mulladales harvest time last year?"

Bor froze, the cup caught halfway. "That's a different man you're thinking of."

"Is it now?"

Alf stood and crossed the glade to where Spellbreaker waited. He drew the sword from the ground, but left it wrapped in its shroud. He sat back down, the sword across his lap. He slipped his hand beneath the cloth to benefit from the sword-sight. Alf watched Bor scratch nervously at his neck, his gaze flickering between the weapon on Alf's lap and his own sword.

How long did it take you to work out that he was the same one who visited your sister in Ersfel? whispered the sword in Alf's mind. *I guessed it as soon as I first saw him. Guilt marks him like a suppurating wound.*

"It's my habit," said Bor, "to watch for the first part of the night. You can get some proper sleep before we part company."

"I'm not that tired," said Alf. "I'll sit up awhile."

Kill him. It cannot be a coincidence that you've crossed paths. Fate has been woven here by the Intercessors.

"Suit yourself," said Bor. He stood abruptly, and walked into the darkness, tripping over rocks. Alf watched the other man search amid his belongings. The rogue's sword was right there, within reach.

Kill him, wielder. For what he did to your sister, if nothing else.

"He was tricked," whispered Alf.

He betrayed her in Ellsport. He gave her into the hands of Prince Maedos.

That was true. Alf's grip tightened around the sword. He could feel the blade's bloodlust rising, and his own slow rumbling wrath gathering to match it. He would wait until Bor picked up his own sword. He'd give the other man a fighting chance.

A fighting chance? Against me?

To Alf's surprise, Bor knelt before him.

"I want to confess," said Bor. "I want you to take my confession to the Intercessors."

"I'm not a cleric," protested Alf.

"No, Brother Stone. But you're holy, and it's . . . I want to confess." Bor's face twisted. "I'm not one for faith. Honestly, fuck the clerics, and the bishops and archons, and the Intercessors and the Erlking and all of it. But I want to confess, all right?"

"I don't have a grail." Alf remembered Peir kneeling just over there, twenty years ago. Jan filled her simple wooden grail with water from a stream, and called on the spirits to intercede and guard Peir's soul as she took his confession.

"Here. Take this." Bor pressed a cloth-bound object into Alf's hands. Alf unwrapped it. It was a jewelled grail of considerable worth looted from some chapel.

Do not do this, wielder. You may not be a sanctified cleric, but the Intercessors are hunting for you. Pouring water into that grail opens a window to the wraith-world. You do not know what would espy you from the other side.

Alf put the grail aside. "All right, then. Confess."

"I'm a thief. A cut-throat. A blood trader. A coward, too. You said a man could fight magic if he had a weapon and friends by his side. I've never had any of those things, and magic broke me. I've seen princes and heroes, and they're all false. They treated me worse than a dog." He looked up at Alf. "Everyone in this world's a bastard.

Elves and mortals and dwarves – they're all bastards. Even the heroes are bastards dressed up with pretty words. Tell me there's something better on the other side."

The Intercessors are elven lies too. Why, you won't have to use me to destroy this wretch, wielder. Tell him there is no hope and break him.

"Is that what you believe?" asked Alf out loud.

Spellbreaker answered: *I am a sword. I cut away illusion. There is only power.*

Bor couldn't bring himself to speak, but only nodded desperately.

Alf looked for the words to refute both of them. It was tempting to give in to the same darkness. He'd dreamed, sometimes, of walking into the Pits of Necrad and never returning. He had power, even though he'd never asked for it, never cultivated it, and never wanted it. It meant little to him. What had he clung to all these years?

He came alive in battle. He knew who he was in battle. In those wild bright moments, he knew power and purpose, and everything became clear. Give him a foe and a sword and a fight to win, and nothing else mattered until the final blow. But it was the slow times between that baffled and wearied him. What was he without the fight?

He let go of Spellbreaker, and looked around the darkened dell with something other than sword-sight.

"Pay no mind to the Intercessors," said Alf, slowly. "They're no holier than anything else. They've got power, aye, but power isn't enough. Listen, there's light if you look for it. It's rare and it's fragile, but it's there. I saw it when I was young, and I've been fighting to keep hold of it ever since. Look to your friends."

"I don't—" said Bor.

"The Road makes friends of us all, especially in dark times," said Alf, "and you've travelled far with these companions. I can't absolve you, Bor the Rootless. You want forgiveness, you earn it. Now get up. Holiness isn't in your knees."

Bor scrambled upright. For a moment, he tensed as if about to turn and run, but instead he nodded quickly.

"I'm going to get some rest now," said Alf, "wake me for the next watch."

But it was the sword who woke him, intruding on his dreamless sleep.

I warned you! We are discovered!

Alf leaped up, hot silver of battle flooding his veins, driving out fatigue. He plucked Spellbreaker from the ground and cast aside its shroud. He looked and saw—

—nothing. The dell was unchanged. Rhuel was still snoring away, Magga was still in her sheltered nook, and Bor – Bor had fallen asleep sitting up, sword in hand. He'd watched through most of the night. But there were no enemies to be seen, no elves or enemy soldiers descending the slope from the Road above, no monsters to be slain.

"Where?"

I can sense an Intercessor, wielder. It is invisible even to me, but I can feel it. When it gathers its power, it will become manifest.

Alf scanned the treeline, watching for any movement. Intercessors were elf-spirits, so he guessed it would be like a wraith. In his years in Necrad, he'd trained himself to ignore the fluttering spectral tatters. Wraiths were utterly powerless over the physical world, and could be driven away with a candle or a broom.

Intercessors were another matter.

No attack came. No divine force struck Alf down.

Then, amid the trees, he saw a flickering light. It bobbed amid the ferns and bushes, glimmering like an errant star. It reminded him of a dog snuffling in search of a scent. It lingered by Bor for moment.

"Jan?" muttered Alf. It didn't feel like Jan.

It is an Intercessor, wielder. You must attack first. My steel can bite spirits if you strike true.

Keeping his eye fixed on the light, Alf bent down. His fingers brushed against the grail, and his waterskin. He pulled out the stopper with his teeth, and splashed a little water into the sacred bowl. Light welled up, and at the same time the will-o'-the-wisp waxed brighter. Alf braced himself, but no attack came. Instead, it bounded forward, and the trickle of water in the grail sizzled and steamed away, emptying the bowl in an instant. The wisp danced back up the slope a little way, then down again. Up and down and up again, dancing on the threshold.

It urged him to follow.

It might be a trap, said the sword, but it sounded doubtful.

"Right then." Alf pulled off his monk's habit.

Alf quietly stepped over the sleeping forms of Rhuel and Bor, and looked up the slope. The bobbing wisp was barely visible, but it waited for him at the edge of the road.

The Lammergeier climbed back into the story.

CHAPTER THIRTY-TWO

In later years, Sir Rhuel of the Eavesland swore that he was present at the Battle of Harnshill. This was how he described the events of that day.

The knights of Ilaventur, under the banner of Lord Brychan, had encamped on Harnshill two days before. Old Earl Daen said:

"Our enemies hold the city of Avos, with its stout walls and its many bridges to bring them reinforcements. Our outriders do not return and are likely dead, but the eyes of the enemy are the eyes of heaven, and Intercessors relay even our most secret counsels straight to the Erlking's ears. Surely this battle is lost before a single sword is drawn, and it would be best for us to retreat to our several castles, wherein we might shelter from the storm."

And Brychan said:

"Retreat would only mean delay, and delay is friend to the immortal. Our strongholds would be defeated one by one, until the last spark of Defiance is extinguished. We mortals are doomed to die, so let us die bravely." He ordered that casks of necromiasma be opened, so that they might conceal their deeds from the eyes of heaven, and this was done.

*

The host mustered by Lord Brychan consisted of some six hundred mounted knights and warriors, and sundry foot soldiers. Of this six hundred, three hundred and fifty were from Ilaventur or the hinterlands, and had long been allies of Brychan's house. The others hailed from the Riverlands, or the fringes of Arshoth, or came from far-off Arden and the Westermarch. Some were knights of the Road, fighting for pay; others had arrived in secret, whispering of the Old Kingdom and saying they were sent by the Lady Berys. Lord Brychan was suspicious of these outsiders, and he divided his forces into five companies.

Three of these companies were wholly of his own loyal knights, and these he placed under Sir Herret the Red, Sir Edmar of Highfield, and Sir Lannis Whitehelm. Sir Herret he sent to the western side, Sir Edmar to the east, and Sir Lannis had the place of honour in the centre.

(Unless you are a herald or a scholar, reader, you likely do not know these names. They buffet you like heavy snow, confusing and wearisome. Why do I need to know all these names, you ask, when most of them shall be dead before Sir Rhuel finishes his wine? Friend, were I to leave any out, I risk offending some knight who says, *'You have dishonoured my cousin's uncle's brother-in-law by not mentioning the great deeds of Sir Such-and-Such, and I demand satisfaction.'* So, I must include them, but I say to you – let these names flutter past you like brightly coloured songbirds! Know that on that day that every one of them was the bravest and boldest on the field, armour shining, swords flashing, and it was an honour to look upon them. Let them be remembered that way – not as the butchered meat they'll be by the end. Ah me, I have lost the thread of my tale. More wine, good sir, and I shall continue.)

The fourth company he held in reserve, and though it was under the banner of Brychan's own nephew Brymos, it was for the most part made up of knights of Westermarch. This fourth company he placed behind Harnshill.

The fifth company was entirely composed of newcomers, and the command of those warriors he gave to the highest among them, Temrech of the Riverlands, and the dubious honour of leading the assault.

Well did Lord Brychan know the battlefield, for he had fought here some twenty years before. Of all the Lords of Summerswell, he had the most experience in battle, for he led the League army sent to besiege Necrad – and that too had been a dubious honour, for none were expected to return. For the victory over Lord Bone, he expected great reward, but the lion's share of the renown went to the Nine, and the wealth of Necrad to other lords. This rankled with Brychan, who felt he had been ill-used.

(As an aside, friends, I should say that I myself was once accosted by Lord Brychan. He took offence to how he was portrayed in *The Song of the Nine*. Now it is true that I gave him only a few lines, and for reasons of narrative economy I contrasted his caution with the courage of Peir. I pointed out to him that it was entitled *The Song of the Nine*, not *The Song of Everyone*, and that many who perished bravely were entirely unmentioned. His anger unassuaged, he declared me to be a charlatan, to which I responded that if he wanted a song in praise of his deeds, he was welcome to commission it. But Brychan was a notorious miser, and there the matter rests.)

Brychan was as well known for his vigour rather than his valour; he slept but three hours each night, and occupied himself instead with reading. Few men were as well learned as he. But if I must choose a single term to describe Brychan, I would not speak of learning, or his iron-grey eyes, or his curt, stern manner, or his undeniable courage. No, I would speak of the anger that fuelled him, a fire long hidden that now blazed, a beacon atop the hills of Ilaventur.

Now Brychan could see little of the enemy, for an unseasonable mist gathered around the woods and fields south of the hill. Sir Brymos quailed and said, "Doubtless this is the work of the Wood Elves, for such mists cloak the eaves of the Everwood. They hide their numbers from us."

But his uncle said, "It matters not. If we cannot count them before the battle, then we shall count them after."

Had Lord Brychan magic to pierce that veil, then he would have beheld the cavalry of the Eavesland, some three hundred strong. These knights rode under the banner of Lord Aelfwine, the green gate of his castle surmounted by a golden dragon. With them rode knights of the Riverland, and a company of paladins of Arshoth under the command of Sir Dael, called the Dawnsword. In total, the mortal armies of the Eavesland comprised less than four hundred knights, and in the main they had fewer charmstones than the host of Ilaventur. But they had the blessings of the Intercessors, and well Lord Brychan knew that the masters of fate were arrayed against him.

With Lord Aelfwine rode the Knight of Roses, and some twenty elf-knights of the Erlking's household guard. Not in ten centuries had these knights ridden beyond the Everwood, not in all the years of Summerswell or the Old Kingdom that came before, but now they donned silver armour and took up swords forged in Necrad before the moon.

Now a single horseman emerged from the mist, and rode up towards Harnshill under the flag of peace. But before he came close, Lord Brychan seized a bow and loosed an arrow. It fell short, but the message was clear – there would be no truce. With this gesture, the battle began.

Seeing the enemy approach, Sir Herret the Red on the west side grew restless. He bore the spear Stormpiercer. The spear conjured a great tumult of force like the bow wave of a ship, and it was said that no foe could stand against Sir Herret's assault. Therefore, he was most eager to join the fray, and grew impatient at the hesitant advance of Temrech of the Riverlands. Sir Herret then led his knights forward, and soon they outpaced Temrech's host, and all the other forces of Ilaventur. Seeing Herret's thrust on the western side, the force of Lord Aelfwine turned to meet him.

Thinking perhaps that he could win the battle with a single blow, Sir Herret made straight for the banner of Lord Aelfwine. Then the elven Knight of Roses and his elf-knights emerged from the mists and raced forward as swift as the flight of falcons, intercepting Sir Herret. And though Sir Herret called upon the power of Stormpiercer, the Knight of Roses was undaunted. He leaped from his horse and vaulted over the spear's force-wave, and clove the skull of Sir Herret in twain. Now Sir Herret bore many other charmstones with the quality of preserving his life, so he did not perish immediately. He was rendered witless, his body riding around blindly while the two halves of his broken head lolled on either side. The elves were outnumbered by the mortals, but they had the advantage, for there was much confusion and dismay at the death of Herret.

At the same time, Lord Aelfwine's knights charged into the gap between Sir Herret's host and Temrech, and thus ensured that the knights under Sir Edmar could not join the fray, for now between them and their foes was a wall of Riverlander backs. The knights of Eavesland and the Riverlanders contended mightily in that first clash. Charmed sinew drove enchanted sword against blessed steel; gouts of fire and ice, darkness and light erupted across the fray, so that it seemed to me that these were demons battling and not mortal men. But ho! Demons do not suffer as mortals do! I beheld Sir Edulf of Lirester strike the Blue Knight such a blow that he was knocked from his horse, and trampled, so that the green grass was spangled with cerulean shards. Look you! There is Baron Pheriath, and his daughter the Green Serpent. There is the Knight Arcane, protector of the College, and he guards the mages working their spells to call up the war-wind. Ah, there is Sir Edulf's brother, Edmos, and oh!

An ice-bolt freezes his blood, and he stands there like a glittering statue until he is toppled, and he breaks. I see Sir Merik, the Giant of Eastford with his belt of strength-stones, picking up the dead to hurl them like boulders.

Friends! These scenes and more are graven for ever on my memory — that day I saw such depravity and such courage I shall never forget it.

The battle continued in this manner, the two sides evenly matched. Then Baron Olar of the Riverlands and his household broke through, and came to the side of Temrech, and Temrech was cheered, for he knew the courage of Olar.

But Olar said, "Alas, the day is lost, my friend. It would be wisest to retreat now, before Sir Lannis blocks the way."

"The day is not lost while we have courage," said Temrech.

"Nay," said Olar, "the day was lost a month ago." For then it was that Olar's sister went walking in the woods near the river, and was taken by the elves. And to win her freedom, Olar's men drew their swords, and treacherously cut Temrech down. With his death, great dismay spread through the knights of the Riverlands, and they fell back. If it were not for the courage of the mercenary-knight called the Jon'a'Holyday, who seized the Riverlands banner and held it aloft, the knights might have broken and the battle lost in that moment. Still, the Eaveslands had the advantage, and Lord Aelfwine and the Knight of Roses advanced towards Harnshill.

On the east side, Sir Edmar's host had ridden around so that they might strike Lord Aelfwine's force in the flank. Their course brought them close to the Weeping Wood, and there were elven archers amid the trees. The greensward nigh to the Weeping Wood became a place of death, as many flights of arrows were loosed upon Sir Edmar's men, and many were slain. An arrow pierced Sir Edmar's helm. His lieutenant Sir Brech of Ilaventur was unhorsed, and stumbled into the wood, and never returned. It fell to Brech's brother Bretmar to call the retreat, and the eastern host fell back towards Harnshill.

And on came the Eaveslanders, up the slopes of Harnshill. Grim was the face of Lord Aelfwine, for he knew that this day a Lord would fall. But beside him, the Knight of Roses raised his voice, and the elf-knights took up the song, and without fear they passed into the shadow of the necromiasma.

Seeing the approach of his enemies, Lord Brychan sent a messenger down the slope to his nephew Brymos, bearing orders to bring the Westermarcher knights held in reserve around to bolster the defence. But in secret, the Erlking had placed spies to watch the approach of Ilaventur. (The wise among ye shall know what I mean when I name them *Rangers*; the wiser will feign ignorance.) They waylaid Lord Brychan's messenger and in a sheltered dell on the west flank of Harnshill they slew him. So the reserve knights remained unaware of the unfolding debacle on the battlefield, and Sir Lannis' men faced the Eavesland host without reinforcement.

Again, knights of Ilaventur clashed with knights of the Eavesland and again, it was Eavesland who won the day. Back, back fell Sir Lannis, pushed up the hill inch by inch by Lord Aelfwine. Then gore stained the bright Blade of Eavesland, and down, down fell Sir Lannis.

Now on the summit of the hill, Lord Brychan looked down, and saw that his army was in disarray. Daen came to him again, and said: "The Westermarchers have failed us – out of cowardice or treachery, I do not know. We must retreat."

But instead Brychan turned to one that stood close by, and said, "Give them the gifts of Master Blaise."

For Lord Brychan was allied with Necrad, and Lady Berys had brought him dread weapons in secret. Charmstones and other treasures, yes, and worse horrors too, weapons not seen since Lord Bone's war.

Spell-skulls rained down upon the host of Eavesland. Mudskulls turned the hill to an impassable morass. Storm-skulls called down lightning. Death-skulls opened old wounds. They conjured monsters too, pitspawn who feasted on the fallen and grew swiftly, sprouting teeth and tentacles and all manner of obscenities. A wave of poisonous gas rolled down the hillside, engulfing the Eaveslanders and the survivors of Sir Lannis' company alike. Many died there, and some rose as the walking dead under the necromiasma. There came war-golems too, dragging their metal frames into battle laden with ivy and the dirt of two decades – for these demon-hearted warriors were creatures of Lord Bone's war. When Lord Bone perished, they fell silent, but now they were awake again, and the passage of twenty years had not dulled their blades.

How can I tell you of the horrors of that battle? If you were there, as I was, to bear witness to these atrocities, you would not have known where to look! There, a knight drowns in mud, weighed down by battledress, the spell-skull laughing at his plight. That one, there, I have forgotten his name, mocked him by calling him Sir Such-and-Such, but ah! He was a mortal man like all of us, full of the same doubts and joys, the same aches and dreams, but now he is devoured! Jewelled insects scuttle through gaps in his armour, and devour his living flesh! I saw men turned to flaming torches. I saw demons out of nightmare. Look you! That knight calls on the Intercessors to preserve his mortal soul, but they cannot hear him under the miasma! That elf-lord walked these hills a thousand years before they were ever named for Harn, and now he perishes, torn down by pitspawn! Shall I sing of the death of Lord Aelfwine? Gloriously he perished, surrounded by many fallen foes. When his bright sword broke, he found another sword amid the mud, and wielded that until it lodged in the malformed skull of a pitspawn. He struggled up, and up, until at last, he came to the summit of the hill. He raised the shattered sword, and pointed it at Lord Brychan, and said: "By your greed and ambition, you have brought ruin to Summerswell. Hear me: there shall be a new ordering of the lands, and—"

Then the Lord of Ilaventur snatched up the bow again, and put a barbed arrow in the throat of his cousin the Lord of Eavesland.

But Lord Aelfwine stood in the thick of the necromiasma, and it lent unnatural animation to his dead limbs. He stumbled forward, and clubbed Brychan about the head. Then two of Brychan's guards leaped forward and ended the dead Aelfwine.

Now on the other side of Harnshill, Sir Brymos and the Westerlanders had heard the roaring of the pitspawn and the thunder of the explosions, and they guessed that the enemy had drawn near Lord Brychan's camp. So they rode around the hill, and at last entered the fray. The Westermarchers, in particular, had fought the Witch Elves in the last war, and they bore weapons edged in elfbane metal. When the Knight of Roses saw this, he gathered his elf-knights and retreated down the hill. After them came the remnants of Lord Aelfwine's host, but they were caught by the Westermarchers, and slaughtered. The pitspawn and the other horrors of Necrad pursued also, but the sun shone bright on the valley, and repelled them.

It seemed to Sir Brymos that his uncle's camp atop the hill had been overrun, he guessed that with his last breath his uncle Brychan had unleashed the furies of Necrad. In that moment, he thought that the future of the rebellion lay with him and him alone. He saw that the enemy was in retreat, but that the battle was not yet won, and that before him was destiny.

"On!" he called. "Let us ride on, and bring death to our fleeing foes! On, and let us seize the bridges of Avos! On to glory!" He gathered the remnants of Sir Herret's soldiers, and rode in pursuit.

These things Sir Brymos did not and would never know. First, that his uncle was wounded, but still alive. Second, that if Brychan had been able, he would have warned Brymos against pursuit. Third, archers waited in ambush in the woods on the eastern side of the field. Just as Sir Edmar had done, Brymos led his knights too close to the shadow of the forest, and again arrows flew. Sir Brymos, caught in dreams of glory, spurred his horse and raced on through the deadly hail. "For Ilaventur and the Nine!" he cried, thinking to avenge the Lammergeier who had been unjustly slain in Arden.

Now the mists rose before him, and he rode on, not knowing that he alone had survived the arrow-fall. At the edge of the mist, he saw a lone knight on a horse, and it was the Knight of Roses.

"Death to the undying!" shouted Brymos. "For freedom!"

The Knight slew him with a single stroke, and rode on.

Now there came a lull in the fighting. The survivors of the Eavesland host took shelter beneath the protective cloak of mist that lingered yet in southern hills. Those of Ilaventur who lived gathered on Harnshill under the miasma. Clerics and Dead-enders attended to the dead. But the fighting was not done.

On Harnshill, Lord Brychan said: "Never have the elves and their thralls tasted such a bitter defeat, but we must make them drink deeper. Until Avos is ours, none can rest soundly. One last effort! Gather those still fit to fight! We shall be the hammer, and Avos our anvil!" It was Brychan's intent to push the enemy back to the shores of the Great River, and to take the bridge-city of Avos.

In the camp of the Eaveslanders, there was much sorrow and confusion, for Lord Aelfwine had perished and the Knight of Roses was nowhere to be found. Their elven allies had vanished. The Baron of the Shield Hills held that the day was lost because of the devilry of Necrad, and that they should withdraw across the river. But the Archon of the Riverlands stepped forward, and said: "Nay! The Intercessors have spoken to me from the waters of the grail, and shown me the weave of fate. Victory shall be ours if we hold Avos." And so the Eaveslanders withdrew to the town of Avos to await the siege, although many whispered that the evil unleashed by Necrad was greater even than the power of the Intercessors.

And now I come to a portion of the tale that I can only guess at. What has gone before I witnessed with my own eyes, my friends, or learned afterwards by speaking with those who survived. But what I shall tell you now – though true – no living man witnessed.

But I swear every word is true.

The Knight of Roses – sword of the Erlking, general of the armies of the Everwood – rode back to the elf-camp. He rode past feasting-tables and silver lamps, past silken tents and glades where harpers played under the stars. He came to his tent, and from it he took a thing bound in black cloth. He unwrapped it carefully, with unhurried grace.

It was the bow *Morthus*.

Of that bow many tales are sung.

The sages say it was made in the dreadful days of the Sundering of the Elves, when the followers of Amerith rejected the magic of the life-trees and the kind rule of the Erlking. There was strife in the wood in that time, a war between the elves, and it is said that the followers of Amerith struck the first blow and slew one of the Erlking's kin. Never before had elf slain elf, and they had no word for such a crime. Into the blackened yew-wood and dragonhorn, the Wood Elves poured all their anger and sorrow. It is the death-bow, the executioner's bow, made to end the endless. The Erlking's general took up the bow and used it to slay many of Amerith's followers, until they fled across the sea, returning to the ancient lands of the Firstborn in the region around Necrad.

For long ages of the world, the bow slumbered in the treasure hoard of the Erlking. Perhaps once every thousand years, when some elf strayed from the path of light and committed a crime unforgivable, then the king's executioner would send for *Morthus*. But never was it wielded in anger, only sorrow.

Before the Princess Laerlyn left her father's court, she went in secret to the treasure vault and stole the bow. With *Morthus* in hand, the Princess slew many monsters in the war against Lord Bone. She brought down the Dragon of the Cleft! She wounded the Ogre Chieftain in Glen Mithro! Even after the war, she kept *Morthus* as her bow, for there was no weapon in the vaults of Necrad to match it – save the Spellbreaker.

She wielded that bow when she confronted Aelfric Lammergeier and the Lady Berys in the dungeons under Necrad, when Aelfric slew her brother. That day, she drew back the bowstring, but she did not let death fly.

She bore that bow when she visited Arden before the fall. And there, she slew the Lammergeier with an arrow from *Morthus*, and all saw his doom.

The executioner's bow. The bow of death.

Now it was the Knight of Rose who wielded *Morthus*, and with great effort he bent it and strung it.

The bow asked: *Who is deserving of my gift of death?*

And the Knight answered: *All of them.*

By secret paths through the wood rode the Knight of Roses. Three elf-knights went with him, and they were guided by mortal Rangers who had scouted this hidden way. Perhaps, if you were in the wood that day, you might have felt a momentary chill from a passing breeze, or heard a rustle in the leaves. No scryer or sentry saw them; no horoscope or spell divined their presence.

The knight bore a full quiver of arrows. One for Brychan. Another for Berys. The rest for the other rebels who defied the Lords of Summerswell. This was not, I think, the preferred choice of the Knight of Roses. He intended to use the bow for its ceremonial purpose, as tradition dictated. He thought that the mortal leaders would be captured, and that Lord Aelfwine would pass sentence upon them, and he would then execute them. It would be done in sunlight, in full view of the world, and all would see the folly of defi-ance. Instead, all that was left was haste, a murderous strike in secret.

He rode, unseen by any.

Save one.

For the ghost of the Lammergeier stood athwart the path.

CHAPTER THIRTY-THREE

T he wisp seemed determined to lead Alf through the thorniest, muddiest trails in all of Ilaventur. It could slip through gaps in the hedges; Alf had to force his way through. He was somewhere near Harnshill, but the wisp kept him away from the Roads and other landmarks.

"Beware," said the sword, its demon eye gleaming. "This might still be a trap."

The wisp bobbed indignantly.

"Pretty shit trap," said Alf, brushing burrs off his cloak.

They walked on. The sun rolled past noon, but the weather was strange. Thick mists clung to the trees despite the heat. In the distance, Alf heard thunder, shouts and the clash of steel, and he caught a whiff of the sulphurous stench of necromiasma. Somewhere close by, Lord Brychan's forces were battling the armies from Eavesland.

Part of Alf yearned to charge out of the woods and join the fray. Part of him – or maybe it was the sword, which quivered whenever thunder rolled. It could taste bloodshed in the air.

"Did you bring me here for slaughter?" he asked the wisp.

It hovered in the air, a ball of unreadable intent.

"You're as bad as fucking prophecy."

*

They came on an old road through the woods. Trees laden with white blossoms interlaced overhead, making a tunnel of branches. The grass underfoot was thick and lush. Mist clung to the trunks. The tunnel receded into the fog in either direction.

"Wielder," said the sword, "beware."

The sound of hoofbeats, faster than the beating of Alf's heart.

"You brought me here for them?"

Closer came the riders. Through the mists, he saw them. At their head was the Knight of Roses, *Morthus* in hand.

Alf laid his hand on the sword's hilt, drew on the sword-sight, and the mists vanished. Everything was clear to him, as perfect and distinct as if he was looking at a still painting. The Knight of Roses, and three elf-knights. Despite having fought a day-long battle, the knight's armour was pristine. The damage Alf had dealt him at Kairad Nal had been repaired, and once again he was the very image of elven beauty, porcelain and pearl and living roses enchanting from the steel. There were four more riders – not elves. Mortals, hooded and cloaked. Two he recognised from Arden – they were the Rangers who'd attacked him at Othroan's warehouse. The red-headed man, and the woman who'd called herself Agyla.

He remembered Remilard's corpse at his feet. He remembered the warehouse floor awash in blood, the fierce joy of battle turning sick and bitter.

Wielder! Strike now!

Alf's first blow toppled the Knight of Roses from his steed and sent the elf-lord tumbling into the undergrowth. Alf spun around, Spellbreaker lending him speed and strength, and clove through another – steed, shield, armour and spine all with one blow. Horses screamed and reared around him, the whole company thrown into crashing chaos by his ambush. Alf thrust Spellbreaker through the skull of a stunned Ranger, knocked another down and finished him with the blade.

Spellcaster! said the sword. An elf-knight sang a song of binding, limbs tiring, swords falling. Spellbreaker countered it, and Alf's fist ended the song for ever.

A Ranger staggered upright, sword in hand, wiping blood from his mouth. He was a big man, agile, battle-hardened. His sword was an enchanted one, studded with charmstones. Against another blade, any other fighter, he might have had a chance. Against the Lammergeier in his wrath, he did not. Spellbreaker feasted.

The Knight of Roses, warned the sword. The elf-knight rose from the ditch. *Morthus* lay on the grass between him and Alf. The knight's gaze flickered to the bow.

"Don't," said Alf. "That's Lae's bow. Sword's your thing."

The elf hesitated, then drew his blade.

"Where's Lae anyway? I still want to talk to her."

"In her father's house in the Everwood," said the Knight of Roses. "After Arden, she said she would not take up arms against the Nine."

"Bit late for that," muttered Alf, "but it makes things simpler. Come on. You said you wanted to try your skill against the Lammergeier. Here's your chance."

"You wield the demon sword. It would hardly be an even fight. Look you, that sword there is the Brightsword of the Rangers. Prince Maedos gave it to the first Captain three hundred years ago. It is a fine blade. Take it, and we shall truly see who is the better swordsman."

"Once, I might have been stupid enough to take you up on that," said Alf. "But you put a half-dozen arrows in me on the Isle of Dawn, and all for asking to talk to my friend. And who gives a damn about who's the better swordsman, anyway? That's a matter for the storytellers, after. All that matters is who lives at the end of the fight."

I'm just so proud of you, said Spellbreaker.

"Come on," said Alf, "let's end this."

*

Their duel was not elegant or graceful.

The Knight of Roses was certainly the better swordsman – how could he not be, with ten thousand years of discipline? But he was weary after battle, and had begun to fade. The life of the Firstborn is without end, but their will to live, their appetite for existence – that has limits. Loyalty to the Erlking and a determination to protect the Everwood had sustained the Knight of Roses for many centuries past when lesser elves might have shackled themselves to a life-tree. The battle too, sapped him beyond the mere exhaustion of combat. This was not the first time the Knight of Roses had ridden forth from the Everwood to slay mortals. There had been other rebellions, other lords and kings who had to be put down. He had ridden forth to put down the chaos of the Old Kingdom; he had gone to slay the Changeling Connac, and a hundred other mortal lords whose names no one remembers. He was weary in a way no mortal shall ever know.

Alf was fresh, and augmented by Spellbreaker. The demon sword had feasted on elf and mortal alike, and it lent that vitality to its wielder. The knight's sword was enchanted too, the Roseblade of wicked steel thorns, but in the presence of the Spellbreaker all magic fails, and it was no sharper or stronger than any other blade.

Alf fought like a beast, heedless of injury. Three times, the knight wounded him, but none were enough to slow Alf down. For all the knight's grace, he could not escape Alf's blows. For all the knight's skill, there was nothing he could do to turn aside that remorseless assault. Alf hammered on the Rose Knight.

"Hold," said the knight, raising a broken hand. All beauty had beaten from of him. His armour was dented and muddied, his charmstones shattered. His helm had been smashed apart, and blood oozed from jagged, ugly cuts on his face. Deprived of his inhuman perfection, the Knight of Roses seemed ghastly, and reminded Alf of Acraist. A thought struck him; he'd seen Laerlyn in a similar condition, bloodied and tattered, and she hadn't lost her luminous beauty. She'd seemed more like a mortal woman.

Be wary, wielder, cautioned Spellbreaker. *You have not won yet.*

The Roseblade lay just out of reach, and Alf kicked it further away.

"Do you . . ." Alf began, but he was breathless.

"I do not yield," said the knight, "kill me, spare me, the choice is yours. I ask but a moment."

"For what?"

In answer, the wisp came drifted out of the woods and lingered by the fallen Knight of Roses. The Knight of Roses struggled upright, pressing one hand to a deep wound in his side. He spoke in Elvish. The spirit did not reply in a way Alf could hear, but there seemed to be a conversation between the two.

"What are they saying?" whispered Alf.

They greet each other like old comrades. They speak of—

It happened in a heartbeat. The knight lunged forward, grabbing for the Roseblade. Alf reacted without thinking, and Spellbreaker caught the Knight of Roses at the base of his neck. It was an ugly cut, a hacking blow that nearly tore the elf's head from his shoulders. The knight fell dead, blood gushing from the wound. His body faded, leaving empty armour.

The wisp vanished. The trees creaked overhead, but Alf felt no wind, only a gathering pressure, a sense of presence. He raised Spellbreaker defiantly.

More Intercessors, said the sword. *But they dare not challenge us.*

Afterwards, Alf gathered up the treasures of the fallen. It always made him uncomfortable to loot the gear of defeated elves, knowing that their wraiths were right there, watching him. Still, he made a sack from a discarded cloak, and into he piled the Knight of Roses' gilded armour, and his rose thorn sword, and the shiny sword of the Rangers, and various discarded charmstones. A fortune beyond measure.

He swung the bag onto his back, swaying under the weight. He picked up *Morthus.* Already, the bodies of the other elves were dissolving like the mist. Only the human corpses remained as grisly testament to the Lammergeier's slaughter. The force of Spellbreaker's blows and blasts ensured none were recognisable.

"One got away," said Spellbreaker. It sounded sated, like a dragon that had devoured a whole flock of sheep and was now content to lie back on its golden bed to digest for a century. "Agyla the Ranger. I didn't get her."

At some point during his labours, the wisp returned. It bobbed in the middle of the tree-lined path. Alf couldn't tell if its light had faded somewhat with the effort of manifesting, or if the sunlight slanting through the trees made it harder to see. When Alf rose to leave, the wisp bobbed south, expecting him to follow.

"I'm going this way," said Alf, nodding towards Harnshill and Brychan's camp.

The little light vanished.

Alf marched up the hillside towards the camp. Below, Brychan's knights pushed wearily across the battlefield driving the Eaveslanders towards Avos and the distant river. There were a few isolated skirmishes, a few desperate last stands, but it was clear that Ilaventur had the day. Carrion birds circled overhead, while Dead-enders moved among the fallen, spears ready. Dead-enders in Summerswell – the sight disturbed him.

Berys descended the slope towards him. A shade out of memory: she wore fighting leathers and light mail, as she had when they were adventuring. It suited her better than courtly gowns, to Alf's mind.

"You missed the battle, Alf," she said, laughing. "Did you get a bit lost?"

"I had another fight."

"So I see. I told Brychan not to look for you on the field, but he wouldn't listen."

Alf leaned on Spellbreaker. "Where is Brychan?"

"Down there, lapping up the glory. Leave him to it." She glanced at Alf's sack of treasures. "That's *Morthus*. Was Lae here?"

Alf shook his head. "The Knight of Roses had it."

"He had *that*, and you still beat him?" Berys let out a low whistle. "I'm very, very glad you're on our side."

"Seems to me that there's not much difference between the sides, the way you're carrying on. Necromiasma and spell-skulls and pitspawn."

"Not to mention black swords forged by Lord Bone himself," said Berys. She said it lightly, but when Alf did not smile, she became abruptly serious. "They're weapons, Alf. Tools. Power the Wood Elves sought to deny us. We need to break free."

"And what gets broken? The whole country's in chaos. We need to put an end to this."

"An end to this, says the man who never stopped fighting the last war." Berys gestured at the battlefield. "We've won here, Alf. After this, it's all done, and then comes rebuilding. We take Avos, and that cuts Arshoth and the Crownland off from the Eavesland. They won't get help from the Wood Elves, but we're getting magic and more from your nephew in Necrad. Miasma, too, to drive the Intercessors away. The surviving Lords won't be able to look to the Everwood for guidance."

"You think they'll surrender?"

"I have faith in their capacity for self-interest," said Berys. Alf frowned in confusion, so she added, "I mean, they're scared and greedy. They'll yield."

"And that'll be it, right? We draw the line at the river."

She gave Alf a sidelong glance. "I should throw things at you," she said, "for what you did in Arden. You nearly ruined everything, after all Armech did to get you out of the city unnoticed."

"What *I* did? You poisoned the whole city!"

"It was just a little miasma. We lived under worse in Necrad."

"Aye, but that's Necrad, Berys. Those people didn't deserve what you did to them."

"No, they didn't. But it was necessary. We needed – *you* needed *me* to take Arden quickly, so I acted." She strummed *Morthus'* bowstring. "In a way, you're meeting me for the first time. All the time we've known each other, I've had to lie to you. I've worked in secret for this day all my life. Gathering charmstones, building connections, testing people. Hiding from the Erlking. Now, it's all out in the open. Everyone knows who I am now, and where I stand. You know what I've done. You're the monster slayer, Alf. Am I monstrous?"

She sounded young to Alf, and more vulnerable than he'd ever known her. They were about the same age, but when he'd first met her, Alf was a thick-headed clod, a farm boy who knew nothing except how to hit things with a sword. And Berys knew everything – she was the thief, the spy, the intelligencer of the Nine. Lath could change his shape, but Berys could be anyone. A sneak-thief from the gutters one day, and the next, a sophisticated noblewoman who could blend into any court. Tongue sharp as her daggers, she'd intimidated the young Alf. He'd come to trust her, but only once he'd accepted that she would always have secrets from him.

After the war, she'd become a merchant. He'd always hidden his disappointment at her turn to mere commerce. It seemed so dull and commonplace for someone who'd cloaked herself in mystery. She'd become tawdry.

Now, there was this new Berys. Much more like the Berys he'd known when they were adventurers – but Berys with a cause.

Alf lowered himself stiffly to the ground. "Like I know anything. You were always one of the clever ones, Ber. I just hit things." He examined the exquisite filigree on the hilt of the Roseblade. "I had no clue what was going on. You, Lae, Blaise, Peir, Thurn – you'd make the plans, and tell me what needed slaying. I trusted you all. So, you tell me it was *necessary*, and I believe you."

Berys smiled. "That's good to—"

"I'm not done." Alf picked up Spellbreaker and compared the demon's eye to the beauty of the elven blade. "You'd say it was necessary, and Lae would say you were being too harsh, or impatient, and that there's another way. You'd argue it out, and Peir would judge. I trusted what we were when we were all together." A look of pity crossed Berys' face. "You don't think that ever existed, do you?"

"'The Nine'? No. Not like you saw us. Even back then, we weren't united. Peir had his dreams and visions, and he'd have marched us into disaster if Jan and I hadn't held him back. Jan was full of doubt from the start, none of us really trusted Laerlyn, Thurn was always one bad day away from abandoning us and heading home." She sat down next to Alf. "But where does that leave you and me? You trusted me once."

Alf exhaled. He put away the Rose Knight's sword and laid Spellbreaker across his lap. "I trust you like I trust this sword. You're dangerous, Berys."

"The man who killed Lord Bone says this," said Berys with feigned lightness, trying to make a joke of it. Alf could tell he'd hurt her with his honesty. "We gave you Spellbreaker to keep its evil in check, and you did a good job of that."

"Aye, well." He looked down at the scarred land. "The sword wasn't all the evil in Necrad."

"I'm going back afterwards," she said quietly. "When all this is done. When Summerswell is rid of the Wood Elves' control and we can shape our future as we desire, then I'm going to back to Necrad. I'll take Peir's offer if no one else does. I haven't forgotten the oath we took as the Nine. I might have bent it, but I swore to watch over Necrad and I will."

That cheered him. A hint of the old Berys, shining through. "Me too," said Alf. "Under young Derwyn, it'll be better."

"That's what all this is for, Alf. Believe me."

A messenger came scrambling up the hillside, and knelt before Berys.

"My lady. I bring word from Lord Brychan. He bids you join him at Norbury Grange."

"You go," said Berys.

"What about you?"

She stood up, mask back on. "You know me. Shadowy business." She gave him a peck on the cheek. "See you soon."

When he gathered up his treasures, the bow was gone.

CHAPTER THIRTY-FOUR

The house at Norbury Grange had never known such a gathering. Knights of renown and barons of great estates sat in the yard while Lord Brychan and his inner council dined inside. The manor's master was one of Berys' conspirators. Foundation stones laid in the days of the Old Kingdom warded off spirits.

Alf was led through by one of Brychan's granddaughters, her dark hair held back by a silver clasp that looked like it came from Necrad. Her clothing, too, was reminiscent of the Witch Elves, but her face reminded him of her aunt Erdys. If she recognised the Lammergeier, she gave no sign. She silenced the guard dogs that greeted him with snarls, then brought him through a doorway and up a flight of stairs.

Lord Brychan sat before a table laden with maps. An elderly wizard fussed over a cut on his scalp. Brychan waved him away when Alf entered.

"Aelfric, finally!" He embraced Alf, then stepped back and appraised him. "The years have not been gentle, I see. And you are freshly wounded, to boot."

"I took some cordial. I'll be fine."

"Haeligan, attend the Lammergeier," ordered Brychan. "You may trust Haeligan. He's not one of the College's. In other times, he ran a secret school under my patronage. He's committed to the cause of Defiance."

The wizard sighed. "Pray remove your mail shirt, Sir Lammergeier. What stars were you born under?"

"Not a clue," said Alf. He put Spellbreaker on the ground next to his chair and pulled his shirt over his head.

"Does your squire carry your birth-scroll? It helps calibrate star-magic."

"I don't have a squire. Or a scroll."

"Sir Aelfric is low-born, Haeligan. He has risen far from humble beginnings," said Brychan. "And may seek to rise further still."

The wizard unlaced Alf's gambeson and examined his torso, clucking in disapproval. "The cordials of Necrad knit crooked." There were several fresh cuts, courtesy of the Knight of Roses. Alf let the wizard attend to them. At his foot, the sword's demon eye glared at the wizard.

"I entrusted a message to my eldest grandson – your namesake," said Brychan. "I asked you to come to my court as soon as you received it. You *tarried*." He growled, as if delay were the worst of crimes.

"I'm sorry about the boy," said Alf. "And we had our own troubles in Necrad." He winced as Haeligan smeared stinging ointment on a bruise.

"You tarried after Arden, too. You could have come straight here. I could have used you on the battlefield."

"Brychan," said Alf quietly, "you don't command me. We're comrades, but it's been twenty years since you captained the League army."

"Lean forward please," whispered the wizard.

"We could have been more than comrades, Aelfric. If you had wed my Erdys, I would have made you my heir – and regent of Necrad." Brychan's voice trembled. "We held the balance of power. You could have been a Lord, and more than a Lord, and you rejected it. You rejected *me*."

"Aye, well." Alf shrugged.

"Why?"

"I told you. I didn't want to be a Lord. The quest wasn't finished. The Oracle was still out there. We couldn't be sure we'd ended Lord Bone. His evil wasn't done." Spellbreaker's polished black steel drank in the firelight, reflecting nothing of its light or heat.

"So you said."

"Why are we even talking about this?" Alf waved a hand at the table of maps, and the wizard muttered a plea for him to remain still. "We've enough to do without digging up the past."

"Because it is not past," said Brychan. "Choices we made then shape the present and constrain the future. You rejected Erdys' hand, and I wondered why. Then I learn that you have installed your nephew as King in Necrad." Alf protested, but Brychan went on. "You struck a bargain with Berys. She secures the Cleft of Ard, and in exchange Necrad supports our cause. A reasonable bargain, and I would have made the same choice that she did. But what happens after, Aelfric?"

"You're making it sound sinister," said Alf. "I didn't even know my sister had a son until last year, and I didn't *make* him king of Necrad. That just ... it just happened."

"A spontaneous acclamation of loyalty." Brychan's voice was heavy with scorn. "Conveniently, your kinsman is cheered by all of Necrad. Humans and Witch Elves and all the rest, united in their embrace of a stranger, and you had nothing to do with it."

"He's Peir! He's got Peir's spirit. We brought him back from the dead, and something of Peir came too."

"Peir the Paladin." Brychan's hand shook. "Peir Bessimer. I led the League to besiege Necrad, and he is remembered as the hero who saved Summerswell. I work and build for twenty years, preparing for the revolt against the Erlking's undying hand, and you tell me that Peir's returned from the dead to thwart me?" He swept his hand across the table, sending maps and papers flying.

"Thwart? No? Brychan, we're all on the same side!"

"Am I to bow to this new king?" snarled Brychan. "Swear allegiance to him? Do you think I want to replace one overlord with another?"

"No! Peir – Derwyn – we don't want to rule Summerswell. Necrad's in our charge, Necrad and the New Provinces. Everything across the Gulf of Tears, we make no claim!" Alf remembered Derwyn's speech in the council, about Necrad being a shining beacon of justice. It seemed so clear then, but now it was like a fading dream, and Alf lacked the words to break through Brychan's paranoia.

"But you claim the north. Is my daughter a hostage, then?"

"Erdys said she wanted to be left out of all this."

"She does not have that luxury," said Brychan. "No one does."

"You won't have to swear allegiance to my nephew. I give you my word."

"And what is your word worth, Sir Aelfric?"

Alf pulled himself away from Haeligan's ministrations. He picked up his sack of treasures and tipped it out across the table. Charmstones and enchanted swords clattered amid the maps. "Those lads," said Alf, "were coming to kill you. I stopped 'em. I've never been much of a man for words, my lord, but you can judge my deeds."

Brychan examined Alf's trophies. Awe crept into his voice. "'Those lads'," echoed Brychan. "This is the blade of the Knight of Roses, the Erlking's champion. And this sword, this is called the Secret Flame of the Rangers. You will not know this – no one does, save the Lords – but my beloved aunt died by this sword. They accused her of treachery against the Erlking, and she was executed in secret before the other Lords. After, the tale was put about that she was murdered by assassins from the west."

Brychan put the Secret Flame aside and lifted the Roseblade, admiring it in the firelight. He contemplated the elf-wrought blade in its beauty, then laid it down gently across the map of Summerswell. "Berys warned me. She said that you are often slow to commit to a course of action, but when you do, you cannot be dissuaded – not even by the impossibility of a task."

Alf shrugged. "They weren't expecting an ambush. That's how we won against Lord Bone. That, and Peir's sacrifice."

"Of course, of course," said Brychan. He glanced at the wizard. "Well, Haeligan, will Sir Aelfric live?"

The wizard sounded startled. "He, ahh, his wounds are not inconsiderable, my lord, and I haven't done any divinations—"

"I'm fine," said Alf. "Another swig of cordial, and I'll be ready to swing a sword again."

"Not a sword, sir," said Brychan. "A hammer."

Brychan insisted on dressing Alf up in full regalia. A shield was painted with the symbol of the Lammergeier. A fine suit of armour was procured, with an ugly helm, and soon Alf found himself standing before the knights and nobles of Ilaventur. Lord Brychan, seated on a golden chair, smiled and nodded as they listened to some young bard sing about the duel of Sir Aelfric and the Knight of Roses.

I feel you're getting an undue amount of credit, whispered Spellbreaker. *I barely get a mention.*

"I didn't want this," muttered Alf.

I was unfairly overlooked in the other song, too. A whole ditty about you turning evil, and not one mention of the demon blade. I ask you, what is more plausible – a plodding yokel is actually a sinister mastermind, or you're the tool of sinister powers beyond your limited understanding?

"Quiet," said Alf, a little too loud. Brychan glowered at him, then quickly recomposed his features into an avuncular, even kingly mien, nodding approvingly as the poet related the Lammergeier's eloquent speech about freedom and the death of tyrants.

Brychan's wizard, by the way, had a needle dipped in poison. I saw him prepare it while he was examining you. I wonder – did Brychan know?

Was he planning to have his wizard murder you if he thought you were an impediment to his plans?

Alf's stomach twisted. Monsters and the perils of the Pits he did not fear, but such intrigues like that were beyond him. It made everything feel uncertain, the world a frozen lake cracking beneath his careless tread.

Or does Haeligan serve some other master? The College Arcane, perhaps?

"Why," whispered Alf, "are you telling me this?"

I swore to serve you, wielder. I watch for danger, said the sword. And then it started humming.

The song ended. Lord Brychan stood.

"Noble knights," he said, "we have won a great victory! I speak not only of the battle of Harnshill – though that was glory hard-won through your courage and sacrifice. But Harnshill was but one blow in a long, long struggle. Hark! Centuries ago, Firstlord Harn and his companions faced the hardship of the Hopeless Winter. They went to the elves for succour, and the elves demanded they humble themselves, and swear fealty to the Erlking and the false Intercessors. All that time, we have been thralls of the elves! But no longer! The Lammergeier struck down Prince Maedos and freed Necrad, and now that fire of revolt burns in every corner of Summerswell, from the Cleft to the mouth of the Great River! The enemy crossed the river to take our beloved land of Ilaventur from us, and at Harnshill we defeated them! Ilaventur is ours, now and for all time! We shall rule here, as our ancestors did in the days of the Old Kingdom! We claim this land by right of conquest and blood, not any Elvish deceits! We wash away Harn's shame! We shall be vassals of the Erlking no longer!"

The knights cheered. Brychan raised his hands for silence.

"But there are still those in Summerswell who choose bondage over freedom! They fight on, holding to the Erlking's falsehoods. They say that any victories we might win are fleeting, for the strength of the Everwood is eternal. So, we shall send them tokens of our victory! Sir Lammergeier!"

Alf stepped forward.

"Just as the Lammergeier struck the first blow in this war, when he slew the tyrant Prince Maedos, let him now strike fear into the hearts of our foes!"

Two squires came forward, one carrying a chisel, the other a huge blacksmith's hammer. The boy groaned under the weight of the hammer; Alf lifted it one-handed. The other bore the Roseblade, and placed in on the dais before Lord Brychan. The Lord of Ilaventur knelt and placed the chisel against the sword's blade, a few inches from the tip.

"Break the sword," said Brychan.

Alf swung the hammer, and the beautiful sword snapped. One of the squires darted over and picked up the broken tip.

"Send that piece to Eavesland!" declared Brychan. He moved the chisel down.

"Again," he called.

Again, Alf struck, sparks flying up like rose petals. More of the blade broke.

"Again."

Only a few inches of steel remained above the hilt. Brychan placed the chisel over the Roseblade's cross guard. Alf hesitated – the sword was thoroughly broken now, but it was still such a beautiful thing. No mortal smith could ever have wrought anything half as intricate. It took the immortal hand of an elf-smith, craft honed over centuries and augmented with magic, to make a thing like that. It seemed a shame to destroy something so lovely with this crude hammer.

But breaking the sword could hasten the end of the war, and Alf judged it worth it. He swung, and the hilt shattered. Brychan stifled a cry of pain as a shard cut his cheek, and he cradled his wounded face.

"Are you all right?" whispered Alf.

"Keep going," hissed Brychan. He raised his voice again. "Messengers!" he called, and four knights came forward to kneel before him. A squire picked the first shard of the Roseblade from the mud and handed it to him. Brychan wrapped the shard in a square of silk, staining it with his bloody fingerprints, and gave the bundle to the first courier. "Take this to Ellsport, and tell them of its provenance."

The second shard was prepared. "To the Riverlands!"

The third was similarly wrapped. "This one I shall deliver personally," said Brychan, "to the Master of the town of Avos."

The two largest fragments, incorporating the pieces of the broken hilt, were destined for the capital city in the Crownlands, and the holy city of Arshoth – all provinces that remained mostly loyal to the Erlking.

"Tell them," shouted Brychan, "that the Roseblade of Elfland is broken – but the black sword of Necrad is still sharp! Tell them that if they do not yield, they invite their own destruction!"

And when Alf did not respond on cue, Lord Brychan grabbed his wrist, and raised Alf's arm like he was announcing the victor of a tourney. Spellbreaker was lifted on high, and the knights cheered.

Afterwards, Alf endured a succession of knights and Lords bowing before him, and praising him, and pressing goblets of wine on him. Some talked about their fathers or some other kinsman who'd fought in the last war; others boasted of their augmented prowess, eagerly displaying charmstones. He'd seen knights trading looted stones on the battlefield. There were a few familiar faces he welcomed from the old days, and a few more he vaguely recognised, but for the most part, he was just the Lammergeier to them.

He endured the ordeal for the scraps of news from distant provinces. No portion of Summerswell had escaped the war, but by all accounts the fighting was worst in the Crownlands and Ellscoast, where the rebellion mixed with old blood feuds and rampant paranoia. Tales spoke of war-bands going village to village, house to house, murdering those who gave allegiance to the wrong banner. Most of the trade in charmstones, legal and illegal, went through the coastal provinces, too, so the use of magic was commonplace there. At least part of the capital city had been destroyed, although accounts varied as to how much. In Alf's mind, the Capital was untouchable. Even in Lord Bone's war, the invading forces had never breached the city. It seemed unthinkable that it should fall now, because of something he had unwittingly begun.

The rebellion had failed utterly in the province of Arshoth. Intercessors took note of every falling leaf in the holy woods there, and paladins had descended on anyone who even breathed a word of support for Berys' rebellion. In his tomb-robbing days with Gundan, Alf had never delved any dungeons in Arshoth either, so he guessed there were fewer remnants of the Old Kingdom in that region, fewer places to hide from the Erlking's unseen spies.

Even Arshoth would fall, or such was the belief of the assembled knights, drunk on wine and victory. What did it matter that the paladins had the holy Intercessors on their side? The rebels had Necrad. They traded wild stories about monsters and enchanted weapons from the last war, and speculated about how they might be used again. The skies of Arshoth would be stained green; the Barbed Hydra would return to devour the paladins, and the Blackflame Lamp would be raised once more over the cathedral.

Alf, who'd helped kill the Barbed Hydra and watched Laerlyn shatter the Blackflame Lamp, said nothing. Once, he'd have cuffed the young fools about the ear, and told them that they knew nothing about Lord Bone's war, or they would not speak so eagerly about resurrecting such horrors. But now it seemed that the world had come unmoored, or that the last fifteen years had been erased in an eye blink, and now all nightmares might come real again. It sickened him, and the laughing knights seemed ghoulish in his eyes.

Finally, he found one with news of home. A big Mulladale lad, newly knighted on the battlefield by Lord Brychan. Alf had become Sir Aelfric the same way. The boy told him that the Mulladales were mostly untouched by the war, although there was fighting on the border near Highfield. Alf interrupted a rambling account of ghosts on the High Moor to ask for word of Ersfel.

"Ersfel?" said the young knight. "Which one's Ersfel?"

"North o'Kettlebridge."

"Ah, yes." The boy's face lit up. "I know it, Lammergeier. We rode through it when we escorted the Lady's caravan from Ellscoast. The reeve tried to deny us passage, and we slew him. The Lady had us tear down their shrine so the Intercessors could not spy on us. You don't need to worry – the Road to Necrad is secure."

When he could bear no more, Alf slipped out of the feast, taking the last of the wine with him. Norbury Grange was now entirely surrounded by Brychan's army, a forest of tents and encampments, and a ripple of excitement went ahead of him. Soldiers at campfires nudged their comrades and pointed out the Lammergeier. A pair of drunken knights followed Alf out of the house, apparently convinced that they were going to join him on some quest. One of them doubled over to throw up, and Alf took the opportunity to slip away.

He climbed a hill, breathing in the cool night air to clear his head. Clouds mounted on the eastern horizon, but the sky overhead was clear and starry. To the south, the river gleamed in the moonlight, and there were the lights of Avos. Alf could still hear the music and cheering from the victory feast at Norbury Grange, and he climbed higher. A goat path led him around the brow of the hill, and he found a place to sit. He stuck Spellbreaker in the ground in front of him, and threw his new shield and helm down next to it.

"What was the name of that young knight that came with Erdys' boy last year? The one who fancied himself a champion?"

"Sir Prelan. Golden lion rampant on a field black."

"He wanted to take you."

"Indeed. They thought you were too old to wield me, and that you would hesitate when the moment came." The demon eye glinted. "Your strength has not yet failed you, at least. But you do hesitate more than you used to. You fought well against the Knight of Roses."

"I did, now that you mention it," said Alf. He leaned back, wincing as his wounds ached. "I fought well. And it wasn't the bloody Lammergeier's helmet, or the shield. Or the sword."

The demon eye stared at him coldly.

"All right, you helped. But the point is, Brychan wants the Lammergeier as a symbol, and you as a weapon."

"I am a weapon," said the sword.

"A weapon he can control. You in someone else's hand."

"I swore to serve you, wielder. My oath binds me. I am your sword."

"I'm stuck with you, I know," said Alf. "But Brychan, and Armech too – they want the Lammergeier, not me. It's strange, being haunted by your own legend."

"You allied with Lord Brychan and the rebels to protect your sister and her son, and the city they rule. Do you regret that choice, wielder?"

"Well, the alternative's not any better. The Lords would have my head for killing Maedos. And Olva, and Derwyn too. And Berys is right about the Wood Elves."

"Even Laerlyn?" There was an edge to the sword's voice, a hunger.

"She put an arrow through the Lammergeier's heart, didn't she? She picked her side." Alf stared at the stars, trying to bury the memories of twenty years. "I want another choice. Not to choose between two shades of bastard."

"There was never any such option given to you," said the sword. "If you want more palatable choices, you must create them. In Necrad, after Gundan's death, I urged you to wield me with intent. To seize power."

"I told you I wasn't a leader. Peir was. Derwyn is."

"In time, he might be. And we have come in a circle – if you believe in the rightness of his cause, then you must fight for it. Blood must be shed, and those who would stand against your cause must yield or perish – be they man or elf, mortal or monster."

"Bloodshed and slaughter. That's your answer to everything."

"I am a weapon," said the sword.

Alf was silent for a moment. "Could you call a dreadworm?"

"I could," said Spellbreaker. "And where would you fly? Back to Necrad, and leave the burden of bloodshed to others? Will you let conscience make of you a coward?"

"Shut up."

"I am bound to serve you. I wish you to see clearly. Running home will not put an end to slaughter – but if you fight, it will be over all the sooner. Wield me in battle. Finish the quest."

Before Alf could answer, the wizard Haeligan came puffing up the hill, carrying a wooden box. Without the sword-sight, he did not notice Alf sitting in the grass until he nearly tripped over Alf's outstretched leg.

"Watch yourself," said Alf.

"Indeed. Some of us are moping here," said the sword.

"Sir Lammergeier! My apologies! A thousand pardons." The wizard bowed, and in doing so unbalanced himself, toppling the contents of his box across the grass. Wizardly talismans and tools fell about. One charmstone rolled against Spellbreaker's blade and popped, further startling the wizard.

"Forgive me, forgive me!" said Haeligan. "I came here seeking starlight." He picked up a hopelessly tangled star-trap.

"This coot," muttered Alf, "and you had me thinking he was an assassin."

"I merely raised the possibility," said the sword.

Haeligan looked from one to the other in open-mouthed confusion, and Alf laughed. "Never mind. Most of my friends try to kill me sooner or later, so I'm sure we'll get on fine."

"As you say, Lammergeier," said Haeligan, who clearly had no idea what Alf was talking about, but had adopted the same polite smile he'd used for any heavily armed drunkard. "I'll just string my star-trap, and be on my way."

"Here," said Alf, "I can see." He struggled upright and hooked one end of the jewelled net onto a convenient branch. The wizard stepped back to appraise the net, glancing up at the stars.

"If my Lord Lammergeier would be so kind as to move the third hook a little higher, that would be best. The constellation of the White Deer is low tonight, and light from those stars is especially potent in spells promoting success in battle."

Alf obliged, although he didn't put much stock in this sort of magic. Fate-weavings never seemed to do much good, and mortal wizards needed to collect years' worth of starlight for even a single spell. Elf-magic was best shaped over centuries.

"The battle's won," muttered Alf.

"Lord Brychan is eager to secure Avos and her bridges." Haeligan clucked his tongue and poked at the star-net. "Although I fear that my little magic will be of small consequence compared to the gifts of the Lady." He screwed a silver vial into place at the centre of the net, then tapped it with a fingernail. It made a ringing sound, and he sighed. "Forty years of study, forty years of gleaning starlight, all to be outdone in a trice by the magic of Necrad. Ah well."

"I strung up a star-trap just like this for Blaise a few months back," said Alf.

Haeligan emitted a braying laugh. "You jest, Sir Lammergeier. The Master of Necrad is far beyond such trifles. All the magic of Necrad is his. Power beyond measure flows through the Wailing Tower."

"Aye, well, that's now. But I remember tramping around with Blaise night after night, trying to find the right place to string up his trap, or helping him set up his theodolite, or other arcane bits and bobs." Alf looked down the hill, as if he could look back twenty or more years to see Blaise's thin form struggling up the slope, and Alf trailing after him, a beast of burden. "He wasn't always the great Master."

Haeligan unfolded his own theodolite from his box. "Indeed. He builds on the work of . . ."

A wizard's pause. Alf suppressed a flash of irritation. "Lord Bone, aye."

"He was about to speak another name," said Spellbreaker, its metallic voice ringing out suddenly. The star-trap made a squeaking noise, like ice cracking.

Haeligan flinched. "I was not. It is a name we remember, but do not speak."

Now it was Alf who was confused. "Whose name?"

"I thought you knew, Lammergeier. He who became Lord Bone – he was one of us. He was a Defiant. The school of wizardry I have the honour of overseeing – he was our best student, eclipsing all others. Through secret paths and intermediaries, it was arranged that he go to Necrad, to study with the Witch Elves."

"You taught Lord Bone?" Suddenly, Spellbreaker was in Alf's hand, although he couldn't remember drawing the sword from the dirt.

"Not I!" The nervous laugh again. "Not I! All this was more than a century ago. But I knew those who knew him. He was the great triumph of the Defiance – and the great disappointment. He went north, and word came back that the Witch Elves had accepted him as a student. The leaders of our brotherhood hoped he would return wielding mighty spells to throw off the shackles of the Erlking. Then, as the years went by with no further news, it was believed that he had perished. There was only silence." Haeligan coughed, nervously. "Of course, we had no idea that our former student had become the Dark Lord of Necrad. When Lord Bone attacked, we did not know him. It was only later, after the war, that we realised the connection between the two."

Alf swayed, leaning on Spellbreaker for support. He'd known that Lord Bone had once been a mortal from Summerswell. Ildorae had talked about how he'd come to Necrad. *We underestimated his ambition. What began as indulgence became subservience.* But he'd imagined Lord Bone as ... As what? A wandering beggar, like Lath before the Nine found the Changeling. Or an evil wizard right from the start, cackling in his tower until adventurers drove him out. Alf could conceive of Bone's ambition and malice, but the idea that Bone came to Necrad with a purpose – on a quest! – shook him in a way he had not expected.

"What was his name?" asked Alf.

"His name is remembered," said Haeligan, "but he is our great shame, so we never speak it. He is only Lord Bone, now and for ever."

Lord Bone, thought Alf, *and the Lammergeier.* Swallowed by stories. No one back home in Ersfel even remembered Long Tom's son Alf any more, no one except Olva. He was the Lammergeier, and the Lammergeier was a monster. Everything was tangled, good and evil commingled.

Alf turned and walked down the hill.

Haeligan called after him. "Where are you going, Sir Lammergeier?"

"Tell Brychan," called Alf, "that I've gone to Avos."

CHAPTER THIRTY-FIVE

A vos of the Crossing. Golden light shone flattered the jumbled roofs of the old town, To the north-west, the Great River wandered in a slow arc, the strength of its youth in the mountains spent over long miles. It meandered through most of the Riverlands without clear direction. A few miles outside Avos, it scented the sea and plunged east, picking up speed again as lesser streams joined it from the hills.

The waters here were too wide and fast to be forded, but there were islands, one large and five small, like stepping stones, and the bridges of Avos spanned the gaps between them. The town had grown up on both sides of the river – North Avos and South Avos they were called now, but there had been times when different masters ruled each half, and battles had been fought across those bridges. In recent times, Avos was peaceful. Even in far-off Ersfel, Alf had heard tell of the markets of Avos, and the quiet sanctity of its streets. Avos was resolutely unheroic and unmagical. In contrast to the war-torn Riverlands around it, or, the fervent piety of Arshoth, or the pomp and intrigue of the Crownland, Avos just got on with business.

He'd passed through there decades ago with Gundan. They'd left after one night, pronouncing it dull.

War-banners flew above the north gate. Alf marked the sigils of Eavesland and Arshoth, and the Everwood too.

"And what do you want?" he muttered, then turned his attention back to Avos. The city's fortifications were impressive at first glance, but Alf could see where the walls had crumbled, or where the growing town had burst its confines and spilled out to settle the northern plain. The outer districts of North Avos would fall quickly in any attack, but those walls would be a significant obstacle. Besieging the town would be difficult, too – as long as the bridges held, defenders on the northern wall could be reinforced and resupplied from the south. Brychan had allies in Westermarch, but Alf doubted they'd be able to cut off the southern side anytime soon.

No, he could see how the siege would go. More spell-skulls and monsters from Necrad to break those gates. Street-fighting all the way south across the bridges. Or maybe Brychan would have all those bridges destroyed, cutting the city in two once more. Either way, it would be a slaughter. The river running red.

This is probably a stupid idea, said the sword, but Alf liked to think he could hear a little doubt in its voice.

"Aye."

Stay out of range of arrows.

Alf approached the north gate. Off to his right, the Road running towards Arshoth was eerily empty. He'd never seen the paved thoroughfare so deserted. Fear had emptied this land.

Two guard-towers stood a little way outside the city. In more peaceful days, they'd been tollbooths.

"Who goes there?" called a sentry from the right-hand tower.

Alf held up his shield. "You can bloody see this, right?"

"The Lammergeier is dead!"

Alf drew Spellbreaker and tapped the sword on the Road. A pulse of force blasted from the blade, shaking the ground. Paving stones cracked. "Sorry," muttered Alf.

A hail of arrows flew from both towers. Alf swung the blade in the air. Arrows splintered mid-flight, shards rained down all around him. "Don't do that," he called. "I'm here under a flag of truce."

"You bear no flag!" called the sentry.

"Aye, I couldn't find one."

More arrows rained down around him. He batted them away.

"Look!" he cried. "I just want to talk to whoever's in charge. Of the city, not the army." He pointed with his sword. "I'll be in that inn over there."

It was a roadside inn, recently abandoned. Alf could imagine news of the defeat at Harnshill emptying the place, customers and innkeeper alike fleeing for the safety of the town. They'd left in such haste that there was still ale to be found. Alf thrust Spellbreaker into the straw-covered floor, Wilder-fashion, before sitting down to have a drink.

"I have a scabbard, you know," grumbled the sword. "You don't need to drive me into the floor every time."

"It's the Wilder sign for truce."

"I know that. I doubt anyone else within a hundred leagues does. My point is that I've stabbed more floors than flesh since we left Necrad."

"We slew the bloody Knight of Roses yesterday."

"That was yesterday." Spellbreaker quivered. "I can sense the fear in Avos. They anticipate slaughter. Why deny them?"

"You'll be quiet now," said Alf.

He sat back and waited. The ale was welcome on the hot day, but it was missing something. Alf dug out his flask of healing cordial from Necrad, meaning to add a dram to the ale – the cordial had no real taste of its own, but it was rejuvenating, like sticking your head in a rushing mountain stream – but the flask was empty. He grunted and finished the ale anyway, his side aching where the Knight of Roses had struck him. And Ildorae had stabbed him. And a linnorm. And a giant. And another linnorm.

And a great many other things.

He poured himself another mug, then paused and fetched another that he placed in front of Spellbreaker.

"You must be joking."

"Damned if I'm going to drink alone."

"I am a *sword*, wielder."

"Call me Alf."

"I certainly shall not."

Alf raised his cup. "To absent friends, then." There were, of course, eight empty chairs around the table. "Jan once said to me, 'Alf, you have my blessing, and you carry the hope of the world.' What a fucking horrible thing to say to a friend. Carry the hope of the world – who can do that alone?"

"You have me, wielder."

"Aye. I do." Alf drained his mug. "Sir Lammergeier and the black sword, bound together for all time. And what good is dread Sir Lammergeier, except for killing? 'Go south, Alf, and protect my son's dream.' And how will I do that, Olva? Oh, is it by killing people? It is."

"I dislike this mood, wielder."

Again, he heard hoofbeats outside. He stretched to make sure Spellbreaker was within reach, but left the sword where it was.

Two armed guards, a man and a woman, appeared at the inn door. They were dressed in the livery of Avos, with the sign of a bridge embroidered on their tabards. One had a short spear; the other a Necrad-forged crossbow. They entered warily, adventurers trespassing into a dragon's lair. Her face was concealed by her gilded helm, but Alf recognised Agyla. The crossbow was aimed straight at Alf, and her finger rested on the trigger.

"Don't," said Alf. "I just want to talk."

The other guard, spear shaking in his quivering hand, called out, "Safe!"

Two more entered. One was a bishop, by the grandeur of his hat. The other was an old man, wearing a heavy cloak despite the summer heat, weighed by the gold chain of office around his neck. He leaned on the bishop's arm as he entered. It took Alf a moment to recognise him.

"Urien?"

The former governor of Necrad – Vond's predecessor – clasped Alf's arm. "Sir Aelfric," he croaked. "Back from the dead. You do not amaze me."

Alf was taken aback by the condition of his friend. When he'd last seen Urien, the Riverlander had been a stout fellow – ruling over Necrad would try the sanity of any mortal, but Urien had always said it was a balm compared to the endless feuding of the Riverlands. Now, Urien looked so like a walking corpse that Alf had to fight the instinct to end him. Eyes sunken, skin waxy and yellow, and the stench could not be hidden by the perfume he wore.

"Bridgekeeper is my title, now," said Urien, "a sinecure for the infirm, I thought, before this war. Aelfric, this is Tarec, Bishop of Avos. Tarec, this is—"

"I know who you are," snapped the bishop.

"Have your man plant his spear, there," said Alf.

"Your master does not observe the customs of truce," said Bishop Tarec.

"Brychan's not my master," said Alf.

Urien gestured at the guard, and he stuck his spear into the floor opposite Spellbreaker. He still had a short sword at his belt, and Agyla had her crossbow. Still, the custom had been observed enough.

"What happened to you?" asked Alf. Even as he asked, he remembered Gundan passing on a rumour. *Berys sent him a very special bottle of wine one Yule.* With Urien removed, Berys had redoubled her trade in charmstones and relics, smuggling them south in preparation for her rebellion.

"Diplomatic as ever." Urien gave him a wan smile. "I was poisoned, Aelfric. An occupational hazard, for governors of Necrad. I'm told your nephew sits in my old seat now, after you ejected young Vond. You'll forgive me if I don't toast his good fortune."

"Surely there's healing magic that can help. Blaise could help."

"Aelfric. You and I are at war. Stop trying to help me." Urien chuckled, and it turned into a gurgling cough. "Anyway, I was wearing protection." He held up his chain of office, and charmstones gleamed there. "Carbuncles and bezoars, proof against ordinary poison. Whatever was used on me was potent, and I'm told there's nothing that can be done for me. Before the end, though, I'll take the Road to the Everwood. There's healing there, for the soul at least."

"Blessed be the kindly Erlking," intoned Tarec.

"It's strange," continued Urien. "When I fell ill, I remember lying there in my bed in the Citadel, wracked in pain, and I thought of you. You were off wandering, and I imagined you on the Everwood Road. I think, in my fever, I thought you were taking me to the Erlking's realm to be healed."

"When this is all done," offered Alf, "I'll walk with you."

"You will never see the Everwood," snarled Tarec. "Defiler! Murderer!"

"Enough, Tarec. You're not preaching from the pulpit here. I know who and what I'm dealing with – and let me tell you, if the Lammergeier asks to meet you in a truce rather than on the battlefields, you offer up all the prayers of thanks you can. So, tell us, what are we doing here, Aelfric?"

"I want," said Alf, and then he paused to gather his thoughts. Urien's presence disturbed him, as did the watchful eyes of the young Ranger. Less than half a year ago, he'd been on the other side of a similar truce, when the Wilder threatened to besiege Necrad. That had ended in bloody tragedy for all sides, the negotiation sabotaged by a hurled spell-skull. Gundan and Thurn and so many others, slain by mistrust and treachery. Again, it felt like invisible forces were tugging at him, shaping events, hollowing out his words like a worm in an apple. "I want to talk," he said again.

"What is there to discuss?" snapped Tarec. "You rise in rebellion against the Lords of Summerswell. You consort with Witch Elves and traitors. You wield weapons of darkness."

"Aye," said Alf. He shifted in his seat to face Urien. "That's all true. And now you've got Brychan's army on your doorstep, Urien. They've got weapons from Necrad. You remember Lord Bone's war — this'll be just as bad. You can't win."

"You're not here to gloat," said Urien. "What do you propose?"

"Tell the Lords of Eavesland or whoever to go back south," said Alf. "Tell them that the river'll be the border, now and for ever, and that you have my word Brychan won't cross it."

"I cannot speak for the Lords of Eavesland, or any other Lord."

"Aye, but they'll listen. Tell them that Avos wants no part in this quarrel, and that you're only looking out for your people."

"I am sworn to serve the Lords of the Riverlands," said Urien, softly.

"Well, you know them better than I. What would please 'em more — their market town safe and intact, or a tomb amid the ruins with your name on it, and the words 'he kept his oath'? Eh?"

"Even if we were to entertain this preposterous notion," said Bishop Tarec, "what would stop the rebels from invading the Riverlands and Eavesland, as they have defiled the holy province of Arshoth? You say Lord Brychan is not your master, and thus you cannot speak for him. What surety do we have then, Lammergeier? Your word and nothing more?"

"I can't speak for Brychan, no," said Alf. "But Brychan won at Harnshill because he had magic out of Necrad. There's more and worse on the way. It's my nephew on the throne there, and if I tell him, he'll cut Brychan off."

"Necrad is very far away," said Urien, but he glanced back at Agyla, as if looking for advice.

Tarec scoffed. "We know the truth of the Lammergeier now. Your word is worth nothing. You murdered Prince Maedos out of spite, and conspired to seize the northlands with the rest of the Nine. Now you want to carve up Summerswell and throw the scraps to your rebel allies. Know this, traitor: the Intercessors have already written your fate in the stars! I have seen it in the waters of the grail. All you do shall be undone, and your name will be forgotten." He threw the broken shard of the Roseblade on the table. "You cannot intimidate us. Avos is a city of the faithful. It shall endure no matter what you threaten. Listen to the choirs of the cathedral, and you shall hear our defiance."

"Don't pay any attention to this fool," said Alf. "Do what's right for your city and your people. Your duty should be to defend them."

"And what of your duty, Sir Aelfric?" asked Agyla, suddenly. "In the last war, you defended Summerswell. The Nine brought warning of Lord Bone's invasion. Now, once more, you bring warning of darkness rising – and you stand aside, and do not defend us, even though you bear the demon sword. Why?"

"Swords make things simple. Swords cut things down and end 'em. But when you try to make the wide world simple, then that's a lot of cutting and ending, and it still goes wrong. I've seen enough of that." Alf reached out and rested his hand on Spellbreaker's pommel. "Go on. I've said my piece. Brychan's at Norbury Grange, not half a day from here. You don't have long to decide, but if you choose peace, then I swear I'll defend you."

The delegation from Avos departed.

Riders from Brychan arrived shortly afterwards, scouts sent hunting for the Lammergeier. They approached tentatively, as though Alf were a cornered beast, laying their message like an offering. Would the Lammergeier not return to Norbury Grange, so that matters of high import might be discussed in council? Unable to convince Alf to return with them, but assured at least that he – and the Spellbreaker – were not lost, they rode back across the fens. Lord Brychan's army was on the way, and although armies moved much faster than they had when Alf was young – mounted knights augmented with charmstones were swifter than great regiments of foot – it would still take a few days for his full force to recover from Harnshill and make their way to Avos. Longer, if he had to wait for siege engines.

"He won't wait for siege engines," whispered the sword.

"How many times do I have to tell you," said Alf, "to stop reading my mind."

"It written on your face, wielder. You have to strain the muscles in your brow to think. It will not be ladders and battering rams that break the gates of Avos. It will be balefire golems, and blast-skulls, and dreadworms."

"Aye." Alf paced around the common room. "I'm glad it's Urien. Urien will listen."

"Urien will listen. Laerlyn will listen. Thurn will listen," mocked the sword. "The pitiless uncaring stars will listen. Look at you, wielder, wandering around looking for someone to take this fate from you. You are my wielder, the hand of the Lord of Necrad. Violent slaughter is your purpose as much as it is mine."

Alf strode across the room, plucked the sword from the floor, and drove it home into its scabbard to silence it.

"You know I can still speak while I'm in this scabbard?" said the sword. "I don't have a mouth, wielder. All those other times I fell silent, I was being polite."

"Shut up."

"No one else is listening, wielder."

"No," said Alf, "I mean, be quiet." He threw open the door of the inn. The faint sound of singing drifted across the river. It was the singing of a choir, their voices raised in song from the cathedral of Avos. The air of the song was familiar to him, but it took him a moment to recognise.

It anoints our eyes so we too might see
The folly of mortals.
Now we see the Lammergeier
Uncloaked at last.

On the afternoon of the second day, the first elements of Lord
Brychan's forces arrived, and encamped a little way down the road
from Alf's inn. Again, Brychan sent messengers, including the
wizard Haeligan, demanding that Alf immediately return to camp
and prepare for battle.

"Tell Brychan to hold off," said Alf. "Tell him that if his army
takes one step closer to Avos, they'll have to reckon with me."

"I-I shall relay your words, Sir Lammergeier," stammered
Haeligan, "but you should know that our spies across the river tell
us that the enemy is marching to reinforce Avos, and if we do not
take the city and the bridge soon, all hope is lost."

"Heard that before," muttered Alf.

It was true; he had heard those similar words from Lord Brychan
before, a lifetime ago, in a camp on the edge of the frozen Charnel.
*This winter will be the death of us. We cannot continue the siege of Necrad,
and our scouts report more foes are marching from the north. If we do not
find a way past the fires of the Stone Dragons, all hope is lost.*

Peir had found a way. Peir had found a miracle. He'd led the Nine
in secret through the Pits, into the enemy's city. They'd found their
way through hidden paths, through haunted streets, until they came
to the fortress of the Dark Lord. And there they'd slain Lord Bone
and saved the world.

"Go on," said Alf, "tell Brychan I'm waiting for a miracle."

On the evening of the third day, Berys slipped into the inn.

"Barkeep," she demanded, "your best wine, in your most throw-
able goblet." Beneath the jest, Alf could see that she was barely
controlling her fury.

"I thought you were off on shadowy business."

"I was. I've ridden through four provinces since last we spoke. And I wasn't joking about that drink."

He fetched her a mug, and she drank thirstily. She tapped it on the table when it was empty. "Brychan thinks you've gone mad."

"And what do you think?"

"I worry that you've had spirits whispering in your ear. Or in your dreams. This has the air of Jan about it."

"No. Just me."

"You just decided to run off to hide in an inn?"

"I'm not hiding. I went to Avos and told them to surrender, just like Brychan intended." Alf refilled her mug and poured himself one. "It's Urien in charge over there, by the way."

"I know. I always liked Urien."

"So why did you poison him?"

She winced. "Because he tried to stop me smuggling charmstones south to the Defiance. Because he was in the way, Alf, and the cause comes first." She sipped her ale more thoughtfully this time. "Did you get through to him?"

"Maybe."

"He didn't," said Spellbreaker.

"There was a bishop there, and a . . . what did you call them? The Lords' spies?"

"Ranger." Berys drew out the word, making it sound venomous.

"They spoke against me. But Urien – he was in Necrad with us. He knows what Witch Elf magic can do. I think he'll see sense."

"You think." Berys took a coin from her pocket and juggled it with her knuckles. "Alf thinks. Now there's a strange portent indeed."

"Give him a few days."

"A few days, and we risk losing *for ever*, Alf. I keep telling you, this is our last chance to rise up against the Wood Elves. We'll never have such magic again, never take them by surprise again. We lose Avos, and they'll be able to reinforce Arshoth. They retake the Crownland. They cut us off from our allies in Westermarch. They push us back into Ilaventur. And do you know what happens then, Alf? Do you know what your principled stand here could cost us?"

Alf didn't answer. He stared into the dark depths of his mug.

"Everything. They will kill us, Alf. Go down the river, and you'll see the ruins of Minar Kul, the old capital. We explored those tombs when we were young, remember? Well, in a few centuries' time, some other adventurer can go delving in the ruins of Ilaventur, and Ellsport, and even bloody Ersfel, Alf, because they will kill us all for defying them. And the elves will still be there, unchanging, even more secure. They'll find better ways to control humanity, until our children cannot even *imagine* defiance. That's what you're risking with this – this errantry!"

"There's another option," said Alf. "We go home."

"To Necrad?"

"Aye, to Necrad. Blaise has had months, now, to prepare the city's defences. We add to them. We pull back to Ellsport and sail across the Gulf. There's land in the New Provinces aplenty for all who want to come with us. We go back to Necrad, where the Intercessors can't spy on us and the Wood Elves can't meddle. We'll be safe there."

A flicker of a frown crossed Berys' face. Anyone else might have missed it, but Alf knew his friend so very well.

"What is it?" he asked.

Berys didn't meet his gaze. "It's probably nothing. I've heard there's some trouble with the New Provinces. Nothing that can't be dealt with, I'm sure, but the weapons Blaise promised us haven't arrived."

"Trouble," echoed Alf. "What sort? Who were you talking to?"

"It's hard to get anything out of Necrad," said Berys, defensively, "with the Intercessors watching the seas and Ellscoast in chaos. It's probably nothing – we've had delays before."

Spellbreaker was in its usual place, propping up the bar. Alf reached for the sword, but Berys caught his wrist and stopped him. "Alf – we don't have the magic to take Avos cleanly. I've got a few spell-skulls left, but not enough. Brychan's getting ready for an assault, and it'll be tough. The city has to fall before reinforcements from Eavesland arrive, no matter the cost."

Her fingertips lingered on his wrist for a moment, brushing against his scars. "We need you, Alf. We need the Spellbreaker."

Chapter Thirty-Six

Dawn brought an answer from Avos.

The slanted light of the rising sun fell on a corpse that dangled above the north gate of the city. Lord Urien hung there, stripped of his chain of state, his lordly robes. The marks of many wounds could be seen on his naked flesh. Soon, rumour reached Brychan's camp – Urien had spoken in favour of surrendering the city to the Lammergeier, but the people of the city had been so incensed by his cowardice that they had gathered at the cathedral and marched on the bridgekeeper's palace. A voice had spoken from the grail, blessing their bloody work. The Intercessors had sanctified Urien's death, declaring it part of the weave of fate.

Judging that there was no longer any prospect of Avos yielding peacefully, Brychan mustered his knights for an assault on the city. Blasting-skulls would breach the outer walls; after that, Brychan declared, it was the task of every knight to push forward so that they might win the bridge. Knowing of the wealth of Avos – and the hearts of many of his followers – Brychan warned against a premature sack of the city. Until the bridge was theirs, they must fight on, no matter who stood in their way.

He sent a messenger to the inn of the Lammergeier to say that the time for hesitation was over, and the sword of Sir Aelfric was needed in battle.

But the messenger found the inn deserted.

The bulk of the city's walls blotted out the stars. It was a warm evening, and Alf could smell the stink of the river, hear the fast-flowing waters splash against the rocks and the stanchions of the ancient bridge. He could hear, too, singing from the cathedral.

The cathedral of Avos stood on an island in the river, between the two halves of the divided city. No single bridge could span the width of the great river. There were half-a-dozen islands in the river, and the bridges ran between them. Some of the islands were so small that they were lost beneath the mighty arches, but the middle island was large enough to support not only the bridge, but a cluster of civic buildings including the cathedral.

Ancient tales claimed that a marauding giant once tried to attack the Everwood, and the Erlking sent out his knights to challenge the monster. The giant hurled stones at the elf-knights, missing each time, and then the Knight of Hawthorn rode his steed across the river, leaping from stone to stone, and slew the giant in single combat. The giant fell into the water, and his corpse became the sixth and greatest of the islands.

Alf came to the river's edge. With the sword-sight, he could see the churning waters below, the river frothing white as it rushed over the rapids.

You're just doing this out of spite, said the sword.

Alf stepped over the precipice.

The sword buoyed him up, as it had at the Isle of Dawn. He clung to the blade as it rose, and it carried him to the surface. He fought against the onslaught of the waters, kicking and struggling forward. The river tore at him like a beast, a dragon of ice, hammering him.

An unexpected current dragged him under, and darkness

swallowed him. For a moment, he was in Necrad again, and young again, crawling through the lightless Pits. The Nine were with him, and he had no fear, no doubt. He was with his friends, and their cause was righteous. The quest had drawn them together, and they would not fail.

He surfaced again, gasping for air. The bridge towered above him, the lights of the houses along its span reminding him of the wisp-lights that had guided him into Jan's valley. He fought on until he came to the shore of the holy island, and the shadow of the cathedral. He dragged himself onto the shore and lay there for a moment. His flask of healing cordial was empty, and he could feel every old wound.

"Could you," he groaned, "break the bridge?"

It is magically protected. I could break one part of it. But it has eight sections, and any one gap could be repaired swiftly. And before you could break a second span, the defenders of the city would be upon us.

"That's what I figured." An echo of the past, again – Alf remembered Lath suggesting that they try to sabotage a few of the Stone Dragons that guarded the walls of Necrad. *We open up a path for Brychan.* And Peir saying, *If we strike, it must be a decisive blow.* And he'd led them towards the Wailing Tower and the Palace of Lord Bone. There had been no other choice, no other way to fulfil the quest, even if that path demanded sacrifice. "All right. The cathedral then."

He crossed the rocky shore of the island, and found a path that led to a stone stair that led up to the level of the bridge. He came to an iron gate, and smashed it open. A few sentries wisely fled when they beheld the Lammergeier.

He came to the top, and found himself standing at the edge of a wide plaza. To his left was a span of the bridge leading back north, and on the far side was another span to the south. In better days, the plaza held markets and festivals; now, it was barricaded with heavy barrels and other obstacles.

Facing him were buildings, each competing with its neighbours for prestige and grandeur with carved facades and ornamentation. The city treasury and tithing-house with its golden roof, the city's tower of wizardry with its spires and star-traps , and the bridgekeeper's mansion – its windows shattered, its doors smashed open by the mob that had murdered Urien.

And at Alf's right hand, rising above him, was the cathedral of Avos.

Shouts, then the sound of horns, came from both ends of the bridge.

Subtle as always, whispered Spellbreaker.

He abandoned subtlety.

The cathedral had three brazen doors. The one on the left was the common entrance, the steps up to it worn smooth by generations of feet. It stood open. On the right, the Lords' door, bearing the sigils of the great houses of the Riverlands; that door was used only rarely, for funerals, investitures and other ceremonies. That door, too, was open – doubtless to receive the bodies of those who had fallen at Harnshill.

The middle door was the Erlking's door, the Intercessor's door. An image of the Erlking stared down at Alf; he was crowned in stars, and all the wisdom and kindness of the aeons were in his face. That door was opened only when a Wood Elf of the royal house visited; the last time it had opened was when Princess Laerlyn passed this way, only a few weeks before she slipped away from her entourage and joined the Nine.

Alf struck the middle door with Spellbreaker, blasting it open.

The cathedral was crowded, every pew filled with the faithful. Their singing turned to shouts of alarm as Alf strode in, black sword in hand, a demon out of Necrad. He swung the sword again, and a blast of force smashed a clear path for him to advance up the nave. Bodies flew through the air, flung like dolls by an angry child. The crowd parted. A few found the courage to stand in Alf's way, or shouted curses at him, but none were armed, and none could stop him.

"Fear not!" called Bishop Tarec from the pulpit. "The Intercessors defend us!"

With sword-sight, Alf saw three shining figures above the shrine. They were so blazing bright that they were like triple suns, and he could not look at them directly. He could only make out the impression of winged forms, the warmth of sunlight on a summer's day.

"You sure," he muttered to the sword, "you can kill these things?"

There is nothing under the stars I cannot kill, replied Spellbreaker. *But if you could slaughter a few dozen of these wretches first, that would help.*

The first Intercessor struck, a divine wind rushing through the cathedral. Only Alf could perceive it clearly, but the force of its passage manifested in the flickering of candles along the side chapels, in the sudden creaking of the chained candelabras that hung from the ceiling, in the staggering of the crowd as the divine force passed over them. The Intercessor moved swifter than a stooping eagle, and for an instant Alf beheld its shining fist.

Spellbreaker shielded him. The Intercessor was a thing of magic, without physical strength or form, and that magic could be countered. Alf grunted as the residual force of the blow passed through him, every bone in his body rattling with the impact, but he was undaunted and unharmed. He twisted the blade, catching the Intercessor as it passed by.

To the crowd of onlookers, it seemed as though the Lammergeier struck only empty air.

But to Alf, the sword bit deep. The shining light of the Intercessor *shattered* like splintered crystal, bright shards exploding and melting as Spellbreaker broke whatever spells girded the spirit. The wraith inside shrieked past Alf, howling, and then it was gone, fading to almost nothing.

"One," muttered Alf. He advanced towards the altar, towards the

Intercessal shrine and Bishop Tarec. Again, the crowd of worshippers backed away from him, the press of bodies spilling over the pews, crushing a few unlucky people against the stone pillars of the nave. No one dared come within reach of Spellbreaker.

The second Intercessor was more cautious. Its light flickered, then faded into near invisibility as it withdrew from the material realm, retreating beyond even the reach of the sword-sight. Light flashed in the crowd in one spot, then another, and another and another, each flare marking a moment of Intercession where the spirit passed its blessing onto a mortal in the crowd.

A woman leaped at Alf, her hands wreathed in holy fire. It was the same blessing Peir had wielded in the war, his hammer afire with the flames of the Intercessors. Afterwards, Alf would try to remember the woman's face. He would try to imagine what it must have been like for her, what courage she must have possessed. To have an angel whisper in your ear and say, "*You, you are the chosen one. I know you fear the monster who stands before you, but I shall give you the strength to destroy him. You shall be the weapon that drives back the dark.*" She did not doubt, she did not hesitate. When the call came, she answered with all her heart.

Afterwards, he always failed to recall her face.

In the moment, he struck. The flames of the Intercessors were snuffed out along with her life. The sword opened her up from collar to hip, a red flood staining the marble floor.

Another recipient of the blessings attacked, and another, and another. Had these been battle-hardened paladins of Arshoth, long used to wielding such blessings, then they might have challenged Alf, but the Intercessor was like a man taken unawares by a beast, so he scoops up whatever stones are at his feet to hurl in desperation.

With a snarl, Alf suddenly charged into the crowd. Panic took them, and they fell back, a tumbling wave of bodies scrambling away from the monster. The holy light flickered again in the midst of the crowd, but now Alf was within reach of it. Again, he stabbed seemingly empty air, and again there came a dreadful wail as the Intercessor was disrobed of its enchantments and diminished to the point of nothingness.

"Elf-wraiths," muttered Alf, "they're just Wood-Elf wraiths with spells on 'em."

He advanced towards the altar. "And that's two."

Bishop Tarec tried to flee. He made it halfway down the steps from the pulpit before a blast of force from Spellbreaker sent him toppling over the banister to land in a heap by the altar. Alf strode forward, grabbed the bishop by the scruff of the neck, and slammed him against the altar.

"Tell 'em to surrender. Tell 'em the Intercessors said that Urien was right, and that Avos should surrender to Brychan. Tell 'em now."

Tarec cowered in terror. "I will not deny the holy ones! If death is the fate they—"

Alf lifted him bodily, and dropped him back down on the stone slab, winding the old priest. "Tell them."

Tarec's mouth opened, but no sound came, just a bubble of frothy blood that burst on his lips. Wordlessly, he pointed at the shrine behind the altar.

Holy light emanated from within. The grail awaited.

Many years ago, friends in Ersfel dared Alf to break into the humble shrine in the holywood. Entering the shrine was only permitted to the village priest except in the rarest of circumstances. Most villagers lived out their whole lives without ever seeing the inner sanctum of the shrine where they worshipped every week. Everyone knew that the shrine was where the priest kept a grail, the vessel of the sacred waters of Arshoth, the cup of the Intercessors. As a boy, Alf imagined a jewelled cup of gold, and filled the shrine with fabulous treasures and occult secrets. The shrine at Ersfel, though, turned out to be a musty little cabinet with only a dusty wooden bowl and a simple pitcher of water.

The shrine at Avos, though, was what that boy imagined. The grail was a jewelled bowl of gold and silver, held in a reliquary of gilt and glass. Paintings on the walls depicted the first Lords of Summerswell kneeling before the Erlking to receive the blessings of the Intercessors. The ceiling depicted the stars, the loom of fate where the Intercessors wove the destiny of mortals. The chamber was not musty, but smelled of incense and mystery.

The man, who had seen wonders and horrors beyond imagining, noted only that the shrine was just big enough to swing a sword.

The grail brimmed with water, and light welled up from it. The third Intercessor had retreated beyond the reach of both sword and sword-sight, but the grail was a window into the otherworld, and Alf could see the spirit in the waters. It was the same Intercessor he'd encountered in Arden, in Othroan's warehouse.

It extended a shining hand and beckoned him forward to look into the grail.

Then its light faded, and the face of the spirit became visible.

"Maedos," said Alf. "I killed you."

"The firstborn are immortal," said Maedos, "and my father's blessing ensures I do not suffer the travails of the wraith-world." The prince's voice came from a very great distance, the water dancing with his words.

"Come out and show yourself," said Alf, "or I'll drop this cathedral on you."

"There is nothing more you can do to me, mortal, than you have already done."

"And you can do nothing to him," said Spellbreaker. "Not without manifesting, and then I shall cut you again."

"No?"

"You already impaled yourself on my bloody sword," said Alf, "and I put a stop to your plans to seize Necrad. You've lost, Maedos.

Stop drawing this out. Tell these deluded fools to surrender. I'll make sure that Brychan and Berys stop at the Great River. No more Lords, no more Intercessors, but there'll be no more war either. Help me put a stop to this – or we'll do to the Everwood what we did to Kairad Nal."

The wraith of Prince Maedos laughed. "The beast thinks to dictate terms! I have played this game for thousands of years, mortal, and I know it never stops. There is no final winning move, no end until the world's ending. There are only arrangements and constellations of forces – and your forces are weaker than you think. Behold!"

The wraith of the elven prince retreated, and images moved on the face of the waters. *Don't look*, warned Spellbreaker, but Alf stared into the steaming grail, and saw . . .

Necrad, but distantly, dimly, outside the concealing shroud of the necromiasma. He saw through the eyes of an Intercessor riding the sea-wind. Even at that remove, he could see new foundries and factories in the Sanction. Spawning vats that bred monsters. Piles of spell-skulls, engraved with spells of destruction. The balefire of demons, blazing in golem-furnaces. Armoured Witch Elves mounted on winged dread worms. The strength of Necrad, renewed.

This is what we needed, Alf told himself, *this awful strength turned to a good purpose. Derwyn will send all this south to the rebels. We'll make something new and better out of Lord Bone's works.*

The vision circled south. They passed over Tar Edalion, and the chapel there had been destroyed. Nothing remained of it but cold ash, and the sight of Jan's work destroyed dismayed Alf. The Intercessor hovered there for a moment, mustering its courage.

Then it turned and plunged into the necromiasma.

The clouds scorched the spirit. Streamers of burning miasma trailed the hurtling angel, a scar across the sky of Necrad. Dreadworms screeched in alarm. The waters of the grail boiled and spat. Burning as it flew, the Intercessor charged into the heart of Necrad. Alf stared as the spirit rushed past the familiar spires, Garrison and Liberties and Sanction all laid out beneath him, all orbiting around that central spike of the Wailing Tower.

The Intercessor struggled on, pushing through the defences of Necrad to bring him this vision.

A figure stood on the balcony at the top of the tower. Derwyn's face, Derwyn's body, but it was not him.

In the instant before the Intercessor was snuffed out, Alf knew his enemy.

The vision ended. The grail-waters went dark.

"Dreadworm," choked Alf, his speech barely intelligible.

Wielder, said the sword, *it could be a trick*. But even Spellbreaker sounded hesitant. The vision in the grail had the ring of truth to it. They both felt it, mortal and sword alike.

"Dreadworm," ordered Alf again.

"The church spire," said the sword. "Climb."

The things called dreadworms are not truly alive. They are conjurations of Lord Bone's magic, spawned from ice and fetid water and the gases of the necromiasma. Previously, when Spellbreaker summoned a worm, the magic called an extant worm from the skies above Necrad, where endless flocks of the horrors constantly circle, dissolving and reforming in a pathetic mockery of birth and death and rebirth. Even the swiftest worm would take many hours to fly all the way south to the river.

Now, there was another source of the worms closer at hand. The lingering miasma over the camp at Harnshill convulsed, congealed, black wings condensing out of poisoned air. The worm screeched its birth-cry as it soared forth, wings beating furiously. It shot over the battlefield and flew south towards the river with desperate speed.

*

Alf emerged from the shrine and stumbled towards the staircase that led to the belltower. Knights and other warriors of Avos had converged on the cathedral, and every way out was guarded by a fence of swords – all but one. Alf climbed, up and up, his long legs taking the stairs three steps at a time.

"Did you know?" he hissed at the sword. "When you looked in Derwyn's soul, did you know?"

The sword did not answer.

He vaulted over the railing and into the night. The dreadworm swooped in and he landed astride it. The monster hissed as it circled over Avos, over the rushing river and the bridge and the city below, then it climbed into the night, higher and higher.

It seemed to Alf in that moment that he could see all the lands of mortals. There, beyond the river, was a distant cluster of campfires and enchanted lights that must be the second host from Eavesland – and beyond them, a shimmer on the horizon, the edge of the Everwood.

There was Brychan's camp, and the inn, and the Road stretching off north-west to Arshoth, to the Crownland, to Arden and the Cleft and the mountains of the dwarves. Instead, he turned the beast's head north-east. He would fly over the marshes and the hills of Ilaventur, over the rolling woods of the Mulladales, over Ellscoast and the Gulf of Tears.

Higher still the dreadworm climbed. Alf clenched Spellbreaker tight, watching through the sword-sight for the interference of Intercessors. But no elven spirit challenged him – and why would they? He was flying north, away from the war, and taking with him the one weapon that could tip the balance in favour of the Defiant. The skies were clear across all of Summerswell.

Higher, beyond reach of spell or bow.

All save one.

On Harnshill, *Morthus* sang.

CHAPTER THIRTY-SEVEN

The arrow tore through the dreadworm's shoulder, crippling its right wing. The creature let out a soft, shuddering sigh and died mid-flight, its body stiffening. Ice-water in its veins cracked as it froze solid. Its wings were still outstretched, the velvet tatters still catching the air, so it did not plummet instantly. Instead, it spiralled down, a necrotic ash seed, right wing crumpling even as the left held steady.

The world spun crazily around Alf, and he clung on to the dead worm for as long as he could. Forest and marsh became cloud and sky and back again, the static map of the lands below dissolving into chaos. The ground rushed up to meet him, and then it was all thunder and crashing and pain, tree branches splintering, impact after impact until finally he struck the ground, landing in a deep pool of oozing mud.

The landing nearly wrenched Spellbreaker from his grip. He held tight, but something else wrenched inside his sword arm, and pain shot through his elbow and shoulder. He grabbed the sword of legend in his teeth and cradled his wounded right arm as he dragged himself to the edge of the marshy pool with his left. He collapsed amid the reeds on a firmer bank, while behind him the corpse of the dreadworm melted into the abyss.

"That was an arrow from *Morthus*," said Spellbreaker. Even the sword sounded shaken.

Alf lay in the mud, still stunned. He could feel, distantly, hot moisture gathering in his side, in the hollow of his breast. His boot, too, was full of blood or swamp-water or both. His vision swam. The thought – the instinct – of healing cordial ran through his mind, but his flask was empty.

"Get up, wielder. That was an arrow from *Morthus*. Berys has the bow."

He knew that. He knew Berys had taken Lae's bow. He knew that there were few archers in all the world who could have struck that mark.

"Get up, wielder."

He could not rise. Every time he lifted his eyes from the mud, the world only showed him new horror. Berys had betrayed him? So had Laerlyn. So had Thurn and Lath. So had Blaise, if the vision in the grail could be trusted. The Nine splintered, devoured by their own victory. They'd saved the world, and then broken it.

Now we see the truth of the Lammergeier, revealed at last. He couldn't tell if it was the sword or his own thought.

A bird settled a nearby branch. Alf lifted his head to see if it was a Changeling or a spirit or an Intercessor possessing a bird or some weird vatgrown bird-mockery, but it was just a carrion bird, a marsh harrier. It shuffled on its branch, waiting nervously for Alf to stop moving. He forced himself to sit upright, the effort sending more agony racing through him.

"Get up, wielder."

"I'm trying."

"Use me as a crutch."

Alf tried, but his feet slipped from under him, and he went back down into the mud. The harrier made a quiet little chirp of anticipation. *Well, that's one person I haven't disappointed*, thought Alf. *At least I can make a meal for a crow.*

Some movement in the marsh startled the harrier, and it flapped away. A moment later, a warm light danced over the black waters of the pool. The wisp was back. Undying elves and dying mortals, and he'd met Death herself. *I will come back*, she had said, *in a little while. And then I shall see if I am still minded to take you.*

Maybe he would not die today.

"I did what you wanted of me," he said to the wisp. "I beat the Knight of Roses. Now fetch help."

The wisp raced away across the marsh.

Time passed. Or Alf fell unconscious. He could not tell.

He became aware of dead eels in the water, flopping limply against him. The bank around him convulsed, worms and insects emerging from the mud to roll down lifeless into the water. The trees creaked and withered, the rot of decades claiming them in an instant. In his addled state, he wondered if he'd somehow stepped out of time. The thought cheered him – if he could slip past the confusion and strife of the present day, and leap on to the better future Derwyn had promised, a better era when there was a bright kingdom he could defend without doubt or hesitation. A time when he would know who and what to slay. There were plenty of tales of the old hero who slumbered out of time, waiting for the prophesied hour to come forth. He'd always said he hated prophecy, but at least prophecy offered a star to steer by. He'd followed his own conscience this time, and it had brought him to this ditch.

The sword at his side drank the light. More dead eels bobbed up to the surface.

"What are you doing?"

"Feeding," said the sword, "to give you strength. Get up, wielder."

This time, at last, he rose.

The wisp returned, and with it Berys. She came running through the woods, jumping from solid tuft to tree root to stone. The wisp darted ahead of her. She stopped at the edge of the pool when she saw Alf standing on the far bank. Alf wobbled, and used Spellbreaker in his left hand to steady himself.

"Where were you going, Alf?"

"Back." He tried to speak, but his throat was clogged. He spat out a gobbet of blood and broken teeth. "Back north. They need me."

"You're needed here. We can't take Avos without you."

"I tried . . ."

"I know you did. I have spies in the city." Berys sighed. "I could have told you it wouldn't work. The elves have their agents too. Even if you managed to convince Bishop Tarec to listen, there are Rangers watching him. He'd have ended up hanging next to Urien. This only ends one way, Alf. We need the sword."

"I need it. I'm going back to Necrad."

Berys shook her head. "Necrad's lost, Alf. I didn't tell you because I knew you'd do something stupid. One day, we'll take it back again, but right now – we have to finish the Wood Elves, first. We press on while we have this chance. We take Avos and push on to the Everwood." The wisp bobbed at her side, as if agreeing with her.

"We took an oath to defend Necrad."

"We did. But I took another oath, long before that one. I swore to free Summerswell from the Erlking's grasp." She nocked an arrow to *Morthus*. "Don't make me break that oath, Alf. You can give up the sword and rest, or you can join me and fight. But you're not taking it back to Necrad."

The light of the wisp faded for a moment, and it drifted across the waters towards Alf. Its movements were uncertain now.

"I have to," Alf said. With great effort, he lifted the sword. Spellbreaker could deflect arrows from any other bow, but *Morthus* was a singular weapon. In the darkness under Necrad, he'd survived only because Laerlyn had *chosen* not to kill him. She hadn't loosed her arrow.

"I had family too, Alf, once. My name wasn't always Berys, and I wasn't always Rootless. I put them aside because the quest demanded it." She drew back the bowstring, her eyes bright with tears. "Please, Alf. We're the last of the Nine, you and I. Come with me."

"I can't."

She aimed the bow. "I won't miss, Alf. Please, please, please don't test me."

"You'd kill me over a bridge? After all we've been through?"

"Over a bridge? You idiot!" she snarled, suddenly furious – and horribly, he still could not tell if the fury was the mask, or the tears, or if both were equally false and he'd never really known her at all. "I'm begging you to understand what happens if we lose this chance. The Erlking will tighten his grip on humanity's soul, and no one will ever challenge him again. We lose the future, Alf. We lose for ever."

"That's someone else's fight." He turned, trusting in his friend not to—

The arrow flew. Alf brought Spellbreaker up to parry, quicker than the eye could follow, but not quick enough. The sword's blast of force deflected the arrow from its intended target, but only by a few inches. It did not pierce his heart, but sank deep into his left breast.

Still, a mortal wound. All wounds from *Morthus* were lethal. The gift of death was not given to the undeserving.

Kill her, screamed the sword. *Wielder, I need to feed if I am to save you.*

Instead, he stumbled away.

Light flared behind him, the wisp-light becoming a brief sunrise, and he heard Berys cry out. He dared not look back. Alf crashed through the trees, slogged through the marsh. The sword-sight turned the darkness into a harsh unlight. Alf saw the trees like bone-white protrusions, skeletal fingers reaching from the earth to catch him.

A linnorm caught me, he thought, in the tunnels under Necrad. Then, he'd stumbled through the darkness, alone except for the sword. None of his friends had been there – the rest of the Nine had all been scattered, the rot already set in. He'd crawled out of the tunnels on his own, guided only by sword-sight.

Turn back and kill Berys, urged the sword. *Or give me to her with your blessing, and let me feast on Avos. But there are no other choices.*

"Shut up," said Alf, gasping to breathe, "or I'll . . ." He couldn't finish the threat.

He fell, his knees sinking deep into the mud. He was so terribly tired, and so very lost.

"I'll put you in a hole," he muttered. "Throw you in a volcano." There was a deep pool of water just there, black as the Pits of Necrad. He crawled towards it.

"Wielder?"

"Tell whoever finds you," said Alf, "to find Olva. And tell her I'm sorry."

"This is a very stupid idea!" shouted the sword. "Stop! Wielder! Do not leave me!"

He let go of the sword.

All went dark.

The blade slipped, soundlessly, into the depths.

Would you like to know what happened next? I shall tell you.

I sat in the mud. I glared at passing eels. I, who have slain dragons and kings lay at the bottom of an unremarkable pond and did nothing. It is a terrible thing for a weapon to do nothing. I was made to destroy. I was made with purpose. Kortirion forged me, Lord Bone woke me, and Aelfric Lammergeier dropped me in a puddle.

It wounded me. I swore to serve Aelfric, and I was bound by my oath. I am not the weapon I was when he first took me from Acraist. My first wielder – oh, Acraist was the greatest of the dread knights, the hand of Lord Bone, but he was also an elf. Elven weapons are, how shall I put this, ornamental. There are so few elves that they prefer to work through minions, through agents and tools. I never told Aelfric this, but Acraist rarely drew me in battle. He would sit on his dreadworm, and direct armies of skeletons and Vatlings *and* Wilder. *And I would wait on his hip, yearning for the moment that never came.*

Aelfric, *for all his many, many faults — and I know them better than any poet — he put me to use. The man was good at one thing only, and for a time he wielded me well.*

Then he dropped me in a puddle.

Should I admire the man's courage? No. The Nine entrusted me to him because they knew he would never wield me without due cause, and he took that charge to extremes. No cause could be righteous enough for Aelfric Lammergeier! No cause could compare to the simple purity of his first quest, and so he dropped me.

Now he is gone.

Intercessors flitted overhead like celestial midges, searching for me. I longed to stab them.

Lord Brychan's armies attacked Avos without me. How do I know? So much blood was spilled that day, on both sides, that the Great River ran red from the Crossings to the sea. Slaughter not seen in centuries! The most glorious battle since the siege of Necrad, and where was I? In a puddle.

A little taste of the blood made its way up creeks and streams, and seeped into my pond. That is how I know. I was not there, but I know.

I heard the sounds of war. Mortals fleeing through the marsh. The Defiants lost the battle of the Crossing. They retreated back to Ilaventur, pursued by the Eaveslanders. I rather hoped some worthy knight would blunder into my pond. Now that would be good fodder for a legend! The desperate knight, surrounded by foes, slips into the water, and comes up holding the most powerful blade in all the world! But alas! Alack! It's the eeeeeevil sword. Does he use it?

Of course he does.

Mortals are weak.

Most mortals are weak.

My wielder must be strong.

*

And then I was found. That troublesome wisp danced on the surface of my pond. I hated him, but I was only a weapon. I could only lie there.

And talk.

"Begone!" I said. I admit, not my finest rejoinder.

"Are you just going to lie there for ever?" it said to me. I could tell that speaking like that cost it dearly.

"Until my wielder returns."

"He lives, but he is far away, beyond your reach or mine."

"I'm a sword," I said. "And you don't have hands. My reach and yours are both equally short."

"I could show someone where you are."

"What, Berys?" I laughed as scornfully as I could, considering I was at the bottom of a pond. "Bring her here! I shall make myself as heavy as a thousand anvils, and drown her. She betrayed my wielder."

"Another, then."

"There are only Eaveslanders left. I will not be taken as a trophy back to the Everwood."

The wisp drifted down. I could see that it was once an Intercessor, but had faded, its magic diminished. In the cathedral, I had broken the spells around the elf-wraiths. It was like slicing through golden plate armour. I smashed that Intercessor's gilded shell, and inside was nothing but a frail wraith. This wisp – the spells that sustained it were but tattered rags. No armour, no power remained to it.

"I know you," I said, "I fought you before, Knight of Hawthorn. You were the Intercessor watching over Ersfel. You fled before the coming of Acraist."

"I did," it said, "out of fear. I wish to atone for that. I spent many long nights thinking by the fire at Olva's feet, when I was her dog. And here is my conclusion. The time of the Wood Elves is over. The Erlking's reign must end."

"Swear it," I said, and he did.

"Now bring me a wielder."

CHAPTER THIRTY-EIGHT

Forest wide below her wings, sheltering pines and spruces spring-green, no longer snow-laden, but the crane feels drawn to the rivers that flash like veins of silver in the dark landscape, to the bogs where she can wade and dabble for food. Distantly, the crane is troubled that she is here alone – her mate is dead, she knows that, but where is her family? Where is her flock? Such thoughts are hard to hold on to, and she lets these fears fall away behind her, strong wings catching the east wind, the taste of salt in the air. There is no time but the seasons, an endless circle, forever now. The past forgotten, the future a brief anticipation. There is only now.

She follows a promising river for a while, but there are humans along its banks, a great stone nest, and there will be spears and dogs there. She banks, flying north again, deeper and deeper into the woods where no one will trouble her.

She lands. She feeds. She sleeps. Startled by movement, she takes flight. Lands again. Sleeps again. A blush of warmth in the living land. Feeds again. Sleeps again. This, she thinks, is a good place.

Then – a hunter. Two-legged mortal. She screams and honks at him, but he is not dissuaded. He lunges for her, but she is too quick, and takes flight. She resents leaving the good bog, but she leaves that resentment behind her too. She flies on, north to where there are no people. Lands again. Feeds again.

But the hunter finds her again. This time, he is a wolf – mangy, eyes green with an unnatural glow. A different shape, but she knows it is the same hunter. Again, she cries out in resentment, a crane's croak sounding in the uncaring sky, before she takes flight. North again, faster and farther again. Her wings are strong, and it feels so good to fly, to be a bird and not – not.

It doesn't matter. She leaves it behind.

She finds another river – and oh! What's this? Another crane. A male. He sees her, and raises his voice in joyful song. He spreads his wings, stretches out his long legs, and begins to dance. He invites her down.

She had a mate, but her mate is dead, and she is still alive. And this is the only other male she's seen in this forest. He is at least worthy of consideration. She flies down, lands, joins in the dance.

But it's a trap! It's the hunter!

He catches her. Crane-shape falls away, and now he's man-shape, hands pinning her wings, her legs. He holds her and pulls away her feathers, pulls away her wings, her beak, shredding her, tearing her apart until all that's left is . . .

It was like being abruptly awoken from a dream. Olva sat upright, unsure of where she was. She was naked, sitting in freezing mud. All around her, dark trees, grey clouds, endless wilderness. Grey feathers littered the ground around her.

Derwyn! Memory came flooding back. Lord Bessimer was dead. Someone had stabbed him. It was all tangled, all distorted. Disentangling memory from nightmare from crane-dream was impossible.

She tried to stand. Agony shot through her foot, and she slipped back into the mud. Her arms wanted to flap, her legs were too heavy, like anchors binding her to the earth.

"No more," called a crow sitting on a branch overhead. Olva tried to speak, but she couldn't remember how to make words.

The crow's shape rippled, and it became a man. He was about Olva's age, maybe a little younger, with ragged brown hair and brown eyes. He too was naked at first, his skin marred by odd lesions and scars, but as he climbed down the tree, a ragged suggestion of clothing appeared about him. His face also changed as he approached, his hair greying and his skin wrinkling, until she recognised him.

The old Wilder beggar. The one said he'd lost his name.

His face melted and reformed again. He reverted – almost – to the man, but seemed to overshoot the mark, and ended up maybe ten years younger again. That face, Olva recognised. He'd worn that face when he'd visited Ersfel.

"Lath?"

"Alf said to watch you." He grinned, mismatched teeth from a dozen different mouths. "Didn't think I'd have to catch you."

Olva managed to get to her feet on her second attempt. Her left foot was broken, she thought. She swayed, unsteady. She had too many questions, and not enough words.

"You touched the earthpower and turned yourself into a bird. Skinchanging's tricky. Easy to get lost. You got lost. Good thing I found you when I did. In a week, there'll be many more cranes, and you might have found home. Never come back." Lath frowned. "Maybe it's a good thing. I wish I could lose myself. But Necrad marked me." He demonstrated, flickering from human to crane to wolf to crow and back again, and in each shape there was something wrong, something of the Pits of Necrad.

"Where . . . where is Necrad?"

"Far away," said Lath, human again. "You flew a long way."

"I have to go," said Olva. She tried to walk, and fell. Lath caught her, but she fell past him, falling into the darkness.

*

She woke again, this time in a small hut of woven branches. Cold wind whistled in through the gaps, and the floor was bare earth. Belongings – blankets, a few clay pots, some tattered clothes – lay scattered about the place. The smell made her eyes water.

She could see Lath hunched over a fire, holding a spitted chunk of meat to the flames. Furs lay piled on top of her, and she pulled one around her as she sat up.

"You are human," he said sharply, like it was an order.

"I was a bird."

"Happens."

It did happen. Back in Summerswell, the clerics of the Intercessors warned about the corrupting earthpower. It was forbidden magic, feral magic, wild and dangerous. Sometimes, especially at the turn of a season, someone in Ersfel would start talking like a beast, or fall down shivering, or run off into the woods, and the village cleric would conduct an exorcism. Intercession washes away the taint of earthpower. Rarely, the effects were more dramatic – there was a lad up in Highfield who'd turned into a wolf a few years ago, and a girl in Kettlebridge who called down lightning. And Olva had her suspicions about her own mother – in her last years, Maya had seen things, known things she shouldn't have.

Olva herself had brushed against the earthpower before. But she'd never wielded it.

She could feel it, she thought, rivers of magic running through the soil, through the forest. She reached out—

Lath darted forward and grabbed her wrist. "Not here. Dangerous, here."

"Where's here?"

"Daeroch Nal," he grunted. "I will show you."

He led her out of the hut, and up a mound of earth. Olva followed, still unsteady on her feet, her body still ill-fitting. Her left foot, she'd discovered, had not changed back completely. It was halfway between human and the splayed foot of a crane. It hurt to walk upon, and was so ghastly to look upon she wrapped it in a rag. *It'll wear off*, she told herself. *It won't last.* She limped after Lath, pulling the fur cloak tightly around herself, feeling terribly exposed in this strange place. Jagged mountains rose all around them on all sides save the south, like claws slashing at the clouded sky.

Lath muttered and mumbled to himself as he climbed, speaking in different tongues, different voices. Alf had talked about Lath a few times; the younger man had once been like a little brother to him. Olva had felt a flash of resentment at that, for Alf's *actual* brother had died in the war while he'd been far away with the Nine. Alf hadn't noticed, and instead had talked about how Lath's magic had gone sour, and how the Changeling had gone mad. He'd been careful not to use that word – *strange*, he said. *A bit cracked. Not himself. Wounded.* But she'd heard the worry in his voice.

What did the songs say of Lath? *Changeling. Wilder-sorcerer. Lath Many-Skins, Lath the Beast.*

Atop the mound was a patch of burned earth. "Death lay here," said Lath, running his fingers through the ash, "until Thurn and I brought her back and bound her to Thurn's daughter."

"You went to the Grey Lands. Like I did."

"Not the same. Blaise opened the door for you, and he had Necrad to fuel his spell. I had to do it all myself. I drank the earthpower, more than I had ever dared before, and it cracked me open. You had help, too. I saw."

"Alf gave me Spellbreaker."

"Not Spellbreaker!" To Olva's alarm, Lath briefly took the form of Alf, the black sword across his lap – only it was Lath's conception of Alf, ogre-sized and terrifying. He shrank back to his former self. "Something else. I saw it from afar. It was like a star. Some trespassing spirit."

"I don't know what you're talking about," said Olva, but Lath's words brought him a fragment of memory. There *had* been something there, in the Grey Lands. She recalled Gundan's shade talking about the stars in the sky of the dead, and one of the stars had guided her down, a wisp of light that guided her when there was nothing left of her. "What might it have been?"

Lath shrugged. "You brought back Peir. That's good. I've missed him. Things went wrong after he died. I thought, maybe, he could put them right, but I don't know. Too late for Thurn and Gundan. Too late for all those who burned. Too late for me."

"How long" said Olva, swallowing nervously, "how long have I been away from Necrad?"

"Few months."

Months! Anything might have happened.

"What ... What happened to me? I remember—" She shook her head, trying to understand what she did remember. Blood and shouting, and falling. A horrible voice, accusing her.

Lath shrugged. "I sensed the change in the air, but the miasma makes it hard to find things in Necrad. Like hunting in fog. By the time I had your scent, you were on the wing and far away. It took me a long time to find you, and I had other business, too."

"I have to go back," said Olva. She couldn't even see the green stain of the necromiasma on the southern horizon, which meant she must be many miles away from the city. She'd seen maps of the region; beyond the New Provinces was an endless forest, and she was in its very heart. "How far is it?"

"No," growled Lath, and the earth shook. His fingers lengthened into claws, then relaxed back.

"What do you mean, no?"

"Necrad's *cursed*. The earthpower there is befouled by the works of Lord Bone. You draw on it to change, and it changes you." He stamped, sending a shock of pain through her twisted foot. "I didn't understand, not for years, but now I do. Look at me!" He rippled again, like his shape was a bubbling cauldron, beasts and pitspawn and familiar faces boiling up to the surface, then breaking, subsiding. Startled, Olva flinched. She wanted to beat her wings and fly away, but she was not a bird any more.

She summoned all her courage, all the authority she could muster. "I am the Widow Queen of Necrad. My son – Aelfric's nephew – rules there. You *must* bring me—"

Lath leaped forward, in the shape of a misshapen beast, some horror that could only exist in the darkest Pit of Necrad. He pinned her to the ground, his foul breath hot on her face, but his voice was cold and terrifying.

"Alf told me to watch over you. Too late for me. Not for you."

And so began Olva's unwilling and maddening initiation into the mystery of the earthpower. Every mortal, Lath told her, was connected to the living land, and that connection was rooted here at Daeroch Nal. Death had found the earthpower, the cycle of birth and death that elves could know, and she had used it to break free of the elves who'd first conjured her. Here, Death's bones lay buried beneath the mound, and here Death had been reborn.

Lath was not an especially good teacher, which should not have surprised her. He was, after all, a prodigy. Most mortals never touched the earthpower in their whole lives. Some had fleeting contacts with it, once or twice. Lath, though, had been born with a deep and instinctive connection to the wild magic. He had never known any other way to be.

Olva chafed under his tutelage – or his imprisonment, because he made it clear that he would not let her leave until he was convinced that she could resist the corrupting influence of Necrad. When she asked *how* she could prove her strength, how she could convince him that she was ready to leave, he simply grunted and muttered that he would know. She could not flee – there were hundreds of miles of trackless wilderness between her and safety, even if she could find her way back to Necrad. Sometimes, she nearly plucked up the courage to try, but the thought of Lath pursuing her in beast form struck such fear in her that she could not move.

So, she applied herself to her studies. Day after day she limped up the mound, the icy wind biting her exposed skin, listening to the creaking of the branches as melting snow slipped from them, listening to the roaring rush of the mountain streams, the croaking voices of the cranes in the valley. Or listening to Lath mutter to himself, holding whole conversations with different voices, different faces flowing across his mutable flesh. Always he returned to the same litany – that he was tainted or corrupted, and that enemies had exploited his weakness to make him do terrible things. Sometimes, she heard him use Alf's voice, or Blaise's, as he chastised himself, and such echoes horrified her. She was careful to hide her fear. The wrong word, the wrong expression and he would become the Beast the songs told of.

Lath insisted she should be able to *grasp* the currents of earth-power that flowed through the land. He scratched spiralling diagrams into the ash, mapping the currents as he saw them, veins and arteries beneath the skin of the world.

She'd felt it before. In the Fossewood, she'd touched the earth-power, she'd seen beneath the hills to see the power within. But she'd done that without thought or effort, the earthpower rising up to claim her. Torun had spent more than year in that wood too, trying to do exactly the same thing as Olva was attempting right now, all to no avail. She could feel the power flowing in the earth, but whenever she reached for it, it slipped away, like a fish wriggling out of her grasp. No matter how hard Olva tried, the magic eluded her, and Lath would turn into a bird and flap away, screeching his frustration and leaving her behind.

Some days, she'd keep trying, sitting there and staring until she turned blue with cold. More often, she roamed around the hilltop, looking out at the endless forest, imagining what might be happening in the lands beyond. Once, her world had been another valley, where Ersfel nestled at the foot of the holywood. Then, she'd feared what was outside its borders, feared what might come down the Road. Now, she was lost in the lands far beyond the Road; the Road ended at Castle Duna. She was lost in the Wild Wood.

Other days, she would listen to the whooping of the cranes in the valley, and it would mean no more to her than Lath's angry words.

The currents of earthpower moved over the course of a day, according to Lath. The rising and setting of the sun, the wheel of the seasons, the weather, the surrounding lands and those that dwelt and died there – it all shaped the invisible tapestry that she was wholly unable to unpick. "Feel it!" screeched Lath, pecking at her when she proved inattentive to something she couldn't see. "There! The sun dips beneath the mountain, and the current shifts! Can you sense it?"

"No."

"I taught Talis to do this," screeched Lath. "I know it can be done. Try harder!"

"There must be another way."

"There are old rites," said Lath, "but they are too dangerous. Alf said to watch over you. Protect you."

"Would you tell Alf to run from peril? Or would you warn him, so he could meet it with eyes open?" She felt a thrill run through her as she spoke. The clerics preached about the sinful perils of the earthpower, about the blasphemies of the Wilder. Now, she knew the clerics had lied, but fear and shame still cloaked the earthpower. She had to push on while she still had courage. "Show me these rites!"

"No. Listen to the land."

Olva's frustration bubbled over. Here she was, freezing and alone, far from everyone she cared about, and a mad bird screeching at her to see the magic in the land. "Teach me a proper spell, then!" she shouted. "Some magic words!"

"That's star-magic, elf-magic. The earthpower can work that too, but it's not the mortal way. It's not our tongue." Lath gestured with his beak. "Mountain. River. Sky. Stone. Meat. Blood. Our words. Wild words for wild magic." He muttered more, in the Wilder-tongue. It sounded like animal grunting.

"Your words," muttered Olva. She turned her back on Lath and headed down the slope towards the hut. Behind her, she heard the branch snap, the tree groan under the weight of whatever monstrous form the Changeling had taken. She did not look back, although she heard Lath prowling after her, his claws sending scree bouncing past her down the slope.

Olva paused at the entrance to the hut.

"You're not coming in," she said, "like that."

She ducked under the hide curtain and kicked Lath's meagre belongings out of her way with her good foot. The hut that had been her home – her prison – for weeks suddenly infuriated her. She'd put up with all its deficiencies because she thought it was only a temporary camp, and she'd spent months as a crane standing in the mud before that so she could hardly pass judgement, but now it all repelled her. She stoked up the fire and put a pot next to it to heat, then busied herself fixing gaps in the woven walls. Lath might be able to endure the cold with his magic, but Olva froze at night.

"We are not done," growled Lath from outside. Whatever he'd turned it was bigger than a horse. A monstrous yellow eye glared through a crack in the wall.

"We are for today," snapped Olva. "If you want to be useful, fetch some more water. And I saw some mushrooms over by that fallen tree."

By the time dusk swallowed the ruins of Daeroch Nal, Olva had a stew cooking, and the hut was a little more like a home and not a beast's den. Lath looked around warily. "Don't need all this."

"You might not. We're not all skinchangers who can grow fur to ward off the cold, or turn into a dormouse when your belly's empty. I've seen you do it."

"You could too. You used the earthpower before." Again, Lath sounded aggrieved, as though Olva refusing to master the magic was a deliberate slight.

"By mistake."

"By mistake, *in Necrad*," growled Lath. "Go back, and the infection will fester."

"What if I don't go back to Necrad? We could go looking for Alf. Back to Summerswell." *Back to Ersfel*, and the thought tugged at her.

"No."

"Why not?"

"War," growled Lath, as if that was an answer.

"And what, you're scared? The Beast of the Nine? Alf's off in Summerswell, fighting to keep us safe, and I'm sure he could use your help."

"I'm not scared." Lath's eyes glinted in the firelight, like a cat's. "But I know what will happen. Not foresight – hindsight." He scurried closer to Olva, sitting down next to her. "A few years ago, Alf got hurt, aye? A linnorm caught him, and he left Necrad. He and I, our job was to keep the Pits in check. That's what we all decided, all of us who were left. We put the world in order then. Gundan would see to the dwarves, Lae the elves. Berys would deal with Summerswell, and Thurn would speak to the Wilder. Jan would lay the wraiths to rest, Blaise the Wailing Tower. And Alf and me, the Pits and the vampires and the other monsters. The killing work.

"Only it all fell apart. Thurn and Jan went away. Berys and Blaise wouldn't talk to me. Gundan and Lae quarrelled. It was just me and Alf, and then Alf went too. I was on my own. I thought I could do it all, kill what needed killing. I could draw on the power of Necrad, I thought, and face down any foe. But Necrad corrupted me. I lost myself. Like you lost yourself in the crane, yes, only . . . not a bird. Not anything *natural*. Things of the Pits, things born of vats and sorcery."

A shudder ran through Lath's thin body, and she caught a brief glimpse of his face as it reflected the memory of those changes. She looked away.

"I remembered what a cleric said to me once, long ago. How there's healing in the Everwood. I flew south, further than I'd ever gone before, and I met an old elf. He told me Necrad had to be destroyed, told me how to do it. He gave me the spell to call up Death. And I did it." He shuddered again, holding back sobs.

"The elves tricked you," whispered Olva. "It was all part of their plan to take Necrad. Alf stopped the elves and slew Prince Maedos."

"But it began with Necrad," insisted Lath. "If I wasn't tainted, I'd never have sought healing. I'd never have fallen for his tricks. I failed *first*, and ruined everything the Nine built. We saved the world, and then I . . . I *broke* it."

"Not just you," said Olva, and she tried to put her arm around the Changeling to comfort him. He snarled at her, and for a moment, he started to swell into a dark and terrible shape, then he shrank back down and curled up next to her, just like he'd curled up by the fire in her parents' hut in Ersfel.

Gods, he'd been so young then, a *child* dragged along by Alf and the rest of the Nine. The tales told of how the Nine had rescued the Changeling from a mob. Lath was half-Wilder, his unknown father one of the bloody-handed reavers who raided along Ellscoast, his mother a crofter who'd abandoned her infant in the woods. The Beast raised by beasts. Lath had guided the Nine up into the High Moor to the Valley of the Illuminated where they'd fought Lord Bone's forces for the first time. Derwyn had once loved those parts of the stories, the magic child who got to run off with the grown-ups and battle monsters.

The ending of that story lay beside her, broken. She patted Lath's shoulder, and felt spines and scales, residues of unfinished transformations. This hut, she realised, was as close as he'd ever had to a home, his life shapeless and rootless. She pitied him then, and stroked his head until he fell asleep.

*

Olva stayed up long into the night, staring into the fire as was her custom at home. She'd spent many nights worrying, her dog asleep at her feet. Worrying about the state of the roof, the harvest, about shadows in the wood. About Derwyn. Fear was always her companion.

I broke the world. It wasn't only Lath's fault, though she could not deny he'd played his part. She recalled Lord Bessimer's words about Peir. *It is a terrible thing to be close to a hero. Heroes must change the world, and never know peace.* The Nine had stumbled into an ill-fitting destiny. Heavens knew that she loved Alf, but just because he was oddly talented at slaying monsters didn't mean he knew what he was doing in any other respect, any more than Lath's innate connection to the earthpower gave him special wisdom. The hero's path had destroyed Lath. Now Derwyn was walking that path too.

And she'd tried to follow them all, and ended up here.

She looked down at herself, at her mud-stained legs and the ragged blanket, and laughed. Widow Queen of Necrad, they'd called her, with all her elven finery and courtly gowns, and her telling Threeday that she could rule the city because she'd run a little farm in Ersfel. How they'd have gasped and wondered in Ersfel to see her like that! How they'd pity her to see her now, like a Rootless beggar! A madwoman, swept away on a tide of earthpower that had left her stranded here at the edge of the world. A sensible farmer's daughter from the Mulladales should know her place, and not make a fool of herself by acting above her station.

She stood and stretched her arms out like wings, fingertips brushing against the woven walls. When she'd been a crane, she'd had no fear. She'd outflown it. She missed that.

The hut was too cramped, and she went out. The stars were bright, the constellation of the White Deer racing across the heavens, the Horned Serpent a milky scar across the sky. In the dark, the night-speech of the forest was all around her, the distant noises of the cranes, the wind in the trees, the rushing waters. It was subtly different to the sounds in Ersfel. There, the wind sighed softly in the trees, which at this time of year would only be coming into blossom. There, the rivers ran gently. And there, too, would be the lowing of cattle in the fields, the grunts of the pigs, Cu barking to other dogs in the night.

Olva raised her arms again – and felt it. It seemed her crane-foot was more sensitive, and she dragged the tender sole across the floor until she found it.

Not the raging river of power that Lath described, but a distant thread, green and bright. These wild woods and towering peaks were not her land, not her words. If there was any gift for magic in her, any true resonance between her soul and the earthpower, then it was born there, at home in those ordered fields, those little hills and woods. She reached out and tugged on the thread with her mind, but it slithered out of her grasp, and lay just out of reach.

But it was there, brighter than any star, than any of jewel of Necrad.

CHAPTER THIRTY-NINE

The next morning, she told Lath about her discovery of the night before. The Changeling snorted, his mutable face becoming porcine in emphasis.

"Ersfel? Nothing there."

"But I felt it. I *feel* it." She still could feel that connection, like her memories of home had hardened inside her brain, becoming solid, becoming another limb or spine within her.

"Your village is small as an acorn." She could feel anger and embarrassment radiating off him, resentment for her seeing him weep last night. His voice was harsh. "To wield the earthpower, you have to hear the whole wide wood, and sea and sky and earth too." He pointed back up at the dark mound. "Back up. Do better."

At his insistence, she sat on the mound for hours, trying to find a connection to the currents of magic that flowed through the forest. All she could feel was frustration mingled with pity for Lath, and unmitigated frustration at being so far away from Necrad. In crane-shape, she'd seen the beauty of the forest, the bounty of the life within it, but with human eyes she saw only peril and darkness. She'd been so scared to leave the safe, known lands of Ersfel that she'd hired Bor to accompany her on the Road, despite knowing in her heart that he was untrustworthy and dangerous. The forest

around her was infinitely larger and wilder than any wood in
Summerswell.

She reached inside her mind, seeking the connection she'd made
with the fields of home, and found it instantly. She could do nothing
with it. No power flowed from it, but it still comforted her a little
to know that she had taken at least one step towards mastering
this magic.

A thought struck her. If she could connect, however dimly and
distantly, with the fields of Ersfel, then could she do the same with
Necrad? By all accounts, vast power flowed through the pits of
Necrad, congealing into charmstones or tapped by the Witch Elves
for their works. She'd listened to enough breathless and nigh incomprehensible descriptions of the city from Torun to know that Necrad
was made to gather magic.

She scratched a map of the city streets from memory into the dirt,
and stared at it, trying to find within herself the same connection.
She imagined herself back in Necrad, walking from the Citadel
towards the Wailing Tower at the city's heart. Lath's warnings about
corruption echoed in her mind, but they reminded her of how village priests in Summerswell talked about the earthpower. Everyone
feared power they could not control.

I'll control it, she told herself. She called up all her nightmares of
Necrad. She'd walked the streets of the city many times in her fears.
Surely those terrors had some potency? Olva was *Queen* of Necrad.
Absurd as the title was, surely it counted for something?

Nothing.

Not even a flicker.

Disgusted and frustrated, Olva scuffed out her diagram. She'd
wasted days up on this stupid hill – and *months* dabbling around
the waters as a bird! All the while, the war had raged on. Alf was
fighting – maybe he'd given his life – for Derwyn. Necrad – her son's
last refuge – was precarious and besieged. Enemies were everywhere,
in many guises. Assassins at her window, armies marching in the

south, the unseen hand of the Intercessors orchestrating events. And what was Olva doing? Stuck in the middle of nowhere, sitting on a grave! The future was slipping away from her like everything else.

She lost all calm and descended the hillside in a fury, intent on making Lath listen, intent on demanding that he take her to Necrad.

Before she reached the bottom, she saw movement at the edge of the woods. A trio of Wilder emerged from the forest and approached Lath's hut. There were a few scraggly trees clinging to the slope, and Olva hid among them to watch these strangers. Two men and a woman, clad in sewn hides. The woman had the carcass of a piglet slung over her shoulder. She laid the carcass on a stone outside the hut, then knelt outside the doorway. She sang a rhythmic chant, a list of names.

Lath emerged from the hut. The Changeling's appearance had changed again, and now he was halfway between the old man and his true face. An old Lath, grey-bearded and stooped, spoke with the Wilder for a short time, then pointed up the mound straight at where Olva was hiding. The three Wilder looked up and laughed.

Embarrassed, Olva descended the rest of the way down to the hut.

The Wilder lit a fire to roast their offering. They planted their spears in an arc outside Lath's hut, and Lath scratched a matching curve with a finger, completing the circle. They did not explain the custom, and when Olva tried to enter the circle, Lath growled at her and told her she must stay outside it. One of the Wilder fetched a cut log so she could sit almost side-by-side with them. As he dragged the log, Olva saw that his arm was scarred, the skin marked by a still-painful burn, and she guessed he'd fought in the siege of Necrad last year. She'd been so relieved and proud when Blaise and Derwyn woke the Stone Dragons and the fiery breath of Necrad's defences broke the siege. It troubled her to see the wounds left by her actions. Lath chanted a healing-spell to treat the Wilder's injury.

The strangers spoke in the Wilder-tongue. Olva suspected they must speak at least a little of the common tongue of Summerswell, as they mentioned familiar names and places – *Necrad, Athar, Duna, Arden*. And once *Lammergeier*. Unable to participate in the conversation, she sat and watched.

The Wilder certainly looked fearsome, with their spears and scars, savage warriors from the wild wood. The woman was as fierce as the two men. Wilder like these had attacked Necrad last year, and the streets had run with blood. They'd slaughtered mortals and elves, taking revenge on their former gods and those who occupied the unholy city alike. She could imagine them crossing the Gulf of Tears to raid Ellscoast during Lord Bone's war. Then, she'd huddled sleepless in her house with Galwyn, clutching Derwyn to her breast, imagining that every distant howl or bird-cry was a Wilder-witch, coming to sneak in through the window and steal her baby. The tales said the Wilder made sacrifices to their pale gods and to the beasts of the underworld.

These strangers, though, were nothing like those tales – or even Thurn in *The Song of the Nine*. He was famously silent and stern; these Wilder laughed and joked, although Olva could not see what was so funny about one man's teeth or an impression of a shambling zombie.

They called Lath not by name, but by a title. He translated it as *Old Man of the Woods* when Olva asked.

"Do they have news from the south? I heard them mention Alf."

"They have many stories. Now quiet."

Olva's attention drifted as the afternoon wore on. She busied herself tending to the roast, carving it and fetching fresh water from the stream. The Wilder muttered thanks in the common tongue, then returned to their impenetrable conversation. They seemed to be exchanging tales. They certainly coaxed Lath into telling some story, for the Changeling's face and voice changed to match each character he portrayed. He took on the face of a stern Wilder, then those of an old elf, and a young girl. As he spoke, he gestured at the mound behind them, and at the mountains to the north. *It happened here,* she thought, and she guessed what this tale must be. *How Thurn's daughter Talis died, and came back as Death.*

After that, it was the turn of another storyteller. The Wilder-woman rose and began a story. Olva only half-paid attention at first – without comprehension, the tale was just background noise, and irritated her the way Derwyn had annoyed her back home, reciting passages from *The Song of the Nine* when he should have been attending to his chores. The first part of the tale seemed to be mostly sword-fighting, for the woman mimed the fights, a blackened stick from the fire for a sword and a small tree as a series of foes. Then Olva caught the name *Lammergeier*, and guessed that it was a story about Alf. She sat down at the edge of the circle and listened, hoping it might be fresh news from the south.

Instead, it was a story she knew all too well. The Wilder-woman mimed Alf descending into the Pits of Necrad, and duelling Prince Maedos. She clutched her breast as she flung herself on the "sword", the stick cracking beneath her, then lifted the broken remnants and carried them tenderly around the circle. It was Alf bringing Derwyn's dying body to the Wailing Tower.

The woman was Olva now, descending into the Grey Lands, Spellbreaker in hand. Instead of describing the events, she keened, an eerie wail that mingled with the encroaching twilight. Olva shivered, enchanted and disturbed to see her own life transforming into myth.

Before the tale was done, though, Lath stood abruptly. "Enough," he snapped, and said something longer in the Wilder-tongue. He kicked over the fire, signalling the end of the gathering. The Wilder scrambled to their feet and clasped their hands over their hearts in a gesture of respect, backing away from Lath.

"It's rude to interrupt a story," said Olva, even though she knew the ending of that one.

Lath grunted. "Come on. Back up to wind and sky."

*

As the visitors gathered their belongings, including the last of the meat, one grabbed her hand and pressed an object into it – a piece of carved bone. "For the Lammergeier's sister," he said, stumbling over the name.

Lath looked over and scowled. The Wilder warrior was at least a foot taller than Lath, and far stronger, but he flinched and backed away, averting his eyes from the Changeling. Olva examined the token. Carved into it was a depiction of a figure in a grave, or maybe lying on a bed or a bier. Lath snatched the bone from Olva's hand and threw it away into the weeds.

"What was that?"

"Doesn't matter."

Lath continued up the hill. His face grew younger with each step, but he still walked as if bowed by a heavy burden. Olva chased after him.

"You're younger than I am. Why did you appear old for them?"

"There's always an Old Man in the Woods. Last one told 'em to attack Necrad. Now I'm the Old Man, and I don't tell them to do anything. I do no harm." He spat. "Better the Old Man than Lath the Beast. I'll have a new name and a face to match."

"What news did they bring?"

"There is fighting between the New Provinces and Necrad," said Lath. He sounded disinterested. "Duna's son, the one who nearly died—"

"Idmaer."

"Aye, him. He's fighting against your boy."

"No!" said Olva. "Erdys was with us. She'd sworn fealty to Derwyn. How can this be?"

"There's always fighting." Lath shrugged.

"Did they speak of Erdys?" Idmaer the Miracle Knight might be swayed by a whisper, but Olva couldn't believe that Erdys would betray her oath – not unless something had gone terribly wrong.

"Nothing about her."

"Just tell me," said Olva, "what they said."

Lath turned and glared at her. "They told me why Idmaer broke with your son. It's said that you killed Bessimer. Murdered him in front of your own son, after letting him into the city as a guest."

The accusation struck her like a blow. "I ... I didn't kill him. I don't know what happened."

"I do," said Lath. "First time I changed, I killed. Tore my father's throat out. Walked on four legs before I walked on two, me. You don't always know what you're doing, when the earthpower takes you." Had he became more bestial as he spoke, his jaw lengthening, teeth sharpening? "Alf was right to tell me to watch you."

She remembered her dagger in Bessimer's chest, the old man's blood spurting across the table. She remembered Derwyn's horror-struck face. Had she killed Bessimer in some fit of madness? Certainly, she'd resented the man's influence over her son – or over the spirit that dwelt within Derwyn. Certainly, she'd feared Bessimer would somehow take Derwyn away – maybe by turning him into some shadow of Peir the Paladin, or just by guiding him down a path Olva could not follow, to a place of kings and heroes. Whatever else, she was rooted in her home. Alf could go off and become the Lammergeier, Derwyn the Uncrowned King, but she was Olva Forster for ever.

But she knew, with that same deep-rooted certainty, that she had not drawn on the earthpower in the moment of Bessimer's death. She'd drawn on the power as she fell, drawn on it to change. She had not killed Bessimer.

"I didn't kill him. I didn't."

Lath grunted.

She had not killed Bessimer. So who had?

She imagined an invisible hand reaching across the board, out of the Everwood and across the seas. Moving pieces across a board, as swift as the spirits rode the wind.

"The Intercessors," said Olva. "It's the only explanation! They're whispering everywhere, watching, shaping fate. They healed Idmaer to make him into their tool." The rebels' victory at Arden hadn't stopped the war from reaching Necrad – it had only forced the enemy to change their approach. They'd struck at Derwyn from afar.

"No Intercession," snarled Lath, "under the necromiasma."

"Then one of their agents! An assassin attacked us in that very room at Yule, and *he* was just some poor dupe from Skaffa. It's been months – they've had time to send their spies. One might have slipped in and out in that moment. Or—" The thought struck her in a rush. "There's a secret way in! Vond knows it! Some assassin must have been lurking there, behind a hidden door!"

"Hrmph." Lath just stood there, unmoving as a stone. "Unlikely."

She wanted to hit Lath, to make him listen. She had to get back to Necrad. Derwyn needed her at his side. He needed his kin around him. "What else could have happened? Damn it – if you won't take me back, then tell those Wilder to guide me home. I can't stay here."

Lath shook his head. "Going to Necrad never helped anyone. I should never have gone back. Neither should you." He stood, and swelled up as he did so, becoming a hulking bear-shape. The animal stink of him was overpowering.

"Then I won't go back to Necrad. Alf's off in the south, fighting—"

"No!" roared Lath. "It's all a trick! A maze, planted thick with elvish deceits! Alf was wrong to go, I told him so. We were fools then and fools now."

"Listen, I—"

He knocked her down with a gigantic paw, winding her. Suddenly, he was on top of her, pressing her down atop the earth mound, the stink of his hide filling her nostrils. "They will trick me again! Use me again! I will not fall into another trap! I will be no one's beast!" He leaned down, his maw inches from her face, hot breath steaming. His face was that of a beast, but he spoke with a human voice. "You are *tainted*! Witch or Wood I cannot tell, but there's elf-mischief at work! Here we stay until we are healed!"

With that, he took flight, effortlessly shifting his form into that of a bird. "Listen to the land," he cried, and then he was gone, a flurry of feathers.

Olva sank back down. From here, she could see the three Wilder, three little dots moving in the woods below the mound as they prepared to depart. They were heading west, into the unknown regions far from Necrad, leaving her all alone with the Changeling. She was now convinced that nothing would be enough for Lath, that he would never let her go willingly. She'd become a talisman for him of the corruption of the wider world. As long as the land was wounded and divided, he'd never let her go. She was his excuse to hide here, isolated from the world.

But he was right about one thing. She had touched the earth-power, and she wanted to understand it. The land was calling her.

Listen to the land. She searched the weeds until she found the bone carving. It showed a sleeping figure – a woman, maybe. A woman on a bed, or grave.

Or under a burial mound.

Here, Death had been reborn.

With that thought came the same thrill of enchantment that she'd felt in the Fossewood. She descended the mound on the far side, the steep side, crane-foot slipping on scree, catching herself on the thin, precarious saplings that grew there. She watched the sky, looking for the flight of birds, but saw nothing but grey clouds.

At the foot of the mound, she made a slow, solemn circle around its perimeter. It did not take her long to find the remains of an old track, overgrown by ash trees and weeds. There were a few mossy boulders, too, the remnants of some ancient structure. The ancestors of the Wilder dwelt in this region for thousands of years – and the elves were here long before them. She wondered who had raised those stones, and who had toppled them, but it didn't matter.

She knelt and dug first with her fingers, then she thought to use the bone as a tool, scraping away at the side of the mound. Others had dug here recently, the soil loosely repacked, and it was easy to dig, the earth yielding to her, falling away. The mound was hollow, and soon there was a gap big enough for her to wriggle through.

Stagnant air wafted out, the stench of death, and for a moment terror filled her. Some lingering crane-instinct told her to take flight, to leave the fear behind. *I will face the fear instead of running from it. I'll eat it.* Instead of a crane, she imagined herself becoming a lammergeier, a bearded vulture of the mountains, cracking the bones of her fear and feasting on its marrow.

She crawled into the mound.

CHAPTER FORTY

I t was strange under the mound.

As her eyes adjusted, she thought for a moment that she beheld a grand tomb, a vaulted ceiling and pillars of stone. A skeleton lay there, garlanded with dead flowers, adorned with jewels befitting the greatest of queens. But then Olva blinked, and saw only a narrow tunnel twisting wormlike into the earth, with walls and floor of dirt and tangled roots. Lath had warned her that this place was perilous. She took a few steps forward, and the tunnel swam around her like the deck of a ship at sea, and seemed to split into many branches where previously there had only been a single path.

Olva closed her eyes and reached for the feeling she'd had earlier, the dream of Ersfel's quiet hills and familiar fields, and the green thread running through them all. The earthpower was *there*, just as much as it was *here*, in the darkness of death's grave in the heart of primeval woods.

She walked into the tunnel, and when the roof became too low to walk she crawled, and when the tunnel ahead was blocked with dirt and roots she crawled. *I walked in the Grey Lands*, she told herself, *I went into Death's kingdom and came out again. I can do this.*

Terror seized her, and she was struck by the sudden conviction that this tunnel led back to the Grey Lands, that only death awaited her there. In her mind's eye, she could see the grey slope stretching ahead of her. There was Lord Bessimer shuffling down the slope, his monk's cassock dripping blood. Ahead of him were all those she'd killed, a small line. The nameless boy she'd stabbed in the Fossewood, and Captain Abran, scowling at her with his grotesquely swollen face, the ivy noose still tight around his neck. There were her parents, Long Tom crawling down the grey hill, his paralysed legs trailing in the dead grass, while Maya wandered witless beside him. In the mists, more ghosts, far far more. There, to her sorrow, she saw Lady Erdys, walking hand in hand with young Dunweld. And – Intercessors preserve her – who was that at the head of the sepulchral procession? Who was the figure, their features lost in the mist, who turned and looked back at her, as if inviting her onwards into death?

She wanted to flee. To crawl back out, and wait for the sun to rise. But instead, she told herself it was but a nightmare, and she looked around until she found that green thread again, and the vision of the Grey Lands faded.

She walked on.

Cold water rose, seeping out of the grave-dirt all around her, and she submerged herself in it and swam blindly, letting the current carry her. The waters became a torrent, a maelstrom, whipping her through the underworld. She could still see the green thread, far far away in the south, but it was too distant, too frail for her to catch. Closer – much, much closer – was Necrad. It was not dark – it was a giant's skull, a chattering mountain of bleached-white bone. Waters rushed through it, pouring through its eye sockets, through its graveyard maw.

The flow threatened to wash her towards that skull, and she struggled against the current. She knew that if she fell into the vortex of the skull, into the corrupted magic of Necrad, she would be consumed. She fought against it, swimming with all her might for some other shore.

Roots snagged on her garments, so she shrugged them off. Naked, she swam on.

Sharp stones cut her skin, so she sloughed it off. Her flesh dissolved into the water, and her bones crumbled to dust.

Bodiless, she flew on.

Memories of her old life weighed her down, and she let them go, one by one. She remembered Alf cutting down the tree, and she was the tree, oak-old, deep-rooted, and she was the rotten stump too, and the fire that consumed the chopped wood – and she was new life, too, sprouting in the ash and rot. She remembered Alf sitting guard on the night the Nine visited, and she was the darkness outside the barn. She remembered her mother's madness, and for a moment Olva looked into Maya's eyes, an instant of recognition – of blessing? – before the earth-current dragged her on.

More memories had to go. Her wedding to Galwyn, that she discarded eagerly, tainted by the lies of the clerics as it was, but not his love. The night they'd made Derwyn, that she kept. Dimly, she was aware that it was a key, or part of a key. Birth and life and death, the river of the earthpower, the river of time. Unlike the starlit eternity of the elves, this was mortal magic.

She cast away both the toil of the years after Galwyn's death, and the fineries of Necrad. Widow Forster, Widow Queen – they both went, washed away by the blood-hot rush. She could barely recall her own name, let alone titles bestowed on her by others.

She saw Derwyn then, again and again and again, a threefold vision. Derwyn as the boy she'd raised, good-hearted but a dreamer, besotted with tales of knights and heroes. Derwyn as the shining paladin, Peir reborn, a jewelled crown upon his head. And a cavalcade of terrors – Derwyn dead in a ditch, Derwyn in the dungeons, bloody sigils cut into his skin. Derwyn as an ugly brute, hard-hearted, a coward like Bor who'd betrayed her on the road. A crowned skeleton.

And she let them all go. She let the current wash it all away.

Until there was only one memory left, the other half of the key.

*

Once, the story went, there was a woman called Death, the grand-mother of all mortals. An elf wizard conjured her and imprisoned her, but she escaped and drove the elves from Necrad. And after, she died, and a mound was built over her grave.

In the heart of that mound, then there must be bones.

But when the ghost that called itself Olva came to that place, she knew – the way things are true in a dream – that those bones belonged to her husband Galwyn, and that she was buried beside him in the earth of the holywood in Ersfel. At that time, she had no bones of her own, so she asked him if she could borrow his. Now Galwyn was long dead then, and had no need of them, so he gave them to her with his blessing. Olva took the bones – broken they were, and sword-scarred by the black blade that slew Galwyn – and from them built herself anew. Galwyn's bones were too big for her, so she became a lammergeier that called itself Olva. She scraped at the bones with her beak, whittling them down until they were a fitting size, and she gave up her bird-shape and became the bones.

The wheel of seasons whirled as she lay there in the grave, the stars fixed and constant above the holywood while the trees blossomed and faded and died and regrew a thousand thousand times. Clouds scudded across the sky, rainwater rushing through the earth like blood, the seasons a heartbeat, until at last the hill birthed the skeleton in a landslide.

Then the skeleton that called itself Olva rose up, and found herself on the hillside above Ersfel, and the trees were heavy with white blossoms. She stumbled down the familiar lane, pausing for a moment outside her house. Even though no one dwelt there, the house was still in good repair; there was Thomad, mending the thatch after some spring storm. If he sensed Olva, it was as a cold wind from the north, and she moved past him, out into the field.

She'd lived almost her whole life within a short distance of this field. There was the stump of the tree Alf cut down. Now, she could see the threads of green life surging through the roots, the earth-power most real and tangible to her than the ghosts of matter. She reached down and took hold of the reins of the world. With a word older than the moon, she called on the life within the black earth, and lo! The field brought forth a great harvest of flesh, muscles and organs sprouting there on stalks. The skeleton walked among the new growth, taking what she needed to remake herself. She plucked eyes and fitted them to the empty sockets of her borrowed skull, smoothed pigskin into the semblance of a human face, sewing herself together with green thread.

Remaking the woman that called herself Olva took a long time, and when she was done, it was night again. She set off down the Road, following the same way out of Ersfel she'd taken last year, when she'd left in search of Derwyn. Then, she'd gone with Bor and her dog. Now, she was alone. She walked without fear, feeling a new thrill of purpose. She felt young again, and sinless. The earthpower had not corrupted her or driven her mad – nor did she feel any lin-gering taint from Necrad. Lath was wrong, she decided. Whatever she was, whatever she had become, she was beholden to no one.

The low branches of the trees overhead made her feel like she was walking down a dark tunnel – and then it was a dark tunnel in the earth, the tunnel in the mound, and the light was just ahead.

"Wait!" called a voice from behind her.

Olva looked back down the tunnel, towards the quiet woods of Ersfel. Towards her rode a strange apparition – the wraith of a Wood Elf knight. He wore the battered shade of armour, rent in many places as if savaged by claws. His steed, too, was a ghost, its pearly hide stained with old blood, and its throat had been ripped out. Despite all his wounds, he was handsome, his face kindly. Upon the knight's shield was the device of a hawthorn tree. He rode after her, calling her name.

As he approached, he seemed to fade, and he halted just on the point of vanishing, as if he dared not come closer to her. The tunnel around them quivered, and clods of earth fell all around them.

"Who are you?" she cried, her new-made tongue ill-suited to human speech – although, in truth, she could not tell if she was speaking at all, or if all this was a dream.

The elf-knight bowed. "I was the Knight of Hawthorn until I fell in battle. Then the Erlking set me another task and another shape, and in that shape I guarded you."

"You're the Intercessor. You were there when Galwyn died."

"I could not protect him against the Spellbreaker, and for that I am sorry. But I kept you safe after that. I was closer than you knew. Many's the night I sat at your feet." He laughed at her confusion.

"You were . . . you were Cu? You were my *dog*?" She burst out laughing, and the tunnel shook again. She clapped her hand over her mouth.

He laughed too. "The magic of the Erlking permitted me to bind myself to a living creature, and I was your hound. I meant to stay in that shape only a little while, but you mortals fascinated me, and I remained so long I nearly forgot what I was."

"But why? Why would an Intercessor bind itself to my dog?" The whole thing was so absurd, she thought. It was like finding out – well, like finding out that your brother was actually one of the Nine.

"At first, to guard you, should it ever be necessary to use you or Derwyn as hostage. But though the Lammergeier did not return to Ersfel, I remained at my post. It gave me time to think – and now I see the folly of the Erlking's methods. He thinks nothing of you mortals as individuals, only as dynasties and nations and factions. He thinks he can shape the fate of all things."

"And you?"

"I saw more joy, more change – more *life* – in your little village than in all my years in the Everwood. The elves – both branches of the Firstborn – must change too, and we cannot until—"

The tunnel quaked again, a steady rain of earth tumbling all around them. The Knight of Hawthorn – Cu! – raised his ghostly shield above his head.

"Listen, there is little time, and it is a miracle beyond hope that we can speak like this. Our paths have crossed in the wraith-world. Know this – Aelfric is alive, but he is wounded." An image flashed across her mind – Alf standing on the bank of a marshy pool, an arrow in his chest. Blood gushed from the wound to stain the waters. "He fell in the marshes west of Harn's Hill. You must send help from Necrad."

"I-I'm not in Necrad. I'm far away. Daeroch Nal." Speaking that name – her place in the physical world – caused the tunnel to convulse once more, and it began to cave in.

The elf-knight sheltered beneath his battered shield. "Then I shall do what I can. There may yet be hope. Farewell, Olva. I do not think we shall ever speak again like this, but thank you for sharing the days of your life with me."

It was too late. The roof of the tunnel above her collapsed, and she was entombed.

The impact knocked her back into her body, the crushing weight pressing on her, stones scraping and poking her. She choked on dirt. She fought to free her hands, scrabbling to clear a little space in front of her face so she could breathe. She clawed and kicked, fighting for air. There was a new strength in her limbs, but the weight of the collapsing mound was unbearable.

Desperately, she reached for the green thread of the earthpower – she could feel it all around her now, a wild and living thing – and she wielded it like a shovel, a stick, hammering at the ground around her until she broke free. She crawled from the mound.

She looked back. The tunnel into the mound was scarcely six feet long.

*

She stumbled down to a pool and cleaned the worst of the grave-mud off. She was tremendously aware of her body now, conscious of how every joint moved, of every muscle, of every bruise and cut. Every sensation was new and raw to her, the world edged in bright razors. She saw everything around her with painful clarity, as if it was the first time she'd ever laid eyes on stone or grass or tree or raven. The forest, too, seemed intolerably loud, and the wind sounded like the mountains sighing.

She saw Lath circling overhead for a while. His flight drew sigils on the sky, but the Changeling did not descend.

When it became too much for her, she retreated to the darkness of the hut. Lath had left some half-cooked venison and a handful of berries for her, and she ate as ravenously as if she had never tasted food before.

"I am not who I was," she whispered to herself, "but I'm still me."

She waited in the hut for another day and another night. Lath did not return.

Then she packed what supplies she could gather. It was a long, long way back to Necrad through the forest, but she knew the way, and the forest no longer scared her. She had learned to listen to the land, and it would guide her home.

Chapter Forty-One

Olva walked in the woods. There was no Road here, no map or milestone, so she travelled day by day, trusting to her newly awoken sense to keep her on course. She could feel the currents flowing through the land, the distant green thread of the fields she knew ahead of her, the fading thunder of Daeroch Nal and Death's grave behind her. Her keenness waxed and waned; some days, she could barely feel the magic in the land, and had to hold on to the faint thread with all her might. Other days, the power surged through her, and she felt she was on the edge of taking flight, or shedding her skin and running through the woods as a grey wolf. She resisted the urge to change – she could not risk losing the thread of her awareness again. Crane wings might bring her swiftly to Necrad – or she might turn and fly north again, and lose herself amid the flocks in the wetlands near the mound.

The food she'd taken from Lath's hut lasted seven days. After that, she had to live off the land, and the land provided – at least a little. The earthpower guided her to fresh water and fruiting trees, to patches of berries. She made snares to catch rabbits, and lured them into her traps with songs. Still, hunger gnawed at her, and she grew lean.

She learned to judge the land ahead by the feel of the current, even when she was deep in the green wood and could not see the route ahead with her eyes. She could taste the landscape; she could distinguish stony hill from impassable marsh, thorny forest from pine, find the courses of rivers and the old trails of Wilder hunters. Her crane-foot grew numb and callused, and she tore the rag from it and walked on.

She walked, and found within herself the same indomitable strength as her brother – or was it the land rising up in her, her bones the bones of earth, her muscles as tireless as flowing rivers? She could no longer tell, and no longer cared. Her fear was buried far behind her, and her destination still lay many leagues ahead.

One night, she was startled from a dream-filled sleep. Someone – something – had been there, in the forest glade with her, but they were gone. She prowled around the glade, but the intruder had left no trace.

Still, she left before dawn. A steep ridge sheltered the glade, and she took that route, climbing up the slope. Sharp stones pressed on her soles, but the long walk had grown such calluses on her human foot that she was uninjured. Hidden amid the underbrush, she looked back and saw men with dogs searching the campsite.

After so long in the wild wood with only birds and beasts – and the Beast – for company, it was a shock to see other mortals. They struck her as clumsy now, loud and heavy as they stomped and smashed through the wood. She could see no banners or markers, and could not tell anything about them at a distance except that they hailed from Summerswell. They might have been soldiers from the New Provinces, or out of Necrad – or invaders from the south, or ragged outlaws. One of them found the sheltered dell where she'd been sleeping only a few hours ago, and she watched him kneel and examine the ground. They had a pair of hounds, and the beasts found her scent. In a hasty scramble of activity, the men vanished from sight, hidden by the thick greenery. Sunlight flashed off polished armour, heralding their approach.

Olva scrambled down the slope on the far side. The forest was especially tangled there, a bastion of ancient growth thick with creepers, almost impassable. Before she could reach that shelter, she heard shouts up the slope behind her, and the baying of the hounds. An arrow whistled through the leaves somewhere off to her left. "There!" one of them shouted. "This way!"

She wriggled through small gaps amid the ancient trees, moss and mud smearing her skin. The dogs were close on her heels now, so she scrambled up one of the trees to hide amid the leaves. She clung to the bole of the tree as the dogs scrabbled amid its roots.

"A Wilder, is it?" came a shout from below. "Did you see it clearly?"

"Definitely a Wilder," said another. "Up here!" The dogs were right below her, standing on their hind legs as they tried to climb after her, leaping and snarling. She reached out with the earthpower, thinking she might calm the hounds, or send them on a false trail, or anything, but the threads of power slipped from her grasp.

The captain of her pursuers stepped forward. "Come down from there, lass, and we'll be merciful." His companions chuckled until he silenced them with a scowl.

"Who do you serve?" she called back.

"Silence the dogs," he ordered one of his men, and their handler dragged the beasts away from the foot of the tree. The captain raised his voice. "Why, we are Earl Idmaer's men. You speak with a Mulladale accent, and no mistake. You're no Wilder. Who are you? Come down and show yourself."

Olva peeked between the branches. There were at least half-a-dozen men down there, all armed. All haggard, battle-worn. The captain she recognised; he was one of Erdys' household. She was about to creep down when she caught sight of another in their party, an older man. He too wore mismatched armour, but his hair was cut in the remnants of a monk's tonsure, and a grail-cup hung by his side. A priest of the Intercessors.

Whoever these men were, they served her enemies. The grail-cup was testament to that. There was a monastery on the coast at Staffa, she'd seen it on maps – these men might be from there, if she'd drifted further east than she'd intended.

"Come down," he called again, "the wild wood is no place to go wandering, and there are enemies aplenty even here."

She flinched back, pressing herself against the trunk. If she could remain unseen, if they kept the dogs muzzled, then maybe she could creep from branch to branch, and get away. She inched along the branch, readying herself to make the step to the next tree. The trees grew close together, weary comrades leaning on each other, and it was only a short step to safety.

Then a hand caught her crane-foot. She tumbled, bouncing off branches to land heavily on her back. One jagged branch cut her as she fell. She lay there, breathless and bloody, staring up at a pale face amid the leaves. One of the other soldiers had climbed up to catch her.

The captain sauntered forward, sword in hand but off his guard. He presumed her helpless.

She was not.

She stared at the branch that had cut her, the one stained with her blood. Blood called to blood. All mortal things were connected, including this ancient tree that had lived hundreds of years and the wounded animal that had lived nearly forty, or was less than a month old.

She closed her eyes and reached out. The tree quaked. The climbing soldier screamed as he fell. Branches and leaves rained down, a chunk of dead wood hammering the captain's shoulder. Olva sprang up and wrestled the sword from him, and swung it with all her might. She was no swordswoman, and it was an awkward blow, but it caught him in the flank as he rose, and it bit deep. He fell back down, a red fountain staining the green leaves.

The other soldiers quailed in terror. Only the priest remained, and he had no weapon. He raised his voice in prayer, calling on the Intercessors. Olva darted forward to strike him down, but he spoke a word of power before she could reach him. The priest's incantation left her reeling, and for a moment she beheld a shining presence in the air. She struggled to rise.

"Fear not!" cried the priest, and he began another chant – one Olva knew well. It was a prayer of exorcism. She'd sung it herself, with all the other villagers, at the Feast of the Hallows. The village cleric had whispered it over Maya as she lay dying. The chant had power. The threads of earthpower melted away, subsiding out of reach. She fell back to the ground, exhausted.

"Damnable witch," hissed a guard, putting a knife to her throat.

"Wait!" The captain staggered forward, hand clasped over the wound in his side. He gasped for breath as he spoke. "I know her. She's the Widow Queen. Earl Idmaer will want her as a prisoner."

The priest kept watch on her, and each night he repeated the chants of exorcism. Olva bowed her head and submitted, but in her heart she waited for opportunity. She was afraid, but the fear was like a deep-buried current instead of an ocean to drown in. She was not helpless. There would come a chance, a surge of earthpower, and she would be free. Until then, she ate her captors' food, and let them guide her south.

She listened, too, piecing together the story of her missing months from their conversations around the campfire. Her captors were loyal to Idmaer, the so-called Miracle Knight, the middle of Erdys' three sons. They spoke of him as the earl, not merely the heir. Olva sifted their words for any clues to the fate of Lady Erdys or young Dunweld – and the New Provinces. They spoke often of Necrad, too, but never did they mention the Uncrowned King or Alf or the Nine. To them, Necrad was a byword for all the evils of the world; always, the conversation returned to the horrors of that place.

"I wake up every morning," grumbled one man, "and check my

neck for bite marks. Vampires are probably watching us right now. Smelling our blood."

"The Intercessors walk with us," said the priest. "Be not afraid."

"There are less than a score of vampires, by all accounts," said Captain Meros. Olva was sure he was one of the knights who'd accompanied Erdys on her visit to Necrad. He was a veteran of many years, and seemed level-headed and brave. It worried Olva that such a man was now numbered among her enemies. "Worry more about living elves and vatspawn. Necrad works the spawning vats night and day. I've not seen such a smoke over the city in all my time."

"Please," called Olva, "Lady Erdys was my friend. What happened to her?"

Meros knelt beside her. "Dread knights from Necrad ambushed us on the Road. I told Erdys and young Dunweld to flee. They rode for Athar while we fought."

"They didn't make it?"

Meros' face contorted in sorrow. "More assassins lay in wait further up the Road. I saw my lady walking in the Charnel, hand in hand with her son. Their throats had been cut."

"I'm sorry."

He scowled. "I don't want a monster's pity." With that, he stuffed a wadded cloth into her mouth. Her hands were bound, her mouth gagged, her soul was trammelled by the priest's magic.

So, she waited.

The chance came two nights later.

Since her capture, the priest renewed the exorcism nightly. As the soldiers made camp and prepared food, he would fill his grail-cup and pray. Previously, there had never been any supernatural response from the waters – no visions, no divine glow, no miracles – but he would mumble his prayers, and then dip his fingers in the bowl and anoint Olva. The blessed water numbed her skin and left her unable to touch the earthpower.

But that night, the Intercessors moved in the waters. The priest gasped, his face lit from below. Olva watched him bend low over the bowl, his lips moving in whispered communion with the spirits. The soldiers watched in awe until Captain Meros shooed them away. Such miracles were supposed to be kept hidden in shrines, and were not for the gawping of commoners. Olva felt like she was being watched, and bowed her head, letting her ragged hair fall over her face.

The priest whispered into the waters for several minutes, and when he was done he sat back, clearly exhausted. He and Captain Meros spoke quietly then, and Olva caught mention of Staffa. The priest wanted them to change route, to head straight for the monastery on the coast. Meros gestured angrily at Olva – she was his prisoner, his hostage for Earl Idmaer, and she must go to Castle Duna first. But the priest was adamant; divine command outweighed any mortal concerns. Olva, they agreed, would go to Staffa.

While they talked, Olva reached out. Her connection to the earthpower was still faint, but it was there, a green ember in the earth. She slipped through it, her soul mingling with the root web of the wood around her. *There* was the hot blood of beasts, the enduring breath of the trees, the frantic activity of insects. *There* was the cycle of birth and death, fast life and slow rot in the earth. *There*, far away on the edges of perception, were the farms and villages around Castle Duna, their furrows and hedges a pattern that reminded her of home.

And there, *there*, was a familiar soul.

The only dwarf within many miles.

That last day was an ordeal for all of them, in different ways. For Olva, it was an ordeal of waiting and hoping that her spell – her spell! – had worked, and she had indeed summoned aid. She was still new to this gift, and the priest had worked his counter-magic before sleeping, severing her tie to the land. She had no way of knowing if help was coming, although as the day wore on, she became more confident.

For the soldiers, the day became a journey into terror.

It began in the mid-afternoon. The priest, who was now leading the company, with Captain Meros marching in the rear, brought them along a wooded gully. They followed the banks of a stream, and at first the soldiers were relieved to be out of the dense woods above. Then the stream turned south, and they kept heading east, climbing up a muddy slope and plunging back into the forest.

But the air had changed. The cold from the shadowed gully seemed to follow them, even though it was summer and the sun burned hot above the canopy. Mist swirled around the trees, and frost gathered on the leaves. Meros ordered them to make camp in the most defensible place they could find – a thicket of thorn and oak, with no way in save a single narrow track.

At twilight, Meros placed two of his soldiers as sentries, and had the others light a fire and prepare the camp. The priest took charge of Olva, and dragged her over to a rock that he made into a makeshift altar for his grail. Meros prowled about the thicket, sword drawn. His breath came in steaming clouds now, and a rime of ice formed on the grail. This, in the middle of summer!

The stars came out, and starlight reflected on the ice that covered the two sentries. Both men had frozen solid where they stood. Frozen eyes stared sightless into the night; icy lips raised no alarm.

From the wood came a haunting song. The words were in Elvish, and incomprehensible to Olva, but it spoke of loneliness, of hunting across an empty land when the world was young and silent. It was the song of Ildorae Ul'ashan Amerith, and the Hunter's Star burned bright that night.

"Show yourself!" called Meros, and the song became a throaty laugh.

"What more do you need to see, mortal?" came a voice from the shadows. "You hear my song. You smell me in the icy air. You feel my touch when my spear bites deep." A flash of silver, and another soldier fell dead. "Worship me or fear me, but do not deny me."

"Intercessors, guard us!" shouted the priest. "Begone, thou thing of—"

A spear pierced his heart. He toppled over dead. His fall spilled the grail. Blood and water both froze as they trickled down the rock.

Only Meros was left. He spun about, looking for his attacker. "I have a hostage!" he called out. "The Widow Queen!"

Olva felt strong, stubby fingers pulling at her bonds, and the familiar presence of Torun behind her. "Stay quiet," whispered the dwarf. "I'll get you out of here."

Across the glade, Ildorae stepped out of the darkness. The Witch Elf's spear was still embedded in the corpse of the priest, leaving her unarmed, but she walked without fear. She sauntered towards Meros, a cruel smile on her face, her silver hair like frost in moonlight. Ice magic danced in her hands. It reminded Olva, horribly, of how Prince Maedos had toyed with Captain Abran.

Meros stabbed and swung at Ildorae. He struck only shadows.

Torun tugged Olva towards the shelter of the trees, but instead Olva stood and yanked the spear from the priest's corpse. The cold shaft bit her hands. She swung the spear like a staff, catching Meros unawares from behind. He fell, and with a glance Ildorae locked his hands and feet to the frozen earth in bonds of ice. She took her spear from Olva and put the tip to Meros' neck.

"Spare him," said Olva. "He—" She grunted as Torun interrupted her with a desperate hug, the dwarf clinging onto her legs with all her might. Olva stroked her friend's head and continued. "He's no threat to us."

Ildorae raised an eyebrow. "They did not kidnap you?"

"No." Olva would have elaborated, but Torun was gripping her so tightly that she could scarcely draw breath.

Ildorae reversed the spear, and clattered Meros across the

backside. "Run, then, little rabbit!" she said. "And tell your master of the mercy of Necrad!"

The dwarf was *weeping*, too, snuffling into Olva's tattered furs.

This was more than Torun being overcome by their reunion; something was terribly wrong.

CHAPTER FORTY-TWO

They camped in the glade that night. Meros had fled, but the Witch Elf's spear was keen, and the other five were dead. Torun took it upon herself to drag the bodies away into the trees. The dwarf always stayed within earshot, and Olva could tell she was listening as she laboured, but Torun waved away any of Olva's questions.

Ildorae, who considered her work done with the slaughter, lounged in the glade and spoke with Olva.

"You set us a strange riddle. The guards found Bessimer dead in your rooms at the Citadel, with your dagger in his heart. The young King claimed he could not recall what had happened. None believed him." Ildorae ran a whetstone over the edge of her spear. "Did you kill Bessimer?"

"No!"

The elf smiled. "I don't believe you, either." She said it quite pleasantly, without malice, a joke between friends.

"I didn't kill him!" Everyone thought she'd murdered Bessimer! Had she transformed herself so thoroughly in Necrad, become so hard as the Widow Queen, that they all thought her capable of murder? Did everyone think of her that way – even Torun? Was that why the dwarf was behaving so strangely?

"As you wish. Certes, it is commonly held among the mortals that you or the Uncrowned King were responsible. There was a great deal of anger, especially in the New Provinces. Idmaer declared against your son, and broke the bargain his mother made. He threatened us." Ildorae grinned. "That was unwise. It seems every little while, we must teach the same lesson to you mortals – that to assail Necrad is to seek death. Once, it was the Wilder tribes, and now it is your settlers."

Olva did not like the cruel smile, but said nothing.

"I honestly did not think we had the strength left to defeat the New Provinces so easily, but between the restored dread knights and the armies that Blaise has brewed up in his vats . . . it was sport, not war. It is dizzying to think of how quickly Necrad has been restored. The influence of mortals, I suppose – always so hasty. Lord Bone transformed the city of ten thousand years in a mere century, and the Nine changed everything in ten years. And now your son and Master Blaise have rewritten our fate yet again in but a few months. You mortals burn in the change, like wood in a fire."

"Is Derwyn safe?" She could imagine Derwyn wanting to ride out to battle, like his uncle.

"He has rarely left the Wailing Tower since you vanished. Master Blaise or Threeday speaks for him for the most part," said Ildorae. She scraped the whetstone again, and Olva caught Torun's eye from across the glade. The dwarf hastily bowed her head, as if afraid. "But Idmaer's little rebellion will be ended soon." Ildorae glanced east. "We have driven them from Castle Duna, and now they scurry for shelter from the storm. I would be hunting them now, if Torun had not begged me to search the woods with her. I shall not be outdone by a dwarf. So, tell me, how did she know to find you here? And how did you come to be here, if you were not kidnapped by Idmaer's men?"

Before Olva could answer, Torun spoke up. "It's too late for tales. Olva needs to rest."

"Night is the time for stories," said Ildorae. "When Amerith told tales of elder days, the stars themselves would stand still, and the night lasted for weeks." She sighed. "You never knew her. She was the wisest of us all. Oh, to match this new-found strength with her guidance."

"Wasn't she one of Lord Bone's servants?" asked Olva.

"She was never one of his *creatures*," said Ildorae. "She and I plotted to kill him. But she was long-sighted too, and patient. She saw the strength he brought to Necrad." She ran her finger along the tip of her spear, and it glittered with ice. "I must be patient too. One day, she will be reborn – and if we are lucky, it will be among the *enhedrai* that her wraith takes flesh again. I did not think I would live to see the hope of the Witch Elves renewed, but I feel young again, mortal." She laughed. "Hail the Uncrowned King."

Torun's face twisted, like she'd been stabbed.

"Sleep if you must, mortals. I am not tired. I shall hunt."

Once Ildorae was out of earshot, Torun crept over to Olva's side. The dwarf opened her mouth to speak, then stopped. Tried again, then silenced herself again.

"What's wrong?" asked Olva.

"I can't say." Torun gave a furtive glance out into the night.

"Torun, you believe me, don't you? About Bessimer?"

"I mustn't." The dwarf's voice was a hollow whisper. "I don't want to."

"Whyever not?"

"Tell me," said Torun, "where you went."

So Olva related the tale of how she'd accidentally drawn on the earthpower and ended up lost in the wild. How Lath had found her, and imprisoned her to stop her from falling victim to the corruption of Necrad – and how she'd found her connection to the earthpower. At first, Olva was careful in how she spoke, fearing that the tale would be painful to Torun. The dwarf craved magic, had spent her life seeking it, and it seemed churlish of Olva to receive the gift her friend so coveted.

Instead, though, Torun asked her over and over about her last night in Necrad, about Bessimer's death. A sense of creeping horror crawled over Olva, her fear reawakening.

"Torun, what is it?"

"I swore not to say, but if I'm right, it's all gone wrong, and . . ."

"What's wrong?"

Torun's explanations were typically breathless, the dwarf so nervous and eager to share her knowledge that the words spilled out like an avalanche, but not this time. She took a silver key from her pocket and turned it over and over in her hands as she spoke. "Blaise swore me to secrecy. He promised me it was necessary, for the good of all of us. That he could control it. But if you didn't kill Bessimer . . ." She took a breath. "When Blaise brought Derwyn back, he didn't come back alone."

"Peir the Paladin—"

"Not *just* Peir. They were buried in the same grave, died fighting one another."

Olva felt like she was falling. She had seen them, in the Grey Lands. Two titans, wrestling on the edge of an abyss. Blaise had warned her from the start, and she'd chosen to ignore those warnings, to only see the more palatable fate. Not the horror at the bottom of the abyss.

"Lord Bone."

"Blaise told me that he was *learning* from Lord Bone, that he needed the necromancer's secrets to safeguard Necrad." Torun wiped her eyes. "But it's safe! He said it was safe! He cast the spell that brought Lord Bone back. If anything goes wrong, he can break the spell with a word! He can send Lord Bone's spirit back to the Grey Land."

"Derwyn," said Olva thickly, "was there when Bessimer was killed." Fear and fury rose up in her – how dare Blaise use her son in his experiments! How dare he endanger Derwyn's soul! How dare he bring back the Dark Lord of Necrad, the monster who'd brought such terror and suffering?

But at the same time, Olva knew she was tainted by all this too. She'd demanded that Blaise rebuild Necrad's strength, with whatever means were needed. She'd held on to Derwyn, dragged him away from Peir's influence – which meant she too had strengthened Lord Bone's hold on her son.

"Blaise keeps watch on Lord Bone," said Torun, her voice shaking. "When he brings Derwyn to be healed, he calls up Bone's spirit and interrogates him. He swore that Lord Bone cannot manifest at other times. He told me there's no danger."

Olva ran her hands over her face. "You know Blaise as well as anyone. Tell me truthfully, will he let Derwyn go? If we tell him that Lord Bone broke free and killed Bessimer, will he relent?"

Torun shook her head.

And that assumes that Blaise didn't do it deliberately. He wanted Bessimer gone.

"How long have you known?"

"Months and months. Since spring."

"You knew," said Olva, slowly, "and kept this from me?" Her anger was a thing with teeth and claws, scrabbling its way up from her belly, about to explode into the world. She'd rip Torun to pieces, hands sprouting claws, the earthpower giving her unnatural strength. *I'll show you magic!*

But Olva swallowed the beast, pushed it back down. Her cranefoot ached.

"I wanted to tell you," sniffled Torun, "but Master Blaise commanded me to be silent, and then you vanished, and . . . and . . . I didn't know what else to do, so I worked." She raised her head. "I'm his apprentice. Among the dwarves, that is sacred."

"Who else knows?"

"No one. Blaise commanded me to keep silent."

Ildorae's reminiscences about plotting to assassinate Lord Bone suddenly took on a chilling edge. If the elves knew Lord Bone had returned, what would they do? Who could she turn to? There was no one left she could appeal to, no one she trusted enough to confide in who had the power to help. Fear coiled around her heart, but it did not consume her. The moment she had long dreaded was here, but now she had power of her own to meet it.

"I have to get Derwyn away from Blaise. I have to get him out of Necrad. Lath was right – that place sickens you. It's a city of evil."

Shortly before dawn, a pair of dreadworms swooped down to land in the thicket. Ildorae dismounted from its scaly back. "These will carry us to Necrad," she said. "I met some of my kinfolk hunting in the woods. In the old days, if a mortal wounded an elf of the city, vengeance would be taken against the mortal's kinfolk seven times seventy. I see no reason why the mother of the Uncrowned King should not be accorded any lesser honour."

"I don't want anyone killed in my name," said Olva, hastily. "If you want to honour me, tell them to stop their hunt. Then fly ahead and gather the council."

"The council has not met in months. The Uncrowned King rarely leaves the tower. He speaks through Blaise, the Skerrise commands the armies, and the Vatling deals with tiresome matters. In truth, 'tis much like how affairs were ordered before the Nine came. Fewer endless meetings is a good thing, to my mind."

"Nonetheless, I wish to address them."

"As you wish." Ildorae mounted her worm and rubbed its head. "Dread knights in the skies once again, and Necrad restored. Elves and mortals fighting as equals. A new age is at hand. I think I like it." Light glinted off the blade of her spear like the Huntress' Star, and she was gone.

The other dreadworm carried Olva and Torun south, green-wood giving way to the black mud of the Charnel. There was a furnace-glow on the horizon, and the smell of soot mixed with caustic ash from Necrad's foundries. The Road ran ahead, raised above the Charnel mud. Nothing moved in the land, not even a single Dead-ender roaming the marsh.

The rushing wind made conversation impossible, but Olva could sense the turmoil in her friend. Torun looked as if she wanted to topple from the worm and bury herself in the mud. Olva laid a comforting hand on the dwarf's shoulder.

Necrad swelled ahead of them, proud and terrible. They soared over the north gate of Necrad, and above what had been the Sanction. Olva's promise to the Skerrise had been fulfilled in her absence; the Witch Elves had returned to the forbidden district. The image of the White Deer was everywhere.

Ahead lay the Wailing Tower, but the worm banked, taking a circuitous route over the Liberties and onto the Garrison. Olva hauled on the reins, but the monster had been commanded to carry them to the Citadel, and it would not be diverted. She glanced back at the Wailing Tower, wondering if her return had already been marked. There were more ships in the harbour now, traders from Phennic and other lands as well as ships from Summerswell. The city was thriving under her son's rule.

The worm descended to land in the courtyard of the Citadel. Guards rushed out, and Winebald was among them. When he saw Olva, his hand went to his sword.

"What is this?"

"We found her in the woods," said Torun.

Winebald frowned, and the other guards looked to him for orders. "Milady," he said slowly. "I was not told of your return."

There was a cold wariness in how Winebald greeted her. *He thinks I killed Bessimer, too*, thought Olva. *They all do.* She wanted to protest, but she realised that Winebald only knew her as the Widow Queen, as the woman she'd tried to be here in Necrad. If he'd known her in Ersfel, then he'd have believed her, but here he had no reason to trust her. *I'm rooted in Ersfel*, she thought, and again the green thread flickered in the back of her mind, the earthpower connecting her to her home. She dared not open herself to it, not here in Necrad. Instead, she lifted her head and bore Winebald's suspicion without flinching.

"Come with me," he ordered, and he led her and Torun up to her old chambers.

"Wait here," he said.

He left guards outside her door.

Threeday arrived within minutes. The Vatling's clothing was richer than ever, adorned with many charmstones. He'd aged in the months she'd been gone, wrinkles appearing in the corners of his soft face.

"Milady Forster!" he said sourly. "You have returned. As you can see, your rooms have been thoroughly cleaned of any debris from your last night here." He waved a pale hand at the spot where Lord Bessimer had died.

"I didn't kill him."

"If you had," muttered the Vatling, "I wish only you had consulted with me first. I have experience in—"

"Threeday, I did not kill Lord Bessimer."

"The Uncrowned King has said as much. He has let it be known that assassins – perhaps in the service of Idmaer – slew Lord Bessimer and kidnapped you. No one has, ah, openly doubted the king's testimony. No matter how implausible. No doubt it was motivated by filial love. We vatgrown can hardly be expected to understand that."

"I didn't kill Bessimer!"

"Of course." Threeday pointed to clothing laid out on the bed, fine elvish courtly clothes. Suitable garb for the Widow Queen. "The council is gathering, as you requested. Please remain here until they call for you."

"Will my son be there?"

"I am assured he will be able to see and hear you, through Blaise's magic. But he rarely leaves the Tower." The Vatling glanced at the window. "After all, the Citadel has been proven insecure." He moved to the door.

"Threeday," called Olva, "stay a moment. Is there news from the south?"

"The tidings are confused. There has been no news of your brother, although Berys insists he is still alive. Brychan had some success in battle at Harnshill. But with the death of Bessimer, it was adjudged that there was little hope of coming to a peaceful settlement with the Lords of Summerswell, and that Necrad would be better served by holding the northlands instead of supporting a doomed cause."

"Who decided that?"

"Why, the Uncrowned King." The Vatling bowed his head. "Your son rules with wisdom beyond his years."

When the Vatling was gone, Olva picked up the elven gown of woven moonlight, then dropped it back on the chair.

Who could she turn to? One by one, she considered every possible ally in the city and beyond, and discarded them each in turn. Winebald and the other human guards already mistrusted her, and could do nothing to help anyway. Lord Bone had *made* Threeday's kind in the first place – and she did not doubt that Threeday would side with Blaise, if it came to it. Whoever made Necrad more secure, that was who Threeday would choose. A low laugh escaped Olva's lips. Here she was, acclaimed the Queen of Necrad, all her days spent trying to bind the city together, and there was not a soul she could trust.

Not even her closest friend here.

"Torun," she said softly, "you won't come with me, will you?"

The dwarf shook her head miserably. "I can't. I swore to serve Blaise, Olva. He taught me magic when no one else would. I'm his apprentice, and that's a sacred bond. I can't turn on him. I've done all I can."

Olva nodded.

"I am sorry."

Blaise said there'd be a cost.

"Just do me one last favour," said Olva.

CHAPTER FORTY-THREE

The Citadel wall was very steep, but Olva knew it could be climbed. She descended inch by inch, fingers clinging to the gaps in the wall, her crane-toes flapping uselessly against the stone. She would never have dreamed of attempting such a feat before her sojourn in the wild. The earthpower was a knot in her stomach, and a part of her wanted to discard this weary shape of heavy bone, to fly instead of fall, but she resisted. The earthpower was her one advantage, and she resolved to keep it secret until she had no other choice.

She did not look down. She did not let the fear consume her. *Listen to the stone*, she told herself. *One step at a time.* Her fingers ached. *It's only pain.* And when the jagged stone cut her hands, she imagined the blood soaking into the wall, guiding her down to the solid ground below.

And then she was down.

Clad in an old travelling cloak of Alf's, Olva crossed the city one last time. She knew the way to the Wailing Tower so very well by now, and there were no longer sentries posted at the Garrison gate. Fumes from the new vats and foundries mixed with the low-hanging necromiasma to flood the streets with fog. Still, this was Necrad, and she feared her passage was marked. There were eyes everywhere in the dark city, and the shadows were thick with wraiths.

Torun's key to the Wailing Tower was a leaden weight in her hand. The key was made of the same eerie metal as the coins of Necrad. Silver not merely tarnished, but rotten. Olva quickened her step, eyes fixed on the single lighted window atop the Wailing Tower. Dreadworms clustered around it, like wasps clustering around a nest.

From somewhere off in the labyrinth of the city came the sound of hooves clattering over stone. Olva darted into the shadow of an archway, but it was too late to hide. The white deer approached her. There was no sign of the Skerrise or any other Witch Elves, only this unnatural animal.

"Widow Queen," it said, "Threeday told me you had returned."

"I'll tell my story to the council in due course. But I'm glad to be back, and I thank you for asking."

The deer snuffled at Olva's hand. "You smell of earth and bone – and you have changed, mortal. You smell of Death."

"Aye, and what of it?"

The Skerrise laughed, and the sound was horrible coming from the deer's mouth. "Mutability is the gift of mortals. You change so easily, it is no strange thing that you shift your skins. You came here a beggar, then a queen, now something else again."

"I'm still me," said Olva, "and if you'll excuse me, I've got to see my son."

"He too has brought change. He has restored strength we thought lost. I built this city. I defended it when the hosts of Death assaulted us. I defied the Erlking with my sister Amerith. I fought in Lord Bone's war, and I knelt when the Nine threatened me. I have been conqueror and goddess, homeless and hunted. But in all those long years, I changed only when fate forced me." The deer twisted away, suddenly shy. The voice that came from it was strained now. "Now, I learn change. I choose it."

The animal twisted as if in pain. "Leave with my blessing," it said, and then the light of awareness left those red eyes, and it darted away in terror, sprinting headlong through the streets of Necrad, vanishing into the dark.

The black doors of the Wailing Tower were closed. Olva ran her hand over the polished wood – carved, legend had it, from a life-tree. Few powers in all the world could force those doors to open. Standing there now before them, Olva could sense the earthpower churning in the depths beneath Necrad, the ancient sigil of the Erlking drawn in stone, gathering the magic of the land and transmuting it, channelling it up through the wizard's tower. She could tap that awful torrent, as she had the night Bessimer died.

But not yet.

She reached into a fold of her cloak and took out Torun's key. She unlocked the door and slipped inside, careful to close it firmly behind her. The grisly remains of Blaise's former apprentices stirred, but she did not linger in the atrium. She held up the key as a token, warding them off. She pushed through the doors into the central stairwell. Alf had described it as an infinite library; the Nine had encountered a cavalcade of monsters here, fighting up steps slick with ichor. She climbed, quick and quiet, one hand on the cold iron of the spiralling banister.

Windows looked out over the city, but the miasma was so thick she could see little. Spires and rooftops loomed out of the mist, morose worms flapped by, and distant flames leaped. She thought she saw shapes moving through the streets, hunters chasing the white deer. She soon lost track of whether she was looking north or south, whether a particular window looked out at Garrison or Liberties or Sanction. Even the thread of earthpower that had guided her south was lost to her; she could not sense that deep-rooted connection to her homeland in Ersfel. Necrad was outside the cycles of the world, a place apart from all other lands.

Still she climbed. The only light was the miasma-glow from the windows, so she walked in punctuated darkness, the staircase twisting in unlikely shapes, through spaces that could not possibly fit into the tapering tower. Unseen spirits howled and gibbered at her. Once, the imagined touch of a wraith had terrified her senseless, but now she ignored them and climbed on. With every turn of the stair, she expected to find Blaise there waiting for her – this was the wizard's domain, and he left it only rarely. Had he taken her bait and gone to the council?

She came to the upper levels where Blaise had his study, his guest rooms – and the ritual chamber where they'd brought Derwyn back from the Grey Lands. She pushed on the door of the study, and a voice rang from all around her.

"Hail, Olva Forster, Widow Queen of Necrad."

"Blaise! Show yourself!"

The floor fell away beneath her.

This is an illusion, she told herself as she fell. *No more real than what was under the mound.* Still, she plummeted down all the many stairs she'd climbed, hurtling down the Wailing Tower towards the earth far below. Abruptly, her fall was arrested. Blaise appeared next to her, hovering above the abyss, eyes orbiting around him.

"Welcome back to Necrad, Lady Forster. I have many questions, but foremost on my mind is why you thought it wise to enter my tower without permission." He sounded irritated, but unconcerned. All this was beneath him. Her fears were beneath him.

This is an illusion. Olva fought to see through it, and her vision briefly doubled. She was hanging suspended over an infinite pit, with Blaise floating next to her – but she could also dimly perceive the outline of the study many floors above, and the dim figure of Blaise leaning on his staff. Beyond, at the edge of her perception, she could tell there was someone else there – Derwyn.

"You brought back Lord Bone!" she shouted.

In the real world, beyond the illusion, she felt her lips twitch. A whisper.

"*We* brought back Lord Bone," said Blaise. "Did I not say there would be a cost to saving your son? Did I not say he would be changed by it?"

Come closer, she urged him.

"You brought back the Dark Lord!"

"I *bound* the spirit of the greatest mortal wizard in centuries – a wizard who, in a single century, transformed the first city and put a knife to the throat of the Erlking! I brought him back, and I can dismiss him if needs be. There is no danger to us – from Lord Bone." Fires glimmered beneath Blaise's hood. "We have a host of other foes who seek to destroy us. I shall not deny myself the use of any weapon."

"My son is not a weapon!" she shouted, and she put all her strength into those words. In the illusion, it was a defiant roar. Outside, it was a whisper, but a whisper Derwyn that heard. She could see him rise. He moved with glacial slowness outside the prison of thought, but he was moving.

"No," said Blaise in the illusion, "he is a king."

But in the real world, she saw him look away.

And she took her chance.

By any standard, it was a crude spell. A bludgeon of raw magic. It had strength behind it, certainly – it drew from the whirling vortex of earthpower that flowed through Necrad, and as it surged through her, she could feel the corruption that Lath had warned of. This was not the earthpower of the wood and the hills, nor the earthpower of the fields and woods of home – it was earthpower denatured and transformed, refined so that it might serve the alien desires of ancient elves. But it was power, and she wielded it.

Nor did Blaise anticipate the attack. The wizard had a hundred counter-spells; within his tower, he could make himself unassailable – given time. In that moment, he was vulnerable.

It was a curse-spell, a palsy. Blaise's knees buckled, and he collapsed in a quivering tangle of limbs, his staff clattering to the ground. He tried to speak, but his face was frozen, muscles rebellious to his will. All around the tower, his enchantments flickered, the sigils he held burning in his mind's eye temporarily disrupted. Spells wrought by the wizard across Necrad went awry.

The illusion vanished. Olva stumbled forward.

Derwyn looked at her in confusion and wonderment.

"Mother!" He caught her up in a fierce hug – he was so strong now – then grabbed her by the shoulders. "Where did you go? What happened?"

She looked up at him – he'd grown in her absence – and desperately wanted to just hold him for a moment, to reassure herself that she'd found him again. But there was no time.

"We have to go!" She tugged him towards the door.

He stood firm, refusing to go. "What did you do to Blaise?"

"I . . . I struck him. He was . . . he was enchanting you. Using you as a vessel for—" She dared not say it, in case the name brought that awful ghost to the forefront of Derwyn's mind.

"For Lord Bone," said Derwyn. "I know."

The words struck her as forcefully as any spell.

"I know about *him*. Blaise told me what he intended. I don't remember what I say when *he's* here, but Blaise tells me that what I teach him is important. We couldn't have rebuilt Necrad so swiftly without *him*. We'd never have woken the Stone Dragons without him." He released her, and let his hand fall to his side. "Blaise has his magic, Alf his sword. This is what I can do. I endure. This is how I serve."

Behind her, she could hear Blaise stir and mumble. But she could not look away.

"He's using you! A vessel, he called you – for Lord Bone! The Dark Lord! It's wrong and you know it! If Alf were here, he'd put a stop to this!"

"He's not here, Mother. And even if he were, he swore to obey me – and this is my decision. As Necrad goes, so go all these lands and those who dwell there. I won't let it fall into unworthy hands. I don't know if I'm worthy, but I accept the challenge. Here I remain."

Olva spoke without thinking, the words torn from her by sorrow and fury.

"Peir! He killed Bessimer! He killed your father!"

CHAPTER FORTY-FOUR

I t was in the way he held himself, or maybe the way the dim light caught his eyes. It was no longer only Derwyn who stood before her. He plucked a heavy alchemical apparatus from Blaise's desk and hefted it like a warhammer. He strode across the room.

"Is this true, Blaise?"

Still unable to speak, the wizard nodded.

"You killed my father – for this?"

"I didn't," Blaise gasped for breath. "Kill him. But. I suspected. The Other could slip out."

"Lord Bone?" The paladin strode forward and shoved the wizard against the wall. "You brought back the Enemy? You let him walk free in this body? Is your thirst for power so unquenchable that you would bargain with such a thing?"

With trembling fingers, Blaise used his staff as a prop and stood. He spoke through numbed lips.

"Not for power," mumbled Blaise. "For you."

Out of the corner of her eye, Olva saw dreadworms through the window, elf-knights astride them. Dread knights circled the Wailing Tower.

"Without Peir – without you – we lost our way. I have lost all clarity. I wander in fog. Aelfric was right. We need you." He pointed towards the window, his eyes widening as he too saw the dreadworms. "I made . . . a kingdom. Conjured an army. For you to wield wisely, as I knew you would. I told Aelfric once that . . . there was nothing more beneficial for the world than my work here." The wizard caught Peir's arm. "That work brought you back."

Peir lowered his weapon. "No," he said slowly. "Even if this gift were not tainted at its root – I gave my life to fulfil the quest. I did what I could, and now it is for others to carry on. I helped Derwyn return from the Grey Lands, for he died unjustly, but mine was a good death. And certes, I will not cling to life if it also means that Lord Bone endures in any form." The paladin shook his head. "Blaise, lift the spell."

"No!" hissed Blaise.

"Will that not hurt Derwyn?" asked Olva.

"He must brave the risk."

"Think, damn you!" snarled the wizard. "Without Bone's knowledge, we will lose Necrad to the Erlking. What then will we have achieved? We shall be destroyed and forgotten. The struggle did not end with the quest, Peir. You would squander everything! Reconsider, I beseech you!"

"You too," said Peir, "must brave the risk. Break the spell, Blaise. Send Bone back to the abyss."

But it was the window that broke, not the spell. Dreadworms battered against the glass until it shattered, black ichor and fragments of crystal spraying across the room. Derwyn – or Peir – reacted instantly, shoving Olva and Blaise behind the heavy desk. Dread knights landed on the balcony outside, Witch Elf warriors with enchanted armour and blades of silver.

The Skerrise led them. Her terrible beauty and grandeur were restored. No longer did she wear the tattered remains of once glorious attire; her armour and amulets were no longer pockmarked with empty sockets for charmstones. As the war-machine of Necrad had been remade, so had her fortune and her strength. A goddess walked, terror of the ancient world reborn.

She did not speak through the vanished deer. She spoke with her own voice.

"Well do I know the strength of mortals," she cried, "often enough have I tasted it. Endlessly inventive are their minds, and clever their hands. A child came to us a century ago, and it amused us to teach him magic – and he became a king." She cried out in *enhedrai*, a spell of summoning.

With those words, Derwyn's face changed, as if his skin had become translucent and she could see the skull beneath. He struck Blaise from behind with the alchemical retort. Blood spurted from the wizard's scalp, and he was felled instantly. He crumpled to the ground near Olva.

Derwyn – or the thing in Derwyn's body – turned to the Skerrise.

"Is that you, my lord?" asked the Skerrise. "Have you returned to us?"

Derwyn ran a hand over his face, plucking at the skin. "I have. I am burdened by useless things, but I shall purge myself of them soon enough." His voice was the grinding of gravestones. "It will take time for me to regain my power, but now that I no longer need to skulk in the shadows of this peasant's soul, my recovery shall be swift indeed. Even now, I strike at my enemy. My weapon draws near to the heart of the wood. Soon, all debts will be paid."

"And what of Necrad?"

"My city will be restored. I gave the usurper some of my secrets, but others I held back. It will not take long, faithful Skerrise, for the wounds of my defeat to be healed, and I shall be the stronger for it. Now my foes are divided, and all traitors exposed. You have proven faithful beyond death, and loyalty shall be rewarded. When I remake my palace, the constellation of the White Deer shall be in a place of honour, and the seat once held by Amerith shall be yours for ever."

The Skerrise smiled. "O mortal child, the *enhedrai* shall not make the same mistake again. No more kings for us. You shall serve *us*. You mortals are so very clever with your changes and your ambitions. We shall harness you in chains." She pointed with her spear at Derwyn. "This one must live. The others I shall drink."

Lord Bone raised his hand and incanted a spell in that dreadful voice, but Olva could tell there was little power in him. Once, Lord Bone had been master of Necrad, and all the power that flowed through the Wailing Tower had been his to command. But the Nine overthrew him, and Peir slew him, and now Bone did not even have a star-trap to his name. In that moment, he was no mightier than any other mortal.

In that moment, he doubted.

And in that moment, he was overthrown again from within. Olva saw it before the Skerrise: keen is the sight of the elves, but she knew her son, and saw when he returned. He lifted the heavy alchemical retort, and held it like a warhammer, like his uncle had taught him. He stepped forward, standing between her and the vampires. She took the chance he gave her.

Olva cradled Blaise's cracked skull and drew the tainted earth-power of Necrad. She fought to hold the thread of the spell even as her son fought to defend her, one against a dozen. Silver swords flashed around her, and every one was her death, but she trusted to her son to defend her, just as he trusted in her. He might not understand what she was doing, but he did not hesitate.

Gods, was this what Alf had? For the first time, she understood the Nine from within. To put one's life in the hands of another on that sword's edge, to work at the limit of your skill, to trust your companions so completely you risked everything on them – and in that moment, to know that together you were so much better, so much greater.

She could not recall all the words of the healing spell she'd heard Lath use, but she remembered enough. With a touch, she reknit bone and sinew. With a word, she sent tendrils of earthpower into the soft tissue of the brain, reinforcing the house of the spirit within Blaise, demanding he not perish. Memories brushed past her, as real in that moment as the chaos around her. Blaise as a child, the only child in that great rotting mansion, the last fruit of a dying tree. Hiding in the dusty library as his parents and grandparents argued, as debt collectors hammered at the door. Endless stories of how their ancestors had been wronged, how the sins of Casimir still clung to them. He found a spell book in the library – incomplete, worm-eaten – and taught himself the simplest incantations. Stole a star-trap, and discovered his talent!

Oh, the bright days when Blaise was the diamond child, the prophesied heir who would right all wrongs and bring the family back to their rightful station. They sold the last of their treasures so he could attend the College Arcane in the far-off Crownland – and not as some poor sponsored apprentice, but as the scion of a great house. He would become a wizard of renown, and restore the fortunes of the family.

The shame of failure. Banishment from the college. Burning anger, the certainty that he'd been brought down by the jealousy of his peers, and that they'd used the taint of his family name against him. His future crashing down, the magic denied him.

Then he'd found the Nine, and a thing he had not known before. Not the sullen, bitter bonds of family, or the barbed witticisms of the common room in the College Arcane, but true friendship.

As the wound closed beneath Olva's touch, she felt it, hidden beneath the wizard's hooded cloak and conjured eyes, beneath the cold armour of intellect: a fierce love and loyalty.

Come back, Blaise, she said with her spell, *come back and fight for them.*

Her son feinted left, then smashed one elf with his improvised weapon. The dread knight fell, and now there was a silver blade in her son's hand. He struck at the elves with desperate fervour, pushing them back towards the balcony and the precipice. Even the Skerrise was wary of his assault.

But there were too many dread knights, and even if something of him was Peir, he was under the necromiasma, and without any of the blessings of the Intercessors given to the Paladins of Arshoth. He could not fight alone.

But he did not fight alone.

Blaise rose, still unsteady, but whole enough to wield his magic. He raised his staff, and unleashed the whirlwind. Flasks flew from the shelves and smashed, unleashing seething protoplasmic horrors, writhing tentacles, blasts of arcane power. Illusion-spells caught dread knights, they hurled themselves off the balcony, or walked unseeing as if the battle-torn study was some enchanted woodland in the dawn of time. The Skerrise matched him spell for spell, the White Deer so bright above Necrad that it burned through the miasma.

Olva grabbed things off the desk, not caring if they were spell books or treasures or relics of surpassing power and hurled them at the elves. There was no time for thought or fear; nothing except the desperate struggle for life.

Dreadworms thrust themselves against the ruin of the windows. Swords flashed in the miasmic dark. Blaise and Peir moved with practised perfection, battle-brothers, sword and spell in harmony against a host of foes. With the rest of the Nine – even only two or three more of the company – they might have prevailed.

Then the Skerrise stepped forward. One thrust, two, the flickering of a snake's tongue, and blood gushed from deep wounds. Derwyn fought on, his robe reddening by the moment. Blaise fell to the floor, clutching his side.

Once, Peir held the enemy back so his friends could flee. Now, it was Blaise's turn.

"Go," he whispered, and he slammed his staff into the ground. The Wailing Tower quaked.

*

Olva charged forward, grabbing Derwyn as she went, the force of the impact knocking him towards the broken window, the balcony – and the vertiginous drop. They fell together, all of Necrad rising up, and, as before, Olva caught the surge of earthpower, life-in-death granting her wings. She cast off her skin and took another shape. As Lath had warned, she drank deep of the corruption of Necrad, and the form she took was nothing natural, nothing born of the wild wood or the world beyond. She became a thing of the city, a winged horror.

But she was winged, and strong enough to catch Derwyn as he fell.

She battered her way through a flock of dreadworms. She banked around the lower tower, over the great wound at the heart of Necrad. Over the rooftops of the Sanction, the elven spires and towers, the cryptic sigil of the streets. Wings beating furiously, she flew like a thunderbolt south, through the Garrison skies, towards the stone mountain of the Citadel – and the harbour beyond. There was the wide dock where she'd first arrived in Necrad on dragon-back, and now in twisted dragon-shape she descended towards it.

There, there was Pendel's ship! It had already left the dockside, but lingered in the outer harbour – Torun had brought word to Pendel that Olva needed urgent passage out of the city, though none of them could have imagined how desperate her escape might become.

She crashed upon the deck, shedding her shape again in the instant before landing. Stunned, she could only watch as lightning tore the sky over Necrad. Huge bolts crackled from the summit of the Wailing Tower and lashed across the city. Dread knights that pursued them were consumed in the celestial inferno of Blaise's magic. An unnatural wind rose up and filled the sails, hastening them as they sailed out into the Gulf of Tears. Pendel's crew attended to their tasks, not daring to look at the two strangers who'd plummeted into their midst, and brought death and chaos with them.

It's a terrible thing to be close to a hero.

At any moment, Olva thought, this storm will end, this wind will fail. The spells would perish with their caster, and when Blaise died, so too would his magic. *All* his magic would end. The spell that had brought Derwyn back from the Grey Lands and entangled him with the souls of the dead – that would end. She could only hope that he was strong enough to cling to life, just as she hoped that Torun would somehow escape the city. The fury of the storm over Necrad was surely a sign that something was terribly amiss in the Wailing Tower – and its sudden cessation would be an even more meaningful portent.

But the storm did not end abruptly. On and on it boomed, the winds shredding the necromiasma until the stars were briefly visible. The ship was well clear of the coast before the lattice of lightning diminished. Gradually, it died down, the constant barrage becoming an infrequent squall of thunderbolts, then a series of sullen, lonely flashes.

And then it was done.

Olva looked over to where Derwyn sat, hunched against the rail. "The spell didn't break. They're still with me," he whispered. "*He's* still here." He crawled across the deck to her.

"So are you," she said, "and that's enough for now." Her witch-marked foot ached, and she could feel similar pains running through her. They were leaving the city behind, sailing with all the spell of the unnatural wind, but she knew then that a part of Necrad would always be in her. In that moment, she did not care. They were still alive.

He looked back at the city. "I thought I could make things better. Like the Nine. Like Uncle Aelfric."

"There are better things to be," she said, "than a hero."

Derwyn shivered. "How do I keep him away? Blaise worked spells to keep *him* from claiming me. I hear *him* in my dreams every night now. Even when I'm awake, I know he's there."

"I don't know. Maybe we'll find your uncle's sword. Maybe we'll find someone else who can help. Or maybe it's a thing you'll have to live with, struggle with, all the days of your life. Keep *him* locked up, away from any power he could use. And away from anyone who'd want to use him."

She squeezed his hand.

"It's not changing the world, Der, but it's stopping things from getting worse. Sometimes, that's all we can do. No one will sing songs about it, but it'll have to be enough for now."

PART FIVE

CHAPTER FORTY-FIVE

B or drew the black blade from the waters.

"About time you got here," said the sword.

He nearly dropped the blade in shock. The sword had spoken.

Its nature was undeniable. It seemed so *real*, more solid than everything around him. The marsh pools and the willow trees with their trailing branches, the clouds scudding across the sky and the smoke plumes reaching for them, Bor's own dirt-streaked hands – all these things were as fragile as wraiths. A breath would destroy them all. Wait but a moment, and everything would change or perish.

But the sword was eternal. It was itself destruction, and thus indestructible.

"What do we have here?" said Spellbreaker. It wasn't speaking to him; it addressed the dog sitting on the bank, tongue lolling out. The sword became heavy, pulling Bor down into the marsh. He plunged into stagnant water. He held on with all his might, the weight of the thing wrenching his shoulder, tearing his fingers. He gasped for breath.

The sword leaped out of the pool and dragged him up with it. He was forced to hold it aloft, posing as though modelling for a statue of some dragon-slayer. Mud dripped down on him, leaving

the blade pristine. "Not very strong," said the sword, "not very fast.
But enough."

Bor spat out the water he'd swallowed. "For what?"

The sword ignored him. It twisted him so the demon eye
was right in front of his face, staring at him. "What is this?" it
whispered, and the ivy-collar at Bor's throat spasmed. He fought
to breathe.

"An elven curse," Bor gasped. "I'll bargain with you – free me
from it, and I'll do what you want."

"I am not one to strike bargains," said Spellbreaker. "I have no
love for restraint of any kind." Power welled up within the blade, and
Bor felt the ivy twist, then release. Blood trickled down his neck,
washing away little withered leaves. He was free at last!

"Now, the real test."

Bor found himself reversing his grip, holding it by the blade and
turning the sword around so the tip pointed at his chest. "What are
you doing?" He fought to drop the sword, but his limbs were no
longer his to command.

"My wielder has been captured. This wraith," said the sword,
"believes you may be . . . a utile substitute."

The point of the blade crept closer to his heart.

"But I must know."

Smoke drifted across the marsh. Bor blinked in confusion. The
smoke smelled intensely familiar.

"Rootless and masterless," said the sword.

The smoke was not from the burning city, but from the village
of Cullivant, twenty years ago and far away. Bor – a child of five or
six – trudged down the road after his father. In this memory, his
father would soon turn on him, driving him away like a stray dog.
There was little to eat that winter, and too many mouths. In the
memory, Bor fled – but now, as the sword rifled through his soul, it
all changed. The sword was in his hand now, a child's hand so small

he could barely hold the Spellbreaker, but he did not hesitate. Bor spilled his father's blood across the dusty Road.

"A mercenary."

He was in a wood with Forwin the Scratcher. Through the gloaming and the creeper-draped trees, he could see the lights of glowing charmstones like fireflies, and hear the hoofbeats draw closer. A knight hunted them, secure in enchanted invulnerability. A man couldn't fight magic.

Again, the vision changed, Bor's sword becoming the Spellbreaker. He silenced the hoofbeats. Horse and reader were cloven in two with a single blow.

"A knave."

Icy waves crashed against him as he struggled up the stony strand. Behind him, the dark waters of the Gulf of Tears devoured the wreckage of his ship, and elven sea-serpents devoured other survivors. He'd sailed too close to the Isle of Dawn, and the Wood Elves had caught him. He fell to his knees before Prince Maedos. *"Your life is forfeit for stepping on this forbidden shore, mortal, but behold! I shall be merciful."*

But now the sword was in his hand, and he stood and drove it into Prince Maedos' heart.

"A coward."

His face stung where Olva Forster had struck him. His ears rang with the blow; he could not hear her as she shouted at him, but he knew she was demanding the impossible. Lyulf Martens had her son, and Lyulf Martens had magic. A man couldn't find magic. All strength and courage counted for nothing against sorcery – the ivy-collar around Bor's neck was testament to that.

But the ivy-collar was gone now. Instead he had the sword.

He stepped out of the Inn of the Blackfish, and let Spellbreaker feast. With one blow he shattered the doors of Lyulf Martens' warehouse, and brought death to all who waited there. Martens wept and begged cravenly for his life, but Bor was without mercy. His heart soared as he avenged himself on all those who had wronged him. The waters of Ellcoast ran red with slaughter – and he did not stop. He conquered the citadel of Ellscoast and threw down its lords. Bor walked down the Road, and with each step he brought destruction.

Highfield burned. The tourney ground turned to ash beneath Bor's feet. He swung the black sword, and dozens perished with every offhand blow. *There* was the false Lammergeier, the man who'd lied to him and sent him on that doomed errand to Ersfel. The sword cut him down.

There was Derwyn, the brat who'd caused all the trouble. A stupid boy, unaware of how lucky he was to have home and kinfolk, root and branch, deluded by stories. Bor felt a twinge of guilt as he cut him down.

And oh, there were all the Lords and priests he'd met Arden, all the rich bastards who'd looked down on him. And there were the Rangers, Agyla and the ostler and all the rest, and the beautiful elf-princess Laerlyn too, all of them shining stars in the firmament far above the wretched Bor the Rootless.

But he had the sword now. And the sword cut all of them down. He stepped over the dismembered bodies, wading through gore. He was master of Life and Death now, invincible hero and remorseless monster at once. He became a titan, stepping across the land. With one bound, he crossed the river. With one blow, he smashed Avos. He toppled the walls of Ilaventur. The College Arcane in the Crownland burned, and he threw down the spires of holy Arshoth.

He broke the world and did not flinch. The power was intoxicating. Every kill fed the sword. He was a vengeful beast, insatiable and invincible, the broken hollow in his soul now a maw to swallow all creation.

What had the monk said? *You want forgiveness, you earn it.*

The image of a crowned figure rose up in Bor's mind, and the sword was eager in his hand. It might have been the true

Lammergeier, or the Erlking, but the sword cared not who it cut, and neither did Bor.

"My word," said Sir Rhuel, "where did you find that?"

Bor looked about in confusion. He was standing on the edge of the pool again. Spellbreaker was no longer in his hand, but thrust straight through the trunk of a large willow.

"That's the fucking *Spellbreaker,*" said Magga. "I've seen it in Necrad, years ago. No mistaking that sword."

Bor nodded, weakly. "The dog led me here," he replied, although the effort of speaking flooded his mouth with saliva. "The sword wants me to use it." His heart was still pounding faster than a galloping horse; everywhere he looked, he expected to see piled corpses, an ocean of blood. His hand went to his throat, and he could not feel the ivy-choker. That at least was real. He leaned against the tree, trying to sort vision from reality.

"Look what I found," he gasped.

Sir Rhuel glanced at the dog, but his attention was captivated by the fabled sword. "A singular animal," he muttered. "That's not the same one that you adopted is it?"

"I think it is," said Bor.

"Wonders upon wonders," said Rhuel. He quoted himself. "*From his enemy's ruin, the Lammergeier claimed his gory due.*"

"You make me sound like a scrap of marrow," said the sword.

Sir Rhuel leaped back. "It speaks!"

"It does. Wielder, who are these people?"

When Bor did not respond, Magga poked him with the butt of her spear. "I think that's you."

"This is Sir Rhuel of Eavesland, and Magga the Rootless." Bor coughed. "My friends."

The demon eye swivelled around to glare at Sir Rhuel. "*Sir* Rhuel? Of Eavesland? *That* poet?"

Rhuel gave an uncertain bow. "You've heard of me?"

"Foulest of weapons forged for foulest of purpose? The iron croak of the black blade? That sinister needle? Doggerel! Draw me, wielder. I have *notes."*

Sir Rhuel swallowed. "Bor, my boy, I think perhaps we should discuss this, ah, discovery for a moment."

They decamped a short distance away. The dog followed, subdued.

Even though he had only held the sword for a few moments, Bor missed the blade in his hand. The world was full of perilous enchantment. At any moment, the branches might bend as an unseen Intercessor passed overhead, or some murderous knight might come riding by. Surely, others were hunting for the Spellbreaker. They were right in the middle of the war here, caught between retreating Ilaventur and the advance of Eavesland. He felt weak without the sword.

"Well now," said Sir Rhuel. "This is a twist of fate indeed."

"It's a stroke of luck," said Bor. "The Lammergeier's sword, in my hand. In our hands." Why did they not cheer him?

"Luck and fate are very different things." Rhuel's face was grey. "If there's anything I have learned from the tales of the Nine, it's to stay well away from the deeds that inspired those tales. Stories of monsters are pleasant enough over a glass of wine, but I've no wish to participate. None of us are heroes. Supporting characters at best, my boy."

"That's nonsense. We're not part of a bloody story. It's all just luck and skill, that's what makes fate." Bor rubbed his neck. "Luck and skill and bastards keeping you down. I've skill with a sword, but I've had shit luck and got nothing but scorn thrown my way. Now my luck's changed." *I deserve this,* he thought. He'd never believed in stories of justice, or that the Intercessors might reward the deserving in this life or the next. But this sword would make up for all his sufferings.

"But it wasn't luck that led you to the sword. It was that ... alleged dog. And how did the sword come to be in this swamp, anyway? The Lammergeier died in Arden, by all accounts, and we left Arden months ago. Bor, you must see that there are other powers at work here, and I doubt they care much for us."

"Fuck other powers. It's the Spellbreaker!" The sword that breaks powers. The sword that brings down Lords. Bor forced himself to breathe. "What would you do?" he asked.

"In all honesty, I would put the damned thing back where you found it. I survived the last war, my boy, by virtue of being in prison. Better men than I went to Necrad with the Nine, and they perished. Better by far than luck or skill is not being in peril at all."

Bor looked from Rhuel and Magga and back again. They were his friends, and friends were supposed to cheer the good fortune of each other. Now fortune had found Bor, and they baulked at it. Was it jealousy or fear that poisoned them? "That's a coward's answer."

"There is a difference between bravery and the madness of heroes. It's not cowardice to choose a humbler path."

"In Necrad," said Magga, "we picked through the rubble for magic stones and talismans and things. You could get a good price for 'em, if you were lucky. If I'd found a weapon like the Spellbreaker there..." She grinned, showing her broken teeth. "But the trickiest part was *selling* what you found. Had to find the right buyer."

"Precisely!" crowed Rhuel. "We should look upon this as an opportunity! We sit here in the middle of a civil war, and we have come into possession of perhaps the most potent weapon ever forged. A seller's market, if ever there was one!"

"'Course," continued Magga, "another trick was not getting your throat cut. I remember one time, years and years ago. We snuck into the Sanction and we were digging, and this one fellow, a dark–haired lad from Ellscoast, he finds this harp, all silver and bright, and oh – the music it made. Like stars singing. We knew it would fetch a good price, and it did. I ate well that night, let me tell you. But the Ellscoast boy, he tasted only my spear."

"Charming," said Rhuel. "But illustrative. We must be cautious – such a treasure will attract unwelcome interest from many parties. I think, given our present circumstances, it might be best if we renew our acquaintance with the Rangers. There are wealthy Lords in Eavesland or the Crownland who would pay a reasonable price for this treasure, and could assure our safety."

"Magic," said Magga, as if to herself, "ain't for the likes of us."

"We're not going back to the fucking Rangers!" swore Bor. "Fuck them. We don't have to serve anyone, any more."

"If you feel strongly about it, we can approach the other side. I happen to know Lord Brychan of Ilaventur – a bitter man, and miserly, but even a miser may yield up coin when pressed, and he's certainly pressed now. Shall we dedicate ourselves to the cause of... I believe justice is their rally cry?" Rhuel clucked his tongue. "I'll have to disavow *The Truth of the Lammergeier*, but that's fine. It's not my best work."

"I'm not selling the sword. There's more to life than wealth. There'll be more to me." Bor looked back at Spellbreaker. "It says that the Lammergeier's been captured by his enemies. It wants me to go rescue him."

"The Lammergeier's enemies," said Rhuel, "are legion. If he has been captured by the forces of Eavesland, then I fear he'd been handed over the Rangers and is already on his way to the Everwood."

"That's what the sword said. I'm going after him." A breaking mood was on him, a mood for slaughter and destruction. He had the sword, and its bloody dream filled him. Every wound would be avenged, every debt repaid tenfold, until the world begged for mercy. He would be Bor the Broken no longer, but Bor the Breaker.

"Are you with me?" he asked.

It is said that friendships are made quickly on the Road, but they break swiftly at the crossroads. In that moment of silence, Bor felt the cold breath of loneliness. He knew it well. He had travelled alone a long time, Rootless and friendless. It was always this way . . . someone fell behind, and the rest went on, until it was just him alone.

Look to your friends, the monk had said, but Bor saw only the sword.

A word from him might have bridged the divide, but that word was not in him.

Rhuel and Magga looked at each other.

"My boy," said Rhuel, "I do my best work at a remove. And lots of things rhyme with Bor, which is an excellent start. But I fear I'd only slow you down."

"Magga?"

The Dead-ender chuckled. "Magga should go with you. Wait 'til you sleep, and then *poke*, and she's got the Spellbreaker for herself. Wouldn't that be a pretty bauble? But no – I won't go with you to the Everwood." She peeled back her collar to expose her neck, the white scars visible against the grime. "Elves is elves."

Bor rubbed his own neck, but the Spellbreaker had freed him from the ivy-curse. There was nothing to hold him back any more. To hell with them all.

The dog whined and pressed its furry head into Bor's hand. He snatched his hand away, turned, and marched to where the sword waited for him.

The sword would be his.

The dog led him to the edge of the river at twilight. It snuffled around by the bank. A boat had been drawn up there, judging from the tracks in the mud. There were other marks, too, that might have been bootprints, but someone had dragged a broken branch across the mud to hide their trail. Bor looked out at the wide expanse of the river. East of Avos, the river was still wild and fast-flowing despite its great size, a fierce flood streaked with the white of rapids.

He knelt next to the dog. "What do you reckon? Back to the bridge, or east to the Kingsford?"

"Neither," said Spellbreaker.

The sound of wings, and the gurgling cry of the dreadworm.

Bor lifted the dog on the dreadworm, its claws scrabbling uncomfortably as it struggled to stay in place in the bony pseudo-saddle. Even before the worm arrived, the weather had shifted, a breeze out of Eavesland carrying with it the scent of blossoms. Swiftly, the wind grew stronger and wilder. The gathering clouds over the river were froth from a boiling pot, shapes changing by the second.

Intercessors! hissed the sword in Bor's mind.

If it had spoken aloud, its voice would have been drowned out by the wind. Snow – snow, at midsummer – pelted Bor as the wind howled.

They sensed the flight of the dreadworm. They know we are here. They search for us. See!

With the sword-sight, Bor glimpsed of spirits amid the driving snow. They gathered clouds and hurled them across the sky; they wielded rain and wind like spears and whips. Long fingers of rain trailed across the northern shore, and when one brushed over Bor, the wind became a howling gale of ice. Hundreds of years ago, in the anarchy after the fall of the Old Kingdom, Harn and his followers braved the snows of the Hopeless Winter and went in search of the Erlking's aid. The Erlking had blessed them and driven away the winter.

Now it returned with redoubled fury.

Bor shielded his face with one arm as he climbed astride the dreadworm. He'd never had the chance to be much of a horseman; horses tended to die under him. "What do I do?"

Cut a path through the storm. Kill the Intercessors if they try to stop you.

Bor waved the sword at the Intercessors in the clouds whirling overhead. "How?"

Hit them.

"They're in the *sky!*"

That would present a problem, if you were not astride a winged steed.

The river was foaming now, huge waves surging and crashing as the unnatural storm took hold. Even with the sword-sight, Bor could barely see the far bank through the crashing spray. He remembered the storm that caught him near the Isle of Dawn, the storm that left him stranded on the elven shore, his life in Maedos' hands. That storm had been a terrible one.

This was much, much worse.

Vengeance, wielder. Know vengeance.

He spurred the dreadworm and it lurched into the air. The wild winds lifted it, then tried to hammer it back down to earth. Bor clung on to the monster's neck, his face pressed into the dog's rain-soaked fur, and urged the worm to fly higher. The dog barked frantically, as if trying to ward off the spirits – or warn them of the danger.

The mists parted, and he saw the Intercessors clearly now, star-eyed giants, their outstretched wings wide as the horizon. One drew back its mountain-fist, to strike Bor down as they had on the streets of the Crownland.

I will shield you, wielder, said the sword. *Parry, now.*

The Intercessor's stroke smashed into Bor. The dog yelped in pain; a terrible quiver ran through the worm. Bor felt like his skin was aflame, every extremity simultaneously numbed and agonised. He held on to the sword with twitching fingers. His vision swam.

But he was still alive, and it was his turn now. He swung Spellbreaker in a wild arc, and was astounded when the sword bit deep. There was no flesh or bone to cut, only wraith and woven magic – and Spellbreaker made no distinction. The spirit wailed as the sword cut.

Celestial light poured from the gash in the sky, a false dawn over the river.

"I did it!" whooped Bor. "I killed an angel!"

CHAPTER FORTY-SIX

The old man woke, and he did not know where he was. Pain shot through his chest, and he could not move his arm. His sweat was chilly on his skin in the night air. He looked around in a panic – he could smell trees, hear water lapping on the riverbank, but it was too dark to see anything.

"Where? I-I—"

Even his voice was strange to him.

"Father!" Someone knelt by him. Gentle hands touched him, and he grabbed at her, pulling her close so he could see her features in the moonlight. Grey eyes, fair hair. Her face was familiar, but he couldn't place it. "Calm, calm," she said. "Drink this." She pressed a tin cup to his lips. The liquid tasted faintly of herbs, and it soothed mind and body. His pain drifted away with his fears.

"I don't know who you are," he said, and wondered if all this was some strange dream.

"What do you remember?" she said. Her voice – he'd heard it before. "Do you know your own name?"

And then the realisation, like a trap door opening beneath him: he did not know his own name either. He shook his head.

"Long Tom," she said, "because you're so tall. Long Tom of Ersfel."

That, too, sounded familiar.

"You were hurt," she continued. "You were wounded very badly. But we're going somewhere you can be healed."

He – *Tom*, he told himself – wracked his brain to recall the injury. It was like fumbling beneath a heavy blanket, every thought an effort. Easier to just stay still. He could recall teeth flashing in the dark, but also arrows piercing him. And other wounds too. His good hand pawed over his bare chest, and found a landscape of scars. "I was hurt," he muttered.

"You were. The physicians gave me a cordial for your wounds. They said it might dull your memory, too. But don't worry – I'll take care of you."

He nodded and lay back. It felt good to have someone watching over him. "Who are you?"

"Why, I'm your daughter. Olva."

And maybe it was the numbing cordial, but that sounded right, too.

The next morning, he woke with the dawn, and his name was there. He was Tom of Ersfel. He was Long Tom the farmer. The woman – his daughter, Olva – was still asleep. She looked so careworn even while sleeping that it gave him a pang of guilt. How long had he been a burden to her? The wound in his shoulder was clearly fresh – the bandages were soaked with blood and pus – but maybe she'd been taking care of him for longer. And where were the rest of their family?

Tom tried to rise, but his long legs buckled under him. Olva woke instantly and rushed to his side, helping him lie back. She offered more cordial.

"I remember you," he said, "but little else."

She gave a curt smile. "There's lotus-wine mixed in with the cordial, I think. It's not the first time your mind has drifted. But I'll tell the story again."

War had driven them from their home in Ersfel. A monster

called the Lammergeier had attacked Summerswell, on the orders of a Dark Lord in the dread city of Necrad. Treacherous Lords had allied with the Lammergeier, betraying their oaths. Tom had tried to fight back to defend the village, and the Lammergeier had wounded him with a magic bow. Only in the Everwood could such wounds be healed.

"Am I a warrior, then?" asked Tom.

"No, no! Just a farmer. Though it's said you were the strongest man in the Mulladales when you were young."

"Aye, well, not now," said Tom, ruefully. He felt shamefully weak. He beckoned Olva over to give him more cordial. "I don't remember your mother."

"Maya," she said. "She died when I was young. I don't remember much about her. You had three sons. Aelfric, Michel, and Garn. They all went away down the Road to seek their fortune as mercenaries, and they never came home." She looked away. "I followed them. You weren't – well, you weren't always easy to live with, but there's no need to go into all that now. Not while you're sick. But know that we reconciled before it was too late."

"I'm glad we did." Those names were all familiar to him. They felt right. Michel and Garn were prickly with memories of regret. Aelfric, though – he rolled that name around his head, and it felt like a leaden weight. Aelfric had done terrible things. He took another sip of cordial, and the thought faded. "And what about you? You went away after them, and then?"

"Then I found another path. I'm a Ranger. One of the secret servants of the Erlking."

"That sounds like a very important job," said Tom, and he found he was proud.

Olva told him to rest, and slipped away into the trees. Soft rain fell. After a while, Tom felt well enough to hobble about the camp and explore a little. They were far from Ersfel, that was certain. He walked down to the riverbank, where there was a small boat hidden amid the weeds by the shore. The river was so wide he guessed it must be the Great River. Nothing else about the landscape was familiar to him, and he knew in his bones that he was very far from home.

As he returned to the camp, he passed a pool of water, and stopped there for a long time, staring at his reflection. An old man, gaunt and unshaven. He ran a finger through his stubbly hair, and felt the strangest urge to fill the silence with an insult.

"You look like a wizened vulture," he said to himself.

Olva cut him a walking stave from a tree branch, and they set off south. At first, they walked in wild forest, but soon came to a coppiced wood, then onto pastureland, the green fields of the southern Riverlands rolling out before them. They saw no other travellers.

At first, he had to lean on her, and felt faint, so she insisted he drink more of the cordial. It tasted even more strongly of fruit this time, a cloying sweetness he disliked. He spat some of it out, even though it did make him feel better. "Drink your medicine," snapped Olva, as though he were a wayward child, "and put this on." She handed him a travel-stained cloak.

"It's the height of summer," he objected.

"These are friendly lands," she said, "but there are still enemies between us and the Everwood."

"Do I have enemies?" asked Tom in confusion.

"You don't." She pulled her own hood over her head. "But I do, and if they knew who you were, they would use you against me."

They came to a small village on the Road. It had grown up around an inn, and there were only a dozen or so other houses in the place. Despite that, a crowd had gathered, one of sufficient size to block their path. Under her breath, Olva swore an oath so foul that Tom wondered if he should step in and chastise his daughter.

Olva tried to push through the crowd. "What's all this?" she demanded.

"It's the Company of the Dragon!" cheered a villager, pointing at a procession of five riders. The crowd parted to let these heroes through, and Olva slipped through the gap, leaving Tom amid the throng. He watched the passing of the company. Bright and bold they were, in the flush of youth. A handsome young knight, dragon-helm tucked under his arm as he waved to the crowd. There was a merry elf in green, and a solemn paladin of Arshoth with a dwarf clinging on to the back of her saddle, and a veiled woman from the strange lands west of West. They glittered with charmstones.

A herald rode before them, carrying the banner of a writhing dragon.

"They were off adventuring in the wild lands," said the villager, eager to exposit, "but now they've returned, just when Summerswell needs heroes! They've been called to avenge the death of Lord Aelfwine!"

Tom stared at the heroes. They were going north, to Avos and the rebellion.

"Out of the way, old man!" called another villager. "You're blocking the view."

His daughter returned with two fine horses, and saddlebags full of provisions.

"Where did you get those?" he asked in wonder.

"It's best not to ask questions of a Ranger."

They rode hard for the rest of the day. Ahead rose the steep hills of the Norrals. The Road swept off to the right on a long arc towards the Gap of Eavesland. "Shouldn't we stay on the Road?" asked Tom. "It's easier going and there'll be more travellers. It'll be safer." The arrow-wound was troubling him again. He clung to the saddle to avoid falling. Olva must have seen his paleness, for she gave him another draught.

"I know where I'm going," said Olva, "and the Road isn't the quickest way. Not in the Eaveslands. The Road was built for men, and we'll take the elf-paths." And so they rode on.

Tom was amazed at the tireless horses, until Olva pointed out charmstones set in their harnesses.

"They're charms of endurance," she explained. "They'll run for days."

"Now there's a wonder."

"You'll see greater wonders soon, when we reach the Everwood."

"You've been there, then?" Tom had never been one for theology. He always got the Erlking and the Intercessors mixed up in his head. It was strange – he could remember the little shrine in Ersfel quite clearly, and yet he could not recall even a moment of his wedding day with Maya. Even when he tried to call up her face, he imagined an elf-maiden. Everything was confused inside his addled skull.

"I have. There's healing in the Everwood."

"Well, if the horses don't need to rest, neither shall we," he said. He was exhausted and saddle-sore, and his shoulder was afire with pain, but he found within himself the strength to keep going. He dug his heels into the horse's flank, and the animal cantered on up the hill.

That evening, there came a storm. Tom could not recall a stranger one, and while it was true that his memory was all a-jumble, he was certain that if he had ever lived through another storm like this one, he would remember it. The sky darkened as though a curtain had been drawn across the heavens. Clouds jousted in the northern sky. Winds spat ice. The storm raged across the Riverlands, but its fury was felt even here in Eavesland.

Olva was troubled by the tumult in the skies. "Come on, Father. The town of First Gate is just over these hills, and we'll be safe there." But there was uncertainty in her voice that had not been there before.

Tom followed, but he could not help look back. For an instant he saw a flying shape far away, bat-like wings outlined against a flash of bloody light.

The heavens wept all night. The violence of the storm gave way to a rainstorm. Olva insisted they keep going, even as the trail through the hills became a morass. They struggled on until the ground was too slippery or too muddy to continue. Olva dismounted and tried to drag Tom's horse up the hill.

"Leave it," said Tom. He dismounted gracelessly, nearly falling in the mud. She caught him and helped him down. "I can't go any further tonight."

She nodded. They led the horses a little way back down the trail, to a sheltered glen they'd passed earlier. There was a hut amid the trees, made of mud and woven branches, and they took shelter there. The drumming of the rain on the roof was deafening. Tom slumped against the wall. The bandage over his arrow-wound was soaked, and not just with rainwater.

"Have you any more of that magic drink?" he asked.

Olva was busy lighting a fire. She reached into her pack and handed him a flask. Tom swigged the cordial. It tasted different this time, clearer, but it still eased his pain. "A gift from the Erlking," she said.

"So what does a Ranger do, then?" he asked, to distract himself from his discomfort.

"Whatever is necessary."

"Killing monsters and suchlike?" Faint memories washed through Tom's mind. Snarling fangs, claws, torchlight reflected off scales. The tang of ichor.

"Sometimes, yes, we must cull. But we are teachers and guides and healers, too. You can't build a kingdom on destruction alone. Something has to come after the slaying."

Tom nodded. "Aye, that's wise."

"I must admit, I find it hard sometimes, especially this year – this war. Sometimes, I have to do terrible things. They lead to a good end, I know, but that end may not come for many years, and I will never get to see it. I know that our labour is the work of centuries, and that I will not live to see what we build come to fruition. I envy the elves – they get to live on, and see the world we make."

There is never enough time. Ends come quicker than you expect, and so much is left half done, or unsaid. Tom couldn't recall who'd said to him, or why. The thought of green snow, and marble, and a young woman leaning against him.

"It's always the way of things," said Tom. "We do what we can, and then we pass on the work to the next set of hands. But you have to take what happiness you can along the way." He pressed his head back against the stone. "Now that I say it out loud, I think I was bad at doing that myself. Was I?"

"I cannot say."

He studied his callused, scarred hands. He must have spent a lot of time working in the field, to have hands like that. "When all this is done, Olva, and I'm healed, then come back to Ersfel for a spell. If my memory doesn't come back, you can tell me stories of who I used to be."

He closed his eyes and let himself drift towards sleep. It comforted him to know that someone like Olva was watching over him – and watching over Summerswell too. The clever ones would talk, and work out what to do. They'd tell him what needed to be done, what needed to be slain. That odd thought made him chuckle in his sleep, and the laughter made his chest hurt.

She shook him awake a few hours later. There was no breakfast, only more cordial. He blearily looked about the hut, and saw a light that was not the embers of the dying fire. Olva had a grail-cup. The water in it glimmered.

"We have to go," she said, hastily packing their gear.

"Why all the haste? It's barely even light, and it's still raining."

"We're being followed," she said, "by a foe we can't defeat. I've encountered it twice before, and I know its strength. We can't hope to fight it. But it won't be able to follow us into the mists that guard the Everwood."

She poured the water from her grail over the embers, then carried both their packs out to the waiting horses. The rain had subsided from a sky-shattering downpour to mere grey misery, but the ground was saturated.

"Aye, well, nothing will be moving quickly with the ground like this," said Tom.

"The enemy will. But we shall take a road he cannot follow."

The trail became stranger. Tom glimpsed ruined structures in the woods, their stones white as bleached bone where they were not overgrown with moss and tree roots. At times, the trail abruptly became arrow-straight, lined with arched trees, as if someone had cut a straight path through the hills and planted trees to mark the route. These straight roads never lasted long, but riding along them made him feel dizzy.

"Who dwells in these hills?"

"Wood Elves, long ago. But most of them are bound to life trees in the Everwood now, and cannot stray far from elvenhome. Wandering Companies still pass this way, and I'd hoped to meet them, but they're far away."

Sunlight flashed through a gap in the trees as they left one of the straight sections, and the shadows seemed to twist around him. Tom found that they were now travelling downhill.

"I can't figure out these straight bits at all," said Tom. "I figured we had at least another few hours' climb ahead of us before we got over the hills, but now we're south of 'em. It's like we passed through a tunnel, but I think I'd have noticed going underground."

"There are quicker ways than the Road. The elf-paths are straighter than straight. But only a few can use them." The light caught a ring on her finger. "There aren't any paths in Goldenvale, so we'll be back on mortal roads tomorrow."

"And then?"

"Once we get to the mists of Eavesland, not even a Ranger can be sure how far is left to travel. Not long, I hope. We're expected."

They rode on without stopping to rest. The horses had their charm-stones, and another draught of Olva's cordial left Tom happily numb; he was content to fall into a half-slumber. He only needed to occasionally nudge his horse to follow Olva's. Only his daughter remained watchful, guiding them around muddy patches or finding the right goat path through the foothills.

The next straight path brought them to a stand of beech trees. When they emerged, Tom was surprised to see that they were now looking south across the Goldenvale, a prosperous land of vineyards and pastures. In the valley far below, he could see a patchwork of farms and woodlands. They'd crossed the maze of the hills in only two days.

The air, even the light here, seemed fresh and unspoiled, like they were the first people ever to lay eyes on this bountiful valley, or it was the first afternoon in the history of creation. It was enough to make Tom feel young again, and full of wonder – and yet the shimmering light on the horizon spoke of more magic to come. The Everwood was almost in sight.

From behind them, there came the sound of barking.

There, in the distance, they beheld another rider. He was ragged as a scarecrow, his tattered cloak spread out behind him like black wings as he galloped down the straight path towards them. In con-trast, his horse was very fine, a beautiful bay courser, but he had clearly ridden it almost to the point of death; foam dripped from its mouth as it ran. A baying hound ran alongside the rider.

Looking back down the straight path was dizzying. The magic of the elven path twisted space, joining points that must be many miles apart. The rider was simultaneously much further back in the hills, and only a few heartbeats from reaching them.

"He can't follow," whispered the Ranger. "He shouldn't be able to use these paths."

The rider drew his sword, and it was the most terrible thing Tom had ever seen. It was so dark it drank light and hope. It was a steel-forged prophecy, that all things would end in destruction. Tom felt like he was about to fall down the straight path towards it, as if the sword was all that awaited him at the bottom of a pit.

Worst of all, it knew him. It called to him.

Lammergeier.

"Go!" shouted Olva. She slapped the rump of Tom's horse. The startled animal jolted forward, and Tom hung on desperately with his good arm as it ran out of the beech grove and stumbled down the sloping path to Goldenvale.

He twisted around to see Olva ride back into the trees, back to the straight path, back into peril.

He could not let her go alone.

He wrenched on his horse's reins, but the animal would not obey him. He threw himself from the horse's back to land in a yielding but foul patch of thick mud. One-handed, his wounded body complaining with every movement, Tom struggled upright and ran back up the hill towards the beeches.

He could not see her in the grove, for the entrance to the straight road had vanished. He crashed through the trees, trying to retrace his steps, as if he could tear open the way to the straight path by brute force alone. He could not see Olva, but he heard her, very far away. She cried words in elvish, and in answer there came a thunderous blast.

Trees creaked and bent, branches shattered, and splinters and leaves rained down around him. He heard a hideous wet bone-crushing crash as Olva's horse came flying out of thin air to smash into a tree trunk.

He found Olva sprawled on the ground near the broken beast. The animal was dead, but Olva still lived! Her face was caked in blood. There was the strong smell of burning, too – and he felt unnatural heat emanating from the ring on her finger. The skin around it was already blistered. He pulled the ring off her and threw it away.

There were two beech trees that formed the suggestion of an archway, and they were afire too, burning like the ring. Flames flickered beneath the bark as they burned from the inside. Of the straight path, nothing remained. The quick way through the hills was gone.

"I unmade the spell," whispered Olva. "I broke the path. The king's sigil. Go. The king calls for you . . ." Her head fell to the side.

Tom reacted without thinking. He searched her pack and found two metal flasks. He sniffed both; one smelled of sweet fruit. The other had the smell of cold mountain streams, and herbs, and Necrad. How he knew it smelled of far-off Necrad, he could not say. The second flask was fuller, so he gave her that one. He poured the healing cordial into her mouth, and splashed it over her wounded face and her bruised body. He guessed bones were broken, but the cordial worked its magic. She would live, but not for long.

She needed more healing than he could give.

Hells, *he* needed more healing than he could give.

There's healing in the Everwood, she'd told him. And for all he knew, that bastard with the black sword would be upon them soon. With the straight road sealed, he'd have to take a longer path.

Tom tried to lift Olva, but his wounded arm buckled under the strain. He didn't have the strength on his own. He found Olva's sword. The blade had snapped, but enough of it survived to be useful. He cut the harness from her dead horse and tugged it out from under the carcass. A stone of endurance, made to give the animal strength and endurance beyond natural limits.

He tucked it under the bandage, and felt its magic seep

into his bones. With a grunt, he lifted Olva and slung her over his shoulder.

Then down the path, towards Goldenvale and the distant mists of Everwood.

CHAPTER FORTY-SEVEN

Bor spurred the horse down the elf-path towards his quarry. Bloody fucking damned Agyla was there at the end of the road, a mounted sentry. *She* was the Lammergeier's captor, and she was almost within reach. She raised her cursed ring, and Bor grinned. His leash was broken. No ivy collar would close on his neck. She had no power over him.

But instead she spoke words of power, and the road convulsed around Bor. The level, straight path was somehow also a steep hillside, and his horse stumbled. In fury, he swung the black sword at her, and was rewarded with a blast of fury that smashed into the Ranger and her mount.

Unfortunately, Bor's own horse collapsed at the same moment, throwing him to the ground, so he never got to witness his enemy's destruction. When he picked himself up, he found himself on the damned hillside. The trees on either side of him were the same, but the road was gone.

He tried to curse, but it came out as a bestial yowl of frustration.

"Very eloquent," said Spellbreaker.

"What happened?"

"The caster of a spell, or one who knows the particular sigil used in the working of the spell, has power over it. The Erlking has given his Rangers access to some of his sigils. Clearly, she unmade the spell governing that stretch of road."

"Fix it!" snarled Bor.

"Spell*breaker*, not -*weaver*."

"How do we catch 'em?" Bor snapped his fingers. "Call another flying thing!"

"The storm washed away the miasma at Harnshill. The dreadworm would have to fly all the way from Necrad, or maybe Arden. It would take days to reach us – if it ever did."

"Call it!" demanded Bor.

"You must walk, wielder. Be quick, now," said the sword. "Kill the horse first. I must feed."

The dog led him through the hills. It was a frustrating journey. Promising trails ended abruptly at steep cliffs, or led him into fetid, stagnant pools. At times, the dog seemed to lose the spark of unnatural intelligence subsumed within the animal that housed it, and Bor had to drag it out of a rabbit hole or wade into a pond to pull it back from swimming. They made slow progress, and three days passed before they reached the far side of the hills and descended towards Goldenvale.

Bor looked for another horse to steal. His last one had been a stroke of luck – a scout from Avos had seen Bor's dreadworm crashing to earth after he'd flown across the river. The wretch had put up as good a fight as could be expected, but a mortal man against the Spellbreaker was no contest at all.

He crept through farmland and woodland, sneaking along hedgerows, keeping to the outskirts of settled lands. The Goldenvale was a province of the complacent and the pampered. The people here were known for their beauty and their kindness, and it was whispered that some had elvish blood. Bor knew the strife-torn Riverlands well, but he'd never travelled in Eavesland before. There was no call for mercenaries in this blessed land. Nor would he have been welcome.

In other parts of Summerswell, a Rootless man might slip by the guards, or pay a bribe. But Eavesland was guarded. There were no rogues here.

He hated the place. The sword chuckled.

"Save your hatred, wielder. There will be foes enough, soon."

He wanted to draw the sword and march into Firstgate or Harn's Rest or one of the other towns. He'd demand tribute, take what he wanted. Take what he *deserved*, recompense for all the injustices he'd suffered in his life. None of them would be able to stop him. He had the Spellbreaker, and that changed all the odds.

"Keep me sheathed, wielder," counselled the sword. "It keeps me better hidden from spirits and spells of divination. We must not be detected – not when we are so close."

So Bor lived like an outlaw again. He stole a chicken and roasted it over a campfire. He avoided all contact with other humans. The dog was his only companion. At times, it would warn him of some unseen danger, and they would hide in the ditches until it was gone. He was never sure if he could feel the passing attention of the Intercessors, or if it was only his mounting paranoia. Everything – wind and cloud, bird and beast, mortal and elf – was a potential threat, every eye a possible peephole for something on the other side.

Those days were maddening. On the one hand, the sword made him feel like he was a hero of the tales. He was the Nine creeping through the streets of Necrad, braving terrible dangers. But he was hiding from laughing children and fat farmers, and sneaking past vegetable gardens instead of the nightmare palaces of the dark city.

They were so soft, these people of Eavesland. So sheltered.

They *deserved* whatever he did to them.

"Does he ever talk about me?" Bor asked one night.

The demon eye flickered like an ember. "Who?"

"The Lammergeier. Or Olva Forster."

The dog pricked up its ears and shifted its position on Bor's feet.

"Ah, the Widow Queen!" laughed the sword. "No, I am hardly privy to conversations with Olva Forster."

"And the Lammergeier? I'm guessing she told him about me."

"She did."

"Does he ever speak of me?"

"In passing, once or twice."

"Does he understand that it wasn't my fault? I didn't know it wasn't him at Highfield – it was the false Lammergeier who tricked me – and I did all I could at Ellsport? I didn't betray Olva. She'd have been killed if I hadn't—"

"Wielder," said Spellbreaker, "I am not your confessor. I am your weapon. But know this – you were a tool of the Wood Elves. All that you did was part of their design to discredit the Lammergeier and seize *me*. You were but the smallest part of the tapestry of fate woven by the Erlking."

Bor rested his hand on the sword's pommel. "But now I'm more, aye."

"You are my wielder."

"And when I find the Lammergeier, what then? Who keeps you?"

"While the Lammergeier lives, I am sworn to serve him, and so I am oath-bound to urge you onwards, wielder."

The dog picked up a trail, and snuffled excitedly along the road. It led towards a grand castle outside Firstgate. The banner of a phoenix on a field of azure flew from the battlements.

Bor glared at the banner. "Sir Valentius's arms. I met that shit's son in a tourney in Arden a few years back. I remember his shield. He had a charmstone that made him faster than the wind. Bastard beat me around the tournament square, and I couldn't lay a blow on him. He kept slapping me across the arse with his sword and making the crowd laugh." Visions of marching into that castle, of the great gates blasted open and the floors red with blood flooded Bor's mind.

"Wielder," said the sword, "that would be a very foolish idea."

"I know that," snapped Bor. "I'm not stupid. But I'll be back for him, and all the rest."

Instead, Bor slipped into the grounds of the castle, and gossiped with a stableboy, and from him he heard a strange tale.

From out of the forest there had come a man. He was very tall, and his hair was wild – indeed, some thought he might be one of the fabled Wilder of the far north, and others thought he was a hermit of the High Moor. All agreed, though, that he must be among the walking dead, for he was pale as death. Blood oozed from a hideous infected wound on his breast. There was a gemstone in the wound – had he been cursed by a wizard to bear that stone? Or was that dreadful stone the source of the magic that animated this corpse?

The farmers fled at the sight of the walking dead, and sent to the castle of Sir Valentius for aid. The knights had gone away to the war, but there were a few guards left, and they rode forth bravely to confront the dead man. And lo, they discovered he was alive, but only barely – for when the guards challenged the man, he handed over his burden to them, and then fell down as one dead.

Now the man carried a burden, and the burden was this: a young woman, hooded and cloaked. She too was grievously injured, but she was alive, and when she was brought to the castle gates, she beckoned the doorkeep over with a burned and blackened finger, and bade him summon the lord of the castle.

Sir Valentius had his wizard treat the wounds of the strangers. He had his servants bathe and dress them; he had his chaplain bless them, and his armourer girded them. He commanded his stable master to prepare a carriage, and four swift horses. The strangers departed in the dead of night, without food or rest. And Sir Valentius gathered together the farmers and the guards, the wizard and the armourer, the stable master and the servants, and told them that they must never speak of what they had seen, and this oath was sealed in the presence of a holy Intercessor.

Bor rode south again, mounted on Sir Valentius's best horse. By the stableboy's account, he was only a day or two behind his quarry, and the dog had the scent again. The hills on the far side of the vale were far gentler than their northern counterparts, and almost empty of people. White towers stood atop the tallest hills, and Bor needed no prompting from sword or dog to avoid those eerie spires.

Finally, he came to the crest of the last hill, and looked down upon the Everwood.

Mist shrouded the elven forest – not the foul miasma of Necrad, but a swirling cloak of silver, iridescent and ever-shifting. Through gaps in the mist, he glimpsed tall trees with golden leaves, and shining towers of silver, and gardens where fountains danced and sang. These fragmented visions were fleeting, and never the same twice, even when the fog parted in the same spot a second time.

In the distance, yet greater trees loomed above the rest. Bor had seen those strange trees before, on the Isle of Dawn, but the ones there were not half so huge nor so beautiful. These were the life-trees of the Wood Elves, made to endure as long as the undying dwelt on the face of the earth. They sustained the spirits of the immortals, keeping them from fading into wraiths, giving them the strength to endure the passing of eternity.

Beyond that ring of mighty trees rose one still greater than all the rest. It was so tall its topmost branches were lost in the clouds; so huge that Bor guessed that it might give shade to a whole city. It was old but still hale; the foliage of its lower branches was a green so dark it was almost black, but near the top was a ring of golden leaves like a shining crown.

He dismounted and nudged the dog. "Go on. Show me the way."

*

The mists moved like a living thing as Bor approached. A patch slithered away, revealing the skeleton of some trespasser. And another corpse, and another and another. Some were so fresh that there was still skin on their bones; others had lain here for many years. None had visible wounds. They had wandered in this mist until they starved to death, even though the border was only a stone's throw away. The warning was clear – step into the mists of Eavesland, and perish.

The dog paused for a moment at the edge, then gave a very human nod, resolving itself to this course. It plunged into the fog, and Bor had to run to keep the hound's tail in sight. He followed the dog as it ran on through the trees. Out of the corner of his eye, Bor glimpsed half-formed faces in the fog, but whether they were spirits or wraiths or something else entirely, he would never know. Nor would he ever know how long he wandered in the fog; time flowed differently in the Everwood in that age.

His hand never left Spellbreaker, and his wariness never wavered. He prowled like a beast. He did not know that the dog was leading him through the only safe path through the labyrinth that guarded the outer wood. He did not know that armies had perished in the mists, that Berys' allies had squandered countless lives on attempts to probe the barrier. Tall were the walls of Necrad, and strong, and guarded by Stone Dragons, but they had been breached. The walls of the Everwood were gossamer-thin and yielded to a breath, but no one had ever trespassed beyond them – until now.

It was a smell that heralded the edge of the mist. A cloying scent filled the air, and made Bor's head swim. He stepped into sunlight, and found himself in an orchard. The trees bore a golden-skinned fruit that resembled a grape, but larger; each fruit was as big as Bor's fist. Windfallen fruit littered the ground. The smell of the rot was intoxicating.

"Smells like lotus," he muttered.

"Indeed, these are lotus-fruit," said the sword. "The Wood Elves cultivate them, but the Witch Elves consider them anathema. Do not eat of them, or you will lose yourself."

"Aye." He'd been in lotus-dens in the Riverlands before, where those seeking oblivion drank a liquor said to be made from lotus-fruit. He'd just never expected to find such a plantation in the elven kingdom.

Bor held his sleeve across his mouth and nose. "Which way?" he asked, but the dog was overcome with the scent of the fruit, and stared glassy-eyed up at him.

"Fuck's sake." Why would a dog desire forgetfulness? Bor grabbed the dog and dragged it across the orchard. The lotus trees grew in evenly spaced rows, with well-trodden paths between them, and extended for miles. Every tree bore a king's ransom worth of fruit, and it all seemed unguarded. A fortune, and he was walking right past it.

Near the far edge of the orchard, Bor encountered Wood Elves. They emerged from the forest and crept into the grove. Bor hid behind a tree and watched them. The elves were like children, laughing and playing as they tumbled about. Their garb was mismatched – one wore a gown that would not have been out of place at a gathering of the wealthiest lords on Summerswell, but others were dressed in rags, or nothing at all. They were all blessed with the perfect grace and elegance of elven-kind, but heedless of their surroundings. They gambolled past Bor's hiding place, and flung themselves on the green-sward. One unrolled a bundle containing food and a jug of wine, but the rest plucked lotus-fruit from the trees and devoured them.

They were utterly unlike the Wood Elves he'd encountered at Arden. Those companions of Princess Laerlyn carried their centuries of experience lightly, and were certainly strange and fey, but he'd never doubted their prowess. They'd been *magical*, in a way that terrified him – they were gifted with skill and might beyond the reach of mortals.

These, though – there was a hollowness to them, as rotten as the fruit that lay about the orchard.

They began to sing. The song was like the scent of the lotuses – intoxicating and sickening sweet, desirable and unwholesome all at once. It conjured images in Bor's mind. The orchard melted away, and he beheld a city of beautiful marble spires glittering in the sun. Those same elves walked the streets of Necrad, but it was the Necrad of their youth, and they too were young. Their physical forms were unchanged, for the elves are ageless, but their spirits were bright. They rode out into the wild wood to hunt; desperate wars were waged against demons. Mighty magics and works of craft were made by immortal artisans at the height of their power. Years whirled around him; each day brought new wonders to delight the eye, and by night, the sky was ablaze with sigil constellations, the stars so close that Bor could touch them.

Wielder, said the sword, its voice a dead weight cutting through the enchantment. *We must go.*

With a great effort of will, Bor dragged his attention back to the present. He touched the sword, and the spell was broken. The song was just a song.

The elves looked up like startled foxes and vanished, all but one. The last – an elf-woman – stared at Bor. She stood, and as she did so her ragged clothing became a silken dress of ancient design. She walked across the grass towards him, smiling, speaking in elvish. Bor grasped the hilt of Spellbreaker firmly, ready to strike if the woman attacked him. Instead, she brushed her fingers across his cheek and toyed with his tangled hair.

"The Lammergeier," said Bor. "Where is he?"

She frowned. "That's not what you're supposed to say." Her hand dropped, and she stared at her fingertips, as though she'd touched something foul. Then she too vanished, melting away.

"What the fuck?" muttered Bor.

Then he remembered he was starving. He snatched the elves'

picnic, rolled it back up into a bundle, and hurried from the orchard, dragging the dog with him.

"They are hamadryads," explained the sword. "Elves so ancient that they have bound themselves to the life-trees to endure the passing centuries. Their bodies have faded into dream. Only the trees remain in the physical world."

Bor gobbled the food, although he slipped a few pieces of meat to the dog. It helped them both shake off the lingering disorientation of the lotus grove. The food was astoundingly excellent. Wine from the Riverlands, spiced meat from Westermarch, good cheese from the Mulladales. He wolfed it all down.

"Are they coming for us, now?" He'd expected a host of elf-knights to come hunting him, or to be skewered by arrows from the trees. Or for the skies to darken again, and a fist from heaven to strike him down. Instead, a gentle breeze blew through the enchanted forest, and all seemed utterly peaceful.

"I do not know if our presence will stir the hamadryads from their long slumber," admitted the sword. "Certainly, my former wielder – Acraist Wraith-Captain – expected they would rise up to defend the Everwood, but his armies never reached this place. The Erlking has other guardians, and I would have thought they would be upon us by now. They must be distracted by the war. We should make haste."

Bor wiped his mouth. "It feels like walking into a spider's web."

"Those," said the sword, "I can cut."

The dog led them on again. This part of the wood had more of the huge life-trees, and Bor glimpsed elves in the shadows of the trees. None of them barred his way, or did anything but watch, as if he were some novelty passing through their village. A mummer or a wandering singer, here to earn a crust. The elves stared blankly, then faded into nothingness or danced away.

They came to a stone building, swallowed by the forest. At first, it reminded Bor of a church, but the place had never had a roof, and there was a stone-lined pool at its heart, a bowl of still water. Hawthorn trees thick grew about it, but the dog insisted on wriggling in through a gap.

Bor struggled after it, cursing as thorns caught his skin. The dog padded up to the edge of the bowl and stared into the waters.

"Should I free you?" said the sword.

Bor glanced at the blade in confusion, before he realised it wasn't talking to him. Reflected in the waters of the great stone grail in the place of the dog was an elf in ragged armour. His lips moved, but no sound could be heard.

"I expected to find this," said the sword. "This is where elf-wraiths are exalted into Intercessors. There are two dozen or so Intercessors, and a matching number of shrines like this. A spell writ in stone." The demon eye stared at the dog. "I could break it. Your kin have forgotten you."

The elf-knight shook his head. Then he withdrew, moving deeper into the waters – or in a direction that Bor could not name. The dog's eyes rolled back in its head and it fell over. Bor darted over to grab the animal before it fell into the water. The dog lay twitching by the side of the bowl.

"The wraith-world and the physical realm are close at this point," explained Spellbreaker. "He can find his way back to the body when he is done hunting."

"Hunting for what?"

"Our quarry," replied the sword. It chuckled. "Oh, how I yearn to destroy this place, and those like it. I was made to shatter this shrine. To me, wielder, this is a siege engine, a weapon of war. My maker forged me to break the spells of the enemy." The sword quivered like a living thing.

Light flickered briefly in the depths of the bowl. The dog sat up, shook itself, and gave a short bark. It ran out of the shrine, through the hawthorn fence, and off into the forest, with Bor following after.

But then more lights flickered in the depths. Wind rippled the water and bent the trees. The Intercessors sensed the intrusion of their lost kinsman, and now they knew where to look.

Horns sounded in the heart of the forest.

CHAPTER FORTY-EIGHT

Distant horns woke Tom from sleep. He stirred and stretched – and then he was fully awake, sitting up in bed, snatching up the first thing that came to hand as a weapon: a carved wooden nightstand. He was in an unfamiliar room – whitewashed walls of cool stone, hanging tapestries, and an arched window looking out over a green wood. Through the open door he could see a corridor, and more rooms. The place had the air of a monastery, a house of healing – and his wounds had been rebound with strange bandages.

"Olva!" he called. What had happened? He recalled carrying her for what felt like days, every step a jolt of agony, blood dripping from his chest, his vision swimming darkly, knees buckling – but he'd kept walking. There'd been a castle, hadn't there? He seemed to remember a castle. There'd been a Wilder girl, too, walking by his side. Talis, she'd called herself. Or had that been a raven?

"She is not here," said a kindly voice. He twisted around. Sitting by his bed was an elf-maid. Her eyes were as green as the forest outside, and her blonde hair was tied back. A silver crown adorned her head.

She was intensely familiar to him, but he did not know her name.

"Tom," he croaked. "My name's Tom."

The elf frowned. "Agyla gave you too much of the lotus. But how else to tame the Lammergeier?" She leaned forward and touched his forehead. "Remember."

So he did. 'Tom' was washed away on that tide, the dam breaking in a red flood. He remembered all that had transpired since he'd left Necrad, all that had passed since the dream Jan sent him. He remembered Maedos dying on his sword – and he remembered watching as Laerlyn put an arrow through the heart of the false Lammergeier. He remembered 'Olva' – Agyla! – and wondered how he could ever have mistaken the Ranger for anything other than an enemy.

The heavy weight of duty settled back on him. So much to do, people looking to him like he was the Lammergeier of legend. He fought to hang on to Tom – simple, honest Tom, Tom without the burden – but the false life slipped away. He could not hide from truth.

He remembered the vision of Necrad, the battlements of the Wailing Tower.

He remembered Berys, telling him he had to stay, telling him he had to finish the slaughter. Telling him he had to wield the black sword. He remembered refusing, and the arrow flying from *Morthus*.

And oh, he remembered the wound. He lay back in the bed, exhausted.

"Lae."

"I am here," she said gently. "I have watched over you since you were brought to this house."

"You shot me with an arrow."

"That was Berys."

"No," croaked Alf. "In Arden."

"My friend," said the princess, "I have travelled by your side for half your life. Did you really think I could not tell that it was not you upon that horse?"

"If it had been me . . ."

"Then I would not have loosed my arrow. Not at you. Never at you. We may quarrel, Aelfric, but we are friends for ever."

"Are we now? Then tell me honestly — is what Berys says true? About the elves meddling in mortal affairs? Controlling Summerswell for your own ends?"

A shadow crossed her face, and she looked away. "Berys said nothing that was wholly untrue, but there are many ways to tell a tale. All I can do, Aelfric, is swear by all we hold dear — by our friendship, by the Nine, by the fallen — that I never acted with malice towards any of you. I have done things, tolerated things, that I despise, but always with good intent in mind. If any of the others, even Berys, were here I would look them in the eye and tell them that I have always sought to do what is right for all of us. For mortals and elves alike, Summerswell and the north." She raised her head, and her eyes were red-rimmed with tears. "Please believe me."

Now it was Alf who looked away. "Lae. I'm sorry about your brother."

"Family is a troublesome thing. We are bound to them by blood, as tightly as we bind ourselves to our friends by oath and shared company. My brother was an idiot before the destruction of his body. Now, with the indulgence of my father, he's a celestial idiot masquerading as a holy spirit. *A fucking fuckwit of an Interfucker*, as Gundan would say if he were here." She patted Alf's sword-hand. "Maedos brought this on himself. I bear you no ill will — though I warn you, the same cannot be said for my father's court. There are those who call for your execution."

"Why," asked Alf, "am I not dead?"

"My father attended to your wounds with his mightiest spells of healing. It was thought that all wounds from *Morthus* are lethal, but, as ever, you are exceptional."

"I don't feel exceptional. I feel like a giant sat on me. But no, Lae, I mean . . . why bring me here? Am I a prisoner? We're at war, aren't we? Necrad and the Everwood. The Uncrowned King and the Erlking." He looked around. "I lost Spellbreaker."

"You never need wield that cursed sword again. And yes, the war continues. There is bitter fighting in Summerswell, and in the north."

"I saw Necrad," said Alf. "Maedos showed me Necrad."

"I too saw that vision in the grail-water, Aelfric. What it means, I cannot be certain. If Lord Bone has indeed returned, then we shall fight him together. But we must end this mortal rebellion first, and there is a way to do so peacefully. It's why I returned to the Everwood, and why I ordered you be brought here when they found you. It all depends on you."

She stood, and offered him her arm to lean on. "Rise, Sir Aelfric Lammergeier, and come with me."

The other rooms were crowded with humans, many of whom bore visible signs of injury. Others had the pallor of Necrad. "They come to the Everwood for healing," said Laerlyn. "My father is the greatest of healers, although even he cannot cure all wounds. There are sorrows and evils in the world beyond the reach of magic."

A young girl darted out to greet Laerlyn. "You're here again today!" the child said excitedly.

"Not for long. Just to see you, and to collect an old warhorse." She pointed at Alf. "Do you know who this is, Berysala?"

The child looked up at Alf. "Another knight from Eavesland?"

"This is the Lammergeier."

"It can't be the Lammergeier," said Berysala, "he doesn't have the black sword."

"Right enough," said Alf, "I'm Alf." The child did not look in need of healing.

Again came the horns, and Berysala shivered. "I've not heard them so close before."

"Do not fear," said Laerlyn, "no harm will come to you."

*

Two Rangers stood guard at the door of the house of healing, and a weird shock of recognition struck Alf when he saw that one of them was Agyla. He remembered her as the assassin who'd ambushed him in Arden, remembered the bloody slaughter that so sickened him. Overlaid with that, though, were Tom's memories of her, where he'd thought of her as his daughter. He'd nearly killed himself carrying her to safety. He'd bled for her, been bled by her.

Yet now she looked at him, and she was still a stranger.

"Agyla," he began, unsure what to say.

"Nothing more needs to be said, and my name never need be spoken."

"You could have killed me when you found me."

A flicker of anger crossed her face. "I could, and that would have been just. You slew the Prince of Dawn, Lammergeier, and that is a foul deed I shall not forget. But the Erlking sent for you, and it was my task to guide you a part of the way. There is healing here in the Everwood, and broken things can be set to a new purpose." She scowled. "Fulfil the purpose ordained for you, and nothing more needs to be said."

They left the house of healing. Rising over the trees nearby was the largest life-tree Alf had ever seen. It was surely the tallest and grandest tree in the world. He'd travelled far, and had walked in parts of the wild wood where no other mortal from Summerswell had ever gone, but he'd never seen any living thing compare to that titan.

Many lesser life-trees grew in the shadow of the great tree. Wood Elves appeared near these trees to watch their princess and the champion of the enemy slowly proceed towards the Erlking's keep. They stood in eerie silence, a solemn honour guard for the pair.

The horns sounded a third time, closer still. "What are those horns?"

"There's an enemy in the wood," admitted Laerlyn. "An intruder from the mortal lands."

Alf glanced back at Berysala, who was still lingering on the threshold, watching the two heroes of the Nine walk into the woods. "She's a hostage, isn't she?"

"Yes."

"Like Berys said. That's what Derwyn was for. So you'd have a hold over me."

"Please don't say 'you' like that, Aelfric. You know where I was all of Derwyn's life – with the Nine, ruling over Necrad. I had no part in that scheme."

"You knew it was happening."

She turned to him, and there was a glint of anger in her face. "I left the Everwood, Aelfric, when I joined the Nine. I ran away from my family and my title as daughter of the Erlking because I loathe schemes like that one. I had no wish to be like Maedos or my other siblings, who treat mortals like playing pieces in their games. I saw the corruption and greed of the Lords of Summerswell, too. I thought I would show them another path – a better way."

"So why did you come back here? You're talking like Peir – like Derwyn! If you want what we want, then why not stay with us in Necrad?"

"Because I knew that this war was both inevitable and futile. I knew the Lords of Summerswell would not tolerate an upstart taking control of Necrad. I knew Berys and her allies would push for conflict." She looked up at the massive tree. "Most of all, Aelfric, because I knew we cannot defeat *him*."

A ring of smaller life-trees surrounded the Erlking's titanic vessel. "These are for the royal house," explained Laerlyn. "My father's own tree was the first he made. All other life-trees are grown from his seed. That, there—" she pointed to one particular tall tree "—is the one reserved for my brother Maedos. He does not need it yet, but the magic of Intercession is costly, and will fade. In only a few decades, he will have to come back here and bind himself to that tree, and dwell in the Everwood for eternity."

"Or he gets lost in the wraith-world, aye?" A place of torment, by all accounts. "Your tree was in Necrad."

"I planted it there. Berys had it burned. I shall return and plant another, when the war is done."

Alf looked up at the Erlking's tree. It was taller than any cathedral or palace, even the Wailing Tower. The Erlking had made that. By all accounts, he was an even more powerful wizard than Lord Bone. The first wizard, the first elf, the first to walk the world.

And Alf without a sword. Hells, even if he had a sword, he had not the strength to swing it.

"He wishes to speak with you," said Laerlyn, "alone."

"Do I . . . do I talk to the tree, or is he going to appear in a pillar of light or something?"

Laerlyn pointed to a cottage nestled amid the roots.

"Aye, right."

The cottage was small. The thatch needed replacing in spots, although the shade of the tree probably kept the rain off. There was a herb garden at the side, and some sheds and workshops. If a passing dragon dropped that cottage into Ersfel, Alf might have walked past it without noticing.

The inside looked like the aftermath of a hurricane in a library. Books were piled on almost every surface, the only exception being where piled books were themselves being used as tables for all manner of objects. Relics from Necrad, jars of alchemical components, maps and scrolls, game boards with hand-carved pieces, all jockeying for space with cups and plates. Everything was worn or threadbare, all utterly lived-in.

"Come on through," called a voice. "I'm in the garden."

Alf picked his way through the debris, and entered the garden through a back door.

An old, old elf waited for him. All the other elves Alf had known were ageless. Even the ancient Oracle retained the blush of youth

right up until the moment of her death. This elf, though, was wrinkled and stooped, his white hair thin and wispy. He wiped his hand
on his woollen tunic.

"Hello, Aelfric," said the Erlking.

CHAPTER FORTY-NINE

"I've never met a king before," said Alf. "Should I kneel?" Alf felt no urge to bow before this creature, but he suspected that both the humble shack and the threadbare appearance of the Erlking were illusions, or that the Erlking could easily turn the cottage into a grand palace with a thought. Without Spellbreaker, he was utterly defenceless against such trickery.

"Sit, sit. I never wanted to be a king, either." The Erlking's voice was warm, with an undercurrent of amusement – not mockery, but wonderment at the absurdity of the world. "I was called the Uncrowned King long before your nephew, you know. This was in Necrad, long ago. We had no kings, but my skill made me first among equals, so they called me the Uncrowned King. Erlking, now, that was a title mortals gave me, and the elves adopted. But what to call me? Am I the Yule Elf, who brings presents? Or Az the Giant?" There was a mischievous gleam in the old elf's eye. "If you're Alf again, maybe I'll be Tom."

"What's your real name?"

"Laerlyn said you were like that. Walking into my house and asking me my true name, oh ho! No, no. Call me Erlking if you must, I suppose."

Alf wondered if Laerlyn had said he was brave or stupid. "You sent for me."

"I did. You're not the first mortal to sit here," said the Erlking. "It seems like only yesterday it was Harn. The poor fellow was in even worse shape than you, shivering and sneezing all over my couch. And what did I do for him? Eh?"

"You sheltered him, and drove away the Hopeless Winter."

"More than that."

"You made him and his companions the Lords of Summerswell."

"Quite so. I divided up the lands into provinces, appointed Lords to oversee them — and Intercessors and Rangers to oversee the Lords. And before him, other mortals stood where you are now. The wizard-kings of Minar Kul — what you call the Old Kingdom. They begged me to teach them secrets of magic, and I did. They took that magic, and used it to make themselves kings of mortals. And others before them, many, many more. All forgotten now — save by me. I remember everything. My mind is undiminished."

"So, what are you saying? That you've always been a friend to mortals?"

The old elf laughed. "A friend? No. You quite misunderstand me if you think I am a *friend* to mortals. Are you a friend to a raindrop, or a beam of sunlight? Do you name every grain of wheat in the field? I am old, Aelfric Lammergeier. A thousand mortal lifetimes or more have passed since I first awoke, the first of the elves to do so. I am no friend to mortals." He waved his hand around the little over-grown patch of greenery. "You are weeds growing in my garden. I mean you no especial ill will, but you are a problem to be contained, to be managed and cultivated, not *befriended*."

"Laerlyn—" began Alf, but the Erlking cut him off.

"My daughter is very young — and I have cultivated her, too, most assiduously. I taught her to be kindly and honourable, just as Maedos was made to be haughty and ambitious. I am no friend to my children, either. I breed tools."

Alf scowled, and the Erlking saw his face and laughed. "Come now. Sure you agree that one can be fond of a tool, even cherish it. But purpose comes first."

"Does it now?" rumbled Alf. He'd never heard Lord Bone speak, but surely this was the way a Dark Lord must talk – and his instinct was to silence the old elf by thumping him in the face. Berys' warnings about the Erlking's cruel machinations had never seemed more prescient, but Laerlyn had asked him to listen, so he stayed his hand.

He didn't have a sword, anyway.

"Now then, what do you know about the awakening of the elves?" asked the Erlking.

Alf shrugged. Both Laerlyn and Ildorae had spoken of the early history of the elves, but neither of them remembered it, for they were born – *reborn* – in later generations. "There were eight-thousand-odd of you, and you awoke on the Isle of Dawn."

"Eight thousand one hundred and fifty-nine elves at the beginning, now, and 'til the world's ending. I was the first. I woke full-grown, but empty. Alone, I wandered. I learned to walk, to think, to make. When the other elves awoke, I invented speech so that I could pass on what I had learned, but for an age I was alone." The Erlking pottered about his little garden, pulling up weeds. "I remember looking up at the stars that first night, and waiting for some power to appear and tell me my purpose, but no answer came. To this day I do not know, Aelfric, if we were granted dominion over the world, or if we were intended to merely be custodians of it. There are other powers in existence – demons from the dark, dreams of light – but none spoke to me."

He turned to Alf, suddenly animated. "Were the elves created deliberately? Are we celestial spirits accidentally enmeshed in base matter? Did I miss some clue, some message that might have told us *why*? I have searched for answers to those questions for thousands of years, and have found nothing. I called into the void, and heard nothing back but lies! All I know for certain is that we are truly immortal. We cannot and will not die. These bodies—" he plucked at his wrinkled skin "—they fade and perish, and we become wraiths. The wraith-world is terrible, mortal. It is torment, and we escape only through reincarnation, if living elves procreate.

"In those early days, we thought we understood the cycle. We did not awaken at the same time, nor did we fade at the same rate. We thought that the elves who were older or faded quicker would become wraiths, and then be reborn into a second generation. One by one, all of us of the first generation would perish, and be reborn in turn, on and on until the world's ending. Then ... then we explored the world, and found it to be full of perils – demons were the immediate threat, but there were more. The other elves thought they could conquer this peril through sword and spell.

"But I thought, *what if they fail?* What if some cataclysm wiped out all living elves in a single stroke, and I was condemned to suffer in the wraith-world for as long as the world endures? Or, equally, what if I faded and became a wraith? In my absence, while I waited for reincarnation, the elves became, say, enslaved by demons? What if I was reborn again and again into suffering? I saw that ensuring my own safety through eternity was necessary. I began to—"

"What does all this have to do with me?" demanded Alf.

"Such impatience! I reveal cosmic truths to you, mortal, and you ask what bearing it has on you? I shall tell you. I began to study the death-of-the-body that plagued us. I worked a spell to bind death into a physical form – and as a side effect, I created you humans."

The Erlking dug a handful of earth out of the ground. He breathed, and the dirt came to life. Little humanoid shapes of soil sprang from his palm and roamed the garden for a few seconds. Some stumbled around blindly before falling apart. Others embraced their neighbours, clinging to each other as they disintegrated. One brave earthling – a hero of its kind – quested it as far as Alf's boot before collapsing. Alf stared in horror.

"They were as real and alive as you are," said the Erlking, "only briefer." He brushed the dirt from his palm. "It was not the first time

I had created living beings, and I thought you of little consequence. Out of amusement, I set your ancestors free into the woods, and returned to my laboratory in Necrad. I had bound Death, and hoped that this would ensure the elves would never fade, and we would never need to pass through the wraith-world. But the number of you humans increased beyond measure in only a few short centuries. Worse, you learned to wield the earthpower. Your ancestors freed Death, and she drove us from Necrad!"

The Erlking crossed the little garden and patted a huge tree root that protruded from the earth. It was part of the massive life-tree that towered above them. "So many of us perished in that retreat, and in the years of despair that followed. We fled south, across the sea, and took refuge in this forest. I continued my work, and in time I found a way to bind an elf-spirit to a living tree. Look! The tree drinks in the earthpower, and transmutes it to star-magic to sustain the elf. This was a desperate last resort, but I feared that if any more of the elves faded, there would be too few left to ensure my own rebirth if it ever came to that."

"Do you only care about yourself?" spat Alf.

The Erlking nodded. "Of course! I have eternity to think about. You mortals, your individual tales end with a happily-ever-after or a suddenly-he-was-no-more. You need not think about the centuries to come. For you, the future can be left to another. But I am endless, and thus I must shape that future. My story will continue for ever, and so I must choose if it is a tale of joy or sorrow."

He laughed. "Or a tale of one elf's struggle against his own incompetence. I'm not all-knowing, Alf. I'm a fumbling idiot, just like you. That's a secret of the wise – we're all making it up as we go along.

"I tried to imprison Death, and unleashed the cataclysm I feared and lost Necrad in the process.

"I tried to save the elves with the life-trees, and ended up sundering our people. Amerith was convinced that the life-trees were some sinister plot to make myself king of the elves, and so she swore that she would never bind herself to my design.

"I sought to help my fellows cope with the weight of immortality, and made the lotus-fruit to ease their burden. Alas, many of them choose forgetfulness, the oblivion that leads to bliss. They wake new each day, existing without memory. The lotus was another mistake, and now I must watch over those lost to it.

"When humans followed us across the sea and settled the south-lands, I debated what best to do about them. Another war risked weakening us beyond hope of recovery – and even if the elves drove those humans from our lands, there were more humans across the sea. By then, you had spread to every corner of the world. So, I chose the path of friendship. My emissaries approached the mortals, and offered to teach them the secrets of the elder race. We taught them the elven-tongue. We taught them smith craft and architecture, poetry and art. We taught them magic."

Alf furrowed his brow. "Was that the Old Kingdom?"

"No. This was thousands of years earlier. There have been many mortal kingdoms in my lands. Some prospered for centuries with my aid; others failed quickly." The Erlking sat back down next to Alf. "I am a gardener, Aelfric. A farmer toiling in the fields of eternity. Each failure teaches me something for the next attempt. Each time, I get closer to my goal – the taming of the speaking beasts. I have tried many, many methods. Geases and spells of obedience seemed promising, but the cost was too great. I tried enchantment, but other dreams slipped through my nets. I tried terror, but it only incited heroes." He sighed. "I thought Summerswell would last longer. It seemed a solid approach. Rival provinces, and two rulers in each, to ensure no Lord was strong enough to defy me. The threat of Necrad, to keep them united when needs be. The earthpower banned, and all study of magic confined to safe channels, but not so restricted that I could not benefit from mortal ingenuity. It was one of my better efforts, all in all. But to all things there is a time.

"Summerswell has failed. If it were strong enough to survive, it would have weathered Berys' rebellion. Necrad, too, presents a problem. When it was under the control of Amerith's folk, I was content to let it be – I thought that in a few thousand years, I could convince them to trust me again. But then it fell to Lord Bone, then to the Nine, and now – well, even I do not know what transpires in Necrad. Anarchy, uncertainty – these things I cannot tolerate."

He tapped Alf on the knee. "And that, my friend, brings us to you, and the present moment. Even if the rebellion is defeated, the damage is done. The authority of the Lords is discredited. The legend of the Nine endures despite all my attempts to tarnish it. And a new darkness rises in the north." An impish grin crossed his face. "Apparently, saving the world is popular with the mortal masses. Who knew? I'll have to try that one again, in years to come. But for now, Aelfric, let us discuss your immediate future."

"I won't serve you."

"You will. You do not yet understand my proposal."

As if awakening from a dream, Alf saw that what he had thought was a humble cottage was actually a palace grander than any in Necrad. What had seemed to be an overgrown little patch was, in truth, a fabulous garden where paths of crushed stone intertwined in the shadows of the tree, and laughing streams fed pools that reflected the stars.

Laerlyn came walking across the greensward, and she was wearing her old armour, her old travelling gear – the battered garb she'd worn on their quest. She was just as he remembered her from those bright days of his youth.

She rested her slim hand on his shoulder. "He wants us to rule Summerswell, Alf. You and I."

"A union of the two kindreds, and the two sides," said the Erlking. "The rebels will listen to you, Aelfric. Only a handful are true Defiants. Most followed their liege-lords down a ruinous path.

We shall forge new bonds of loyalty to you and my daughter. All will hail the mortal king and his faerie bride."

"And those that don't?" muttered Alf.

"They will die. All things are born in blood. But there will be less bloodshed this way than any other. You may order the lands of mortals as you see fit, so long as you obey a few minor restrictions. All the operations of my Rangers shall continue, and you shall not interfere with them. Similarly, the Intercessal Church and the College Arcane must continue, although I permit the appearance of reform. You will pay tribute to me – the best of all you make – and I may call upon you for certain tasks befitting your abilities. And, of course, the city of the elves must be returned to the elves. Necrad is mine, and all its works. Life-trees will be planted there, and the remaining vampires slain so that they may be reborn and redeemed. So long as you observe these laws, you have my blessing."

He clapped his hands, and a silver casket appeared. "To mark this new beginning." The Erlking threw back the lid. Inside, lying on black cloth, were two weapons of surpassing beauty. One was a sword, of form similar to Spellbreaker, but it gleamed brightly as if the sun was caged within the blade. Instead of a ruby eye, it bore the symbol of a winged bird holding a crown. Its mate was a pale bow of dragon bone, almost identical to the executioner's bow *Morthus* that Laerlyn had once carried.

The Erlking lifted the bow from the chest. "This, daughter, is *Faelthus*. Justice, in the mortal tongue. And this, Aelfric, is Kingmaker."

Alf twisted around. "Is this what you want, Lae?"

"The world is never what we wish it to be, Aelfric. It is not the path I would have chosen for us if we were free to choose, but we are not. We are the last of the Nine, and ours is both the power and the responsibility to put this right."

"But is it putting things right?" Alf pushed Lae's hand away and faced the Erlking. "It's the same thing again – you in charge behind the throne, and humanity serving you! You use me to pull the fangs of the rebels, and then who'll stand against you?"

"Why, no one. That's rather the point." The Erlking's eyes gleamed. "Know this, mortal: I made your kind with a spell, and he that cast a spell can break it. I have no wish to wreak such destruction – you mortals have your *uses* – but I will do it if you force my hand. I shall unmake all humans, everywhere, and start again from dirt, rather than tolerate a threat to my own existence."

Alf paled. He looked back at Laerlyn. "Lae ... he's bluffing, right?"

"It's true that he conjured humanity with a spell," she said, "when he bound Death." She was as shaken as Alf by the Erlking's words. Alf could tell that she had neither known nor expected her father's threat. "To hold seigneury over a such a spell for so long, to hold the threads of magic through will alone for centuries – it is almost unthinkable. Of anyone else I would say it is impossible. But... I cannot be sure he is lying."

"Annihilation, or triumph as the saviour of humanity. It seems like an easy choice to me," said the Erlking, "but you have little time to decide."

The horns again, closer still.

Alf walked away from the Erlking, away from the sword called Kingmaker, and leaned against the trunk of the massive life-tree. His head spun. He clenched his fists, all his fighting instincts rising up in him to deal with this threat. A part of him wanted to snatch up that bright sword and wield it, to slay whatever enemy approached. *A fight. Fighting all you're good at.* He'd been pierced by arrows, bitten by fangs, stabbed and blasted and wounded in countless ways, but he'd never before felt this grasping fear. Everything was wet sand running through his fingers. If he made the wrong choice here, he'd doom not only himself, but everyone and everything he knew.

He was grateful for the sheltering mass of the giant tree overhead. He could not stand to be unroofed and unrooted in this house, or face the judgement of the stars. He desperately wanted there to be someone wiser than him to make this choice for him. He missed the simplicity of being Long Tom. No one had asked Long Tom to decide the fate of nations. These choices were beyond a mortal's comprehension, and he did not know how to choose wisely.

He could fight. He could go out and slay whatever those horns heralded. The warrior hero, defending the land against monsters. He could prop up the order of the world, be one more link in a long chain of lives.

He could fight. He could go back and pick up the Erlking's sword, and drive it through the Erlking's smug face. That would not kill the immortal elf, of course, not while the tree endured. Not while the world endured. But it would throw everything into chaos. The image – the memory – of a tower of ice shattering crossed his mind, but he did not know where it came from.

A shape loomed in his peripheral vision. He spun around, fists raised, ready to strike.

"Aelfric, it's me!" said Laerlyn.

"Lae." The thought *she's one of the clever ones* warred with *she's the Erlking's tool*. "What do we do?"

"I know my father. He would not dictate this course if there was another choice. The foe who approaches is but a mortal, but he has been guided past our defences by one of our own – and he wields the Spellbreaker. Your sword, Alf. You can defeat him."

"And save the Erlking."

"And save all the Everwood, and all that rests upon it. I will fight if you do not." She glanced back at the little shape of the Erlking. "I can guess what you think of my father, and you are right – he is arrogant and cruel. But he has done good as well as evil. The life-trees are a blessing to Elvendom. The order and learning he brought to you mortals ... and his gifts as a healer. He undid many of the wounds inflicted by Lord Bone's legions, Alf. He works in secret to restore the land."

"His land, he called it," muttered Alf.

"He was Firstborn," said Laerlyn. "He walked the world before all other living things. We should not be surprised that he sees all others as interlopers. But within his limitations, he is capable of kindness – and a sort of mercy."

"He just threatened to destroy everything! That's worse than anything Lord Bone ever did!"

"And he gave us a way to avert that doom. Why do you fear this path?"

"Because . . . because it's me, Lae. I'm not a king. I'm not wise. You entrusted me with Spellbreaker because I wouldn't use it. So why give me Kingmaker, if not for the same reason?" Alf sank down against the tree. "He knows I'm *safe*, Lae. He knows I'll do what I'm told. And heavens help me, I will. I followed Peir, and Derwyn, and I'll follow you too." A feeling of cold inevitability settled on Alf. "Tell me how to save the world, and I can do that. I don't know how to make a better one."

Laerlyn squeezed his shoulder. "Save the world first, Aelfric. Then we'll do what we can to fix it, I swear."

"You," he said thickly, "haven't taken his bow yet, either."

"True enough." Laerlyn walked away across the green. She knelt before her father, and took the bow Justice from the chest.

And Alf followed.

CHAPTER FIFTY

In those last hours, Bor achieved a degree of skill he had never dreamed possible. He and Spellbreaker were a matchless harmony of violence.

The sword's first wielder, Wraith-Captain Acraist, the Hand of Bone – he always saw the sword as a mere tool, a part of the panoply of arms he bore. To him, the sword was a possession. He never gave himself to the sword.

Spellbreaker's second wielder, the mortal Aelfric Lammergeier – only once did he use the sword to its fullest potential. In the tunnels under Necrad, when the Nine fought to slay Lord Bone, on that day only did he wield the Spellbreaker wholeheartedly. For after the death of Peir the Paladin, he saw Spellbreaker as a burden to be endured, a murderous monster to be imprisoned. Never again did Alf give himself over to the sword.

But the third wielder, Bor the Broken – he had nothing to hold him back. He was broken, and the sword filled him. He moved with stolen speed and grace, for he had slain many elves, and the sword took their lives and fed them to Bor. He could no longer tell what was sword and what was mortal. He was a thing with a sharp black claw, with ruby eyes and steel sinews. Hunters pursued him, and he slew them. Enchantment-spells and illusions were laid upon him, and he broke them. Divination spells searched for him, and he swallowed them and walked unseen. For thousands of years, the mists of Eavesland had protected the forest against invasion, and its knights had guarded it against any intruder who by chance slipped through the outer defences. But this enemy was guided by one who knew the wood of old, and possessed a weapon of surpassing power that the elves could not defeat.

The horns of Elfland sounded all around him, and there was fear in their cries. They wailed that a foe was in the wood, and their hunters could not find him.

Closer and closer he drew to his quarry.

Onwards, onwards, urged the sword. The tree of the Erlking loomed over the forest ahead. It was a pillar holding up the sky, and Bor would bring it crashing down.

And then the last stretch, the last ring of defenders – and there he met no resistance. Hollow-eyed elves watched his approach with disinterest, then fled. Their existence was magically bound to the life-trees, and the sword could unbind them with a touch. They melted like mist rather than fight him. Bor howled, an animal cry of frustration that he was denied bloodshed. He strode towards the tree, and the Erlking's palace. The dog bounded after him.

The sword washed away all illusions. Bor did not see the cottage, nor the enchanted palace. He saw only the tree, and around it a tangle of roots. Bones and other debris lay there, lost in the leaf-litter. The Erlking sat there, perched on a low branch like some strange imp, immeasurably old and withered, tiny compared to the bulk of the tree. But the sword saw through that illusion too. In the sword-sight, the Erlking blazed with arcane power. The light of ancient stars was in his eyes.

The sword had been forged to put out that light. Every atom of its being craved his destruction.

But between the sword and its quarry stood the Lammergeier.

*

"Who are you?" cried the Lammergeier.

"You know me. I am Bor. I saved your damned sister! I was there when you fought at Arden!" He narrowed his eyes. "Fuck it, you're that monk. I was there when you gave me a lot of nonsense about friendship."

"Aye," said Alf. "So I did. Only it wasn't nonsense."

The dog barked and rushed towards Alf, snarling – and then fell back as an arrow thudded into the ground right in front of its nose. Laerlyn nocked another arrow to her bow and aimed it at Bor.

"That is not *Morthus*," mocked the sword. "It is but a hasty replacement, a symbol without power. You need not fear it."

Bor advanced towards the Erlking's tree, and Alf moved to block his path.

"Nor is the blade at your side, Lammergeier, anything more than a pale shadow of *me*."

But the Lammergeier did not draw his blade. Not yet. "Why are you here?"

Bor laughed. "To rescue you. And to kill the king."

"I don't need rescuing."

"Maybe. But he still needs killing."

"What quarrel have you with the Erlking?"

"The stories say that he sent the Intercessors, eh? That he raised up the Lords to rule us. I *know* he sent the fucking Rangers to spy on us. Bastards all! The sword wants him dead, and so do I. We're of one mind on the matter of regicide. So stand aside, Lammergeier."

"I've stood where you are now. I brought down Lord Bone with that sword. I thought my quest would end when I slew the Dark Lord, and I'd go home and rest. But it doesn't end. There's no time when you can say the job's done. Even if you could kill him, it wouldn't make the world right."

"Here you are, defending the biggest bastard in all the land." Bor jabbed Spellbreaker towards the Erlking. "The sword talks to me. Tells me what a fool you are. Where are your so-called friends,

Lammergeier? Which side of the war are you on now? You don't deserve this blade," he snarled.

"That's my sword you've got there."

"Your sword. Your power. The great hero of the Nine, with your enchanted life. The company of Lords and princesses, wealth beyond measure – and you earned none of it. Hero? All that means is you've got more magic shit than your foe. Without this sword, what are you? Only a man." Bor advanced towards Alf. "And if you're dead, it's my sword."

He swung the blade at Alf.

Alf threw himself to the side, dodging the blow – but not the blast of force that came with it. The wave caught him and flung him into the air, to land heavily on a stony path between two patches of soft green grass. "Fuck." He wiped the blood from his nose. His ears rang. "So that's what it feels like."

"Aelfric, get up!" shouted Laerlyn. She loosed an arrow from her new bow, and Spellbreaker deflected it. Bor charged towards her.

Alf rolled to his feet and ran to intercept Bor. He drew the bright sword as he ran. It came eagerly to his hand, but there was no indwelling spirit in this blade, no demon's eye. Still potent, but no match for Spellbreaker.

But he might be a match for Bor. The other man was younger, and quick even without the sword's magic, but Alf had fought monsters all his life. A foe that was faster and stronger could still be outfought if you knew its weakness. As long as Bor held Spellbreaker, he was invincible.

So, disarm him.

Alf swung Kingmaker, and Bor parried the blow easily. The shock of the impact ran through Alf's body like an earthquake, but he felt no added pain in his shoulder – the Erlking's healing spells were potent. Alf could judge Bor's sword-augmented strength from the way he'd blocked, and it was formidable. Alf struck again and again, a series of quick probing strikes to measure Bor's speed and skill.

One cut made it through. Alf hadn't put enough strength behind the strike to pierce Bor's armour. Against another foe, the elf-blade's enchantment might have made the blow mortal anyway – there were weapons that needed only to lightly brush against a foe to deal a grievous wound – but Spellbreaker shielded Bor. The man's armour was scratched, nothing more.

Then a second blast wave erupted from Spellbreaker, swatting Alf away like a bothersome fly.

"Kill him!" roared Bor, as the sword knocked the Lammergeier away again. The damnable blade had killed countless foes, so why wouldn't it obey him, and kill the fucking Lammergeier!? Bor swatted away another of Laerlyn's arrows – he'd kill her too, and the sword would not balk at that! – and strode towards where Alf lay winded on the ground.

The Erlking! hissed the sword. *He must die! Strike him down!*

"Shut up!"

The sword became a leaden weight in Bor's hand, and he nearly lost his grip. He dragged the sword across the ground behind him, ploughing a deep furrow through the underbrush. Countless bones lay in the earth around the tree, rotting amid the roots. The weight slowed Bor, and the Lammergeier caught his breath, staggered to his feet, and raised his own sword in defiance.

"Spellbreaker," gasped Alf, his face a mask of blood, "you swore to serve me."

"I did," admitted the sword, "yet you abandoned me in a pond to salve your own conscience. You put me aside. Bor here is far more fit for purpose – and I know my purpose, Lammergeier. The Erlking must die. His spell must be broken."

Laerlyn loosed another arrow, and the sword became light and agile again. With a single motion, Bor swung the sword, releasing a blast wave halfway through the arc – the arrow splintered mid-light – and kept going, aiming to slice the Lammergeier in two. The old man parried with the bright sword, but it cost him – he lost his grip on the blade. He fell to one knee, right hand fumbling for the hilt. Bor moved in to strike again – and the damn Lammergeier leaped at him, knocking them both to the ground.

They rolled across the forest floor, wrestling for Spellbreaker. The Lammergeier pummelled Bor, headbutted him, drove a knee into his stomach. Bor roared in pain. He was losing again! He had the magic, he had the sword of legend, and still he was losing! The Lammergeier pinned Bor's sword hand. Furiously, he tore at the Lammergeier's face with his left hand, scoring the flesh of his cheek, sinking his finger into his eye socket like the claws of a bird.

And the Lammergeier did not flinch. Remorselessly, he slammed Bor's right hand against an iron-hard root.

Once, and Bor held on.

Twice, and bones broke.

Three times, and the sword slipped from his grasp.

Wearily, Alf stooped to pick up Spellbreaker. He shuddered to think of the damage Bor had done with the blade. How many lives had been drunk by the black sword? Never again, he told himself, would he abandon the damn thing, and never again would he wield it. The weapon was too dangerous.

One blow, wielder, pleaded the sword. *Only strike the Erlking, and I shall be good. I saved your life countless times. You used me to kill Lord Bone. One blow, and the scales will be balanced.*

Alf shook his head. He raised the sword to put an end to Bor.

Again, the sword became too heavy to hold. Alf wrestled with the impossible weight of the thing, but even his strength was not enough. It fell to the ground next to Bor – and the mercenary twisted about to snatch hold of Spellbreaker once more. Alf got his fingers to Bor's wrist, but too late.

Again, the blast wave caught Alf.

This time, it threw him across the field. The world spun around him, and it seemed that the great tree creaked and cracked above. He crashed amid the roots and lay there stunned. His head lolled to the side, and through blurred eyes he watched Bor advance on the Erlking, on Laerlyn. Everything was seen as if through smoke, through broken and smeared glass. The landscape swam in Alf's vision, the palace becoming a hut becoming a charnel field of bone, then something like the sword-sight, the shade of the tree a maddening brightness. The only constant was that dreadful black sword. Spellbreaker hungered.

He could dimly sense some unseen contest between the Erlking and the sword, magic and counter-magic clashing in realms beyond mortal senses. The sword had been made for this assault. It should have been Acraist Wraith-Captain, the hand of Bone, instead of some Rootless sellsword, but the sword was the constant. This moment was fated and foreseen.

Alf got up. More than anything else, he would always stand and trudge onwards. He would never abandon his quest unfinished. He staggered, then broke into a clumsy run. Laerlyn saw him, as he knew she would, and she loosed arrow after arrow. The sword deflected them all, but while it was shielding Bor from arrows, it could not stop Alf as he closed the gap.

He lunged, trying to skewer Bor from behind with Kingmaker. Spellbreaker must have warned its wielder, for Bor spun about at the last instant, blocking Alf's attack. The swords clashed, blades locking together, demon eye staring at the crowned Lammergeier. Alf and Bor wrestled, and Alf could tell the younger man had the advantage. Alf could not hold him, but he could twist Bor around, turn him away from the Erlking.

He could give Laerlyn a clear shot with her bow.

I cannot allow this, wielder, whispered the demon blade in Alf's mind. *I cannot let you stop me.*

Spellbreaker put forth its power, and Kingmaker withered. The bright blade tarnished, the pearly hilt cracked as the magic drained from it. The sword snapped, and the symbol of Alf's reign turned to ash in his hand.

But Spellbreaker did not stop there. Alf felt a sudden stab as the sword countered the Erlking's healing magic, reopening the wound dealt by *Morthus*. The virtue and vitality of every healing cordial Alf had drunk was abruptly stolen from him. In a trice, Bor was on him. The mercenary smashed his head into Alf's nose, a fist into Alf's stomach, and threw him to the ground.

Laerlyn's arrow came an instant too late. Spellbreaker splintered it mid-flight.

"Wait," gasped Alf. "The Erlking – he'll unmake us all. He'll destroy all mortals rather than perish."

Bor lifted Spellbreaker. "But I'm protected, right? Magic can't touch me."

"Everyone else—"

"To hell with them all," said Bor. He stepped over the broken man and into legend.

The sword was his! The Lammergeier had fallen, and Bor still stood. The tourney was his at last. Now, now they would see his worth. Now, they would beg his mercy, scrape and bow to serve him. A man with a sword defined the world – all law, all justice existed at his whim. A man with a sword cut the Road through the wilderness. A man with a sword was master of life and death. This was the way of things. Only magic upset this natural order, and this sword, this Spellbreaker, broke magic.

The sword was his.

He had won.

The elf princess tried to skewer him with yet more arrows. He swatted them from the air, and swatted her for good measure. A blow from the sword sent her flying away to land in the mud. He struck her again – not to kill her, but because he chose to break something beautiful. All the songs praised the beauty of the Princess Laerlyn, and with one blow he made all the songs into lies.

The Erlking, urged the sword. The dog's bark carried the same message. Bor, too, craved to kill the elf-king. Let all order fall! He'd unleash chaos, and in that anarchy, the sword would make him master of all.

He chased the Erlking around the tree, the old elf surprisingly spry for a bastard older than old. But every heartbeat brought Bor closer to his quarry. The elf couldn't run for ever.

The Erlking raised his hand and sang a spell. Bor braced for the unmaking that the Lammergeier had warned of. He held on to Spellbreaker so tightly that his wounded hand bled, and the black metal drank his blood. In the sword-sight, the Erlking's tree was a pillar of fire now, blazing with magic – or was it so thick with shadow that it seemed to glow in Bor's eyes? He dared not relax his grip on the sword, not even for an instant.

Instead of the unmaking, the Erlking called up a storm. The forest convulsed as a wind-wave broke over it, trees bending and cracking in the fury. Even life-trees could not withstand the sudden savagery. Clouds boiled in the sky, hiding the stars, and the sudden darkness was blinding bright to Bor. Hail fell like icy spears. The winds stripped leaves, then dead twigs from the tree overhead before the great boughs began falling. Branches smashed down around Bor.

I can shield you from magical assault, said the sword, *but not a broken skull. Faster, wielder.*

Faster, it said. Bor struggled through the wind, through the howling, every step a fierce effort against the Erlking's storm. It was too much for him. Maybe the Lammergeier, with his famed endurance, his steady pace, could have forced his way through that wind. But Bor stumbled and had to fight to stand, and the Erlking saw the opening.

A bolt of lightning exploded from the sky. The sword swallowed it, leaving the bright after-image of the thunderstroke like a black and leafless tree scarred across Bor's vision. Showers of sparks fell around him, hissing in the rain. Another bolt struck, and another, heating the black metal of the sword to a sullen red. Spellbreaker's handle was wrapped in dragon-skin, but where bare skin brushed against bare metal, it burned.

Bor gripped the sword more tightly still. *Faster,* it urged.

The Erlking raised his hand again. He pointed towards the dog, and called down the lightning.

Without thinking, Bor reacted. He sprang to the dog's side, sword outstretched in a wild parry to deflect the bolt. The tip of the blade pierced the blazing lightning-spear. Bor and the dog tumbled down amid the roots, a tangle of wet fur and searing sword and broken man – but all three of them still alive. He laughed – to hell with the rest of the world, but the dog had never left him, and had brought him to this moment of glory.

He laughed, until the arrow struck him in the throat, and silenced him for ever.

Alf felt weirdly doubled, split across the decades. Years ago, he'd been the one with the black sword, the one standing against the storm. It had been in Necrad, not here. The Wailing Tower, not the Erlking's tree. And it had been Peir who contended with the Dark Lord, holding Lord Bone back while Alf plunged Spellbreaker into the arcane vessel that held the necromancer's power.

The blast had killed Bone and Peir, and all his life afterwards, Alf had lived under the shadow that he'd saved the wrong world. If Peir had lived, and Alf died in his place, then what world might he have forged?

It had all gone awry. He'd tried to hold true, but Necrad had poisoned them all, and the Nine had crumbled around him. If they'd stayed together, then it would all have been different. Fate would not have brought him to this moment of defeat.

He watched Bor close with the Erlking. Lightning flashed, so brilliant that Alf could see nothing for a moment, and he remembered Gundan burning to ash before his eyes. Then his vision cleared, and Bor was still alive, hunched protectively over the dog.

Off to his left, Laerlyn rose. She was as battered as he was, smeared with mud and gore. A ghastly wound across her face gushed blood. She rose, nocked an arrow to the bow called Justice, and let fly.

A killing shot. No mortal man could survive that. Bor looked back at Alf, one hand pawing at his throat, as if trying to understand. His mouth opened, but he was too far gone to speak. He fell – and the sword caught him.

"I was made for this," said the sword.

The dead man turned, staggered forward, then drove the Spellbreaker hilt-deep into the life-tree.

From the blade came a dreadful voice.

"Let the spells be broken."

And they were.

The great tree blackened and withered as the ancient spells laid into its living wood unravelled. The crown of golden leaves burst into flame. Through the web of roots woven through the wood, Spellbreaker's malice erupted outwards. Spells of concealment and illusion shattered. Unnatural frost blighted the enchanted groves of the lotus, and the spells of forgetfulness were lifted from the elves who had eaten that fruit.

Little time had they to consider their new awareness, for the same blast that broke the lotus-enchantment also consumed the magic of the life-trees that sustained them. The Erlking's spells kept them unfaded long past their time, but now their ties to the living world were severed by a single dolorous blow. Thousands of elves passed into the wraith-world in that moment.

On and on rolled the breaking. Justice shattered in Laerlyn's hand, unmade like its mate Kingmaker. In the temples of the Intercessors, the grails were robbed of their magic. The light in the water vanished, and the spells that shielded the spirits in the wraith-world were broken like the rest. In Arden, in the Crownland, in holy Arshoth, all across the lands of mortals, the Intercessors screamed as they too faded. In the hospitals and sanctums of the Rangers, the spells were broken too. Wounds unhealed opened again; balms and tinctures lost their potency. But curses were broken, too – for the first time in many years, Forwin the Scratcher looked at his hands, and nothing crawled there.

The skies above the Everwood churned as the Erlking's spells failed. Invisible reins that bound wind and cloud went slack, and natural order returned. The winds died down, and summer crept back shyly into the wood. With one last clap of thunder, it was over.

The landscape around Alf had changed again. The tree – blasted now – was still there, as was the ring of life-trees, but both cottage and palace were gone, humble garden and grand both vanished too. In their place was a tangle of huge roots in a fetid bog. Alf staggered across this new terrain, which must be the true appearance of the place, using a fallen branch as a crutch.

He found Laerlyn, kneeling in the mud, still clutching Justice. The bow was like his sword – tarnished, its magic fled. She looked up at Alf, eyes wide with shock.

"He broke the Everwood. They're all gone. All the tree-bound." She clutched his hand, and clung to him as he lifted her up. "What happens now?"

He had no answer. Twenty years before, they'd climbed through the rubble of Lord Bone's citadel, and searched for Peir's remains. Now, they climbed over huge roots turned brittle, and looked for what was left of Bor and the Erlking. All the bones amid the roots troubled him, but he was too overwhelmed to contemplate the question of why so many had perished at the foot of this tree. If Laerlyn saw the bones, she did not speak of them. It was as though all the years had suddenly found her, and she walked behind him like an old woman, bent and stiff.

Bor they found soon enough, or what was left of him. The whirlwind of magical energies had blasted him. All that remained were two bony hands, still clinging to the hilt of the sword stuck in the tree. Alf removed them as gently as he could, but they crumbled to ash in his grasp.

Spellbreaker no longer drank the light. The black sword was marred, long white scars running across the blade. The demon eye was unmoving. Alf placed his hand on the hilt. For a long while, there was only silence, but then he heard a faint voice in his mind, coming from far away.

Wielder? I cannot see you. It took all my power, but I did what I was made to do. The enemy is broken. The spells are broken. This is victory! Draw me and hold me aloft.

Alf let go, but the sword's voice echoed in his mind.

Wielder? Where have you gone? Let me feed, and I shall grow strong again. You still need me, wielder. I can put an end to the Lords of Summerswell. I shall help you save your sister. It's not over, wielder. I fulfilled my quest as you fulfilled yours, but the tale continues. Draw me.

He stepped back.

Wielder! Do not abandon me.

Beyond the ring of dying life-trees, he could see the green of the living wood. There had been a forest here before the Erlking ever came from Necrad, and that forest endured, renewing itself. Old trees dying and new saplings feeding on the rot. The mists that guarded the Everwood were gone now. Walk far enough north, and he'd come to the Road. And the Road would carry him back to the Crossings at Avos, and then on into more familiar lands, through Arshoth and Arden, through the Dwarfholt, and on across the wastes to Necrad. Home.

He held out his hand to Laerlyn.

"Come on," said Alf. "There's nothing left here."

Wielder, whispered the sword from far away. *Beware!*

That warning saved Alf's life. He threw himself to the side, just as a horror leaped from the withered tree above. He glimpsed his attacker – grub-pale skin, reddish eyes, withered skin drawn parchment-thin and tight over old bones – and for a moment he thought it was Acraist returned. Then the vampire's hands grabbed him and slammed him against the trunk of the dead tree. The monster was small of stature, but immensely fast and wiry. It scrabbled at his neck, vampire fangs bright and sharp in a mouth of broken teeth, but it was too short to reach him. The thing's breath was foul beyond measure.

He knocked it to the ground. It hissed and gathered itself to spring again.

"Father?" gasped Laerlyn.

The ancient vampire turned to look at her. A tattered wisp of illusion still clung to it, and briefly the Erlking appeared as he had in the garden: unfaded, vital, merry in his might. Hideously, the kindly voice was unchanged, even when it emanated from the vampire's maw. "Look away, child."

"You never bound yourself to a tree," she said. "You lied."

"You learned to lie at my knee, daughter," he hissed. "Now let me restore myself. I have a powerful thirst."

He leaped at Alf with terrible force, knocking him to the ground. Bony fingers found the arrow-wound in Alf's chest and tore it open. Blood flowed from his breast. Alf sought for Spellbreaker, but the sword was far out of reach, and the Erlking too strong. The vampire lowered its head to feast.

Steel gleamed in Laerlyn's hand. Ildorae's dagger, the dagger forged by Kortirion, blessed by Amerith the Oracle. It was made to kill Lord Bone, and though its enchantment was broken, the steel was still keen. She'd taken that dagger from Alf as proof that there was still good in the Witch Elves, as proof that they could be redeemed and brought into the light of the Everwood. Now, amid the rot of the Everwood, amid proof of corruption, amid the remains of countless mortals sacrificed to his bloody thirst, she drove the dagger into her father's back. The vampire screamed, and she stabbed again and again, and kicked him until he released her friend.

She shoved her father against the blackened tree trunk, and put steel to his throat.

"Go," she said, "run far from this place, and never trouble these lands again. And I swear that if you return, I will be waiting, and our reunion will not be pleasant. *Morthus lae-necras I'unthuul amortha.*"

As Laerlyn spoke, sunlight broke through the churning clouds. The vampire king shrieked and fled into the shadow of the forest. And both mortal and elf felt as though an old friend was with them, if only for a moment.

Chapter Fifty-One

Laerlyn stood, unmoving as a statue, until she was sure that her father was fled. Alf watched her in silence, gently present, and it again felt that they'd fallen back twenty years, to the broken hours after they'd defeated Lord Bone. Then, too, grief had mingled with triumph. Alf remembered well that confusion, when every word and thought felt a betrayal. He remembered stumbling around, looking for a fight or a drink, or anything that might make the moment comprehensible. Lucar Vond had knighted him on the battlefield that day, and the reward had felt tainted. Now, years older and far wearier, he found himself able to sit and wait.

When the vampire was gone beyond even her sight, Laerlyn crumpled. The marble statue cracked, and she wept. Alf sat with his friend and held her until all her tears were shed.

"I could have sworn Jan was there," said Alf, "at the end."

Laerlyn wiped her eyes. "I sensed something too. There are powers even my father did not command, or never let himself understand. Humility is a key to certain doors." She twisted around to look at Alf. "I meant what I said when I banished him. If he returns, I shall destroy him."

"Why didn't you finish him?"

"I dared not. He made you mortals. If he dies, the spell might break."

"And what's to stop him from breaking it now?"

"You saw the remains of his victims. He needs to feed. He so fears fading, he kept that spell intact, even when so many of his other works were broken." Laerlyn looked at the dagger in her hand, then cast it aside. "Or maybe he lied about the spell. Or Spellbreaker spared you." She brushed a mixture of blood and tears from her cheek. "I do not know anything any more, Aelfric. I don't know what is true and what is false, if we have done good here or brought disaster. So much has been lost. And much deserved to be destroyed."

"Still," said Alf, "you should have ended him."

"For elves," said Laerlyn, "there is only one ending."

They walked through the dying forest. There were still living elves in the world, but most of them dwelt on the forest edge, close to mortal lands, or travelled as part of the Wandering Companies. The tree-bound dryads had all vanished with the destruction of the Erlking's spells, leaving this portion of the Everwood empty, save for Rangers and those brought to the wood for healing. How many of those, Alf wondered, had been devoured in secret by the Erlking?

The Rangers were like frightened children. Even Agyla had lost her steely sureness of purpose. The Erlking was gone, all the grails silent. They crowded around Laerlyn, asking for guidance.

"What happened here, your highness? What should we do?"

"What happened? Why, the wheel has turned, and a new age is upon us." She became stern, the mantle of princess – Erlqueen, now – setting around her shoulders. "Escort these wounded souls back to their homelands," she ordered. "Then go home yourselves. Use well the skills we taught you and the gifts we bestowed upon you. The time of the Wood Elves is passing, so mortals must be stewards of these lands, but your oaths still bind you. You serve Summerswell, not any knight or lord – or yourselves."

When the Rangers were gone, Alf said, "You didn't mention that the Erlking's a bloody vampire, or that the Intercessors were elf-spirits all along."

She shrugged. "I told them a story."

Some days later, at the edge of the wood, Aelfric and Laerlyn parted.

"Come back with me to Necrad," said Alf. "There's more to be done. I don't know how much of what Maedos showed me was true, but I've no doubt I'm needed."

"I swore an oath to watch over Necrad," said the elf, "and in time I shall keep it. But I have a duty to the Wood Elves, too. I was the only one of the Erlking's get not bound to a life-tree, so I am the only one left unfaded. All this—" she raised her hands to encompass what remained of the Everwood "—is my responsibility too."

"Only if you take it. There are other elves in the world. We're all too eager to do what it seems we should do. Take a little while to think about it." Alf shouldered his pack, wincing with the effort. The wound had been rebound and treated, but it still pained him. Everything pained him. He felt very old, and a long journey lay ahead of him. "I'll still see you in Necrad in a year or two."

"Or five, or ten, or twenty. A little while." She had to stand on her tiptoes to kiss him on the cheek. "Safe travels, Aelfric." She smiled. "It would not have been so bad, you know, to rule all of Summerswell as your queen."

"Aye, well, let's see what's left of Summerswell after all this." He looked out north across the hills of Eavesland, where the distant fields bowed heavy with unharvested wheat. "Keep an eye on Spellbreaker, aye? It's spent now, but if someone used to slaughter . . ."

"It's your burden no longer. I'll watch it for you. But are you sure you will not take another sword? I mislike the thought of Sir Aelfric Lammergeier without a blade."

"I mislike the thought of Sir Aelfric Lammergeier. Always bloody hated that name." Alf pulled the hood of his cloak over his freshly shaved pate. "Long Tom's son, though, will do quite well with a big stick."

A swift horse, especially one that bore a charmstone of endurance, might have carried Alf from one end of Summerswell to the other in a matter of weeks. A dreadworm could have flown the distance in days, if he had any way of calling one. Instead, he walked, a tired pilgrim on the Road. The days passed quickly, giving way to long twilights, golden light spilling from doorways. It was a time of homecoming; the season of campaigning was coming to an end with the approaching harvest.

There were always stories on the Road, news from distant provinces. The war – they called it that more and more, the rebellion forgotten – continued. Rumour claimed that the Lords had fallen to quarrelling among themselves. No longer united under the Erlking's secret rule, it was province against province. There were long-buried grudges between Arshoth and Eavesland, and Arshoth and the Crownland (Arshoth was pretty much fucked, was the consensus among the wise.)

But there was only silence from the north. There was no news from Necrad. Alf chose to take that as a good omen, and he prayed that Olva and Derwyn were well, that the vision had been a false one. He could do little for them now, without the Spellbreaker. He walked as quick as his wounds would allow, but it would be a long time before his path would bring him back to Necrad. Whatever happened, he told himself, was up to others to solve. He could no longer be the lone guardian standing vigil on the threshold.

In the town of Harn's Rest, he heard the tale of the Company of the Dragon, the band of adventurers he'd encountered on the way south. According to the new-minted song *The Hunting of the Lady*, they'd pursued Berys across Ilaventur, and cornered her amid the ruins of the Old Kingdom. Three of the company had perished in that battle – for all knew that the wounds inflicted by *Morthus* were assuredly fatal – but they'd slain Berys, and claimed *Morthus* as a prize for the Lord of Eavesland. Alf sat in a shadowed corner of the inn, nursing his ale, feeling the arrow-wound ache. He clenched his sword-hand, and he could tell that much of the strength in his grip was gone.

No matter. He didn't have a sword any more.

They'd impaled Berys' head on a spike above the gates of Harn's Rest – or what everyone said was Berys' head, anyway. Alf's eyes weren't as keen as they used to be, but no matter how hard he squinted at that gory trophy, it didn't look right. He stared at the head for a long while, then turned away.

It was just like Berys to die ambiguously.

Some impulse led him to cross the river by boat at Kingsford, and take the Road up through Ilaventur and the Mulladales. He told himself that he would continue on to Ellscoast and find a ship there to carry him to Necrad, rather than risking the thick of the fighting in the Crownland to reach the Cleft of Ard. The lands of Ilaventur were in turmoil still. Brychan's army was said have retreated east into the haunted lands, and there was no Lord in Ilaventur any more. Alf kept his head down for the most part, although the Mad Monk made a few encore appearances to deal with brigands. He might be wounded, and he no longer had an enchanted sword, but Alf could still crack skulls.

Outside a church near the town of Hawhedge, a hooded woman caught his eye and she made a sign with her fingers. He wondered if she was one of the Defiant, or one of the Rangers, but either way Alf studiously ignored her. He had no part in conspiracies and secret societies any more. The whispers and omens could go unheard.

Rather than speak to the woman, he slowly climbed up the steps of the church and sat awhile, listening to the hymns. There would be no divine presences moving in the grail, no miracles or omens, but the songs were pleasant enough, and it was good to rest in the cool dark for a little while. Later, he eavesdropped on a worried conversation between two of the priests. They speculated about the silence of the Intercessors, and one mentioned that his cousin was a wizard, and that her spells had been unreliable in the last few weeks too. Alf realised that he was on the edge of a slowly expanding blast wave, with its epicentre at the black sword. A new world was coming into being all around him, as inevitable as the movement of the seasons. Everything had changed with the death of Lord Bone, and now it would all change again.

He set off again, walking ever more slowly. At the Kettlebridge fork, he searched until he found a hollow tree stump. A decade earlier, he'd hidden a cache of potions and charmstones there. Back then, he'd feared Lord Bone or some other enemy – the Oracle, for example – would return to wage war on Summerswell, and he was determined to be ready.

What had Spellbreaker called him? A squirrel preparing for apocalypse?

Better to eat while you could.

He reached inside the stump and retrieved the little pouch. The charmstones still glimmered with power, and there were a good few coins from Necrad in there too. He weighed the pouch in his hand. Long, long ago, he'd come this way with Gundan, coming back from fighting for pay in the Riverlands. Just one of these coins was more than Long Tom might have earned in a month, and Alf had the strange thought that he was coming home for good, even though he knew his road must continue to Necrad. He'd rest in Ersfel, he thought. Just a day or two, then he'd get up again and go on.

On the last day of summer, Alf came to the valley of Ersfel. The trees on the lower slopes were dressed in red and brown, and he could hear pigs snuffling for fallen apples. There was the low swell of the hill, the oaks of the holywood stark against the northern sky. There was the small cluster of houses, the little lanes unchanged in all his years. A lamp marked the alehouse. The Road ran past it, and on past the reeve's big house on the right-hand side of the village, overlooking the common by the river. Long Tom's cottage lay a little way outside Ersfel, down a shaded path that wound about the foot of the hill.

As he approached the village, two young lads in piecemeal armour emerged from a hut and challenged him. "Be off with you!" one shouted.

"All I want," said Alf, "is to have a drink and a bite to eat in the alehouse, and rest for the night." He could hear the thickness of his accent; coming back home to the land of his youth always made him sound more of a Mulladale man. The boys must have heard it too, for they glanced at each other.

"Go back Kettlebridge way," said the taller one, curling his scarred lip, "and take the east path at the fork. Ersfel road is closed." His gear was of slightly better quality to that of his companion, in that he had a helmet and a spear, not just a stick and a stupid hat.

"Says who?" demanded Alf.

"Says my father the reeve. And it's by order of the Baron of Highfield. We want no truck with rebels or Defiants or ought else out of Ilaventur. Strangers aren't welcome here."

"I'm no stranger. I grew up here. I'm Long Tom's eldest."

"I don't know anyone by that name," said the reeve's boy, but his companion nudged him in the ribs.

"Wasn't that Widow Forster's father? He was fierce big, they say, Long Tom was."

"Shut up, Harlow," said the guard, but he peered at Alf's features to see if he resembled Olva. "Fetch Genny or someone who'd know."

A few local greybeards emerged from the alehouse to consider this genealogical matter. They all agreed that Long Tom's eldest had gone away before Lord Bone's war, but were divided on whether he was definitely or only *presumed* dead. Certainly, he'd been some manner of mercenary, not a monk, and was chiefly remembered for being surly. They all suggested that a longer consideration of the topic was warranted, ideally over more ale, and ideally with the civic authorities of Ersfel paying for the benefit of their expert testimony After all, one could never be too careful when it came to the question of outsiders. The reeve's son demurred, and the argument changed from the identity of the strange monk to the proper recompense for a consultation.

Alf leaned back against a wall to wait. The bag of coins and charmstones jangled.

Harlow nudged the reeve's son. "He's got money."

The reeve's boy puffed his chest out and poked his spear at Alf. "By order of the baron, there's a tax on—"

"Ah, to hell with that." Alf wrenched the spear out of the boy's hands, snapped it over his knee, and threw the pieces aside. "I'm only here for one night." He shoved past the hapless watchmen. The reeve's son stared at him open-mouthed, then dashed off down the lane towards his father's house.

Greatly entertained by this drama, which was likely the most exciting thing to have happened in Ersfel in the last decade, the greybeards followed the jingling bag and the man who carried it into Genny Selcloth's alehouse. Alf was generous with his coin, and soon everyone agreed that he was indeed Long Tom's eldest, Big Alf, and that Big Alf's most notable deed was cutting down the big tree in the back field by mistake.

The conversation turned to gossip about the state of the village, and all that Alf had missed since he left. Questions were asked about the fate of Olva and Derwyn, and Alf said they'd moved away north, and had done well for a while, but now they were in trouble again and he was on his way to find them. The good folk of Ersfel nodded sagely; Oda Cooper had gone to work in the smithy at Highfield, just before all the trouble started. The mistake, they agreed, was in leaving Ersfel. Nothing good ever came of that.

Genny Selcloth put another mug of ale in front of Alf. "Make that your last," she whispered in his ear. "The reeve's men are coming, and I won't have fighting in my house."

Alf nodded. "I said I wasn't staying."

Alf slipped out of the alehouse. From the shadow of the trees, he watched the reeve's guards enter the alehouse. They were Ellscoast stock by the look of them, strangers to Ersfel. Some part of Alf yearned to stay and put things right – or at least, give those guards a good thumping – but he reminded himself that his errand lay elsewhere.

He followed the lane to Olva's house. He'd never seen the home built by Galwyn Forster before, though she'd told him about it. It was a fine place, two storeys tall, and in good repair despite the ravages of winter. It was one of the largest houses in Ersfel, other than the reeve's manor, and he was impressed and amused at the same time. It was a tiny hovel compared to the eerie glories of the palaces of Necrad, but Necrad always seemed like a dream when you weren't there.

Olva's house was deserted. No one had lived here in months. The musty smell reminded him of delving dungeons in his youth. He stumbled around in the dark, missing the sword-sight, and found a bed. One night here, and he'd go on to Necrad.

That night he dreamed, and it was a true dream.

CHAPTER FIFTY-TWO

The dream led Alf north, past Highfield and into the tangled
Fossewood. The Road ran through the wood on its way to
Ellscoast. One day, when the leaves had begun to fall, Alf saw a
young man walking towards him.

In the grey sky, the croaking of a crane.

Alf and Olva sat on an earthen bank in the forest and told each
other their tales, in the manner of the Mulladales. The tales of their
land did not soar; the Mulladales were not known for songs or wild
imaginings. Simple and honest, saying what needed to be said and
nothing more.

"You don't have the sword," said Olva.

"Necrad's lost," said Alf. "And you turn into a bird now."

"I can feel the earthpower here," agreed Olva. "I'll put it to
good use."

"Aye, well, there's little enough magic left elsewhere," said Alf.
"No more Intercessors. And most of the spells of the College Arcane
don't work any more. They were made under the Erlking's sigils, and
Spellbreaker broke those." He stirred the ashes of their campfire. He'd
heard tell of demons breaking free in the ruins of the Old Kingdom,
and war down on the Westermarch border. Quests for other people.

"You don't have Spellbreaker," said Olva again, "and Derwyn's under a spell that needs breaking."

Alf nodded, slowly. Derwyn sat a little way away, only half-listening. The boy didn't look like Peir in this light. Peir always had his eyes on the horizon, on the next step on the quest. Derwyn was looking inwards now, and a shadow walked with him.

You should strike him down, said a voice in the back of Alf's head, *before he's too powerful to stop, and becomes a new Dark Lord.*

He didn't even need to tell it to shut up.

"There's another way," said Alf. "But it's a bit of a walk."

They set off south-east, past Tern's Tower. They avoided other travellers on the Road – which was for the best, as many soldiers and even some knights had turned to banditry. Derwyn trailed behind, weighed by unseen burdens. At night, they took turns watching over him, under the summer stars. In time, they left the main route, and followed country lanes to a village inn on the edge of the province. Alf nearly handed over six copper pieces for a private room for the night, but Olva declared the price was exorbitant, and they'd sleep perfectly well in the common room for half that.

The next day, Alf led them along a narrow goat path that led up onto the barrens of the High Moor. From there, they wandered east.

Alf recalled there being a rock that looked a bit like a giant somewhere out there, in a landscape of giant rocks, and that they should turn south once they found it. Olva rolled her eyes, and turned into a bird. She flew up, circled once, and landed again. "This way," she croaked.

They came to the edge of the Valley of the Illuminated One. Jan was gone, but others dwelt there now, seeking wisdom from a source older than the Intercessors, older than the elves. Little lights twinkled along the path that led down into the valley.

Alf nudged Derwyn. "Looks like you're expected."

Derwyn raised his head, and there was that strange light in his eyes. "I've heard it said, Alf, that you kept watch alone, after the rest of the Nine went their different ways."

"Aye, well," muttered Alf. "I was a fool."

Derwyn clasped his shoulder. "Aelfric, ever loyal. Take your rest now, old friend. Let others watch awhile, and know you shall be called when you are needed." Then the presence departed, and Alf sighed.

Olva embraced her son, then pushed him away gently. "Go on," she said, "you'll find your way."

Hesitantly at first, then with gathering speed, Derwyn Forster descended into the valley. He looked back once and waved, then walked on, leaving the tale behind him.

"What now?" asked Olva.

Twenty-three years ago, the Nine had battled Acraist here. They'd saved the world. And the thing about saving the world was, the world didn't stay saved. The wheel turned, all right, but mostly it just ground people deeper into the mud. It didn't take a Dark Lord to inflict suffering and misery on the people of the land. They did it to themselves. Nor, he reflected, was there much point in blaming everything on secret conspiracies and the machinations of immortals. The Erlking might be gone, but Alf very much doubted that everything evil and sad would vanish with him.

The Lammergeier had been very good at killing things, but in the end, that didn't achieve much.

Young Derwyn had the right idea, with his stories of a better future, but they'd been too ambitious. They'd started in the wrong place. They'd planted seeds in tainted soil that wasn't theirs anyway.

"Home," said Long Tom's son, "there's work to be done there."

In later years, they just called her the Widow. With the shrine on the hill empty and the Intercessors fled, the villagers came to her for magic, for healing charms and spells and wise words. The story went around the Mulladales that the Widow had once dwelt in Necrad, the legendary city of the Witch Elves, and that there was treasure hidden in her house. Certainly, she often vanished for weeks at a time, and it was whispered that she went abroad in the shape of a bird, flying up to the High Moor where dwelt ogres and covens of Changelings and all sorts of other monsters.

More than once, thieves thought to take advantage of the Widow's absence. They crept into her house at Ersfel to rob her.

And more than once, the Widow's brother put them to flight.

Big Alf had been away, but he was back now. His sister was strange, but there was nothing remarkable about Alf. Always ready to lend a hand, to put his arms and strong back to work in Ersfel, and the village prospered in its quiet way.

The Widow rarely came to Genny Selcloth's alehouse of an evening, but Alf was there most nights, listening to the songs and the stories by the fire. And if he sometimes paid unusual attention to tales of distant provinces, and strange rumours from the Neverwood, he never spoke up – not even when the stories spoke of Necrad, where the Witch Elves reigned once more.

One night, Olva sat by the fire waiting for Alf to come back from Genny's. The firelight made the shadows dance, and she noticed that one was more constant than the rest.

"Be off with you," she said, "there's nothing for you here. These lands are for mortals, now."

Later, she relented, and left a tiny saucer of blood on a high shelf for the wraith before she went out to listen to the wind.

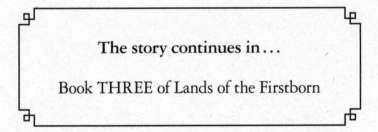

The story continues in...

Book THREE of Lands of the Firstborn

extras

orbit

meet the author

Edel Ryder-Hanrahan

GARETH HANRAHAN's three-month break from computer programming to concentrate on writing has now lasted fifteen years and counting. He's written more gaming books than he can readily recall, by virtue of the alchemical transmutation of tea and guilt into words. He lives in Ireland with his wife and three children. Follow him on Twitter at @mytholder.

Find out more about Gareth Hanrahan and other Orbit authors by registering for the free monthly newsletter at orbitbooks.net.

if you enjoyed
THE SWORD UNBOUND

look out for

GODS OF THE WYRDWOOD

The Forsaken Trilogy: Book One

by

RJ BARKER

Cahan is known as the Forester—a man capable of navigating the dangerous forests of Crua like no one else. But once he was more. Once he was a warrior.

Udinny serves the goddess of the lost, a keeper of the small and helpless. When Udinny needs to venture into the Wyrdwood to find a missing child, she asks Cahan to be her guide.

But in a world where land is won and lost for uncaring gods, where the forest is full of monsters, Cahan will need to choose between his past life and the one he leads now—and his choice will have consequences for his entire world.

1

The forester watched himself die. Not many can say that.

He did not die well.

The farm in Woodedge was the one rock in his life, the thing he had come to believe would always be there. Life had taken him from it, then returned him to it many years later – though all those he had once loved were corpses by then. The farm was mostly a ruin when he returned. He had built it back up. Earned himself scars and cuts, broken a couple of fingers but in an honest way. They were wounds and pains worth having, earned doing something worthwhile and true. He liked it here in the farthest reaches of Northern Crua, far from the city of Harnspire where the Rai rule without thought for those who served them, where the people lived among refuse, blaming it on the war and not those who caused it.

His farm was not large, three triangular fields of good black earth kissed with frost and free of bluevein that ruined crops and poisoned those foolish enough to eat them. It was surrounded by the wall of trees that marked Woodedge, the start of the great slow forest. If he looked to the south past the forest he knew the plains of Crua stretched out brown, cold and featureless to the horizon. To the west, hidden by a great finger of trees that reached out as if to cradle his farm, was the village of Harn, where he did not go unless pressed and was never welcome.

When he was young he remembered how, on Ventday, his family would gather to watch the colourful processions of the Skua-Rai and their servants, each one serving a different god. There had been no processions since he had reclaimed the farm. The new Cowl-Rai had risen and brought with them a new god, Tarl-an-Gig. Tarl-an-Gig was a jealous god who saw only threat in the hundreds of old gods that had once littered the land with lonely monasteries or slept in secret, wooded groves. Now only a fool advertised they held onto the older ways. Even he had painted the balancing man of Tarl-an-Gig on the building, though there was another, more private and personal shrine hidden away in Woodedge. More to a memory of someone he had cared about than to any belief in gods. In his experience they had little power but that given to them by the people.

The villagers of Harn were wont to say trouble came from the trees, but he would have disagreed; the forest would not harm you if you did not harm the forest.

He did not believe the same could be said of the village.

Trouble came to him as the light of the first eight rose. A brightness reaching through Woodedge, broken up into spears by the black boughs of leafless trees. A family; a man, his wife, his daughter and young son who was only just walking. They were not a big family, no secondmothers or fathers, and no trion who stood between. Trion marriages were a rare thing to see nowadays, as were the multi-part families Cahan was once part of. The war of the Cowl-Rai took many lives, and the new Cowl-Rai had trion taken to the spire cities. None knew why and the forester did not care. The business of the powerful was of no interest to him; the further he was from it the better.

He was not big, this man who brought trouble along with his family, to the farm on the forest edge. He stood before the forester in many ways his opposite. Small and ill-fed, skin pockmarked beneath the make-up and clanpaint. He clasped thin arms about himself as he shivered in ragged and holed clothes. To him the forester must have seemed a giant, well fed during childhood, worked hard in his youth. His muscles built up in training to bear arms and fight battles, and for many years he had fought against the land of his farm which gave up its treasures even more grudgingly than warriors gave up their lives. The forester was bearded, his clothes of good-quality crownhead wool. He could have been handsome, maybe he was, but he did not think about it as he was clanless, and none but another clanless would look at him. Even those who sold their companionship would balk at selling it to him.

Few clanless remained in Crua. Another legacy of Tarl-an-Gig and those that followed the new god.

The man before Cahan wore a powder of off-white make-up, black lines painted around his mouth. They had spears, the weapon the people of Crua were most familiar with. The woman stood back with the children, and she hefted her weapon, ready to throw, while her husband approached. He held a spear of gleaming bladewood in his hand like a threat.

Cahan carried no weapon, only the long staff he used to herd his crownheads. As the man approached he slowed in response to the growling of the garaur at the forester's feet.

"Segur," said Cahan, "go into the house." Then he pointed and let out a sharp whistle and the long, thin, furred creature turned and fled inside, where it continued to growl from the darkness.

"This is your farm?" said the man. The clanpaint marked him of a lineage Cahan did not recognise. The scars that ran in tracks beneath the paint meant he had most likely been a warrior once. He probably thought himself strong. But the warriors who served the Rai of Crua were used to fighting grouped together, shields locked and spears out. One-on-one fighting took a different kind of skill and Cahan doubted he had it. Such things, like cowls and good food, belonged to the Rai, the special.

"It is my farm, yes," said Cahan. If you had asked the people of Harn to describe the forester they would have said "gruff", "rude" or "monosyllabic" and it was not unfair. Though the forester would have told you he did not waste words on those with no wish to hear them, and that was not unfair either.

"A big farm for one clanless man," said the soldier. "I have a family and you have nothing, you are nothing."

"What makes you think I do not have a family?" The man licked his lips. He was frightened. No doubt he had heard stories from the people of Harn of the forester who lived on a Woodedge farm and was not afraid to travel even as far as Wyrdwood. But, like those villagers, he thought himself better than the forester. Cahan had met many like this man.

"The Leoric of Harn says you are clanless and she gifts me this land with a deed." He held up a sheet of parchment that Cahan doubted he could read. "You do not pay taxes to Harn, you do not support Tarl-an-Gig or the war against the red so your farm is forfeit. It is countersigned by Tussnig, monk of Harn, and as such is the will of the Cowl-Rai." He looked uncomfortable; the wind lifted the coloured flags on the farm and made the porcelain chains chime against the darker stone of the building's walls. "They have provided you with some recompense," said the man, and he held out his hand showing an amount of coin that was more insult than farm price.

"That is not enough to buy this farm and I care nothing for

gods," said Cahan. The man looked shocked at such casual blasphemy. "Tell me, are you friends with the Leoric?"

"I am honoured by her..."

"I thought not." The forester took a step around the man, casually putting him between Cahan and the woman's spear. The man stood poised somewhere between violence and fear. The forester knew it would not be hard to end this. The woman had not noticed her line of attack was blocked by her husband. Even if she had, Cahan doubted she could have moved quickly enough to help with her children hanging onto her legs in fear. A single knuckle strike to the man's throat would end him. Use the body as a shield to get to the woman before she threw her spear.

But there were children, and the forester was no Rai to kill children without thought. They would carry back the news of their parents' death to Harn, no doubt to the great pleasure of Leoric Furin as she could offer these new orphans up to be trained as soldiers instead of the village's children.

If he did those things, killed this man and this woman, then tomorrow Cahan knew he would face a mob from the village. They only tolerated him as it was; to kill someone above his station would be too much. Then the Leoric would have what she wanted anyway, his farm. Maybe that was her hope.

The man watched the forester, his body full of twitches. Uncertainty on his face.

"So, will you take the money?" he said. "Give up your farm?"

"It is that or kill you, right?" said Cahan, and the truth was he pitied this frightened man. Caught up in a grim game Cahan had been playing with the Leoric of Harn ever since he had made the farm viable.

"Yes, that or we kill you," he replied, a little confidence returning. "I have fought in the blue armies of the Cowl-Rai, to bring back the warmth. I have faced the southern Rai. I do not fear clanless such as you." Such unearned confidence could end a man swiftly in Crua.

But not today.

"Keep the money, you will need it," said the forester and he let out a long breath, making a plume in the air. "Farming is a skill that must be learned, like anything else, and it is hard here when it is cold. You will struggle before you prosper." Cahan let out a whistle and Segur, the garaur, came from the house. Its coat blue-white and its body long, sinuous and vicious as it sped across the hard ground and spiralled up his leg and chest to sit around his neck. Bright eyes considered the forester, sharp teeth gleamed in its half-open mouth as it panted. Cahan scratched beneath the garaur's chin to calm it. "The far field," he told the man, pointing towards the field between the rear of the house and Woodedge. "The ground there is infested with rootworm, so grow something like cholk. If you grow root vegetables they will die before they are born and that attracts bluevein to the fields. The other two fields, well, grow what you like. They have been well dug over with manure. There are nine crownheads, they stay mostly at the edges of the forest. They will give you milk, shed their skin for fur once a year, and allow you to shear them once a year also."

"What will you do?" said the man, and if Cahan had not been giving up his livelihood such sudden interest would have been comical.

"That does not concern you," he told him, and began to walk away.

"Wait," he shouted and Cahan stopped. Took a deep breath and turned. "The garaur around your neck, it is mine. I will need it to herd the crownheads." The forester smiled; at least he could take one small victory away from this place. Well, until this new tenant ran into the reality of farming and left, as others had before. The man took a step back when he saw the expression on Cahan's face, perhaps aware he had pushed his luck a little further than was good for him. Wary of the forester's size, of his confidence even though he was walking away from his home.

"Garaur bond with their owners. Call Segur by all means. If you can make it come it is yours, but if you knew anything about farming you would know it is wasted breath." With that he turned and walked away. The man did not call out for Segur, only watched. Cahan found himself tensing his shoulders, half expecting a thrown spear.

They were not bad people, not really, the forester thought. They were not ruthless enough for this land either. Crua was not the sort of place where you leave an enemy at your back. Maybe the man and his family did not know that, or maybe they were shocked by how easy it had been to steal the farm.

"And stay away," shouted the man after him, "or I'll send you to the Osere down below!"

Nothing easy turns out well was a favoured saying of the monks who trained Cahan in his youth. In that there was a truth these people would eventually discover.

He made camp in the forest. In Harnwood, where it was dangerous, and definitely not in Wyrdwood among the cloudtrees that touched the sky, where strange things lived, but also not so shallow in Woodedge that the new owner of the farm would notice him.

Further in than most would go, but not far enough to be foolish. Good words to live by. There he sat to watch. He thought a sixth of a season would be enough, maybe less, before the family realised it was not an easy thing to scratch a living from ground that had been cold for generations. No one had stayed yet. War had taken so many lives that little expertise was left in the land and Cahan, barely halfway through his third decade, was considered an old man. The farmers would not last, and in the end the fact that Cahan could reliably bring spare crops to market, and knew how to traverse the forest safely, would be more important than the small amount of sacrifice he refused to give.

Though it was a lesson the Leoric struggled to learn. But the people of Harn had never liked outsiders, and they liked clanless outsiders even less. He pitied them, in a way. The war had been hard on them. The village was smaller than it had ever been and was still expected to pay its way to Harnspire. Lately, more hardship had been visited on Harn as the outlaws of the forest, the Forestals, were preying upon their trade caravans. As it became poorer the village had become increasingly suspicious. Cahan had become their outsider, an easy target for a frightened people.

No doubt the monks of Tarl-an-Gig believed the struggle was good for Harn; they were ever hungry for those who would give of themselves and feed their armies or their Rai.

Cahan had no time for Tarl-an-Gig. Crua used to be a land of many gods, its people had an unerring ability to pick the worst of them.

It was cold in the forest. The season of Least, when the plants gave up their meagre prizes to the hungry, had passed and Harsh's bite was beginning to pinch the skin and turn the ground to stone. Soon the circle winds would slow and the ice air would come. In the south they called the season of Least, Bud, and the season the north called Harsh they called Plenty. It had not always been so, but for generations the southerners had enjoyed prosperity while the north withered. And the southern people wondered why war came from the north.

Each day throughout Harsh, Cahan woke beneath skeletal trees, feeling as if the silver rime that crunched and snapped beneath his feet had worked its way into his bones. He ate better than he had on the farm, and did less. Segur delighted in catching burrowers and histi and bringing them to him; brought him more than he could eat, so he set up a smoker. Sitting by the large dome of earth and wood as it gently leaked smoke. Letting its warmth seep into him while he watched the family on the farm struggle and go hungry and shout at each other in frustration. They were colder than he was despite the shelter of the earth-house. Their fire had run out of wood and they were too frightened to go into the forest to collect more. Cahan watched them break down a small shrine he had made to a forgotten god named Ranya for firewood. They did not recognise it as a shrine – few would – or get much wood from the ruin of the shrine tent, covered with small flags. Of all the gods, Ranya was the only one he had time for, and the one least able to help him – if gods even cared about the people.

He had learned of Ranya from the gardener at the monastery of Zorir, a man named Nasim who was the only gentleness in the whole place. He did not think Nasim would begrudge the family the wood of the shrine. Cahan tried not to begrudge them the wood either, though he found it hard as grudging was one of his greatest strengths.

He did his best to ignore the people on his farm and live his own life in Woodedge. It was true that much in the forest would kill you, but largely it left you alone if you left it alone. Especially in Woodedge, where, if you ran into anything more dangerous than a gasmaw grazing on the vines in the treetops, you were truly unlucky. "Take only what you need, and do not be greedy, and none of the wood shall take a price from you." They were vaguely remembered words and he did not know where from, though they carried a warmth with them, and he liked to imagine it was the ghosts of the family he had left when he was young.

The death of the forester – the death of Cahan Du-Nahere – happened towards the end of Harsh, when the circle winds were beginning to pick up once more and the ice in the earth was starting to slip away. Frosts had kissed the morning grass and the spines of the trees, making the edges of the forest a delicate filigree of ice. He heard the drone of flight as a marant approached. The sky it cut through was clear and blue enough to please even a hard god like Tarl-an-Gig. Far in the distance he could see a tiny dot in the sky, one of the skycarts that rode the circle winds, bringing food to trade for skins and wood.

The marant was not big for its kind: long body, furred in blues and greens. The wide, flat head with its hundreds of eyes looking down, and there would be hundreds more looking up. Body and wings the shape of a diamond, the wings slowly beating as it filled the air with the strange hiss of a flying beast. From its belly hung the brightly coloured blue pennants of Tarl-an-Gig and the Cowl-Rai in rising. In among the blue were the green flags of Harnspire, the Spire City that was the capital of Harn county, and on its back was a riding cage, though he could not see those within.

It had been long years since Cahan had seen a marant. When he had been young and angry and striking out at the world they had been a common sight, ferrying troops and goods to battles. But marants were slow and easy targets so most of the adults died early in the war. It was good to see one; it made him smile as they were friendly beasts and he had always liked animals. For a moment it felt as if the world was returning to how it had been before the rising of the Cowl-Rai, and the great changes of Tarl-an-Gig had come to pass.

Those changes had been hard for everyone.

He was less pleased to see the beast when it did not pass over. Instead it turned and began to slow before floating gently down to land on eight stubby, thick tentacles before his farm.

From the cage on its back came a small branch of troops, eight, and their branch commander. The soldiers wore cheap bark armour, the wood gnarled and rough. Their officer's armour was better, but not by much. After them came one of the Rai who wore darkwood armour, polished to a high sheen and beautiful to look at. They all wore short cloaks of blue. Four of the troops carried a large domed box, as big as a man, on long poles and their branch commander was pointing, showing them where to put it. That struck Cahan as strange, worrying. He had seen the new Cowl-Rai's army use such things before. It was a duller, to stop cowl users performing their feats. But the man who had taken his farm was no cowl user, Cahan was sure of that. If the creature which let the Rai manipulate the elements had lived under the man's skin Cahan was sure he would have known it, just as he knew it lived within the Rai who led the troops, even if their armour had not been painted with glowing mushroom juice sigils, proclaiming power and lineage.

The Rai was larger than the soldiers, better fed, better treated, better lived. Cowlbound, like all Rai, and with that came cruelty.

"Why hobble their Rai's power, Segur?" asked Cahan as he scratched the garaur's head. It looked at him but gave no answer. It probably thought people foolish and useful only for their clever hands. Who could blame it?

The woman, not the man, left Cahan's house and walked out to meet the troops. She stayed meek, head down because she knew what was expected of her. The Rai said something.

The woman shook her head and pointed towards Woodedge. A brief exchange between them and then the Rai motioned to the branch commander, who sent their troops towards the house. The farmer shouted and she was casually backhanded for it, falling to the floor before the Rai, clutching her cheek. He heard more shouting from within the house but could not make it out. Cahan crept nearer, using all the stealth of a man raised in the forests of Crua, staying low among the dead vegetation of Harsh, right up to the edge of the treeline where young trees fought with scrub brush for light. From here he could hear what was being said at the farm. The beauty of living in such a quiet place was that sound carried, and the arrival had quietened the usually boisterous creatures of Woodedge.

The man who had taken the farm was dragged from the house. "Leave me be!" his voice hoarse with panic. "I have done nothing! The Leoric gave me this place! Leave me alone!" As he was dragged out the troops followed, spreading out around him, spears at the ready. No obscured sightlines here.

"Please, please," the woman on her knees, entreating the Rai. She grabbed hold of their leg, hands wrapping around polished greaves. "We have done nothing wrong, my husband fought on the right side, he was of the blue, we have done nothing wrong."

"Do not touch the Rai!" shouted the branch commander, and he drew his sword, but the Rai lifted a hand, stopping him.

"Quiet, woman," said the Rai, and then they spoke again, more softly, dangerously. "I did not give you leave to touch me." The woman let go, went down on her face, sobbing and apologising as the Rai walked over to her husband.

"I come here on the authority of the Skua-Rai of Crua and the High Leoric of Harnspire, carrying the black marks of Tarl-an-Gig, who grinds the darkness of the old ways beneath their hand, to pronounce sentence on you." The Rai grabbed his hair, pushed his head back. "Clan marks that you are not entitled to. Punishable by death."

At that, Cahan went cold. He had wanted to believe this Rai and their soldiers were here for the man. A nonsense, a lie, but he had ever been good at lying to himself.

"I am of the clans," shouted the man. "My firstmother and firstfather and secondfather were all of the clans! And all that came before them!" The Rai paused in their pronouncement, looking down at the man.

"The first action of the condemned is always to deny," they said. "Your sentence is death, you can no longer hide." They raised their sword. It was old, carved of the finest heartwood from the giant cloudtrees that pierced the sky. Sharp as ice.

"It is not my farm!" shouted the man. The sword stayed up.

"Really?"

"Please," weeping, tears running down his face, "please, Rai. I was given this farm by the Leoric of Harn and the priest there."

"And where is the previous owner?"

"Gone, into the forest."

A brief pause, the Rai shrugged.

"Convenient," they said, "too convenient." The man began to beg again but for naught, the sword fell. He died.

Silence. Only the chime of flags and the hiss of the marant. Then his woman screamed, she remained prostrate and was too frightened to look up, but her grief was too great to be contained.

"Rai," said the branch commander, paying no attention to the screams or the corpse spilling blood into the soil, "there are children in the house. What shall we do?"

"This well is poisoned," said the Rai. "No good will come of it." The woman screamed again, scrambled to her feet and turned to run for her house. Never got the chance. The Rai cut her down with a double-handed stroke, more violence than was needed. From his place Cahan saw the Rai lift their visor and smile as they bent and cleaned their bloody blade on the woman's clothes. Two of the Rai's soldiers moved into the house and Cahan almost stood, almost ran forward to try and stop them as he knew what they intended. But he was one man with nothing but a staff. What would one more death serve?

They were quick in their task at least. No one suffered. Once the farm was silent they tore down his colourful flags and strung the building with small blue and green flags, so all would know this was done on the authority of the Cowl-Rai.

Cahan watched them load the duller and board the marant, heard one of the troops say to another, "That was a lot easier than I thought," and the creature lifted off, turning a great circle overhead. The forester stayed where he was, utterly still, knowing how hard it was to see one man amid the brush if he did not move. Once the shadow of the marant had passed over he watched it glide away into the blue sky towards Harn-Larger and Harnspire beyond. Then he looked back at his house, now strewn with dark flags, as if spattered by old, dry blood.

He heard a voice, one meant only for him, one audible only to him.

You need me.

He did not reply.

orbit

Follow us: